NAO DE CHINE
TREASURE OF
THE MANILA GALLEON

ROBBIE JOHNSON

DownWind Press

ISBN: 0615782795
ISBN-13: 978-0-615782799

DEDICATION

For my amazing daughter, Dawne Rose Michael,
a loving mother of my three terrific grandchildren,
and a dedicated Registered Nurse (RN) BSN.

CONTENTS

ACKNOWLEDGMENTS

Every author who devotes the time and energy to writing a full-length novel incurs the debt of many, many kind and generous persons without whom the novel would have never been realized. Each person contributed something essential to the tale, a piece of the puzzle that the author wove into the overall fabric so that the finished work would delight and entertain readers. Sometimes a timely cup of hot coffee can be as generous a gift as a suggestion for a character, or a resolution to a situation in the story. Who can say which contribution was the greater? I cannot. I can only express my deepest appreciation to all of those who helped my on this long journey. All of you know who you are, and it unnecessary to proclaim your names and your love to strangers. I look forward to the next voyage and sharing the ride with you.

HISTORICAL PREFACE

Each year for two and a half centuries the *naos de chine*, or China Ships, as the galleons were called in their time, crossed the Pacific Ocean between Acapulco, *Nueva Espana*, present-day Mexico, and the Spanish colony at Manila, Philippines in what was the longest navigation ever attempted by mankind—over 9,000 miles of open ocean. The first *nao* sailed in 1565, when Philip the Second was king of the Spains, and Elizabeth Tudor was queen of England. The last crossed in 1815, when the new republic called the United States, was not yet 40 years old.

No other ships sailing upon any of the oceans of the world, then or since, carried greater riches than the *naos de chine*. In the early years, the *naos* were smaller than those that would follow them in later decades as the volume of trade with China increased. But even these first galleons, as we call them today, carried fabulous cargos whose value in modern-day currency boggles the imagination. In the course of two hundred-fifty years of cross-Pacific voyages, dozens of the *naos* were lost, along with thousands of men, women and children—and unfathomable millions in treasure. Some sailed away and were simply never heard from again; some foundered on remote islands and reefs, some were seized by enemy ships, and others endured hardships beyond imagining, like the *San Jose*, found drifting off the coast of California in the mid-17ᵗʰ century, her sails aback and not a living soul found alive of the original 450 passengers and crew who had boarded her in Manila a year earlier.

The galleons were the lifeblood, the vital jugular vein of trade for the remote Spanish colony in the Philippines. Loss of the annual galleons to storms, disease, pirates, or enemy naval vessels brought great suffering and economic strife. Following the consecutive loss of two galleons in 1638, a writer of the time wrote, *"There is a universal sorrow and gloom over all the country such as it has never known before."* The numerous losses of galleons in the closing years of the 17th century caused *Manilenos* to lament, *"The resources of our citizens are exhausted, their daughters are without dowries... the wives of those who went down at sea are in miserable widowhood and their children in helpless orphanages. Priests, soldiers, maidens and widows, whose sustenance was secured by the charitable foundations, are perishing."*

The westward-bound galleons typically departed Acapulco in January or February, loaded with silver and hundreds of ambitious Spaniards bent upon achieving great wealth from the galleon trade with China. These Conquistadores labored under no benign intention of developing the Spanish colony's natural resources. Quick wealth was their only aim, and they brought with them millions of pesos in minted silver coins and tons of silver bullion from the mines of Peru, Bolivia and the silver mines of Zacatecas, Pachuca and Guanajuato in present-day Mexico. The mere act of transporting the silver from *Nueva Espana* across the Pacific to the Philippines doubled the silver's value when used in trade with the Chinese.

But the richest of the *naos de chine* were the east-bound ones. From Manila, the *naos* bound for Acapulco departed ideally in June or July, just before onset of the annual monsoons, and were crammed with the finest Chinese silks and brocades in existence, exquisite Chinese porcelain, gold bullion, hand-fashioned gold chain necklaces and jewelry of every description made from the purest 22.5 carat gold transshipped from India; pearls, diamonds and semi-precious stones from Siam (Thailand), Ceylon (Sri Lanka) and Burma (Myanmar); delicately spun silver and gold filigree boxes, buttons, buckles, broaches, and crucifixes of both gold and silver, many of which were mounted with faceted and polished jewels of every description; intricately carved jade and ivory statuettes, and a variety of spices to please the palates of European royalty and the well-to-do of Iberian society.

In terms of navigation and general suffering of crew and passengers, the westward-bound *naos* had the easier passage. From Acapulco, the cross-Pacific voyage to the Philippines was normally completed in roughly 3 to 4 months, the westward track being as much as forty degrees of latitude south of the colder and stormier *tornaviaje*, or return route, taken by the eastward-bound Manila *naos*.

Leaving Acapulco at approximately sixteen and a half degrees north latitude, the *nao* sailed south and west, dropping down to the tenth or eleventh parallel in order to fall in with the steady easterly trade winds that bore her across the "Spanish lake," as the boastful Spaniards sometimes called the 70,000,000 square miles of the Pacific Ocean. After sixty or seventy days under sail, the Acapulco *nao* changed course slightly to carry her up to the thirteenth or fourteenth parallel to intercept the *Ladrones* (Marianas Islands), where she dropped off official mail and supplies at Guam or Saipan, watered and took on fresh provisions.

On average, two to three weeks more of downwind sailing and the *nao* would spy Cape Espiritu Santo on Samar, Philippines. From there, the *nao* began the tedious and exceedingly dangerous navigation among the treacherous tides and currents in the confined passages of the San Bernardino Straits to reach her home port of Manila Bay and Cavite harbor, which were located on the opposite or western side of Luzon island.

Although the weather and distances were more favorable for the Acapulco-to-Manila crossing, that is not to say that those westward voyages were easy and uneventful. If the departure from Acapulco was delayed by more than a couple of months, contrary winds and oppressively hot weather were likely to be encountered, inviting starvation and epidemics to strike. Weather and sea were not the only dangers to a westward crossing. The passengers and crew were an eclectic mix, and not always a congenial one. Jesuits, Dominicans, Augustinians and Franciscans of the Roman Catholic Church, hardened soldiers and sailors from the vicious and bloody civil wars of Peru, companies of uniformed veteran infantry serving the Spanish Crown, royal appointees and their families and retinues, political exiles and conscripted Mexicans conspired to foment mutiny on more than one occasion. The *San Geronimo,* which cleared Acapulco for the Philippines early in 1567, experienced no less than 2 mutinies before reaching Manila, and ended up abandoning one of the mutiny leaders and twenty-five of his companions on an island in the Carolines, never to be seen or heard from again.

But it is the sagas of the east-bound *naos* that capture our imagination; struggling to make their way back to *Nueva Espana*, and the annual *feria*

5

in Acapulco, where their cargo was to be sold at enormous profit and all labors and dangers rewarded.

A well-traveled and oft-quoted Italian of the late 17th century, Gemelli Careri, described the Philippines-to-Americas voyage thusly:

> *"the longest and most dreadful of any in the World.... because of the vast Ocean to be cross'd, being almost the one-half of the Terraqueous Globe, with the Wind almost always a-head; as for the terrible Tempests that happen there, one upon the back of another, and for the desperate Diseases that seize People, in 7 or 8 Months, lying at Sea sometimes near the Line, sometimes cold, sometimes temperate, and sometimes hot, which is enough to Destroy a Man of Steel, much more Flesh and Blood, which at Sea had but indifferent Food.... Many galleons are lost, and others, having spent their Masts, or drove by contrary Winds, return, when they are half way over, after losing many Men at Sea, and the best but ill condition'd.*

> *"there is hunger, thirst, sickness, cold, continual watching, and other sufferings....Abundance of flies fall into dishes of broth, in which there also swim worms of several sorts....On fish days the common diet was old rank fish boil'd in fair water and salt; at noon, we had 'mongos,' something like kidney beans, in which there were so many maggots, they swam at top of the broth, and the quantity was so great, that besides the loathing they caus'd, I doubted whether the dinner was fish or flesh."*

Unlike the faster 3-to 4-month average of the Acapulco-to-Manila voyage, the *naos* bound from Manila eastward with their holds and decks stuffed to the bursting point with treasures of China and the East, and loaded with hundreds of passengers anxious to return with their wealth to the Americas or Spain, endured passages that frequently took 6 to 8 months or more, testing ship and passengers to the breaking point. The route of the *tornaviaje* back to Acapulco required the *naos* to sail northward from the Philippines, passing to the east of Japan to reach the higher latitudes above 30 to 40 degrees North before finally turning east to ride the prevailing easterlies and the Kuroshio current across the cold and stormy northern Pacific Ocean.

The grim sufferings of passengers and crew usually began as the *nao* reached the six-month period of time at sea. By this time, all of the fresh provisions including the live hogs, chicken and cattle, as well as most of the sea biscuits, dry garbanzos, smoked fish and salted meat had been eaten. The cold and wet weather, the monotony and unhealthiness of confined quarters, the violent storms and constant sea motion, lack of food and fresh water, the increasing population of rats and roaches, all conspired to open the flood gates of disease and madness. Again, the Italian traveler, Gemelli Careri describes it best:

> *"There are two dangerous Diseases of this Voyage, Berben which swells the Body and makes the Patient die talking. The other is the Dutch Disease, or sea-scurvy, which makes all the Mouth sore, putrifies the Gums, and makes the Teeth fall out.*

> *"The Ship swarms with little Vermine, the Spaniards call Gorgojos, bred in the Biskit; so swift that they in a short time not only run over Cabbins, beds, and the very dishes the Men eat on, but incessantly fasten upon the Body. There are several other sorts of Vermine of sundry Colours that suck the Blood."*

In the closing weeks of a protracted voyage, passengers and crew were overcome with physical collapse, madness and desperation, unable to bear any more the starvation and diseases that racked their bodies and minds. Some simply jumped overboard, others slit their throats, or just crumpled to the deck to expire where they lay. Following his agonizing cross-Pacific passage from Manila, Gemelli Careri wrote from Acapulco,

> *"But for my own part, these nor greater hopes shall not prevail with me to undertake the Voyage again, which is enough to destroy a Man, or make him unfit for anything as long as he lives."*

Dcuments on deposit at the *Archivo General de Las Indias* in Seville, Spain, suggest that dozens of the *naos* were lost during the two and one-half centuries of the long and deadly Pacific navigation. Of those whose fate we know for certain, their tragedies can only leave us in awe of the relentless and unforgiving forces of wind and sea. The *Espiritu Santo* departed Cavite, Philippines, in 1604, and was within sight of Cape Mendocino, California, when assaulted for 12 days by a monstrous gale, then twice struck by lightening, killing 3 and injuring 8 on the first strike, and stunning sixteen on the second. In February 1746, the *Santo Domingo* barely made it into Matanchel harbor, *Nueva Espana*, after weathering no less than sixteen storms during her crossing of the great Pacific Ocean. And then there is the *Santa Margarita* of 1600, that beat about through 8 months of storms, only to founder on one of the *Ladrones* (Marianas), losing all but fifty of the original 260 who had boarded her in Manila. Her fate was learned only when another *nao*, the *Santo Tomas*, passed through the *Ladrones* months later and a former crewman of the *Santa Margarita* paddled out in a native canoe to tell the tale of her final moments.

The roll call of tragedies goes on and on: The *San Felipe*, her passengers and cargo lost in 1596; the *San Nicolas* lost in 1621, with 330 souls aboard; the *San Ambrosio* wrecked in 1639 with a loss of 150 persons; the *Santo Cristo de Burgos* lost in 1693, and her fate not learned until 2 years later when pieces of charred wood washed ashore in testimony of her burning on the open sea; the *San José*, the largest galleon built to date, lost in 1694 almost within sight of Manila Bay with over 400 persons drowning, described by Padre Casimiro Diaz as, *"No larger or richer galleon had ploughed the sea, for the wealth that she carried was incredible;"* the first of the two *naos* named *La Nuestra Senora de la Concepcion*, with a cargo valued in the tens of millions of dollars, driven ashore on Saipan in September 1638, where most of the survivors were killed by the island's natives; and the second *La Nuestra Senora de la Concepcion*, largest *nao* ever built and with a cargo manifest documenting the greatest treasure ever carried by a single *nao*, simply sailed into the Pacific void never to be heard from again.

As if natural disasters were not peril enough, the hated English, both privateer and commissioned man-o-war, stalked and sought to seize any unwary galleon. Capture of a *nao* burdened with cargo was considered the greatest prize by the English, whether privateer, pirate or commissioned naval vessel of the Crown. Thomas Cavendish, sailing under a protective royal warrant was the first Englishman to take one of the *naos* enroute from Manila to Acapulco. In November 1587, he took the *Santa Ana* off Cabo San Lucas, at the tip of present-day Baja California. Although the *Santa Ana* was a small *nao*, Cavendish reaped a great reward for his audacity. The royal treasurer at Manila valued the *Santa Ana's* cargo in Mexico at more than 2,000,000 pesos. The galleon was also believed to carry a large amount of undeclared gold. When Cavendish sprung open one of the chests of gold, he is reported to have exclaimed, *"Now we are rich!..."* He read from the Santa Ana's cargo manifest: *"To wit, an hundreth and 22 thousand pezos of golde; and the rest of the riches that the ship was laden with, was in silkes, sattens, damasks, with muske and divers other merchandise..."*

But the best known of the captures by the English, was Commodore Anson's seizure in 1743 of the westward-bound Acapulco galleon, *Nuestra Senora de Covadonga*, just as she was ending her long westward crossing of the Pacific and beating for the Embarcadero off Cape Espirtu Santo, Philippines. After a brief battle, Anson's frigate, the 60-gun Centurion, prevailed. The *Covadonga's* immense treasure in Mexican silver was transferred to the Centurion, and Anson escorted the *Covadonga* to Macao on the China coast where he sold her for six thousand pesos to a private merchant. During the trip to Macao, his officers and men continued to find contraband secreted in virtually every corner of the *Covadonga's* vast interior. Anson and the Centurion then continued around the world by way of the Indian Ocean and the Cape of Good Hope to England, arriving with a treasure of 1,313,843 minted silver pesos and more than 3,000 pounds of silver bullion. It took 32 horse-drawn wagons to haul the treasure from Spithead for safe-keeping at the Tower of London.

In 1811, the last of the *naos* entered the port of Acapulco. Political turmoil and revolution throughout Mexico had led to rebels seizing the silver that had been set aside to be embarked on that year's galleon, the *Magellan*, named in honor of the famed navigator and seaman who had first brought the Spaniards to the Philippines. Two years later, on October 25th 1813, King Ferdinand VII, by royal decree suppressed the line and the *Magellan*, last of the great *naos*, cleared Acapulco for her homeport of Manila, completing the final voyage of the longest navigation in the world.

EXTRACTS FROM THE PERSONAL JOURNAL OF THIRD LIEUTENANT SAMUEL WHITE, HMS CYGNET, a 56-gun British man-of-war

May 24th, 1699

Western Pacific, Lat 27° N, Long. 154°, 09'W

Hove-to

A remarkable day. The foremast lookout spied a low-lying island in the northern quarter shortly after daybreak and Master Greene ordered a change of course to bring us closer. The island did not appear on our charts and we began soundings while still several leagues distant. Captain Wellcome, indisposed with gout, was informed of the change in course but remained in his cabin. Winds being light to moderate, upper courses were shortened, sheets eased, and we closed carefully. To our surprise, a plume of thick smoke suddenly rose from the island. Climbed the starboard main ratlines along with Bosun's Mate Harper with spyglasses to survey the island and determine the source of the smoke.

The island was sharply pointed, thick with trees and

scrub brush and a thin scattering of wind-whipped cocoanut and palm trees at the edge of a bright coral beach being pounded by a large surf. Only a single person was seen on the beach. He appeared feeble and seemed to stagger about rather than walk. On orders from Master Green, launched the starboard cutter at 10 AM with Sergeant Burton of the marines in command, accompanied by six crew, all armed. Signals from Sgt. Burton on landing confirmed the presence of only one person and the request to bring him to the ship was granted by Master Greene.

After some difficulty getting the cutter through the surf, ship's party and castaway arrived alongside. The frail condition of the castaway occasioned his being brought on deck by a quickly improvised canvass sling. The ship's surgeon gave the poor soul's emaciated body a quick going over. The obvious effects of starvation and exposure, plus numerous pus-oozing infectious cuts about the feet and legs led the surgeon to declare that the castaway would not survive more than a day or two at the most. The surgeon was also able to decipher from the castaway's feeble whispers that he was speaking Spanish. Our Spanish guest was transported below decks to be ministered to by the surgeon. Officers of the deck took the noon latitude, checked the log to advance the previous evening's lunar observations and recorded our position. Top gallants were restored, our course regained, sheets tightened and we bore away from the tiny island, losing sight of it within the hour.

Summoned by Captain Wellcome to his cabin, which was attended by First Lieutenant Shaw and several other ship's officers. Captain Wellcome asked of my rumored proficiency in speaking the Spanish language. I acknowledged a minuscule ability, informing Captain Wellcome of my having a Spanish-speaking nanny for five years of my youth. Captain Wellcome ordered me to confer with the ship's surgeon and at first opportunity to question the Spanish castaway as to how he came to be a castaway. Special attention was to be given to any information regarding Spanish trading galleons, their harbours and recent naval activities.

I repaired immediately below decks to the surgeon's cabin. Looking over the shoulder of the ship's surgeon, I gained my first close look at the poor devil, writhing and moaning as he lay in a canvass hammock. He was in a terrible state, sun-burnt skin stretched tautly over a rib cage made prominent by the rigors of starvation. Some of his lacerations had already been bandaged, and the surgeon had coated him from head to toe in lard. His eyes were closed and he strained at the rope restraints about his wrists as the surgeon cut foul flesh from his legs and swabbed his many wounds with a coarse cloth. The surgeon informed me that he had administered a fair measure of laudanum earlier and said questioning would have to wait until the morrow—if the Spaniard made it through the night.

May 25, 1699

Western Pacific, Lat 27°N, Long. 154°, 50'W

All sails set in light winds with a large following sea. Great curiosity among the crew regarding the Spanish castaway who had been heard moaning and occasionally screaming during the night. Returned to the sick bay to find the Spaniard's eyes open but he still under the effect of the laudanum. The surgeon had retired to his bunk after a long night of attending to the Spaniard's wounds and his assistant said the Spaniard had been given small amounts of water throughout the night and had consumed a teacup of broth just before dawn. But lest I be encouraged, the surgeon's assistant shook his head as he lifted a corner of the cloth covering the Spaniard's right leg revealing a swelling and putrid mass of decaying flesh extending from toes to kneecap. *The surgeon's assistant said the leg would come off that evening as soon as the surgeon was restored. It was his estimation that the Spaniard would not survive the procedure. When I glanced at the Spaniard's face, his black opal eyes were fixed on me with a distant curiosity. All I could manage was to wish him good luck.* "Buena suerte, senor." *With either a grimace or a resigned smile, I could not tell which, he closed his eyes.*

May 26, 1699

Western Pacific, Lat 27°N, Long. 156°, 25' W

Winds rising but are abaft the beam. We make good eastward progress. Informed that the ship's surgeon removed the Spaniard's right leg above the knee. Unfortunately, other infectious cuts and the results of his protracted deprivations have left the Spaniard at Death's door. I reported same to First Lieutenant Shaw. Visited the surgeon's cabin after change of watch, but the Spaniard was unconscious.

May 27, 1699

Western Pacific, Lat 27°N, Long. 158°, 10'W

Moderate gale in the first half and later calming. Captain Wellcome called for gunnery practice. Competition among the batteries was lively, the starboard Red Crew's 24-pounders winning. Guns were swabbed and secured. Captain Wellcome well pleased with the gunnery and ordered the opening of a bottle of Spanish carrack which we had taken from a coastal schooner off Guam and saw it distributed to the crew. Repaired to the surgeon's cabin for a look at the Spaniard. He seems improved but is barely lucid. Attempted a conversation but he whispers weakly and the noise of the ship makes it impossible to understand him. He made gestures for a quill and paper. I am encouraged at this possible line of communication and provided the necessities but the Spaniard's frailty and the ship's motion conspired to render his penmanship illegible. He does convey

14

that his intent is to write a farewell letter to his family in Spain. I am persuaded that he is aware he will not likely survive his present calamity. We agree to try again on the morrow. Later, joined Lieutenant Shaw and junior officers of the first watch for an evening of whist. Continued my winning streak.

May 28, 1699

Western Pacific, Lat 27°N, Long. 160°, 25'W

Fresh breeze with large following sea. All courses set and topside crew put to repairing cordage and running rigging. Overseeing the securing of our first bower when interrupted by the surgeon's assistant. The Spaniard is again asking for writing materials. In the surgeon's cabin I am informed by the surgeon that the Spaniard's remaining leg is worsening but the loss of blood in removing the right leg prevents its immediate removal. He fears the Spaniard will soon succumb to his wounds no matter the effort to save his life. He says he will no longer administer laudanum, saving his meager supply for our own crew. I attempt a conversation with the Spaniard, asking the name of the ship from which he was stranded. Unable to make out his speech, but he writes, "Santo Nino." I ask her port of origin and destination and he writes, "Ladrones," then, "Acapulco." I ask his name and he writes, "Capitan Emilio Bustamente de la Vega." I ask the nature of his voyage and he writes that he has been transferred to the military garrison at Veracruz. When I ask how he came to be a castaway, he whispered feebly, "Una tormenta terrible." The best I could muster in Spanish was to ask the equivalent of "The sea, you were pushed into it?" No, he said, the boat was lost. I asked how many were aboard and where they are now. Again he chose to speak rather than write: "Setenta," seventy, he says. "Todo son murio." All are dead. It was then that he grasped my wrist and said, "Soy un Catolico. ?Y usted?" I am a Catholic. And you? I tell him I am Protestant. Church of England. He smiles and says, "Pero un Dios, para nosotros, si?" But only one God for us both, yes?

I agreed, then he spoke more urgently, telling me that he was sure he did not have long to live and wanted to write the Catholic Pope to convey his prayer for absolution of his earthly sins. He beseeched me in the name of our mutual love for the Savior to make every effort to see it delivered. I gave my word as a naval officer that I would see the letter was sent, but that he must understand the current state of hostilities between our respective countries may cause some delay. He smiled and said that in this matter, time was of no consequence. Then he asked if it would be less difficult for me politically if I sent his letter to the Church in Rome via a Catholic priest in England. I told him I saw no great difficulty in sending a copy to both. I arranged with the surgeon for quill, ink and paper.

Reported immediately to Captain Wellcome, telling him that the Spanish castaway's name was Capitan Emilio Bustamente de la Vega, that he was a military officer but not a naval officer and that he had been a passenger aboard a Spanish trading schooner named Santo Nino enroute from the Ladrones to Acapulco, and that seventy souls had been lost when the schooner was overcome by a storm. Captain Wellcome inquired as to the Spaniard's state of health and I told him there was little hope for his survival. I was dismissed without further comment from the Captain and returned to my duties.

May 29, 1699

Western Pacific, Lat 27°N, Long. 162°, 50' W

Barometer falling steadily and winds increasing to near 40 knots. All topsails furled and secured. Following morning watch, visited the Spaniard Bustamente. Found him to be only mildly improved in his physical condition and disconsolate over his inability to write legibly. I notice he is writing in Latin with what was once an impressive court hand, but I agree with him that it is difficult to read. Fortunately my schooling included lessons in Latin, so I offer to transcribe in my own hand. He accepts and I begin to read his text back to him, he correcting me as necessary. He asks if I know the name of the island where he was stranded. I tell him it was uncharted and therefore had no name. He asked if I knew the charted position and I gave him the latitude and longitude as I had entered it in my log. He repeated the coordinates, then remarked that it still seemed a long way to Acapulco. I agreed. He signs his name to the transcription with a great flourish and appends beneath his signature, in Spanish, 'Loyalty to the Crown and Defender of the

Faith', which he explains is drawn from his family crest. I take the letter to my own cabin for later transcription of the second copy.

May 30, 1699

Western Pacific, Lat 27, Long. 165°, 00' W

Strong gale out of the northwest. Large seas and considerable motion. All gun ports battened and secured. Only fore and aft sails set and these deeply reefed. Visited the Spaniard and was startled to see the extent of the downturn in his condition. The surgeon showed me the Spaniard's remaining left leg and explained that its decaying flesh was poisoning the Spaniard's blood. In his estimation, the Spaniard would die before the next dawn. I gained the Spaniard's attention, but he was feverish and seemed to implore me, saying something about "la carta al Padre." The letter to the Catholic Pope. I assured him I would make every effort to see that it was conveyed, either through a priest in England, or courier to Rome. He attempted a smile, gave a great chest-heaving sigh, then closed his eyes.

April 1, 1699

Western Pacific, Lat. 27, Long. 167°, 20' W

Gale is moderating but seas remain large and confused. The Spaniard Bustamente has died and his mortal remains are trussed in a piece of salvaged sail and secured beneath the windward bulwark. As soon as weather permits, he will be committed to the sea. Captain Welcome has approved only a three-gun salute since we were never apprised of the Spaniard's military rank beyond his referring to himself as "captain". I am copying below the Spaniard's letter to the Catholic Pope and at first opportunity will transcribe his final words into letters which I will post upon my return to England.— End of Extract

HMS Cygnet plunged ahead in its eastward journey toward the West coast of the Americas, then south along the South American coast and through the Straits of Magellan to the Atlantic Ocean, stopping only briefly in the Falklands for watering and victualing before carrying on across the Atlantic to her home port in the Solent, adjacent to the Isle of Wight, England. There Third Lieutenant Samuel White disembarked with his sea chest, registered his arrival in the naval hall, then engaged a carriage to transport him to his family home in nearby Lymington.

On arrival, his sea chest was carried joyfully to his bedroom by his two younger brothers. The following day while enroute on horseback to the local market, Lieutenant White was thrown from his horse when it was spooked by a village dog. His head struck the top of a stone wall and he never recovered consciousness. His naval officer's uniform was removed from his sea chest and he was buried with honors in the small village cemetery. Following his burial, his mother and brothers read each and every page of his personal sea log, marveling at his adventures. They read of the Spanish castaway, and puzzled over the Latin of Bustamente's letter. But curiously, there was no evidence among the sea chest's contents of the two letters Lieutenant White had promised to send to Spain and Rome. They assumed he must have made arrangements for them sometime between his arrival at the Isle of Wight and the carriage trip home. In any case, Lieutenant White's log was returned to his sea chest which in turn was moved to the attic for storage.

The Lymington property of the White family remained in the family's possession until the end of World War II. That war took the lives of the three remaining male members of the White family line. Corporal Gerald White died of gangrene on the beaches of Dunkirk while waiting his turn to cross the Channel. Reginald White, a Royal Air Force navigator, went missing on an RAF raid over the industrial plants of the Ruhr Valley, and Dudly White, midshipman, was lost on *HMS Hood* in its fateful clash with the German battleship, *Bismarck.*

In 1947, the family estate was auctioned off and purchased by a London banker. Either following that purchase, or perhaps in a subsequent change of ownership in later years, Lieutenant White's sea chest containing his personal log from *HMS Cygnet* were removed from the attic, and along with other memorabilia and tattered household effects, made their way to various and sundry second-hand shops in the greater London area.

In 1999, a buyer from Boston purchased a large lot of period furniture and nautical items that included sextants, barometers, chronometers, ship's bells, and old ship's logs. Banded together with several dozen other ship's logs, both military and commercial, was the personal log of Third Lieutenant White, containing the final words of Capitan Emilio Bustamente de la Vega, sole survivor of the greatest treasure ship ever to sail upon the oceans of the world. Unbeknownst to any and all who handled Lieutenant White's personal journal from the voyage of *HMS Cygnet*, was the fact that the letter Capitan Bustamente dictated to Lieutenant White in May of 1699, contained a secret message encrypted using a simple substitution cipher keyed to Busatamente's family coat of arms. The cipher had been provided to his family a hundred years earlier by the Church in Rome to permit secure communications between Bustamente's powerful Andalusian family and the head of the Catholic Church. When deciphered, the message would read:

Concepcion of Manila lost. Cargo saved. Buried in cave.

Latitude 27° 15'N, Longitude 154W.

CAPITAN DON EMILIO BUSTAMENTE DE LA VEGA

"Each Chinese appears to be the devil incarnate, for there is no malice or deceit which they do not attempt. Although here in Manila they do not rob or plunder the foreigners openly, yet they do it by other and worse methods."

— Hernando de los Rios Morga, 1598

August 30, 1698

Lat. 14° 35' N, Long.121º 00 E'.

Manila, Philippines

One)

Don Emilio Bustamente de la Vega, capitan of the Manila military garrison, stomped off an agitated pace along the upper fighting platform atop the three-sided fortress wall surrounding Manila. Below him, a mean-spirited crowd of furious *Manilenos* filled the *Plaza de Armas* in front of the governor's palace. Manila's Spanish citizenry was in a mutinous uproar over the royal governor's heavy-handed edicts apportioning the "*piezas*," or shares of cargo space, aboard the soon-to-sail royal *nao, Nuestra Senora de la Concepcion.* Most were armed with machetes, knives, pikes and clubs; a few had firearms.

In response to the growing furor, *His Excellency Gobierno Julio Ruiz Obando* had ordered his personal guard of twenty arquebusiers to take up positions around the plaza and his residential palace. A contingent of Manila's military garrison under the command of Capitan Bustamente also ringed the plaza, their black-barreled arquebuses and gleaming 12-foot battle pikes sending a chilling message to the crowd. An ugly and likely bloody confrontation was building, and only the anticipated appearance of Manila's archbishop was holding events in check.

Capitan Bustamente was both angered and saddened by the events unfolding beneath him in the plaza. Normally, the impending departure of the annual galleon was cause for great cheer and endless rounds of fiestas, but the last two of the annual galleons had disappeared in the vast blue of the Pacific Ocean somewhere between Manila and Acapulco. As a result, the Spanish colony was now suffering a deep melancholy and fatalistic gloom.

The first of the missing galleons had departed Manila for Acapulco a year earlier in June 1697, laden with a great fortune in trade goods and 420 souls aboard. It should have made port by the end of the year. And the returning Acapulco galleon bearing the minted silver coins and silver bullion in payment for the earlier shipment which should have cleared Acapulco no later than January or February 1698, had failed to arrive in Manila during the normal April-to-May period. Whether the earlier Manila galleon had arrived safely in Acapulco after a typical 6-month voyage, or whether the returning Acapulco galleon had sailed on schedule, but was merely delayed by some misfortune, was unknown. The Spaniards of Manila, living at the farthest edge of the Spanish empire, knew only that hundreds of loved ones and a vast fortune were missing and unaccounted for.

Capitan Bustamente knew that if these two galleons were indeed lost forever, then some of Manila's oldest and most prominent Spanish families were near financial ruin, if not completely bankrupt. The future of these families, and indeed, the colony itself, was in great jeopardy.

The ensuing fight for survival was pivoting around the allotment of *boletas*, or tickets, that represented portions of each *Manileno's pieza*, or space reserved for shipping cargo aboard the annual galleon. The disappearance of the two galleons had left many *Manilenos* so destitute they couldn't afford to buy and ship goods, and thus were reduced to selling their *boletas* to the highest bidder. But Capitan Bustamente knew also that it wasn't a fair trade market. It was becoming increasingly obvious that the religious orders, especially the Jesuits, were cornering the market and attempting to control the value of the surplus *boletas*.

Over the past decades Manila had become an *almacén de la Fe,* or "warehouse of the Faith," bursting with a population of more than 1,500 Catholic priests, who outnumbered the total Spanish lay population. In spite of a long-standing royal edict that all Spanish citizens of Manila were to be allowed to participate in the galleon trade, the religious orders, along with a few dozen of the wealthier Spanish families, were beginning to dominate the apportioning of the galleons' precious cargo space. Corruption was rampant and to make matters worse, the royal governor, Obando, was in the forefront of those seeking to exploit the galleon trade to their own personal ends.

From his elevated perch atop Manila's fortress walls, Capitan Bustamente had a commanding view of the beleaguered city. Fronting on the *Plaza de Armas*, in addition to the governor's palace, were the prominent stone buildings of the *Cabildo*, or city hall, the colony's main cathedral, the royal treasury and various arsenals. Around and behind these impressive edifices were the monasteries and *residencias* of the Catholic religious orders, the Jesuits, Augustinians, Dominicans and Franciscans. Further down the compact cobble streets of the *Intramuros*, or walled city, were the royal hospital for Spaniards, the charitable hospital, *Hermandad de la Misericordia*, richly-endowed by the *obras pias* charity organizations to care for the children and widows of Spaniards lost on earlier galleons, and the Hospital of *San Juan de Dios* for treating the natives.

The fortress-walled *Intramuros* also contained the spacious homes of some 600 Spanish families. Since the devastating fire of 1603, most of the houses were now built of stone and topped with red tile roofs.

However, a few still had the traditional *nipa* thatch roofing. All of the residences within the *Intramuros* belonged to Spanish citizens. No Chinese or Filipino natives lived within the fortress walls of the city unless they were attached to a Spanish family. Their residences were in the villages outside the fortress walls and across the Pasig River.

Capitan Bustamente's own home, along with his mistress and their three children, was located in the *Intramuros*, and he was decidedly unhappy about the civil disturbance forming in the *Plaza de Armas* below. He was even less happy at his being summoned by the governor at a time when his most pressing concerns lay with protecting the huge fortune already aboard the new galleon lying at *Cavite*, and maintaining order along the approaches when the passengers began boarding the galleon in the coming days.

Turning his attention from the angry crowd in the *Plaza de Armas*, Capitan Bustamente looked over the fortress parapets across ten miles of Manila Bay toward the headland of *Cavite* where the new *nao de chine* was taking onboard the last of its water supply and provisions. He could not see the great galleon itself, of course, but in the fading tropical twilight he could see the soft yellow glow of hundreds of torches lighting the approaches to the galleon and the wharf alongside which it was moored.

His troops had begun guarding the huge *nao* from the moment the chests of gold bullion belonging to the royal crown had been lowered into its cavernous hold. As the hundreds of additional chests belonging to the colony's wealthiest merchants and the religious orders were secured in the lowest depths of the hold, the guard had been doubled, then tripled. Troops were now stationed not only in the *nao's* below-deck levels, but at every hatch leading to the main sailing deck and along the full length of the wharf.

But Capitan Bustamente's attention was not captured solely by his responsibilities toward protecting the *Nuestra Senora de la Concepcion* and its swelling fortune. He shifted his gaze to look down at the swarm of flickering lanterns that hung in the rigging of more than 30 *Sangley* (Chinese) junks anchored in Manila Bay immediately in front of

Manila's fortress walls. Many of the junks, perhaps twenty of them, had arrived laden with precious trade goods to be sold in exchange for Spanish silver.

However, it was the remaining junks that worried Capitan Bustamente the most. He was fully aware that they were war junks, bristling with powerful bronze cannons and each crammed with 400 or more armed *Sangley* warriors. If these dangerous military forces united with the large *Sangley* and *Moro* population that lived in the villages surrounding Manila, there was a strong likelihood that the Spanish colony could be overwhelmed and sacked.

And somewhere among those darkened war junks was Ling Po, the Chinese pirate-trader who most likely commanded the combined fleet. In recent years Capitan Bustamente's fate had become increasingly entwined with Ling Po, the two of them increasing their personal fortunes through a strange relationship between heathen and Christian that was now being tested by what appeared to be the total loss of their mutual investments aboard the previous year's missing galleon.

Don Emilio Bustamente de la Vega's family, his wealth and his future were all at extreme risk, and no matter which strategy he might employ to recoup his losses, Ling Po lay at the heart of each. Would the *Sangley* pirate continue their commercial relationship in spite of their strained financial situation, or would he cut his losses by dumping Bustamente and form some other alliance? Capitan Bustamente was roused from his troubled thoughts with a hail from one of his lieutenants standing below in the *Plaza de Armas*. "El gobierno!" shouted the lieutenant, pointing to the entrance to the Governor's palace.

Bustamente quickly descended the stone staircase that led from the upper fighting platform to the *Plaza de Armas*. At the bottom, he was immediately surrounded by a squad of his own militia, each man with a drawn sword, or brandishing a black-barreled arquebus. They moved as one into the hostile crowd and ascended the palace's stone stairs.

(Two)

Upon entering the palace salon, Capitan Bustamente was obliged to leave

24

behind his personal escort and follow the gobierno's aide down a long, candle-lit hallway leading to the governor's private office. The thick, iron-strapped doors to the official office of Manila's governor were thrown open by guards as Bustamente approached, and he strode forcefully into the elegant and spacious surroundings of Manila's absolute royal power.

Gobierno Julio Ruiz Obando, richly clothed in garments made of the finest Chinese silks colored in the scarlet and gold of Spain's royal house, sat regally behind a grand desk of polished Philippine mahogany. But Bustamente quickly saw that the colony's governor was not alone, and the makeup of the group surrounding his desk gave Bustamente's chest cause to tighten. The Archbishop of Manila, and the heads of each of the Catholic Church's religious orders, all in their dark cloaks with gleaming silver or gold crosses hanging prominently from their necks, stood together at Obando's right looking to Bustamente like black crows on a country fence surveying the landscape for a quick meal. In addition, five Spanish gentlemen from some of the wealthiest families in Manila sat before Obando's desk in sumptuous hand-carved chairs upholstered in brightly colored Chinese brocades. Each turned his head to acknowledge Bustamente's arrival.

To the royal governor's left stood two men whom Bustamente had come to dislike intensely; Capitan Luis Torres, captain of Obando's personal guard, and Capitan Juan Calderon, the newly appointed captain of the *nao de chine, Nuestra Senora de la Concepcion,* now lying at Cavite. The week before, Gobierno Obando had abruptly and with no explanation removed Rodrigo de Morga as captain of the new *nao* and replaced him with Calderon, who had arrived in Manila the year before by way of the Indian Ocean and Malaysia. Bustamente was highly suspicious of Calderon's credentials as a sea captain as well as his personal integrity. Calderon had already run up a considerable debt owing to his compulsive gambling habit, and he had been seen in the company of several widows whose husbands had been lost in earlier galleons.

Granting appointment to the captaincy of the annual galleon was a privilege of Obando's office, however, and thus sanctioned by the

Spanish crown. Bustamente could only wonder at what lay behind the sacking of Capitan Rodrigo de Morga, a respected seafarer and navigator with a reputation for keeping order aboard his ship, especially during times of trial and suffering. But Bustamente was sure that Calderon's appointment and de Morga's sacking contributed in some way to fattening the royal governor's purse.

Not until Bustamente had brought his gaze full circle did he become aware of the gathering's final member. Standing alone in the shadows of the room's far side was a tall, slender figure that he recognized instantly as a *Sangley* — a Chinese. He was dressed in the traditional black gown and high round hat of woven horsehair that signified his rank and trade. Despite the deep shadows forced by the day's failing light, Bustamente was stunned when he recognized the austere countenance of Ling Po. And though he looked overlong in his direction, as far as Bustamente could tell his gaze was not returned, the Chinaman's coal-black eyes being invisible in the darkness.

!Que Diablo! Bustamente's mind reeled. *How is it that this heathen pirate, granted my business partner in many past ventures, was included in this august gathering of Manila's most powerful?* Before he could give further thought to the matter, Governor Obando rose from behind his desk and greeted Don Emilio Bustamente de la Vega, with all the accord due a respected member of the colony's *Audencia* and Bustamente's office as Capitan of Manila's militia, the colony's largest military force.

"Buenas noches y bienvenidos, Don Bustamente!" Obando said in a booming voice with a broad smile. "We are all acquainted here, please take a seat," he said, indicating the sole remaining empty seat before his desk. "We have been discussing the unfortunate disturbance in the plaza. The Archbishop is expected to speak momentarily, so we must waste no time."

After the briefest of greetings to those assembled, Bustamente took his seat, shifting his heavy battle sword to ride alongside his left leg, and listened as Obando outlined his solution to the insurrection building in his plaza.

26

"Every effort must be made to prevent violence, at least until the *nao de chine* has sailed," Obando explained. He pointed out that an unruly crowd, particularly if aided by the Moros and Chinese in the villages, could conceivably torch the new galleon and sink her before she sailed, ending all of their prospects for financial success. Indeed, the city itself was at risk of being sacked. Therefore, Obando reasoned, some accommodation must be reached with those *Manilenos* who felt they were being excluded. Rather than relenting to their demands for a redistribution of the *boletas*, he proposed to offer those who had no money to buy trade goods be granted an extension of credit.

"We have obtained a source of credit, Don Bustamente," Obando announced with a sly smile of satisfaction crossing his face. "Our Jesuit brothers in Christ have offered to provide the funding that will permit all Manilenos to participate in the new *nao's* profits. An accord has been struck with our Sangley trading partners," Obando explained, nodding in the direction of the shadowy figure of Ling Po. "And the Jesuit order has asked for only a small consideration, one which I am confident everyone here will agree is of minor inconvenience, and will in the bargain bring our colony ever higher esteem in the eyes of the Mother Church in Rome." Obando's beady black eyes shifted to the assembled clergy. The Jesuit priest, Nicolas Vende, took the cue to speak.

"We are blessed to have the close relations with our Sangley brothers in China, to arrange a transfer of trade goods and forego payment until the return of the *nao* with its silver from *Nueva Espana*," Friar Vende began silkily. "In return we ask only that a very special gift from our Order to the Holy Father be given cargo priority aboard the *nao*. At great sacrifice and considerable cost, we have at long last prevailed upon the great Khan in China to permit the firing of a porcelain table service in the Khan's own kilns. The special kaolin clay and use of the Khan's kilns, as well as the best of his artisans, have produced a table service bearing the Holy Father's own crest that is unique in the world."

At this, Friar Vende reached behind him and removed a shimmering platter from a purple velvet sack and handed it to Obando. "This piece is from the same firing and lacks only the Holy Father's crest. The rim, as you can see is gilded in gold. We commissioned a small assortment of vases, tureens, serving dishes, and table fare of this quality to sell at the *feria* in Acapulco to pay the Khan's fee for producing our gift to the Holy Father. Our terms for the credit extension to the citizens of Manila require the inclusion of these wares aboard the *nao*."

While Friar Vende spoke, Gobierno Obando examined the porcelain platter, then passed it to one of the Spanish gentlemen seated before him, each of whom in turn passed it along until finally Don Emilio Bustamente held it in his hands. It was without question the finest piece of porcelain he had ever seen transshipped through Manila. It was incredibly light in weight and the color was an almost translucent blue-white. The gilded edge was faultlessly thin and delicate. It was the quality of table fare destined solely for the royal houses of Spain, and Bustamente knew such a shipment would bring a fortune at Acapulco's *feria*.

Clever, Friar Vende, very clever, thought Don Emilio Bustamente. The amount of space aboard the *nao* that such a shipment of porcelain would require would normally mean a tariff payment to the Spanish crown costing Manila's Jesuit order many thousands of pesos in gold. This financing arrangement with the Sangleys, really nothing more than a deferred loan payment, gave the Jesuit's cargo a free ride to the market in Acapulco. The profit from the additional porcelain was pure windfall. Well, maybe not all of it. Bustamente was confident that Gobierno Obando had a piece of the action.

Obando resumed command of the meeting. "There is one final but critical item to be addressed," he announced. "The Sangleys also require a consideration for the extension of credit," he began, once again nodding in the direction of Ling Po. "This is a difficult matter as you will soon see. The Sangleys want a representative to accompany the *nao* to Acapulco, for the purpose of overseeing the sale of goods with the understanding that their profits will be distributed to them first and then held apart from the rest of the sale. A great sum is owed them from the previous two shipments that now appear to be lost. They are unwilling to await distribution when the *nao* returns to Manila. And finally, to recoup some of their losses, they insist upon being able to use their profits at Acapulco's *feria* to buy additional silver at the same market price enjoyed by Spanish citizenry."

Obando gave the assembled members a moment to digest all of that then said, "Our Sangley guest, Ling Po, known to most of you as a trusted merchant in his own right, has volunteered to serve as the representative of the investment offered by our Jesuit brothers."

Obando had barely finished speaking before the first of the merchants rose in fury against the proposal. The very idea of a Sangley transshipping to *Espana Nueva* aboard a *nao* was itself unimaginable! And to allow a Sangley unfettered access to Spanish silver, silver that once brought to Manila, would compete against the silver held by the merchants themselves to buy Chinese goods! That was blasphemy in the highest degree!

The centuries-old racial hatred and cultural disgust of the Spaniards for Sangleys was more than evident in the heated exchanges of the other Spanish merchants as they each rose in turn to protest against Obando's announcement. Don Emilio Bustamente turned his head in Ling Po's direction to gage his Sangley partner's reaction and was not surprised to see that Ling Po was no longer hovering in the shadows, but had already exited quietly and quickly.

Obando pleaded for silence, but was shouted down by the rising emotional exchanges of the five merchants. Finally, Obando gave a nod to Capitan Luis Torres, who grabbed a battle pike from one of the guards, and struck the flooring with great force.

"You forget yourselves, Senores," Gobierno Obando said in a commanding voice. "I am the King's appointed servant in this matter, and it is I who will decide. Obando then lowered his voice and spoke conspiratorially, an oily smirk spreading across his face. "Of course, no *Sangley* will accompany the *nao* to Acapulco, much less be allowed access to the *feria*. I have spoken at length with Ling Po, and we have reached a compromise. I will choose one of our own to represent Ling Po at the *feria* and watch over his investment, as well as the credit expenditures in behalf of Manilenos, and Ling Po will be allowed to approve or disapprove of my selection."

(Three)

Don Emilio Bustamente was furious. No, it was more than that. He was apoplectic to the point of contemplating murder of the first *Sangley* he laid his eyes upon. His jaw was so tightly clenched in anger that every jolt his carriage received when it hit a rut in the road struck painfully at the base of his skull. He was being propelled through the early dusk down the road leading from Manila's fortress, across the Pasig River, to the Parian wherein resided Manila's Chinese and Moro population. Behind the carriage, nine mounted and well-armed militiamen under Bustamente's command rode to protect their leader against whatever the tense tropical night might throw against them. In the present circumstances, anything was possible.

Gobierno Obando had terminated the earlier conference with a royal command that he, Don Emilio Bustamente de la Vega, was to sail to *Nueva Espana* on the new *nao* to represent Ling Po's investments. Capitan Luis Torres would assume temporary command of the Manila militia during Bustamente's year-long absence as he sailed across the Pacific to Acapulco, and back to Manila next year. A perilous journey beyond description, and his family unprotected in Manila. It was inconceivable!

As Bustamente's open carriage clattered across the bridge into the Parian, he was acutely aware of the heightened activity among its residents. Hordes of Chinese and Moro natives were scurrying to and fro in every direction; the din was deafening, the smell was overpowering, and every house and building was alight with lanterns and candles. Bustamente's carriage and mounted guard drew little attention in the melee, but Bustamente knew from long experience living in Manila that his every move was being watched by the Moros and the *Sangleys*. He also knew with the certainty of a seasoned soldier that his puny force of mounted militia would be quickly overcome if a confrontation with the *Sangleys* broke out. He was not looking for a confrontation; but by God he was determined to have an explanation from Ling Po, and a sorting out of just where their relationship stood.

In the course of the past couple of decades, the population of "Christian" Chinese had risen to more than fifteen thousand, with another five or more thousand of dubious conversion. The size of the *Sangley* population, when compared to the Spanish population of only a couple of thousand, gave Spaniards cause for considerable concern of an uprising against their colony and their small numbers. It was not an unwarranted fear. Several times since the founding of Manila, the Chinese had attempted to overrun the colony. In 1574, a fleet of 70 war junks had descended upon Manila to kill all Spaniards and seize the town, but had been turned back at great loss to the desperate Spaniards. The Spaniards had then proceeded to slaughter every *Sangley* in sight, thousands and thousands of them. Just a few years later, in 1593, the Spanish governor at the time, Gomez Dasmarinas, was murdered by the *Sangley* rowers of his galley. The hatred and suspicion of the two races for each other only heightened; ten years later, in 1603, another uprising that resulted in the slaughter of an estimated twenty-three thousand *Sangleys*. There had been less than 700 Spaniards in Manila at the beginning of that particular insurrection, and more than half of them were dead or wounded at its conclusion.

When Bustamente's carriage pulled up to the broad porch of a large, two-story stone warehouse, one of the oldest structures in the Parian, his escort remained mounted. No sooner than Bustamente exited the carriage, Lingo Po stepped onto the porch holding an exquisite mother-of-pearl lacquered tray bearing a steaming porcelain teapot and three delicately crafted cups. He bowed gracefully to Bustamente, waved a hand of dismissal to over a dozen Chinese attendants on the porch to clear the way, and greeted Bustamente warmly, but formally. "Buenas noches, Your Excellency. Mi casa es tu casa," he said with a thin smile, and gestured with the teapot to an elegantly upholstered sedan chair and polished mahogany table.

It never ceased to irk Bustamente that this heathen Chinese spoke

Bustamente's native language so well and that Bustamente, despite the many years of their association, had mastered only a few very basic Mandarin expressions. But he acknowledged grudgingly that the progress of their partnership would have been seriously hampered without Ling Po's fluency. He took the steps up to the porch two at a time, holding his battle sword in its place and returned Ling Po's bow, saying "El gusto es mio, Senor. Bien venidos a Manila. ?Como te vas?"

"I am well, but troubled, my friend," Ling Po responded. "But no less so than you, I am sure. Gobierno Obando is a dark spirit. It is not my doing that he sends you to Acapulco. We must talk further on this matter, but I think we must include someone else in our conversation." With that,

Lingo Po motioned toward the dark interior of the building, and from its shadows stepped a grim-faced Capitan Rodrigo de Morga, former capitan of the soon-to-sail *nao*, *La Nuestra Senora de la Concepcion*, who had been relieved of his command without explanation by Gobierno Obando.   .

PORTER & THE SEA BONES

October 27, 2000

Lat. 26º 4' N, Long. 77º 2' W

Harbor Point Yacht Club, Ft. Lauderdale, FL

> "Captain Porter of the *Sea Bones*. Captain
> Porter of the *Sea Bones*. You have a UPS
> delivery at the office."

Jake Porter was wrestling the new 25-horsepower Mercury outboard
motor onto the transom of the *Sea Bones*' fiberglass tender, a 13-
foot Boston Whaler, when the announcement came over the
marina's public address system.

"Got to be the transducer," he said aloud and to himself.

He tightened the last of the lugs securing the motor to the Whaler's
transom, then jumped onto the *Sea Bones*' slotted teak swim
platform. From there he passed through the yacht's open transom
doors, past the two fighting chairs and up the starboard
companionway to the boarding ramp leading to the dock.

The 72-foot long *Sea Bones* occupied a slip just inside the T-head at the far end of the Harbor Point Yacht Club's Pier A. Jake grabbed a dark green, short-sleeved knit shirt that was draped over the *Sea Bones'* rail and slipped it over his head as he made his way to the marina office. Club decorum decreed shirt, trousers or shorts, and deck shoes—no tank tops, cut-offs or flip flops. Jake's shirt was custom-embroidered with a leaping silver marlin over the pocket. Across the top of the marlin was the name, *Sea Bones*, and below it, *Captain*.

It was a short walk of some 200 yards down the dock to the marina office, passing along the way many millions of dollars in members' yachts. The UPS package sat on the counter top at the receptionist's desk. "I signed for you, Jake," said the middle-aged woman sitting behind the desk, a telephone headset draped around her neck. "The driver was running behind," she added. The return address on the package confirmed the sender was the Texas manufacturer of *Sea Bones'* transducer.

"No problem, Millie," Jake said. "I've been waiting two weeks for this sucker."

"Are you still planning to top off your fuel before six this evening?" Millie asked. Club policy prohibited fueling after six o'clock for safety reasons.

"Yes," Jake answered. "Doctor Ambrose and his party want an early start tomorrow. And would you let the guard at the gate know that a truck from the Fresh Market will be arriving sometime after four o'clock? Just have them use one of the club's dock carts to haul it all down alongside the *Sea Bones*. I'll take it from there. Nobody's to go aboard. I don't want any dirty shoes tracking up the deck, okay?"

"Will do. And if I don't see you before you leave, have a safe journey," Millie said. *And if I were twenty years younger, you handsome devil, I'd be working some kind of an angle to be bedding down with you during that wicked voyage.*

Jake left with the package under his arm, and half-way back to the

Sea Bones, he used his cell phone to call the *Sea Bones'* owner, Dr. Jerome Ambrose. He left a message with Ambrose's office that the transducer had arrived and everything was on schedule for tomorrow morning's departure.

Back aboard the *Sea Bones*, Jake carefully removed the transducer from the styrofoam peanut packing. It looked to have survived the journey from Texas intact. Jake then called a local diver to arrange for the transducer's installation beneath *Sea Bones'* hull. The installation was a simple procedure and under other circumstances, Jake would have grabbed a SCUBA rig and done it himself. But he had his hands full handling the logistics involved in taking a 72-foot luxury motor yacht to sea for a week with eight guests and two crew aboard.

Jake had spent the past week putting all of *Sea Bones'* shipboard systems through operational tests, beginning with oil and filter changes for the two 350-hp GM diesels that drove her at up to 22 knots, and the Kohler auxiliary power unit that supplied electrical power while away from shore power. All pumps had been put through their paces, from electric discharge pumps for the four heads, to emergency bilge pumps, galley fresh water and seawater pumps, and even the seawater pump for washing down the decks topside. Filters were changed, diaphragms lubricated, hose clamps checked and through-hull seacocks rotated through open and closed positions.

Next came the electronics. VHF marine radios, GPS navigation receiver, weather fax machine, depth finder, autopilot, radar, hailer, spotlights, running lights and the stem-to-stern stereo system. At present, the *Sea Bones'* electrical systems were being supplied with shore power, but before leaving the dock Jake would fire-up the Kohler generator as well as the two main diesels, each of which had belt-driven 220-amp alternators to keep the battery banks fully charged.

The moment of truth would come when he disconnected the two large yellow power cords from shore power and the *Sea Bones'* shipboard power grid took over. Jake would take that leap when all the fresh provisions were onboard, and he was ready to move the *Sea Bones* from her berth to the club's fueling dock.

Jake was making his way aft down the *Sea Bones'* starboard side to continue preparing the tender for the coming voyage, intending to snap on her weather cover and lift her out of the water with the electric-powered davits when his cell phone rang. It was Cindy Wright.

Cindy was the young woman whom Jake usually called on to serve as cook and galley maid for Dr. Ambrose's impromptu Bahamas voyages. She was a bright-eyed, good-looking, sandy-haired blond and was a graduate of the Culinary Institute of America in New York. After graduation from the CIA, she had migrated to the swanky eateries of Miami Beach and environs. From there it was a small leap to become the personal chef of a wealthy Cuban with a 20-million dollar, 210-foot yacht. During a port-of-call in the British Virgins aboard the Cuban's floating palace, she had fallen in with a bunch of hard-partying sail boaters and been swept off her feet by a handsome, sweet-talking yacht captain from Galveston, Texas. Cindy jumped ship and she and her captain-lover bought a 57-foot Summers-designed cutter, teamed up as captain and first mate/galley maid and chartered throughout the Caribbean to Yankee snowbirds.

Each year they brought their sailing yacht to south Florida for an annual haul-out and refitting. While ashore, Cindy left the boat maintenance to her lover-captain, and kept the cash flowing by cooking and catering parties for assorted clients. She had first met Jake, and later Dr. Ambrose, at Sammon's Boat Yard where the *Sea Bones* had been hauled out alongside her own cutter. She would never forget the first time Jake had asked her to go on a "special cruise" to the Bahamas. The "special" translated into some pornographic filming. The "actors" and filming crew would join the boat in the Bahamas for a week of cinematography porn and partying. Jake had been careful to spell out Cindy's role as solely chef and crew. And the generous tips had been forth coming as Jake had promised.

"'lo Cindy. What's up?" Jake asked.

"You're going to want to kill me," Cindy said in a tone of voice that was clearly distressed. "Dan and I were moving our 100-lb. Luke anchor dockside this morning for scraping and painting. The damn thing flipped over and one of the flukes landed on my left foot. No broken bones, but my foot's as big as an ice chest. I can't even stand up. I am *so* sorry, Jake, I know this puts you in a bind."

"Yeah, trying to find a gourmet chef between now and tomorrow morning's kick-off is going to be a bit of a problem," Jake said with heavy resignation in his voice.

"I have an idea, if you're interested," Cindy said.

"I'm all ears," Jake said.

"You know Brenda, the gal who paints boat names over at Sammon's? You've seen her around, I'm sure."

"Yeah, a real looker and hangs out with a big bruiser of a guy," said Jake, "but can she cook and serve? More to the point, can she handle a galley and a half-dozen or so crazies for a week in the islands? And is she available on short notice—like tomorrow morning?"

"The 'bruiser' is Dwight something. I don't remember his last name. He was a football player with the Miami Dolphins for a few seasons until he was cut after being arrested at a brawl at a South Beach watering hole carrying a gun. As to Brenda, I'm not very tight with her, actually. But we've chatted a few times at some of the evening get-togethers at Sammon's. She's pleasant to be around and sharp topside. More to the point, she went to some chef school in San Francisco, as I recall. And she worked the crewed charter scene in the Virgins for several years. I figure she's seen her share of bare-butt crazies, so I don't think the Doctor's filming project will freak her out."

"Okay, I'll check her out," Jake said. "But I've got to run, Cindy. I have a diver coming over to install a transducer, and perishables will be arriving dockside soon, and I still need to top off the *Sea Bones'* fuel. Take care of that foot. See you when I get back." He disconnected with Cindy, then called Sammon's Boat Yard and asked if Brenda was working on any boats in the yard. He realized he didn't even know her last name. The answer was yes; she was working on *Beelzebub*, a black-hulled 47-foot Hinkley yawl.

Jake headed for his vintage Volvo station wagon and when he passed through the Harbor Point Yacht Club's gate, he told the guard to expect a diver and that he would find the new transducer waiting for him in *Sea Bones'* port side fighting chair.

The drive to Sammon's Boat Yard was little more than ten minutes. Jake drove past the two huge, rusting anchors in front of the sagging chain-link fence that more or less surrounded the boat yard and parked alongside the largest of three World War II steel Quonset huts that served as the yard's office and parts department.

It looked like the yard was having a good season. Jake noted more than three dozen assorted power boats and sailing yachts out of the water surrounded by an impressive gaggle of boat people of every size and description massaging their boats in one fashion or another.

Sammon's Boat Yard was a cultural phenomenon as much as it was a boat yard. One of the few remaining do-it-yourself yards that permitted owners to do their own repair work, Sammon's was the gathering place of one of the most eclectic boating communities anywhere. At one time or another, just about every type of sailor and adventurer passed through. Charter boat crews, round-the-worlders, Caribbean lay-a-bouts, pirates and mercenaries, salvers and treasure hunters, modern-day pirates, hustlers of every description, and plenty of just plain folks who had discovered the magic of living and traveling on the ocean.

Jake had no trouble finding Brenda. She was perched atop a folding ladder, straddling its top with long, perfectly tanned legs and stretching with a brush to put a final touch to *Beelzebub's* transom. Beneath her a bunch of appreciative male yachties lounged casually about the base of the ladder sitting on or leaning against some old 55-gallon steel barrels to either side of Beelzebub's stern. With beers in hands, they were chatting up Brenda over her artistic endeavors, while soaking in eyefuls of Brenda's very brief shorts stretched tightly over a perfectly formed derriere.

Beneath a broad-brimmed Bahamian straw hat, Brenda wore a bright orange kerchief blouse that barely contained a bosom of the kind that most men only dreamed of caressing. Each time she leaned toward *Beelzebub's* transom to apply a stroke of paint, her breasts strained against the kerchief and her shorts rode up to reveal the juncture of legs and derriere. It caused the beers to stop in mid-lift and the conversation to stammer.

Jake had stopped some fifty feet away to watch, and after a few minutes strongly suspected Brenda was playing to her audience. Some of those moves just didn't seem all that related to the painting. No doubt about it though, she was a looker. *Christ! If only she can cook, and if only she will agree to joining the Sea Bones for a week.* Then he realized the greater challenge. How was he going to explain the filming? That sort of action wasn't everyone's cup of tea. He headed for Brenda's audience feeling little prospect for success.

"Hey, Jake! What's up mate? Come down from your fancy yacht club to slum with some real boat people for a change?"

The hail came from a smiling Aussie by the name of Archie McGruder, who lived aboard a converted wooden sailing fishing boat built in the 1930s near Breton, France. Jake knew him from the anchorage where Jake kept his own boat. He was an amiable sort with a rough sense of humor who had already sailed around the world once and was now working at Sammon's to pad his traveling budget for the next leg of a second circumnavigation. No doubt he would soon be heading south to transit the Panama Canal.

"I see you still have an eye for more than shear lines, Archie. When are you casting off for the 'Canal? Jake said.

"Just as soon as I sign up Brenda here for a First Mate berth that I just happen to have vacant." Archie grinned and looked up at Brenda, "What say there, Brenda, how about Tonga or the Fijis by December?"

Brenda swung a shapely leg from over the top of the ladder and began to descend, brush and pallet in hand. "Somehow, Archie, I have the feeling there isn't enough deck space aboard your boat for me to escape your lecherous clutches."

Everyone laughed including Archie. "Spoken like a true Sheila, my love, and you know you're breaking my heart," Archie said.

"I'm sure you'll find a cure for what's ailing you on one of those South Pacific islands, Archie. You'll just have to take matters in hand until you get there," Brenda smiled sweetly. Again the assembly laughed, and when it tapered off Jake took the opportunity to speak to Brenda.

"Brenda, my name is Jake Porter. I'm captain of the *Sea Bones* and I would appreciate a moment of you time.

"Careful there, Brenda," Archie McGruder said with a sly grin, "Just because he's good looking and running a millionaire's fancy power boat don't mean he ain't after more than your time."

"The *Sea Bones*? I don't believe I know it," Brenda said, ignoring Archie's crack. She had turned to face Jake and liked what she saw. He was nice looking with an open, engaging face and a body that was naturally muscular. He stood six feet in his deck shoes and wore khaki cargo shorts and a green knit sport shirt monogrammed with a leaping silver marlin, and *Sea Bones* above it and *Captain* beneath it. His sunglasses rode atop light brown hair that was thick, wind tossed and bleached nearly blond from the sun. In short, just what you'd expect the captain of a fancy power yacht to look like.

"It's a 72-foot Bertram LRC berthed at the Harbor Point Yacht Club just off the Intracoastal."

"LRC?"

"Long Range Cruiser. Extra fuel bunkers for longer trips. Bertram turned them out semi-custom for a few years. Forgive me if I seem abrupt, Brenda, but I'm in a real time crunch and I'd appreciate it very much if we could talk privately for a few minutes."

Actually, Jake was feeling that this was all a waste of his time. There was just no way this lovely young woman was going to drop everything and leave tomorrow morning for a week-long outing with total strangers. And there was the matter of the filming, too. How to broach that particular topic and not sound like a grease ball? He was already resigning himself to driving the *Sea Bones* and handling the galley duties as well. God knows, he'd done it many times before.

"Of course," Brenda said. "Could you grab my ladder for me? She turned to her admirers and said, "See you later, boys."

Jake collapsed the aluminum ladder and followed Brenda to a panel van with a rack on top. The sides and rear doors were painted with advertising for Brenda's yacht lettering business. She opened the doors and put her brushes in some jars sitting in a wooden crate.

"So, how may I help you? The *Sea Bones* needs to have her name changed or refreshed?" She took a seat on the edge of the van's cargo deck and crossed a pair of legs that Jake found hard not to look at. The deep cleavage and twin nipples pressing against the orange kerchief were compelling as well. *Have a good look, Captain Jake Porter. You're not such a bad sight yourself. Love those green eyes, too.*

"I wish it was that simple," Jake began, making every effort to ignore a pleasant warmth spreading across his thighs. "Actually, I'm looking for a galley mate for a week-long cruise to the Bahamas. She's got to be an above average cook, a chef really. I heard you went to a cooking school in California, and have worked the charter trade in the Virgins. The *Bones'* owner, Dr. Ambrose, his personal guest and a party of six plus you and me will be aboard. The pay is good. Five hundred dollars a day, and from previous experience I believe you may be assured of handsome tips along the way.

"That's a large party, especially if they're expecting three meals a day."

"Breakfast will be light duty, if at all," Jake said. "I'll help you as much as I can. And the *Bones* has a walk-in freezer that Doctor Ambrose keeps stocked with flash-frozen gourmet meals from his favorite New Orleans restaurant. At least half of the evening meals will require only microwaving. We'd serve those along with a fresh salad or fruit, followed by drinks." Jake was feeling like a sales representative or cruise director, and in truth, felt like he was wasting his time. He unconsciously glanced at his wristwatch, then back at Brenda.

"Hmm. And when does the cruise begin?" Brenda saw that Jake was making a concerted effort to maintain eye contact and avoid looking at her cleavage.

"That's the tough part. We're committed to a departure tomorrow morning. I've been busting butt for the past week to get everything ready. But my regular galley mate mashed her foot with an anchor this morning and can't walk."

Jake thought he sounded pathetic and he wished only to get this over with. He decided to bring his misery to a quick end. "I know it's probably impossible for you, or anyone really, to drop everything and tear off to the Bahamas on such short notice, especially with total strangers. But I thought I'd give it a try."

"When are you going to tell me about the fuck flicks?" Brenda asked smoothly. She had a hard time keeping a straight face when she saw Jake Porter's jaw drop. *Gotcha there, Captain.*

42

"How the hell...?"

Brenda smiled innocently. "Cindy Wright called me and told me about her accident. She said I should expect you. I have the impression that she holds you in high regard.

"For Pete's sake." Jake was at a loss for words.

"She also gave me the low-down on your Doctor Ambrose's cinema projects, but she said I could expect you to be a perfect gentleman. Brenda paused, then said sweetly, "If that will be the case, I accept your offer to man the galley."

"There'll ...be...no problem with the Doctor," Jake stammered, relieved at the prospect of resolving his galley mate problem, but still recovering from the 'fuck flick' comment.

"There is just one thing, however, since this is on such short notice," Brenda said with a smile.

Uh oh, here comes the deal breaker. Jake waited in anticipation.

"My van, as you can see, is filled with the tools of my trade," Brenda said. "I need to take a quick shower here at the yard and change clothes, then I need a 5-minute ride just up the river to take a look at some old British naval stuff at a nautical boutique. I'm interested in brass chronometers and old ship's bells. I want them for my houseboat. The owner of the shop is a friend and she just got in a shipment from a Boston antiques dealer. She always calls me when she has something special. If I take off for the Bahamas for a week I'm afraid all the good stuff will be gone by the time I get back. It shouldn't take more than an hour including the shower."

Still counting his good fortune, Jake said, "You've got a deal. I'll wait for you at my car. It's a white Volvo station wagon parked next to the yard office." He put Brenda's ladder on the van's roof rack while Brenda grabbed a towel and beach bag and headed for the shower.

"'Fuck flicks', for Christ's sake," Jake mumbled to himself as he headed back to his car, shaking his head in disbelief.

Jake got on his cell phone and called the Harbor Point Yacht Club to see if the diver had installed the new transducer on *Sea Bones'* hull. Good news. It was done. Jake then called the Fresh Market to get an update on the arrival of the fresh produce and meats. Four o'clock was the estimate. Plenty of time to make the trip to the boutique with Brenda. And now that Brenda was on for the trip, she could put away the food while he took the *Sea Bones* to the yacht club's fueling dock. Everything was back on track.

Jake made one more call, this one to Doctor Ambrose's office to leave a message about Cindy Wright's accident and that a new galley mate with chef credentials would be making the trip. He indicated, cryptically, that she was cool with the filming.

The ride up river to the nautical boutique was brief, but it gave Jake an opportunity to learn that Brenda's full name was Brenda Kate Warren and that she had indeed graduated from the San Francisco School of the Culinary Arts. He also learned that she had completed her Junior year at Stanford University studying psychology, but had made the mistake of having an intimate relationship with a married professor, which resulted in the two of them leaving the university. Brenda told the story in a lighthearted shorthand fashion, indicating that it was only so much water under the bridge and just a bit of youthful folly.

Brenda also confirmed that she had worked the charter boat scene in the U.S. and British Virgin Islands, mostly cooking and entertaining guests on large, fancy sailing yachts. One of them had been a 65-foot Gulfstream masthead ketch named *Backdraft* that was jointly owned by five retired New York City firemen.

"Well, then," Jake said, "you're definitely prepared for Doctor Ambrose. Cindy Wright probably told you about his lecherous ways, but I can tell you that he will mind his manners if you let him know where you stand. If you have any difficulties with him, just let me know, okay? I'll straighten it out and keep things on an even keel."

"I'm sure I can handle it," Brenda smiled. "Oh, here's the place, on the right." Jake turned his Volvo into the crushed-coral parking area of the nautical boutique.

Brenda went into the shop ahead of Jake. Jake stopped to look at an old bronze ship's binnacle on the shop's sagging front porch. When he finally went inside, he saw Brenda was talking with her shopkeeper friend and looking at a turn-of-the-century British Navy barometer and matching brass chronometer. Brenda looked up, waved him over and introduced him to Sara, the shop's owner.

"Oh, I know you," Sara said. "Well, not really you, but your boat. I saw it at the annual blessing of the fleet at the municipal marina. You and a bunch of people were on your boat. The one with the Chinese sails. The Witch, or something, she's called right?"

Jake Porter smiled. "The *Giggling Witch*."

"Oh, I just loved those dark red sails and that Chinese junk rig. She looks so exotic. Not like most of the fiberglass production boats," Sara gushed.

"She's a 'Gazelle', a Tom Colvin design. Forty-two feet. Welded steel construction. Built in the bayous of the Mississippi delta area for the owner of a company that builds steel shrimpers," Jake said with obvious pride.

"Everyone was snapping pictures of her. And that cute little dinghy you were towing, the *Wiggling Bitch*, right? We cracked up over that one. There were lots of 'ohs' and 'aahs' when you passed by the pier. Where do you keep her?"

"Most of the time she's anchored out at the Wilshire bight off the Intracoastal where the transients hang out. But when I'm occupied with the *Sea Bones*, I put her in a slip at the marina behind Sammon's Boat Yard. That's where she is now." Jake said.

"I know the *Sea Bones*, too," Sara said. That doctor who owns her has been in here a few times. He has a different woman with him each time and it seems like he is always helping them decorate an apartment or condo."

"That's my doctor," Jake smiled, giving Brenda a quick, furtive look.

I'll just be a few minutes more, Jake," Brenda said with a friendly wink. "Sara has a couple of ship's bells on the back porch she wants me to see."

"Make yourself at home, Jake," Sara said. "If you're interested in old British naval stuff, I just got in a shipment. It's spread all over the floor in the next room. Go take a look."

Jake crossed to the room Sara had indicated and went in. The room's floor was covered with all sorts of nautical junk, and the crates in which they had been shipped. On top of one of the crates was an untidy pile of old nautical charts topped by what appeared to be twenty or so ship logs in varying sizes and condition. Although relatively new to the sailing game, Jake had developed an affection for nautical charts and began to thumb through some of them, but quickly saw that they were mostly of the Mediterranean area and the Indian Ocean, and quite old. Good for framing or decorating, but of no practical use in navigating.

He then picked up several of the ship logs and thumbed through a few of them. Most of them were captains' logs of old whaling ships chasing whales in the north Atlantic, and a few merchant vessels that were plying the west coast of Africa at the turn of the 18th century. Then there was an odd one in the lot, a personal journal of an officer in the British Navy, a Third Lieutenant Samuel White. It stood out from the rest because its cloth cover had been shellacked, probably to waterproof it. The shellac was cracked, peeling and dark brown from aging. The pages inside also reflected the passage of time and were yellowed and dog-eared. But the India ink script had held up and, for the most part, was still legible.

Lieutenant White's log was written in a large, flowing script with elaborate flourishes and exaggerated ascenders and descenders. Although the lines on the pages were hand-drawn and fairly close together, it was not difficult reading. Since it was the personal log of a naval officer and not an official British Navy ship's log, it was written in a casual, almost conversational narrative style. As he thumbed through the first half of the pages covering about two years of sailing, including a passage around the Cape of Good Hope and across the Indian Ocean, he came upon a page that differed from the others. Centered in the lower half of the page and immersed in the author's narrative were two brief paragraphs written in Latin.

The Latin script stood out from the rest of the writing and caused Jake to pause. He backed up and read the portion of the log immediately preceding the Latin script. There he read the description of the rescue of a Spaniard castaway, Don Emilio Bustamente, from a Pacific island. Jake was still reading the fascinating tale of the surgery to remove Bustamente's leg and his subsequent death and burial at sea when Brenda and Sara came alongside him.

"Ready when you are, Captain," Brenda said brightly. "Find something interesting?" she asked.

"Yeah, an old British sailing journal," Jake said. He turned to Sara. "How much?"

"Those were kind of thrown in with all the other stuff I bought," Sara answered. "How about twenty dollars?"

"Deal," Jake said and fished a twenty out of his wallet.

They loaded Brenda's new purchases into the Volvo and drove to Brenda's houseboat, a well-kept 50-foot Gibson with a Bimini steering station and sun deck topside. Jake helped Brenda put her purchases on the houseboat's foredeck and offered to take her back to Sammon's to pick up her van. Brenda pointed to a bright yellow Karman Ghia and said, "That's mine. My van is safer at Sammon's if I'm going to be gone for a week. I just need to put together some clothes and stuff and then I'll drive my Ghia over to Harbor Point."

"Sounds like a plan," Jake said. "I'll leave word with the club's security guard at the gate to expect you. Tell him you're crewing on the *Sea Bones* for a week and will need a parking lot pass. Just put the pass on top of your dashboard so they can see it when they make their rounds, okay?"

"Got it," Brenda replied. "See you in a few." And with that, she disappeared into her houseboat.

(Two)

When Jake pulled into Harbor Pointe Yacht Club's parking lot, the Fresh Market truck was parked alongside the ramp leading down to the dock. He saw that one of the dock carts had already been commandeered by the driver and was on its way down to the *Sea Bones* loaded with fresh produce and galley supplies. Fresh fruit and vegetables are at a premium in the Bahamas, and priced dearly. From long experience, Jake had learned there would be no service stations or supermarkets along the way. The accepted wisdom was: bring it with you, or do without.

Besides, if the filming scenario was to be anything like the last trip, the *Sea Bones* was going to have to be self-sufficient. There would be no hanging-out at yacht clubs with shoreside facilities and prying eyes. They would be underway a lot, or for additional privacy, anchored at one or more of the tiny uninhabited cays south of Bimini. But the *Sea Bones* was well equipped for offshore cruising and hanging out in remote places. She was air conditioned throughout, had hot and cold running water in the galley and staterooms, 12-volt DC and 120 AC electrical systems, and a huge walk-in freezer and double-door refrigerator with a separate icemaker. As long as the twin-diesels purred and the Kohler generator pumped out electrical power, life aboard the *Sea Bones* would be sumptuous indeed. And it was Jake's responsibility to see that that was the case.

Jake came up beside the dock cart, stepped aboard the *Sea Bones* and went into the main salon. He tossed Lt. White's sailing journal atop the galley counter then returned to the deck outside and began stacking the boxes in the cart onto the dock. The Fresh Market's driver brought two more cartloads and helped with unloading them. After the full load was alongside the *Sea Bones*, Jake began to remove all the canned goods and stacked them in rows. Then he took the cabbages, tomatoes, lettuce, broccoli, and other fresh produce from the cardboard boxes and plunged them in a bucket of Clorox bleach-treated water to kill any bugs, roaches or spiders. He placed the loaves of bread in neat rows on the *Sea Bones'* deck. As he moved through the groceries, he carefully checked what had been delivered against his list of what Cindy Wright had ordered. It would be up to Brenda to store the supplies so she would know where everything was when she was preparing meals.

And with perfect timing, Brenda came down the dock, rounding the *Sea Bones'* bow. Jake liked what he saw. Not only was a stunning young woman approaching, she was a seasoned sailor as evidenced by the fact that she carried only one canvas duffel and a tie-string shoulder bag. Brenda was wearing a thin, pale-blue Indian madras blouse and very brief white shorts. She had a soft-brimmed sailor's hat atop her short, French-cut blond hair, and dark aviator-style sunglasses. From the gentle jiggling beneath the blouse Jake surmised correctly that her ample superstructure was standing proud and unaided by artificial support. *Damn! It's going to be a long week,* he thought, and not unpleasantly.

"Ahoy, captain! Galley slave reporting aboard," Brenda said with flashing white teeth.

"Ahoy, yourself," Jake replied, smiling and still not believing his good luck in coming up with a for-real chef, and a good looking one at that, on such short notice. "Perfect timing. I've just about got the victuals sorted out. Everything's accounted for, at least all of what Cindy ordered. Let me give you a quick tour and you can start putting things where you can find them later, okay? If there's anything missing or that you feel you will need, we can make a call to Fresh Market and have it delivered.

"Is the doctor aboard yet? Brenda asked.

"No. I expect to get a call from him within the next hour or two. Usually he has dinner downtown with his female guest and doesn't show until after 10 PM. But that's always subject to change. We'll all probably have drinks together at the club's lounge before they retire. I'll let you know as soon as I know.

"Fine," Brenda said. "I'm looking forward to meeting him. I've heard quite a bit about him today."

"He's okay really," Jake said somewhat defensively. He just likes to party and chase skirts after a hard day in the operating room."

"And the filming crew and...uh... actors?" Brenda inquired with an arched eyebrow.

"We pick them up at the Cat Cay Yacht Club on the other side of the Gulf Stream," Jake answered a bit self-consciously. "They're flying down from New York to Miami, and will take one of Chalk's amphibians to Cat Cay," he added.

Jake stepped onto the *Sea Bones'* deck, slid open the companionway door to the main salon and waved Brenda inside with a "Welcome aboard."

For a semi-custom yacht, the *Sea Bones* was nothing less than elegant. Her first owner had been a General Motors executive with a young trophy wife who spent his money with abandon. The main salon's bulkheads and cabinets were soft, rosy Honduras mahogany with solid brass fittings. The sofas and chairs were plush and covered in bright tropical hues, and the sole was topped with an immense Oriental carpet of contrasting reds, oranges, greens and gold. The wet bar was ten feet long and backed by a huge faceted mirror. There were five swivel seats with shiny brass pedestals fronting the bar.

A large athwarthship galley of bright stainless steel occupied the main salon's forward bulkhead with a 4-burner stove and oven, an open-flame grill with hood, microwave oven, double-door refrigerator, stainless steel double sinks and built-in cutting boards. A blender and food processor were also built into the counter top. All in all, it put many a Manhattan apartment to shame. It was definitely a place to party.

The *Sea Bones* had three levels not counting the sun deck atop the main salon. Forward of the upper level's main salon was the helm and engine controls, steering compass, navigational gear and radios. Directly behind the helm was a large upholstered seat against the bulkhead for sitting while the autopilot did the steering. At the forward end of the main salon, a companionway staircase led down to the mid-deck level.

Aft of the salon on the starboard side was a companionway ladder to descend to the after cockpit where the fighting chairs for sport fishing were located. A second and smaller wet bar was installed against the forward bulkhead of the cockpit.

The mid-deck level could also be reached through a doorway leading from the aft cockpit. This level contained Doctor Ambrose's master stateroom and four double staterooms. Each had showers and heads. All the way forward, in the bow, was a seldom-used crew quarters and forepeak head. Forward of that was the chain locker where the *Sea Bones'* ground tackle was stored.

Jake conducted a brisk tour, pointed out the stateroom that Brenda would use during the crossing to the Bahamas, and deposited her bags there. Then he took her down a companionway to the third and lowest level. Forward of the companionway ladder was the walk-in freezer and opposite it a washer and dryer and dual utility sinks. The athwartship bulkhead was covered by a large double-door pantry filled with canned goods, sauces, canisters with dried beans, rice, pasta, flour and various condiments. Aft of the ladder was the engine room. They half-squatted to pass through the engine room's forward bulkhead. The engines weren't running, but Brenda could sense the power of the two massive marine-green GM diesels. Jake pointed out the Kohler power generator, the power distribution panel and the bilge pumps.

It was not lost on Brenda how tidy the engine room was. Most of the other boats she had been on, albeit most had been sailboats, the engine rooms were grimy, smelly, overly-moist denizens rank with drippings and untidy bundles of wiring. Jake definitely had his act together, and strangely, it was seeing the engine room that erased any doubts Brenda may have had as to Jake's character.

When they returned to the main salon, Jake went aft and led Brenda up a ladder to the sun deck and topside steering console. Complete with a helm and a set of engine controls, running lights panel, compass and VHF radio, and shaded by an enormous blue-and-white striped Bimini top, this was the *Sea Bones'* fair-weather steering station. Only if the weather became rainy or cold, or the sea state too rough, would Jake shift to the interior helm at the forward end of the main salon. A vinyl upholstered seat with a teak divider along the back and an aft-facing seat for guests complimented the steering station. The sun deck aft of the steering console had four sizable chaise lounges for sun worshipping guests and a cradle for storing the *Sea Bones'* tender.

When they passed to the main deck again, Jake and Brenda transferred the groceries from the dock into the main salon and Brenda began to store things in the galley's cabinets. She unpacked two Styrofoam containers topped with dry ice covering dozens of frozen T-Bone steaks, rib eyes, filet mignon and roasts. When the galley freezer was filled, she put the remainder in the big freezer down below.

Jake, in the meanwhile, fired up the diesels and the power generator, turned on all the radios and other equipment to check their operation, and lifted the Boston Whaler tender to its topside cradle with twin electric-powered davits. He then made a quick trip to the engine room to see that all was well there since starting the engines, then went to the dock and unplugged the shore power cords. He checked all equipment again to make sure the switch to the onboard power grid was successful.

A half hour later, Jake stepped gingerly to the dock, cast off the forward, stern and spring lines, jumped lightly onto the deck and climbed up to the topside steering console, then backed the *Sea Bones* out of her slip. He used the VHF radio to call the yacht club office to ask for a fueling attendant. Just as the *Sea Bones* snuggled up alongside the fueling pier and the club's attendant was securing the stern line, Jake's cell phone rang. It was Doctor Ambrose checking in.

"Jake, I got the message about Cindy's accident. I also got your call about the replacement. You say she's a chef, right?" Ambrose inquired cautiously. Doctor Jerome Ambrose was not into 'roughing it.' And with guests aboard, especially a new lady friend, he expected uncompromised service and no unpleasant surprises.

" I haven't actually eaten one of her meals, Doc, but she has the credentials. Graduate of the San Francisco School of the Culinary Arts and quite a few years running the galley on some big yachts in the Caribbean. I think she's definitely up to it," Jake said with confidence.

"Well, sounds like we got lucky. Especially on such short notice," said Ambrose, mirroring Jake's own feelings of good fortune. " Personality's important, too, you know. What do you think of a meal aboard the '*Bones* before we cast off? A week at sea, especially with those cinema nuts aboard, it would be hell if the galley wasn't tight."

"I don't see a problem," Jake said. "I believe you will find her personality compatible." *Not to mention her impressive physical attributes.* " We've just taken on stores so the menu is wide open. What would you like, and what time?"

"I'm bringing a guest, Margaret Swell. You haven't met her yet. Let's keep it simple. How about steaks, a veggie or two, and a salad. And bring up a bottle of that Australian *Shiraz*. We'll come

53

aboard between eight-thirty and nine. How does that sound?" Ambrose asked.

"No, problem, Doc," Jake said. "I'm fueling now. Why don't we just kick off in the morning from the fuel pier?"

"Sounds good, Jake. See you shortly," Ambrose said and hung up.

Jake climbed down from the topside steering station, stepped onto the fueling dock and took the diesel hose from the attendant, then inserted the nozzle into the fueling port and gave the attendant the go ahead to start pumping. He then stepped into the main salon and relayed the news to Brenda about Dr. Ambrose's request for a meal aboard that evening.

"Putting me to the test, is he?" she asked with an impish grin, handing Jake a slice of cold cucumber with a deliciously tangy dip of her own concoction slathered on one end.

Jake glanced at his watch and said, "We have about four and a half hours before the good doctor and his female friend show up. Let me finish with the fueling and topping off the fresh water, and then let's sit down for a chat. I'd like to fill in the blanks on Ambrose and the 'fuck flick' situation, as you have so eloquently described it."

"I'd like that," Brenda said with a laugh. "I'm going to marinade the steaks and prep the veggies while you finish your chores. And I'd like to take a shower and change before the doctor arrives."

"Me, too," said Jake. He turned to leave, but paused. " You got another one of those cucumbers?"

(Three)

October 28, 2000

Lat. 25° 44' N, Long. 79°15' N, Cat Cay, Bahamas

In spite of it being late Fall, the day was one of bright sunshine, cloudless sky and a gentle, caressing breeze from the southwest that smoothed the ocean's surface. The *Sea Bones'* fine bow cleaved a broad rooster-tail of spray as she came off the dark blue depths of the Gulf Stream and entered the pale turquoise-green shallows south of Bimini Island.

Dr. Ambrose was at the topside helm, bare-chested and wearing swim trunks with Margaret Swell sitting beside him in a purple bikini, long-billed sport fisherman's cap and dark sunglasses. Her lovely tanned legs were crossed with her feet atop a corner of the steering console. They were a happy couple. From the sounds that had emanated from the master stateroom the evening before, Jake concluded the sex had been good.

Jake had just visited the engine room for a quick survey and was now on the foredeck readying the ground tackle and laying out the lines for docking at the Cat Cay Yacht Club. They were still a good quarter-hour's run from the club, so the pace was casual. Brenda was squaring away the galley and straightening the staterooms in preparation for clearing Bahamian customs.

The dinner of the previous evening had gone, as they say, famously. Doctor Ambrose and his guest had arrived promptly at 8:30, and were greeted by the handsome couple that were crewing his boat. Introductions were made and it was evident that Brenda more than met Dr. Ambrose's expectations. And Margaret Swell did not conceal her pleasure over the lean, muscular young man with the genuine smile and firm handshake—a delightful bonus to the upcoming cruise in her opinion. Jake and Brenda made such a nice couple, she thought, and immediately wondered if they were lovers.

The main salon table had been set for dinner for two, complete with candles. Jake explained that he and Brenda had already eaten. Soft music played on the stereo system and as Doctor Ambrose and Margaret (she insisted they all call her Maggie) took their seats, Jake popped the cork on the Australian shiraz and Brenda delivered a cold, crisp salad, steaming vegetables and two marinated steaks smothered in rum-sautéed Portobello mushrooms; all of it broadcasting a most pleasant aroma. Jake and Brenda then left the couple to their meal and went aft to sit in the fighting chairs and finish off their own drinks.

Prior to Dr. Ambrose's and Margaret Swell's arrival, Jake and Brenda had showered then sat at the main salon bar sipping wine spitzers while Jake outlined what to expect on the upcoming filming session. He explained that the "actors" were usually two well-endowed couples and were accompanied by a cameraman and what passed for a director. The story lines were simple, idiotic really, and mostly set up the situations for raw sex in all the imaginable positions possible given the normal number of arms, legs and orifices. The *Sea Bones* and some deserted beaches at one or more of the small uninhabited cays strung along the eastern edge of the Gulf Stream south of Bimini would serve as exotic backgrounds for the filming.

During the filming, Jake explained, he would be called upon to maneuver the *Sea Bones* for best orientation to sunlight and island backdrop. If the *Sea Bones* was anchored and late afternoon shadows were a problem, he would take a line from the *Sea Bones'* stern and with the other end fastened to the Boston Whaler tender pull the big yacht's stern in one direction or another to improve the light or the position of the island backdrop. Brenda, Jake explained, would only have to keep food and drinks flowing from the galley, and maybe occasionally hold a piece of off-camera prop while scenes were moved. After a day's filming, there was swimming, drinking and getting high, followed by an evening meal if anyone was left standing. All in all, Jake said, with the exception of the sex filming it was really just like any other boat charter.

"Why the Bahamas?" Brenda asked, visualizing what might be entailed in the production of the sort of pornographic films she had seen in the firemen's video library aboard the *Backdraft*.

"Keeps the Doc's hands clean when it comes to federal or state laws on pornography. The filming is done digitally, and the Director will download the week's work via the Internet to Holland before we leave. Everyone connected with the actual filming arrives in the

Bahamas via Chalk's airline, and leaves the same way. There's no official connection with the Doc or the *Sea Bones*. Ambrose has never given me any details, but I assume he receives a sizeable chunk in an offshore bank account somewhere, Caymans maybe. He makes it a point to give me a nice bonus, and we make it a point to never discuss it afterwards in case of any kind of surveillance. You will get a generous bonus, too, and Ambrose has left it to me to explain the necessity for secrecy. You okay with that?"

"No problem, Captain," Brenda smiled. "My lips are sealed." She rose and stepped over to the galley stove, lifted the lids of a couple of stainless steel pots, stirred the contents and returned to her seat at the bar. An enticing aroma wafted across the bar and Jake found his mouth watering. "May I ask how you came to be running the doctor's boat?" Brenda continued.

"When I mustered out of the Marine Corps, I didn't want to return to my hometown. I'd put away a good part of my pay, and as a veteran I was eligible for free tuition to college. It was wintertime, so I bought that Volvo station wagon from a used car dealer outside of Quantico, and headed south to Florida. I'd already finished two years of undergraduate studies through correspondence courses and attending University of Maryland classes on base while in the Corps. The plan was to finish my degree and get into some kind of business. But in the interim I needed an income of some sort. I kind of fell into boat work and did some freelancing at Sammon's Boat Yard. I met the Doc when he had *Sea Bones* hauled out for annual bottom painting, and he hired me to help with installing a new water-maker. Later, he invited me to help with handling his boat on several of his regular party jaunts to the Keys and the Bahamas. Next thing I knew, he hired me full time. I got my U.S. Coast Guard Captain's license at his insistence because it lowered his insurance rate."

"Doctor Ambrose is a party animal?" Brenda asked innocently.

"Let's just say he knows how to have fun, okay?" Jake answered. "I'm not going to talk out of school about him. He's a respected surgeon and the *Sea Bones* is his toy. We have a good relationship and he's always treated me fairly. You'll have plenty of opportunity over the next few days to see what he's all about. He's been married and divorced three times, but continues to value the company of a woman."

"And you? Brenda asked.

"And me what?"

"Still value the company of a woman?" Brenda was pleased to see a bit of color rise in Jake's cheeks.

"Hey, haven't you heard? Marines are legendary lovers from the halls of Montezuma to the shores of Tripoli," Jake said with a grin. And on that note they heard Dr. Jerome Ambrose and his female guest step onto the *Sea Bones'* deck.

(Four)

Now, as they approached the Cat Cay Club's dock they could see some kind of commotion. First of all, there was a dark gray Bahamian marine patrol boat occupying the end of the dock, and as the *Sea Bones* drew closer, two black Bahamian police officers, one with a semi-automatic rifle slung across his chest, moved quickly down to the end of the dock and waved the *Sea Bones* off. Standing on the bow, Jake was able to exchange words with the officers then went to Dr. Ambrose at the topside steering station.

"They want us to anchor off, and wait for a launch to bring Customs aboard," Jake announced.

"That's strange," Ambrose said. "Can you make out what's going on? Hell, I'm a member of the club."

"No," said Jake. "Maybe a drug bust. There's a lot of police over there by that sailboat on the other side of the dock. Anyway, I've got the Danforth ready, so we can just backdown a ways and set it."

"Oh, all right," Ambrose snorted. "But as soon as we're set, put the

Whaler in the water. I'm going to motor over and see what's going on. I want to be done with Customs before the Chalk's flight arrives. It's not a good idea to have our actresses waving their tits and asses around these native lawmen any longer than necessary. " Ambrose turned to Margaret Swell and said, "My apologies. No offense intended." He gave her a peck on the cheek.

"None taken," Margaret answered, clearly excited about being in the Bahamas and already something exciting going on.

Ambrose put the *Sea Bone's* diesels in reverse and slowly backed away from the dock. Jake stood on the forward deck and at the appropriate time stepped on the deck switch to release the anchor. Ambrose continued in reverse until a hand signal from Jake that he had halted the run of chain rode. Ambrose allowed the *Sea Bones* to drift further aft until a second hand signal from Jake that the anchor had snagged the bottom and the chain had lifted from the water. Ambrose then engaged the diesels again to give the anchor a strong tug and set it. Jake gave a cut-the-throat signal, and Ambrose shut down the diesels. The *Sea Bones* turned and swung gently into the wind. Only her generator purred, and spat cooling water from a through-hull exhaust.

Jake climbed to the upper steering station and crossed over to the starboard side to undo the straps lashing the Boston Whaler in its cradle. He swung the motorized davits outboard, pressed an electric switch lifting the tender and swinging it over the side for lowering. Margaret had come up behind him and was peering over the side as the tender settled into the crystal clear Bahamian water.

"The water is like glass!" she exclaimed. "Oh, look! There's a sting ray," she said, pointing to a dark gray shape gliding beneath the boat.

"Jake!" Dr. Ambrose yelled up from the starboard deck. "Give me some slack here, and let's get over to the club." Ambrose had already made the tender's painter fast to one of the rail cleats and was pulling on the davit straps to set the tender free.

As soon as Ambrose had the two straps loose, Jake tripped the electric motor to draw the straps back into their housing. Then he sprinted down the after companionway and joined Ambrose at the rail. Jake didn't like the idea of not waiting for the Customs boat to come out to the *Sea Bones*. There was something serious going on at the club, and he felt it was best to wait and see. But then, he didn't own the boat.

"You know, Doc," he began in the diplomatic fashion that was characteristic of his approach when he differed with Ambrose's handling of the boat. "The presence of women can soften an encounter with officials. Those marine patrol guys seem a bit uptight right now. Might be a good idea for all of us to go in."

"Fine with me, Jake," Ambrose said, climbing onto the Whaler and starting the new Mercury outboard motor with a soft roar. He called up to Margaret, who was still in her purple bikini and leaning over the side to watch the launching of the tender. Her full breasts were barely contained by the skimpy bikini top. "Maggie, how about changing into shorts and a blouse, and you and Brenda go with us?"

"You got it!" Margaret answered excitedly and danced away to go below for a change.

Grinning broadly, Ambrose turned to Jake. "Damn! That woman's got a fine rack, Jake! And everything that goes with it! Never underestimate a recent divorcé, Jake. I was looking for the handlebars all night!" he said with a conspiratorial grin.

Jake had never been comfortable talking about women's physical attributes or their sexual performance. In response to Ambrose's assessment, he just nodded in agreement.

"I haven't had a chance to say much about our new chef, but that dinner last night and the breakfast this morning were more than wonderful. Hell, if she puts out like she cooks, she's a keeper, Jake."

Again, Jake just smiled and said only that she certainly was a fine chef.

"Jake, you're just too damn reserved for your own good," Ambrose said good naturedly. Then added, "You met her only yesterday, right?"

"Right," Jake said.

"Well, we'll see how she holds up under a lot of close-up naked sex," Ambrose grinned.

"Cindy Wright gave her the low-down on the filming and what to expect," Jake said. "She's well aware of what the trip's all about. Cindy mentioned that Brenda was galley mate for a big charter sailboat owned by five retired New York firemen. I got the feeling that she had no trouble keeping their fires under control," Jake said.

Brenda and Maggie arrived alongside the tender and were helped in by Jake. Individually, they were beautiful. Together, they were almost more than the eyes could behold. Dr. Ambrose immediately saw how right Jake had been. No amount of officialdom could overcome the boatload of tits and asses he was bringing ashore.

By the time they pulled alongside the Cat Cay Club's dock, only one of the two Bahamian marine policemen was still standing at the end of the dock. He looked uncertainly back toward the Club, then reached down to take Brenda's extended hand and helped the beautiful young white woman onto the dock. Brenda greeted him with a soft thank you and wide smile, followed by Maggie, who bestowed the same. But Ambrose broke the spell.

"I'm Doctor Jerome Ambrose," he called up from the tender. "I'm a member of the club here. Is there a problem why we can't dock?" He said it pleasantly enough, but with unmistakable authority.

"You are a *medical* doctor?" the young policeman asked.

"Yes, that's right" Ambrose answered.

The policeman turned quickly toward the clubhouse and gave a sharp whistle. "A *doctor* here!" he yelled excitedly.

Out of the clubhouse came the policeman with the automatic rifle, followed by a short, rotund and very black Bahamian officer with a gold star on his shoulder boards. The officer came on rapidly and when within twenty feet exclaimed in recognition, "Doctor Ambrose! Mercy! Is that truly you?"

"Hello, Chief Tommy," Ambrose answered, extending his hand. Chief Tommy's marine patrol office was located on Bimini just north of Cat Cay, but he spent lots of time chumming around the wealthy tourists at the Cat Cay Club. He had shared many a drink with this Fort Lauderdale surgeon, who seemed to have an endless supply of beautiful women aboard his yacht. "What's going on here, Chief?" Ambrose asked.

"Please come, Doctor!" Chief Tommy said with great emotion, taking Ambrose's hand. "We have a terrible situation. A man is dead and his wife is in very bad shape. I think she has lost a lot of blood."

Jake heard all of this even though he was still standing in the Boston Whaler. "I'll get your kit," he yelled to Ambrose, and fired up the Mercury.

"Jake!" Ambrose yelled after him. "Bring the white plastic box, too, the locked one in my stateroom closet with the red cross. I've got plasma in there and an intravenous kit." As Jake sped away, Ambrose followed Chief Tommy to the clubhouse and was met with a grim scene. A male corpse was lying partially covered on the floor, the right arm almost completely severed at the shoulder. On a tropical rattan couch lay a naked woman, modestly covered with a bright yellow table cloth. The tablecloth was soaked in blood. Ambrose quickly took her vitals and saw that she had indeed lost a lot of blood. The pulse was weak, and the woman was in shock. A quick examination left no doubt that she had been viciously raped and brutally beaten.

"Chief, you'd better call for a helicopter fast. I don't know how long we can stabilize her without trauma support," Ambrose said.

"I have already sent for it, but it is coming from New Providence," Chief Tommy answered, speaking of the main island where the capital, Nassau, was located.

At that moment, Jake ran up with Ambrose's medical kit and the box containing plasma. Jake glanced at the male corpse and noted the nearly severed arm dangling alongside it. Then, he saw that the battered young woman had once been a lovely blond, but was now slashed with ugly, dark red cuts over her arms, legs and torso. *What animal could have done this?* he thought with controlled fury.

As if reading his thoughts, Dr. Ambrose spoke to Chief Tommy while rigging the IV. "She's been raped, you know. And these slashes all over her body didn't have anything to do with restraining her. Who could have done such a cruel thing?"

Chief Tommy sucked in his breath and said with utter disgust. "Haitians, Doctor. They are like cockroaches these days. We patrol the Windward Passage and all of our islands nearest Haiti, but there are so many of them. They come over on anything that floats; truck inner tubes, old fuel drums, wooden fishing smacks, you name it. They are desperate people. Life on their island is worse than you can imagine. The poorest of our poor here in the Bahamas are wealthy by Haitian standards. They come to steal boats and rob our people. It is an even bigger problem for our government when they harm tourists like these poor people."

After Dr. Ambrose got the plasma IV started, he elevated the woman's feet and covered her in a shiny foil emergency blanket, then went to the corpse and lifted the cover from it. "This was her husband?" he asked.

"We believe so," said Chief Tommy. "Their passports are gone and the sailboat's registration is missing also, but we checked the address on the radiotelephone certificate and have made an inquiry with the U.S. Coast Guard. We should know more soon."

Ambrose lowered the cover and glanced over at Jake. He was taken aback by what he saw. He hardly recognized his captain's face. Jake's jaw was clenched so tightly and his lips pulled so thinly that Ambrose thought he resembled a snake ready to strike. But it was Jake's eyes that were the most unnerving; they had gone all dark and squinty. "You all right, Jake?" he asked carefully.

"Yeah, I'm okay, Doc" Jake answered mechanically. "I thought I'd check out the sailboat if that was okay with the Chief."

"Best you don't go on board, Captain Jake," said Chief Tommy. "Those Haitian scum may have left something of theirs or a clue that will help us to identify them."

"Right," said Jake. "I'll just look from the dock." Jake went outside and was met by Brenda and Maggie, who had been prevented from entering the clubhouse by the marine patrol policemen. He met their eyes and said simply, "Yachting couple. Husband dead and the wife may not make it. Chief thinks it was Haitian thugs. I'm going to take a look at their sailboat. A helicopter's on the way to pick up the wife." The women meekly followed Jake to the sailboat, disinclined to ask any questions. They both had noted the severe change in Jake's demeanor.

Alongside the sailboat, as Jake walked the dock from the bow of the boat to the stern, the two women were stricken by the blood; not just the amount, which was startling in of itself, but by the haphazard fashion in which it appeared all over the cabin top, the cabin trunk, the decks and the cockpit. It spoke of a furious struggle, or an act of mayhem beyond imagining, or both. Jake also noted a streak of blue-green paint beginning at the starboard edge of the sailboat's transom, and skipping unevenly along the hull at about the height of a native-built sailing canoe's hull. Then, they heard the distant and unmistakable whumping sound of a large helicopter approaching from the southeast.

Jake and the two women stood alongside the bloody sailboat while the Bahamian government helicopter hovered to a landing on the broad green lawn of the Cat Cay Club, barely missing the club's flagpole. More police officers, two carrying a stretcher, plus two men and a woman in light-green medical garb all clambered out of the helicopter and ran for the clubhouse. Moments later, the medical staff, two policemen and a stretcher bearing the injured woman went aboard. They were followed by four policemen, each holding one corner of a black body bag. The bag was placed gently in the rear of the cargo compartment, then the four policemen stepped back as the helicopter rose to a hover, rotated in place, then tipped forward and raced away toward New Providence.

As the diminishing speck that was the helicopter finally disappeared in the distance, Doctor Jerome Ambrose, Chief Tommy, and a slender black government officer with twin silver bars on his blue uniform's lapels came out of the clubhouse and walked over to where Jake, Brenda and Maggie were standing. Doctor Ambrose made the introductions.

"Brenda, Maggie, this is Chief Tommy of the Bahamian Marine Patrol, an old friend. And this is Captain Jones, a criminal investigator with the Bahamian National Police. And Captain Jones, this is my captain, Jake Porter." Everyone shook hands, but the mood was somber.

"I am most regretful, ladies, that your welcome to our fair islands was so unpleasant," began Chief Tommy. "These are trying times. I have explained to Doctor Ambrose our problem with Haitian bandits. I feel sure this is their work, and we will not rest until we have these savages in custody. Captain Jones is our most experienced investigator. He will pursue every avenue to locate and apprehend those who committed this tragedy."

"I understand you are waiting for the arrival of the rest of your party?" Captain Jones said, turning to Doctor Ambrose.

"Yes," Ambrose answered. "Four friends from New York and two from Montreal. We were planning to do some snorkeling and underwater filming. A five-day island-hopping get-away for some otherwise very busy people."

"I understand," said Chief Tommy. "I sincerely hope you will not let this unfortunate happening spoil your holiday. This is the perfect time of the year to putter about our lovely islands and enjoy yourselves. It is most definitely better than New York or Montreal at this time of the year," he smiled. "We will be vigilant in our search for the wrong-doers. Don't you worry about that. You have only to focus on having fun,"

"I'd like to bring the *Sea Bones* alongside the club's dock now, if that is permissible," said Ambrose. "Our guests arrive on the afternoon Chalk's flight from Miami."

"Permission granted, dear friend," Chief Tommy said expansively. "I am indebted for your very fine medical assistance. I am certain you saved a life today." He turned to Captain Jones and asked, "I assume you will want to keep the sailboat secure, but have you any reason why my friends cannot continue with their vacation plans?"

"None whatsoever, Chief," replied Captain Jones. "We must continue with our investigation of course, and the sailboat will be sealed off. He turned to Dr. Doctor Ambrose and said pleasantly, " Simply advise your guests when they arrive that they have the run of the club grounds with the exception of where the sailboat is docked."

"Thank you, captain," said Ambrose. "Actually, once we have everyone aboard we will be casting off and proceeding south in the direction of Andros Island. We plan to stop in several places along the way over the next few days for some swimming and diving."

"That sounds wonderful! Now, I believe a round of drinks is in order," said Chief Tommy, "and I am confident the club manager will refuse our money," he said with a wink. "I will see that your entry into our waters is properly cleared by the resident customs officer. He's my cousin, you know," smiling again.

(Five)

Two hours later, Chalk Airlines' vintage twin-engine Grumman Mallard splashed gently into the crystal clear water behind the Cat Cay Club, and taxied noisily to the club's ramp. With a burst of power from each of its 12-cylinder Pratt & Whitney radial engines, the stubby amphibian surged up the ramp and the engines were cut. The passenger door aft of the overhead wing opened and a stewardess lowered the door. The first passengers out were without doubt the guests of the *Sea Bones*. The two women were gorgeous; a fiery redhead with flashing green eyes, lush pouting lips and a superstructure that would stop a stampede. She was followed by a blonde Nordic-looking blue-eyed beauty, equally well-endowed with long, faultlessly tanned legs. Behind them came a balding, slightly overweight man dressed in a black sport coat, black sweatshirt and black trousers wearing Gucci sunglasses and a gleaming Rolex Submariner. Next off were two lithe, athletic men in colorful knit sport shirts stretched across muscular chests and wearing pleated tropical-weight trousers, each with thick manes of hair and deeply tanned faces behind stylish sunglasses. Last off was unmistakably the cameraman, a youngish man in his late twenties with an SLR camera case strung around his neck and carrying a polished aluminum valise that almost certainly contained his digital camcorder and lenses.

"Maggie whispered to Brenda, "I think I've seen this movie."

"Maybe the plot will thicken," Brenda said with a knowing smile.

Doctor Ambrose introduced everyone and was successful in getting all the new arrivals and their luggage aboard the *Sea Bones* and clear of the Cat Cay Club without their being aware of the earlier unpleasant happenings. The Bahamian customs officer dutifully stamped everyone's passport, and within the hour all the guests were acquainted with their staterooms and the *Sea Bones* cast off its lines. Jake took the helm, Brenda mixed drinks and set up a colorful buffet of snacks on the bar. Dr. Ambrose put a lively Brazilian meringue on the stereo, then he and Maggie assumed their roles of host and hostess.

The redhead with the fiery green eyes had introduced herself as Rikki, and the Nordic blond asked to be called Magda. They were in high spirits and obviously excited about being aboard such a beautiful yacht in the Bahamas. It was a welcome change from most of their filming sets. The two swarthy young men with Roman noses, flashing white teeth and thick black manes called themselves Romulus and Remus, and announced that they were first cousins from Romania. Both had taken note of Brenda, and flashed winning smiles her way. Louie Levy, the balding and rotund director, introduced himself and his cameraman, Stevie, with a theatrical flourish and immediately turned to the bar to ask Brenda to fix him a double martini. Soon, everyone had a drink and was filling their plates from the colorful buffet.

With Jake carefully steering the *Sea Bones* slowly through the shallow water on a southerly course, the newly arrived guests stripped to the briefest of bikinis and Speedos to catch the last rays of the day's sun, sitting either in the fighting chairs in the after cockpit or stretched out on the chaise lounges on the topside sundeck. Brenda had already pulled frozen New Orleans Creole-style gourmet dinners from the main freezer and defrosted them with the microwave. The basics of a fresh salad were atop the galley cutting board awaiting a final toss, and a large pitcher of iced tropical punch was riding in the bar's sink. She came topside and climbed to the steering console where Jake sat at the helm.

"So, how am I doing, Captain," she asked, handing Jake an ice-cold Heineken and a piece of toasted French baguette with some kind of spicy butter topping."The Doctor is impressed," Jake said." He thinks you're a keeper."

"That's nice to hear," Brenda said. "Maggie's all right, too. She's a radiology department manager at the hospital where Ambrose does his thing. She was divorced recently and this trip is just what she needed," Brenda said. "Where are we stopping for the night?" Brenda knew you didn't go motor boating about the Bahamas banks at night unless it was your intention to tear the bottom out of your boat on a coral reef.

"Another hour maybe. Dunbar Cay is just south of us. It's deserted and has a few palm trees and a nice beach. We can anchor behind it to get out of the swell, and it'll make as good a place as any to start filming in the morning,'" Jake answered. "To tell you the truth, I could use a couple of stiff drinks after we're battened down for the night."

"Me, too," said Brenda. "I saw enough blood today to last a lifetime. Your request is duly noted Captain. I'll fix up a whizzer or two for you after dinner that's guaranteed to take the edge off."

A little before sunset, Jake eased the *Sea Bones* behind Dunbar Cay, went to the foredeck and lowered the anchor himself, then went to the main steering station to back down the *Sea Bones* and set it. He shut down the diesels then went to the engine room to see that all was well, and check the oil level on the Kholer generator since it would run all night.

By the time Jake got back to the main salon, Brenda was setting the evening meal on the table and everyone was raving about the sumptuous buffet she had served earlier. Jake poured the iced punch for those that wanted it, or freshened up the drinks from the bar. After captaining the *Sea Bones* for countless trips to the Bahamas and the Florida Keys, Jake knew the routine well, and it looked like these folks were going to party most of the night. It was good that the newly arrived guests had been spared the gore and tragedy at the Cat Cay Club earlier. He was only beginning to recover himself from what he had seen. He was glad to finally slip into his bunk in the forward crew quarters at 2AM having gratefully consumed the promised 'whizzers' from Brenda, a rum-based drink made even smoother with a tart fruit punch mix.

For the next five days the *Sea Bones* and its contented crew and guests basked in sunny, cloudless weather, each day beginning with one of Brenda's sublime breakfasts followed by three or four hours of filming, then a mid-day break for a buffet lunch. Then, three more hours of filming before calling it a day. The closing hours of daylight each day were devoted to snorkeling the reefs, water skiing behind the Boston Whaler and diving from the *Sea Bones'* bow into the flawlessly-clear water. Jake moved the *Sea Bones* to a different anchorage each night, always choosing a deserted cay for maximum privacy. Once the boat was settled in for the night, and while the guests were swimming or motoring up to the cay to take a walk along the beach, Brenda would turn out another of her multi-course meals and Jake would man the bar.

Several times during the cruise, when time permitted, Jake retrieved the sailing log of 3rd Lieutenant White from his berth in the forward crew quarters and thumbed through the pages reading at random. He chuckled at the young sailor's tale of his first sexual encounter while the *HMS Cygnet* was anchored before Table Bay, South Africa. He had gone ashore with another lieutenant and a couple of midshipmen. True to fashion, they had wound up in a whorehouse and Third Lieutenant White had lost his innocence. His sixteenth birthday was the following week. It was clear from this and other candid stories in his log that it was not the young lieutenant's intention for anyone else to ever read his log.

Interesting as Lt. White's narrative of his journey across the Indian Ocean and through the treacherous waters of Indonesia into the Pacific was, Jake found himself always coming back to the pages with the Latin text and the tale of the Spaniard Bustamente's amputation and subsequent death. There was something in the young lieutenant's narration that didn't square up quite right, but Jake couldn't put his finger on it. On one occasion he showed the journal to Dr. Ambrose in hopes that the doctor could read the Latin text, but Ambrose demurred saying his Latin was restricted to medical terms and had not been his favorite subject in med school.

When Jake returned the log to his bunk in the crew quarters, he resolved that once back in Fort Lauderdale, he would find someone who could translate the Latin. Maybe, he thought, that would explain everything. And he was particularly curious as to what north Pacific island was located at Lat 27 N, Long 154W.

(Six)

The next day, the sixth and last day of their Bahamas sojourn, called for only a half-day of filming. The first half of the day would be spent retracing their route to spend the last afternoon and evening at their first anchorage, Dunbar Cay. Jake took the *Sea Bones* out into the Gulf Stream several miles west of the line of cays they had been visiting and set up fishing poles in the fighting chairs. Maggie strapped in and was the first to catch a fish. Screaming in delight, she hauled in a 60-pound gleaming gold-and-green dolphin, the fish the Hawaiians call the Mahi Mahi. Jake brought the fish over the transom with the gaff, a foot-long galvanized hook with a half-inch thick shank that was attached to a thick wooden handle. He planted the hook deep into its gills, and as it landed on the deck of the cockpit, he grabbed a small bottle of alcohol and gave a strong squirt into the fish's gills on both sides to shock the fish into submission.

Jake returned the gaff to a plastic tube holder just inside the starboard quarter and expertly removed the lure from the fish's mouth. Maggie had her picture taken with the fish. Doctor Ambrose, smiling broadly, stood beside her, one hand holding up the fish's tail and the other resting on Maggie's rear end. Rikki, the red-head, was the next lucky angler, snagging a shiny black-and-silver tuna of about twenty or thirty pounds. Equally proud of her catch and wanting a picture, too, she held the tuna to one side, almost squeezing her breasts out of her bikini top. " I definitely want a copy of that one!" laughed Dr. Ambrose, and took a good-natured elbowing in his side from Maggie.

71

Once anchored behind Dunbar Cay and the filming underway, Jake took the Boston Whaler and snorkeling gear over to a nearby reef. Within an hour he had bagged seven nice- sized spiny lobsters and picked up three large conchs. He trolled slowly back to the *Sea Bones* trailing a bright yellow lure and was rewarded with a two-foot-long barracuda. Jake's return brought the filming to a temporary stop as everyone came to the Sea Bones' stern rail and looked down into the Boston Whaler to admire the lobsters and the razor-toothed barracuda. Brenda announced that Maggie's mahi mahi and the lobsters would be the main course for dinner, and both the barracuda and conch would soon be reduced to a spicy Bahamas-style ceviché, flavored with fiery red Bahamian "bird' peppers. The tuna would be served sushi-style for pre-dinner appetite-whetting as soon as the filming was done.

After the filming resumed, Jake carried the lobsters, conch and barracuda to the galley in a nylon net bag and placed them in the double stainless steel sink. Brenda came in behind him and between the two of them the fish were quickly and expertly filleted. Brenda focused on the special sushi-style slicing and rolling of the tuna and Jake reduced the mahi mahi to nice-sized steaks, then skinned the barracuda and diced its flesh into small chunks which he dumped into a bowl and covered with fresh-squeezed lime juice, a diced purple onion and half-a-dozen Bahamian "bird" peppers. He covered the bowl and placed it in the refrigerator.

"You're pretty good with that filleting knife, Captain," Brenda said. "Learn that in the Marine Corps?

"No, but I'll take that as a compliment seeing as how it's coming from a graduate of the San Francisco School of the Culinary Arts," Jake said with a smile.

Brenda's cooking and serving for ten people, plus Jake's involvement in running the boat, had not left much time for he and Brenda to become better acquainted, but Jake had come to appreciate Brenda's talents in the galley as well as her graceful manner in dealing with the *Sea Bones'* current guests. And he knew the good doctor was equally impressed. Jake sensed that Ambrose would be inclined to hire Brenda rather than Cindy Wright for the *Sea Bones'* next cruise. Which was fine by Jake. He was definitely inclined toward getting to know her better. Even in the company of the two porno-pros aboard the *Sea Bones* at the moment, Brenda was a stunningly good-looking woman. And he had noticed her looking at him numerous times, especially during some of the more steamy filming sequences. And to be perfectly honest, he knew she had caught him several times studying her.

"I have an idea, Jake," Brenda said, almost reading his mind. "What would you think of the two of us having dinner on the beach over a driftwood campfire? Kinda get away from the crowd for a bit." Pause. "Followed by skinny dipping under the full moon?" This last added with a slightly raised eyebrow and an impish smile.

"Sounds like one of the scripts we've been filming this week," Jake said in jest. But he hastened to add in case Brenda mistook his meaning, "I'm all for it. Let me run it past the doc, okay? I think we've put enough points on the board that it will be no problem."

"I'll put two of the lobsters aside for our pot and bring along some ceviche and fixings," Brenda said with a soft smile. "After we've fed the troops and got them into the sauce, we can slip over the stern and make our getaway. How does that sound?"

"I especially like the 'slipping over the stern part'" Jake said with a chuckle, and went to clear the plan with Ambrose.

(Seven)

"It appears there's been more going on in the galley than I was aware of," Doctor Ambrose said good naturedly with another of his conspiratorial winks. "You have my blessings, Jake. And any private services you can deliver to convince that young lady that she should consider another cruise on the 'Bones', I will take as a special favor to me. She's one hell of a chef, not to mention being easy on the eye."

"Thanks, doc. We'll make sure everything's together before we leave. The beach is only a hundred yards away anyway," Jake said.

"We'll be fine, Jake. You just concentrate on having a good time. You've earned the break," said Ambrose.

As planned, Jake and Brenda stepped through the *Sea Bones'* transom doors onto the teak swim platform and into the Boston Whaler shortly before nine o'clock. No one even noticed their departure. The main salon table had been covered to over flowing with large platters of marinated and grilled mahi mahi steaks, multiple platters of tuna sushi and small bowls of spicy ceviche, surrounded by larger bowls of steaming vegetables and a huge tossed salad with Brenda's own version of a Caesar's dressing. And the guests, including their hosts, Doctor Jerome Ambrose and Maggie Swell, were well on their way to being pleasantly plastered. The drinks had been kept flowing from Jake behind the bar until just before he grabbed the large lobster pot and net bags that Brenda had filled. As he lowered it all into the Boston Whaler, Jake noticed Brenda had placed an unopened bottle of 150-proof Jamaican dark rum on top. Could be a long night, he thought, reflecting only briefly upon his total inability to anticipate women.

With Brenda aboard, Jake motored the short distance to Dunbar Cay's tiny beach and nosed the tender's bow up onto the sand, jumped ashore and tied the painter to a palm tree. Brenda stacked the lobster pot and dinner fixings atop the tender's port rail and Jake relayed them to the beach. The two of them quickly gathered up ample driftwood for the fire. For a seat, they rolled a storm-shattered palm tree log to the shallow fire pit that Jake had dug in the sand, and in a few minutes a knee-high fire was working its way down to red-hot coals. Jake took the lobster pot to the surf's edge and filled it three-quarters with saltwater and set the pot on the edge of the fire. Brenda retrieved ice cubes from a cooler and mixed their drinks making liberal use of the 150-proof Jamaican rum. Then they both sat down on the log and looked out on the anchorage where the *Sea Bones* floated serenely, her interior lights reflecting brightly off an ocean shimmering beneath the soft glow of a full moon.

"Not a bad way to make a buck, huh?" Jake said, surveying the quiet anchorage, then turning to the very beautiful young woman sitting ever so seductively in her bikini bottom and kerchief-tied blouse.

"Here's to fair winds and safe harbors," Brenda said as she leaned toward Jake to clink her glass against his, making sure Jake had a clear shot of her cleavage. After all, she thought, there's been nothing but naked women and lurid sex acts dancing before his eyes all week and he may be a bit desensitized.

But Jake was far from being desensitized. Beneath the full moon and the warm tropical night, not to mention the rising heat from the 150-proof rum, he was fully expectant of being seduced. He rose to push the lobster pot more squarely over the fire, and Brenda stepped alongside him to lift the lobsters from their bag. Their shoulders touched first, then Jake placed a hand in the small of Brenda's back and kissed her fully on the lips. Brenda responded in kind and pressed her softness into Jake's recesses. Then, they stepped back and looked at each other.

"I figure one more rum drink, then dinner, then a swim," Brenda said, her voice catching slightly.

"You're one hell of a tour director," Jake laughed. "But I *am* hungry, and I may need my strength later."

"You can bet on it," Brenda said, taking his glass and planting a juicy kiss on his cheek.

They ate slowly, savoring the quiet of the deserted cay, watching the fire burn down and the moon pass overhead. They made the kind of small talk that people make to build the bridges of intimacy and fill in the necessary spaces. Among other things, Jake was curious as to why Brenda had taken up painting names on yachts when she was obviously such a great chef. And Brenda asked how Jake had come to own the *Giggling Witch*. Brenda said she was just looking for a temporary change of pace until she found the next yacht to crew. The crewing involved living in close quarters with the owners, and finding the right situation was not easy. Jake nodded in understanding; yacht owners had a tendency to expect their galley slave to also do duty in the master stateroom.

Then Jake told of how he had gone to a government auction in Fort Lauderdale about six months after leaving the Marine Corps. The auction was mostly used military equipment, vehicles, boats and assets seized for non-payment of taxes. As a military veteran, he got extra points in the bidding process and was surprised to find himself the owner of much more than he thought he was bidding on.

The *Giggling Witch* had been stored in a wooden cradle and was covered with greasy-looking tarps. She had no masts, the propeller was missing, and there was no ladder to board her for a look around; a real pig-in-a-poke. He was as surprised as anyone when he learned that he had been the high bidder.

He hired a tractor and low-boy trailer to haul her to Sammons Boat Yard. As he was about to pull out of the auction area, he was directed to a steel hangar and shown a huge pile of equipment that belonged to the *Giggling Witch*. Atop it all were the two masts, the missing bronze propeller, bagged sails, coiled anchor line, anchors, propane bottles for the galley stove and a host of other equipment that would have cost thousands to replace. It was the one time he felt the Marine Corps had come through for him.

SNAPPER

August 1990

Latitude 28º 26' N, Longitude 48º 30' E

Saudi Arabia

At 1AM, August 3ʳᵈ, 1990, three Iraqi Republican Guard divisions crossed the frontier into the emirate of Kuwait with nearly 1,000 tanks. The Al Jahra heights overlooking Kuwait City were quickly seized while the Madinah Division steered west to block the border with Saudi Arabia. Within the hour, Iraqi special forces entered Kuwait City by helicopter assault and seized government buildings. Sheik Jaber Al Ahmed Al Sabah, the Kuwaiti emir, fled for his life to Saudi Arabia, and by early evening Kuwait City had fallen even as Iraqi tanks sped south to capture Kuwaiti seaports on the Persian Gulf.

Within 72 hours of crossing the border, elements of eleven Iraqi divisions occupied Kuwait. Saddam Hussein announced that the former emirate no longer existed, and was merely "the 19th Province, an eternal part of Iraq." Saddam now controlled one-fifth of the world's trillion-barrel oil reserves.

When news of these events reached Corporal Jackson T. Porter at the

United States Marine Corps Sniper School in Quantico, Virginia, Jake knew with a certainty that his four-year enlistment, due to end next month in September, would be extended. But he had no idea how fast it would happen.

Within three weeks of the Iraqi assault on Kuwait, General Norman Schwarzkopf had gathered together a relatively small reaction force to protect the Saudi border against any further expansion ambitions of Saddam until greater forces could be assembled to take the war to the Iraqis. That initial force of what came to be called Desert Shield included 17,000 U.S. Marines, and among them, the newly-extended Corporal Jake Porter.

Jake arrived in Saudi Arabia in the cargo bay of a C-141, and stepped down the plane's loading ramp into the hellish desert heat of late summer to join a line of other Marines where he picked up two-days of MREs (Meal-Ready-to-Eat), a standard issue M16 with two bandoliers of ammunition and two canteens of water, then boarded a six-by-six truck in a convoy that transported them at breakneck speed to a featureless piece of Saudi desert thirty miles south of the so-called "boot heel" of Kuwait, and some twenty miles inland from the Persian Gulf coastline.

The hastily-assembled desert bivouac of the First Marine Division offered all the traditional discomfort and physical misery to be expected of a Marine Corps combat staging area: little protection from the 100-degree-plus heat and blowing sand, no showers for weeks on end, no hot meals and living under the stress of knowing that positioned just a few miles away on the other side of the Saudi-Kuwaiti border was an overwhelming force of two Iraqi armored divisions, two mechanized infantry divisions, and eight divisions of Iraqi infantry composed of hardened veterans of Iraq's earlier 8-year war with its neighbor, Iran.

As a corporal with four years of service and a sniper billet in one of the division's Surveillance and Target Acquisition (STA) (pronounced 'stay') platoons, Jake's skills as an armorer and marksmanship instructor were put to work fine-tuning the shooting skills of his battalion's snipers. When 20 of the newly-adopted .50-caliber (12.7 mm) Barrett Model 82 "Light Fifty" sniper rifles arrived under an ALLMAR disbursal order,

Jake was assigned to a team to set up a 1,000-yard firing range, select the division's 20 best marksmen to trade in their standard-issue M40A1 sniper rifles for the new Barretts, then conduct full weapon familiarization of the Barrett rifle.

The Barrett "Light Fifty" was not new to Jake. While serving as a marksmanship instructor at the sniper school in Quantico, VA, he had followed its development. At the time, he was training Marine Corps snipers in the use of the M40A1. Based on the commercially-designed Remington Model 700, the 7.62 mm M40A1 had an octagonal barrel fitted with a flash suppressor, a 5-round magazine, weighed 14 and one-half pounds, and had a muzzle velocity of 2,550 feet per second with an effective kill range of 880 yards.

But continuing Marine Corps interest in the greater range and destructive power of the .50-caliber round led to research and development efforts to produce a sniper rifle in that caliber. The U.S. Marine Corps' most famous sniper, Sergeant Carlos Hathcock, had pioneered the use of the .50-caliber round for sniper missions during the Vietnam War. One of Hathcock's more spectacular feats with the .50-caliber round was the confirmed kill of two NVA regulars at the phenomenal distance of more than one and one-half miles (3,000+ yards).

Testing of the new .50-caliber Barrett rifle was conducted at the Marine Corps Marksmanship Training Unit in Quantico, Virginia. Two other .50-caliber rifles were being evaluated at the same time, the McMillan ELR and the bolt-action Haskins Model 500. The Haskins rifle, with its fluted barrel to reduce weight and a muzzle brake to diminish the teeth-jarring recoil of the .50-caliber round, was 8 pounds heavier than the M40A1, and the .50-caliber ammo was heavy, too. At over 40 grams, a single round weighed four times as much as the 7.62 mm round of the M40A1. But traveling at 900 meters per second (about one mile in two seconds) in a near-flat trajectory, the .50-caliber projectile exited the Haskin's muzzle with five times the energy of the 7.62 round, and arrived at the target with a destructive power second only to 20mm cannon fire. And when depleted-uranium, armor-piercing incendiary ammo was used, it could penetrate 4 inches of hardened armor and bring death and destruction to crews of just about every armored military vehicle except a main battle tank.

Jake had an opportunity to fire several thousand rounds in the Barrett rifle as well as the McMillan and the Haskins. Several months later, in reward for placing first in an inter-service marksmanship competition at the U.S. Army's Marksmanship Training Unit (MTU) in Fort Benning, Georgia, Corporal Porter was given the blessing of the Quantico school's commandant to select his rifle of choice and he chose a SOPMOD (Special-Operations Peculiar-Modified) Haskins .50-caliber sniper rifle. The Special Ops modification was a noise and flash suppressor version that reduced the noise of the Haskins' report by about 50 decibels. At eight hundred yards out, the Haskin's report was an almost inaudible pop; beyond that it was totally silent. A notation in Jake's service jacket validated his authority to use the non-issue weapon.

During the time Jake spent in his first weeks in Saudi Arabia indoctrinating the STA snipers in the Barrett rifle, he took the opportunity to retrieve his Haskins SOPMOD from the battalion's armory and raised quite a few eyebrows with the exotic-looking weapon when he took his turn on the range to fine-tune the Haskins. Among these best-of-the-best Marine Corps marksmen, Jake demonstrated many times over on the 1,000-yard range how he came to be an instructor at the Corps' Marksmanship Training School in Quantico. They particularly marveled at how smoothly and rapidly he worked the Haskin's bolt action, ejecting the spent shell casing and returning the telescope's cross-hairs on target in the blink of an eye. Alongside the other snipers using their new Barretts, Jake shot tight groups at 1,000 yards that rarely exceeded 5 inches, and he did it almost as fast as the semi-automatic Barretts with their 5-round magazines.

But for the greater part of Jake Porter's first five months in Saudi Arabia, the Haskins rifle was stored in the battalion's armory, and Jake was provided with the standard issue M-16. As a member of the First Marines' *Task Force Shepherd*, a lightly armed force of twelve hundred Marines, Jake spent most of his time on small reconnaissance teams observing Iraqi troop and tank movements, or crawling on his belly at night with a bayonet clearing and mapping paths across mine fields with a GPS receiver. It was miserable, bone-wearying duty that had no call for use of the Haskins rifle. The only up-beat news during this time came when the battalion's Sergeant Major told Jake he was on the division's recommendation list for promotion to Sergeant. Jake had to bite his tongue to keep from saying that he'd gladly trade the promotion for an honorable discharge. The Corps and its ways were beginning to wear on Jake Porter, and he was chafing deeply over the extension of his enlistment just one month before his separation date.

Then in mid-November, while still a corporal, he was given command of a six-man STA sniper team and rotated with two other teams to man an observation post (OP) north of Khafji, a scruffy now-deserted Saudi border town situated alongside the Persian Gulf, seven miles south of the Kuwaiti-Saudi border and some 50 miles south of Kuwait City. The bulk of *Task Force Shepherd's* Marines were thirty miles further south.

In the closing months of 1990, U.S. and coalition forces had grown to over 400,000 men, and it was clear that all-out war was near at hand. Iraqi armor and infantry were in constant motion and sporadic artillery fire was occurring daily. Marine Corps surveillance and target acquisition teams, including Jake's, were being deployed to keep track of last minute shifts in Iraqi forces.

In the third week of December, after returning from a two-day stint at his team's "hide" on the rooftop of the desalination plant north of Khafji, Jake was told to report to his company commander. *Probably going to present me with those damn sergeant stripes.* But when Jake saw five other STA team members being held in a group in front of the command post (CP) by the company's first sergeant, he figured he had it wrong. Something was up. With Jake's arrival they were all summoned into the CP tent.

Captain Zeke Murray, USMC, a hard-core Citadel graduate from Sumter, South Carolina with a thick southern accent, announced to the six Marines assembled before him that they would make up the three sniper teams that were to be "vertically deployed" (insertion by helicopter) the next evening in the vicinity of Kuwait City and the International Airport. The mission was to stir-up entrenched Iraqi armor and aviation assets and draw them out of their positions within the city and the airport proper so they could be destroyed without collateral damage to the city's buildings or the airport's facilities. General Swartzkopf had promised Kuwait's emir that he would return Kuwait to him with a minimum of damage to the country's infrastructure.

"It's gonna be like poking a beehive, Porter," drawled Captain Murray as his gaze singled out Jake. "And when the bees come out of their hive to sting you, they're gonna be met by some tank-killing Marine Corps A-10 Warthogs and Apache gunships. You'll have a front-row seat to a massacre, *Sergeant*," Murray smiled broadly. He picked up a manila envelope with Jake's promotion orders and a pair of sergeant stripes, handing them to Jake and offering his hand. "Congratulations, *Sergeant* Porter. Let's have those on your sleeves by the time you saddle-up tomorrow night."

"Aye, aye, sir," Jake said mechanically, bracing to attention.

Captain Murray turned back to the assembled snipers, "Ops briefing will be at 1600 hours tomorrow, men. The battalion S-2 (Intelligence) will fill in all the blanks. That'll be all. Good luck and good hunting."

"Aye, aye, sir," the gathered snipers replied in unison. They all did an about-face and left the company commander's tent with haste. Barely out of the CP tent, the band of snipers swarmed around Jake to punch the arms of the new buck sergeant. Jake took the painful, time-honored ritual good-naturedly, but his mind reeled at the prospect of being dropped behind enemy lines to "poke" at a fanatical enemy's armored might with his single-shot rifle. It was not lost on him that this could well be his last evening as a living, breathing human being among his comrades.

MURDER & MAYHEM IN PARADISE

Date: November 6, 2000

Lat. 24º 15' N, Long. 76º 00'W

Dunbar Cay, Bahama Islands

Their drinks finished and the small talk waning, Brenda rose and walked over to the Boston Whaler untying her kerchief blouse as she went. When she turned, now bare-chested, to look at Jake, he had just shucked his swim trunks and was standing naked alongside the palm tree log watching her place her blouse on the Whaler's bow. Smiling, she pulled the strings to her bikini bottom.

The scream pierced the night calm with a penetrating suddenness. It was a primal scream, the kind that makes the heart of any animal skip a beat and the hair to stand on end.

Jake went from pleasantly drunk to stone cold sober in the space of a microsecond. Brenda grabbed her shoulders, crossing her arms over her breasts and turning toward the *Sea Bones*, the direction of the scream. Jake ran past her and jumped into the Whaler, flipped the cover off the Mercury outboard and yanked free the ignition harness. He handed it to Brenda as he jumped back onto the beach. Not yet comprehending what was going on, she watched Jake snatch up the large kitchen knife she had stuck in the sand earlier when preparing their dinner.

"Take this!" Jake said forcefully, putting the knife in her hand. "Go to the end of the cay and squat down in the brush. Don't move about. Don't come out to the boat. Wait for me!" Then he dived, totally naked, into the dark water and began swimming rapidly toward the *Sea Bones*.

Jake made powerful strokes, but was careful to not make splashes with either his feet or his arms and he kept his head above water, eyes focused on the deck of the *Sea Bones*. If he was spotted, there would be little he could do. He heard several more screams, muffled this time. Then a pistol shot, followed closely by a second shot. *Damn! They found the doc's pistol.* He had recognized the sound. Ambrose owned a U.S. military-style Colt .45-caliber automatic that he kept in a bedside table. The doctor had fired it many times while aboard the *Sea Bones*, usually at sharks that had been snagged on a fishing line by one of his guests.

Jake was sure it was the Haitians, and had hoped they were armed with only knives, machetes or clubs. The pistol, he knew, diminished his odds of a successful intervention. He wondered who had been shot and what kind of carnage he would find on the *Sea Bones*. When he reached the bow, he paused to gather his breath, then slipped underwater and followed the *Sea Bones'* hull until he reached the teak swim platform. The platform rode about a foot above the water's surface and Jake rotated beneath it and peered up through the slots. No one was on the platform, but he could see that a wooden native craft was floating aft and was tied to the *Sea Bones'* stern.

Silently and with the greatest care, Jake eased onto the swim platform and from the far starboard quarter lifted his head only for a moment to scan the aft cockpit. A shirtless Haitian in ragged shorts was standing in one of the fighting chairs bathed in light from the *Sea Bones'* main salon. Machete in hand, he was looking forward into the *Sea Bones'* main salon intent on the action taking place there. Jake reached over the transom and silently slipped the gaff hook from its holder. Crouched on the swim platform, he took a tight grip on the gaff's wooden handle, drew a deep breath, then in a single motion threw a leg over the transom and in one leap was behind the Haitian. The Haitian had begun to turn, but the huge hook slammed over his shoulder and into his neck. Jake gave a furious yank that buried the hook deep into the Haitian's throat. The yank pulled the gargling Haitian clear off his feet and he sailed over the transom into the water. Jake let go of the gaff as the Haitian arced through the air. He picked up the Haitian's machete from the cockpit's sole and as an afterthought snatched the bottle of alcohol from its holder. Then he moved crab-like up the starboard side of the *Sea Bones* toward the forward deck.

Not until he passed the companionway door did he dare to take a quick look inside. He saw Ambrose and the four other men trussed up and lying facedown on the salon sole. There was a woman on her knees surrounded by the Haitians, but Jake couldn't see who it was because his view was blocked by the Haitians. He didn't see the other women at all, and it looked like there were three Haitians. He couldn't make out which one had the pistol either. Jake continued forward to the *Sea Bones'* foredeck, slowly lifted the hatch and eased himself down into the forward crew quarters. Then, he made his way aft along the companionway toward the steps leading into the main salon, the bottle of alcohol in one hand, the machete in the other.

For those who can appreciate such things, it was both horrible and beautiful at the same time. Jake's tactical surprise was complete. The Haitians were engrossed in their evil deed and had no time to appreciate or evaluate the sudden and unexpected appearance of the screaming, naked white man. They didn't see the small plastic bottle in his left hand, and they didn't see their comrade's machete in his right. And they were paralyzed by Jake's maniacal battle scream. From beginning to end it was all over in less than eight seconds.

Three of them. One with his back to Jake, grabbing a handful of Margaret Swell's lovely blond hair, using it to pull her mouth back and forth over his erection. The other two, one standing with a foot on Dr. Ambrose's neck, guffawing and shouting encouragement in an incomprehensible Haitian dialect while waving his machete, the other holding Ambrose's Colt 45 automatic pistol at his side, also shouting excitedly.

Everything changed when they saw their friend's head leap from his shoulders followed by a gushing fountain of arterial blood. The fury of Jake's swing with the machete had cleanly parted the Haitian's head from his body. The wooly head tumbled to the cabin sole, the face frozen in wide-eyed surprise. Then the headless torso collapsed behind it revealing the charging white man screaming at the top of his lungs. The Haitian with Ambrose's automatic pistol took a jerky half-step back and was raising the pistol to fire, but he was too late. The naked white man sprayed his eyes with stinging alcohol, flung down the bottle, and was upon him with an excruciatingly painful grip on his wrist forcing the pistol down, followed by a knee to the groin then a slicing elbow to the nose that drove cartilage into his brain ending his life. The third Haitian had his machete in full swing with every intention of splitting open Jake's head, but he, too, was late. Jake rolled under the swing, smashing the Haitian's knees with his left shoulder, hearing them snap and crumble under the impact. The Haitian screamed in agony and made to stab downward knife-like with his machete into Jake's exposed back, but the force of his thrust only drove his chest more solidly onto Jake's upraised machete. The razor-sharp point pierced the Haitian's heart and he sank with an eruption of blood

86

from his mouth.

Jake came from beneath the hemorrhaging Haitian and scrambled for the 45 automatic, quickly snapping back the slide and watching a fresh round seat itself in the breech. "Are there any more? Where are Rikki and Dagmar?" he shouted as he came to his feet.

"GOD ALMIGHTY, JAKE! GOD ALMIGHTY! Doctor Jerome Ambrose yelled. "CUT ME LOOSE. CUT ME LOOSE!" he pleaded.

Jake stepped over the headless torso and cut Ambrose's bonds with the machete, but pressed for an answer to his question. "Where's Rikki and Magda/" he repeated forcefully.

"In one of the staterooms," Ambrose answered. "Locked in, I think," Ambrose added in a squeaky and frantic voice. He crawled on hands and knees to Maggie Swell who had collapsed groaning incoherently, her hands tied behind her back.

Jake picked up a machete from the salon floor, dropped it in front of Ambrose and ordered, "Cut the others loose, doc," and charged back down the companionway, the .45 automatic pistol held firmly in front of him. The first stateroom on the starboard side was locked, the key still hanging in the lock. Jake opened the door and found Rikki and Magda, naked, bound head and foot. They yelled in simultaneous joy, "Jake! Jake!" He cut them free, but spun quickly out of the stateroom and back to the main salon.

When he re-ascended the companionway stairs to the main salon, Ambrose had already freed Louie, Stevie, Romulus and Remus and was kneeling alongside Margaret, holding her tightly. "There's one more, Jake!" he yelled. "There's four of the bastards!"

"Got it covered, Doc," Jake said.

Rikki and Magda stumbled into the main salon reeling from the shock of their experience, but ecstatic to see that everyone was still alive. They had heard the gunshots and feared the worst. They witnessed a sight that they would never forget for as long as they lived. The salon sole was awash in blood. A severed head lay in the open, its eyes still open. A headless corpse and two more bodies lay motionless, one of which was bleeding copiously from a machete stuck in its upper chest. And there stood Jake, completely naked, streaked with blood from head to toe and holding a pistol in his right hand like some kind of avenging angel. Then, a distant scream.

"Christ! Brenda!" Jake yelled and dashed outside to the deck. He ran forward to the bow and leaped into the water feet first, pistol in hand and began to swim furiously toward Dunbar Cay's beach.

The full moon was now low on the horizon and the beach was dark. As he came to his feet and stepped out of the surf, Jake yelled "Brenda! Brenda!" It was then that he saw a human form lying on the beach alongside the Whaler and his heart skipped a beat.

"Jake! Here!" Brenda called out as she stepped from the brush beyond the Whaler, kitchen knife in hand. "Watch out! There's one of them here!"

With pistol hand extended, Jake stepped toward the body next to the Whaler and saw that it was the Haitian he had gaffed earlier. The gaff was still firmly embedded in his throat, the wooden handle riding over his shoulder atop his back. Apparently he had remained alive long enough to thrash his way to the beach.

Brenda ran up to Jake and grabbed him tightly. She had put her blouse and bikini bottom back on. Jake put an arm around her and asked, "He give you a scare?" indicating the very dead Haitian.

"More than a scare," Brenda shivered. "I heard gun shots. What's happened? Was it the Haitians?" Then, an observation: "Jake, you're naked!"

The swim to the beach had washed the blood from Jake's body and there was nothing to suggest he was any different from when he had dived into the water barely 10 minutes earlier. "Yeah, I thought I was going to get laid. You got the wiring harness?" he asked as he picked up his swim trunks and tee shirt and put them on.

"Yes, here," Brenda said, handing it to him. "Are you going to tell me? Is it that bad? Who was hurt?"

"Nobody you know," Jake said as he stepped into the Whaler and reinstalled the Mercury's wiring harness. "Let's get back to the 'Bones and straighten things out. It's a real mess there."

"What about him?" Brenda asked, pointing at the gaffed Haitian.

"He's not going anywhere," Jake said. "Come on. Let's take care of business."

They were in the Whaler only long enough for Jake to tell Brenda that only Haitians were among the dead, but the scene aboard *the Sea Bones* was not going to be pretty, and that everyone was pretty shook up. He said he and Brenda needed to move everyone out of the main salon and up to the topside sundeck or the aft cockpit. The fresh air would help and maybe Brenda could get some coffee going. It was another five hours before first light and it was going to be followed by a long day for everyone. Jake made no mention about any of the particulars concerning the fate of the Haitians. He figured she'd get that soon enough.

When they boarded the *Sea Bones* and stepped into the main salon, Brenda gasped and Jake asked, "Where's the doctor?"

Louie answered first. "He's sedating Maggie. They're in the master stateroom."

Jake, still carrying the Colt .45 automatic, crossed the main salon and went down the companionway to Ambrose's master stateroom.

Brenda was frozen in place. She couldn't take her eyes off the severed head staring at her.

Jake saved our asses big time, Brenda," Louie said, the tone of his voice strangely hollow.

"Jake?" Brenda said dazed, finally willing her eyes to leave the severed head and encounter the three corpses, one of them headless and another with a machete sticking out of its chest. And the blood! It looked like buckets and buckets of blood had been poured over everything.

But it was the greatly altered demeanor of the *Sea Bones'* guests that struck her the most. When she had last seen them little more than three hours earlier, they had been laughing and cutting up; the women in bikinis and the men in bathing trunks. They were finishing the second round of drinks and swarming over the feast Brenda had prepared and spread over the main salon table. The work of filming was behind them; it was party time and they were aboard a luxurious yacht loaded with booze and food.

Now, Brenda saw, they were subdued and traumatized. They had been to death's door, in the hands of merciless savages armed with razor-sharp machetes bent on mayhem and murder. None had expected to get out alive. They had been suddenly overwhelmed by the intruders, then bound hand and foot, and made to watch the first of their company, poor Maggie Swell, dragged to her knees, stripped and forced to take the Haitian leader's erection into her mouth.

"Man," Stevie said, his voice, too, kind of off-key and squeaky, "if I'd had a camera going from the time Jake came up those stairs screaming like a demented banshee and lopping the head off that fucking Haitian, I'd have footage that would guarantee me an income for life."

And then they told her how it went down, blow by blow. Rikki and Magda heard it all for the first time, too.

When Jake returned from checking in with Doctor Ambrose, he announced, "Maggie's going to be fine. She's shook up and the doc is going to hang in with her for a bit. I'm going to radio the Bahamas Marine Patrol on Bimini and see if we can get some cops down here. It'll take several hours for them to get here. Let's move topside and get out of this mess." He turned to Brenda, in full command of events and said, "Round up some blankets and get everybody covered up and stretched out on the deck chairs. Then, brew up some coffee and bring up a bottle of brandy."

With that said and without waiting for a reply from Brenda, Jake went to the forward steering station and fired up the marine VHF, calling on Channel 16 and requesting emergency assistance. Jake identified himself as captain of the motor yacht *Sea Bones*. The Bahamas Marine Patrol operator came on immediately and asked the nature of the emergency. "Our vessel is not in danger, but we have fatalities on board. No medical assistance is required, just police officers." Jake was careful to not mention pirates or having been boarded by Haitians. He knew Channel 16 was monitored by hundreds of boats and shoreside facilities; no sense in spreading panic throughout the island community. He gave the GPS position for the *Sea Bones* and signed off without giving the operator an opportunity to ask for further details.

When he returned to the main salon, the last of the guests were passing through to the main deck and up the companionway to the topside sundeck. Brenda came up from the staterooms companionway with an armful of blankets and gave Jake a look as though she had never seen him before in her life. She was struggling to put it all in perspective, trying to reconcile her first

91

impressions of Jake as a good-looking, soft spoken yacht captain, and now the fact that he had just killed—no, slaughtered—four men. Louie's and Stevie's descriptions of their rescue by Jake, and the brutal savagery of it, left Brenda in an incomprehensible daze. *Christ! I almost made out with this guy! What was I thinking?*

Jake either ignored Brenda's look or was unaware of it and crossed the main salon to the bar, grabbed a bottle of brandy and went topside. Once he saw that everyone was settled into a deck chair and covered with a blanket, he handed the bottle of brandy to Brenda.

"Take a swig of this and pass it around," he said. "I'm going to go back down to brew the coffee and check on the Doc and Maggie. It's best that you don't go back down unless it's absolutely necessary, okay?"

Brenda took the brandy without comment and just nodded.

(Nine)

The eastern sky had only begun to lighten slightly when the *Sea Bones'* passengers and crew saw the brilliant spotlight of the Bahamas Marine Patrol boat sweeping across the night sky, a red light also flashing from atop its communications mast. Doctor Ambrose had come up to the sundeck to join the others, leaving Maggie Swell sedated in the master stateroom. He had gone to each of his guests, including Brenda, and asked after their health and whether they required any medication. But the coffee and brandy had done the trick, and now they were waiting submissively for the police. No one wanted to return to the main salon.

Jake had crossed to the topside steering console and called the patrol boat on the VHF radio informing them he had them in sight. The patrol boat also acknowledged having sighted the *Sea Bones* and was now negotiating the shallow cut at the northern end of Dunbar Cay. Jake and Doctor Ambrose stood apart from the others to watch the patrol boat's approach.

"There are no words, Jake," Ambrose said in a flat tone of voice. "I don't believe what has happened. And all I can say is Thank God you were here. I have no doubt those bastards would have killed us all."

"Their killing days are over, Doc," Jake said. His voice was even and without emotion.

"I believe that's Chief Tommy at the bow rail," Ambrose said as the gray-hulled Bahamas Marine Patrol boat powered down to slow its approach to the *Sea Bones*. There were at least ten marine patrolmen scattered about the patrol boat's deck, automatic rifles slung across their chests.

The squat black officer, dressed in his short-sleeved blue shirt, gold star gleaming from its epaulets, a black Sam Browne belt crossing his chest supporting a sidearm, and matching blue shorts with black knee-high socks, gave a tentative wave to Ambrose and Jake.

Once the patrol boat was made fast to the *Sea Bones'* starboard side, Chief Tommy and the phalanx of patrolmen swarmed aboard. It had not escaped Chief Tommy's observation that a Haitian-style sailing craft with an outboard motor was tied to the *Sea Bones'* stern.

"It is good to see that you are not among the fatalities that Captain Jake radioed us about," Chief Tommy said. A very conservative smile crossed his face. He took Ambrose's hand first, then Jake's, squeezing them firmly.

"We have been fortunate, Chief Tommy," Ambrose said, equally subdued. "We owe our lives to Jake. We were boarded," at which point Ambrose nodded toward the Haitian boat, "and at their mercy in moments. Three of them are in the main salon, and the fourth is on the cay's beach."

Chief Tommy gave a curt nod to two marine patrolmen with sergeant stripes on their sleeves and followed them into the main salon. A motor launch was put over the side of the patrol boat and sped away with three patrolmen to examine the body on Dunbar Cay's beach.

Three hours later, the *Sea Bones* was underway, trailing the Bahamas Marine Patrol boat and headed for Bimini. Jake was at the helm accompanied by seven of the marine patrolmen, but everyone else including Doctor Ambrose had been transferred to the patrol boat. The main salon's crime scene had remained undisturbed to await the forensic experts from Nassau, who were now enroute to Bimini by helicopter. As it turned out, a Superintendent from the Ministry of Defense was said to be aboard the helicopter as well.

At Bimini, everyone from the *Sea Bones* was given a room at a small tourist hotel to freshen up and await interrogation. Dr. Ambrose stayed with Maggie Swell, who was slowly recovering from her ordeal. Rumors were spreading fast among the islanders, and there was a small group of onlookers at the marina to witness the bodies of the four Haitian pirates placed in black plastic body bags and taken ashore. Jake was transported to the Bahamas Marine Patrol headquarters building by Chief Tommy where they were met by Captain Jones, the homicide officer Jake had met at the Cat Cay Club six days earlier.

That afternoon, with Chief Tommy, Captain Jones and the Defense Ministry Superintendent in tow along with a crime scene photographer, Jake walked them through the previous evening's events aboard the *Sea Bones*. He took the opportunity to point out that the yellowish-green paint on the Haitian's boat looked like the same color on the stern of the sailboat at the Cat Cay Club. Captain Jones made a notation in his notebook. The two gunshots, it turned out, were fired into the ceiling of the *Sea Bones'* main salon mainly to frighten and intimidate the hostages. The .45 slugs had been stopped by the thick insulation and multiple layers of fiberglass-covered plywood of the topside sun deck. A crime scene tech was standing on a short stepladder digging them out with a thin-bladed knife.

The Superintendent, after having seen the aftermath of Jake's assault upon the Haitian pirates and heard his rendition of events felt compelled to ask, "Captain, have you had any special kind of training in the martial arts?"

"Only in the Marine Corps, sir," Jake answered cautiously.

"Ah, the United States Marine Corps," the Superintendent said with an appreciative smile. "A fine organization, without doubt. Doctor Ambrose and the others aboard the *Sea Bones* are indeed fortunate you paid attention to your training." And he left it at that.

"You heard the scream from the beach and heard the pistol shots while you were swimming to the yacht," Chief Tommy summarized. "What were you thinking, Captain Jake? You were surely outnumbered and out-gunned. Why did you continue to the boat?"

Jake answered, but slowly and deliberately. "I didn't like the likely consequences if I didn't. It wasn't really a matter of choice, Chief."

"Quite," Chief Tommy said. "A matter of necessity, I think. It is as the Superintendent has said, your friends were very fortunate you had the will and the way."

(Ten)

Two days later everyone but Jake and Brenda boarded a Chalk's Airline amphibian for a flight to Miami, and then on to their respective destinations. Dr. Ambrose wanted to accompany Maggie back to Fort Lauderdale, and he had asked Jake if there would be any problem in Jake taking the *Sea Bones* back across the Gulf Stream to Florida. To Jake's surprise, Brenda volunteered to help with the crossing. She had had little to say to him since arriving in Bimini, avoiding his eyes when he glanced in her direction. In some ways her silence didn't surprise Jake at all. If anything, it just confirmed some vague assessment he had about his own character that he was still working out to his personal satisfaction.

Jake was informed that no charges would be pressed. The entire incident was being handled as one of self-defense. The Superintendent from the Ministry of Defense, Whatley was his name, had made a point of asking Jake to realize that this sort of incident could reflect badly on the Bahamas' reputation as a tourist playground. It could also impact on the already strained relations with the Haitian government, and he implored Jake to do his best to keep the whole affair to himself. Keeping it a secret was out of the question, he admitted, since local islanders had seen the four black body bags coming ashore and rumors were already speculating as to what had happened on the big power yacht. Jake assured Superintendent Whatley of his cooperation and said that he, too, hoped the news could be contained.

Chief Tommy and Captain Jones accompanied Jake to the Bimini dock and wished him well. When they had left, Jake hired a couple of Bahamians to help him roll up the blood-soaked Oriental rug in the main salon and drag it outside to the aft cockpit. He then fired up the *Sea Bones'* twin diesels to let them warm up and went through the boat to secure everything for sea. When he came topside to walk the decks and check the mooring lines, Brenda was standing alongside with her two bags.

"Unless you have some reason to hang out here any longer, Jake said, "I figure we're ready to cast off."

"I'm ready to go home," Brenda said. She tossed her bags onto the deck and went to the dock cleat holding the *Sea Bones'* bowline. She uncleated the line and looked at Jake. "Whenever you're ready, Captain," she said.

Jake cast off the stern and spring lines, then climbed to the topside steering station and engaged the engines. Brenda stepped aboard bringing the bow line with her and the *Sea Bones* eased away from the dock making her way to the channel that led to the Gulf Stream. Within twenty minutes Bimini had disappeared beneath the eastern horizon and the *Sea Bones* plowed gracefully toward her berth at the Harbor Point Yacht Club.

(Eleven)

It was a strained trip. Brenda spent most of her time sitting on the upholstered sun bench on *Sea Bones'* forward deck while Jake sat at the topside steering station. About mid-day, with the boat on automatic pilot, Jake went down to the galley to grab a beer, then went to the forward crew quarters to retrieve the battered log of Third Lieutenant White and took it back topside. An hour or so later, while he was flipping through the log's pages once again, Brenda appeared at his side with a platter of fruit and sandwiches.

"I've noticed you reading that quite a few times over the past week. Is it that interesting? she asked.

"Yeah. Take a look at this," Jake said, handing Lieutenant White's log to her. "Start reading here where they come upon an island with smoke, and read to here where they put the Spaniard over the side."

Brenda took the log, sat down on the steering station bench seat next to Jake and read the log. "Poor guy," she said when she had finished. "I wonder how long he was stranded on that island. He must have been real glad to be rescued even though it was the English who saw his signal. How about the confession in Latin. Can you read that part?" she asked.

"No," Jake answered. "I was hoping you might know someone who writes Latin, like a priest maybe."

Jake brought the *Sea Bones* alongside the Harbor Point Yacht Club's fueling pier and idled the engines while the yacht club's attendant took the bowline tossed by Brenda and secured it to a cleat. Brenda meanwhile had moved quickly down the port side and picked up the stern line. She climbed over the transom and stepped from the swim platform to the dock and made up the stern line to a cleat. Watching from the topside steering station, Jake then shut down the engines.

"Top her off, Timmy, port and starboard tanks only," Jake called down. And by the time he had gained the main deck, Brenda had her two bags in hand. She looked at him with steady eyes and considered that just eight days earlier this handsome young man had offered her a Bahamas cruise aboard a luxury yacht owned by a prominent surgeon. True, there was that slightly kinky part about the sex filming, but all in all a straight-forward job at a good wage. And under a soft Bahamian full moon she had come close to making out with him. Not the way it worked out.

"Jake, you look like a yacht captain," she began, "but there's more to you than that. That's for damn sure. You took out four killers in less than 10 minutes; one of them, you chopped his head off," she recapped it slowly. "I've been hanging out with yacht captains for years, and I've never met one with that particular talent. You're one scary guy, Jake Porter, and I don't know what to make of you. I don't want to seem ungrateful. I'm glad you were there for us." When Jake offered no immediate comment and only stood looking at her through dark sunglasses, she said, "I'll see a priest I know about getting that translation for you." With that said, Brenda turned and walked away.

An hour later, with the fuel tanks topped off, Jake moved the *Sea Bones* from the fueling dock to her berth at the end of the T-head.

He called the marina office on his cell phone and asked Millie if she knew of a reliable firm that could clean a deeply-stained oriental carpet from the *Sea Bones*. He added that it was an antique, one of Dr. Ambrose's favorites, and quite valuable. Millie answered in the affirmative, and Jake asked her to contact them, tell them the carpet was in the aft cockpit of the *Sea Bones* ready for pick-up.

Millie asked, "What's it soiled with?

"Blood, Millie. Lots and lots of blood," Jake replied, then hung up before a startled Millie could respond. He went below, gathered his belongings into his sport bag, including Lt. White's shellacked and battered sea journal, connected the *Sea Bones* to shore power, and secured all hatches. He then made his way to his Volvo station wagon, and drove to the marina behind Sammon's Boat Yard where the *Giggling Witch* was berthed waiting for his return.

OF CHARTS AND A FARAWAY ISLAND

Date: November 15, 2000

Lat. 26º 4' N, Long. 77º 2' W

Fort Lauderdale, FL

(*One*)

The *Giggling Witch* bobbed gently at her berth in the marina behind Sammon's Boat Yard. As Jake came down the dock, he was pleased to see that all was well with his sailboat. The surprise, however, was that the berth next to her, one that had been empty when he left for the Bahamas with the *Sea Bones*, was now occupied by Archie McGruder's ancient French fishing boat, the *Waltz'n*, and McGruder himself was standing on the dock in front of his boat resting a hand on the end of her long bowsprit.

"What say there, Cap'n Jake?" hailed McGruder when he spied Jake coming down the dock.

"You've become a neighbor, I see," Jake replied, lowering his sport bag to the dock in front of his own boat's bowsprit. He and Brenda had departed Bimini early that morning, bringing the *Sea Bones* across the Gulf Stream in record time. It had been a long day. It was now early evening and he was thinking of nothing more than climbing aboard the

Giggling Witch, having a stiff drink, and turning in for the night.

"Moved in early this morning, Jake. 'Thought I'd class up the marina a little with a real sailboat," McGruder said. With a wide grin, he offered his hand.

"I just got back from the Bahamas charter, and I'm beat," Jake replied, taking McGruder's hard, calloused hand. "Had the owner and his personal guest, six passengers and one hired galley chef to watch after. It was a handful."

"I'm guessing that galley chef would be Brenda. Her truck's been parked at Sammon's ever since you snatched her away last week."

"I didn't snatch her away, Archie," Jake said. "I lost my regular galley chef to an accident. Brenda was recommended to me, and you happened to be at Sammons when I came along to recruit her. She did a good job, by the way, and she's made a nice piece of change for a few days of entertaining."

"Well, I'm hoping you haven't spoiled her. I'm still campaigning her for a cross-Pacific trip. What do you think are my odds?" Archie asked.

"No idea, Archie, but as I recall she turned you down the last time you asked," Jake said.

"They always say 'no' the first time around, Jake. Sheilas like to be coy, and they're as fickle as the wind," Archie responded with a wink. "But look here, I can see you're sagging. Step aboard *Waltz'n* and I'll set you right with a tip of 20-year-old Irish malt, then see you to your bunk all safe and sound. I'm hauling tomorrow at Sammons. I'll be so busy fixin' and repairing for the next five days that I won't have time for a decent conversation."

"You're on. Let me toss my kit aboard the '*Witch*, and pop the hatches."

(*Two*)

Descending the companionway into the *Waltz'n's* main salon was like going back a hundred years in time. Originally designed and built in rugged workboat fashion on the north coast of France between the two World Wars, the interior of *Waltz'n* had originally been a fish hold. With no engine, and fitted out with a gaff rig of main and mizzen, and a huge foresail hanked onto the jibstay at the end of her long wooden bowsprit, she had plied the cold waters of the north Atlantic for weeks at a time, her owner and one or two crew tossing their salted-down catch into the hold until it was full. The years of accumulated salt had pickled the hull, and preserved the boat from freshwater rot, the deadly disease of most wooden boats.

Waltz'n had survived the destruction of World War II because she had joined the fleet of boats that carried the survivors at Dunkirk across the Channel to safety in England. A one-way trip for her; she spent the war years on the hard, up a small creek, and was eventually bought by an English couple who converted her fish hold to a small cabin with two comfortable bunks, a tiny galley with a Tilley kerosene stove, and a folding table that served for plotting courses on charts as well as a surface for eating. She remained engineless, and relied solely upon her sails for propulsion.

After his first circumnavigation around the world, a voyage that took Archie McGruder seven years to complete, he arrived back in England with about the same amount of pocket money he had when the started. He sold his little 26-foot cutter, *Songbird*, and began a search for his next boat, something a bit larger, and not requiring all the cosmetic fussing of a yacht. He found *Waltz'n* near Brighton, England, and the aging owner, a former British Spitfire pilot, anxious to sell. The deal was quickly closed.

For the next two years, Archie worked in various jobs as a welder, ship fitter and general laborer at boatyards along England's south coast, saving his money and bringing *Waltz'n* up to ocean voyaging standards; new sails, stainless steel standing rigging, an illuminated compass with an easy-to-read 5-inch card, two new anchors and 300 feet of chain and another 600 feet of half-inch, 3-strand nylon cordage. He kept the old boat's kerosene running lights, but added an electric tri-color masthead light just to be on the safe side. Then, he cast off for warmer climes, going through a succession of young women from port to port, each of whom lost their starry-eyed ideas of long-distance ocean sailing when they realized that it was a lot of hard work, and scary, too.

He spent a couple of months at Gibraltar freshening up his stores and chasing tourist skirts, then sailed solo across the Atlantic from the Cape Verdes off the northwest coast of Africa, and made into Barbados, West Indies 31 days later, then cruised leisurely through the Caribbean for the next 6 months, taking in the Caymans and Jamaica, the Turks and Caicos, and the Bahamas before crossing the Gulf Stream to Fort Lauderdale. He had no trouble finding plenty of boat work in a place that has more boats per square mile than any other on the planet. At Simon's Boat Yard he had found all the work he could handle. Now, with his cruising funds restored, he was hauling his boat to clean the bottom, paint it with two generous coats of anti-fouling paint and replace the old iron pintles and gudgeons that held *Waltz'n's* rudder to her hull. Then, it was off to the Panama Canal and a transit across the isthmus to the wide Pacific Ocean.

Archie had plunked down two Old Fashioned glasses in the middle of the main salon table and poured two fingers of pale bronze Irish malt whiskey into them. He took his seat on the starboard side of the table and Jake slid into the port side. Archie raised his glass in a toast, "Salud y pesetas, amigo." They clinked glasses, then Archie asked, "So how did the charter go, mate?

"Rich folks from Montreal and New York," Jake answered, with no intention of discussing the actual events of the Bahamas trip. " Two lookers, and the Doc's new girlfriend not bad at all in bikinis. Lot's of drinking, some swimming and a little fishing," Jake added, finishing his drink and accepting Archie's refill.

"Brenda looking good in a bikini, too? Archie grinned.

"Brenda, too. But she was kept busy cooking for that gang and didn't get to play all that much. Turned out some fantastic chow though. I'm pretty sure the Doc will want a repeat performance."

"So I'm competing against the Doctor, too, eh?" Archie asked.

"You're not competing against anybody, Archie, as far as I know," Jake said. "If I've heard right, Brenda's already got a beau. Ex-pro football player, I believe." *No sense provoking Archie with a description of Brenda shucking her blouse and untying her bikini bottom for a skinny dipping with him at Dunbar Cay. Just muddy the water.*

"Oh yeah. I've seen him. Talked with him a couple of times at the weekend parties at Sammon's. Doesn't strike me as too bright. Follows Brenda around like a puppy dog on a leash."

As they talked, Jake looked around the main salon of *Waltz'n* and took in all the artifacts and souvenirs that Archie had accumulated during his last circumnavigation. One of the most impressive was the upper and lower jaw teeth of a Great White shark that were mounted on the forward bulkhead. There were also many strands of beautiful South Pacific seashells, and a huge pink conch shell, and a barbed native fishing spear. Photographs were everywhere, mostly of Archie and young bare-chested native women in colorful sarongs with wide, toothy smiles; a few were of fellow sailors and their boats anchored in palm-fringed lagoons somewhere in paradise. Beneath the shark jaws was a map showing the round-the-world route that Archie had sailed in his sloop, Songbird, the route indicated by a thin red line.

As Jake's finger traced Archie's route across the Pacific Ocean, the longitude increasing with the westward progress, he remembered the position given in Lt. White's sailing log: Latitude 27º North, Longitude 154º West. Without pausing in his tracing of Archie's route, and giving no indication that he was scanning the scale across the top of the map, Jake scoured the ocean beneath the given position and —no island!

"You've got a lot of sea miles under your belt, Archie," Jake said in admiration, but mildly disappointed that he had not seen an island depicted on Archie's chart where he had expected it.

"That I have, Jake, lad," Archie said. "And if the sea gods are kind, many more to go."

"I've been considering a voyage myself, believe it or not. Tending to the Doc's boat has been okay, but not much money. It fit in with my life after mustering out of the Marine Corps, and while I was finishing off my college degree, but I'm feeling an urge to move on. Change of scenery, if you know what I mean."

"Well, you've got the boat for it. The *Giggling Witch* belongs out on the open ocean, mate. She'd take care of you no matter where you went. That steel hull will keep you snug and dry, for sure. You thinking about any place in particular?"

"Cross the Pacific I think," Jake said, purposely vague. "I spent 6 months on Okinawa while I was in the Corps. Great diving there. And I've always had an interest in the Philippines. Good looking women and easy living from what I hear."

"Now you're talking, Jake! Never made it to the Philippines myself. Took the more southern route through the Marquesas, Societies, Tonga, Fijis, New Caledonia, then south of New Guinea, and the Torres Strait across the top of Australia into the Indian Ocean," Archie said as he poured another two fingers of the Irish malt into their glasses.

Jake was mellowing under the influence of the liquor, but his head remained clear. "You wouldn't happen to have a small scale planning chart of the Pacific would you?" He thought: *I really want to take a closer look at Latitude 27º North, Longitude 154º West on a nautical chart with a proper scale. Large scale to depict a small geographical area, small scale to depict a large area, he remembered from his Marine Corps surveillance training and map reading classes.*

"That I would, mate." Archie rose, turned to his navigation table, lifted the top and quickly thumbed through a thick stack of charts. He laid a folded and well-worn chart in front of Jake. "You're welcome to keep that one, Jake. I know my next route like the back of my hand. By the way, have you picked up on the use of a sextant yet?"

"Actually I bought one of those fifty dollar plastic ones to practice with when I went over to the Bahamas the first couple of times with the *Giggling Witch*. Learned the basics from Blewitt's book, *Celestial Navigation for Yachtsmen*; got a copy of HO 249 sight reduction tables, a current almanac, and used my Sony shortwave to pick up the time signals from Greenwich.

"Good show. But you really need a better sextant than that plastic one, Jake, especially a better telescope. I just happen to have an extra one that I can let go for a good price. Weems & Plath, cast aluminum body and a solid brass arc with a micrometer drum and a four-power scope. Got a steal on it from a sailor down on his luck in Tobago. It's yours for $300.00, and really worth closer to $500. Take a look at it, give it a try and let me know by week's end before I shove off." Archie pulled a slightly scratched mahogany case from a locker behind his seat, opened the top to reveal a polished sextant, and set it in front of Jake.

"I'm expecting a bonus from my Bahamas guests of the past week, and if it turns out they are as generous as usual, you've got a deal," Jake said, lifting the sextant from it's box, knowing Archie was giving him a good price.

"Crossing the Pacific east-to-west is trade wind sailing, mate. You'll need a copy of *Ocean Passages of the World* to plan your sailing route to take advantage of favorable winds and currents. It's published by the British Admiralty, but you can buy it in the larger chart and marine stores here in the U.S. There's also *Admiralty Chart 5308, The World Sailing Ship Routes*, sometimes called Chart 7, that you'll find handy. The most important charts are the Pilot Charts and Sailing Directions for the specific areas and ports you intend to visit. They're pricey, but you gotta have 'em if you're gonna go poking around in coral-infested waters. No slight intended against the Americans, but in my opinion, the British Admiralty pilots are the best."

"I'm much obliged, Archie, for the info, the sextant offer and your Irish whiskey hospitality, but if I don't start making my way back to the *Giggling Witch*, I may need more than a chart to find my bunk," Jake said, feeling slightly rubbery around the knees.

"Right you are, Jake," Archie said with a laugh. "I'll just see you off *Waltz'n* to the dock and across to your boat. Wouldn't want to lose you right here in the marina before you have a chance to use that new sextant."

Back on the *Giggling Witch*, Jake laid the sextant on his navigation table, and before collapsing on the main salon settee, he unfolded the planning chart and quickly scanned across the longitude scale at the top of the chart, then ran his finger down to Latitude 27. There, not exactly at Longitude 154º, but maybe a hundred miles to the east of it, was a tiny dot of an island. Beside it was labeled *Marcus I.*, and beneath that in even smaller italicized script was *Minami Torishima (J)*.

I'll be goddamned! A Jap island. Wouldn't you know it? And Christ! Out in the middle of nowhere. Not a speck of land within hundreds of miles of it. Easily more than a thousand miles east of Japan. All alone in the cold waters of the north Pacific...waiting.

(*Three*)

The bright shaft of morning sunlight pierced one of the portlights of the *Giggling Witch's* main salon and came to rest on Jake's face and chest. He stirred fitfully under the bright light and heat, then rolled over and groaned at the unwelcome intrusion. He had never made it to his bunk in the aft cabin, but had passed out on the couch in the main salon. Grudgingly, he sat up, pawed at his hair, yawned deeply, then gripped the edge of the table and pulled himself to his feet. Woozy from the Irish whiskey of the night before, he stumbled to the head and relieved himself, then made his way to the galley and set a pot of water to boiling for coffee.

While the coffee seeped in the French Press, he sat at the table and gazed at the Pacific Ocean chart spread across it. He reached for the sextant box, opened it and lifted the instrument out. Holding it in his left hand, he put the telescope to his eye and squeezed the index bar trigger, sliding the bar smoothly across the polished brass arc, then put the sextant back in its box. He unzipped his sport bag and retrieved the English lieutenant's weathered sailing log. He ran his hand over the rough cover, the darkly browned shellac peeling at the edges. He thumbed the log open to the page with the Spaniard's confession, looked again at the Latin text, then laid the ancient, weathered log atop the chart.

After pouring a cup of steaming coffee into a large ceramic cup, Jake climbed the companionway stairs and went topside. He stepped over the lifelines onto the finger pier alongside the *Giggling Witch* and walked to the main dock, passed in front of his boat, then turned back to look at her, admiring her lines every bit as appreciatively as if he were checking out a young woman strolling through a shopping mall. But his mind was elsewhere.

The island is real, by god! Just like the young lieutenant's log described it. And now, 400 years later, a Jap island. Out in the middle of nowhere. Is it inhabited? With no water, not likely. So damn small and inhospitable, no way it was an intended destination. More likely some kind of accident, a grounding on the reef in the dark of night, or a storm. And how is it that a Spanish don was stranded there? And what's happening on that island today? Lots of questions. Time for a bit of reconnaissance. Library first, then maybe the Internet.

NEW BEGINNINGS

Date: November 16, 2000

Lat. 26º 4′ N, Long. 77º 2′ W

Fort Lauderdale, Florida

(One)

Within the hour, Jake was halfway to the county library to begin his research of the nameless island in the young British lieutenant's sailing journal when his cell phone rang. It was Millie at the Harbor Point Yacht Club.

"Jake, the cleaners called. Your rug is ready. Do you want to call them, or should I have them deliver it directly to the *Sea Bones*?" she asked.

"Well, that was fast service. They said it would take a week. Anyway, I need about an hour or hour and a half, and I can be at the marina," Jake said. "That thing is really heavy, Millie. Is Jimmy working the fuel dock today? If possible, I could use his muscle to help me wrestle the rug onto the 'Bones."

"Yes, Jimmy is working today. I'll give him a heads-up. Why I don't I call the cleaners for you and have them deliver it, and Jimmy can help the delivery people get it alongside the Sea Bones. Then, it can wait until you arrive."

"That's a good plan, Millie. I appreciate your help," Jake said.

"Are you going to tell me how it got covered in blood," Millie asked sweetly, curiosity oozing through the innocent inquiry.

"You don't want to know, Millie," Jake said. "Believe me, you don't want to know."

Jake decided to take care of the rug situation on the *Bones* first, then tackle the research at the library, so he turned around and headed for the yacht club. Jimmy, the club's fuel dock attendant, was standing alongside the *Sea Bones* when Jake arrived.

The carpet was bundled in a thick cargo paper, the waxed side out, and trussed up with manila cordage. The two of them half-drug, half-carried the heavy carpet into the *Sea Bones'* main salon, removed the cargo paper and unrolled the carpet into place. Jake slipped Jimmy a twenty dollar bill and sent him off with his thanks.

Barefoot, Jake walked the carpet, then kneeled and smelled it. Fresh and clean. Not a hint of the gore that had covered it just a few days earlier. When he stood, he noticed for the first time that the red message light was flashing on the telephone atop the galley counter.

The message was from Cindy Wright. "Ahoy, Jake! Heard you and the *'Bones* were back. My foot is on the mend. Another week and I'll be good as new. How did Brenda work out? Did she tell you I called her to present your bonafides and give her a heads-up on Ambrose? Give me a ring first chance you have, okay? By the way, there's a going away party shaping up for Archie McGruder, the Aussie, this weekend at Sammons. You planning on going? Maybe next week I can fix a dinner for all of us. Either our boat, or the *'Bones*. We'll talk, okay? Later, captain."

(Two)

Jake secured the hatches of the *Sea Bones* and headed for his Volvo and the county library. His cell phone rang once again and this time it was Doctor Ambrose.

"Hullo, Jake. Did I catch you at a good time?" he asked pleasantly.

"Good a time as any, Doc. I was on my way to the library. How are you doing, and how is Maggie?"

"I'm fine, Jake, thank you," Ambrose said. His voice had a somewhat solemn tone. "Maggie is in a psychiatric clinic, and under professional care. She'll eventually come out of it, the doctors say, but those damn Haitian thugs took her to the edge." There was bitterness in his voice, also. "By the way, Chief Tommy gave me a call, and confirmed your suspicions that the paint on the Haitian's skiff matched the paint marks on that young sailing couple's sailboat at Cat Cay. Same bastards that killed her husband and slashed and raped her are the same ones that boarded the *'Bones.'*"

"They were a bad bunch, Doc. No doubt about it, but they're off the board now forever," Jake said.

"Thanks to you, Jake. Thanks to you," Doctor Ambrose said. "I have never met anyone in my entire life who would have stepped up and done what you did for us We will be in your debt forever, you know that. And actually, the main reason I called was to let you know that I've got a paycheck and a couple of bonus checks for you, and a check for Brenda, too. I was wondering if we could meet at the *'Bones* late this afternoon around four o'clock and let me give those to you. How does that sound?"

"Sounds fine, Doc," Jake said. "I'm just grateful that everyone got out of it with their lives. I'm really sorry to hear the news about Maggie, but time heals all wounds they say. I'll be happy to visit her at the clinic anytime you say if you think it would be of some help."

"I know she'd like to see you, Jake," Ambrose replied. "But right now they've got her on some medication and are restricting visitors, especially anyone that might trigger memories of that horrible night in the Bahamas. I'm sure you understand."

"Of course, Doc," Jake said. "Just let me know when's a good time. She and Brenda got along well, too, and I'm sure Brenda would like to see her when the time is right. Anyways, I'll see you at the *Bones* at four."

"Fine," Ambrose said. "See you at four, then" and rang off.

Jake checked his watch. Plenty of time for a quick trip to the library before returning to the *Bones* to meet the Doc.

(Three)

At the library, Jake went to the reference area first and pulled out the National Geographic's World Atlas, turned to the index in the back and looked up Marcus Island. There it was, and he also noted that an alternate name was *Minami Torishima*, with the letter "J" following to indicate that it was a possession of Japan.

He turned to the page indicated and checked out the map that depicted most of the western Pacific Ocean. Marcus Island was an obscure, tiny, incredibly remote island east of Japan. Not another island or landmass within hundreds of miles. At least a thousand miles east of Tokyo.

At the reference desk, he asked for help finding out more about the island, and got more than he bargained for. The librarian found several books on Pacific Ocean history, including the official Department of Defense history of the Pacific war of WWII by Samuel Eliot Morrison. Apparently the island had played a role during the war. There was also a monograph written by an ornithologist, named Bryan, who had visited the island before World War I, and described its topography and bird population. Some of the material was not available for checkout, but Jake made a note of what he couldn't take with him, and checked out the remainder.

(Four)

Jake returned to the *Sea Bones* just before 4 o'clock, went aboard and began to open hatches, and the companionway doors to the aft cockpit. The mustiness, and a strange odor that he couldn't identify, were quickly swept away. He went down to the engine room, checked oil levels, and fired-up the two diesels. He had just returned to the main salon when Doctor Ambrose arrived. The Doc was dressed in light beige tropical trousers, a brightly printed silk short-sleeved shirt, and wore canvas deck shoes. A pair of Gucci sunglasses rode atop his shaved head. Despite the finery, he looked a bit haggard.

"Welcome aboard, Doc," Jake said. "All systems up and running."

"Good to see you, Jake," Ambrose said, taking Jake's hand and pulling him closer for a manly touching of shoulders. "You've taken good care of the *'Bones*, Jake, and you're a fine Captain. This is difficult, Jake, but I have to tell you. I'm thinking of selling the *'Bones*. In fact, I called a couple of brokerage firms yesterday to get a feel for the market. The bottom line is that I don't think I'll ever be able to forget that Haitian bastard's foot on my neck and me watching helplessly at what they were doing to Maggie. All of us so close to death."

"I understand, Doc," Jake said.

"It's not going to happen overnight, but I wanted you to know my plans. I realize you have your own live-aboard boat, but you are welcome to stay aboard *'Bones* whenever you want; use the telephone, the Internet connection, whatever. I'll call if I intend to visit so I won't interrupt any love making," Ambrose said, smiling. "And you may entertain on her, and take her out for a run if you want. It's better that she not sit idle at the dock for too long. Should a potential buyer, or a broker want a demo, I'd appreciate you taking her through her paces for the broker and prospective buyers. Just keep me informed. I'll keep you on the payroll until she sells and the papers change hands."

"I appreciate that, Doc," Jake said. He was touched by Ambrose's generosity, appreciating how difficult it was for him.

Ambrose reached into his hip pocket and brought out two envelopes. "These are for you and Brenda. You'll find several checks in yours, one for your regular captain's pay, the bonus for the filming venture, and two additional ones in gratitude from Louie and me. I know there's no way to place a value on what you did for us, but we just wanted to make some kind of expression of thanks for giving us our lives."

Jake took the envelopes without opening them and put them in his own hip pocket. "Thanks, Doc," Jake said. "I didn't have a choice in the matter, you know. I was running on pure adrenaline that night, and thinking about that sailing couple at the Cat Cay Yacht Club. No way was I going to let that happen again, especially to friends and crew under my responsibility. No way."

"Well said, Jake," Ambrose answered, looking his captain and friend squarely in the eyes. "Let's say no more about it, and let the evil die on the vine, okay?"

After Ambrose had left, Jake shut down the engines, checked the bilges, then closed the companionway doors and the hatches. Topside on the dock, he looked the *Sea Bones* over, then headed for his car. He looked at the pile of library books in the front passenger seat and had a definite sense that a new chapter of his life was unfolding.

Back on the *Giggling Witch*, Jake spread out the books on the main salon table and began to sort through it all. No way had it formed in his mind just yet that he might one day sail to this forbidding place on the other side of the world, but nevertheless, he was curious about the identity of the island that bore no name when the Spaniard castaway was recovered from it. And even more curious as to why the Spaniard would be abandoned and alone on the island to begin with.

MARCUS ISLAND

Lat. 22.17 N, 153.58 E Lon.

Western North Pacific Ocean

(One)

Rising barely 200 feet above the heaving blue surface of the great Pacific Ocean, the island is a curiously shaped, near-perfect triangle of barely one-half square acre in total area, sparsely covered in scraggly trees and thick, low vegetation. Its three-sided beach perimeter can be walked in less than 15 minutes. It is most definitely not the common image evoked by the expression, 'Pacific island.' This is no exotic coral atoll populated by friendly, brown-skinned natives. There is no flashing white surf smashing against a reef-enclosed lagoon of quiescent turquoise beauty. Rather, it is only the tip of an ugly, black volcanic spire topping a Central Pacific seamount that begins 2,500 feet below on the ocean floor. It is forbidding, uninhabited, lacking in fresh water and continually assaulted by fierce seasonal typhoons and frequent north Pacific storms. It is girded on all three sides by a coral reef necklace and off-lying rocks ready to gut the bottom from any vessel foolish enough to be caught in the relentless ocean swell passing around it. There are only two small breaks in the coral barrier, one on the northeast side, and one on the southern side, neither of which affords a safe all-weather anchorage. To say that the island is inhospitable is not overstating the facts.

This tiny speck of island is so insignificant against the vast ocean that surrounds it that its depiction on the nine-square foot area of British Admiralty Chart #5257 is little more than the span of the head of a pin. Identified on the nautical chart as Marcus Island, it lies at Latitude 24 degrees, 17 minutes North, 153 degrees, 58 minutes East, over 3,100 miles west of Hawaii, and more than 1,000 miles east of Tokyo. Alone in the vast reaches of the north Pacific, its nearest island neighbor is the East Island of the Maug Islands of the Mariana Islands Group which is 631 miles (1,015 kilometres) west south-west of Marcus Island. Wake Island is roughly 760 nautical miles to the southeast. However, it is not the remote geographical position, but rather its remoteness from the affairs of mankind that has made it a true enigma.

There is no agreement whatsoever among historians as to who was the original discoverer of the island. The date upon which the first human stepped onto the island and his name or nationality are lost to us. Some scholars have tried to establish Spaniards of the mid-seventeenth century as having first come upon the island, but there is absolutely no documentation to support those claims. In fact, no one even knows who is the Marcus-person after which the island was named in modern times. Various suggestions as to who this modern era discoverer might have been have included New England whaling captains and Hawaiian missionary priests. But no one knows for sure.

OPNAV 50E-9, a civil affairs handbook produced by the Office of the Chief of Naval Operations of the United States Navy and dated 10 July 1944, states that Marcus Island "escaped discovery until 1896." It goes on to say that the island "was discovered by the Japanese navigator Shinroku Mizutani [who] came upon the uninhabited island in the course of an exploratory voyage to Kulaunus Island and claimed the island for Japan."

But the Navy had it wrong. There is absolutely no documentation to support the claim that the Japanese were the first to discover the island, and in fact, there is ample evidence in proof of the exact opposite. For one, Marcus Island was depicted on British Admiralty and U.S. nautical charts long before the 1896 date of "discovery" attributed to the Japanese by the U.S. Navy's handbook.

(Two)

On the evening of December 16, 1864, some 32 years before the asserted 1896 date of discovery attributed to Japanese navigator Mizutani, a Hawaiian missionary ship named the Morning Star was returning from Micronesia, and Captain Gelett reported sighting the island and claimed it to be a new discovery. The discovery was reported in the Daily Evening Standard of New Bedford, Massachusetts on March 17, 1865:

> "A New Island. — On the passage of the missionary packet *Morning Star* from the Micronesian Islands to this port, Capt. Gelett discovered a new island located in North latitude 24, 4, and East longitude 154, 2, or about 800 miles N.N.E. from Guam. On the evening of December 16, he observed numerous land-birds, which increased in number the next morning and remarked that land must be near by, which was discovered at 3 P.M. of the 17th. The island is about five miles long, densely covered with trees and shrubbery, with a white sand beach, and rises in a knoll at the center, perhaps 200 feet above the sea. The brig passed within three or four miles of it about sunset, and breakers were seen all around. There were no signs of inhabitants living on it, though all hands on board kept a close lookout. A reef extends to the north of the island. On the old Admiralty charts a doubtful island is noted in the vicinity of the one discovered, but on Wilke's American chart and on Luray's London chart none is laid down within 100 miles of the spot. The discovery of this fertile island is important, and is reliable. We propose to name it Gelett Island, in honor of the Captain of the brig. It ought to be visited by some war vessel and fully explored. It lies directly in the track of whalers bound from the Ascension to the Ochotsk or Arctic." —

However, Captain Gelett's claim of discovery was short-lived. Three days later, the following announcement appeared in the Daily Evening Standard of March 20, 1865:

> "Notice to Mariners — The island reported as being a new discovery, by the master of the brig *Morning Star*, is undoubtedly the same as shown on the English charts as Marcus Island, the position of which (not accurately determined) is placed in Lat. 24, 20 N, Lon. 153 50 E, and differing but little from Capt. Gelett's report. "Messrs. E. & G.W. Blunt state that this island is, and has been for years, on their charts of the North Pacific Ocean."

There is further irrefutable evidence of the island's existence being known prior to the asserted

Japanese "discovery" of 1896. On April 10, 1874, twenty-two years earlier, the USS Tuscarora, under the command of Commander (later Rear Admiral) George E. Belknap, passed the island while surveying the ocean bottom for the world's first trans-Pacific communication cable. Official logs and soundings of the USS Tuscarora noted the island's existence and gave the position as Lat. 24º 02' N, Long. 155º 08' E.

It is reported in numerous sources that the USS Tuscarora "visited" Marcus Island in 1874 during her trans-Pacific voyage from San Francisco to Yokohoma. However, a detailed accounting of the Tuscarora's voyage compiled by Henry Cummings, aboard the Tuscarora at the time, and set forth in his "Synopsis of the Cruise of the U.S.S. Tuscarora," gives the following account of the Tuscarora's actual encounter with Marcus Island:

> "Cast No. 47 was taken while within a few miles of a small, uninhabited island, designated on the chart as Marcus Island, and, as it lies directly in the range with the sub marine elevations before and afterwards found, it is fair to conclude that it is one of a range of sub-

marine mountains more fortunate than its companions,
in that its cap rises above the ocean's surface."

The depth of Cast No. 47, the nearest to Marcus Island that was taken, was 1,499 fathoms, and the character of the bottom was recorded as "Coral Limestone, with specks of Lava."

The first record of a Japanese landing on the island is another story. In November, 1883, nine years after the USS Tuscarora sailed past Marcus Island, the first Japanese landed on the island, and, ironically, they arrived on a British ship, the Eta, which had been leased by the Yokohama Konshiro Company. Their purpose was to survey the island's guano deposits and bird populations for exploitation. It was the opening chapter in the story of Marcus Island's destruction at the hands of human beings.

(Three)

The island was visited in July 1902 by William T. Bryan, a well-known orinthonolgist. He was accompanied by Japanese military personnel, who watched him closely while he was on the island, and even forbade the American party of scientists to use shotguns to collect bird specimens. Bryan reported that the island was without fresh water, that the highest elevation was about 21 meters, and the primary vegetation was a large tree (tournefortia) species that grew to a height of about 35 feet, and a tree of the order Rubiaceae which averaged about 30 feet. Bryan reported coconut palms (cocos nucifera) "of a great age," many of them 60 feet or more high and "were well established in the larger of the four dry lagoons in the centre of the island." Bryan also noted that " a hundred and fifty yards from the coast line on every side the whole surface of the island is heavily wooded, with the exception of irregular patches...which are entirely destitute of trees and shrubs... "The density of the vegetation at times made it impossible to see at any distance, and at all times rendered locomotion difficult."

The bombings by U.S. Naval forces during World War Two would alter that condition dramatically. In fact the island would be virtually flattened above ground, and its subsurface lava structure severely fractured below.

(Four)

MINAMI TORISHIMA AND WORLD WAR II

On June 30, 1886 a Japanese named Shinroku Mizutani led a group of 46 colonists from Hahajima in the Ogasawara Islands to settle on Marcus Island. The settlement was named "Mizutani" after the leader of the expedition. They were there to harvest the huge guano deposits that had collected there over the centuries, and bird feathers from the migrating flocks of sea birds.

The Empire of Japan officially annexed the island July 24, 1898, ignoring the previous United States' legal claim from 1889 according to the terms of the Guano Islands Act. In 1902, the United States dispatched a warship from Hawaii to enforce its claims, but withdrew on finding the island still inhabited by Japanese, with a Japanese warship patrolling nearby. The Japs essentially stole the island in blatant disregard of the legitimate terms of an official international act to which it was a signatory, and then re-named named it "Minami Torishima," or "South Bird Island," placing it administratively under the Ogasawara Subprefecture of Tokyo. It became the most eastern territory of the Japanese empire.

In 1933, by orders of the Japanese government, the civilian inhabitants of Minami Torishima were evacuated. In 1935, the Imperial Japanese Navy established a meteorological station on the island, and began to build an airstrip barely 3,000 feet in length. In 1937, the first of the Imperial Japanese Army troops arrived. Seven hundred forty-two men of the Minami Torishima Guard Unit, commanded by Rear-Admiral Masata Matsubara came first, followed by the 12th Independent Mixed Regiment led by Colonel Yoshiichi Sakata, a 3-battalion force of 2,005 men that brought with them 9 Type 95 Light Tanks, 3 Type 38 75mm Field Guns and a Signals Company.

Following the attack on Pearl Harbor, the United States immediately accelerated construction of a new fast aircraft carrier, the Essex Class, to take the war to the Japanese. The United States Navy bombed the island repeatedly in 1942 and 1943 with the new Hellcat aircraft operating from the flight decks of the Essex carriers, but never attempted to capture it. The long-term American strategy at the time was to by-pass selected islands and allow them to wither on the vine from lack of logistical support. Though isolated, the Japanese were able to resupply the Marcus garrison by submarine, using a channel cut through the reef on the northwest side of the island. That channel is still visible today.

The US Navy's first WWII combat bombing using the new Essex carriers and the Hellcat aircraft was the March 1942 attack on Marcus Island:

EXTRACT

AFTER-ACTION REPORT/Bombing Squadron Six, USS Enterprise (CV-6)

Lt. Cdr. W.R. Hollingsworth, Commander,

4 March 1942

Lat. 22º 17" N, Long. 153º 58' E

Central Pacific Ocean

"In the pre-dawn darkness, the 17 aircraft of Bombing Squadron 6 took off from the flight deck of the aircraft carrier, USS Enterprise (CV-6), and on a bearing of 251 degrees, climbed through a heavy cumulus cloud cover running from 4,000 to 10,000 feet, heading for Marcus Island, 128 miles distant. The mission: a two-squadron dive-bombing attack on the Japanese airfield believed to be under construction there. The sea was calm, surface winds at 8 knots from 170 degrees, and there was a full moon at an elevation of about 30 degrees that provided considerable illumination above the clouds, but left it comparatively dark below. The sky to the east was beginning to lighten at the time of the attack, twenty-three minutes before sunrise.

At 0630, the tiny triangular-shaped volcanic island was spied through a hole in the overcast. Starting from 16,000 feet, the squadron divided into 3 groups and began high-speed approaches from the south and west. The dives varied in steepness from 045 degrees to 070 degrees, and bomb releases were in ripple drops from 3,000 to 2,000 feet; pullouts were at 1,000 feet followed by continued power glide until retirement from the attack. The attack was delivered from 0640 to 0645 hours.

Each aircraft dropped a single 500 lb. MK12 bomb with a 2.1-second delay fuse, and two 100 lb. bombs with similar delayed fuses. Less than 300 rounds of .30 cal. and .50 cal rounds were expended in strafing due to a large volume of Japanese 20mm or 37mm rapid anti-aircraft fire that hastened departure from the island. Limited large caliber (3-inch) fire was also observed. Planes retiring 5 miles away saw tracers close aboard. The island seemed to be ringed with the light batteries, with strongest concentrations at the three corners of the island. This high volume of AA fire made it impossible to adjudge the raid's damage, but several buildings or hangars on both sides of the field were on fire and several explosions at short intervals occurred in one group. A hit on and subsequent fire in what appeared to be a fuel storage tank was witnessed by the attack's spotter aircraft. Two large fires visible from 20-30 miles out were still burning brightly at 0705.

No enemy aircraft were seen on the ground or in the air during the attack. The airfield appeared to be still under construction. By 0845 hours, all aircraft of Bomber Squadron 6 were landed safely aboard the USS Enterprise."

The island has one last claim to fame before sinking into obscurity after the end of World War II: The most famed bomber in aviation history, the Boeing B-29 Enola Gay of the U.S. Army Air Force, destined to drop the first atomic bomb on Hiroshima, plastered Marcus Island on July 7th, 1945, with a load of 500 lb. conventional bombs. Flying from Wendover Army Air Field, Utah, to Tinian Island in the Marianas, the soon-to-be-famous bomber had arrived at North Field on Tinian Island on July 2, 1945. It made a return raid on Marcus on July 21, 1945 under the command of Captain Robert Lewis, dropping another bomb-bay load of 500 lb. bombs on the tiny island.

When the Japanese Imperial government finally recognized the futility of continuing hostilities and surrendered unconditionally to Allied Forces, Rear Admiral F.E.M. Whiting aboard the USS Bagley (DD-386) arrived offshore of Marcus Island and took the formal surrender of approximately 2,500 emaciated Japanese troops on the last day of August 1945.

(Five)

Following the war, Minami-Torishima began to slowly sink back into obscurity, but it continued to be shown on U.S. and British charts as Marcus Island.

On April 30, 1952, not quite seven years after the Japanese surrender in August 1945, ending World War II, a small group of ornithologists from Hokkaido University boarded the "Kuroshio-maru," a 450-ton supply ship, for what was described as a scientific trip to study the bird population of Marcus Island, now named Minami-Torishima. Curiously, the trip occurred at a time when the Black-footed Albatross, Storm-Petrels and Skuas had already completed their migrations to the cooler areas, and tropical species such as the Puffinus nativitatis and Pterodroma had already gone to their breeding islands. Strange timing indeed for Japanese bird scientists seeking to record bird populations at a time when their own island nation was struggling to recover from nuclear holocaust and the devastating wartime losses of resources and population.

Whatever the true purpose of the Japanese visit, the voyage of the

"Kuroshio-maru" from Tokyo Harbor on April 25, 1952, until its arrival at Marcus Island on April 30th, was occasioned by rough seas and strong N.N.E. winds. Upon landing, the expedition's leader, Nagahisa Kuroda, described Marcus Island as he found it:

"The whole island is formed of coral gravel...and the island is surrounded by scattered coral rocks about 200 meters offshore, especially on the northern coast. Now being totally disfigured, [by the bombings of WWII], Minami-Torishima, which lies peacefully and beautifully with green cover and white beach surrounded by deep-colored semi-tropical ocean, impressed us as a disappointment as soon as we landed upon it. Everywhere on the island are to be found residues of war. All along the coasts are trenches, with [concrete emplacements] here and there on which rusted anti-aircraft guns are still pointing to the sky...the ruins of United States camps and trucks are scattered everywhere. Almost all of the southwesterly one-third of the island is left as it was, devastated by [an earlier] typhoon.

"The only trees are of two kinds of small, tropical bushy ones, and though they make a rather thick jungle, it is too simple a cover without any big trees which will offer a good, cool shelter for arboreal birds. The central cover is a dense creeping undergrowth of Gunbaihirugao and a few grasses. There were a few poorly grown papayas and five banana plants. Minami-Torishima seems to be visited by only a few of the migrant shore birds in very small numbers. Land birds are totally lacking...and this is easily explained by the lack of fresh water and foods such as fruits and a variety of insects. We found scant animal life; small land crabs, locusts, skinks and geckos, and an unhealthy species of Rattus alexandrinus."

Kuroda and his fellow bird-watchers embarked on May 7, 1952, for their return to Tokyo.

Afew years later, the U.S. Coast and Geodetic Survey placed a seismic monitor on the island. The U.S. Coast Guard followed with the installation of a LORAN-C navigation signal tower on the island in 1964, but with the advent of satellite navigation systems, the tower was disassembled and hauled away. The same with the seismic monitor. The island was returned to Japanese control in 1968.

Finally, abandoned by humanity, its overt usefulness to any military or civilian purpose gone, Marcus Island began to slowly sink back into its former obscurity; a pitiful one-half square mile (1.2 sq. kilometers) of scruffy, water-less coral sand-covered lava with a billion-dollar secret.

THE TRANSLATION

Date: November 17, 2000

Lat. 26º 4' N, Long. 77º 2' W

Fort Lauderdale, Florida, USA

(One)

After a long night spent pouring over some of the books, maps and research material he had checked out of the library, Jake called Brenda on his cell phone. She answered on the second ring.

"Hey there! I was going to call you today. I've got something for you," she said brightly.

Jake laughed. "Well, I've got something for you, too. A paycheck from the good doctor. Want me to bring it over?" He was relieved to see that she was in a better frame of mind than when they had last parted at the Harbor Point Yacht Club after returning from the Bahamas.

"Actually, I'm not home at the moment. I'm at Sammon's meeting with some of the sailor folk. We're trying to put together a send-off for

Archie McGruder this weekend. Boy, will I be glad to see that character gone. He's worse than a blood hound."

"Yeah, his boat was in the berth next to the Witch when I got back, and he asked about you," Jake said. "He wanted to know what I thought his chances were in winning you over for his upcoming voyage. I told him I thought you were already taken by a retired football player, but nothing seems to discourage him."

"Well, I am not 'taken by a retired football player,' as you so graciously put it, but thanks anyway for trying to put him off the trail. We're all trying to round up some available women for the party to give him a shot at landing crew," Brenda giggled. "You're invited to the bash, you know," she added.

"Thanks. I'll make it a point to be there. I agreed to buy a used sextant from Archie yesterday, and after cashing my paycheck, I'll have the bucks to pay him. I'll probably do that at the party. So what do you have for me?"

I got a translation of the Latin text from that sailing log you bought. Father Dominguez at my parish did it for me. I drop in from time to time to confess my sins, but since I don't have many, I'm an infrequent visitor," Brenda laughed.

"Glad to hear you're such a good girl," Jake replied, laughing as well. "So, when would be a good time to get your check to you?"

"How about my houseboat at five o'clock? I can make us a sundowner, and maybe dinner. But since we're both loaded with fresh cash, maybe dinner out would be better, you think?"

"Sounds good. Let's work it out when we get together, okay?"

(Two)

Jake opened the envelope that Doctor Ambrose had given him. There were three checks, one for his monthly captain's salary of $1,500 plus

$2,500 for his usual bonus for a Bahamas filming trip, and another from Ambrose for $5,000 drawn on a different account that had a notation at the bottom, "For services above and beyond," and a third from Louie, for $5,000. The check from Louis had a brief note attached saying Stevie, Magda and Rikki had each contributed $500 to the total. He added that Rikki said she had something special for him should he ever visit New York. Jake was overwhelmed, and somewhat embarrassed by their generosity. Fourteen thousand dollars! But on reflection, with unemployment looming, he was grateful for the windfall.

When Jake arrived at Brenda's houseboat, the day's light was fading fast. Brenda had turned on the houseboat's deck lights, and an antique brass kerosene globe lamp hung over the table, glowing warmly on her front deck. The table had a tropical-yellow linen tablecloth, and two wine glasses, a quarter round of cheese, some crackers and an uncorked bottle of Portuguese red table wine.

"Ahoy the boat!," Jake called out as he came down the boarding plank, a bottle of imported Spanish Sangria in one hand, and an Italian salami in the other.

"Come aboard, Captain!," Brenda hailed from the galley. "Be with you in a second. The translation is on the table."

Jake took a chair, laid the salami and sangria on the table and picked up the folded paper with the Spaniard Bustamente's prayer for absolution, now translated into English. He read it quickly. It seemed a bit wordy, but nothing stood out as unusual, unless maybe the fact that it was addressed to the Pope himself. If anything, it was less exotic in English than Latin.

"Father Dominguez was very, very curious about the prayer," Brenda said as she stepped out onto the deck. She was ravishing, and Jake swallowed deeply as she came to the table, bent over and bussed him on the cheek. She wore a simple summer dress that hung from her shoulders by thin spaghetti straps, the top falling a good two inches below the beginning of her cleavage, and the bottom ending considerably higher than midway between her knees and her crotch. No bra either. As if that were not enough, she smelled wonderfully fresh and floral.

"In fact, when I told him it was quite old, several centuries, and probably written by a Spanish nobleman, he became quite excited. He pleaded with me to find out when it was written and who was the author. I told him the original was not in my possession, and I was not sure if I could do that." she smiled, and licked her lips slowly before pouring wine into the two glasses.

Without taking his eyes off of her, Jake handed her Ambrose's envelope.

Brenda opened it, and exclaimed, "Oh, my! How wonderful!" She handed the check to Jake.

Brenda's check was for $5,000; $500 per day for the 8 days aboard the Sea Bones, and an additional $1,000 bonus. A note from Ambrose explained: "My deepest apologies for the stress of our Bahamas voyage. Thank God Jake was able to intervene and change the course of events. You are a marvelous chef, and a graceful hostess. Should I require culinary services aboard Sea Bones in the future, you are my first choice. I will gladly prepare a letter of reference for you at any time. Finally, thank you for your friendship with Maggie. She is undergoing some clinical therapy at the moment, but the prognosis is good. Call me when you have a spare moment." The note was signed with Ambrose's illegibly-scrawled signature.

"Nice," Jake said, handing it back to Brenda. "Here's to flush times," he laughed, lifting his wine in a toast. Brenda clinked her glass to his, and they settled into snacking on the cheese and crackers, finishing off the Portuguese red in short order, then opening the Sangria.

"What did you think of the translation," Brenda asked softly, beginning to feel the wine.

"Well, I'm not Catholic, and I've never seen a prayer for forgiveness of one's sins. But it seems rather ordinary except for the fact that it is addressed to the most powerful person in the world at the time, at least in the Western portion of the world."

"That was my feeling as well," Brenda said. "Do you have any idea why he was stranded on that island?"

"None," Jake replied. "I'm really curious though. I visited the library yesterday and checked out a few history books and some government publications to get some feeling for what was happening during that period of time. A Spanish don stranded all alone on a Pacific Ocean island in the seventeenth century stuck me as really odd; there just has to be a story behind that, and the one given in the English lieutenant's log seems too pat. I've just begun reading, but the one thing that seems interesting is that the Spanish had a colony in Manila, Philippines, and were doing a lot of trading with the Chinese; porcelain, jewelry and silk stuff that was probably worth a lot of money.

"There were some aerial photos of the island in the stuff I checked out of the library; taken during naval air raids during World War Two. And there were some hand-drawings by the aircrews and a rather precise engineering drawing of the island done by the U.S. Coast Guard. It's a very strange-looking island, shaped like a triangle and only a half-square acre in total area. Very small, and there's an old airstrip and a few temporary buildings that haven't been used since the late 1960s. We gave the island back to the Japs in 1968."

"The island is near Manila?" Brenda asked politely, but was really thinking, *What next? Where are we? Did the Bahamas voyage begin something, or end something?* Reading Jake was not easy.

"Actually, no," Jake said. "The island sits off all by itself. One of the books I checked out has a map showing the routes taken by Spanish trading ships between Manila, and Acapulco. Most of them stayed way south and east of my island, down between the Marianas and the

Bonins. They needed the tradewinds to carry them across the Pacific to Acapulco, so they turned east before reaching the latitude of my island."

Brenda looked deeply into Jake's eyes and reached over to place her hand atop his and stroke it softly. He was truly handsome and so content with himself, it seemed. She dropped her eyes to his hands. They were ordinary in every way, yet with them he had killed four men, three of them in less than ten seconds. She was alive today because of those hands.

"Jake," she began, "I want to apologize for my unpardonable behavior following the Bahamas...incident." She didn't know what else to call it. "I thought you were just a nice looking yacht captain. It was very superficial on my part, I know. But when I came into the *Sea Bones* salon with you and saw all the blood, the decapitated head, the machete sticking out of the chest of one of those thugs, it just disconnected me in some way."

Jake smiled and placed his hand atop the one Brenda had on his. "A good looking yacht captain, you say?" he grinned, leaning across the table to kiss her. She met him halfway, lips parted, and pulled him closer, placing a hand behind his neck to whisper in his ear.

"I'm not wearing any panties, you know."

(Three)

Jake woke to the sounds of Brenda taking a shower. He was stretched out across her bed, naked. He had gotten little sleep the night before, but he wasn't complaining. He glanced over to a clock on the nightstand: nine o'clock.

The water stopped running in the shower, and Brenda stepped out naked, rubbing her hair dry with a beach towel. She caught his eye immediately and, teasingly, began to turn slowly in place, giving Jake a 360-degree view of a flawless body. "You like, goodtime sailor boy?' she mimicked in an oriental voice.

"I like," Jake laughed. "But I no damn swabbie. I'm a Marine. Comee here. I've got a message for you."

"I can see message you have for me, Marine," Brenda giggled, observing Jake's manhood slowly assuming a more erect posture. She cocked her hip, jutted her dark delta forward, put a hand beneath one of her breasts and lifted it. "You maybe want more good time with party girl?" Brenda giggled girlishly, dropping her towel to the floor.

It was eleven o'clock before Jake cleared Brenda's houseboat. After almost two hours of languorous late morning sex, she had fixed a Mexican-style scrambled egg torta with sautéed mushrooms, chopped onions, fresh tomatoes, and green peppers served atop hot corn tortillas, along with a large mug of Jamaican Blue Mountain coffee. As breakfast concluded, Jake announced that he was going to see if he could find someone with a knowledge of codes and code breaking, and was going to start with a local Marine Corps Reserve unit.

"You think the confession has a code in it?" Brenda asked while she stroked Jake's inner thigh beneath the table.

"There could be," Jake replied, taking her hand in his. "Then again, maybe not. But I've got a funny feeling about it."

When he climbed into his Volvo, Brenda had come to the doorway of her houseboat, stepped half-way onto the porch, pulling her beach robe back to expose a proud breast, a hint of her delta, and a long, shapely leg. "You come back soon, happy time Marine?" she asked with a smile.

"You betcha, China babe," Jack said with a laugh, and drove off.

MARINE INTELLIGENCE

Date: November 18, 2000

Lat. 26º 4' N, Long. 77º 2' W

Fort Lauderdale, Florida

(One)

The U.S. Marine Corps Reserve detachment located on Fort Lauderdale's Vicente Reale Boulevard was a plain-looking concrete-block building painted a nondescript beige color. It sat in the middle of a ten-acre lot surrounded by a twelve-foot-high chain-link fence topped with three strands of gleaming razor wire. The entrance and corresponding exit was a u-shaped drive that arced in front of the building framing a large concrete pedestal that supported a flagpole flying the flag of the United States of America at the top, and the U.S. Marine Corps flag directly beneath it. There was a highly polished bronze dedication plaque centered on the flagpole's pedestal honoring Marine Corps dead in WWI and WWII. To the left and right of the pedestal were stout black granite obelisks of about 4 feet in height bearing the incised names of local Marines who fell on the battlefields of Korea and Vietnam.

The parking lot extension of the entrance side of the drive contained a couple dozen or so civilian vehicles, mostly pick-ups and SUVs. The parking area that extended off the exit side of the driveway and continuing around the back of the building was filled with an eclectic mix of military vehicles: Humvees, Bradley Fighting Vehicles, 4-by-4 and huge 6-by-6 trucks with canvas covers over their beds, an armored communications truck bristling with all sorts of antennae, and even a bulldozer atop a low-boy trailer, all of them painted in the light tan-and-brown colors of desert camouflage.

Jake Porter passed through the gate and turned into the parking area for private vehicles, got out and was making his way toward the detachment's main entrance doorway when a short, stocky Marine in fatigues, laced combat boots and wearing a billed field cap rounded the far corner of the building. He was carrying two eight-foot guidons, their banners neatly wrapped and secured around their poles. As he came closer, Jake saw from the insignia inked in black on his sleeves that he was a Master Gunnery Sergeant. Jake also noticed the grey hair around his temples, his leathery tan and that his fatigues were heavily starched with ruler-straight creases. They met at the doorway, the Master Gunnery Sergeant eyeing Jake with small, black piercing eyes.

"Good morning, Gunny," Jake began. "My name is Jake Porter. I'm an ex-Marine sergeant from the Second of the First, and I'm looking for some help." Jake glanced quickly at the inked name above the Marine's right breast pocket and saw that he was talking to Master Gunnery Sergeant Sweikert, G. W.

Without so much as a blink of an eye, Master Gunnery Sergeant George

Washington Sweikert turned to enter the building and said over his shoulder, "Come."

The entrance hallway was waxed and polished to a high gleam. A long glass display case was centered against the wall. At one end was a ramrod-straight mannequin dressed in U.S. Marine Corps dress blues with a gleaming sword in a white-gloved hand held against its right shoulder. At the other end of the display case stood a similar mannequin only this one was in a menacing crouch dressed in full combat gear complete with a camouflage net hanging over its face topped by a floppy field cap, and the hands holding at the ready an equally camouflaged M4 special operations carbine with a noise suppressor and starlight scope. The image was clear: this is what a professional killer looks like. Choose sides carefully, or you may find this guy looking for you.

"Wait here, *Sergeant* Porter, while I stow these pig stickers," Master Gunnery Sergeant Sweikert ordered with the authority of a Paris Island drill sergeant speaking to a raw recruit, then strode down the hallway toward a pair of double doors that Jake could see opened to a large meeting room.

Jake watched the crisp straight strides that Sweikert made down the hallway, then turned to look at the contents of the glass display case. The three shelves contained a variety of booby-trap devices used by the North Vietnamese against U.S. troops during the Vietnam War. There was an SKS 7.62 mm rifle of the type carried by NVA regulars. On a lower shelf was a Russian AK-47 captured in the first Gulf War and an RPG (rocket-propelled grenade) launcher with *"Allah akbar,"* God is Great, painted on the tube in Arabic script. Placed in and about the weaponry were a number of unit patches taken from the uniforms of either killed or captured Iraqi Republican Guard units in Operation Desert Storm. There were also some Iraqi knives and short swords on display.

Jake was just beginning to look at the photos on the wall above and behind the display case when he heard the click and snap of Sweikert's boots returning. He had enough time to see a photo of an awards ceremony, the local Marine Corps detachment being recognized for its success in achieving a high state of combat readiness. Jake suspected that Master Gunnery Sergeant Sweikert had something to do with that. Everyone in the photo including the Marine Corps colonel making the presentation was wearing his medals, and in the quick glance that Jake gave the photo, he saw that Sweikert had five rows over his left breast plus the dangling silver marksmanship bars that attested to his mastery of infantry weapons.

"Let's take it inside, *Sergeant*," Sweikert said, and led the way down a hallway leading off the main entrance. They passed several offices with glass windows and Jake saw enough Marines going about their business to suggest that a weekend drill was in progress. He followed Master Gunnery Sergeant Sweikert into his office. Sweikert closed the door behind them and went behind his desk, still standing.

"To begin with, Sergeant Porter, there is no such thing as an *ex*-Marine. In case you've forgotten, the United States Marine Corps is not plumbing that is turned on and off. Now as you can see we have a drill in progress, but in deference to your being a former Marine, although not of my acquaintance, I am giving you the benefit of the doubt that the matter which has brought you here today is worthy of my very valuable time."

It took only a fraction of a second for Jake to realize that that was the only introduction this salty old bastard was going to give him and he was now waiting for a reply. Jesus Christ! Where do they get these hard cases? No doubt this son-of-a-bitch has been down the road and seen his share of killing. Those five rows of medals confirm that, but what keeps them in this eternal tight-ass state of mind?"

"I apologize for showing up unannounced, Gunny, and on a drill weekend. I'll be brief. I'm hoping you might be able to help me hook up with a Marine Corps intelligence officer."

Master Gunnery Sergeant Sweikert squinted at Jake with a focused intensity, as if he were trying to read Jake's mind, or remember something just out of his mind's reach. "What's this officer's name, rank and outfit?" he asked evenly, not taking his steely eyes from Jake's face.

"Not a particular intelligence officer, Gunny," Jake replied. "I'd be happy to talk with any Marine Corps officer with a background in intelligence." *Please, dear Christ, don't make me have to tell him what I'm trying to do. He will toss me out on my ear.*

"Sergeant Jake Porter. Second Division of the First Marines, I believe you said," Sweikert said slowly, continuing to study Jake's face. "What were your service dates, sergeant?"

"June 1986 to July 1991," Jake answered, wondering what this was all about.

"Five years, not four. You were extended for the Gulf War?" Sweikert began closing in.

"That's right, Gunny," Jake answered.

"What was your duty in the Gulf, Sergeant Porter?"

"I was on a STA team, Gunny," Jake said, pronouncing STA as 'stay' and still not comprehending where this was going.

Well, I'll be damned! A thin smile crossed Master Gunnery Sergeant Sweikert's weathered face. "Wait right there, Sergeant. I want to get something." And with that, Sweikert left the room. When he returned in less than a minute, he held a small booklet and handed it to Jake. "Page 11, Snapper," was all he said.

Jake felt his neck muscles tense when Sweikert called him 'Snapper.' The last time anyone had called him that was fellow Marines in Iraq. And he hadn't taken kindly to it even then. He took the booklet from Sweikert without breaking eye contact. Sweikert looked like the cat who had just swallowed the bird.

Jake glanced at the cover of the booklet and saw that it was Marine Corps recruiting material. There was a photo collage of combat scenes on the cover, the Marine Corps emblem in full color at the upper left, and the title, "Marine Heroes That Made a Difference" in large type across the center. The booklet was a collection of After Action Reports, the kind that are gathered by intelligence officers immediately following combat operations.

Jake opened the booklet to Page 11 and there was a picture of Marine Corps sniper Sergeant Jake "Snapper" Porter receiving the Silver Star, the Marine Corps Medal for gallantry, and Purple Heart from Lieutenant General Walt Boomer, commander of the 1st Marine Expeditionary Force in Iraq. Beneath the picture were verbatim abstracts from the After Action Report for each of Jake's combat exploits at Khafji, and the Kuwait City airport, complete with the story of how his "specialty" of getting off the second round before the report of the first round reached his target led his comrades-in-arms to bestow upon him the nickname, 'Snapper.'

When Jake looked up from the booklet, he saw that Master Gunnery Sergeant Sweikert, for the first time since their meeting, was offering his hand. Somewhat taken aback, Jake took it automatically and was not surprised that the grip was hard and leathery.

"You want a favor, Snapper? So do I," Sweikert said in a tone only slightly more friendly than his earlier communications. "Come with me." He turned and headed back down the hallway, then down to the large room that lay beyond the double doors.

Jake followed in his wake, wondering where all this would lead, and still not happy at being called 'Snapper' again, even if was by this hard-assed old Marine with three times his medals.

Jake could see immediately that the room was being prepared for a ceremony of some sort. There was a podium and a long table at the front of the room with U.S. and Marine Corps flags to either side. A couple of Marine privates were setting up rows of folding chairs, leaving a center isle leading to the podium.

"We're burying one of our own, Snapper," Sweikert began. "A dyed-in-the-wool, give-no-quarter Marine. The kind they don't make any more." He went to a small table beside the doorway and picked up a single sheet of paper from a stack and handed it to Jake.

While Jake looked at the color photo of Marine Corps Master Sergeant William "Willy" Coleman in dress blues with more medals than Jake had ever seen on a single Marine Corps tunic, Sweikert spoke reverently.

"Willie Coleman cut his combat teeth at the Chosin Reservoir in Korea when he was just 7 months into being seventeen years old. He killed over thirty Chinese in less than twenty-four hours and was wounded twice. A week later, he was knocked unconscious by a Chicom mortar round while mowing down more Chinese, and his position was overrun. The Chinese thought he was dead at the bottom of the ravine where the mortar blast had thrown him and passed him by.

"Willie regained consciousness later that night and fought his way back to friendly lines killing a half-dozen more of the enemy with his knife and bare hands, bringing their weapons with him. He left Korea on a stretcher with two Purple Hearts, two Bronze Stars and the Marine Corps Medal. Later, he went to Vietnam for three tours and came out with two more Bronze Stars, a Silver Star and the Navy Cross for unspecified gallantry behind enemy lines. Oh yeah, and another couple of Purple Hearts," Sweikert said.

"Well, gunny, I'm not sure I under..." Jake began, but was cut off by Sweikert.

"I know a Marine Corps intelligence officer, a top graduate of the Navy's cryptology school actually, who saw duty in the first Gulf War just like you. He took a fair measure of shrapnel in his back and legs from an Iraqi mortar round, so he's been there. He has a Master's degree in mathematics from Georgia Tech and teaches at the University of Florida. I can set up a meeting for you," Sweikert offered.

"And in return?" Jake asked warily.

"You attend Master Sergeant Willie Coleman's funeral in dress blues with your medals. I want some brother warriors to send him off."

Sweikert said it simply, with a chiseled face that was completely devoid of emotion.

"Geez, Gunny," Jake said. "I don't know if my blues are even fit to wear. I live on a sailboat and most of my stuff's been in dry storage for years."

"Come," Sweikert said, and spun on his heels. He led Jake to a large closet, flung open the double doors and there hung maybe thirty dress blue uniforms in assorted sizes. An upper shelf bore a dozen or more dress white covers with gleaming gold Marine Corps emblems, each wrapped in clear plastic. Rows of shiny black dress shoes lined the floor.

"Go check on yours. Run them through the cleaners. If there's a fit problem, I'm sure we can find something that will work. I will call my Marine intelligence officer and set up an introduction. I won't even ask what numb-nuts thing it is that has brought you off civvy street to ask for the personal services of a United States Marine Corps officer. Deal?" Sweikert said, offering his hand to seal the bargain.

Jake had been out maneuvered and knew it. He simply couldn't refuse Sweikert's hand.

"The funeral service is here at 1600 hours next Sunday," Sweikert said with authority. "Here's my cell phone number. The detachment building will be manned 24 hours throughout our weekend drill. All of the detachment's troops will attend the funeral services next weekend. Just let me know if you hit a snag of any kind, okay? I'm going to take care of my end of the bargain right now."

And with that Jake knew he had been dismissed as he watched Master Gunnery Sergeant Sweikert's back recede down the hallway.

(Two)

Back in his office, Sweikert checked his Rolodex file and dialed a number in Gainesville, Florida. When a male voice answered, Sweikert began with, "Gunny Sweikert here, Major. How you doing, sir? Fine, fine. Sir, you won't believe who just left my office." A pause. "Sergeant 'Snapper' Porter, the Gulf War sniper who was written up in that Marine Heroes recruiting booklet. The one who nailed Saddam's cousin, the defense minister. You got a copy of it? Good. Well, you can do me a big favor, sir, by chatting with him. Pause. No, no idea what he wants to talk about, but he's doing me a turn and I'd appreciate it if you would give him a few minutes of your time. Fine sir, fine. I'll have him call you direct. My compliments to your fiancé, Stacy, sir." Master Gunnery Sergeant George Washington Sweikert put the phone down with the satisfaction of a job well done.

(Three)

Jake left the Marine Corps Reserve Center still pondering the consequences of his encounter with Gunnery Sergeant Sweikert and the upcoming funeral services. He turned his Volvo toward the Atlantic Self-Storage lot where he kept a rented locker, and wherein lay his Marine dress blues uniform. He plowed through his storage locker with a vengeance, working his way to the very back where the earliest of his gear had been stowed when he had first moved to Fort Lauderdale after mustering out of the Corps.

Over the past years of working at Sammons, he had accumulated an impressive inventory of marine and boat-related stuff; anchors, radios, life preservers, bilge pumps, seat cushions, etc., etc. For some of it he had traded his labor, some of it had been given to him by boat owners simply wanting to lighten their load.

Now he had to move the greater part of it out of the way and stack it in front of his locker to make his way to the military footlocker with his uniform. He stepped into the uniform trousers then slipped into the tailored blouse, buttoned up the front, and then put on the dress tunic. Everything still fit, and that brought a smile to his face. The boating life and the rigorous physical demands of marine maintenance beneath the hot Florida sun had kept the fat at bay. Jake grabbed his shoes, black socks, tie, and the boxes with his medals. He tossed it all in a cotton laundry bag and put it in the Volvo. It took another hour to restack all the stuff in the locker before he could lock the door and head for a local drycleaners.

A GATHERING OF WARRIORS

Date: November 23, 2000

Lat. 26º 7' N, Long. 80º 8' W

Fort Lauderdale, Florida, USA

(One)
The following Sunday, Jake showed up at the Marine Corps detachment looking like he'd never mustered out of the Corps. His brass gleamed, his jet-black shoes were polished to a high gloss, his uniform creased in all the right places, and his medals hung impressively over the left breast pocket of his tailored tunic. This is not to say that he wasn't uncomfortable. He sensed it most as he walked into the detachment building and came under the scrutiny of other Marines standing in small groups in the hallway. The young ones in particular eyed the array of medals stacked over his left breast pocket, especially the Bronze Star and the two Kuwaiti and Saudi Arabian medals with their gaudy golden medallions and broad, brightly-colored ribbons.

But Jake soon saw that he was not the only battle-tested Marine attending the funeral services for Master Sergeant Willie Coleman.

There were over a dozen Corps veterans of Korea, Vietnam, and the Persian Gulf War in attendance, officers and non-coms alike. He also noticed several U.S. Army Rangers and Special Forces-types with their Green Berets, who had apparently crossed paths with MSGT Willie Coleman in the course of their military service. Without exception, every one of these non-Marines wore the Combat Infantryman Badge (CIB) over the top of their rows of medals in testimony to having fought hand-to-hand with the enemy. Just about all of them also had Purple Hearts among the medals dangling over their left breast pockets. It was truly a gathering of warriors. Gunny Sweikert would be pleased.

Master Gunnery Sergeant George Washington Sweikert entered the building with a small gray-headed Negro woman dressed in black. With his white cover tucked securely under his left arm, he held her hand in the crook of his right arm, gently leading her down the hallway. Sweikert was impeccable in his Marine dress blues. When he came abreast of Jake, he stopped and addressed Master Sergeant Willie Coleman's widow. "Ellie, this here is Sergeant Jake Porter, known to his Marine Corps buddies as 'Snapper.' He's the Gulf War sniper I was telling you about."

"Hello, Sergeant," Ellie Williams said in a soft voice. "George tells me that you volunteered to escort me today. I am most thankful for your courtesy. I regret you were not able to know my

Willie. He was a Marine's Marine, as they say. I know you would have liked him." She said it sweetly and sincerely, then placed her black-gloved hand on Jake's forearm.

"Mam," Jake said deferentially with a polite nod of his head, then turned to lead Master Sergeant

Willie Coleman's widow to hear the eulogies for her husband, but not before cutting a withering look in Sweikert's direction. Sweikert responded with a thin smile and a sly wink.

Master Sergeant William Coleman's funeral service played out in accordance with strict and time-honored Marine Corps precision. Over a half-dozen of his former comrades-in-arms took the podium in front of his metallic-gray military-issue coffin to recall exploits of battles gone by which they had shared with "Willie" Coleman. A Brigadier General, a full-bird Colonel, a former company commander, a leather-faced Marine Corps Master Sergeant and two U.S. Army Green Berets who could only hint at a covert mission in Cambodia in which the now deceased Master Sergeant Coleman had distinguished himself, all had their say.

Their tales were not without a touch of humor at times, and many of those in the be-medaled audience nodded their heads and chuckled at the special brand of battlefield humor that is shared only by those who have slugged it out in hand-to-hand struggles to the death.

Finally, a short and balding Baptist minister in a rumpled dark blue suit and striped tie rose and stood beside Willie Coleman's coffin. Clutching a well-worn Bible in one hand, he spoke softly of the life of this hero as a loving husband and father. He told of the great personal tragedy that had struck Willie and Ellie Coleman when their only child, Tommy, had died in an automobile accident at the age of 16, while Willie was in Vietnam, fighting for his country. In a voice slowing rising in intensity, he gave assurance to the assembled heroes that the same God who had kept them safe in battle, the same God who had whisked their many fallen comrades to his heavenly embrace, and the same God who had comforted Willie and Ellie in the loss of their son, now welcomed Master Sergeant William Coleman to life eternal as just reward for his fidelity in this world.

Through it all, Willie Coleman's widow had listened to her husband's comrades speak of his ferocity in battle, his loyalty to the men under his command and his strict adherence to the highest traditions of the United States Marine Corps. But it was the closing words of the country preacher that seemed to affect Ellie Coleman the most. In a small, plaintive voice only Jake could hear, she sighed, "Oh, Willie," and placed her hand atop Jake's arm, patting it softly.

(Two)

The ride to the cemetery in the black stretched-Cadillac hearse was short, barely fifteen minutes. Jake and Master Sergeant Coleman's widow sat alone together in the rear compartment. They were separated by a darkly tinted window from the two forward compartments occupied by some of the escorts and honor guard. Ellie Coleman sat with her gloved hands crossed in her lap. She turned to the window on her right and watched the streets, traffic lights, and fields go by slowly. Her gaze was broken only when one of the police motorcycle escorts sped ahead to stop traffic at the next intersection. She began speaking without any preamble.

"My Willie said his duty to the Marine Corps was a calling; a special calling that only a few could answer. Me, I was just a simple country girl with no education from the hills of West Virginia, when I met Willie sitting in the "White's Only" section of the railroad station's coffee shop, and not a soul daring to tell him to get up and go sit in the section reserved for Coloreds." She paused and turned to give Jake a wink.

"He had just returned from Korea, and was on his way to Parris Island to be a Drill Instructor. He looked so smart in his green uniform with all his new medals. He was so confident, so sure of who he was even though he had only recently turned nineteen years old. It was a thrill to sit down with him in the railroad station's forbidden territory, but I had no idea what meeting him that morning would lead to. He said nothing about all those Chinese people he had killed, some of them with his bare hands and a knife. There was no way I could understand at that time what it would mean to be the wife of a Marine. When he returned each time from a tour with new medals across his breast pocket, and new stripes to be sewn onto his sleeves, I was so very proud of him. But when I read the citations detailing how he'd come to be decorated, I was devastated. I wondered if he cared to be alive, and whether he

146

came home to me because he loved me, or because other than a Marine Corps barracks, he had no other place to call home."

Ellie's gaze had never left the hearse's window, only the side of her face visible to Jake, who sat quietly as Master Sergeant Willie Coleman's widow reminisced. There was a soft, dreamy quality to her voice that seemed to address no one in particular, not even Jake, the only other occupant in the rear compartment.

"Terrible as Korea was for Willie, Vietnam was even worse," she continued. "Willie and I weren't able to sleep together anymore after his first tour there. He tossed and turned so much and was given to yelling in the middle of the night. 'Ghosts,' he'd tell me in the morning. 'Nothing to worry about. Happens to everybody,' he said. But I knew better; the killing was changing him and he was going down a road that I didn't know where it was leading. And by the time our son, Tommy, was killed, Willie was on his third tour in Vietnam and so far down that road that he had gone all hard inside and I felt more lonely than ever."

Ellie sighed deeply, then continued, still looking out the hearse's window. "It broke completely for me when Willie couldn't come home for Tommy's funeral. His only son. Can you imagine? The Marine Corps said they couldn't get to Willie; that he was on a mission of great importance in a place they couldn't name and that lives depended on him. They sent a full-bird colonel and a general's aide-de-camp to stand in his place. When Willie finally came home three months later, he couldn't look me in the eye. Didn't matter any. I'd already moved to the second bedroom, and we never slept together again. When the Veterans Hospital found the cancer, Willie took to drinking and we didn't hardly talk any more. Today they're putting him in the ground and giving me that damn folded flag." She finally turned from the window and looked at Jake with soft dry eyes and a smile of resignation.

"End of story, Jake," she said, then added, "I see from your own medals that you've been in the thick of things yourself. Gunny Sweikert says you distinguished yourself by knocking off the Iraqi defense minister all by yourself."

"Much like your husband," Jake began slowly and with some trepidation, "I played the cards the Corps dealt to me. As you know, the Corps doesn't give you much say in the matter. They don't ask if you feel like killing that day. They just point you to the enemy and tell you to go get them. To tell you the truth, at the time, I just wanted out of the Corps. I was a bitter teenager when I signed up, but I'd done a lot of growing up in the four years I'd been in. I'd been taking college classes by correspondence whenever I had the opportunity. I wanted to get on with my life after the Corps. I wasn't too happy that my tour had been extended and sent to Iraq. I guess you could call me a reluctant participant," Jake said.

"As far as these medals go, I was trying to stay alive as much as I was trying to put a hurt on the Iraqis. I was one of three teams sent out that night to give the Iraqis a hard time, and I had a spotter with me that called the shots. It could have been anybody in my sights. What I saw in my rifle's telescope was a heavy hitter in Arab dress receiving military salutes and boarding an executive jet at an enemy airfield. By the rules of engagement, he was a fair target. It was just the defense minister's unlucky day, I guess," Jake said, feeling somewhat self-conscious in discussing his exploits in the company of a woman whose husband they were burying this day.

"Yes, of course it was, Jake." Ellie Coleman nodded in understanding. "And who knows what decisions he may have made, or commands he may have given the next day that could have resulted in the deaths of many Marines, or innocent civilians, in the coming days of war," she said with a mixture of conviction and compassion. "You did what you were called to do, Jake. It's of no help to second guess your superior's orders. Every Marine knows that in his bones.

"Besides, there's more than enough evil afoot in the world today. I'm sure you know that, too. Sometimes good people are called to intervene, or stop something, to set things right. It's nothing to be ashamed of, Jake, to have been called to protect others. No matter how much blood may have been spilled, if it was for the right cause, that's all that matters. My Willie lived and breathed by that creed."

"Yes, mam," Jake replied, and opened the limousine's door as it came to a stop alongside Master Sergeant Willie Coleman's final resting place.

VOYAGE TO NOWHERE

Date: August 20, 1698

Lat. 14º 29′ N Long. 120º 55′ E

Cavite Harbor, Luzon, Philippines

Ling Po's carriage led the way to the wharf. Capitan de Morga rode alongside him. Capitan Don Emilio Bustamente de la Vega rode in his own carriage immediately behind them, closely followed by the nine mounted soldiers that had accompanied him from Manila's fortress. They rode with their sabers unsheathed, the blades resting against their right shoulders, ready to strike. Ear-shattering shouting and violent gesturing preceded them. The hordes of Chinese and Moro natives pressing for access to the great *nao* parted reluctantly to allow them to pass.

The wharf was illuminated by hundreds of tar-and-straw torches, each placed exactly ten feet apart, and a Moro standing fireguard with two buckets of water between each of them. A contingent of Manila's militia under the command of Bustamente was spread across the wharf just in front of the main gangway leading to the *Concepcion's* main deck. They stood three-deep, the first row with lances lowered to belly-level, and the two rows behind them armed with arquebuses. The Royal Fiscal sat at a table at the sally port with three deck officers attending him to keep order.

Bustamente stepped from his carriage and mounted the gangway, followed by first, Capitan Rodrigo de Morga, then Ling Po. Ling Po's hands were tucked into his sleeves in the Sangley fashion, his horsehair hat atop his head, and his head and eyes lowered in respect. At the sally port, Bustamente saluted Spain's Royal Banner and announced himself. The Fiscal jumped to his feet and saluted in kind. Bustamente introduced Capitan de Morga, and he, too, exchanged a salute with the Fiscal. Ling Po was not introduced. Bustamente asked for the Capitan of the Guard, and informed the Fiscal that he was there to conduct a final inspection. The Captain of the Guard had been down below when Bustamente arrived and he now came at a near-run to give his report. Bustamente dismissed him and said that he was going to pass through the various deck levels for an eyeball inspection, and was not to be disturbed.

Once below decks, Capitan Bustamente turned to Ling Po and asked, "Now, tell me why we are here."

Without a word, Ling Po went to the port side of the hull and placed his hand on one of the eight-inch thick *molave* frames. He placed a foot on a horizontal stringer and reached up to the shelf where the frame disappeared on its way to the upper deck. He pulled on something, and a ceramic jar with a top sealed in wax tumbled out. Ling Po drew one of his long fingernails across and around the stopper, then lifted it free. He handed the open jar to Bustamente with an elegant bow.

Bustamente sniffed the jar, recognizing the smell of pickled cucumbers and ginger, one of his favorites.

"The greatest danger of your long trip to Acapulco, my friend, is lack of water and lack of food. We all know the stories of agony and suffering

151

when the voyage to Acapulco becomes overly long and supplies are exhausted. Don Bustamente, it is I who chose the work gangs that built this *nao*. It is I who picked the crew leaders. It was I who directed the construction these past three years. Our mutual future rests on the success of this *nao,* and I wanted nothing less than the best. I arranged for every third of these," he indicated the frames, "to have a compartment with either food or water."

"Why am I not surprised? Bustamente said.

Ling Po smiled and again bowed his head. "There's an old saying that fate favors the prepared." At that, he reached within the folds of his silk gown and retrieved two silk purses, giving one to Bustamente and the other to de Morga. "I ask no more than our usual arrangement. An even split, fifty-fifty of the profit."

Bustamente hefted the purse, then drew apart the string enclosure. He tipped a portion of the contents into his hand. It was a collection of more than 50 cut and polished stones, some of them diamonds, some rubies, others sapphires. A handsome stash that would bring a good price at the *feria* in Acapulco.

"I will be candid, my capitans. Recent losses, especially the loss of last year's *nao* and its cargo, have strained my resources. I imagine the same is for you, Don Bustamente. In addition, there is great turmoil in my country. Violence is spreading across the countryside as factions fight for a transfer of power. I have temporarily moved my home to a small coastal island in order to be closer to my fleet should I need to depart hastily."

"I am grateful for your concern for my health, Ling Po," said Bustamente. "It is true that my financial condition is strained just like yours. But that is not what is occupying my mind at the moment. Gobierno Obando is a devious, crooked bastard. He is sending me to Acapulco to get me out of his way. I cannot leave my wife and children in Manila, unprotected."

"I have given some thought to that, my friend," Ling Po said. "You do not need to worry about your wife and children. With your permission, I will take them with me when I depart. They may stay in my home for as long as necessary until your return."

Bustamente had long suspected that his wife was Ling Po's daughter since it was he who had provided her. The children would be Ling Po's grandchildren. To some extent it was a natural offer of self-interest on the part of Ling Po, but Bustamente was not offended and glad to receive the offer.

"Capitan Rodrigo, has Don Bustamente ever told you the story of how we met and came to be business partners?" Ling Po asked. "No? Then let me tell you, because it is a lesson in the role of fate in our lives.

"Eleven years ago, I was returning to my country after a successful trading session in Manila, and my junk was loaded with Spanish silver. As we passed the big island of Mindanao , we were becalmed between summer squalls when suddenly a dozen native pangas loaded with hostile Moro pirates came charging from behind a small neighboring island and were suddenly upon us. They swarmed over us with their spears, knives and machetes. We were fighting for our lives and losing the battle when Don Bustamente came upon us. He and fifty of his men armed with arquebuses were making a routine scouting trip aboard a coastal sailing vessel. They could have left us to our deaths. They were under no obligation to intervene. But my friend here, no lover of Muslims and worshipers of Mohammed, ordered his men to fire upon the Moros. The Moros fell like flies, and when they saw their advantage disappear, the survivors leaped into their pangas and fled into the island's jungle."

Bustamente picked up the story: "I saw Ling Po wielding a battle sword like a scythe. His bald head was covered in Moro blood, and he was naked to the waist. I never saw anyone fight more fiercely, but the deck of his junk was overrun with Moros. The issue was going to be decided in the next very few minutes. I ordered my men to fire, and be careful not to hit any Chinese. The Moros were easily identifiable because they were very dark skinned and naked except for loincloths. We made short order of them. When I boarded Ling Po's junk, he graciously made a gift of his sword to me. It is this sword I carry today. When Ling Po returned the following season with trade goods for Manila, he invited me aboard his junk and made me a present of a flawlessly beautiful girl of fifteen years age. She is today my wife, and the mother of my three children."

Ling Po smiled. "Capitan de Morga, you should have seen the look of utter surprise on Don Bustamente's face when my gift spoke perfect Spanish. She had been schooled by Jesuit priests in my country, and could quote from memory many passages from the Christian Bible. She was not only beautiful to the eye and gracious in her movements, she could sing like an angel and was also an accomplished cook with a mastery of both Chinese and Spanish cuisine."

"Maria speaks Chinese, Spanish, and several of the local Moro dialects," Bustamente said proudly. She teaches in our school. I have never heard her utter a word of complaint in all our years together. Tonight, I am calling a priest to my home to marry us. I am ashamed that I have not done it sooner. Ling Po, you must attend this ceremony, I beg you. I will arrange for Manila's main gate to be opened for you, with an escort to my home. Rodrigo, I am hopeful you will stand as a witness to the ceremony."

"I am honored, dear friend," Ling Po said, bowing deeply. "I will be there."

"And I as well, my capitan," said Capitan Rodrigo de Morga, also bowing respectfully.

(Two)

Don Bustamente's home in the Intramuros within the fortress walls of Manila, was brightly lit. When his carriage deposited him and Rodrigo de Morga at the courtyard entrance, his wife, Maria, stood in the double-door doorway smiling. She raised her arms in greeting. He crossed the courtyard briskly and took her in his arms. They kissed and Maria said, "You are hungry? I have kept our dinner warm. The children have already eaten and are ready for bed. Welcome, Capitan de Morga."

"Forgive my late arrival, Maria, my love," Bustmente said. "I have been with Ling Po making final arrangements. We went aboard the *nao* to see that all is well."

"Do not trouble yourself over telling me the news of your being sent to Acapulco, my heart. Everyone in Manila has heard of it."

Bustamente took Maria in his arms again and squeezed her to his chest. News and rumors traveled fast in the tiny Spanish community of Manila. He had wanted to be first to tell her of this latest change in his fortunes, but was secretly glad he had been spared the pain. He whispered in her ear, "Ling Po will visit us here tonight. Arrangements have been made for you and our family's safety. Have no fear."

"Come, let us sit for dinner and a glass of wine," Maria said. Holding her husband's hand in hers, she led the way to the dining room. Rodrigo de Morga followed.

Before they could reach the dining room, Bustamente's three daughters came bounding down the stairs yelling, "Papa, Papa!" Bustamente gathered them up in his arms and gave each a kiss on the forehead. He noticed that his youngest daughter, Teresa, barely three years old, had tears in the corners of her eyes. "?Que pasa, mi amor?" Bustamente asked her. Teresa pointed at her foot, then lifted it for him to see. Bustamente took her tiny foot in his hand. Teresa turned it so her father could see the new tattoo on the bottom. There, newly-inked in the instep was the double-circle tattoo with the family's sign within. Bustamente's chest tightened. Maria, sensing up-coming change and uncertainty, had ordered the tattooing of her youngest child, the only one remaining without it. If ever she was separated from her children, she would always be able to identify them no matter the length of time a search might take.

Bustamente took Teresa's foot and kissed it multiple times. He spoke softly to his daughter. "Now you have our family's mark, just like your sisters and your mother. Your mother received her's when she was a small girl in China, just like you. It keeps you safe in the world, and connects you with your family. Understand?" Teresa nodded shyly, wiped away the tears and kissed her papa. Then she bounded up the stairs along with her sisters to their bedroom.

Bustamente turned to his wife, who had been listening to his talk with their youngest daughter and said, "All will be well, my love. Now let us eat."

With dinner behind them, Rodrigo diplomatically filled his pipe with tobacco and strolled into the courtyard. Bustamente took Maria's hand and walked into their garden, taking a seat on a polished teak bench surrounded by sweet-smelling tropical flowers. The next half hour was one of the most difficult in Bustamente's life. He was pressed to tell of his love for Maria and all that she had meant to him over the years. He acknowledged that he had been a difficult person to live with. He praised her forbearance, and the gift of their children. Through it all, Maria sat silently with watery eyes, holding Bustamente's hands in hers and preparing to be told that she and her husband were soon to part forever.

Finally, he came to the point. He asked her to take him as her husband, and begged her forgiveness for taking so long to acknowledge his love in a proper way. When he said it, he saw first surprise and joy, then fright in Maria's eyes, and realized his confession of love was overshadowed by his being sent to Acapulco. Silently, in his mind, Bustamente cursed Gobierno Obando.

Maria leaned forward releasing Bustamente's hands and placed her own hands behind his neck. She kissed him full on the mouth, eased her grip, then pulled him to her and kissed him again. "You are my husband. My children are your children. My life is your life. Your life is my life. I want nothing other than what I have with you."

Bustamente held her tightly, his mouth just above her ear. He whispered, "I have asked Friar Nicolas to marry us tonight. Forgive me for the hurried preparations, but I believe the *nao* will sail tomorrow night, or the following day for certain."

Maria smiled. "Friar Nicolas christened our children and is a welcome guest in our home. He has never spoken a word in rebuke for my Sangley birthright, or our living outside the marital dictates of the Roman church. If he is willing to sanction our marriage, then I have only one question to ask. What did you pay him?" She could not suppress her laugh.

Bustamente laughed, too. "The going rate, my love. Priests do nothing for free. I made a small donation to the Augustinian treasury, and gave my promise to be a better Christian."

There was a call from the front gate, and word was passed that there was a Sangley waiting in a carriage, and a priest as well. Bustamente ordered them admitted, and rose from his seat alongside Maria. She stood, tipped her face to him and he gave her another long kiss.

The ceremony was simple, yet dignified. Ling Po had given Bustamente a cast gold ring that he placed on Maria's finger at the appropriate moment, promising his faithfulness until death should part them. Rodrigo de Morga presented her with a small leather-bound Catholic missal with pressed gold corners, and Ling Po gave her an exquisite set of matching porcelain jars for her paint brushes, along with two of the finest ox-hair brushes, one trimmed broadly, the other tapered for fine pointing. Maria kissed each of them on the cheek, thanking them. They were the three most important men in her life, and she knew that her own life and the lives of her children were in their hands.

(Three)

The frenzy around the *Nuestra Senora de la Concepcion* grew in intensity as Manila's Spaniards escorted their loved ones to board the great ship. Men, women and children swarmed the sally port, showed their boletos to the Fiscal and made their way to their cabins. The confusion of the arriving passengers seeking their allotted living space and the ship's crew hurrying about their tasks to prepare for departure created mayhem both above and below decks. The arrival of Capitan Juan Calderon brought no relief.

The capitan that Gobierno Obando had chosen to replace Capitan Rodrigo de Morga was still recovering from a night of debauchery with a local widow. Before retiring to his cabin he gave few orders, and they were as confused as his crew. When Capitan Bustamente arrived wharfside, he was unable to get his carriage to the gangway. He drew a pistol, fired it to get the attention of the squad of his militia, and they quickly beat their way through the crowd to escort him. Once on the deck, he asked for Calderon, but was told the Capitan was attending to ship's business and was unavailable. One of the senior bosun's mates saw Bustamente's plight and formed up a crew to ferry Bustamente's personal trunks to his cabin.

Once settled into his quarters, Bustamente regained the deck to observe the chaos. He had said his goodbyes to Maria and the children earlier that morning, a tearful affair the memory of which still constricted Bustamente's chest. Ling Po had met Maria's carriage just outside the fortress walls of Manila, shortly after noon and escorted her and the children to a small wharf where they and their possessions were ferried out to one of the Sangley war junks riding at anchor. They were received with great deference by the fierce-looking warriors and taken to their cabin.

Only moments later, a porcelain jug filled with lemonade was brought to the cabin along with some freshly baked sweet cookies with chopped dates and nuts. It was made clear that Maria had only to ask and her needs would be met. After a brief snack, Maria put the children in their bunks for a late afternoon nap, then sat at a porthole and looked out on

Manila Bay wondering what the next chapter of her life might hold. She absently fingered the corners of the missal that Rodrigo de Morga had given her and said a silent prayer for her husband, Emilio Bustamente.

(Four)

Five weeks! Five weeks! Bustamente fumed in frustration. Five weeks at sea and they had only this morning spied the first channel through the treacherous San Bernardino Straits leading to the great Spanish Lake. The voyage had thus far been cursed with the squirrely light winds, near-constant rainsqualls and thundering lightning typical of the early typhoon season.

The *Concepcion* had cast off her lines at Cavite a full month late for a favorable passage. Bustamente had watched Ling Po's war junk bearing his wife and children sail off to the north and west of Manila on a course for China. The distance had been too great to afford a glimpse of his family. He prayed for a safe journey for the junk under Ling Po's command, and once again cursed Gobierno Obando for his treachery. Now, the *Concepcion* wallowed fitfully in a short sea whipped by an earlier late-evening squall. The rolling and pitching motion had brought many of the passengers to the leeward rail to throw-up their dinners. Two infants had already died, several of the small children were sick, their mothers in despair and the passengers in general were moody.

Most of the men spent their days topside on the deck, drinking, joking and cursing the distance yet to be traveled. Capitan Juan Calderon was a frequent butt of their jokes. They had already picked up on some of the crew's comments about Calderon's indecision in ordering timely sail changes, and noted his obvious discord with the ship's navigator, Friar Miguel Ortiz. The Jesuit priest was a veteran of the Pacific crossing, and had successfully steered other vessels of the Spanish crown's fleet in the Mediterranean and along the coasts of Africa. They had observed his skillful use of the Jacob's staff to determine their latitude, and the smooth way in which he deployed the chip log over the stern rail to measure their speed through the water. They noticed, too, that Capitan

Rodrigo de Morga also took the latitude with his own Jacob's staff, and observed the casting of the chip log and recorded the speed in a personal logbook. What faith the passengers lacked in Capitan Calderon was more than made up in the presence of de Morga and Friar Ortiz.

Bustamente watched with apprehension as the passengers and crew mindlessly ate their way through the fresh provisions. The slaughter of the cattle, pigs and chickens would start soon. In less than two months at sea, by his estimation, they would be reduced to salted beef and pork, and tasteless ship's biscuit. *Gracias a Dios!* that Ling Po had provided for he and Rodrigo de Morga in the event.

After another two weeks, the *Concepcion* finally broke free of the reef and island-strewn San Bernardino Straits, poking along at less than three knots into the Spanish Lake. It had been a tension-filled passage, the strait's strong currents and tidal races frequently tugging the ship off-course and toward razor-sharp reefs during maddening periods of calm, forcing the crew to take to the ship's cutter and small boats to row the *Concepcion* away from lee shores and impending dangers. The hot, humid and windless days and nights in the straits had left the passengers and crew in an ill mood.

Now, when a brisk and constant wind arose from the south and the sails filled and the rigging hummed, all seemed to turn for the better. But the wind continued to rise in strength and drove an ever-steepening sea before it. Fortunately the wind came over the starboard stern, and the *Concepcion* rose gallantly to ride atop the growing sea, driving a huge bow wave that hung momentarily above the bow, then collapsed to the foredeck washing the deck all the way to the mainmast. By nightfall, the wind was shrieking and with the exception of a spanker forward, all sails had been struck. Capitan Calderon was seen only briefly on deck, preferring to leave the handling of the *nao* to his sailing master.

The weather abated by dawn and fears that the blow was the forerunner of a typhoon were dismissed. Course was set to proceed north by northeast to pass within sight of the coast of Japan, until a latitude of 30º North was obtained, at which time, the *nao* would bear off to starboard and ride the current and northeast trades across the cold waters of the north Pacific.

But the progress was slow because of the tardiness of the departure from Manila. Another month and a half passed and the *Concepcion* was still south and east of the coast of Japan. The weather was becoming cooler and rain more frequent. It was miserable for the poor passengers. Several more children had succumbed to the rigors of the voyage, along with a few older women and an elderly Spanish soldier returning at last to his homeland intending to live out his retirement in sunny Alicante on Spain's Costa del Sol. All were wrapped in old sailcloth and committed to the dark ocean, Friar Ortiz usually officiating. The last of the cattle and pigs had been slaughtered. Only a few dozen chickens remained.

The sudden appearance of a school of sperm whales brought a mixture of fear and awe. The passengers huddled together on the deck, holding on to one another, gaping wide-eyed at this never-before-seen phenomenon. The whales were longer and larger than the *Concepcion*. They passed close enough that everyone could smell the foul fishy breath emanating from their spouts. They effortlessly passed the *Concepcion* as though she was anchored, and it was not lost on anyone the consequences should these grey behemoths turn in anger and smash against the *Concepcion*. It made them all feel small and inconsequential. On returning down below to their cabins, many reached for their Bibles and invoked Jesus' name and favored saints in long and fervent prayers.

Another month of damp northward sailing and Capitan Calderon called for a course change to east by northeast. The heavy mists and rain had joined to form an impenetrable curtain between them and the coast of Japan. The coast was never sighted. Days had passed without a clear sky or sun to take a reliable latitude sighting. Calderon's dead reckoning, derived from course steered coupled with the running of the chip log, suggested they were north and west of the Bonins, far enough north to clear them for the approaching turn to due East. But no sooner than the course was changed, the wind shifted to southeasterly and began to increase until it was blowing a full gale. The *Concepcion's* motion became violent. The sailing master called for reduced sails. By nightfall, the ship was plunging and rolling under bare poles. There was nothing left to do but endure the ocean's fury.

This time it was serious. The storm did not lessen its violent grip on the *Concepcion*. For five days and nights, the seas and winds were relentless; the topmasts on both the main and mizzen snapped under the strain of the whipping, crashing to the deck in a pile of Manila hemp rigging and broken spars. Two of the crew were crushed to death beneath the shattered wreckage and another three received broken arms or legs. The severe pitching and rolling of *Concepcion's* hull tossed the passengers below decks like marbles in a tin can. Heads were smashed against bulkheads, bodies tumbled through the air to crash against bunks and other passengers.

The injuries began to mount, and the screaming and moaning never ceased. The galley stoves were cold, impossible to use while the storm raged. Hard ship's biscuits and salty strips of tough beef jerky were all that could be served under the existing conditions. That diet increased the demand for drinking water and soon all of the water-filled bamboo *bombones* were exhausted, leaving only the clay *tibores* stored in the lower decks to slake their thirst.

When the storm finally relented, the clouds parted and the sun shone once again. The weary and battered passengers stumbled onto the deck, some crawling with bandages wrapped around their heads, or dragging broken legs, many bringing with them their decomposing dead family members. Friar Ortiz moved gently among them, offering prayers and encouragement. He helped bundle the corpses and carry them to the leeward rail. Later, giving the last rites for burial at sea, he beseeched God for mercy for the living and a welcome into heaven for the departed.

Don Bustamente stood in a daze watching the pitiful proceedings. Not a seaman, he had suffered no less than the passengers, being tossed about endlessly and dry-retching an empty stomach. Rodrigo de Morga had been sympathetic to Bustamente's seasickness despite his own immunity to the sea-going malady. He had insisted that Bustamente take small amounts of water to stave-off dehydration, and he had lashed Bustamente to his bunk to prevent him being thrown about the cabin. De Morga had gone to the stormy deck many times during the tempest to observe the crew and offer advice, being careful not to intrude upon the authority of Capitan Calderon's sailing master. On more than one occasion the sailing master had offered his thanks for de Morga's comments and acted upon them.

With the storm relenting, the galley fires were finally lit and a hot bean soup with floating chunks of salted beef and biscuit was distributed to crew and passengers alike. But the meal was spoiled when it was learned that one of the women had slit her wrists and silently bled to death in her bunk. Her husband went berserk and had to be subdued, tied and taken to the deck. Only after being forced to drink a strong liquor did he become calm. He moaned and cried until he passed out. De Morga confided to Bustamente, saying that the worst was yet to come.

Prophetically, the sky clouded over, the warm sun retreated, and by dusk the wind began to rise in tempo. Unfair! Unfair! the passengers screamed. Had they not suffered enough? How much more were they expected to endure? The dark grey sea, its furrows growing deeper and steeper, the white froth on the face of mountainous waves like saliva dripping from a rabies-crazed dog, offered no answer.

The deck crew heard it first, staring anxiously aft into the black night to see what was approaching. An ominous, moaning roar the only warning given as a great rogue wave, so large that it loomed over the tops of the masts. It surged under the *Concepcion*, lifting her violently, twisting her in a sickening corkscrewing motion, then shoving her bow down into the sea to cause the *nao* to trip on her own bowsprit and pitch-pole end-over-end. Upside down, shoved deeper into the sea, the *Concepcion* regained the surface minus all of her masts and sails, and not a single human being left on the deck, all washed overboard. Below decks, water sloshed from compartment to compartment at waist level drowning many; the weight of the water in the hull causing the *nao* to wallow deeply and dangerously, her gunnels barely two feet above the ocean's boiling surface. Pieces of masts and rigging dragged through the water, beating against the side of the hull and causing her to skew sideways against the waves, inviting even more water to enter the hull. A precarious situation that must be remedied immediately, or the *Concepcion* would surely sink.

Bustamente waded through waist-deep water, climbed a short companionway and made his way to the main deck. He was appalled by what he saw. The sky was open above him; no masts, or sails or rigging. The *Concepcion* had been reduced to a floating hulk at the mercy of the elements, not even a rudder to steer a course. Worst of all, his companion, Rodrigo de Morga was gone, presumably flung overboard with all of those who had been topside at the time of the pitch-poling. He soon discovered that Capitan Juan Calderon was a casualty as well, his cabin empty and awash in seawater.

The pounding of the rigging against the hull caught his attention and he quickly saw the danger. He hurried to his cabin, retrieved the battle sword that Ling Po had given him, then went to the rail and began hacking away to free the rigging. Two or three men, seeing what he was about, came to assist. Once that was done, he stepped back to gage what should be done about the seawater down below; it had to be pumped out, and fortunately there were several crewmen who knew the location of the pumps and how they worked. Bustamente ordered them to begin pumping and set up a temporary watch schedule to relieve those at the pump every hour.

The storm raged for another two days, driving rain and fierce winds forcing the *Concepcion* on her beam's end and rolling her so violently that it was impossible to stand up without holding onto something.

When the weather cleared, the two days of near-constant pumping had removed most of the seawater, and the *Concepcion* rode high in the water, but completely out of control. Bustamente knew with a certainty that his and Ling Po's fortunes were gone. The *Concepcion* would never make Acapulco, they would never sell their precious stones in the *feria*, and in all likelihood, he would never see his family again. The only chance that he might come out alive was the very slim possibility that a passing vessel would come to their assistance, or they would drift onto an island with a friendly population. He thought of the vast fortune that lay within the *Concepcion's* hull. What would become of it, he wondered. Already some of the passengers were looting the family chests of fellow passengers that had died or disappeared. He went to Rodrigo de Morga's bunk and quickly found the purse of precious stones that Ling Po had provided for sale at the *feria*. He promised himself that if he survived the present ordeal, he would see that the stones were sold and the money sent to de Morga's family in Seville.

Entering the eighth month since departing Manila, the *Concepcion* floated aimlessly across the Pacific Ocean, drifting south by southeast with the current. Following the pitch-pole capsizing two months earlier, a little less than one hundred of the original seven hundred seventeen passengers and crew remained alive, and many of them injured. Some died every day, and Friar Ortiz was a common sight among the survivors. He had broken his left arm and also received a nasty bump on the head during the capsizing that had left him slightly fuzzy in the head for over a week. Bustamente had decided to donate Rodrigo de Morga's share of their secreted food and water to the survivors, but it was not enough to sustain them all. He was determined to keep his share to maintain his own life; Maria and the children deserved no less, he argued with himself when his conscience provoked him.

Finally, it was down to six men, counting Bustamente, and Friar Ortiz was not among them. The compassionate friar and skilled ocean navigator had died quietly in his sleep two weeks earlier. Despite his secret stores, Bustamente was constantly hungry, thirsty and lacking in energy. Despondent in the extreme, he was barely hanging on. When the sun set that day, he made no effort to leave his place alongside the starboard bulwark where he had made a pallet to lie beneath the stars. He was awakened by a strange bumping and a motion unlike any of the past months since the capsizing. The *Concepcion* tilted strangely, and even though it was dark, dawn still another three hours away, Bustamente forced himself to his feet to look over the rail.

Mother of God! An island! They had grounded on an island! The surf was small, driven by a light wind from the south, and the *Concepcion* was lying on her starboard beam, grinding on the sandy beach. Bustamente croaked out a yell, "Tierra, tierra! Gracias a Dios!"

Bustamente ran forward to the bow and played out a Manila hemp line over the side until it touched the island's beach. He climbed over the rail and lowered himself until he set foot on the island. He fell to his knees and touched his forehead to the sandy beach, praising the heavens for his deliverance. The other passengers, two of them former ship's crew, followed him laughing hysterically. They moved deeper onto the beach, turned and looked back on the stricken *Concepcion*, now firmly aground. They hugged one another, clapped each other's backs and began to walk down the beach toward the southwestern point. The island's interior was wild with tough, prickly bushes. A few cocoanut trees could be seen in the early morning light. They continued along the beach because it offered the least resistance, and were startled to come upon the *Concepcion* from the opposite direction barely thirty minutes later! It was a sobering discovery. Their new-found world was a tiny world. The next question was whether there was water, or anything to eat.

Bustamente used Ling Po's sword to hack a path toward the center of the island. A small, shallow depression in the middle of the island held some brackish water that was probably the product of recent storms. The island, on first inspection, had no underground spring. They had found land, but the prospects looked bleak for long-term survival. Returning to the beached *Concepcion*, Bustamente and his fellow survivors began to discuss their options. One of the first considerations was what to do with the *Concepcion's* cargo. It must be moved before the arrival of a storm that would break-up the wreck and wash everything away. The sheer bulk of it was intimidating; could the six of them in their weakened condition move it all ashore to a safe place? Then, the question of rescue. What could they do to attract the attention of a passing ship?

The conversation went on all day with no resolution. Finally, Bustamente announced that as a King's Officer, he was obliged to at least attempt to preserve the gold bullion from Manila's treasury. It belonged to the King. He said the obligation was his alone, and no one else had to participate. He left the group to their deliberations, climbed the rope to the *Concepcion's* deck and made his way deep into the interior. When he had been down below for several hours, slowing removing decking and cargo to get to the gold, one of his fellow survivors arrived and said they had decided to begin collecting driftwood to build a huge signal fire. They agreed to take turns watching the horizon for a ship and be prepared to light the fire when one was sighted. They remained undecided about the *Concepcion's* cargo.

By nightfall, Bustamente had reached the first of the wooden chests with the gold from Manila's treasury. He determined there were twenty-five of them. They were heavy. It was really a two-man job to lift one. The survivor who had brought the message bent down and grabbed the rope handle of the first chest and the two of them ferried it to the deck. By this time, the others had re-boarded the *Concepcion* and announced that they would help transfer the cargo to the beach until their strength wore out or they were rescued, whichever came first.

The following morning, Bustamente scouted some of the lava caves that dotted the island's southeastern shoreline. Only one of them was big enough to hold most of the cargo, and Bustamente was not really sure of that one. The plan was to put the chests of gold in first, spread them out on the bottom of the cave to create a sort of floor for the crates of porcelain to rest upon. Should tidal water rise in the cave, the gold and porcelain would be unharmed. Atop the porcelain they would place the individual family cargo chests, most of them made of wood or bound in leather, and on top of them the skeins of silk and the bundles of woven tapestries.

They spent most of the next day on the island capturing as much as they could of the water caught in the island's depressed center. They brought porcelain jars, clay pots and cooking pans from the galley, anything to pour the water into. Then they ferried the containers to a small lava cave directly opposite where the *Concepcion* lay on the beach. The water was brackish, but drinkable. They prayed for more rain to restore the water level in the depression, but the day was bright and cloudless. For the next three weeks, they lifted the *Concepcion's* cargo from its hold, drug it across the canted deck and over the side onto the beach. From there, they dragged or carried each box or bundle to the large cave. A storm finally blew up a huge surf and the *Concepcion* was soon pounded into an unrecognizable debris field that slowly floated away on the tide.

In the end, it was the lack of water that finished them. One by one, they collapsed and died, leaving the survivors thankful for one less person to consume what little water there was. It did rain two or three times, but the amount was not sufficient to keep them alive. Finally, Bustamente was the only one left, and he was more dead than alive. He had cut his feet and scraped one of his shins on coral while fishing, and the cuts were festering painfully. His time, too, was coming to a close and he knew it. He had been a soldier too long to not recognize the first signs of gangrene.

Among the family chests, he found a scrap of paper, some ink and a quill, and composed a note to Maria and his children. Then, he folded it and placed the note and the battle sword given him by Ling Po atop a large crate of porcelain, then closed the cave's entrance. He slept in the open alongside the pile of driftwood that was to serve as a signal. But no ship appeared, and he had little hope for one. He prepared himself to accept death.

The early morning sighting of the bright white sails of a ship shook him from his death meditations. He quickly lit the signal bonfire and tossed wet kelp on it to make smoke. He held his breath in anticipation of his signal being seen, and was stunned to see the vessel strike its upper courses and launch a cutter. Salvation! *Gracias a Dios! Gracias a Dios!*

THE SHOESTRING OPERATION

Cryptology was used quite widely [in Europe during the 17th and 18th centuries]. Nowhere is this more evident than with Spain. Her ascent to power can be traced in the proliferation of her ciphers, and these project an interesting image of the cryptology of the day, as practiced by the richest and mightiest nation in Europe.

Date: November 25th, 2000

Lat. 26º 4' N, Long. 77º 2' W

Fort Lauderdale, Florida

(*One*)

Jake and Brenda cleared the front gate of the Harbor Point Yacht Club just after 7 AM. Brenda steered her canary-yellow Karman Ghia convertible across town to the intersection of the Florida Turnpike. They stopped at a Famous Amos restaurant for breakfast, then took the turnpike north as far as Wildwood, before leaving it to take Interstate 75 to Gainesville, home of the University of Florida. With the windows and top down, the road noise was just loud enough to discourage long conversations. Brenda, however, did manage to ask about the Marine Corps major they were going to visit, and Jake told her what little he had learned about Major Taggart from his conversation with Master Gunnery Sergeant Sweikert. He mentioned that Taggart had suffered war wounds during Operation Desert Victory in Iraq. He also told her that Taggart had a Master's degree in mathematics from Georgia Tech and had served in Marine Corps Intelligence, including being a graduate of the Navy's cryptology school.

Once they reached the exit off Interstate 75 for Gainesville, they proceeded down University Avenue and entered the campus of the University of Florida through the main gate. The perfectly manicured campus was bustling with students of every size, shape and color, some hustling to their next classes, others gathered loosely in small groups frivolously bantering and laughing the day away as only college students can.

Following the instructions Taggart had given Jake, they finally parked in the visitors' area alongside Morehead Hall. Inside, on a hallway directory, they confirmed Taggart's office location on the Third Floor and took the well-worn marble staircase. Jake knocked twice on the door and when he heard "Come" from the inside, he held the door open for Brenda and followed her in.

Major Bryce Taggart, USMCR, rose from behind a cluttered desk fronted by an exotically-carved teakwood sign that read "Professor Bryce L. Taggart." He smiled pleasantly and greeted the very good-looking young woman and the strapping former Marine sergeant who followed behind her. *So this is 'Snapper.' He's tall for a sniper, but he definitely has the eyes. He's stayed lean, too. And Jesus, this is one bitching fine-looking woman with him.*

"Bryce Taggart," he introduced himself with a refined southern accent, offering his hand first to Brenda, then Jake. "And this is the sad end to those who don't publish often enough, or not at all," he said lightly, gesturing to indicate his tiny, sparsely furnished office.

"Jake Porter, Major. And this is Brenda Warren." Jake surprised even himself when he elected to call Taggart 'Major' rather than 'Bryce' or maybe 'Professor Taggart'. Old Marine Corps habits don't die easily. "Gunny Sweikert at the Corps' reserve detachment in Fort Lauderdale asked me to send his respects, sir."

"Well, thank you, *Sergeant* Porter," Taggart answered, "Gunny Sweikert and I met in the Iraqi desert once upon an evening a long time ago. He was probably too humble to mention that he saved my life that night. Anyway, *Jake*, since we will be in the company of a couple of civilian women for lunch, let's suspend the 'Major' shall we? My friends call me 'Tag.' I think the ladies will find Marine Corps etiquette tiresome, at least I know my fiancé will. And Stacy will tell you that she has heard enough Marine Corps tales to last a lifetime," Taggart chuckled. "My reserve outfit meets once a month, and sometimes a few of us gather afterwards for beers, barbecue and combat stories. The exploits and derring-do grow with each telling of course. Stacy has now suspended her belief of any war tales told by Marines."

But she was very impressed, Snapper, when I showed her the recruiting booklet with the After Action Reports of your sniper exploits in Kuwait City and the Iraqi desert. I must admit I was a bit jealous of the time she spent reading it and marveling over your feat of arms.

"I understand, sir, uh, Tag," Jake said. "I've tried to spare Brenda the finer details of life in the Corps myself."

"Yes. I'm not surprised," Taggart replied, searching Jake's face for any hidden message and finding none. "Well, let me give Stacy a call to let her know you are here. We've planned to meet in the faculty cafeteria, if that's okay with you. The food is decent, definitely better than Marine Corps fare, and the price is right."

"Fine by us," Jake said, glancing quickly at Brenda, who nodded in agreement.

"Stacy has a Ph.D in European Studies from the University of Chicago," Taggart said with obvious pride as he picked up the telephone receiver. "She's fluent in three languages besides English and teaches early

European history. As a matter of fact, she may be of some help with that text message you're looking into, Jake." He dialed a number and spoke briefly with a department secretary who connected Taggart with his fiancé. Stacy said she would meet them at the faculty cafeteria.

They joined up in the hallway outside the cafeteria and Taggart made the introductions. Stacy Burns was a pert brunette with large brown eyes, full lips and a wide smile. Although she was considerably shorter than Taggart's six feet, she was nicely setup and curved in all the right places. She was clearly in love with Bryce Taggart, but touched his hand only briefly in deference to campus decorum for faculty in public. The four of them made their way down the cafeteria line, then took a booth along the wall with long windows looking out over the campus.

They exchanged the usual getting-to-know-you pleasantries as they ate, and it was clear that the two college professors found Jake and Brenda's lifestyles intriguing. Under friendly prodding, Jake told of how he came to buy his sailboat at a U.S. government auction after migrating to Florida following his mustering out of the Marine Corps, and how he had first met the surgeon Dr. Jerome Ambrose at a boatyard and later became captain of Ambrose's yacht, the *Sea Bones*. He mentioned somewhat self-consciously that he had recently finished off his Bachelor's degree in Business Administration at the University of Miami's campus in Fort Lauderdale, feeling it was small potatoes when compared to Stacy's doctorate, and Taggart's Master's degree.

Brenda gave a shortened version of her stint at Stanford University and migration to San Francisco and the culinary school. She breezed over the chapters covering her travels aboard several yachts and how she wound up in the charter trade in Antigua in the West Indies. Neither she or Jake mentioned her working on the *Sea Bones*, or anything about the recent bloody trip to the Bahamas.

As they finished eating, the conversation finally turned to the reason Jake had asked Gunny Sweikert to set up a meeting with Taggart. Jake handed Taggart a hand-written copy of the English-translation version of Bustamente's confession along with a photocopy of the original Latin text from Lt. White's log book. He had opted to leave off Bustamente's signature.

"You say the original was written in the late seventeenth century, and you know the author to be Spanish, right?" Taggart asked as he took the text from Jake.

"Yes, that's right. The original was written in Latin, and from the context in which I found it, I believe it was like a deathbed confession. He had a leg amputated two days before it was written, and he was dying from gross infection of his other leg. In fact, he died two days after writing it."

"I see," said Taggart.

"Why, it's absolutely fascinating is what it is," Stacy chimed in, whisking the copy gently from Taggart's hand. "Are you sure of its authenticity? How did you discover it?" The excitement in Stacy's voice was evident, and she clearly meant no offense in questioning the message's authenticity.

"I have no reason to doubt it's authentic," Jake smiled. "I discovered it in an old sailing journal. The journal belonged to a young naval officer aboard a British warship that came upon a castaway on a remote Pacific island. The author of that text," Jake said, indicating the one Stacy was holding, " was the castaway and is clearly identified as Spanish by the British officer in his journal. This text was his last message, and as you can see, it is addressed to the Pope, and is a confession and plea for absolution of his sins. He prevailed upon the English naval officer's honor to see it delivered."

"Well, if I recognize the look on Stacy's face, I'd say you have an intriguing piece of history here, Jake," Taggart grinned.

"Oh, cut it out, Tag," Stacy said with a smile and turned to Jake. "Was the message actually delivered to the Pope, Jake?"

"I don't know," Jake replied. "From the naval officer's journal, the last entry confirms his arriving at the fleet's anchorage in the Solent adjacent to the Isle of Wight. So he made it that far. Since there are no more entries, it's just speculation what he did when he went ashore. Whether he carried through on the promise to send the message to the Pope, I really can't say. He may have started a new journal with his next vessel, or he may have never returned to sea. I used the Internet to contact the British Admiralty's historical center to see if it was possible to locate individual officers and their ships. I gave them the name of the warship and the young lieutenant's name. But I'm afraid it's worse than looking for a needle in a haystack. Four centuries have passed now. Identifying crew below captain or flag rank that far back, or trying to find the ship's official log, would be quite a research project. Besides, I don't have the financial resources to do that."

"Maybe I can help you in that area. In the course of my academic studies I've spent quite a bit of time in museums and government archives in England and on the Continent as well. What I'm not clear about though is why you're sharing this with Tag," Stacy said with a puzzled look.

It was Brenda who answered. "I took a copy of the original Latin text to a Catholic priest that I know and asked him to translate it into English. He saw that it was addressed to the Holy Father and became really excited when I told him it was written several hundred years ago. He has called me several times since. He seems to be particularly interested in the exact time period in which it was written and who was its author."

"Actually, he drove across town twice and left messages for Brenda at her houseboat asking to see the original message," Jake said. "It may be nothing, but it got me curious."

Talk about curious!, Stacy thought. *Jake is an ex-Marine sniper with a chest full of medals for heroism and drives a wealthy surgeon's yacht. Brenda is a gourmet chef who lives on a houseboat. And they're both here talking with my Marine Corps intelligence officer/mathematician husband trying to figure out a centuries-old Spanish message that was addressed to the Pope by a castaway who had his leg chopped off just before writing the message and then dying. What an interesting couple!*

"Hmm," Taggart mused, "I would not presume to second-guess the motives of your priest, Brenda, but if he knows his history, then he certainly is aware that most people living three or four centuries ago could neither read nor write. Reading and writing were reserved for the clergy, royalty, and a small population of powerful intelligencia."

Taggart reached across and retrieved the copy of Bustamente's text from his fiancé's hand. "So, given that the author of this text most likely belongs in that small and exalted company of the literate people of his time, coupled with the fact that this is a death-bed message addressed to the Pope himself, who was arguably the most powerful and influential person on the planet at the time, I can understand the heightened curiosity of a Catholic priest about the identity of the author."

"Tag, darling? Would you hold that thought for a moment? I'd like to visit the ladies' room," Stacy asked sweetly. She turned to Brenda and said, "Morehead Hall is one of the older buildings on the university's campus and the route to the ladies' room is quite tortuous. Would you like me to show you the way?

"Yes. A good idea," said Brenda with a smile and followed Stacy out of the cafeteria.

Jake and Taggart watched the two women exiting the dining room and were pleased to see a number of the male diners turning their heads to look at the two exceptionally good-looking women.

"I'm wondering what is so important to the priest about knowing the date and author of the text," Jake began. "I mean, he made the translation from Latin into English, and now has his own copy of the text. What more does he expect from the text beyond the Spaniard's confession? Would knowing when the message was written and who wrote it tell him anything special, anything *additional*, other than just satisfying his personal curiosity?"

"Hard to say, Jake," Taggart answered. "One possibility, of course, is what you are no doubt suspecting, that there is some other message buried in the text. If that is the case, then knowing the date of the message would give some insight into the sophistication of encryption used. The science of cryptology is centuries old, and as codes are broken, cryptologists are kept busy creating new ones. The encryption techniques become increasingly complex over time and that is where knowing the date would help. I'll have to refresh my memory with a bit of research, but I believe the era in which your message was written, late seventeenth century, the use of a nomenclator and ciphers involving simple substitution were in vogue."

"I don't have a clue what you're talking about," Jake said with a hapless smile.

"Don't worry about it," Taggart said smiling. "When I attended the Navy's cryptology school, I was provided with an excellent text on the history of cryptology. Written by a fellow named Kahn, I believe. And he makes a good job of explaining the basic encrypting and decrypting process. I'll review it and fax you copies of the relevant pages and you can tackle your Spaniard's message yourself to see if there's more to it than meets the eye."

"I'd be very grateful," Jake said, but still feeling a little out of his depth. "And there's no way to just look at this text," he indicated the translation that Taggart was holding in his hand, "to say whether there's a hidden message or not?"

"Unfortunately, no. You have very little text to work with here, and you have no history of previous messages. If this text were more voluminous, you could examine it for repetition of vowels, or other clues that might suggest text substitutions," Taggart explained. "What you need here is the cipher, the key upon which the hidden message, if there is one, is based. The cipher will be known only to the party sending and the party receiving the message. It could be a quotation from the Bible, the name of a saint, or maybe a religious celebration. Those are the more common ones of that era as I recall. The more you know about the backgrounds of the sender and receiver, whether their power lay in military feat of arms, or the politics of the Catholic Church, or Spanish royalty, the better able you will be to uncover the cipher.

"It's a minor event in the greater story of the discovery of the New World, but in 1498 Christopher Columbus used a private family code provided by the Vatican to write a letter from the New World to his brother in Spain to fight off a governor sent by the Crown.

Unfortunately, the code was broken—we call that decrypting. When Columbus's secret message was revealed, he was placed in chains and sent back to Spain for trial. It is a well-documented fact that the Vatican provided ciphers to most of the wealthy and politically influential families so they could communicate with Rome without fear of their messages being read by their enemies. Your castaway could be from a prominent Spanish family that used a cipher provided by the Vatican."

(*Two*)

Stacy was bubbling with chatter as she and Brenda made their way to the restroom. "You have no idea, Brenda, how interesting all of this is to a couple of university types. We live such a cloistered existence compared to you and Jake. Mind you, I'm not complaining. It's a very rewarding life we have here at the university, but it just doesn't have the level of excitement that yours does."

"The excitement factor for me has increased dramatically since I met Jake. He's a magnet for action, I can tell you," Brenda said, and was tempted to say more, but did not.

"He's quite a man. You must be very proud of him," Stacy said.

Puzzled, Brenda asked, "How do you mean?"

"Did he ever show you this?" Stacy asked, reaching into her purse and pulling out a copy of the Marine Corps recruiting booklet, 'Heroes Who Made a Difference.' The section relating Jake's Iraqi exploits and photos of the awards ceremonies was marked with a slip of paper.

"Tag showed this to me after his conversation last week with Gunny Sergeant Sweikert when they were setting up today's meeting. Tag was very impressed, I can tell you. It's the sort of thing that Marines hold in very high regard," Stacy said.

Brenda took the booklet from Stacy and read the after-action reports, noting in particular the final line which estimated that Jake had killed over twenty of the enemy on the Kuwaiti airport mission, and another ten to fifteen at the Khafji desalination plant. It put the deaths of the four

Haitian pirates in a completely different perspective. On impulse, she decided to tell Stacy about the bloody Bahamas trip—all of it, right down to the wooly, wide-eyed head rolling on the blood-soaked salon sole of the *Sea Bones*.

"Dear God!" Stacy exclaimed when Brenda had finished. "You could have been killed that night, Brenda! And all those other people, too, if Jake hadn't done what he did," Stacey marveled.

"Yes, we were very fortunate," Brenda admitted, reinforcing a growing guilt on her part in the way she had treated Jake on the return trip across the Gulf Stream aboard the *Sea Bones*.

"But how is it that this has never made the newspapers, or TV? I mean, this was a major happening. A U.S. citizen killing foreign mercenaries, saving lives, and practically right next door, in the Bahamas of all places," Stacy asked incredulously.

"We were sworn to secrecy by the Bahamian government," Brenda said. "We were told that our release was conditional upon our cooperation in keeping it quiet because of the effect it would have on tourism and Bahamian-Haitian relations. Had we not agreed, we could have been detained for God only knows how long until all the legal proceedings were concluded."

"So, no charges were brought against Jake, and all of you were released?

"That's right," Brenda answered. "A government minister from Nassau and a senior police officer conducted an investigation on board the *Sea Bones*. The Haitian pirates' bodies were taken to a morgue on Bimini. Each of us was placed in a motel room and questioned separately. Then, the next morning, we were told we were free to go if we signed a statement agreeing to absolute silence about the incident. Needless to say, every one of us just wanted to get out of there as quickly as possible. Doctor Ambrose was feeding Maggie some pink pills to keep her together until he could get her to a clinic in Fort Lauderdale to deal with the shock. It was so sad; her vacation turned out to be a journey through hell. We all signed. Jake and I brought the *Sea Bones* back to 'Lauderdale. The others flew out on Chalk's to Miami."

When Brenda and Stacy returned to the table, there was a subtle shift in the meal's ambiance and the men sensed it.

"So what did we miss?" Stacy asked brightly with a smile, doing her best to give no sign of what Brenda had revealed about Jake's encounter with the Haitian pirates. She didn't miss the exchange of looks between Brenda and Jake as Brenda took her seat. *Damn! Me and my big mouth. Why do I have the feeling it was a big mistake to mention Jake's Gulf War exploits to Brenda? But then, why hasn't Jake told Brenda about his combat exploits in Iraq? Is he ashamed of them—or what? Will she tell him that I told her? And what have I done to the relationship between Jake and my husband? Damn, Damn, dammit!*

Bryce Taggart arched an eyebrow in Stacy's direction noting her preoccupation, but let it go. "Nothing, really," he said. "But I've probably disappointed Jake by telling him that it's going to take some digging to uncover any coded message in his Spaniard's text, if there is one."

"To tell the truth," Jake said, "I'm really kind of poking around in the dark. When I first read the passage in the journal about a Spanish castaway on an island in the Pacific Ocean almost four hundred years ago, I had no idea what a Spaniard might be doing on an island in the Pacific Ocean in the 17th century, or for that matter, why a British warship would be there either. Nautical history is not my strong suit," he said modestly.

"But I would guess you've done some research since then, right?" Stacy asked, trying hard to pick up the relationship she had with Jake before learning that he had killed four men just days earlier with practically his bare hands. "You know about the galleon trade between Manila and Acapulco? You're thinking there might be a connection between the Spanish castaway and a trading galleon?"

"Well, in the past couple of weeks I've read a few of the popular history books about the galleons and the treasure they carried. But I haven't been successful in connecting my Spanish castaway with any galleon. In fact, the opposite. The island he was rescued from is not only extremely remote, it is well off the traditional route that the galleons sailed between Manila and Acapulco. Once a reliable return route across the north Pacific was discovered, the Spanish government discouraged deviation from it. The route that was used for over 200 years didn't come anywhere near the island position identified in the Lieutenant's log. Also, the Spaniard says he was aboard a vessel called the *Santo Nino* that was sunk by a storm. He says there were seventy people aboard, and all of them were lost at sea.

"There's a place in Seville, Spain," Jake continued, "where they keep all the records of the galleon trade. I e-mailed them and they said there was no record of a vessel named *Santo Nino* sailing the Pacific during that time frame, certainly not one of the royal galleons. They have a fairly complete record of the galleons because they were owned by the Spanish crown, and there's a lot of paperwork that goes with that. And the treasure galleons usually had several hundred people on board anyway, not seventy."

"The *Archivo General de las Indias*," Stacy said. "It's called the 'AGI'. That's where you sent the e-mail. I know it. I visited there several times while conducting research for my doctoral dissertation. It's one of the few historical repositories where researchers are entrusted with the original documents. You go up to the counter and place your research request on the computer. Men in dark suits bring the documents to your table. They are usually bound in bundles with linen straps called a *legato*, and when you open the embossed covers, you have in front of you original documents that are centuries old. Believe it or not, some of them still have grains of the sand between the folios that was scattered over the ink to blot it. It is so exciting to touch them.

"The AGI is a lovely old building," Stacy continued, slowly regaining her composure. "The outer structure is made of stone, and the inner casing is of polished marble. The study hall has thirty-foot high ceilings, and there are usually a couple of dozen or more people in the main study hall pouring over old documents and manifests researching the history of Spain's adventures in the Americas and the Pacific Rim. Dozens of the Acapulco and Manila galleons were lost in the course of two and a half centuries, and there's apparently quite a market in trying to pin down where their treasures might be."

"That's the place," said Jake. "I'll probably be talking with them again soon. I thought I'd get the names of the galleons sailing in the years immediately prior to my Spaniard being found, then check the passenger manifests to see if any of the crew or passengers have the same name as his. The way I figure it, the Spaniard may have lied about the name of the ship he was sailing on. Especially if he was sailing on the annual Manila galleon and it had foundered on the same island where he was rescued."

"How do you mean?" asked Taggart, leaning forward in renewed curiosity. He was beginning to see that there was more to this former Marine Corps sergeant than met the eye.

"Well, the Spaniard was Catholic. He was rescued by Protestant Englishmen, arch enemies at the time. I'm pretty sure he was both surprised and real disappointed when he realized who had responded to his distress signal. The Spanish called the Pacific Ocean their 'Spanish Lake', and the presence of an English man-o-war in the western Pacific was rare for those times. The Spaniard was dying and he knew it. If he had been aboard the Manila galleon, it is not likely that he would have provided that bit of information to his English rescuers, especially if the galleon's treasure was on the island where they found him."

"So in a nutshell, Jake," Bryce Taggart said, "you're thinking there may be a hidden message in the Spanish castaway's death bed confession to the Pope that reveals the treasure's location."

"Something like that," Jake replied, "Of course I already know the location of the island from the sailing journal. Each entry in the British officer's journal is accompanied by a notation of the vessel's approximate geographical position. It's connecting the Spaniard with a galleon that's the trick. If he was a passenger on the annual Manila galleon and the galleon foundered on the island where he was picked up by the British, then the galleon's treasure would be on the island, too."

"Wow, like an 'X marks the spot' treasure map," Stacy said, glancing to her husband, Tag.

"Not to put a wet blanket on all of this," Taggart said, "but two things come to mind. The Spaniards had sailing vessels of all sizes plying the Pacific Ocean, and the one your Spaniard says he was on may have been a smaller inter-island commercial vessel of little or no consequence, so that would explain why no records were found in the *Archivo General de las Indias*. Secondly, even if he had set sail on a Manila treasure galleon, the galleon could have sunk at sea and your Spaniard could have washed up on the island in a ship's cutter or hanging onto a piece of flotsam. His presence on the island doesn't necessarily mean the galleon's treasure arrived with him," Taggart reasoned.

"You're right. But there's one odd thing," Jake replied, smiling. "In the sailing journal that I found, the British officer writes that the Spaniard asked for the longitude and latitude of the island. Now, why would a dying man who's about to write his spiritual confession to the Pope want the precise geographical location of where he was found?"

The question hung in the air like a dead goose on Thanksgiving morning.

"Jake, I may be jumping ahead somewhat, but I'm curious," said Stacy, a slight frown forming across her brow, "If you find out that the Spanish castaway was actually on board one of the Manila galleons, and that the galleon's treasure might be on the island from which he was rescued, what do you intend to do?"

"Why, go get it, of course," Jake said.

There was a pause, and then they all laughed in unison. It seemed so preposterous to hear it said out loud, but no one doubted that Jake was serious, certainly not Major Bryce Taggart, USMCR. *And I'll be damned if I don't believe you will, Snapper! Damned if I don't.*

"So what can we do to further this enterprise? Stacy asked brightly and quite seriously.

"I'm working two angles," Jake said, "both of them focused on connecting the Spaniard to a Manila galleon. The Major, uh…Tag, has offered to help me with checking the Spaniard's confession for a coded message. Then I'm going to see if any of the records at the AGI in

Seville indicate my particular Spaniard was aboard one of the galleons that would have been sailing around the time he was rescued. If either of those pan out, then I'm going to have to decide how to go about reconnoitering the island."

"You mean actually sail to the island?" Stacy asked. "Your sailboat can do that?"

"Yes," Jake answered. "My sailboat is probably better prepared to do it than I am. I'm not exactly a seasoned blue water sailor, and the voyage would be dicey in a number of ways. From what I've been able to uncover so far, the island has no water and no natural all-weather harbor. Once on the island it could take weeks to locate the treasure and excavate it—if it's still above water— and I don't know how I would keep my boat safe while I'm ashore. If she should drag anchor and drift away, or be driven up on the coral reef by an unexpected squall, it would definitely be bad news to find myself stranded there. I would have no way to contact anyone, and no water or food. I'd be in the same situation as the Spaniard castaway."

"An island on the other side of the world," Bryce Taggart mused. "And the treasure would have arrived on the island almost four centuries ago. What do you think the odds are that it would have gone undiscovered for so long a time?"

Jake turned pensive for a moment and did not answer quickly. Then said, "I'm assuming some effort was made by the galleon's survivors to conceal the treasure, burying it or something so you couldn't just stumble upon it. That seems only logical. Then, the island itself is so incredibly remote and off the beaten path that I think it unlikely someone would have come upon it in the first couple of centuries. It's World War II that's the unknown factor. Just about every square acre of all of the Pacific islands were occupied at one time or another either by Japs or the Allies. This island was no exception. But even so, I'm fairly certain the war didn't uncover the treasure," he said with conviction.

"Why is that?" Stacy asked, now thoroughly entranced by the prospect of recovering some fabulous hoard of long-lost treasure, even if the expedition was led by a machete-waving Marine Corps sniper named Jake Porter.

"Because of the size of the treasure and the nature of it," Jake said. "The facts are well documented. The Manila galleons carried tons of exotic Chinese silks, crates of Chinese porcelain, hundreds of chests containing a fabulous amount of jewels and gold, and all sorts of other stuff. If it had been found, even by the Japanese military, it would have certainly been reported and would have raised worldwide attention when the cargo hit the market for sale."

Up until that moment, Brenda had not said anything since returning to the table with Stacy. Now she said, "Jake has had me spend a few hundred hours on the Internet scouring world news reports and auction activity from Sotheby's and Christie's in London, to every other major gallery and auction house from Singapore and Hong Kong, to Monaco," Brenda said with a smile. "He recruited me for this little adventure after we returned from the Bahamas. Sort of a Marine Corps bonding ritual, I guess," she added. She cut a quick glance to Stacy, and smiled again.

"I asked Brenda as a favor to survey world news beginning with the year 1930, until present," Jake said almost defensively. "So far, nothing to suggest an event as monumental as recovering a treasure worth hundreds of millions of dollars."

"Why 1930?" Bryce Taggart asked.

"That would pretty much be the earliest date that the Japs put troops on the island," Jake said. "From what I've been able to find out so far, the Japs pushed around a bit of dirt while they were on the island, built a small runway for aircraft and some gun emplacements. If one of their bulldozers had unearthed the treasure, I'm sure it would have hit the news big time, especially in Tokyo. The island also endured some pretty fierce bombing as well."

"Playing the Devil's advocate again," said Taggart, "Couldn't that also suggest the treasure isn't on the island?"

Again, Jake was slow to respond. "That the treasure is not on the island is always a possibility. Four centuries is a long time for any one of a number of things to happen. The island is pounded every year by typhoons, for instance, and they could have washed away a portion of the island and the treasure with it. But until I can confirm that my Spanish castaway was aboard a galleon, there isn't anything to even talk about. However, if he left Manila on a galleon, and the galleon's treasure was secreted on the island, then I understand why he wanted to know the precise location of the island before he died. He wanted to get the news back to Spain or the Vatican, and since he was dying, the only way he could convey the location was through the so-called confession he was dictating to the young British officer.

"As to the Japs, they arrived on the island to build an airstrip and prepare for war, not to find a buried treasure. I've studied aerial photos taken of the island during the war that show where they did their digging for gun emplacements and building the runway. They worked where the ground was the flattest and easiest to prepare for an airstrip, and avoided the only elevated area on the island, a volcanic hump about two hundred feet high and a quarter-mile in length. That's where I think the treasure will be found."

"Jake, you've got my heart pumping!" Bryce Taggart said. He was grinning like a 5-year old.

"Oh! It's a wonderful adventure!" Stacy said excitedly. "I feel like we're a bunch of pirates!" *I just pray to God we won't be called to join Jake in any killing!*

"Speaking of pirates," Jake said, "there are people out there with lots of money and state-of-the-art technology who work the year 'round looking for treasure. Like you said, Stacy, there were researchers at the *AGI* in Seville looking for clues about lost Manila galleons. There's no telling who's funding that research, but you can be sure they're serious about what they're doing. They'll spend any amount of money and break every rule in the book, moral or otherwise, if they think it will bring them closer to the treasure. It's a no-holds-barred deal and the only winner is the one who comes up with the treasure."

"Finders keepers, losers weepers," Stacy said, looking again to her fiancée, Tag.

"Right. If you read the stories of modern-day treasure salvers," Jake continued, "just about every one of them cites instances of pirates trying to rip-off the treasure. Mel Fisher, the guy who found the wreck of the *Atocha* in the Florida Keys did his research at the *Archivo General de las Indies*. Fisher ended up fighting everyone from Florida government officials to thieves invading his dive sites trying to grab the treasure.

"And the guy who led the multi-million dollar consortium that recently recovered the hundreds of millions in gold from the *S.S. Central America* that went down 200 miles off Cape Hatteras, followed all the rules and even had a Federal court order protecting his recovery operations. But would-be pirates used the court papers to find out where the wreck was located and tried to grab the treasure anyway. I think it's important to realize that what we're dealing with here today demands absolute discretion. The market value of this treasure is more than the annual budget of most of the countries on the planet."

"Yes, I can see that," said Bryce Taggart. "And I've noticed that you've been very circumspect in what information you've shared with us. I don't believe Stacy or I have knowledge of anything yet that would compromise your search, Jake."

"Well," Jake began with a smile, "I did show you the Spaniard's message, didn't I? But yes, I am being cautious. The single most important piece of information is the name and location of the island. If that ever got out, all would be lost. But knowing the name of the Spanish castaway and having access to his final message could be equally devastating if it turns out that his message does contain a code revealing the treasure's location. So far, I am the only one with access to the sailing journal revealing the exact location of where the Spaniard was rescued, and has his final message. And I am the only one who knows his name. There may come a time when I will have to reveal some of that. But for the moment, I have placed the sailing journal in a safe place out of harm's way. My goal now is to take any path that leads to connecting the Spanish castaway to a Manila galleon. That's what brought me here today. I need help with research, and I've got to keep everything low-key to prevent inviting trouble."

"And for what it's worth," Brenda chimed in, "I can tell you that life around Jake is never dull," catching Stacy's eyes with her own. *That's your cue, honey,* Brenda thought, *if you want to announce what I just told you in the restroom. But if you don't do it now, I know you'll tell him the first time you're alone with him. Cat's out of the bag, as they say.*

"Well, this has been without a doubt the most memorable lunch that Stacy and I have shared in quite a while," Bryce Taggart said. "Don't you agree?" he asked, turning to his fiancée.

Stacy nodded. "It's going to be hard going back to my afternoon class on the political parties of post-Napoleonic France," she said. "Jake, I believe I can help with the archival search of the AIG's records in Seville to identify the crew and passengers on the Manila galleons. I have access to the university's computer system and I can make a relatively anonymous search. I can do the same with the British Admiralty archives. You want to give me some instructions along that line?"

"That would be great," Jake said, relieved to see that he wasn't being seen as a nut case. "To keep the search as obscure as possible, inquire about any Acapulco-bound Manila galleons from 1695 to 1700 that didn't make port. That would cover the time period that is reasonable for the castaway to have survived on the island. Ask only for the passenger manifests. That may throw off anyone who's curious. Treasurer salvers usually want the cargo manifests so they can gage the payoff and what the recovery logistics might be. They hardly ever show any interest in who was aboard."

"Speaking of cargo logistics, Jake," Bryce Taggart said, "how are you going to haul it back to the States? It must weigh tons and take up hundreds of cubic yards of space. Surely you can't do it with your sailboat"

"Now there's a problem I'm looking forward to solving," Jake answered with a laugh.

"He's already promised me a piece of the haul for my help," Brenda interjected.

"On that note and at the risk of sounding somewhat presumptuous, I'll say this. Any help I may get, especially if it leads to actually recovering some or all of the treasure, will put me in a position to be very generous. I hope I have an opportunity to make all of us very rich."

"Well, it looks like we have a plan," Bryce Taggart said. "I'll round up some code information to help with evaluating the Spaniard's message, and Stacy will begin some historical inquiries. How shall we communicate with each other? I appreciate the fact that we must be very circumspect."

"Let's avoid the Internet completely," Jake answered. "I have access to the telephone aboard the *Sea Bones*. I'll give you the number and you can leave a message that you're trying to reach me. I'll return your call from some other telephone, probably using a pre-paid phone card. If there's important information to swap, I'll drive to Gainesville, so we can talk under controlled circumstances.' Jake paused, then added, "I know this sounds a bit melodramatic, but like I said, given the value of what we're pursuing, there are people who will spend a lot of money and do just about anything to cut us out of the action. Our best weapon is secrecy, believe me."

"Loose lips sink ships," Stacy said brightly, but never more seriously in her life.

"Exactly," Jake said.

(*Three*)

They parted in front of Morehouse Hall, Jake and Brenda heading for the Karman Ghia, waving as they drove away. Bryce and Stacy stood side-by-side watching the yellow convertible make its way off the campus.

"What an afternoon!" Bryce Taggart said, looking down affectionately at his fiancé. "What do you think, sweetheart? Is this too real, or what? Think Jake's up to this?"

"I have no doubt that Jake is capable of whatever may arise," she answered, visualizing the bloody scene aboard the *Sea Bones* that Brenda had described, "Be it pirates, storms, or whatever. In fact, my love, there's no way I can go back to my class today. I'm too stirred up. I'm calling my intern to cover for me. You don't have any classes until tomorrow as I recall. Let's go home. I think we need to talk," she said, taking his hand in hers, rising on tip toes to give him a kiss on the cheek.

NUESTRA SENORA de la CONCEPCION

Date: July 27, 1698

Lat. 14º 29' N, Long. 120º 55' E

Cavite Harbor, Luzon, Philippines

It is not given to us to know our final fate in advance. And that is the way it should be, of course. But if the passengers and crew making their way to board the great galleon had been aware of what awaited them in the coming voyage, they would have flung down their every possession, abandoned without a second thought their closest and dearest companions, and fled in frenzied panic as fast as their feet, horses, or carriages could take them. For every man, woman and child boarding that magnificent vessel would soon perish, and the galleon, along with all of its fabulous cargo, would vanish from the reckoning of mankind before ever reaching its destination on the far side of the Pacific Ocean.

The galleon itself inspired every confidence; it was three years in the building, and at 190 feet in length, a beam of 53 feet, with a draft of more than 20 feet, and displacing over 2,300 tons, she was the largest galleon ever built for the trans Pacific trade between Manila, Philippines, and Acapulco, *Nueva Espana*. Built at Cavite by Chinese and Moro natives, her frames, knees, buttocks, deck beams, shelves and keel were sawn from invincible tropical *molave*. The decks, cabins and bulkheads were of flawless, fine-grained teak harvested from local forests, and the hull's planking was of *lanang* wood so thick and hard that even the 24-pound cannon balls of the hated English would bounce harmlessly into the sea.

She slid gracefully down the ways and splashed into Cavite Bay the first week in July, and completed her sea trials in local waters barely two weeks following her launching. Everything was new, from her cast iron ground tackle of anchors and chain, to Manila hemp cordage and hand-carved lignum vitae blocks for running rigging and sail-hoisting, to cotton sails meticulously cut and sewn by dozens of Chinese women in the nearby province of Ilocos.

The man who would command her, Capitan Rodrigo de Morga, was a veteran of three Pacific crossings; two westward voyages from Acapulco, to the colony in Manila, and one difficult *tornavieja*, or eastward return from Manila to Acapulco. The principal navigator for the coming voyage would be Friar Miguel Ortiz, equally skilled and a devout servant of God and Church in the bargain. Good omens all, but nevertheless it was destined that all 711 of those who sailed on her would never see their homeland again. And everything that they, the Spanish Crown and the Catholic Church had so carefully secreted aboard the royal *nao* would be lost to them forever.

The loading of the galleon began within hours of her return from sea trials, for the season was well advanced and it was imperative that she clear the islands for the open sea before the arrival of the annual monsoons, which were expected within a few weeks. Ten-inch thick hemp hawsers secured her snugly to the wharf just inside the headland of Cavite harbor, her bow and fifty-foot long bowsprit pointing resolutely seaward. The tons of ballast stones that were used to temporarily simulate the weight of her intended cargo and set her trim for the sailing trials were removed by gangs of Chinese laborers and carted away. That task alone took almost a week.

As the weight of the ballast stones came off, the hawsers leading to the wharf were eased and the galleon rose slowly out of the water until the tops of her bulwarks towered more than 60 feet above the wharf, and her masts soared another one hundred twenty feet beyond that. When fully loaded and down on her lines, *Nuestra Senora de la Concepcion's* towering sterncastle would still rise 65 feet above the waterline. As she now lay alongside the wharf with bare innards, the galleon's physical bulk dwarfed the tiny humans and draft animals scurrying back and forth along the broad wharf bringing the first of her cargo.

The heaviest of the cargo would be loaded first and secured in the lowest portion of her cavernous hold to serve as the ballast necessary to keep the galleon upright against the pressure of the winds and seas against her towering sails and immense crescent-shaped hull. The loading began when twenty-one stout wooden chests of gold bullion belonging to the Spanish Crown were brought aboard and carefully centered fore-and-aft directly atop the keel. This gold represented an entire year's worth of the customs duty and port fees that the Spanish government had collected piecemeal from the Chinese merchants bringing their wares to Manila for sale, and from Spanish merchants who were paying for the transshipping of their wares aboard the royal galleon. It was of the purest 22.5 carat quality, and had been melted down, purified and poured into uniform ingots at the royal customs house within the walled fortress of Manila, each ingot struck with the royal insignia to claim ownership, along with an individual number for accounting purposes.

Next came almost 500 chests of varying sizes and weights belonging to the wealthier merchants and trading combines, royal functionaries, religious orders, senior military personages, and the charitable organizations like the *obras pias,* among others. Most of the contents of these hundreds of chests were of gold, diamonds and semi-precious stones, some polished and faceted, others uncut and unmounted. For the most part, the gold in these chests was not cast in bars of bullion. Instead, the bulk of the gold was in the far more valuable forms of

Chinese-crafted jewelry, tableware, buttons, combs, chains, and religious objects such as crucifixes, reliquaries and rosaries, plus diverse other finished forms that greatly multiplied the gold's base value.

The cargo manifest of *Nuestra Senora de la Conception* that would one day reside in the *Archivo General de las Indies* in Seville, Spain, reflects that when she set sail on August 1, 1698, among these hundreds of chests stored deep in her hold were 120,000 gold filigree combs; more than 250,000 gold chains in lengths of 5 to 20 feet each; 3,000 jewelry boxes and snuff boxes of differing sizes in intricately-spun gold and silver; 500,000 gold filigree costume buttons and jewel-encrusted broaches; plus dozens of gold and silver sword hilts intended for the dress swords of European royalty. In addition, the cargo manifest chronicles over 5,000 separate pieces of gold or silver dinnerware, fruit plates, tureens, vases, serving trays and cups fashioned by Chinese, Siamese and Indian metal smiths into a host of exotic and eye-pleasing styles. Because space within the chests was at such a premium, virtually every one of the aforementioned boxes, tureens and vases was stuffed with diamonds, rubies, topazes, sapphires and pearls.

But the official cargo manifest falls far short of recording the true inventory of wealth brought aboard the *Concepcion* in these first chests. Most of these chests also had cleverly concealed secret compartments designed to pass the cursory inspection of the royal government's *Fiscal* when they were brought aboard and thus escape paying duty to the royal crown. These compartments were of necessity small and since space within them was at a premium, they usually contained small jewelry such as rings, broaches, buckles and filigree dress studs mounted with diamonds, rubies, sapphires, topazes and a host of other semi-precious stones including strings of pearls as well as a variety of objects carved and fashioned of the finest jade, ivory and tortoise shell.

Once these heaviest-of-the-heavy chests were stoutly lashed with hemp ropes and secured by boards to prevent their shifting, 90 thick-walled jugs, kiln-fired in China and filled with mercury, were secured in place. Mercury was highly prized in the silver mining regions of *Nueva Espana* for purifying the silver being mined there. Half of the galleon's 120 bronze cannons were also lowered into the hold and secured along with several tons of cannon balls to add to the ballast that would stiffen the *noa* against winds and sea. Then came the crates of Chinese porcelain, carefully packed in straw, each crate containing an assortment of full table settings, vases and jars; many of the pieces were in the post-Ming style, but most were Shunzu and Qing period, characterized by bright colors of red, orange and yellow to depict all manner of exotic creatures and landscapes. Several of the Spanish merchants and senior Catholic priests had private trading connections in China, and had arranged for the manufacture and purchase of several hundred pieces of the rarest of Chinese porcelain, these fired in the Chinese emperor's own imperial court kilns.

Next, the first of the galleon's water supply was lowered into the hold. At this lowest of the galleon's four deck levels, over 1,000 earthen jars called *tibores*, each filled with almost 30 gallons of water at eight pounds to the gallon, were carefully and tightly secured to prevent movement. Several hundred gallons of oil and vinegar in similar Chinese-made stoneware *bojitas* were also stored in this lower bilge level. Most of the galleon's dry and preserved foodstuffs, however, would be stored in the next two upper levels because it was the lower bilge portion of the galleon's interior that was most susceptible to flooding from leaks and foul weather.

With the heaviest of the cargo now secured evenly both fore-and-aft and athwarthships, thick boards that had been carefully measured and fitted were placed over all of it to create the deck for the second level. These boards were cut and placed in a pattern that would permit access to the water, oil and vinegar in the latter weeks of the voyage as they were needed. Most of the second deck level was still below the galleon's water line, but regular pumping of the lower bilge would keep it dry except in the most dire of circumstances.

Into this second deck level was stored the bulkiest of the galleon's cargo, principally the priceless Chinese silks and brocades, Persian rugs and exquisite tapestries, more crates of Chinese porcelain plus the personal chests belonging to the hundreds of passengers. Many of these personal chests also had secret compartments containing small fortunes in gold and silver jewelry, diamonds, pearls, and semi-precious stones. Other crates belonging to the merchants, religious orders and royal appointees were stuffed with indescribable beauty and craftsmanship in the form of escritoires, boxes and desks of aromatic woods, some having lacquered surfaces with exotic inlaid designs of shimmering mother-of-pearl. Most of these smaller boxes also contained contraband jewelry and precious stones.

The second deck level also carried the largest concentration of the galleon's water and foodstuffs for surviving the 6-to-8 month voyage. Some 2,000 fired-clay *tibores*, were lowered into the hold and secured, along with 700 *bombones*, bamboo cane in lengths of 8 spans and thick as a man's thigh, also filled with water and sealed at the top. Next came 4,510 pounds of salted beef, 3,550 pounds of salted pork, 45,000 pounds of sea biscuit, 2,700 pounds of dried fish, 400 bushels of rice, hundreds of pounds of garbanzos, 700 cheeses, and 350 pounds of onions and garlic. Additional stoneware vessels carried hundreds more gallons of oil and vinegar. All of these provisions were carefully recorded in the *Concepcion's* cargo manifests.

The third deck level, the level immediately below the main sailing deck, was divided into tiny living spaces for the 700-plus passengers and crew. But lashed in and amongst these spaces were more *tibores* of water, plus packages of preserved foodstuffs and passengers' luggage, even a few hundred more skeins of Chinese silk. Every cubic inch of the galleon's interior was precious.

The sailing deck mounted the galleon's remaining bronze cannons, reduced to half the number in favor of additional cargo stacked in and about the deck on the galleon's centerline, leaving only tight passageways for the crew to hoist the sails and trim the running rigging.

More *tibores* of water hung from the ratlines. And at the after-end of the sailing deck rose the huge sterncastle. Here ship's officers, royal appointees and a few selected wealthy had tiny sea cabins in the main deck level of the castle, and the Captain's cabin rode supreme at the top.

And so, as the doomed crew and passengers made their way down the wharf to board the great galleon to join their possessions and fellow *Manilenos*, the heavily burdened *Nuestra Senora de la Concepcion* squatted ever lower in the water awaiting her *capitan* and her *zarpe* or port clearance for Acapulco, *Nueva Espana* on the far side of a more than 9,000 miles crossing of the northern Pacific Ocean— a world and a lifetime away.

A CAESAR'S SHIFT & THE VIGENERE CIPHER

Date: November 27, 2000

Long. 29º 39' N, Lat. 82º 19' W

Gainesville, Florida

(One)

"Tag, darling, could you tear yourself away from your code books for a minute and take a look at this?" Stacy sat behind her large screen Apple computer with a half dozen windows open on the monitor, most of them attached to academic research sites. One of them was the *Archivo General de las Indias* (AGI) in Seville, Spain.

Bryce Taggart was stretched out on their leather sofa, barefoot and head propped up by a couple of fringed decorator pillows. On the coffee table at his elbow were spread close to twenty books, three notepads filled with hurried cryptic scribbles, and an Apple laptop computer connected to the Internet through their apartment's wireless router. He rose from the sofa, brushed his hair back from his forehead, and went to stand behind Stacy.

"Whatcha got, doll?" he asked, placing his hands on her shoulders and flexing his fingers.

"Ummm, that feels good, " she sighed, then raised a finger to point to one of the open windows, stroking the image to a larger magnification. "These are PDFs of the passenger and cargo manifests of the three Manila galleons that went missing in the last four years of the 17th century. The images and files are too large to print copies here. I'll send them to my desktop at the university. We have a large format printer there that I can use to make copies for Jake, but I don't think he will be able to read the Spanish script in the passenger manifests to find his castaway.

"I was lucky to get these. The AIG is digitizing all of its documents, and has put on hold any external research support. Fortunately, I know one of the assistant curators there, a Dr. Silva. He is Portuguese by birth, and he remembers me from when I was doing research at the AIG for my master's thesis. He was also kind enough to send along some administrative correspondence files that are related to the galleons. This is a letter I found in a file folder on the galleon that departed Manila in late Summer of 1698, and is one of the missing ones. Her name was *Nuestra Senora de la Concepcion*."

"So what's it say? Tag asked impatiently. "I'm not very good at reading 400-hundred-year-old Spanish, you know."

"Don't be such a pill, darling. It's a letter from the newly-appointed royal governor in Manila, writing to Spain's royal treasurer in Madrid, explaining discrepancies among the cargo entries in the galleon's manifest. Apparently the previous governor, Julio Ruiz Obando was his name, was relieved of his office and ordered to Madrid for an accounting. Looks like he got caught dipping his hand in the Royal till.

"What's particularly interesting is the explanation given for not including in the galleon's manifest an accounting for a large cargo of Chinese porcelain. The new governor explains to the royal treasurer that the porcelain shipment in question was deemed non-taxable by the former governor of Manila because it was a gift to the Pope from Manila's Jesuit order, and the Jesuits in turn had arranged for a line of credit for disenfranchised citizens of Manila during an especially stressful economic time."

Stacy paused to allow that to sink in, then continued. "The new governor of Manila goes on to describe this special shipment by the Jesuits: It is a 100-place banquet setting of porcelain that was fired in the Chinese Khan's personal kiln of the finest kaolin clay. It was trimmed in gold, and the Pope's crest was hand-glazed on each piece. Can you imagine what that set of Chinese porcelain would be worth today?" Stacy exclaimed.

"I think you can be sure the Vatican would be at the head of the line when bidding at an auction for it," Tag chuckled.

"Millions, probably tens of millions," Stacy mused. "Just for that one part of the cargo the galleon was carrying. It's almost too much to imagine what the entire cargo would be worth. Look at the pages of cargo entries. There are thousands of items. If Jake is able to recover just a fraction of these things, he will stun the antiquities market worldwide. It's almost too much to imagine."

"The only thing is," Tag responded, "we don't know for certain if the treasure Jake is after is from that particular galleon. And we don't know if the treasure of that galleon is on the island where the castaway was found. It makes the point that we need to put the arm on Jake and explain to him some of the realties of the kind of research that is needed if we are to pin his Spanish castaway to a treasure galleon. I can appreciate his being very cautious about what he tells anyone about what's in that English lieutenant's sailing journal, but we need to know at least two specific things: the exact date that the Spanish castaway was recovered, and his name."

(Two)

Five days earlier, as Jake and Brenda drove away from the university campus, Stacy had turned her classes over to her graduate intern, and she and Tag had driven home. On the way, Stacy told Tag what had happened when she and Brenda had gone to the women's restroom at the campus cafeteria. She told of how she had shown to Brenda the Marine Corps recruiting booklet describing Jake's combat experience in Iraq and crediting him with the deaths of twenty to thirty Iraqi soldiers. Her intention was to impress Brenda with Jake's bravery. But Brenda had topped the recruiting booklet with a blow-by-blow description of Jake's killing of 4 Haitian pirates in the Bahamas just 3 weeks before.

She told it all: the headless corpse, the two other dead in the *Sea Bones* salon, one with a machete sticking out of his chest, and the one on the beach with a steel gaff through his throat. All dead at the hands of former U.S. Marine Sergeant Jake Porter. She mentioned the pistol and the shots fired, and how they had all been interrogated by the Bahamian officials and signed documents swearing to secrecy. She also mentioned the incident at the Cat Cay Club and the sailor who had been killed, and his wife raped and brutally slashed by suspected Haitian pirates.

"Damn!" Tag had said in response. "He must have been out of his mind. Taking that Haitian's head off was not very Marine-like."

"What do you mean, 'not very Marine-like'?" Stacy had replied in complete puzzlement.

"Our training teaches us to stab, not slash," Tag said. "When approaching an enemy from behind, we stab directly into a vital organ, usually the kidney if we want to prevent an outcry that would alert the enemy."

"Oh, God, Tag! I could have gone the rest of my life without hearing that!"

"Sorry, but you asked."

Brenda's revelations of the Bahamas incident had underscored Tag and

Stacy's initial assessment of Jake Porter: he and his inquiries were not to be discounted out of hand. He was a determined, battle-hardened young man, fully capable of taking care of whatever needed to be done to complete a mission. They had no doubt that he was prepared to sail his boat to the other side of the world to search for treasure if he had reasonable evidence to support the venture.

Now, five days later and many conversations later about Jake and the whole treasure adventure, they had devoted most of their spare time to investigating any and everything they could that might help Jake. Stacy was accessing any resources that might reveal the identity of the Manila galleons lost in the late 17th century, and Tag had begun to gather information that could help Jake decrypt any secret message that might be contained in the Spaniard's last words. He had gone into the attic of their apartment to retrieve his many textbooks, class notes and instructional materials from his attendance at the U.S. Navy cryptology school.

"I think we might have enough progress to justify inviting Jake for a meeting to share our findings, and in the process convince him why we need more information from him," Tag said to Stacy. "The only thing Jake has at the moment is a hunch. The only facts he has are that a Spaniard castaway was recovered from a Pacific island. He has the castaway's name and the longitude and latitude of the island's location, and the date, but no connection whatsoever to a galleon treasure. That's why he has come to us.

"Let me show you something." He went to the coffee table and brought back a computer printout and a yellow writing pad. The computer sheet was titled "The Caesar Shift" and showed a single horizontal line of English alphabetic characters from A to Z. Two spaces below and to the left, in a vertical line, the characters of the alphabet were stacked one over the other, beginning with the letter A at the top and descending vertically to the letter Z.

"The letters in the first horizontal line represent the plaintext letters of a message," Tag explained. "Now, beginning with the letter B in the vertical column, the B would shift to beneath the plaintext letter A, and the rest of the alphabet following the B would also shift one character to the right. That's the idea of the Caesar's Shift. Now, if one dropped down the vertical alphabet to the letter N, for instance, and placed it beneath the letter A, then each letter in the encrypted text would shift 14 characters to the right because the letter N is the 14th character in the alphabet. The letter A in a plaintext message would be encrypted as an N." Tag demonstrated the process for Stacy using the plaintext word 'money' and the 'N' cipher. The word 'money' when encrypted read, 'ZBARL.'

"I've been trying to figure out how to explain cryptology to Jake, and what's involved in deciphering a hidden message," he began. "Jake tells us the approximate date: late 17th century. The castaway is European, a Spaniard, and a Catholic. I've been reviewing my study material from the Navy's cryptology school, and I believe I can say with some degree of certainty that if there is a hidden message in the Spaniard's prayer for absolution, it calls for a Caesar's shift, which is a simple substitution cipher like I showed you with the word 'money'. But the Caesar's shift alone was known to be too vulnerable to frequency analysis, and in all probability was combined with a polyalphabetic substitution cipher using a keyword known only to the sender and the receiver. The Vatican made considerable use of this kind of encryption system for centuries. It's much like the one-pad systems used by spies during World War II.

"The most likely polyalphabetic choice during the time period we are looking at," Tag continued, excitement rising in his voice, "was the Vigenere tableau. It is simple and portable in the field. Remember, Jake's Spanish castaway was in great pain and near death; the encrypting process had to be easy. Blaise de Vigenere was at the court of Henry III of France during the 16th century when he devised his method of encryption. He turned to the Caesar's shift to set up the first cipher-text alphabet, then incorporated a second alphabet that encrypted the first through the use of a keyword, or cipher. If you knew the keyword, all you had to do to encrypt and decrypt a message was repeat the keyword as many times as necessary above the characters in the plaintext message. To derive the cipher-text using the Caesar shift tableau for each letter in the plaintext, one finds the intersection of the row given by the corresponding keyword letter and the column given by the plaintext letter itself to pick out the cipher-text letter."

"Dear God, Tag! How can you expect anyone to understand all that?" Stacy exclaimed.

"Well, I can draw it out in charts and give Jake some practice," he responded, somewhat deflated. "If he doesn't feel like he's up to it, he can lighten up a bit and let us have the name of the Spanish castaway. The challenge here is to uncover that cipher, the keyword known only to the sender and receiver. Knowing the identity of the Spaniard, his family, what part of Spain he came from, the name of his village's patron saint, all that kind of stuff, because that is typically where a cipher is drawn from. That's why I think it would be a good idea for us to meet and talk about all of this."

"You've been at this cryptology and intelligence business for so long, sweetheart, what seems very straight forward to you can be impossible for someone who didn't receive the Navy's professional training."

"My reserve unit's monthly training is this coming weekend. What do you think of us inviting Jake up, ask him to spend the night with us. We'll have a nice dinner, show him what we have so far. Maybe I'll ask him if he would like to visit our reserve center. My boys would really like to meet the sniper from the recruiting booklet," Tag said with some enthusiasm returning to his voice.

"I have the feeling Jake is not particularly interested in having a bunch of young Marines probing him for war stories," Stacy said.

"Why do you say that? Tag asked, a bit perplexed.

"Well, for starters, I'm pretty sure he didn't laud it over Brenda. And you know Marines; they love to impress their girlfriends with their feats on the battlefield, real or imagined," Stacy said with a smile.

"Well, I'll give him a call and run it past him. I think with your letter about the Pope's Chinese porcelain and the PDFs of the passenger and cargo manifests, plus my cryptology deductions, we have a good trade for his time.

THE PIRATES' ROUND TABLE

Date: November 18, 2000

Berne, Switzerland

46° 95' N Lat., 7° 44' E Long.

The video conference was assembled from Berne, Switzerland. Its purpose was to bring the participants up to date on developing inquiries concerning what was looking more and more like the forming up of a new treasure-seeking venture. All of the participants to the conference were well acquainted with one another and each knew that one of the first and most reliable clues to the launching of a serious treasure quest was activity revolving around historical research. Each also understood the importance of quickly identifying the main principals behind such a project in order to understand what financial and technical resources were at the disposal of the recovery organization.

The understood goal was to make every effort to thwart the recovery effort of others and seize the treasure for themselves. The reward was typically calculated in the tens, if not hundreds, of millions of dollars. Morality was not an issue—they embraced the concept that a lost treasure, until found and recovered, was free game. And the victory laurels of the quest went to whomever got the treasure first.

After a brief welcome acknowledging the presence of the participants, Berne began with a summary of events:

"Our first alert came from one of our permanent sources, in this case, an assistant curator at the *Archivo General de las Indies* in Seville. He reported that *"un Norte Americano"* had called from Florida, USA, and asked if he could get a photocopy of the passenger list of a Spanish sailing vessel named the *San Pedro*, which he said sailed from the *Ladrones*, present day Marianas, in the western Pacific Ocean, and was lost at sea sometime in the period 1697-99.

"A search was conducted of the archives and no evidence was found of a Spanish vessel named the *San Pedro* sailing during that period of time in the Pacific Ocean. The *Norte Americano* was so informed.

"The first curiosity at this point is why was the *Norte Americano* interested only in the *passenger* list of the *San Pedro*? Treasure seekers typically show greatest interest in the *cargo* manifests. Is it because his research has already revealed the extent of the cargo? Or was he just being clever? As you will see in a moment, this same *Norte Americano* will cease inquiring about the *San Pedro*, and begin inquiring about Manila galleons in general that were sailing in the same time period of 1697-99. We must first ask ourselves, how and why it is that the *Norte Americano* has focused his attention on this specific time period. What has he found that so precisely fixes the date? What is behind this very narrow interest?

"At any rate, our next alert comes again from the *Archivo General de las Indies* in Seville. This time, little more than two weeks after the first inquiry, *una Norte Americana, una professora* at the University of Florida in Gainesville, Florida, is inquiring about names of Manila galleons 'that were lost at sea during the late 17th Century.' Notice that she is interested only in the eastward bound galleons from Manila, and only those that were lost at sea. She asks for no specific dates, just late 17th Century. The curator provided her with a list of five eastward-bound galleons lost during the period 1650 to 1700.

"Our inquiries have revealed that the professora's name is Stacy Burns. She has a Ph.D from the University of Chicago in European Studies and teaches early European history at the University of Florida in Gainesville, Florida. We have obtained a copy of her college transcripts and *curriculum vitae*. She is fluent in French, Spanish and German, in addition to her native tongue of English. We have no documentation indicating that she has ever participated in research endeavors for treasure-seeking operations. However, as you know, she is the very type of academic person typically recruited to conduct preliminary research for a treasure recovery operation.

"Now comes our third alert. A *Norte Americano* contacts the *Archivo General de las Indies* via the Internet. He logs onto the *Archivo's* Website and inquires about purchasing photocopies of the passenger lists for galleons sailing eastbound from Manila, but were lost at sea during the years 1697-99. That was a short list—three galleons, all lost at sea without a trace. The failure of the last of the three, a galleon named *La Senora de la Concepcion*, to make port in Acapulco made it three losses in a row. It was one of the most financially disastrous periods in the 250-year history of Manila's galleon trade.

"The e-mail box from which the Internet inquiry came belongs to a Doctor Jerome Ambrose, a surgeon in Fort Lauderdale, Florida. Copies of the passenger and cargo manifest of the three missing galleons were e-mailed to the doctor, but the payment for the copying services was made by a Visa credit card belonging to another *Norte Americano*, Jackson T. Porter, who according to his driver's license is also living in Fort Lauderdale, Florida. Taking advantage of the Freedom of Information Act, our preliminary investigation revealed that Porter holds a U.S. Coast Guard Captain's License. We do not know as yet how it is that Porter has access to Doctor Ambrose's e-mail box. We believe Porter was the *Norte Americano* who made the initial inquiry about the *San Pedro*, but we have been unable to confirm that at this time.

"So, what do we have here? A surgeon, quite possibly the project's financial resource, a university history professor who is almost certainly handling the research, and a boat captain, who would have the ability to direct the recovery vessel's operations, and all of them living in Florida, and all interested in the same part of Oceania, same time span, and with the exception of the first inquiry, all looking for information about galleons eastward-bound from Manila, and only those that were lost at sea."

The conference attendee in Monaco offered his thoughts. "It sounds like something is definitely being investigated, but it seems amateurish, and they're obviously in the early stages of the venture. I'd be interested in knowing whose money is behind it—if it really is a serious treasure quest. And what was the research development that moved the inquiry from a vessel named the *San Pedro*, to the three galleons? That seems to suggest that some kind of evidence has been found and starting from that point, the *San Pedro*, it is leading them to a broader inquiry about the missing Manila galleons. Where and how did they first learn of the *San Pedro* and what is the connection?

Singapore chimed in. "I agree. I believe there is more than coincidence here. Amateurs or not, we are seeing only the level that is being revealed to us through their initial research. Who knows what other research they are conducting? I think it would be interesting to have a closer look at the participants. Nothing too intrusive, mind you. Just a cursory look to see if they've been careless and laid some of their research about unguarded, enough to give us a clue as to what has piqued their interest in the *San Pedro* and lost Manila galleons."

Berne responded. "I have forwarded to each of you a copy of the cargo manifests of the three missing galleons. At the moment, we do not know which of the three is being pursued. But the last of the three to be lost at sea was built in the Philippines, in Cavite, and it appears she was the largest built to date. Her name was *La Senora de la Concepcion*. Examine her cargo manifest and I believe you will agree that the declared cargo alone will approach a half-billion U.S. dollars in today's currency. And if the history of the galleons' reputation for undeclared cargo holds true with the *Concepcion*, it is not unreasonable to estimate a total value exceeding one billion dollars. And that's discounting the total loss of all silk, fabrics, tapestries, lacquer ware and other items that would be destroyed by exposure to light or water during the course of four centuries.

"On that note," Berne continued, "I believe it is worth mentioning that there was extensive correspondence between the court of Philip V and the Manila governor following the realization that the *Concepcion* was indeed lost. A number of investigations were conducted, and there is a most interesting letter from Manila's archbishop in which he informs the Spanish king that Manila's Jesuit order had placed aboard the *Concepcion* a full 100-person table setting of gilded Chinese porcelain that was fired in the Chinese emperor's personal kilns in Xhiang Province. It was intended as a special gift to the Pope. Each piece bore the Pope's personal crest. Can you imagine what the Vatican would pay for that set of tableware?"

"You have made your point," said Singapore. "The matter is definitely worthy of further inquiry. It's a small investment to conduct a preliminary investigation into the principals. We need to know what is fueling their interest, and which of the galleons has caught their fancy. It appears we've come upon them in the early stages of their research. They are most vulnerable to a search now, while their guard is down."

"I agree," said Monaco. "And that will also give us an opportunity to look for money transfers and financial resources, as well as telecommunications traffic linking to their research."

"Good. We are agreed then. I will arrange for a two-person team to be sent to examine the principals," said Berne. "It will be non-intrusive, nothing to alarm them. The team's report will be forwarded simultaneously to each of you upon their return. We will have another conference after everyone has had an opportunity to review the report."

The screens in each city went blank and only a steady dial tone remained.

MEET THE HASKINS

Date: November 28, 2000

Lat. 82º 19' N, Long. 29º 39' W

Gainesville, Florida

(One)

The phone call from Bryce Taggart, Major, USMC Reserves, came just as Jake Porter was scanning color photos of Marcus Island with a large, rectangular magnifying glass. The photos showed the tall counter-poised LORAN tower that had been installed on the island in the early 1950s. He could also see the several rows of WWII military trucks, lots of 55-gallon fuel drums, and a number of small structures scattered here and there, and no idea as to their purpose. The two breaks in the reef that surrounded the island were also clearly evident. Just about every document pertaining to the tiny Pacific island that he had garnered through the local library and their interlibrary loan system was spread out on the *Giggling Witch's* main salon table.

"Hello, Jake," Bryce Taggart greeted. "Am I interrupting anything? I can call later."

"No, sir, uh, not at all Tag," Jake answered.

"Well, in keeping with our telephone security protocol I won't mention anything specific, but Stacy and I have some information for you that I think will be very helpful. Stacy is actually bubbling all over the place with some of the stuff she has uncovered, and cannot wait to lay it all out for you. I have made some progress myself and believe it will prove useful. We'd like to invite you up for dinner and a skull session, and we'd like for you to plan to stay overnight so we can put away a bottle or two of some wine. How does that sound to you?"

"You've got my antennae buzzing, Tag," Jake said. "You're talking about this coming weekend, right?"

"Right. And bring Brenda with you if you like. I'm assuming you're keeping her in the loop on all of this," Tag said, then added diplomatically, "Or if that is not the case, we can have separate social and data-sharing sections for your visit."

"I will probably come alone, if that's okay with you," said Jake.

"Whatever you prefer, Jake. Stacy and I have been completely swept away with all of this. The research she has been doing is making it all so real. We haven't had so much fun in a long time. But I also have a special favor to ask, and you just let me know if I am imposing too much on you. My reserve unit meets on Saturday next weekend. I've got a fine bunch of young Marines that I'd like for you to meet. I'd also like for them to meet the fellow Marine that knocked off Saddam's defense minister from a mile away. We can keep it short and sweet, nothing elaborate."

Jake was tempted to demur, but then considered the time and effort Tag and Stacy were putting into his treasure quest, if that's what it was, and he graciously accepted the invitation. "How about a 'show and tell' and I bring along my Haskins?"

"Your Haskins?"

"My sniper rifle. The one that did the deed," Jake chuckled.

"Holy smokes! That'd blow them away, Jake" Tag said. "But how the hell were you able to keep your weapon? You don't have the thing illegally do you? I wouldn't want to encourage violations of Corps regulations."

"All above board, sir," Jake said. "My Haskins was non-issue. I was granted possession by the Corps' Commandant as a reward for winning a marksmanship contest against the U.S. Army. It was surveyed by the Corps as non-serviceable at the time of my discharge, and I had it shipped back to the States with my locker."

"I know some young Marines that are going to be blown away, Jake. I am mightily appreciative."

"No problem, maj...uh, Tag. If you have a range, we could fire it if you want. It's a pretty impressive piece," Jake offered. "I have about a hundred boat-tail rounds that are getting some age on them."

"My reserve unit uses the county sheriff's office firing range for weapons familiarizations. I'll have to check on availability and let you know about any live fire stuff, okay? But your offer blows me away. Thank you again."

"No problem. So we're on for next weekend then? I'll plan to arrive on Friday around six o'clock if that works."

"Six is perfect. I'll get word to Stacy and we'll have some grilled meat and fixings ready for you," Tag said and signed off, a very happy man.

(Two)

"Come on in, Jake. The door's unlocked," Stacy called out when he pressed the doorbell. Inside the hallway, he smelled cooking going on and followed the enticing aroma to a spacious, brightly-lit kitchen. Stacy was at the stove stirring with a wooden spoon. She was dressed in a white blouse and beige shorts, and wore a bright orange apron. She laid the spoon on the stovetop and came over to receive a peck on her cheek. Jake obliged her and remarked on the tempting aroma.

"I'm doing Tag's favorite mac-and -cheese dish, and I have a mixed-greens salad cooling in the fridge. Tag is on the patio," she said, nodding across the living room. "He went to our favorite butcher this afternoon and bought a huge Chateaubriand that must be a foot-and-a-half long, three-quarters of a foot wide, and two inches thick. He massaged it with crushed garlic cloves and a Texas dry rub. Its been soaking up the spices all day. Tag is very good at the grill," Stacy said smiling, returning to the stove. "Go on out and let Tag know you're here. I'll bring a glass of chilled Spanish sangria in just a minute.

Jake crossed the living room and stepped out onto the patio. Tag was lifting one corner of a huge piece of meat checking for doneness.

"Looks about ready to me," Jake said.

"Hey! Jake. Good to see you. How was the drive?" Tag said, wiping his hands on an apron that proclaimed him as a Master Chef not to be tampered with, and gave Jake a firm handshake.

"Easy drive. My Volvo is a veteran," Jake said. "That's an impressive piece of beef you have there."

"We are in a celebratory mood, Jake. All the stops are out. Stacy is busting a gut to show you what she has uncovered from that 'archivo' place in Spain. Once we get through dinner, you need to brace yourself for a major presentation," Tag said with a laugh.

"I can't wait. Can you give me a .quick briefing? I haven't been able to sleep since your phone call."

"Stacy would kill me if I stole her thunder, " Tag said. "For my part, I will say this: I believe I have determined the encryption mode used by your Spanish castaway to secret a message in his prayer for absolution, if there is one. I'll show you how it works. Stacy's contribution is far more exciting, I think. She has downloaded and printed full-size the cargo and passenger manifests of three galleons, and they tell a fantastic story. And there's some royal correspondence she's acquired that's quite interesting, too. But that's all I'm saying at the moment."

Stacy came onto the patio holding a glass of sangria for Jake. "Everything's ready on my end. How's the cow doing?"

"Jake has proclaimed it done, and I agree," Tag said. "Let me slide it onto a platter and I'll meet you at the table."

The stereo system played light Argentinean tangos, the lights were turned down and a large green candle floating in a crystal bowl completed the ambiance. Once they began eating, Stacy began explaining how an academic colleague at the Archivo General de Las Indias, a Portuguese, had helped her get downloads of the galleon documents she was seeking. She had then gone to the graphic arts department at the university and printed them out full size. She nodded her head at the large sheets of paper draped over the back of the big sofa in the living room.

"We still don't know which of the galleons your Spanish castaway was on, if any of them. The next step is to examine the manifests for his name, something you will have to do yourself since Tag and I don't know the name. If his name is on one of the manifests, then that is pretty conclusive evidence of how he came to be stranded on the island. As Tag pointed out when we first met at the university cafeteria, whether the treasure accompanied him is another issue."

When dinner was over, they moved to the living room and Jake got a closer look at the manifests. They were a work of art and lovely to behold. The treasury scribe had drawn an elaborate and fanciful façade imitating a Catholic cathedral, then surrounded it with cherubs blowing trumpets to chase away billowy clouds. Starting at the top of the edifice were proclamations of the Royal Court stating its authority to rule followed by a naming of the prime court personages appointed to managing the Spanish crown's far-flung territories. Beneath that began a series of names that started with the Royal Governor of Manila, and his military staff, then the Capitan of the Vessel, the Sailing Master, and so on down through the ranks.

Next came the names of the Church's representatives, and finally, each of the individual passengers, grouped under heads of families. The list was huge. Hundreds and hundreds of names. All written in tiny Spanish cursive characters. Jake realized immediately that he'd never be able to read them. They may as well have been written in Egyptian hieroglyphics.

"These three are the manifests of the cargo," Stacy said as she draped them across the back of the sofa, the excitement in her voice growing." The bulk of the cargo in all three galleons is the same: porcelain, silk tapestries and raw silk skeins, plus the personal family chests. Those chests will contain hundreds of different types of jewelry, precious stones, and reliquaries; a small fortune in each one. Each galleon also carried hundreds of bars of refined gold belonging to the Spanish crown. These were stacked in wooden chests. The wood will have deteriorated after 400 years, but the gold will be like new, of course. Each piece of the cargo was numbered, and where it was stowed on board is numbered, too. The gold was at the very bottom, in the bilge. The silk brocades and family chests were stored higher in the hull to be safe from sea water."

"Mind boggling, Jake!" Tag said, picking up on Stacy's excitement. "Can you imagine coming up on something like this?"

Jake laughed. "I'm trying. I'm trying." And truly, he was. He pictured in his mind the *Giggling Witch* stuffed with the treasure; every nook and cranny taken up by bars of gold, priceless Chinese vases, bags of diamonds and rubies, and long chains of gold. Then sailing across the Pacific in glory and wealth.

"The hardest part for the two of us," Stacy said, "is imagining how you are going to pick and choose among the treasure which things to bring back. You can't get it all into your little sailboat."

"When Stacy translated portions of the manifest for me, calling out loud the description of different pieces of the treasure," Tag said, "I tried to picture you holding each one up to the light and saying, 'Yep. This is a keeper', then tossing it in a bag to take to the *Giggling Witch*."

"I think I'm going to need a coach," Jake said in a slightly more serious tone. "From a practical viewpoint, I need to maximize the value of the cargo that I can reasonably stow in my boat. I was thinking about recruiting an antiquities expert to our group."

"Good idea!" said Stacy as she turned one of the pages of the cargo manifest. "Just look at this list of porcelain. It's thousands of pieces. And one of the most valuable is not even listed. Here is a translation of a letter between Manila and the Spanish crown's Treasurer in Seville." She handed it to Jake. "A complete set of porcelain tableware for 100 guests fired in the Chinese Khan's personal kilns, laced with gold and hand-painted crest. Commissioned by the Jesuits and a gift to the Holy Father. The historical value multiplies the base value a thousand times. It's truly priceless in the sense of the term."

"I'm not sure there's enough room on the *Giggling Witch* for just that one piece of the treasure. I guess if I could get it all aboard and fill all of the soup bowls with diamonds and pearls, I'd be in pretty good financial shape when I returned," Jake said.

"You'd be set for life, no doubt," Tag volunteered. "Now before we drift off the planet with our pirate dreams, let me show you my progress with the search for a hidden message in your Spaniard's prayer for absolution. Here's my feeble attempt to present for you an explanation of the system I believe was used to encrypt any message during that time period."

For the next hour, Tag took Jake through the encrypting and decrypting process using the Caesar's Shift and the cipher of Blaise Vigenere. Once he got the hang of it, Tag handed Jake some sample messages to break, and in short order, Jake modestly proclaimed himself a code breaker.

"Just remember, Jake, "Tag cautioned, "I made it easy for you by giving you the cipher to use with Vigenere's scheme. The tough part is going to be the uncovering of your Spaniard's private cipher. If you ever reach a point where you're comfortable revealing the Spaniard's name to us, Stacy and I can work on that part. Who knows what the message may contain, if there is one. It could be the very key to locating the treasure, especially if it's not on the island where he was recovered."

Jake realized he had already reached that point. One look at the hundreds and hundreds of names on the galleons' passenger manifest, and the pages and pages of tiny scribblings in ancient Spanish language describing the cargo, and he knew he had bring Tag and Stacy fully on board.

"I want to give you the name, and in the same breath, I want to emphasize the absolute secrecy we must maintain. The text of the Spaniard's prayer is already in the hands of a Catholic priest. Brenda has seen it and probably has a copy of it somewhere on her houseboat. God only knows who else has it. The one thing I know for sure is that until right now, I am the only one who knows his name. Putting his name together with the text of the prayer could tell the wrong people where the treasure is, and create a very dangerous situation, or at the least, the loss of the treasure to us. I am asking that you never repeat his name outside of the company of the three of us, until I say differently, and that you never, never write it down or enter it into a computer."

"Done, Jake," Tag said, Stacy nodding in assent as well. "We are honored that you take us into your confidence, and we will keep the name secret to us three, so help me God."

"His name is Don Emilio Bustamente de la Vega," Jake said.

"A Spanish Don!" Stacy exclaimed with delight. " A member of the Spanish aristocracy! His family will almost certainly have a crest, property records, and marriage records, and a relationship with the church in Rome!"

Jake and Tag burst out laughing. It was as though Stacy had just opened a present beneath the Christmas tree. The prospect of ferreting out everything she could about this mysterious Spanish Don stretched out before her, and she couldn't wait to tackle the project.

"Just remember, Stacy." Jake cautioned. "Your research inquiries must not give any hint of his name."

"Believe me, Jake, I know how to do that. The competition among academics has taught us all how to protect our research from those who would plagiarize our efforts to create something original for a thesis or dissertation."

"And on that note, "Tag said, I would like to suggest we have one last glass of wine and retire. Jake and I have a full weekend drill day tomorrow with my young Marines."

(Three)

It was the smell of bacon frying that dragged Jake from slumber to full consciousness. After a quick shower he was at the table with Tag and Stacy. Stacy was bubbling with energy as she put a tall glass of orange juice in front of their plates. She informed them that she had been up before first light to begin scanning the passenger manifests for the name of the Spanish castaway, Don Emilio Bustamente de la Vega. "The penmanship is terrible, the lines cramped and there is no sensible order among them," she said. "But I'll know soon enough," she pronounced with a certainty.

"We have every faith, my love," Tag said, giving his fiancée an affectionate pat on the behind. "Jake and I will get out of your hair and leave you to your musings. We're going to muck about at the armory, introduce Jake and his Haskins to my men, and maybe visit the sheriff department's firing range."

"Will Gunny Sweikert be there as usual?" Stacy asked.

"Probably, but I haven't heard from him," Tag said. "We were scheduled for some hand-to-hand combat drills today. He's always game to show the younger troops that he hasn't lost his touch at putting an adversary on the ground. Now that Jake is here with his Haskins, I'm diverting from the usual schedule. If we're able to get permission to use the sheriff's range, that will probably blow the rest of the day. I'm sure Gunny will be interested in Jake's Haskins, too."

"He's hard core, Tag," Jake said, not sure he really liked the idea of spending a day with the hard-nosed Marine, but resolved to deal with it out of respect for Tag and Stacy's help with his treasure project. And after all, Sweikert had made the connection between him and Taggart.

"Yeah, he's the real thing, Jake," Tag said. "I owe my life to him for some help in Iraq. But if you're ever in a tight spot and Gunny Sweikert is on your side, you've got a good chance of coming out on top."

On that note, they left for the armory, Jake grabbing his Haskins and a small bowling bag that contained some ammo and a cleaning kit.

The Marine Corps Reserve building outside of Gainesville was similar, but smaller in size than the one in Fort Lauderdale. The compound's yard was already filled with civilian vehicles, and there were groups of young men standing around knocking off their last cigarettes before going inside the non-smoking area of the building. When they saw their commander arrive, they quickly doused their cigarettes and headed inside before Tag and Jake stepped out of their vehicle. Inside, they were all standing in the main assembly room and waiting for the command, 'Atten -hut! Officer on Deck!"

The command was given and Major Bryce Taggart, USMC, gave the order, "At ease, men. Take your seats."

ll eyes were on Jake and the old leather shotgun case that held the Haskins. Everyone in the room had read the Marine Corps recruiting booklet that described Jake's heroic acts in Iraq, and his killing of Saddam Hussein's cousin, the Deputy Defense Minister. Before them stood an authentic role model for every Marine, a 'hero', if you insisted on the term.

"Men, as promised, here is Sergeant Jake Porter, Second of the Third, and a veteran of the first Gulf War in Iraq. Jake has kindly offered to show us his Haskins rifle, the one he used to take out an important member of the enemy's government. Now Jake is going to assemble his rifle, take you through the nomenclature, brief you on its capabilities and tell you how he came to be carrying a non-issue weapon in a combat zone. At the conclusion of the show-and-tell, I will call a brief recess so you can each come up and introduce yourself to Jake and offer your thanks for his time. I have met Jake's girlfriend, or at least one of them, and I can assure you Jake has better things to with his time than entertain you jarheads on a Saturday afternoon." The men all laughed in unison just as a Corporal walked in and passed a note to Major Taggart.

Taggart held the note up and said, "Good news. We have permission to use the county firing range this afternoon. Jake has brought along a few boat tail rounds in case any of you would like to experience the recoil of a .50-caliber sniper rifle. Any takers?" he asked. The room erupted with hoots and laughter. At that same moment, Gunny Sweikert entered the room without fanfare and took a seat at the rear of the room.

I thought so," Taggart said. Okay, Jake, the floor is yours."

Jake pulled the Haskins from the old shotgun case, unwrapped the oiled gauze covering it, snapped the barrel into the receiver, dropped the bipod down and slid the Utel telescope into its grooves atop the receiver. You could have heard a pin drop to the floor. When Jake snapped the bolt back, the crisp metallic sound echoed from wall to wall of the assembly room. He then opened the bowling bag and brought out a single .50-caliber round, and sat it upright on the table. It was a huge round, more than twice the size of the ones they used in their M-14s, and the assembled Marines saw that it was an armor-piercing, incendiary one; one bad piece of business if it was making its way toward you in combat.

As a skilled Marine Corps armorer and marksmanship instructor, intimately familiar with all of the infantry combat arms employed by the Marine Corps, Jake had taught hundreds of officers and enlisted Marines in all aspects of weaponry and marksmanship. He breezed through the presentation, did a quick field stripping of the Haskins, and once it was reassembled invited the young Marines to approach the table and heft the Haskins for themselves. They rose in enthusiastic unison, and Jake stepped back to give them room. It was then that he noticed Gunny Sweikert at the back of the room. Sweikert rose and approached.

"How ya doin', Snapper?" he grinned, offering his hand.

"Gunny, if you don't mind, I'd appreciate you calling me 'Jake', 'Porter', or 'Sergeant Porter', as you prefer," Jake said, taking Sweikert's hand, but not returning the smile.

"No problem. Then Sergeant Porter it is," Gunny Sweikert replied, still grinning and not missing a beat. "I appreciate your time motivating these young Marines. Also, I didn't get a chance to thank you for attending the funeral. Willie Coleman's widow said some very complimentary things about you, and I got the impression the two of you had a mutually satisfactory conversation on the ride to the cemetery. Changing the subject, you mind if I come along for the shoot-out at the county range?"

"I'm just a civilian, Gunny, here at the invitation of Major Taggart," Jake said evenly. "I've brought along about a hundred rounds of ammo for the Haskins. 'Should give everyone an opportunity to make two shots each, including you if you're so inclined."

"I'll take you up on that," Sweikert said, turning to return to his seat at the back of the assembly room.

"Alright, men," Major Taggart said, "Here's the program. We'll make best use of our invitation to use the county firing range. Gather your rifles from the armory and board up by squads on the four-by-sixes for transport to the range. Sergeant Nixon will manage the ammo and targets. You'll fire for the record and the results will go down on your personal jackets. Jake will manage the firing of the Haskins. Any questions?"

(Four)

When the two Marine Corps trucks arrived at the firing range, two county sheriff's department cruisers were parked at the entrance and waved them in. One of the officers was the Chief. "Good morning, Major," Chief Benton greeted Major Taggart. "I understand we have something other than small arms fire planned. That right?"

"Good morning to you, Chief," Major Taggart answered. "Yes, I called your office. I thought it best to give you a heads-up that we have a large bore sniper rifle being demonstrated for my men. It makes a hell of a noise, and has a one-mile range. Just wanted to make sure you approved of our safety practices."

"Thank you for that courtesy, Major," the Chief replied. "I have full confidence in the United States Marine Corps' ability to conduct safe weapons training. The 800-yard range in on the far end and below the lip of the quarry. You'll see the sand bags set up there. No problem with the sniper rifle. I'm guessing it's one of your .50-caliber Barrett light-fifties. We have two prior military sniper-trained officers on the force, and their rifles are fifty caliber, too "

"You're right about the caliber, Chief, but the rifle being demonstrated is a Haskins special ops model and is the weapon that took out Saddam Hussein's cousin, his deputy defense minister. The young man firing it today is the Marine who took that shot. I'd be pleased to introduce you," Major Bryce Taggart said.

"That's mighty kind of you, Major," Chief Benton said with a smile. "I'd be honored to meet that young man. I remember reading the news about how Saddam was going to take revenge on the Marine Corps for the killing of his cousin."

Jake was standing with a group of Taggart's Marines, one of them cradling the Haskins in his arms. Sergeant Nixon was handing out targets and ammo. When he got to Jake, he gave him a dozen or so of the new color targets depicting a snarling, turban-headed jihadist running with an AK-47. Jake had never seen the new targets, and only smiled as he rolled them up. He saw Major Taggart approaching in the company of the county's chief law enforcement officer.

"Jake, I'd like you to meet Chief Benton of the county sheriff's office," Taggart said.

Chief Benton extended a beefy hand and pointing to the Haskins, said "That your rifle, sergeant?"

"Yes, sir," Jake answered respectfully, turning to the young Marine holding the Haskins, lifting it from his arms and handing it to Chief Benton.

Chief Benton grunted as he took the weight of the sniper rifle. "Heavy son of a gun, ain't she?"

"Yes, sir. Twenty-three pounds, sir" Jake answered. "The ammo is heavy, too. The magazine holds 4 rounds. The business end of the bullet weighs 1.5 ounces and comes out of the barrel at 4 times the muzzle velocity of the 7.62 NATO round of the M-16."

"And I see you have a silencer and flash suppressor mounted as well, plus the scope," the Chief said, handing the Haskins back to Jake. "That's quite a package. Well, let me show you the 800-yard range we have for our SWAT snipers," he said with a smile and turned to walk down behind the firing line for the lighter weapons.

"I'll get our squads firing, Jake, then come down to see your set-up, okay?" Major Taggart said.

Jake and two Marines, one of them again carrying the Haskins, followed Chief Benton to the bottom of the sand quarry and stopped at a pile of sand bags set up to steady the heavy weapons of a SWAT team. Jake took the Haskins and set it atop two of the bags, slid behind the rifle and adjusted the bipod for height. He then took two of the paper targets and a roll of tape down range. On the way, he noticed a shot-up old Buick that had taken a few hundred rounds of rifle and pistol fire. Cops playing 'Bonnie and Clyde', he guessed.

Once the targets were set up, Jake returned to the Haskins, inserted the magazine into the Haskins leaving the bolt back, and turned to the Chief. "I'll spot for you, Chief, "he said.

"Well, now, Sergeant Porter, if you don't mind I'd like to see you take a shot just so I can get the feel of the recoil. I understand that thing has quite a kick."

"No problem, Chief," Jake said. "The Haskins does have a punch, but not much more than a 10-guage shotgun. There are two hydraulic cylinders in the stock that take some of the sting out of it. Maybe you could man the scope here and call the shots for me?"

"Okay," said the Chief, dropping first to one knee, then spreading out into a prone position behind the spotter's telescope. The two Marines stepped back graciously to give the sheriff plenty of room.

"Ready on the right! Ready on the left! Ready on the firing line," Jake called out, then put his eye to the Haskins' telescope. He had already adjusted the scope for the range, and now centered the crosshairs on the forehead of the Jihadist charging with the AK-47.

KA-BOOM! The Haskins roared and every bird within a quarter mile took flight. The Marines behind Jake both jumped at the ear-smacking sound and recoil. Further up the quarry where Taggart's Marines were firing their M-16s, the Marines turned their heads quickly at the sound of the Haskins discharging.

Chief Benton shook his head, and grunted appreciatively. "That's a hell of a cannon, Sergeant Porter." He looked downrange through the scope and noted the neat round hole centered in the neck of the Jihadist, reporting to Jake its exact position.

"A little low," was all Jake said as he reset himself and pulled the scope to his eye again. Again, the Haskins roared, and this time Chief Benton reported a new hole, this one in the left eye of the Jihadist.

"Want to give it a try, Chief?" Jake said. "You can borrow my padded shooter's jacket if you like."

"I'll take you up on that Sergeant," the Chief said, swapping positions with Jake after putting on the padded shooter's jacket. "I'm going for his center chest," he announced.

Chief Benton took his two shots and was rewarded with a high right shoulder hit and lower abdomen hit. Both equally fatal to the target, and given the Haskins destructiveness, either would have reduced a real jihadist to a bloody, unrecognizable pulp.

Jake motioned to one of the Marines standing behind the firing line and pointed to the Haskins. He then slid into a prone position alongside the Marine and adjusted the eyepiece of the spotter scope. Jake spoke softly with instructions on trigger pressure and pivoting the Haskins' barrel around its bipod, and mentored each of the Marines that followed. He called their shots and congratulated each on their marksmanship irrespective of how well or poorly they did, explaining that it took a couple thousand rounds with the Haskins before reaching a consistent accuracy.

"You see what I see, Major?" Gunny Sweikert asked. He and Taggart stood about twenty feet behind the firing line, observing Jake's management of the marksmanship instruction, and the attentive demeanor of the Marines waiting their turn to fire the Haskins.

What's that, Gunny?" Major Taggart replied.

"He's a natural born leader, sir," Gunny Sweikert said, indicating Jake.

"Look at them," Sweikert gestured toward the Marines. "He has them eating out of his hands. Every one of them, even your corporals and sergeants, are just waiting for him to say 'Jump!' "

"Jake does have a presence, Gunny," Taggart said, smiling.

"You never did mention why he was trying to hook up with an Intelligence Officer," Sweikert said.

"No, I didn't, Gunny," Taggart responded. "Sworn to secrecy."

"I'm just trying to figure him out, sir. You mentioned that he completed his college education after mustering out of the corps. He's been screwing around working on boats and driving a doctor's yacht. A waste of talent in my opinion, sir. The Corps is looking for officer material, sir. And a former combat experienced Marine with a degree puts Porter at the top of the recruiting list," Sweikert said, explaining his thinking, and a bit put off by Major Taggart's disinclination to discuss his relationship with Porter.

"I don't want to dissuade you in your recruiting efforts, Gunny, but I can tell you that Jake has a lot on his plate these days, and signing up for another tour in the Corps is very near the bottom of his interest list. I agree with you most heartedly that he would make an excellent Marine Corps officer, but the timing is not right in my opinion."

As the last of the Marines had filtered down from the M-16 firing line and taken their shots with the Haskins, Jake walked over to Chief Benton, pulled from his pocket the depleted uranium, incendiary round and held it up for the Chief. "This would make a bang-up of a finale for the Haskins demonstration, Chief. I was wondering if maybe I could take a shot at the old Buick."

"Don't see why not, Sergeant Porter. Let's clear the lower end of the quarry, and you just give me a signal when you're ready, okay?" The Chief waved his arms and motioned all observers to the upper end of the quarry, announcing that Jake was going to demonstrate the true purpose of the Haskins, the destruction of armored vehicles. The Buick didn't quite meet that description, but it would serve.

A corporal met them enroute and announced to Major Taggart, "Miss Burns is here, sir. 'Looking for you, sir."

"Stacy?" Taggart said, puzzled as to why Stacy would come out to the range. He looked uphill and saw her, waving, a big smile on her face and kind of dancing on her tip-toes. "What in the world?" he said aloud to no one in particular. He came up to her and gave her a quick kiss, aware that his Marines were all looking in his direction. "What's up, doll?" he asked his obviously excited fiancée.

"Where's Jake? Stacy asked almost breathlessly.

"He's taking a last shot with his Haskins at the old automobile down at the bottom of the quarry. What going on?" he asked impatiently.

Before Stacy could answer, the Haskins roared once again, and to the complete amazement of everyone, the riddled old Buick took the shot in the grille, through the radiator and the cast iron V-8 engine exploding into dozens of pieces, the Haskins round continuing on through the firewall and the incendiary element exploding to ignite the whole thing in a great ball of flame. The Buick 's front end lifted upward and the whole car took a backward flip, exploding in mid-air and coming to rest upside down in roaring flames and black smoke. Nothing was left that resembled an automobile.

The Marines hooted in excitement and slapped each other on the back. A single rifle shot had brought total destruction. As professional riflemen, what they had seen was a testament to the power of a single infantryman and his weapon. They all applauded and whistled as Jake picked up the Haskins, folded the bi-pod and came up the hill, a boyish, triumphant grin on his face.

After some hand-shaking and congratulations, Jake was able to separate himself from the Marines and police officers to join Taggart and Stacy.

"Mighty impressive, Jake," Taggart said, a broad smile crossing his face.

"Jake, Jake, Jake," Stacy burst out, totally uninterested in talking about a rifle, Haskins or no. In a terse, but subdued voice, she announced to her fiancée and Jake: "It's the *Concepcion*, Jake! Don Bustamente was on the *Nuestra Senora de la Concepcion*! There's your connection to the treasure!"

PALM BEACH SHOPPER

Date: November 30, 2000

Lat: 26º 42' 54" N, Lon. 80º 32' 22"

Palm Beach, Florida

(One)

Somewhere over the last 24 hours since returning to Fort Lauderdale from his visit with Tag and Stacy, Jake realized he had passed a Rubicon of sorts. He had been galvanized by Stacy's announcement that the Spanish castaway, Bustamente, was aboard a Manila treasure galleon that most likely foundered on the Pacific island where Bustamente was stranded. Jake's suspicions were confirmed that Bustamente had lied about the vessel he had been sailing on, the *San Pedro*, and had asked the young British officer for the charted position of the island so he could convey it to the Pope in Rome. There was no doubt in Jake's mind that he was headed across the Pacific Ocean in search of the treasure of *Nuestra Senora de la Concepcion*. But the breath-taking ramifications of that commitment were only just beginning to register in his mind.

During the drive back to Fort Lauderdale, Jake had played over and over in his head the look of excitement in Stacy's face when she told him that Bustamente was on the passenger manifest of the *Concepcion*. He mentally revisited Stacy's earlier recounting of the treasure that was listed in the cargo manifest, and tried to envision what it would look like in a cave on a remote Pacific island. And he tried to picture the *Giggling Witch* stuffed to her gunnels, winging her way back across the Pacific to land the haul and convert it into cash.

By the time he arrived back in Fort Lauderdale, Jake had decided that his next task was to get some help in evaluating the treasure aboard the *Concepcion*. Given the small interior of the *Giggling Witch*, Jake knew he could haul away only a tiny fraction of the treasure. It was crucial to the success of his voyage that he maximize the available space and select the most compact items with the highest market value. At the moment, he had no way of knowing how to do that. A bar of gold in one hand, a Chinese porcelain jar in the other: which to take, which to leave behind? The decision could make tens of thousands of dollars in difference.

It was the vision of the *Giggling Witch* hauling away from the island with the treasure that propelled his thinking. He needed an antiquities expert, someone who knew porcelains, especially very old Chinese porcelains. The cargo manifest Stacy had read aloud to him also named dozens and dozens of different types of artifacts, jewelry and precious stones. Where could someone with that kind of information be found? After some thinking, Jake realized the answer was closer at hand that he might have thought. Palm Beach! Home of some of the wealthiest people on the planet. Old people and estate sales came to mind. Auctions to peddle anything of value.

Jake stopped at the Harbor Point Marina and went aboard the *Sea Bones* to use Doctor Ambrose's Internet connection. He Googled and pulled up the names and addresses of a half-dozen jewelry and antiquities dealers in Palm Beach whose Internet ads and websites suggested they also had worldwide connections with major auction houses.

(Two)

The drive north up Interstate 95 from Fort Lauderdale to West Palm Beach was a short one. Jake crossed over the bridge onto the island of

Palm Beach, and took the drive down Royal Palm Way. The prominence of wealth was everywhere, especially in the parked automobiles; RollsRoyce, Bentley, Lamborghini, Ferrari, Aston Martin, Porsche, stretched Cadillac limousines and just about every other luxury vehicle worth over a hundred thousand dollars were in evidence. Jake elected to pay ten dollars for a half-day's parking in a commercial lot. He gathered up a manila folder and his copy of *Nuestra Senora de la Concepcion's* cargo manifest, then headed down South Ocean Boulevard to the first store on his list.

'THE LEFT BANK', the polished silver sign across the long expanse of clear plate glass proclaimed, and in smaller letters, 'ANTIQUITIES - JEWELRY - FINE ARTS.' The impressive storefront occupied the corner of Royal Palm Way and South Ocean Boulevard, and was situated as the first story of a 10-story luxury apartment building. A uniformed security guard strolled the sidewalk, a Glock 22 automatic pistol strapped high on his hip, a radio transmitter in his left hand. He gave Jake a close look as Jake crossed the street and stepped onto the sidewalk. Jake had dressed for the part. He wore dark blue summer-weight wool slacks, a pale ivory silk shirt beneath a blue Harris Tweed sport jacket, and highly polished maroon Bass loafers. His chrome Omega chronometer was visible just below his left sleeve; a pair of Gucci sunglasses were pushed back atop his perfectly trimmed hair. His barber employed a nail tech, and Jake had his nails trimmed and polished while his hair was shampooed and cut. He could have been anything from a well-kept boy-toy to an architect with his drawings going to make a presentation. The Left Bank's sidewalk security gave Jake a smile and a tip-of-the-hat salute as Jake made for the door.

Alongside the double-door glass entry, Jake saw a stack of international cities listed in gold leaf: Beirut, Paris, Monaco, New York, San Francisco, Stockholm, Tokyo, Berlin, Zurich, Hong Kong and Singapore, among others. Once inside, he was immediately met by a smiling and impeccably dressed concierge with a fresh red rose in his lapel who approached to inquire of his needs. Jake returned the smile and eased into the role he had prepared for this moment.

Jake had spent some considerable time determining just exactly how he was going to present his situation. His goal was primarily to gain some insight into the value of the *Concepcion's* cargo, and how to recognize the more valuable pieces. His secondary goal was to build a relationship that would facilitate the sale of any treasure he was able to recover from Marcus Island. The treasure would be valued in the millions of dollars, and he knew that one of the main vehicles for selling art and collectibles was through international auctions. He needed a respected antiquities firm to manage the sale. He told The Left Bank's concierge that he wished to speak with an authority on ancient Chinese porcelain.

With a respectful bow, the concierge led Jake past several rows of glass counters displaying a dazzling array of jewelry interspersed with Egyptian and African sculptures atop swatches of colorful Indonesian Batik prints. They stopped at a large mahogany desk behind which sat a perfectly-coifed and well-dressed matronly woman of about fifty years of age. The concierge made the introductions and left gracefully.

"Is there a particular period of Chinese porcelain in which you are interested, Captain Porter?" Grace Chandler asked, quickly getting down to business.

Jake presented his business card announcing the fact that he was Captain of the Motor Yacht *Sea Bones,* and a United States Coast Guard Captain. His USCG license number and his Fort Lauderdale address at the Harbor Point Yacht Club were below his name. At the same time, he presented the business cards of Dr. Stacy Burns, PhD, Professor of European History, University of Florida, and Major Bryce Taggart, USMC (Ret.), Professor of Mathematics, University of Florida. Jake immediately launched into his spiel, announcing that he was the point person for a treasure salvage operation seeking a firm to represent the sale of a considerable quantity of Chinese porcelain, jewelry and other antiquities. The two college professors, he explained, were members of the consortium's research team. He partially unrolled the beautifully inscribed cargo manifest of the *Concepcion*, explaining that the cargo was described in detail in the manifest, but unfortunately in four centuries-old Spanish.

"Oh, my!" Captain Porter," the woman exclaimed. "How exciting! But this is beyond my expertise. You need to speak with Rebecca. She is the daughter of the The Left Bank's owner, and a graduate of the Sorbonne. She speaks five languages, and she has handled Chinese porcelain sales in the past. Please give me a moment and I will let her know you are here."

Within five minutes Grace Chandler returned, accompanied by one of the most beautiful women Jake had ever seen. Five feet six inches of exotic European polish, flawless tawny skin, full lips with just the right amount of lipstick, perfectly arched eyebrows and dark, flashing oval eyes; modest cleavage emphasizing a firm C-cup size, tiny waist, and a not-quite-to-the-knees length dress from one of the high-fashion runways of Paris. Several loose bangles of gold and silver on one wrist, a large opal-mounted silver ring on one finger, no wedding ring on the left, and a Swiss watch encrusted along two sides with small yellow diamonds with a narrow brown alligator strap. Every item exquisite in detail and each perfectly in place.

"Captain Porter?" she asked. "I am Rebecca Fontaine. Grace tells me you are marketing some Chinese artifacts." She offered a soft but firm handshake and smiled sincerely revealing perfectly formed white teeth.

"My pleasure, Miss Fontaine, Actually I am looking for two things: a resource for identifying ancient Chinese porcelain and other period artifacts, and also someone to represent our finds at auction," Jake began. "We have positively identified the vessel and its location, and we have a manifest that details the cargo. *No sense mentioning it's located on a Japanese island on the other side of the world and I have yet to get there.*" You can appreciate, I am sure, that I must be very circumspect in what I share with you and ask for your absolute discretion."

Rebecca smiled. "Please call me Rebecca, Captain Porter. May I call you Jake?" Her voice was soft and flowed like honey. "Have you had lunch?" she asked. "The Left Bank has a reserved table at The Breakers. We like to begin new relationships with a bottle of wine and a meal. My family is Lebanese, and it's a tradition."

Taken aback by the friendly gesture, Jake smiled and accepted the invitation. "This is an exact copy of the vessel's original cargo manifest," he added somewhat lamely, indicating the rolled-up document in his hand. "I brought it along to help in identifying what we are recovering," Jake said. The truth was, he didn't know whether to bring it along to lunch, or leave it in Rebecca's office.

"Let's take it with us," Rebecca said, fully in control and appreciative of the rugged good looks of this well-built young man, whom she noticed did not have a wedding ring. "Grace, would you please have my car brought from the garage? And tell Papa that I will be at The Breakers with a new client."

Rebecca's bright maroon and highly polished Bentley convertible was delivered curbside in front of The Left Bank. The valet held the door for her, and Jake climbed in on the opposite side. Once seated and buckled in, Rebecca flipped a switch and the top folded into the trunk. She handled the automobile expertly as they made their way down a busy South Ocean Boulevard. "I know Doctor Ambrose, Jake," she announced with a smile. "He visits our auctions every now and then, usually in the company of woman, a different women each time I might add," she said with a low chuckle, cutting him a quick glance. "I believe the silver setting for the *Sea Bones* was purchased at The Left Bank."

Jake laughed. "That's my doctor, Rebecca. He's a three-time divorcée, and he does get around. It has been quite an experience running his yacht for him." *Not a chance that I will mention the hijacking of the Sea Bones in the Bahamas just a few weeks ago, or my eliminating those murdering Haitian bastards.* "I will soon be leaving his employ though in order to fulfill my responsibilities in the recovery of this treasure and ensuring its safe passage to the auction halls. *"Just me and the Giggling Witch sailing across the whole of the Pacific Ocean. Not going to mention that either. "*I will tell you very frankly, Rebecca, I am in awe of the value of the *Concepcion's* treasure. It is beyond my imagining. I'm just a country boy from North Carolina, who joined the Marine Corps at the age of seventeen. If we can come to an agreement, we will be depending on The Left Bank to accurately assess each piece of the treasure, and conduct auctions or individual sales until the last piece has been sold."

Rebecca was impressed by Jake's humility and sense of humor. As she pulled into the drive in front of The Breakers and turned her Bentley over to the valet, she realized that she was very much looking forward to lunch with this handsome, self-effacing young man. "Here we are! Bring your manifest. I'll get us a table large enough that we can unroll it."

Inside the foyer they were greeted like royalty by the restaurant's staff. It was obvious that Rebecca was well-known and a frequent customer. She asked for a private dining area near the pool, one with a table for ten guests. The shift was handled expertly by the staff, and in short order a platter of fruit, followed by an assortment of fragrant Spanish tapas were placed at one end of the long table. Rebecca asked Jake for his preference in a wine cooler and Jake deferred to Rebecca's selection. Jake, in the meanwhile, unrolled the *Concepcion's* cargo manifest and placed empty glasses on the corners to hold it in place. Rebecca rose, wine cooler in hand, and began to examine the document.

"Fascinating, Jake!" she exclaimed. "Dear God at the sheer bulk of it! This is the dream of every auction house in the world to manage a haul like this!"

"You can read that?" Jake asked.

"Yes, of course," Rebecca replied, running a perfectly manicured finger down the rows of tiny Spanish script describing the treasure stored aboard the *Concepcion*.

"Well then, there's something additional you might find interesting." Jake pulled from the manila envelope the copies of the correspondence between Manila's new governor and the Royal Treasury in Madrid, discussing the Jesuit's gift of a 100-place setting of Chinese porcelain to Pope Innocent XII.

"This is on the vessel, too?" Rebecca asked in astonishment.

"Yes. The majority of the cargo in terms of volume is Chinese silk and tapestries. The next bulkiest is the Ming china, and the least bulky is jewelry, loose precious stones and gold bars from the Manila treasury."

"Ming china?" Rebecca asked.

"Yeah, crates and crates of it," Jake replied.

Rebecca laughed heartily, much to Jake's confusion. "I may have a surprise for you, Jake," she said. "Look. This is the sailing date of the *Concepcion*," she said, pointing to the date clearly written at the top center of the cargo manifest: 22 de Agosto 1698. "The Ming dynasty ended over fifty years before that date. There may be a few Ming-era pieces aboard the *Concepcion* that were from some merchant's private collection, but the bulk of the porcelain production on the *Concepcion* is probably Shunzhi or later, the period immediately following the overthrow of the Ming dynasty. Collectors call it the 'Unknown Reign' because the violence that followed the Ming collapse brought such chaos to porcelain production. The Shunzhi period is generally said to run from 1644 to 1661. That was followed by the Qing dynasty from mid-to-late18th century during the reign of the fourth emperor, Qianlong. Many of these pieces aboard your galleon most probably resided in the Chinese Royal Palace, and were fired in the Khan's personal kilns. Shunzhi porcelain in particular is extremely rare. Most of it never left China. There are some major collectors of Shunzi among the very wealthy Chinese on mainland China and Taiwan. It is very prestigious among the Chinese to collect porcelain and other cultural things from that era to preserve China's heritage. The best news for you is that certain pieces of Shunzhi and Qing dynasty porcelain are worth five times as much as Ming because of the scarcity."

"Well, Rebecca," Jake said with chuckle, "That's why we need someone like you and The Left Bank to take care of that end of things."

Their food arrived and the two of them sat down to eat, Rebecca changing the subject and wanting to know more about Jake Porter. She questioned him very gracefully and was rewarded with a somewhat self-conscious recounting by Jake, beginning with his Marine Corps experience minus the Iraqi war tales, his migration to Fort Lauderdale and the encounter with Doctor Ambrose and becoming the *Sea Bones'* captain.

"My brother, Abraham, was in the Marine Corps," Rebecca said softly. "He was a Second Lieutenant. He was in Iraq for only a few weeks before he was killed by a roadside bomb near Fallujah. It devastated my family, my father more than anyone else. He had vehemently opposed Abraham going into the military, especially the Marine Corps. But Abraham was determined to be his own man. Following his death, I found it impossible to continue living at home. I took a scholarship from the Sorbonne and spent the next three years in France. My father begged me to return and play an active role in The Left Bank. So, here I am," she smiled. "I live in a condo penthouse on top of The Left Bank under the watchful eye of my father. He's determined to prevent me from running off with a Marine!" she smiled, fluttering her eyes and lowering them in a way that made Jake catch his breath.

"I'm sorry for your loss, Rebecca," Jake said solemnly and with sincere compassion. "Iraq was a bitch." He decided to quit right there.

"You were in Iraq with the Marines?" she asked, looking closely into his eyes.

"Yes, but it's not my favorite topic of conversation," Jake responded as diplomatically as he could.

"Sorry," Rebecca said. "I didn't mean to pry." She turned to the *Concepcion's* cargo manifest and continued to read aloud items she thought interesting. Finally, she said, "I have an idea, Jake, if you're game."

"I'm all ears," Jake said, stuffing the last of the lunch into his mouth and finishing his glass of wine.

"How would you like to hold some ancient Chinese porcelain in your own hands? I think you would find it much more interesting than looking at the pictures I have in auction catalogs and art history books."

"Absolutely!" Jake said. "That's what I've been doing the last couple of weeks. Just looking at pictures and trying to get a feel for the real thing."

"Well, let me make a phone call. There's a very special client of The Left Bank who lives here in Palm Beach, and she's a collector of all things Chinese, especially porcelain. She's quite elderly, but very spry for her years. I think she could be one of your first customers when you bring the *Concepcion's* cargo to market." Rebecca did a quick dial with her cell phone, speaking with whoever answered on the other end. "Yes. This is Rebecca Fontaine from The Left Bank. May I speak with Miss Hattie? We are old friends. Tell her it's about Shunzhi porcelain. Yes, I'll wait."

Rebecca covered her cell phone and whispered to Jake. "Harriet Heinz, as in the ketchup family. Married to a member of the Dodge automobile family before that. 'Loaded' is a modest word to describe her wealth. Long time resident of Palm Beach. Used to be an active socialite, and major contributor to worthy causes. She's in her eighties now, I'd guess, but a darling.

"Yes. Hello, is that you Hattie?" Rebecca said into her cell phone. "I'm so glad to hear it. I know you will be interested in my find. And I'm bringing along a very handsome young man, a former Marine, by the way." Pause. "Hattie! You are positively shameful! I just met him today, and we've talked about nothing but Chinese porcelain. I haven't even held his hand." Pause. "Thank you, but we have just finished lunch at The Breakers. Your name came up as we were looking at a 400-year old cargo manifest for a lost Manila galleon circa 1698. You won't believe what was aboard. I'll give you a quick hint: a gift of the Jesuit order in China to Pope Innocent XII." Pause. "Very exciting. And from what I can decipher from the cargo manifest, there will be some magnificent Shunzhi and Qing pieces. It will set the market on fire!" Pause. "Yes, of course. You're always at the head of the line, Hattie, you know that. That's why I thought you'd like to meet the young Marine who's heading things up. You could use your charms to convince him we are his best resource for buyers before an auction." Pause. "Hah, Hah! I thought so! We'll be there in about twenty minutes if that's okay with you. And we'll bring the galleon's cargo manifest. It's quite beautiful, and a work of art in itself." Pause. "Wonderful! See you in a few. Bye-bye."

(Two)

As Rebecca steered her Bentley into the palm tree-lined drive of the huge Palm Beach mansion, she warned: "Hattie's home is guarded like Fort Knox. You'll see security people everywhere. It could easily qualify as a national museum. Her collections are valued in the hundreds of millions of dollars. Once a year. she hosts a public viewing of her treasures in sponsorship of a worthy charity. Thousands of visitors come. No cameras allowed, and the private security detail is tripled. Palm Beach Police Department officers manage the traffic and surround her property's perimeters to keep the crowds from trampling over her flowerbeds."

They pulled up to the security booth, its steel boom lowered, and two uniformed private security types inside the air-conditioned cubicle. One of them stepped outside, tipped his hat to the strikingly beautiful driver of the polished maroon Bentley, recognizing its driver immediately. "Hello, Miss Fontaine," he greeted. "Miss Hattie is in the arboretum inspecting her orchids. She said you should meet her there. You know the turn around the back?"

"Yes, Harry. I do," Rebecca said, flashing a wide smile. Thank you."

The guard smiled appreciatively at Rebecca's remembering his name. He turned and waved to his shift partner to raise the boom. Jake was impressed as well. Rebecca traveled in some exalted company for sure. When they parked alongside the arboretum, a slender, silver-haired woman who looked to be in her late seventies or mid-eighties, waved a gloved hand to invite them in.

The interior of the arboretum was a tropically hot and humid environment filled with orchids of every description, some potted and sitting on long benches, others hanging from wire mesh stuffed with sphagnum moss. The spectrum of colors was phenomenal, and Jake was caught off guard when Rebecca tugged him forward to meet one of the wealthiest women in the world.

"And this is the young Marine I mentioned, Hattie. His treasure expedition is onto a major find of Chinese antiquities aboard one of the 17th century Manila galleons. Jake is looking for assistance in marketing the cargo. He's brought along the cargo manifest of the vessel, and I believe you will find it to be nothing less than jaw-dropping," Rebecca said.

Hattie Heinz gracefully pulled off her glove, and with a delicate smile offered her hand to Jake. "Rebecca, you have a major find here, and I'm not just talking about Chinese treasure," Hattie said, laughing softly while giving Jake an appreciative head-to-toe assessment.

"Oh, don't you start, Hattie," Rebecca laughed. "You'll just embarrass Jake."

"Rebecca, dear, I haven't even gotten started," Hattie said, turning to Jake. "Jake, are you by any chance familiar with the work of Georgia O'Keeffe, specifically her painting of lilies?"

"Only from pictures in an art textbook from a class in art history. It was a required course for my degree," Jake answered, returning the smile. "I believe her paintings of lilies were compared to the female sex organs, and some people put a Freudian interpretation on them. Other than that, and the fact that she was married to a famous New York photographer, I don't know much more about her."

"Now, see there? Rebecca, your young Marine is much further along than you might have thought," Hattie said triumphantly. "I'm not at all surprised that a young Marine would know something about female genitalia. Jake, let me show you something." She led them out of the arboretum across a stone pathway to the main house and into a great hall with a vaulted ceiling. Rebecca had taken Jake's hand and given it a squeeze. When he looked at her, she was rolling her eyes in amusement. At an intersection, Hattie Heinz paused and directed Jake's attention to a large oil painting that he recognized as the one he had seen in his college textbook.

"This is Georgia O'Keeffe's 'Black Iris'. She painted it in 1926," Hattie said proudly, then added, "Did you know she lived to the age of 98? It makes my 81 seem more bearable. If I were twenty years younger, Jake, I would be working on some way to get rid of Rebecca and invite you up to my bedroom to see my etchings."

Jake flushed red and didn't know what to say. Rebecca said it for him. "Hattie, darling, you would have a hard time separating me from my find. Finders keepers, and Jake is all mine. He's not interested in looking at your etchings," she laughed. Jake could see that this was all just friendly sparring from two women who were well acquainted and enjoyed poking fun at men.

"What Jake really wants to see are your Chinese porcelain pieces. He needs to become an expert really fast, and I told him your collection was unsurpassed for a private collector," Rebecca said, again squeezing Jake's hand.

"Very well then, let's get on with it, but you better keep a close eye on your young Marine. He's a dish, as they used to say in my time." Hattie put her arm into Jake's and led him across an immense living room to a long hallway lined with glass display cases. She stopped in front of one of the cases displaying a slender Chinese vase no more than 16 inches high. A sparse mountain scene with a waterfall, trees and a small landing with a tiny boat tied to it covered the surface of the vase. The background was a pale, delicate white that was almost blue.

"Rebecca says your recovery vessel has limited space and that you need to initially recover pieces that are small, light in weight, but worth a lot of money. Take a close look at this vase, Jake. Which would you rather have, a thousand pounds of gold bullion, or this rather small piece of oriental ceramic?"

"I have this feeling, Hattie, that I had better choose the vase, but I don't know why," Jake said.

"This is a Chi'ing-era piece and was purchased at auction in Paris for $2.8 million dollars. As you can see, it takes up a lot less space than a thousand pounds of gold, and is much easier to tote around."

"The cargo on our galleon will have thousands of pieces of porcelain, Hattie" Jake said. In choosing which to recover first, is it size, or style, or color or function that I should focus on?"

"A little bit of each, Jake," Hattie said. "Let's do a tour of some of my pieces and I'll give you some pointers. We'll call it Ancient Chinese Porcelain 101. Is that the cargo manifest of your galleon that you're holding? Bring it along and we'll take a look at it later."

Jake, with Rebecca at his side, followed Hattie from display case to display case, still reeling from the fact that such a tiny piece of porcelain could bring over two million dollars. He envisioned the *Giggling Witch* filled with such pieces and tried to calculate the impossible: hundreds of millions of dollars in treasure.

"Now here is a piece that I am sure you can identify with, Jake," Hattie said. "It was recovered by the Australian salvage diver, Mike Hatcher, in

1987. It's from the wreck of an old Asian trading boat that struck a reef in the South China Sea and sank. Hatcher was looking for World War II ship wrecks and came upon this instead." Hattie pressed a handheld buzzer disarming the display cover. She lifted it clear, then picked up the piece saying it was a pot for paint brushes, and handed it to Jake. "Hatcher sold only a portion of the cargo at Christie's auction house in Amsterdam, in 1987, but walked away with about $20 million dollars. He kept the remainder for his private collection to finance future treasure hunting expeditions. No way to know the total value of his haul, probably one hundred million dollars or more. Hatcher was very tight-lipped like most of you treasure hunters. Anyway, Rebecca handled the purchase of this piece for me, I believe.

We bought that one for less than $20,000 as I recall," Rebecca confirmed. "If re-sold today, it would probably bring $40,000 to $50,000. A very nice investment, don't you think?"

"Rebecca says the cargo of the vessel you are recovering most probably consists of Shunzhi and Qing pieces," Hattie said. "Very rare. I have only one Shunzhi piece, but it is marvelous. And I have three porcelain pieces from the Qing-era that followed. They are equally exquisite.

"In the antiquities market, Jake, one of the most difficult challenges is separating the fake from the real. You are spared that ordeal because you are recovering the objects in situ, undisturbed since their loss. Treasure salvers like yourself are what keeps the antiquities trade so exciting. If your treasure is accompanied by sufficient provenance to authenticate its history, you will have the world's antiquity dealers at your mercy.

"Anyway, let's go up to the second floor of my home and take a look at something special. The first floor has become more a museum than a home because of the security people. They roam the first floor at all hours of the day and night. They can come up to the second floor only by invitation, or if an intrusion alarm goes off." Hattie turned into a shallow alcove. "Come, we can take the elevator. Believe it or not, Jake, this house has 24 bedrooms!" she said, cutting a mischievous eye toward Rebecca.

Arriving on the second floor of the huge Palm Beach home, Hattie led the way down a thickly-carpeted hallway, then swung open the glass-paneled French doors to a large parlor decorated in the art nouveau style of the 1920's . "Here's my beauty, Jake!" she said, stopping to stand in front of a glass display case containing a highly decorated squat pot about twenty-inches in height. To Jake, it seemed little different from most of the porcelain that he had already been looking at. Hattie disarmed the security, then Rebecca lifted the glass cover and sat it on the floor. Hattie picked up the plump vase and handed it to Jake, saying "Carefully, please, Jake."

Jake accepted the vase, holding it away from himself, turning it slowly, then tipping it upside down and looking at the base. He had heard that inscriptions and marking on the base went a long way toward identifying and proving the authenticity of a piece of antique porcelain.

"You're headed in the right direction, Jake," Hattie observed. "See the six Chinese characters stacked in two vertical columns within a circle? That's a clear sign that this is a Shunzhi piece," she said. "A Chinese potter working in the Imperial kilns in Jingdezhen, created this piece sometime around 1645, about 355 years ago."

As Jake turned the vase in his hands, Hattie described its features. "The landscape is painted on top of a blue underglaze, and it is copied from a 15th century scroll. It was a common practice in those times to use old 14th and 15th century woodcuts and drawings lifted from manuscripts for inspiration. The lions circling the bottom of the vase are Buddhist, and the plants are stylized decorative themes of that era."

Jake handed the vase back to Hattie, who then returned it to the display case. "It's very beautiful, Hattie. I can see why you're so proud to own it. During our recovery operations, I'll keep an eye out for pieces like this one," he said.

"Why don't we take a look at that cargo manifest from your lost galleon and let Rebecca tell us what you've got? We can go into the drawing room and spread it out on the table" Hattie said.

With the intricately-drawn manifest unrolled and its corners held down by salt and pepper shakers and a sugar bowl, Rebecca began to read the disposition of the cargo throughout the galleon. The manifest described the exact location within the *Concepcion's* hull where each piece of treasure was stowed and who was the owner. She made the point that the galleon contained many thousands of pieces of treasure, *objects de arte* that were not necessarily porcelain, specifically the hundreds of pieces of jade sculptures, ivory carvings, and jewelry mounted with precious and semi-precious stones. An auctioneer's dream.

When she reached the accounting for the Jesuit's table setting for Pope Innocent, Hattie leaned forward to follow Rebecca's fingertip tracing the script. "I wonder what kind of claim the Vatican will make for that table setting," Hattie said.

"What do you mean, Hattie?" Jake asked.

"I can hear the Vatican's lawyers ranting and raving in international court proceedings right now," she said, "claiming that the recovered table setting is clearly owned by the Church. The fact that the galleon sank enroute is only a minor footnote, and that it was not delivered to its rightful owner four hundred years ago in no way alters ownership. You're going to have to be very careful in marketing that piece of the galleon's treasure, Jake."

"In fact, Jake," Rebecca said, "The Chinese government may declare all cargo aboard your galleon as cultural property of the Chinese people. The fact that it was sold to the Spaniards in Manila, may dilute that claim, but that means that the Spanish government could also make a claim in behalf of the Spanish citizens who owned it and lost it. A very sticky affair, Jake, which is why letting The Left Bank work as your agent is a smart move," Rebecca said.

"My! All this talk about treasure and court battles has made me thirsty and a bit hungry. I'm going to order up some victuals from the kitchen and have it brought up by dumbwaiter. What does your palate have to say?" Hattie said.

Hattie called down to the kitchen and ordered dinner for three. She specified blackened Chilean sea bass, fresh butterbeans in garlic-infused butter, jalapeno cornbread and an ice-cold Caesar's salad, and iced green tea. "While the food's underway, kids, let's have a libation. Cuban-style Mojitos, okay with you two?"

The mojitos arrived iced in a large glass pitcher on the dumbwaiter, a copious amount of fresh mint leaves swirling around the ice. Rebecca brought glasses from a teak sideboard, and Hattie poured.

"This treasure hunting business seems to me to be a dangerous one, Jake. The amount of money involved, the remote lawless places where it all takes place, and the various kinds of foreign low-life that call themselves 'pirates' trying to grab what they can. Are you and your consortium prepared to deal with the ugly side of things?"

"We would prefer that no one gets hurt, Hattie," Jake said evenly. "We are keeping a low profile, presenting as small a target as possible. We aim to recover the treasure quietly, protect the artifacts from damage, and see them to auction intact."

"You were in the Marines, right?" Hattie said. "May I ask you a personal question?"

"Ask away, Hattie. I am deeply in your debt for your hospitality today and the assistance you have provided me."

"Have you had to kill someone, Jake? On a battlefield with the Marine Corps?"

"I have, Hattie," Jake said. "I was a sniper in the Gulf War. I shot a number of Iraqi enemy, mostly in their backs, or when they were

247

unawares. It was done at a great distance. That's the nature of a sniper's killing." Jake had no intention of mentioning his deadly hand-to-hand encounter with the Haitian thugs aboard the *Sea Bones*.

"Would you do it again if the enemy was people trying to take the treasure from you, or preventing you from getting to it?" Hattie asked.

"There's a lot of grey area in that question," Jake said. "And like I say, I would try to do things without loss of life, but if the interference was from non-government types, or plain thieves, I would have no hesitation in removing them from the equation," Jake said.

"Hmm, 'removing them from the equation'. That's an interesting expression, Jake," Hattie said.

"Ah, here's the food," Hattie said when the dumbwaiter bell sounded. "Let's eat."

Rebecca moved the *Concepcion's* manifest to a sofa and set the table. When she began to pour the iced tea, Jake said he'd continue with the mojitos. Rebecca said she would as well. Before they sat down to eat, Hattie said, "I have something beautiful we can look at while we eat." She left the room and came back moments later carrying a jade carving mounted on a polished teak platform. The carving was about eleven inches high, eight inches long, and maybe 4 inches deep. The center of the jade was a mottled green that changed gradually into a near-white along the outer edges of the carving.

"Your galleon's manifest mentions 'jade carvings' or 'jade statuette' many times. I thought you might like to see what they may be referring to. This is a 16th century jade carving, dating to about 1565. As you can see, it is the very rare 'applewhite' jade, and the Chinese sculptor did a superb job of representing a crouching Tibetan tiger on a mountain cliff. I believe Rebecca can confirm that there is a very active market for jade carvings of this type, especially if they date back several centuries. I bought this one at a gallery in New York about 20 years ago, and I believe it was over $100,000. So, in addition to porcelain, I would be very interested in purchasing any jade *objects de arte* that you recover."

"My consortium's relationship with Rebecca guarantees that you will be at the head of the line, Hattie. You will have first refusal on anything on the manifest that we recover."

"Wonderful!" Hattie exclaimed. "I have deep pockets, Jake, and I'd rather have beautiful art than stacks of corporate bonds and dollar bills. When I buy an artifact, I really haven't spent any money. I've just exchanged ugly money for beauty. The value of the art far exceeds the money spent. So, I wait with bated breath, as they say, for you to deliver. And I have this feeling that you will indeed deliver."

Rebecca laughed. "I knew the minute he walked into The Left Bank that this was going to be an interesting day. When he unrolled that cargo manifest at The Breakers and I saw the extent of what was being recovered, my heart did a flip-flop, Hattie. We are going to set the world's antiquities market on its heels! I can't wait to tell the Vatican's curator that he has 72 hours to say 'yea' or 'nay' on buying Pope Innocent's tableware setting, before I sell it outright to a Chinese billionaire in Taiwan, where it will be lost to the Vatican and the Western world forever."

"Well, let's don't start World War Three, Rebecca," Jake said. "There's plenty to go around."

"And on that note, I must announce my retirement for the day. I'm an old lady, you know, and I must have my rest. It's late and both of you have been consuming a fair amount of alcohol. You've no business out on the streets driving an automobile. I insist you stay for the night. Like I said, there are 24 bedrooms here, so you have plenty of choices. Rebecca, you've stayed here before, so just take Jake down the hall and see that he's comfortable." She gave a wink, then patted Jake on the shoulder. "See you in the morning, kiddos."

(Three)

Jake Porter was a happy man as he crossed the bridge from Palm Beach to West Palm Beach the following morning. Mission accomplished, he thought. He had a firm arrangement with a respected antiquities firm to market any treasure he recovered from the *Concepcion's* cargo. That would not only spare him the agony of peddling and haggling with collectors, but more importantly, would provide a buffer of safety for his own person. To that he added the bonus of making the acquaintance of one of the world's wealthiest women, who just happened to be an ardent collector of ancient Chinese porcelain, and was now waiting in the wings with unlimited funds to buy any treasure he had to sell.

And then, there was Rebecca. An incredibly beautiful, cultured woman whom he had almost made love to. Jake smiled to himself as he recounted the previous evening at Hattie Heinz's Palm Beach mansion. He and Rebecca had continued to sit in the parlor after Hattie retired for the evening. They had returned to the *Concepcion's* manifest while finishing off the pitcher of mojitos. Standing closely shoulder to shoulder, Rebecca's perfume working its magic, Jake had followed her finger, mesmerized as it moved from compartment to compartment of the *Concepcion*, describing, it seemed to him, his future wealth. Rebecca lifted her finger from the manifest, placed her hand atop Jake's and said in a slightly husky voice, "Let me show you the bedrooms."

Jake followed her down a long hallway, Rebecca stopping to open bedroom doors at random and peeking inside. "This one is yours," she finally said. "Mine is next door." She raised up on tiptoes and gave him a light kiss on the cheek, then went into the adjoining bedroom, giving Jake a quick glance before closing the door.

Jake went immediately to the big king-sized, canopied bed, flipped the covers back and flopped onto the bed. For a moment he considered whether he should go to the interconnecting door to Rebecca's bedroom and make some sort of effort at deepening their relationship, but the mojitos prevailed and he fell asleep. A short while later, the interconnecting door opened quietly. Wearing a black thong and bikini bra, Rebecca stepped inside Jake's room She tiptoed over to the bed, saw that Jake was passed out on the bed, and sighed. *Guess I'll just have to settle for the treasure.* She unhooked her bra, let it drop to the floor, and crawled under the covers to snuggle next to Jake's back.

LOOSE LIPS SINK RELATIONSHIPS

Date: December 1, 2000

Lat. 26º 4' N, Long. 77º 2' W

Fort Lauderdale, Florida

(One)

As he drove south to Fort Lauderdale, Jake checked his phone messages and saw that he had a call from Brenda. Her message said that the Saturday evening bon voyage party for McGruder was shaping up and asked if he intended to come.

"Yep, I'll be there," Jake said when he returned her call. "I need to pay him for the sextant he sold me. Did he recruit you for his Pacific voyage?" Jake teased.

"Give me a break," Brenda said. "No way. Besides, I've found a loose sailor who may prove to be a keeper."

"That right? Anyone I might know?" Jake asked.

"I'm keeping my cards close to my chest on this one."

"And a nice chest it is, I might add." Jake said.

"Thank you. See you tonight at the party?" she asked.

"Don't see why not," he said.

Now, a couple of hours later, Jake found himself arriving at Sammons Boat Yard in the late afternoon, several hours before the party for McGruder was scheduled to start. McGruder's boat, the *Waltz'n,* had been hauled out for several days and lacked only a painting of the bottom with anti-fouling paint before re-launching her. Jake went straight to McGruder's boat and knocked on the hull. McGruder came up from behind him and said, "The Captain's not aboard, mate. Can I help you?"

Turning around, Jake said "Actually, you're the guy I'm looking for. I came to square-up with you on that sextant. My boat came in and I'm flush."

"Good on you, mate," McGruder said. "Come on up and we can have a wee taste of that Irish brew before the party gets going." He climbed up the ladder resting against the *Waltz'n* hull and Jake followed him.

"Your other galley gal, CIndy, and her guy were looking for you earlier. Looks like her foot is repaired except for maybe a slight limp. She told me the inside story of that charter you just did to the Bahamas, too."

"What inside story? Jake asked.

"Well, when we last talked over at the marina, you kind of left out the part about the Haitians. I can appreciate your not wanting to make a big deal of it, but you have to admit it wasn't your usual charter."

"Exactly what did Cindy say, Archie?" Jake asked.

"Just that you were boarded by some murderous Haitian bandits and that you....eliminated them. Saved the lives of everyone on board, she says."

"For Pete's sake!" Jake exclaimed. "We were sworn to secrecy by the Bahamian government. Where in the hell has she gotten this information?"

"No idea, mate. I didn't know it was such a secret when she told me. She didn't tell me it was a secret either. I've mentioned it to a couple of others here in the boatyard. I wouldn't have done that if I had known it was that important to you. I'm really sorry, mate."

"It's not your fault, Archie," Jake said. "But it's a serious breach of faith between me and the Bahamian government, and I'm not sure what will happen when the word spreads. Christ, when news reporters get hold of it, they will swarm my boat. Hell, the FBI or the U.S. State Department may want to interview me. Damn! I can't believe it. Any idea where Cindy is right now? I want to get to her as soon as I can and find out how she found out about this and let her know that spreading it around can cause me a lot of trouble."

"She and her guy were carrying some platters of food, so they are probably over at the barbecue area setting up the tables. I'm really sorry, Jake. I will keep my mouth shut and act like I've never heard anything."

"Thanks, Archie," Jake said. "Look, here's the bucks for the sextant. I appreciate you giving me such a good deal. I'll put it to good use. Let me go see if I can find Cindy."

Jake crossed the boat yard to the barbecue pit area and saw Cindy standing with a half-dozen other yachties. He gave her a wave, beckoning her to separate herself from the crowd and come over.

"Jake! How great to see you and that you're all in one piece," she said, giving him a big hug. "I can't believe it! I really can't believe it. Man, am I glad I missed that charter."

"Cindy, how did you find out about the Haitian thing?" Jake asked. He was not smiling, and Cindy saw that something was wrong.

"Brenda told me. I was asking her about how the charter went and did she take a liking to you. She told me the whole thing. Then, she told me not to say anything to anybody about it, that it was a secret. The only one I've told was Dan here," she said, indicating her lover and partner.

"Did she tell you we took an oath with the Bahamian government officials to not breathe a word about this. Did she tell you that we were released from custody only on the condition of that promise?"

Looking severely chastised, a stricken look crossing her face, Cindy said, "No, she didn't. It was like we were just not to say anything to anybody. I thought it was just the regular kind of secret, not an important government thing."

"Look, keep this under your hat, okay? Not another soul. Not a word to another person, okay?" Jake said. "How's your foot?"

"Tender, but at least I'm mobile again," Cindy said. "I'm so sorry about this, Jake. I just didn't have any idea the seriousness of it. Are we still friends?

"Yes, we are definitely still friends. I am just blown away that Brenda takes this so lightly. I've got to find her and put a clamp on this. Do you know where she is?"

"Several hours ago she was on her houseboat making up a couple of dishes to bring to the party. Why don't you call her on your cell?"

"I'll do that," Jake said.

Jake moved away and called Brenda. She answered on the first ring.

"Are you at your houseboat?" Jake asked abruptly and coldly.

"Jake? Is that you? You sound strange," Brenda said.

"Don't go anywhere. I'm on my way there."

"No, Jake. Don't come right now. Meet me at the party. There's someone...." But Jake had already hung up.

"Shit!" Brenda said into the dead phone.

When Jake arrived at Brenda's houseboat, her yellow Karman Ghia was parked in front. There was also a sleek black Mercedes alongside. As Jake approached the ramp, Brenda stepped out onto the front deck, and right behind her was a brutish-looking guy with a neck as thick as Jake's thigh. He had a huge chest and massive biceps The only thing tiny about him was his pig-like eyes, and they flitted side-to-side like enemy radar.

"We need to talk, Brenda," Jake said.

"Jake, you hung up before I could tell you that I had company. Let's meet at the party, okay?"

"Brenda, this is important. It can't wait," Jake said.

"The lady said it can wait until the party," the monster at her side said. "Now, go along, and we'll see you shortly."

"Like I said, this is important. I don't know who you are, but this is none of your affair. So butt out."

"Jake, please...." Brenda started to say.

"Wait a minute. You're not the character who beats up on little island niggers, are you?" the monster said. His mouth was twisted in a snarling kind of grin.

"You told him, too?" Jake said to Brenda.

"That's right, bozo. Brenda and I are old friends. She tells me everything, and your best bet is to shag out of here pronto in that beat-up old Volvo of yours. Otherwise, I may have to put a little wrinkle in your departure."

"You're starting to annoy me, big boy," Jake said. There was pure menace in his voice. "I need to speak with Brenda alone."

"Not going to happen, cowboy," the monster said.

"Dwight, please," Brenda implored, but it was already too late. The ex-football player had stepped down off the houseboat, his fists clenched, and was heading in a straight line for Jake.

Jake back-pedaled and side-stepped slightly to change the rhythm of Dwight's approach. Then, he sprang up on top of the hood of Dwight's impeccably polished Mercedes. He jumped up and down crushing the hood beyond repair. Dwight cursed with a fury and climbed up on the hood to do battle. That was all Jake needed. He nimbly jumped to the ground and grabbed Dwight's ankles, yanking his legs out from under him. Dwight fell heavily, hitting the ground head-first. Jake stepped around the front of the Mercedes and gave Dwight a judicious karate kick square in the face probably breaking his nose, then stomped on one of his knees, hearing a satisfying snapping of cartilage. Dwight screamed in pain, rolling on the ground, unable to stand up.

"Stop it! Stop it!" Brenda yelled, jumping in between Jake and Dwight.

Jake grabbed one of her arms and shoved his face in hers. "Have you any idea what you have done to our personal security? Did your swearing of that oath of silence in the Bahamas mean nothing to you? Are you really that stupid? We will be lucky if the Bahamian government doesn't call our FBI and ask for extradition. How do you feel about some jail time in a nasty little Bahamian prison serving time for conspiracy to murder? Brenda, I swear to God, if I ever have reason to believe you have mentioned that Bahamian incident to anyone else, I will make you regret it." The coldness in Jake's voice left Brenda in no doubt of dire consequences.

Jake got into his Volvo and slammed the door. Then he got out with a tire tool in his hand. He came over to Dwight, still writhing on the ground. Jake tapped Dwight on the head with the tire tool. "As for you, dipshit, if you ever see me again, you better reverse direction, because if I see you, I will make sure that you spend the rest of your life in a wheelchair, and no sex till you die. "Comprende, asshole?" He climbed back into his Volvo and left.

Although definitely not in a party mood, Jake returned to McGruder's send-off at Sammon's mainly to gage the extent of the damage Brenda had caused. He knew most of the sailors there. He worked his way among them, explaining the need for keeping the Haitian incident quiet. He received many pats on the back for taking out the Haitians and saving the lives of those aboard the *Sea Bones*. Everyone promised to keep the story to themselves and not offer any help to the media. He asked McGruder to go to the people he had told of the Haitian incident and explain to them the necessity of not discussing it with anyone else. Knowing human nature, Jake knew his efforts were futile in the long run. He just hoped he could get out of town before it all blew up in his face.

As the party progressed it became obvious that Brenda was not going to show up. Probably in a hospital emergency room somewhere with Dwight, Jake concluded. He located Archie McGruder in a group of women enthusiastically pitching the idea of a south Pacific cruise. He didn't seem to be getting any takers. Jake gave him a come-hither gesture and McGruder broke away from the women. Jake could see that McGruder had consumed a bit more of the Irish malt whiskey and was feeling no pain.

"Archie, I need to talk with you," Jake said. "Can we go aboard the *Waltz'n* for a brief chat?"

"You got it, mate," McGruder said, and crossed the yard to his boat, climbing the ladder somewhat unsteadily.

Once down below, Jake said, "Remember when we were on your boat at the marina right after I returned from the Bahamas charter, and we were talking about crossing the Pacific, and you gave me a chart? I said I was giving some thought to taking off myself."

"I remember," McGruder said.

"Well, Archie, my timetable on that has sped up. I figure to leave ASAP, before the news of the Bahamas thing spreads. As it turns out, I have a plan for a cross-Pacific sail that's a little more detailed than I indicated."

"Mate, you are just one bundle of secrets after another, aren't you?" Mc Gruder said with a bleary smile. "So, tell me."

"Here's the deal, Archie. I have a lead on some sunken treasure, and I am going to go take a look. There's nothing sure about it. It's all based on a tale I came across, and it may come to nothing. But I have a question that you may be able to help me with."

What's the question, Jake?"

"Here it is: if I should get lucky and recover some valuable stuff, how do I get it to market without some government, including the U.S., ripping me off? U.S. Customs can grab anything over $10,000 when you're passing through to leave or enter the country. What's a better way?"

"I must say you are an interesting guy apart from your martial talents in dealing with pirates. First of all, if it was me, I wouldn't even try to bring the stuff Into the United States. No need to, really. You Just want to sell it to the highest bidder and let the buyers deal with any customs and import duties. If you have just a few small items, they are best traded one-on-one to individual buyers. If you have a larger haul, you need a safe place to set it down, then have the buyers come to you. There's a treasure hunter from Australia, name of Hatcher. Mike Hatcher. He found some big wrecks in the South China Sea, but didn't take any of it back to his home country. Stashed the loot offshore and had an international firm auction it off by telephone and closed circuit television. A place I'd recommend for that would be the Zona Libre, in Panama. You can enter Panama with sealed boxes, declare the cargo in bond and have it transported into the Zona Libre. The customs people, the Adjuana they call them, ferry the sealed boxes into the Zona Libre. What you do inside the Zona Libre is your own business. But anything that leaves the Zona Libre is sealed and escorted by the Adjuana either to an airplane, a truck or a boat, all of them leaving the Republic of Panama. You pay a small fee for taking the boxes in and out. The important thing is that no government or anyone else gets to see what's in the boxes. The Zona Libre is what the Panama Canal is all about. It doesn't take much imagination to see the possibilities."

"So, putting the treasure in the Zona Libre, conducting an auction from inside, and let the buyers move the stuff out of the country? Have I got that right?" Jake asked.

"That's it, mate," McGruder said. "Get yourself a reliable auction firm to handle the transactions and put the money in your bank account. Keep all the valuables and money outside the United States. Set up an offshore banking account in Panama. There's no great secret to how it's done. Your auction firm will know the ropes."

"Archie, you're a warehouse of information," Jake said.

"Glad to oblige, mate," Archie said. "Seeing as how you're going to be spending some time among some Pacific islands, many of which have very little rainfall and no natural springs, I have something you will find useful." He went forward to the *Waltz'n's* forecastle, opened a locker and returned with a plastic-sealed package of about one-foot square. "This is a surplus U.S. Air Force desalinator from an aviation survival kit. I bought three of them at a military surplus store in Miami, and I'll make you a present of this one.

The instructions for use are on the inside. Really simple. Just blow-it up like a balloon. It creates a dome inside for condensed water to slide down into a collector. Just pour salt water into the reservoir and put out in the sun. Depending on salinity of the water and how hot the sun is, it can produce about a gallon of fresh water a day."

Thank you, Archie. Now, let's get on with this party."

UNINTENDED CONSEQUENCES

The Law of Unintended Consequences is an idiomatic warning that an intervention in a complex system always creates unanticipated and often undesirable outcomes. — Wikipedia Encyclopedia

Date: November 24, 2000

Latitude: 25°47'16"N Longitude: 80°13'27"

Miami, Florida

(*One*)

"Garcia Investigations. How may I help you?" Maria Torres answered the telephone anxiously, but it was not the call she was expecting from the fertility clinic with news of whether or not she was at last pregnant. It was instead a clerk at the Miami branch of Banco Santander, Madrid, asking to speak with Mr. Benito Garcia.

"Mr. Garcia is not in the office at the moment, may I take a message?" Maria Torres answered, switching to speakerphone mode and looking across the room at her boss reading the sports section of the Miami Herald. The bank clerk, announcing the arrival of a priority courier package and speaking in flawless English, but with a definite Latina accent, recited a claim number and explained that the package could be delivered solely to Mr. Benito Garcia, proprietor of Garcia Investigations, and that Mr. Garcia must identify himself with the claim number, a passport, a driver's license, and proof of ownership of Garcia Investigations, preferably with a copy of his business license. She added that if the message was not picked up in person by Mr. Garcia within 48 hours, the package would be shredded and the sender notified to that effect. Did she require the address of Banco Santander's Miami offices?

Benito Garcia, lowering the sports section of the Miami Herald and meeting Maria Torres' eyes, shook his head. He raised one finger, then returned to his reading.

"Mr. Garcia will pick up the message within one hour, Maria Torres said. "Thank you."

(*Two*)

The bank clerk returned Benito Garcia's identification documents and led him to a spacious office with a large mahogany desk and floor-to-ceiling bookcases filled with mortgage law books. She laid a thick manila-colored envelope on the desk, then peeled off the courier certification label and Benito signed a receipt stating that the envelope had been delivered to him with the security seal intact. Once the clerk had left the room, Benito broke the seal, opened the envelope and spread out the various contents. The cover letter explained that on recommendation from a former client of his, Benito was being offered a substantial fee to undertake a surveillance assignment in Fort Lauderdale and Gainesville, Florida. The objects of the surveillance were a doctor named Jerome Ambrose, one Stacy Burns, a professor at the University of Florida, and an individual named Jackson T. Porter.

Ambrose was the owner of a yacht named *Sea Bones*, located at the Harbour Point Yacht Club in Fort Lauderdale, and was a practicing physician at Mercy General Hospital. Porter was believed to be the captain of the yacht, and a copy of his Florida driver's license complete with photo, and his U.S. Coast Guard Captain's license were provided.

The letter went on to explain that for reasons not to be revealed in this letter, Dr. Ambrose, Professor Burns, and Captain Porter were believed to be involved in a research and recovery operation of a sunken vessel. It was suspected that they had falsely obtained access to proprietary information, and the purpose of the surveillance was to determine if that was true, and obtain photographic copies of any materials in their possession pertaining to the sunken vessel. It was imperative that the subjects be unaware of the surveillance, and nothing was to be taken from the premises, or any property damaged. Benito was not fooled for one moment. "Surveillance" in this case was in reality a breaking and entering, a B&E, as the police would call it.

The final document was a sealed envelope, and when Benito opened it, he whistled softly. An international draft drawn on Banco Santander in the amount of $25,000 U.S. dollars was enclosed, payable to Garcia Investigations for "Services Rendered." An additional draft in the amount of $5,000, marked "travel expense," and drawn on a bank in Liechtenstein was also enclosed, and an accompanying note instructed Benito to keep track of any costs above and beyond this initial payment if he expected reimbursement, but to request permission to spend more should it exceed $10,000.

(*Three*)

"We have an assignment," Benito announced to his secretary when he returned to the office. Maria stopped typing on her computer and immediately picked up a notepad knowing her boss's tendency to launch into rapid-fire instructions for assembling a new investigation. But this time, he surprised her.

"That cousin of yours, Paco? What's he up to these days? Last I heard from you he was still unemployed after that bust-up in Little Havana."

"I haven't spoken to him for a couple of weeks. He was at Bayside Hospital for almost a week, then he did some rehab at a community clinic for his arm and leg. They really worked him over at that bar, but I think he's pretty much mended now. You want me to call him for you?" Maria asked, wondering what use Benito would have for her oldest brother's wayward son, a smart-mouthed Miami hustler with a knack for getting into trouble. Why Benito Torres would think of him to help out with something, she had no idea.

"Yeah, give him a call and see if he's got a week to spare for an out-of-town job. Light duty, no rough stuff. I just need somebody to carry my stuff and watch my back for a few days. Pay's $100 per day with food and lodging." Benito was already thinking ahead. He wanted someone who would have no problem with a slightly illegal project, burglary plain and simple, and preferably with a rap sheet that would divert the cops away from himself in the event of trouble.

Maria called the last number she had for Paco, but the person who answered said she thought he was dead. "Got mixed up in a bar fight about a month ago, I heard," she said with the slurred speech of an alcoholic. "But the one to check on that is his asshole buddy, Domingo, down at the Cantina Refugio on the river."

"The bartender at the Cantina Refugio announced, to Maria's relief, that "Yeah, Paco's playing pool right now."

"Please, this is very important. Tell him his tia, Maria, needs to talk to him. It's a family emergency, Maria said in a voice she contrived to be one trembling with concern.

"!Hola, tia mia," Paco answered. "?Como te vas?"

Speaking in Spanish, Maria answered, "I'm fine, Paco. Still praying for a baby, but other than that all is okay. Listen, mi amor, I have some good news for you. My boss has an out-of-town job and needs some help carrying his camera and doing some of the driving. He's paying $100 per day plus food and hotel."

"Where out of town, and how long the job?" Paco answered suspiciously, always on the lookout to avoid anything that resembled honest labor and no chance to hit on chicas.

"Why don't you come by Benito's office this afternoon and let him give you all the details. That'll give me a chance to give you a get-well hug, too," Maria said affectionately.

"Okay, tia mia," Paco said. "I got some business to take care of, but I'll be there about four o'clock, okay?"

"Si, esta bien. Hasta a las quatro," Maria said and hung up. She turned to her boss, who had been listening to everything, and raised an eyebrow.

"Good," Benito said. "Now, round up my photo gear including the camcorder, check the batteries and spares, and put it in my kit bag. I'll need the laptop, too. I'm using the Camaro for this one, so call Manuel and have him pull it out of storage and freshen-up everything. Top off the tank, and fill the two ten-gallon plastic containers in the trunk, too, in case I don't want to stop for fuel and service station security cameras along the way, okay?"

(Four)

The Camaro hummed with authority as it sped up Interstate 95, now half-way to Fort Lauderdale, Benito at the wheel puffing on a contraband Cuban cigar that Paco had presented him earlier with great fanfare and a wink suggesting international connections. Benito had not seen Paco for over a year, but his assessment had not changed: Paco was a loser; a motor-mouth braggart who thought he was a gift to the opposite sex. He dressed like a pimp in Benito's opinion, and already he was wishing he had taken more time to look for a better bag boy for this job. But what was done was done, and he would have to make the best of it.

"Paco, this is a simple job," Benito began, "I've been hired to check out some people who may be collecting some information about my client's business, and I'm looking for documents that might prove that. I'll be looking for printed stuff on paper as well as computer files. Just so we're clear, I will be entering some premises without the permission of the residents. The single most important thing is that there must be no evidence of my having been there. Alerting anyone to having been searched will be as bad as getting caught in the act. Secrecy is everything, got that?"

"That $100 dollars per day don't cover exposure to burglary charges, Benito," Paco said sourly.

"Who said anything about you being a burglar?" Benito said. "You're along just to watch my back while I'm inside taking a look, and to help with my photo gear. I don't want you anywhere near my targets, particularly with that shit neon shirt and gay pantalones you're wearing."

"Hey! These pants cost over a hundred bucks, and this shirt is from Paris, France, man," Paco said, clearly offended.

Benito turned off I-95 north to head into Fort Lauderdale, working his way east toward the Intracoastal Waterway. "Our first stop is to take a look at a marina where one of my subjects has a yacht," Benito said, changing the subject. "I want to see where the boat is situated and what sort of access problems we might have. The boat's name is *Sea Bones*. It's a powerboat about seventy feet long at the very end of one of the piers. The marina is called *Harbor Point Yacht Club* and you can be sure there's security foot patrol as well as closed circuit TV cameras, no doubt. We're not touching her this time, just looking over the access situation. We'll go on board it on our way back from Gainesville."

From the parking lot of the Harbor Point Yacht Club, Benito could see that the security shack was positioned to control foot traffic only. Members and guests parked their cars, then walked to the security shack to pass through the 10-foot high chain link fence protecting the club. Members with cooler boxes and gear picked up a wheeled dock cart and loaded it while still on the parking lot side of the fence, then went down a ramp to the main pier paralleling the parking lot.

Finger piers jutted out from the main pier along its entire length, and Benito figured there were over 300 boats in the marina. No way he could spot the *Sea Bones* from the parking lot, so he presented his identification at the security shack and explained that he was looking for a berth for his boat, a 50-footer. The guard directed him to the marina office, and Benito walked down the ramp into the plush, air-conditioned office. He was greeted by woman behind a desk who wore a name tag identifying her as "Millie Watson, Client Services Manager."

Millie gave Benito a fold-out color brochure describing Harbor Point Yacht Club's amenities and asked about the kind and size of boat he had. Benito gave her the information then asked for a tour of the facilities. Millie used the intercom to call one of the dock attendants. When the dock attendant arrived, he introduced himself as Jimmy and led Benito down the dock to look at the facilities. It wasn't long before they reached the T-head of Pier One and Benito saw the *Sea Bones*. *Damn! Big son-of-a-bitch, and nice looking, too. Kind of old fashioned 1950s style. Just what you'd expect a flush doctor to be sporting around in.*

But, he'd already concluded, no way he and Paco could get to the *Sea Bones* undetected by strolling down the pier. He'd spied two CCTV cameras mounted on slender aluminum poles that monitored the pier from end to end. However, the *Sea Bones* was at the very end of the pier, and the entrance from the river into the club was just behind her. A rubber dinghy or small rowboat could conceivably round the end of the T-head and come up behind the *Sea Bones* and board her there. The security cameras were focused on the pier, not the seaward end of the T-head. Dicey, but possible, thought Benito. *Gonna have to get a boat somewhere, dammit,* he thought. It was not an inviting prospect. Benito hated the water, was afraid of it, really. He'd never learned to swim. The thought of paddling out on the water in the dark of night was not a pleasant one.

When he returned to the Camaro, Paco was leaning against the front left fender puffing on a cigar and looking like a tourist on the make.

"Let's mount up," Benito said, tossing the car keys to Paco. "You're driving. Time you started earning your wages. Let's pick up the Florida Turnpike and head for Gainesville."

(*Five*)

Once they were on the turnpike, Benito climbed into the back seat and took a nap. It was a long haul, 315 miles and almost five and one-half hours of driving time. They stopped once for lunch. When the Turnpike ended at Wildwood, they exited onto Interstate 75 and continued north to Gainesville, home of the University of Florida.

The information package that Benito had received from the Banco Santander contained the address of Professora Stacy Burns, and with a city street map of Gainesville, Benito had no trouble locating the two-story condominium complex on the outskirts of town. *Alhambra Estates* it said on the entry portal, and from the few automobiles parked in the covered garages, just about everyone was at work, or out shopping. After a couple of circuits of the complex, Benito drove away and parked a couple of blocks away. He turned to Paco.

"Our target shares a condo with another professor. According to my instructions, both of them have classes this afternoon. They shouldn't be returning to their condo until after 5 PM. I should be able to do what I got to do in less than a half-hour. Your job is to park so you can see our target's front door and the garage. If they return early, or you see any activity around the condo, call me on the cell. I will exit the complex at the back. You drive around and pick me up. Got all that?"

"No problem, jéffe," Paco said. There was an obvious tinge of excitement in his voice.

"That's all you do, Paco," Benito said sternly. "Don't get creative. Don't do anything other than keep a low profile. Be inconspicuous and be at the back of the complex after you see me leave. ?Compréde?"

"I got it. I got it. No problem," Paco said, feeling Benito was speaking down to him as though he were a child.

Benito grabbed his briefcase and strolled down the block toward the *Alhambra Estates*. The briefcase held his laptop computer, a separate hard drive with USB connector cables, and a small leather bag with an assortment of keys, flexible plastic shivs, a steel punch, two fine-tooth files, a glass cutter fastened to a suction cup and radius arm, and a case-hardened steel hammer with a very short handle. Tools of the trade for a professional burglar. Benito had been taught by the best, a Miami-based cat burglar who specialized in second-story entries and heisting very expensive jewelry.

He had no trouble disabling the burglar alarm, a pedestrian mass-market model at least 10 years out of date. The deadbolt lock surrendered quickly to a pick and the lower lock answered with no protest to his factory-produced master key. He left his briefcase on the hallway floor, bounded up the stairs to check out the bedrooms and baths. Then returned to the first floor and located the office den with the computers. He had no intention of spending time to analyze the contents of the computers to see if they contained files relating to sunken boats. He would just download the computer's entire system, forward that in its entirety to his clients and let them do the analysis.

He went to Stacy's desktop computer first, plugged in his hard drive, accessed the Preferences option in the system, selected the 'BackUp' function, indicated the hard drive as the data destination, then pressed 'GO.' There was a huge amount of data on the system and it took all of 15 minutes to capture it. Then he went to the laptop on the coffee table, saw that it belonged to "Taggart" and performed the same data capture from it. While the hard drive was guzzling the information, Benito rustled through some loose papers laying about, saw some strange mathematical-looking columns of what appeared to be random alphabets, and took photos of them with his Minolta digital SLR.

When the download to the hard drive was completed, Benito packed everything back into his briefcase and left the condo, re-engaging the burglar alarm as he left. He peeled off the neoprene painter's gloves that had prevented any fingerprints being left behind, and strolled casually to the back of the complex. He breathed a sigh of relief when he saw that Paco had the Camaro waiting exactly as he had instructed.

"How'd it go, mano?" Paco asked as he drove the Camaro out of the residential area and toward I-75.

"Like it was supposed to," Benito replied, a bit of tension remaining in his chest. *Damn! I'm getting too old for this shit.* "Let's find a good motel. One with a Wi-Fi Internet connection so I can send this data off to my client. I need a shower, too, and I'm hungry as hell. Dinner is on me."

They picked a Ramada Inn on I-75 south of Gainesville. Within minutes of checking in, Benito had his computer hooked up with the Internet and the external hard drive plugged in. He brought up the URL that had been provided by his European client, clicked first on the download file from the professora's desktop computer, then clicked on 'Send.' He watched the counter wind down as the data fed magically across the ether to its destination. When the dialog box signaling 'File Transfer Complete,' appeared on the screen forty-five minutes later, he repeated the procedure for the 'Taggart' laptop data. That was done in less than 25 minutes. Next, he downloaded the dozen or so digital photos of the documents he had shot with the Minolta SLR. That done, he wiped clean the hard drive's memory and disconnected his computer. No connection now between him and the burglary. Time for that shower, then dinner. He and Paco would head back down for the doctor's yacht in Fort

Lauderdale after a good night's sleep.

Climbing out of the shower, Benito was feeling more of himself. As he grabbed one of the motel's thick towels and began to dry off, he heard the unmistakable metallic *snick-snick* of an automatic pistol chambering a round. *What the hell?* His heart in his throat, and he unarmed, naked in the shower. He slipped alongside the bathroom door, slowly eased the handle and opened the door a crack. He saw Paco acting out a James Bond posture, brandishing what looked like a 9mm Beretta. When he flung open the door, Paco shoved the pistol beneath the bed covers, but knew instantly that Benito had seen the weapon.

"What the fuck you got there, Paco?" Benito asked coldly. "I thought I told you no guns. This is just a look-see operation, not a combat mission. Let me see it." Benito thrust out his hand.

"I just brought it for protection, Benito," Paco said lamely. I'll keep it in my bag and out of sight, okay?

"Give it, you dumb shit," Benito snarled, snatching the pistol. "And a silencer to boot! Have you any fucking idea what you've got here?"

"A Beretta 9 mil, with a custom Czech silencer," Paco answered meekly.

"No, stupid!" Benito said with barely suppressed fury. "This is 10 years in a Florida State prison with no parole. Just for possessing a silenced weapon. You don't have to be caught using it. Do you have any idea what a cop will think when he catches you with this? You're a hired killer. Where did you get this, Paco? Who sold it to you?"

"Just a guy. A Cubano. It's a $900 dollar pistol, not counting the silencer. The silencer is another $1,000. But I got both for only $700," Paco said.

"You are one pathetic asshole, Paco," Benito said. "And incredibly stupid to boot. Why do you think you got such a deal? Your seller wasn't just peddling a pistol, stupid. He was passing on the history of this pistol to an unsuspecting numb nuts like you. Putting somebody between him

271

and the last person this gun killed. A ballistics check of this pistol will probably match a hit, and since you're the one carrying it around, the cops won't look any further for the killer. What you have here is a one-way ticket to the gas chamber, or at a minimum, 10 years of hard time in a state prison."

"I don't think..." Paco began, but was abruptly cut off by a furious Benito.

"I don't care what you think. You've put me in a real bind, Paco, and you've jeopardized my operation. Bring your bag over here."

Paco picked up his bag and laid it on the bed. Benito wiped the Beretta with the bedsheet, then handed it to Paco. "Let's see that shooting posture again, Paco." Satisfied that Paco's fingerprints would be all over the pistol, Benito said, "Toss it in your bag and throw your shirt over it."

Paco did as he was told.

"You got a couple of pieces of ID with your name on it? Not your driver's license, asshole."

Paco brought out a Miami social club membership card, a bank deposit receipt and a couple of other items with his name on them.

"Toss 'em in the bag and zip up the bag," Benito commanded. "Now pick up the bag and follow me out to the car. When I open the trunk, you toss the bag in like you just caught a ride with me. Understand?"

Paco followed Benito to the Camaro and when the trunk lid raised, he tossed the bag in. Benito slammed the trunk shut and turned to Paco, his voice cold and threatening. "If your Aunt Maria was not such a valued friend to me, I would drive away and leave your dumb ass standing in this parking lot with that assassin's pistol in your bag. You would probably try to hitch a ride back to Miami, and the odds are the highway patrol or a local cop would stop you between here and there and check out your bag. From there you would be history. Handcuffed, hauled to the local lock-up, arraignment the next day, appointed a free sell-out lawyer and shortly after that you'd be on a prison bus headed for the state prison in Starke. No pussy for at least ten years, if you're lucky, or death row for the next ten or 20 years while the appeals play out.

"But I'm giving you the break of your life. Paco. Out of respect for your Aunt Maria, I'm going to keep you onboard and off the road. You're going to help me in any way I say in 'Lauderdale while I scope out that doctor's yacht. You will not open the trunk of this car and you will not touch that pistol until I leave you on the sidewalk in Miami. If we are stopped by the law and they elect to go into my trunk and take a look at your bag, you will tell the truth: that the bag and everything in it is yours. You will also confirm my story that I just picked you up and gave you a ride. We have never met before. You got that?"

Paco, head down, nodded glumly in assent, shoved his hands in his pockets and headed back to their room.

"Hold up," Benito called after him. "We're having dinner in the motel dining room. Like I said, I'm buying."

"Not hungry. I'm going to bed," Paco said over his shoulder.

"Suit yourself. Just stay in the room and don't wander off. If you're not in the room when I get back, I'm tossing your bag into the bushes and leaving your ass here in Gainesville," Benito warned, then headed for the restaurant.

(*Six*)

They left early the next morning, Benito doing the driving, stopping at the first McDonald's they spied from the Interstate for coffee and egg sandwiches. Neither spoke to the other. The tension between them was palatable. The silence suited Benito perfectly. He really had nothing to say, preferring to give his thoughts to how he would gain access to the doctor's boat, and not relishing the thought of using a boat to get there.

273

They arrived in Fort Lauderdale a little after one o'clock in the afternoon. Benito drove past the Harbor Point Marina and pulled into the parking lot of a marine store next door. "Stay in the car. No need for us to be seen together. I'm gonna check out buying a small row boat," he instructed. No reply from Paco. He was still pouting, staring in the opposite direction out the window.

The marine store clerk showed Benito a half-dozen models of small dinghies and rowing craft. He emphasized the fact that the inflatables were the more stable. "Can't flip those over, and even if they do, they still float. They come equipped with rowing paddles and a foot pump for inflating. "

That was what Benito wanted to hear even though the inflatables were more expensive. He paid cash and had the clerk put the boat in the Camaro's trunk. He learned from the clerk that there was a pubic boat ramp just a few hundred yards further down river from the store, and Benito could launch the dinghy into the river free of charge. Leaving the marine store, Benito drove down to the boat ramp and reconnoitered the ramp and parking lot, then drove to a Howard Johnson's motel and checked in.

The plan was to rest and wait until the early hours of the next day, sometime around 3-4 o'clock in the morning, and row in behind the *Sea Bones* to board her. Benito needed the rest, too. The tension between him and Paco had drained a lot of energy, and he had not gotten any sleep the night before.

(*Seven*)

Paco pumped up the inflatable using the foot pump, and attached the oars. Benito was surprised to see that he and Paco were not the only ones using the ramp at such an early hour. A couple of crabbing boats, chicken-wire traps stacked all over the decks with large registration numbers painted on the sides of their hulls, and a pair of guys launching a 20-foot bass fishing boat with a half-dozen rods and reels poking over the bow. Once the ramp was cleared, Benito and Paco each grabbed a side of the inflatable dinghy and carried it down the ramp to the water and pushed off, Paco rowing.

They made their way slowly up river toward the Harbor Point Yacht Club, and when they reached the riverside of the pier's T-head, they paddled in quietly and came up behind the *Sea Bones*. Benito grabbed the bag with his laptop, hard drive and SLR, and stepped gingerly onto the transom teak ramp, breathing a sigh of relief.

"Remember," Benito whispered to Paco, "Don't let go of our boat. Keep it tight against the yacht. Stay down low and don't stick your head above the rear of the boat. Security walks the dock. If they see you, we're in deep shit. Got that?"

"Yeah, I got it," Paco answered.

Benito climbed over the transom and made short work of the lock on the door leading from the fighting cockpit into *Sea Bones'* main salon. It took him a while to figure out the layout of the interior, discover the staterooms down below, and do a methodical search. He found a laptop computer on a countertop in what was Doctor Ambrose's cabin, and immediately married his own computer to it and the external hard drive. He was just finishing up disconnecting it when he heard voices, a male and a female, and a door being opened upstairs. *Damn!* He picked up his bag with gear and slipped into a closet. His mistake was that he forgot to shut down the Doctor's laptop. Its monitor was still glowing in the dark.

Paco, sitting low in the dinghy, holding onto the *Sea Bones'* transom, heard voices coming down the dock and tensed up. Clearly a male and female, laughing and sounding a bit tipsy. No way to warn Benito. He heard the visitors enter the boat and saw lights come on. Uncertain of what to do, he elected to climb over the transom and crawl silently to the salon door. He pushed it open a few inches so he could hear what was going on inside. Almost immediately he heard the male voice exclaim, "Somebody's been on the boat! The computer's on!" Then he heard a scramble, something like a drawer being pulled open, then the male voice again, "Don't move you son of a bitch! This forty-five'll put a hole in you a car can drive through! Call 911!"

Paco entered the *Sea Bones'* main salon quickly, at the same time reaching behind to lift the back of his shirt and draw his Beretta. He had recovered it from his bag when he and Benito unloaded the dinghy for inflating. In the dark Benito had not noticed him retrieving it. No way, Paco thought, was he going to participate in Benito's burglary without some kind of protection. He now moved purposefully across the main salon following the voices emanating from the staircase. Stopping the 911 call was uppermost in his mind as he went down the stairs.

"There's another one!" the woman's voice yelled.

Paco could see the male turn, waving a large automatic pistol, and without thinking any more about it, lifted the Beretta with its Czech silencer and squeezed the trigger. The Beretta spit silently and the male dropped to the floor almost soundlessly. The woman, getting a good look at Paco and her mouth forming to begin a scream, choked on the 9mm bullet that entered just below her chin, lodging in her spinal column. She, too, collapsed to the floor.

Benito stepped into the hallway holding his computer in front of him, looking down at the two bodies. "Holy Christ almighty, Paco! What have you done?"

"Saved your ass from a few years of prison time for burglary," Paco answered, his heart beating fiercely. "Fucker had a Colt 45 automatic on you."

"What a fuck-up! Let's get out of here. Move it!" Benito ordered. "Keep it quiet and move slowly when we're outside. Check the pier for the security people."

They mounted the transom and dropped into the inflatable dinghy.

Benito dropped his computer into the bottom of the dinghy and took the oars, rowing frantically from behind the *Sea Bones* and around the T-head into the river.

"Give me that damn pistol," Benito ordered.

"No way, Benito," Paco answered. "I'm covering my ass all the way back to Miami with it." He held it tightly against his chest.

Benito lunged forward and grabbed for the pistol. "Give me the goddamn pistol!"

The Beretta silently spit again, the bullet passing through the dinghy's inflated chamber. With no air, the chamber collapsed and the two men were dumped into the river. Benito grabbed the now collapsed dinghy to stay afloat, but it slid under water leaving him to thrash helplessly. Paco surfaced coughing violently, and no swimmer himself, wrapped his arms around Benito's shoulders.

The two of them sank in a burst of bubbles and frantic splashing. The remains of the ruined dinghy floated away with the river, soon to pass into the ocean and ride the Gulfstream north. Benito's briefcase slowly filled with water and sank, joining the Beretta at the bottom of the dark river.

PIRATES' ROUNDTABLE -

A SITUATION OF CONCERN

Date: November 26, 2000

Lat. 46° 95' N, Long. 07° 44' E

Berne, Switzerland

The teleconference began as arranged at 1200 hrs. Zulu, and originated as usual from Berne, Switzerland.

"Gentlemen, we have a real breakthrough in information on the Florida-based treasure venture, some of it good and some of it puzzling, if not troubling.

"First things first: Per our earlier agreement, we hired a private investigation firm in Miami to take a look at the residences of Doctor Ambrose, the venture's suspected financial resource, and the husband-wife team in Gainesville, Florida, that has been conducting historical research, and the US Coast Guard-licensed captain, Jake Porter, probably the operator of any research vessel to be used in the treasure hunt. The mission of our operatives was to surreptitiously examine the premises of each of the participants and look for evidence of research that would reveal the specific vessel being sought and possible location of a wreck site. Particular attention was to be given to any maps or chart lying about, computer files, and print-outs of any data relating to Spanish vessels and treasure.

"We emphasized the importance of giving no hint of our intrusions; nothing was to be taken or disturbed. Our investigators did a superb job at the home of the husband-wife team. Their computer files were downloaded and transmitted to us. I am forwarding those to each of you as I speak so you may examine them at your leisure. As you will see, the professora has downloaded many files from the *Archivo General de Las Indias* in Seville, most of them relating to the nao de chine called *Nuestra Senora de la Concepcion* that set sail from Manila in August 1698, although she also examined two earlier lost galleon as well. Her files contain both the passenger manifest as well as declared cargo. The professora emailed a copy of both to Captain Porter, but not to the doctor. No explanation for that.

"A bonus find was evidence of attempts to break a code. Evidently they have recovered some document that holds a key to either the location of the treasure, or some piece of information necessary to the recovery. Apparently they believe the document contains a code. We have learned that the husband of the chief researcher is a former crypto-analyst for the US Navy, and he is lending his expertise to decrypt the code. He has narrowed his research to the Caesar Shift and the Vigenere Cipher, and some of his notes that were photographed by our investigators indicate that he was teaching or demonstrating how the encryption process works. But unfortunately, there was no evidence of the document or text that they are trying to decrypt."

"If I may interrupt," said Singapore. "Has the captain made any attempt to lease or charter a recovery vessel large enough for this venture? The Lloyd's Register agents and brokers around the world might have some information we could use."

"A good idea," replied Switzerland. "When our investigators visited the boatyard where we supposed Captain Porter could be located, he was not present. There was talk around the yard that Porter was thinking about trucking his own sailing vessel to San Diego, and proceeding across the Pacific. Unlikely, but it bears watching. He may be thinking of a reconnaissance mission to the wreck site to verify their research."

"Anyway, as I said, there is also some news of concern. Our investigators seem to have disappeared. They planned to drive north to Fort Lauderdale to reconnoiter the doctor's marina first and determine the best method for entering the yacht undetected. Next, they were going to the boat yard in Fort Lauderdale where Porter hangs out, then on to Gainesville for a look at the professora's computer files and anything else that was laying about. They planned to enter the doctor's yacht on their return to Fort Lauderdale. But we have received no information from a search of the doctor's yacht. Two days have passed since receiving the download from Gainesville. We made indirect contact with our investigator's office in Miami, and the secretary is also concerned. She has not heard from her boss or his assistant. She insists that this is very unusual."

"A couple of thoughts here," Monaco chimed in. "What's the possibility that our investigators stumbled onto the very thing we are looking for: the location of the wreck site, or something equally valuable unknown to us, and have decided to keep it for themselves, or hold it in ransom for some additional reward."

"A possibility, of course, but I think unlikely," replied Berne. "But you said a couple of thoughts."

"Yeah," Monaco said. "This captain with a boat of his own. I think he's the one we should watch the most carefully. He's the tip of the spear, so to speak. He's the one most likely to make the first move. Those boatyard people mentioned that there was talk of this guy taking off to San Diego, and heading out across the Pacific. If he actually does that, then I think that is a clear sign that this group has some solid evidence of a find. Maybe the captain is going to reconnoiter the site, maybe grab a piece of the treasure if he locates it. But no way is he going to make-off with the bulk of a treasure that filled an almost 200-foot long vessel with a 50-foot beam and more than 20-foot draft. We need to track this guy when he sets out from San Diego. Why not put a birdie on board and let him lead us to the wreck?"

"You're way ahead of me, but I think you make a good case for watching this Captain Porter," Berne said. "However, the disappearance of our investigators has me more concerned at the moment. When they reestablish contact with us and forward information from their search of the doctor's yacht, we will have more information to work with. We could also send a GPS transponder, a "birdie" as you call it, to them and instruct them in how to secret it on Porter's boat while he's still available in Fort Lauderdale. I suggest we give it another day or two before we undertake an alternative plan. One thing is evident from what we know so far: these people are onto something solid, but they are amateurs. They are not our usual competitors. Nevertheless, they may get lucky, and we want to make sure their luck is our luck.

"I'll contact a supplier in the United States and purchase a 'birdie' just in case. Let's keep our fingers crossed for an early reconnect with our investigators and more data from the doctor's boat. I'll contact you as soon as there is anything to report."

Singapore and Monaco agreed and signed off. The conference screen went blank.

ACROSS THE SPANISH LAKE

Alone, alone, all, all alone

Alone on a wide wide sea!

And never a saint took pity on

My soul in agony.

Samuel Taylor Coleridge, Rhyme of the Ancient Mariner

December 6, 2000
Lat. 32° 44'N, Long. 117° 10'W
San Diego, California, USA

(One)

Jake returned from the nearest supermarket with the last of his provisions. The basket attached to the handlebars of the marina's bicycle was stuffed chest-high, and the short luggage carrier over the rear tire had a plastic box lashed with a bungee cord that was stuffed as well. He transferred the load to one of the dock carts and pushed it down alongside the *Giggling Witch*.

By late afternoon, everything was stowed, water topped off, including the four extra 5 gallon plastic jugs, and he was standing on the dock with nothing to do but cast off the lines. He pulled the short list of "things to do" from his shirt pocket and saw that every item had been struck through. Time to go.

He went below to the navigation table, pulled the San Diego harbor chart from the chart drawer and spread it atop the table. He turned on the VHF radio to monitor Channel 16 for boat traffic, started the engine and set it to idle. Then he went topside to cast off the lines. The marina dock was empty; no one to say goodbye to, or to wave him off. He removed the spring line first, then the aft line, and tossed them onto the deck. Then he uncleated the bow line, grabbed the bow pulpit with both hands and pulled himself aboard, giving the dock a bit of a kick to send the *Giggling Witch's* bow away. He returned to the cockpit, placed the engine in forward gear and steered toward the channel. In less than an hour, the *Giggling Witch* was passing through the breakwater and rising to a gentle Pacific swell as the approaching evening's darkness descended over the ocean.

(*Two*)

The telephone in Switzerland rang only once before it was answered with a non-committal "Yah?"

"You should be getting movement on the GPS."

"One moment, please, sir" Pause. "Yah. We got him. Data's coming in fine. He's heading south-southwest at about 5 knots."

"I will be back in Berne tomorrow night. Call me only if there is a fault in the GPS's signal. Understood?

"Yah. Understood, sir."

(Three)

Jake brought the *Giggling Witch's* bow around to head south-southwest on a course of 220 degrees, trimmed the sails, set the autopilot, and made himself comfortable in the cockpit, binoculars near at hand, with the Channel 16 ship-to-ship chatter for company. By one o'clock in the morning, the lights of San Diego had slid below the horizon, leaving only a soft yellow glow. The temperature had dropped sufficiently that he went below to grab a light windbreaker. Returning to stand in the cockpit, he scanned the horizon with the binoculars, pausing to study the red, green and white lights that marked the progress and direction of dozens of commercial vessels approaching and departing one of the busiest ports in the world. Only five thousand miles to go.

PIRATES' ROUNDTABLE - MURDER BY TWO'S

Date: December 7, 2000

Lat. 46º 95' N, Long. 7º 44' E

Berne, Switzerland

(One)

"Gentlemen, a great deal has transpired since we last met. We have some very serious developments. To begin, I flew to Miami, Florida, via New York, then drove a rental car to Fort Lauderdale, with the goal of placing a passive GPS device, what everyone calls a 'birdie", on board the sailboat belonging to Captain Jake Porter so we could track its movements. We got very lucky with the timing. We came close to missing Porter altogether.

"When I arrived at the boat yard, Porter had already hauled his boat, painted the bottom, and hired a trucking firm to transport the boat to California. Porter and his boat had left three days before I arrived. I was able to get the name of the trucking company from the boat yard office under the pretext of needing the same service. I called the trucking office and got the destination of Porter and his boat, a boatyard in San Diego, California, saying I was a crew member joining up with the boat later. Porter's road trip across the country took five days, but after flying to San Diego, I got there the day before Porter arrived. In fact, I was waiting in a rental car at the yard when the boat transport arrived in the late afternoon. Porter's boat was immediately lifted from the transport with the yard's hoist. The mast was unstepped at this point, and as luck would have it, the yard decided to step the mast the next morning just before launching the boat.

"That night, after the yard had shut down, I epoxied the 'birdie' to the top of Porter's mast, right next to the mounting for his masthead light. It was practically invisible. I sat in my car until morning and watched the yard crew hoist the mast into place, secure the rigging, and lower the boat into the water. Porter was standing right alongside his boat while all this was going on, and I was afraid he would see the 'birdie', but the crew had already lifted the mast from the horizontal, and Porter didn't see a thing. It was a close thing, friends, and I can tell you I am not suited for this sort of action.

"So, all of that was successful, but there is other news, very disturbing news. While I was at the boat yard in Fort Lauderdale, I heard people talking about the mysterious disappearance of Doctor Ambrose and a young woman named Brenda Warren, who worked at the yard painting names on sailboats. The talk was all about the discovery of the bodies of Ambrose and this Brenda aboard the *Sea Bones*, the doctor's boat. They had been murdered. Both shot at close range.

"Needless to say, that was unsettling to hear since Ambrose is the principal that we have identified as the most likely financial source behind the Florida-based treasure recovery effort we have been following these past weeks. But it gets worse. The local newspaper also reported the local police discovering a vehicle belonging to our detective. Our detective's secretary had filed a missing person's report for the detective and an acquaintance of his believed to be in his company. The automobile was found parked at a public boat ramp just down the river from where Doctor Ambrose's body was discovered. In the front set of the detective's car was a receipt from a nearby marine store indicating the purchase of an inflatable rubber dinghy. The dinghy and the two men are missing.

The police have not made any connection between the murders and our detective. But it is not difficult for us to realize that there is definitely a connection. Four people dead, and what exactly transpired is a complete mystery. Why our detective would kill someone is beyond me. If it turns out he did not kill them, then who did, and why? And where is our detective and his acquaintance? He is most likely dead since his car has been abandoned and he has not called in to his office. But who killed him, and what were the circumstances? Is it possible there are other players of whom we are unaware? Lots of questions, but no answers. Any comments from you gentlemen?

Singapore: "From the very beginning, this Florida thing has been kind of screwy. No corporate names. No heavy hitters. No history of marine salvage work. No past treasure hunting experience. Just a series of strange, but focused research and well-informed inquiries about specific Manila galleons that were lost at sea. Then those photographs taken in the professora's apartment indicating that they were trying to break a Viginere-coded message. What message? What have they found that has them so motivated? Now, we see that Porter has crossed the country, launched his boat into the Pacific with the obvious intention to sailing to the treasure. Does he know the Doctor and this Brenda are dead? Did he kill them and is now escaping across the Pacific? Is any of this making any sense?"

Monaco: "Well, we had them figured for amateurs, and I don't see anything to change our minds about that. This thing with the deaths of 4 people is the really puzzling part. Two of theirs, two of ours. But what's the connection? It looks to me like we have nothing left to do but follow Porter and his boat and see where he's bound for and what he's up to."

Berne: "I agree. We are receiving updates of Porter's progress across the Pacific. His boat is making about five-and a-half knots. It appears he is following the same trade route taken by the galleons. We can only wait to see what direction he ultimately steers for. He has a plan, this Porter. Of that I am sure. I'll keep you informed. Given the distances, our next news is probably a month or two away at the earliest."

End of Transmission

CRUCIBLE OF DEATH

15 June 1944

Lat. 15º 15′ N, Long. 145º 45′ E

Saipan Island, Northern Marianas

Lieutenant General Yoshitsugu Saito, commander of the 43rd Division of the Japanese Imperial Army swallowed deeply as he scanned the western horizon from a cave above Garapan, the largest town on the island of Saipan. Although the enemy's entire invasion fleet of 535 warships was not visible to him, he was awed by the hundreds that were spread before him as far as he could see. He knew with a fatalistic certainly that today was the day the round-eyed Yankees would storm ashore.

Their arrival was not unexpected. Saipan had received a wake-up call four months earlier with a ferocious aerial thrashing by U.S. Navy carrier-based aircraft on February 23rd. Over one-hundred Japanese aircraft were destroyed on the ground, and of seventy-four other aircraft that got airborne to meet the enemy, only seven retuned safely to their bases. That brought an end to the quiet life that Saipan had enjoyed for the two years of war following the attack on Pearl Harbor.

General Saito had received the last of his reinforcements in late May. Although tiny Saipan was only 13 miles long (about the length of Manhattan Island) and ranged from barely two-and-one-half to 5 miles in width, a sparse total area of 85 square miles, it now teemed with almost 32,000 Japanese defenders, including 800 elite Imperial Navy Marines, all ready to die for their emperor.

The island's rugged volcanic topography with thousands of caves and 70 percent of its surface area covered by dense sugar cane fields made it a defender's paradise. In the center of the island, a jagged ridge dominated the space between 1,554-foot Mount Tapotchau and Mount Marpi at the northern end, this ridge punctuated by deadly peaks and escarpments.

But General Saito's battle strategy called for repulsing the enemy at the beaches, not within the rugged interior. From the village of Charan Kanoa in the south, to the town of Garapan and the village of Tanapag in the north, all artillery, mortars and machineguns were zeroed in on the reefs and approaches to the western side of the island. The general smiled; the Yankees would be mercilessly slaughtered.

A few days earlier, on June 11th, the huge American invasion armada that was approaching Saipan struck airfields on both Saipan and nearby Tinian island with 208 fighters and 8 torpedo bombers. General Saito had also been informed that American demolitions teams, "frogmen," were observed scouring the reefs in front of Saipan's western coastal towns of Charan Kanoa and Garapan. As the cane fields above Charan Kanoa blazed from the recent aerial bombardment and thick smoke descended the slopes toward the beaches, General Saito finally decided to move the troops he had positioned at Magicienne Bay on the eastern side of the island where he originally thought the enemy would come ashore. All available forces now faced west. Two days later, on the 13th, the enemy's battleships began to bombard the island's west coast. But the Americans were new to the game of naval warfare and their gunnery for all its ferocity was having very little effect on the well-entrenched Japanese.

Offshore on D-Day, June 15th, the invasion fleet formed up while the final shelling and aerial bombardments pounded the four-mile assault front stretching from Charan Kanoa to almost five miles north to Garapan. To the U.S. Marines of the 2nd and 4th Marine Divisions, Saipan itself was barely discernable through the glowing red smoke and burning buildings. They clambered into their amphtracks, rapidly chewing gum and glancing nervously toward the dark purple shape taking form in the early morning light, waiting for the huge LSTs to ferry them into hell.

At 0700 hours, Vice Admiral Richmond Kelly Turner, commander of the Joint Expeditionary Force, gave the order, "Land the landing force!" The naval bombardment was lifted, and two miles from the beaches, 34 LSTs crammed with eight battalions of Marines drew up to their lines of departure. They disgorged 719 amphtracs which spun away toward the village of Charan Kanoa like crazed water beetles, and all went well until they were about 800 yards from the beach. Then, a concentrated fusillade of Japanese mortar fire and artillery descended upon them; several amphtracts received direct hits and sank immediately with all hands. The remainder, along with 18 amphibian tanks, clambered over the reefs to reach the beach. Within 20 minutes, eight thousand Marines were ashore and fighting for their lives as pre-sighted Japanese artillery and withering machinegun fire raked their ranks.

The Marines quickly realized that Charan Kanoa was not a paper and bamboo native village covered by blooming bougainvillea, but rather a deadly complex of one and two-story concrete buildings with interlocking fields of fire from automatic weapons and countless dozens of one-man "spider holes." On the first day of the battle, two thousand Marines, mostly teenagers, were killed or wounded before even half of the assault front was secured. Once the beachhead was in hand, the Marines were joined by soldiers of the U.S. Army's 27th Division and pushed inland, cutting the island in half on the third day, June 18th.

But splitting the island in two was only a momentary chapter in the bloody agonies that both the Japanese and the Americans would inflict upon one another in the coming weeks. Fierce, savage fighting would continue yard by yard as the Americans drove the Japanese toward Marpi Point at the northern tip of the island. Thousands of Japanese civilians were also being driven before the onslaught, and when they reached the end of the island at the cliffs of Marpi Point, they began to commit suicide by leaping onto the rocks and surf almost a thousand feet below. Men threw their children off the cliff, then followed. Mothers leaped to certain death with their babies in their arms. Later, a U.S. Navy lieutenant aboard a minesweeper told of seeing a pregnant woman's nude body with her newborn's head protruding from between her legs, and floating bodies so thick that it was impossible to steer the boat without running over them.

On July 9th at 1614 hours, almost a month after the initial assault of June 15th, Admiral Turner declared Saipan secured, but in fact there remained thousands of deadly fanatical Japanese soldiers hiding in caves who would have to be rooted out one by one in the coming weeks. In the end, over 30,000 Japanese soldiers, almost the entire garrison, died at the hands of the United States Marines and the U.S. Army's 27th Division. Two out of three Japanese civilians, at least 22,000 of them, also died. Lieutenant General Yoshitsugu Saito, Major General Keiji Igeta, chief of staff of the 31st Imperial Japanese Army and ironically, disgraced Vice Admiral Chuichi Nagumo, commander of the Japanese fleet that had attacked Pearl Harbor, all committed *seppuku* (slicing open their stomachs) and had junior officers shoot them in the back of their heads, then burn their bodies.

For the Americans, the less than 4 weeks of fighting for control of the island's pitiful 85 square miles of land resulted in over 14,000 killed, wounded or missing, most of them Marines of the 2nd and 4th Marine

Divisions. It was more than double the earlier losses at Guadacanal. But now the Japanese homeland was vulnerable to airstrikes; the airfield at the southern end of Saipan would begin immediately to serve as the jumping-off place for B-29 bomber raids on Tokyo. And from Tinian, the slightly smaller Marianas island just three miles away, the most famous of all B-29 Superfortress bombers, the *Enola Gay*, would soon deliver to the Japanese homeland the atomic holocaust answer for Pearl Harbor and all the misery that the Japanese Imperial Empire had brought upon so many millions of innocent people throughout Asia and the rest of the world.

SAIPAN

Date: February 25, 2001
Lat. 15º, 15' North
Long. 145º, 45 East
Saipan, Northern Marianas

(One)

Mount Tapotchau, Saipan's highest elevation, was the first to poke its nose above the western horizon. The 1,554-foot peak rose slowly, an indistinct bump whose dark base grew and broadened imperceptibly as the *Giggling Witch* rode the rising Pacific swell pushing her westward. Within the hour a second peak came into view, the top of Mount Tipo Pale breaking the surface to the left of Mount Tapotchau.

Jake had been scouring the horizon in anticipation of the island since first light. He had passed from the navigation table to the cockpit a dozen times in the past few hours. The GPS receiver showed he was a little over 40 miles east of the island. Earlier he had taken his brass dividers, set them to the *Giggling Witch's* speed of 7 knots, then walked them across the chart from the latest GPS position to Nafutan Point, Saipan's southernmost tip. Jake calculated that he would enter Saipan Channel between Tinian Island and Saipan, then round Agingan Point about mid-day. As the morning light strengthened, he saw the minute silvery flash of an airliner descending steeply toward the island from the south. The island grew over the next several hours until its burgeoning green bulk eventually filled all of the horizon to starboard of the *Giggling Witch's* bow. Small houses with shiny tin roofs began to appear sprinkled among the lush, dark-green foliage. Another airliner, its gear extended for a landing, passed ahead of him and he heard the faint roar of its engines.

Then, for the first time since the evening lights of San Diego had slipped below the horizon two and one-half months earlier, Jake changed course and trimmed the mainsail sheet. He brought the *Giggling Witch's* bow to point slightly higher to starboard, then went below to retrieve a slice of bread from the galley. He smothered it with orange marmalade, poured a fresh cup of coffee and returned topside to sit atop the *Giggling Witch's* cabin trunk, his back against the mainmast and his bare feet propped against the starboard lifelines. A school of twenty or more dolphins sped silently alongside, crisscrossing and feinting gracefully in front of the bow just beneath the surface.

A short while later, as the *Giggling Witch's* bow came abreast of Agingan Point, Jake left his perch atop the cabin and settled in behind the helm. He disengaged the windvane's automatic steering, tightened the mainsail, forestaysail and jib sheets and felt his sailboat settle into her new course to parallel Saipan's reef-strewn west coast. As he passed into the lee of the island, suddenly his senses were assaulted by the luxuriant, earthy smell of vegetation and he saw the beginning of the off-lying coral reef protecting Saipan's western beaches.

The surf foamed brilliantly white as it smashed against the coral barrier; seaward of the reef the water was a vibrant emerald green, while the sheltered lagoon-side was a deep sapphire blue. Beyond the piercingly-white beaches the island rose steeply, the slopes covered in a profusion of blossoming bougainvillea and bright vermillion flame trees. The shoreline was bustling with local traffic, small autos and microbuses, motor scooters, bicycles and pedestrians. Jake scanned the activity hungrily with his binoculars.

Having reached Agingan Point, Jake was able with the binoculars to peer the two miles ahead to see the tightly clustered village of Charan Kanoa sprawling up the slopes, and four miles beyond it the taller buildings of Garapan. Half-way between Agingan Point and Garapan, the shoreline jutted seaward to form Afetna Point where Jake spied the rusty hulks of two American amphibious tanks hung-up on the reef, their gun barrels askew but still pointing toward an enemy long since defeated.

The closing hour of his voyage brought him into the company of dozens of brightly colored windsurfers, darting in every direction in front of Garapan's reef. A number of them sailed alongside the *Giggling Witch* for a closer look at the graceful sailboat with the strange maroon-colored sails and Chinese junk rig.

Tourists, Jake realized, *and damned if they weren't Japanese!* One particularly attractive woman with slender, shapely legs and wearing the briefest of bikinis came abreast of the cockpit to wave. Jake, smiling, doffed his visored sailing cap and self-consciously rubbed his two-month growth of beard. The Japanese windsurfer, her breasts squeezed seductively together by her grip on the sail's wishbone, smiled shyly then shifted to the opposite tack and sped away.

The first break in the reef opposite Garapan was marked with a large steel buoy painted black and white. Jake steered the *Giggling Witch* into the lagoon, slacked all sheets as he rounded the buoy and surveyed the shoreline for a marina or anchorage. Two steel island freighters with rusty topsides, one of about 150-feet in length and the other perhaps 90 feet, were anchored before the town, and behind them was a small marina with maybe a couple of dozen small power boats, and a few sailboats.

Further up the shoreline, toward the village of Tanapag, Jake could see another gathering of sailboat masts and for no particular reason headed that way. Closing with the shore and approaching the cluster of sailboats, he saw lying alongside the marina's longest pier a broad-beamed, double-ended ketch flying a New Zealand flag from its mizzenmast. Jake started up the diesel engine and let it idle while he went forward to douse the sails. The *Giggling Witch* slowed, and after securing the sails, Jake slipped the engine into forward gear, letting his boat idle slowly toward the opposite side of the pier with the New Zealand ketch.

A sandy-haired and deeply-tanned young boy of about 10 years of age stepped from the New Zealand ketch onto the pier to take the *Giggling Witch's* bow line that Jake tossed to him. He was followed by a lean and equally-tanned sailor, barefooted and with a floppy handmade canvas hat topping long sun-bleached hair. He caught the stern line and made it fast to one of the pier's large galvanized iron cleats.

"Welcome to Saipan, Yank," said the smiling New Zealander, offering his hand as Jake stepped onto the pier.

"Thank you. Jake Porter," Jake replied, taking the New Zealander's hand while savoring solid land for the first time in over two and one-half months.

"Malcom Lassiter, and this is my son, Liam," he said, putting his hand on his son's shoulder. Liam, wearing a Maori-patterned bathing suit and a black coral necklace with a white shark's tooth hanging from the center, smiled brightly and shook Jake's hand just as his father had.

"Unless I miss my guess, mate," Malcom said, " you'd be game for a cold beer. What say?"

"You'll get no argument here," Jake said.

Malcom Lassiter turned to his boat and called out, "Hallo, Lizzie! A beer for our new neighbor."

A trim brunette in her mid-thirties came up the ketch's companionway, stepping expertly into the cockpit and over the coaming with three beers in hand. She wore a brightly patterned native-style wrap-around and was also barefoot and tanned. "I'm well ahead of you, luv," she said with a smile, and handed beers to the two men.

Malcom Lassiter introduced his wife, and no sooner had Jake taken the beer in his hand than he saw the head of a young girl of about seven or eight years old pop up through the ketch's fo'c'sle hatch, see the activity on the pier and come bounding down the deck, over the lifelines and onto the pier.

"And this is our daughter, Tess," Malcom said proudly. "Tess, this is Captain Porter."

"Pleased to meet you, sir," Tess said brightly. "What's your boat's name?"

"The *Giggling Witch*," Jake answered.

"Oh, that is so funny!" Tess said with a wide smile. "Is she named after your wife?"

"Tess!" her mother exclaimed, then turned to Jake with exasperation in her voice. "Children growing up on sailboats can be so precocious. Please excuse my daughter."

Jake was laughing. Turning to little Tess, he said "Actually I've thought that might have been how the former owner came to call her that myself. But I really don't know, Tess. That was her name when I bought her. And as you know, sailors say it's bad luck to change a boat's name."

Little Tess beamed at Jake's coming to her defense. He had won her heart in a single stroke.

"Where have you come from?" her brother Liam asked politely.

"San Diego, California," Jake answered.

"Non-stop?" Malcom Lassiter asked, appreciating from a small boat sailor's perspective the great distance such a voyage involved.

"Yes," Jake said. "Actually I began the trip from Fort Lauderdale, Florida. I wanted to catch the season's southeast trades, but I made the decision too late to go via the Panama Canal. So I had my boat trucked to the West Coast, and left San Diego 79 days ago. It's been a long haul."

"Most sailors take what they call the Milk Run, across the southern Pacific through the Marquesas, Tahiti and the Society Islands, and Tonga," Malcom observed. "But you sound like a man on a mission. You wouldn't happen to have been a U.S. Marine, would you?" he asked.

"Yes, I was in the Marine Corps," Jake said, "But why do you ask?"

"I thought you might have been trying to get here in a hurry because of the ceremonies scheduled for the American Memorial Park next month," Malcom said.

"And the rededication of the church," Malcom's wife, Lizzie, added. "It was the only church on Saipan when the Marines landed to take the island from the Japanese, and it was destroyed during the battle for the island. The Marines made a $5,000 donation toward having it rebuilt. There are some Marine Corps veterans of the Saipan invasion coming for the ceremony next week."

"Right you are, Lizzie. The Santa Remideo Catholic Church in Tanapag. It's just a short walk from here," Malcom said. "By the way, Jake, this is the Micro Beach Marina. It's owned and run by the local government.

299

And if you just walk across that road," he said, pointing to the busy road at the far end of the pier, " you're in the American Memorial Park. That's the Beach Road, it's called."

"The park is so lovely, Jake," Lizzie said. "So many Americans lost their lives here, mostly Marines, and they've built a beautiful memorial. There's the Court of Honor and the Flag Circle with the dedication plaques and names of those killed or missing in action. But my favorite is the Carillion Bell Tower. It's made of speckled black and pink marble, and tolls every half-hour. At different times during the day it plays the American and Marianas national anthems, then the Marine Corps hymn and other patriotic songs. At the end of each day, it plays Taps. It's very moving."

"Sounds great," Jake said with a smile, "But to tell you the truth, the only thing I have on my mind right now is checking into a hotel for a hot fresh water shower, a steak dinner prepared by someone other than me, and a good night's sleep on a non-rocking bed."

Malcom and Lizzie laughed together. "We know that one, mate. That's for sure."

"We recommend the Dai Ichi," Lizzie said. "It's more intimate than the Hyatt and not quite so pricey. It's just down the Beach Road in Garapan. The service is terrific, the water hot, and massages in the spa are heavenly."

"It's less than a half-mile to the hotel. You can use one of our bikes if you want," Malcom offered.

"What's the drill on checking in with Immigration and Customs?" Jake asked.

"You're a U.S. citizen and Saipan's a part of the U.S. Commonwealth of the Marianas. So there's not much to it. Immigration and Customs are both located at the airport, but you can leave your passport with the marina office and they'll call the officials for you," Malcom said.

"Well, I'm off then. I'll take you up on the loan of the bike," Jake said. He went below on the *Giggling Witch* and tossed a change of clothes and his toilet kit into a canvas sport bag, returned topside, closed all the hatches and walked the bike down the pier to the marina office. The pretty Chamorro desk clerk took his passport and gave him a key to the marina's shower. She explained that laundry could be left in the morning and would be returned in the late afternoon. His bill could be paid upon his departure, or once a week, whichever occurred first. Before Jake could turn and leave, the clerk asked, "Are you a Marine?"

"I was, yes," Jake answered, perplexed as to why she would ask.

"Welcome to Saipan, Marine," she said, with a thoroughly sincere smile.

(Two)
When Jake awoke, his first thought was one of incredulity, that he was actually no longer on a tiny sailboat in the middle of the Pacific Ocean, but had arrived safely and was now lying on a queen-size bed in an air conditioned hotel located on a 13-mile-long tropical island 3,500 miles downwind from San Diego. The Dai Ichi was everything Malcom and Lizzie had described. After checking in the evening before, he had gone immediately to his room and taken the longest shower of his life, luxuriating in the hot, stinging spray of fresh water.

Refreshed and with a change of clothes, he went down to the hotel's restaurant and wolfed down a magnificent steak tenderized in the Japanese Kobe-style and served by a graceful Chamorro waitress with a flaming red blossom in her long, shiny black hair. He spied a barbershop across the hotel's lobby and went in for a haircut and shave. When he returned to his room, he took another shower, not so long as the first and then collapsed on the bed to instantly fall asleep.

Now, the following morning, Jake picked up his wristwatch from the night table. It read 9 AM. Surprised that he had slept so late, he got out of bed and threw open the room's curtains. The view took him aback. He was on the hotel's fourth floor, and as far as he could see was the deep blue of the great Pacific Ocean. It rose to meet the horizon in a clean, sharp line against the sky's lighter blue; a massive, dominating presence not in the least troubled by the island upon which Jake stood. Below, the smaller of the two freighters that had been anchored in the lagoon when he arrived the day before had cleared the reef and was now steaming slowly toward Tinian Island in the near distance. To his right, looking north, was what Jake knew from his nautical chart to be Managaha Island, a tiny coral island less than a half-mile off Tanapag's beach. The day's windsurfers were already zipping back and forth to its broad white beach, and a small ferry boat was hauling tourists out for a picnic and swim in the azure waters surrounding the island.

Directly in front of the Dai Ichi and across the Beach Road was what appeared to be Garapan's main marina, filled mostly with small fiberglass runabouts. The exceptions were about a half-dozen 40-foot sport fishers with high Biminis topped by VHF antennas, and a couple of rather large multihulls, one a trimaran and the other a catamaran. The night before, Jake had picked up a color brochure from a rack in the Dai Ichi's lobby that advertised sightseeing and diving trips. One of the boats featured in the brochure was a 70-foot trimaran called the *Titan III*. There being only one tri-hulled vessel of that size in the marina, Jake correctly guessed the green-hulled trimaran with the orange trim and green-and-white striped cockpit shade to be the *Titan III*.

Jake took one last shower, put on a pair of light tropical trousers, a short sleeved sport shirt and his reef-walker sandals, then went down to the Dai Ichi's lobby to check out. He grabbed breakfast in the hotel's restaurant and read the day's copy of the *Saipan Tribune* that had been left at his room's door. He was amused to see that for all its tropical beauty, Saipan had not escaped the trials and tribulations that beset a modern society. The *Tribune* reported of government chicanery and

302

missing funds, citizens protesting the rise in prostitution and the growing number of poker parlors, and the current plunge in tourism dollars owing to the collapse of the Asian economy. There was an article about Japan Airlines promising to bring more Japanese to visit the island and spend their money there. In another article, Saipan's garment industry, employing mostly Chinese workers, was credited with keeping the local economy afloat during the current economic crisis.

Before paying his bill, and after some thought, Jake decided to place a telephone call to Bryce Taggart's university office in Gainesville; just a heads-up in case there was a breakthrough in their research. He left a message on Tag's answering machine. He purposely didn't call Bryce and Stacy at home because with the time difference it was the middle of the night there. The message he left said simply, "I've arrived in Saipan. Long trip, but all is well. Beautiful island. I will refresh supplies, and wait for a turn of weather next month. I'll call before I leave. You can leave a message for me at the Micro Beach Marina in Tanapag. I'm made up to the dock there."

With that done, Jake paid his hotel bill, retrieved his borrowed bicycle from the rack in front of the hotel and walked across the Beach Road to the marina where the *Titan III* was berthed. The morning traffic was brisk and Jake was amazed at the cultural diversity of the pedestrians; native Chamorros and Carolinians, Filipinos, Thais, Chinese and countless American and Japanese tourists. The Japanese tourists were easily identified by their Hollywood-style sunglasses and the Nikon cameras hanging around their necks. Most of the Americans were older males, a few accompanied by their wives. They tended to be wearing bright, flowery Hawaiian shirts and Bermuda-style shorts.

Once in the marina, Jake laid the bike against one of the pier's pilings, and walked down the dock toward the big green trimaran. The closer he got, the rougher the boat looked. It was obvious that the charter trade was banging her up pretty badly. Dive charters in particular are hard on a boat; all the diving tanks, weight belts and gear take a toll. But for all her cosmetic bumps and scrapes, the *Titan III* still looked more than seaworthy.

A small group of American tourists was gathered at the boarding steps alongside the trimaran and being ushered aboard by a stocky, barefoot Chamorro wearing baggy canvas sailing shorts, an orange tee-shirt with big green letters spelling "Titan III Charters" across the front, and a dark blue New York Yankees ball cap. He greeted Jake with a wide, toothy smile.

"Going sightseeing with us today? We're takin' in what we Saipanians call 'Laderan Banadero,' or 'Suicide Cliff' where the Japs jumped to their deaths during the battle for Saipan. Four hours dock to dock, and my wife fixes a dynamite lunch along the way. Name's Sammy T," he said, extending his hand.

"Actually I've had enough boat and water for a while. Just spent two and a half months getting here," Jake answered with a smile.

"Hey, that wasn't you that came into the harbor yesterday afternoon in the boat with the Chinese lug rig, was it?"

"That was me," Jake said.

"Man, that's a fine looking boat. You up at the Micro Beach marina?" Sammy T asked.

"Yes. I crashed last night at the Dai Ichi and I saw your brochure in the rack in the lobby. I'm interested in doing some diving while I'm on the island. Awhile back, I read a National Geographic article about a Spanish galleon that went aground here," Jake said, taking an immediate liking to this friendly fellow sailor.

"I have to tell you, there's not much to see where the galleon came ashore," Sammy T said. "And it's a rough place to dive, too. You have to pick the weather for it. Even when it's calm, there's a heavy surge and undertow. And right now, I expect to be booked 'most every day taking War Two Marines and their families to the north end of the island to see where the Japs made their last stand."

"Well, it's not exactly at the top of my list, so there's no big rush," Jake said. "I'll stop by from time to time to see how your schedule is going," Jake said, offering a handshake in departure.

"I forgot to ask where you sailed in from," Sammy T said, taking Jake's hand.

"San Diego," Jake answered.

"You sailing solo?" Sammy T asked.

"Yeah, just me and the autopilot," Jake said.

"You pushing to get here for the ceremonies at the American Memorial Park next month?" Sammy T asked, then added "You a former Marine?"

"I just found out about the ceremonies yesterday when I arrived," Jake answered. "And yeah, I was in the Corps."

"Me, too," Sammy T said, lifting the left sleeve of his tee shirt to expose a tattoo of the Marine Corps emblem with 'Semper Fi' beneath it. "Kind of a family tradition. My Dad was in the Corps and my younger brother is in right now. Me, I just wanted to be able to vote in the stateside presidential elections."

"Well, Paris Island boot camp and four years in the Marine Corps is a hell of way to win the vote," Jake said with a smile.

"I did my boot camp at Camp Pendleton in California. Actually, I had pretty easy duty in the Corps compared to most. They sent me to the

Navy's culinary school and I ended up cooking for the brass on troop transports. Cooked for the First Marine Division commander's mess tent in the Gulf War. You catch any of the Iraqi deployment?" Sammy T asked.

"Yeah, a little piece of it," Jake said. "I was in the Second Marines," he added.

"What was your duty?" Sammy T asked.

"I was assigned to a STA team," Jake answered, pronouncing it 'stay'.

"Surveillance and Target Acquisition, right? Sammy T said. "Damn! That's hardcore. You were a sniper?"

"I had easy duty like you in the beginning. I got good scores on the weapons range and I made the Corps' rifle team. Traveled a lot representing the Corps in competition matches. Then I was teaching marksmanship to officers at Quantico, and taking college classes at night. Saddam screwed that up and I went to Saudi Arabia with the Second Marines. Fortunately, it was a short war," Jake said. Then to change the subject, "I get asked a lot here about whether I am or was a Marine. That a holdover from World War Two?"

"Yeah. Memories run strong here. The Japs were bad news during the occupation. They also brought a lot of Japanese civilians to Saipan before Pearl Harbor, and pretty much took over things," Sammy T said. "But most of the Jap civilians were killed or committed suicide when the Marines came ashore. Lots of Chamorros died during the invasion, too. Everybody on the island lost someone. It's not the sort of stuff that's easily forgotten."

"No, I guess not," Jake said. "For such a small island I notice there seems to be quite a diversity in cultures."

"The island of Guam, 300 miles south of us, is where you'll find the real melting pot. Just about every Pacific Rim culture is represented there. Guam was U.S. territory before War Two and the Americans still have a huge military presence there," Sammy T said. "Saipan is so small and so far off the beaten track of Pacific commerce that we are kind of a backwater. Government payroll, tourism and garment manufacturing are about all that's happening here these days. Our language is Chamorro, but English and American History are required subjects in school. Depending upon their ancestry, some islanders speak Carolinian. A few of the grandparents speak a little Japanese they learned during the war, but the language is not taught here. Hotel employees and some of the retail business owners speak a little Japanese, too."

"Do many of the Japanese tourists charter your boat?" Jake asked.

"Oh yeah," Sammy said. "The Japs have plenty of money. Most of them want to drop flowers in the ocean off Marpi Point to honor their war dead and take pictures of the cliffs. But the last three or four years I've been getting more and more Navy and Marine Corps veterans. The War Two veterans are in their 70s and 80s now and dying off fast. I read somewhere that about a thousand War Two veterans die every day. They'll soon all be gone. Looks like the Japs will take Saipan after all," he said with a rueful smile.

"The difference though," Jake observed, " is that they'll be passing through Customs bringing Japanese Yen and not rifles, and they will be customers, not oppressors."

"Yeah, you're right. And the Marines had a hand in that, didn't they?" Sammy said proudly with a wide grin.

"Yes they did," Jake said, curiously pleased with the thought.

Two more American tourist couples came down the dock and Sammy T, looking over Jake's shoulder, greeted them. "Good morning, Marines," he said jovially.

"How'd you know we were Marines," growled one of them, both of his forearms heavily tattooed and his plump wife tugging at his flashy Hawaiian shirt.

"Just a guess, sir. Just a lucky guess," Sammy T answered. "You looking for a boat ride to Suicide Cliff?"

"Yeah, that's right," the other age-weathered Marine answered in a slightly less gruff tone. "The last boat ride I had off this frigging island was taking Jap machine-gun fire and I didn't have much of a chance to look around."

"Well, the only thing you'll be dodging on this ride is my wife's buffet lunch," Sammy T said. "Step aboard." He gave Jake a surreptitious wink.

"Well, I'll be off as well," Jake said. "Stop by the *Giggling Witch* when you have a chance and I'll give you a tour. I'll check in with you from time to time to see if a dive charter is shaping up. I expect to be around for the next month or so until the weather changes"

"Okay, Jake. Always glad to have another jarhead around," Sammy T said.

(Three)
As he turned off the Beach Road in front of the Micro Beach Marina and dismounted from the bicycle, Jake saw that Malcom and Lizzie were entertaining some other boat folks, and several of them were standing on the dock alongside the *Giggling Witch*. As he approached, pushing Malcom's bicycle, little Tess came running down the dock. She did a quick double-take at Jake's freshly shaven face, then yelped.

"Oooh, you're so handsome, Captain Porter. You look different without the beard," she said in a squeaky voice.

Jake couldn't help laughing. "Thank you, Tess. What's the happening at your boat?"

"Oh, just the usual," she sighed. "Yachties coming over to chat. But no one's got anybody my age, or Liam's. It's so boring. Charts and weather and harbors and sailing routes are all they talk about. We want to toss our Frisbee, but mom and dad won't let us go into the park without an adult. Would you go with us?" she beseeched in a plaintive voice.

"I don't see why not," Jake said. "Let me drop off my kit and open the *Witch's* hatches first."

"Oh goody!" she squealed and ran to her boat yelling for her brother.

Malcom Lassiter stepped onto the dock and took the bicycle from Jake. "All right, mate! You look like a new man without that beard," he said pleasantly, offering his hand.

"Tess says I'm downright handsome," Jake answered.

Malcom laughed. "She's growing up fast, that one," he said. "Thanks for taking the heat off of us on going to the park. The kids have been bugging us all morning to go play Frisbee with them. But as you can see, we've been descended upon by our marina neighbors. The two English boats are leaving on Monday, so we're having a bon voyage gathering."

"No problem," Jake said.

"Have a beer with us before you go to the park. By the time you get back, Lizzie will have a decent meal together. We bought two huge mahi mahi from a fisherman this morning. Lizzie is going to grill them with a pineapple and soy sauce marinade that is simply fabulous " he said.

It was more than an hour before Jake, Liam and Tess could clear the marina for the American Memorial Park. No sooner had Jake opened the *Giggling Witch's* hatches and rigged the sun awning with the help of the kids, than some of the sailors at Malcom and Lizzie's party spilled across the dock to strike up a conversation with the new arrival and take a closer look at the steel sailboat with the Chinese rig.

Jake patiently answered their questions about his experience with steel boat construction and maintenance, and the inevitable questions about the sailing performance of the Chinese lug rig. But noticing Liam's and Tess' growing impatience with the adult boat talk, Jake excused himself, explaining his promise to play Frisbee.

The three of them crossed the Beach Road and entered the American Memorial Park. The first thing Jake noticed was the immaculately trimmed grass, a thick golf course-type of Bermuda. The memorial itself was perhaps a hundred yards or so into the park, prominent for its gleaming white marble countenance and the ring of flags flying from its top. There were a couple of dozen people gathered around the memorial, mostly in groups of two or four. Several were sitting on the broad steps, leaning forward deep in thought or subdued conversation. A few sat alone, heads in hands, or simply staring across the park. The clusters were mostly centered around the dedication plaques reading the inscriptions.

Liam and Tess had sprinted ahead in youthful exuberance, laughing and slinging the Frisbee out ahead of them, then racing to catch it before it hit the ground. Jake followed them until they had gone well past the memorial and circled to toss the Frisbee to each other. Jake joined the circle and became absorbed in the kids' enthusiasm.

For the next hour, the three of them ran and tossed the Frisbee with abandon. Little Tess, for all of her 8 years of age, had the technique down pat and was as skillful as her brother, lacking only Liam's strength for distance. They formed now a large circle and were alternating turns when a strange thing happened.

Tess had just thrown a high-speed zinger to Jake, heading straight for his head. In the moment just before he would have reached up to snatch the Frisbee, Jake was taken by an irresistible urge to turn to his right. What he saw, at a distance, was a native woman bending gracefully at the knees to lay a bouquet of flowers on the ground. Two children of about Tess' age stood beside her. Just as Jake's gaze fell upon her, she stood up and turned to look in Jake's direction as if suddenly sensing his attention. The children followed her gaze and each instinctively took one of her hands.

At that moment, the Frisbee struck Jake squarely in the back of his head. But Jake never took his eyes from the woman who, seeing the Frisbee strike Jake, raised her hand to her mouth.

Jake couldn't tell if the hand-to-mouth gesture was to cover a laugh, or one of surprise, or perhaps bewilderment. But before he could give it any further thought, Tess had run up and grabbed him around the waist.

"Oh! I'm so sorry, Captain Porter. I thought you were ready," Tess said. A frown of genuine concern crossed her brow.

Jake broke his gaze and looked down at Tess, smiling. "My fault, Tess. I wasn't looking," he said.

"I know," Tess giggled. "You were looking at that pretty native girl."

"I guess I was," Jake said, returning his gaze in the direction of the distraction, but all he caught was a glimpse of the young woman's back and the two little girls trailing her as they hurriedly left the park. He was left with a puzzling sense of loss, of disappointment, and didn't really understand why.

They made their way back across the Beach Road and onto the Micro Beach Marina dock. The bon voyage festivities for the departing English couples were well underway; the smoky aroma from the mahi mahi steaks on the grill was thick and inviting. All the adults had a beer or a glass of wine in hand and the conversations were animated.

"Hey, Jake!" Malcom yelled from the grill waving a spatula, "What'll you have, mate? Beer or a wine cooler?"

"A beer for me," Jake said. "Let me change into a clean shirt. The kids have me sweating like a pig." Jake crossed the dock and went down below on the *Giggling Witch*. He sat on the salon settee for a moment and thought about the young woman he had seen in the memorial park. Why he was so drawn to thinking about her was a mystery. The way he had been enticed into looking at her was also strange. An irresistible impulse of some kind.

And the way she had looked at him, as though she was as taken by the moment as he. But why did she leave so quickly? And were those her children? It just didn't make any sense, but he was nevertheless left with a sense of incompleteness. He pulled on a tee-shirt and crossed over the dock to the party, taking a beer from Lizzie and sitting down on the cockpit coaming next to little Tess and her brother, Liam.

The bon voyage party lasted until a little after midnight. Tess and Liam had long since been put to bed when Jake stood to leave. Malcom crossed the dock with him to the *Giggling Witch*. "You seem to have been a bit distracted this evening, Jake."

Jake recounted the incident in the American Memorial Park earlier in the day, and the strange feeling he had when he first saw the young woman with the two children leaving flowers at the grave site.

"Sounds like one of those 'thunderbolt' encounters you read about in romance novels," Malcom said. "The children with her were not necessarily her own, you know. And that grave you're talking about belongs to the Saipanian fellow who helped the Marines find the hidden Japs during the World War II invasion. I can't pronounce his name in Chamorro, but he's the only non-American buried in the park. There's a movement afoot to create a larger memorial for him. Something you might want to think about is the re-dedication of the Santa Remideo Church this coming Sunday. That will be a huge event. This is a small island and just about everyone on

Saipan will be there. There will be a U.S. Marine honor guard and a presentation of some sort as part of the festivities. Your young lady might attend and then you'd have an opportunity to re-start your acquaintance."

"Not a bad idea," Jake said. "Give my thanks to Lizzie for a super meal." He shook hands with Malcom and said goodnight. But sleep was not in the offering. Jake brewed a cup of coffee and with cup in hand, strolled down the dock, crossed the Beach Road into the American Memorial Park and went to the gravesite where the young woman had been laying flowers. It was too dark to read the inscription on the flat marker, but the flowers were still fresh. He bent to touch them, thinking maybe he might experience a flash of some sort, some kind of repetition of the feeling he had experienced earlier in the afternoon. But nothing happened, and he felt a bit foolish. He turned and left the park, finishing off his coffee as he returned to the *Giggling Witch*.

(Four)

Three days later, the Sunday morning of the re-dedication of the Santa Remideo Church, Jake was on his second cup of coffee and just finishing up an omelet when he heard the sounds of a marching band. Going topside, he looked down the dock toward the Beach Road and saw what appeared to be a high school band marching toward Garapan. Tess and Liam were standing just inside the marina entrance watching the band pass by.

"Hey, Jake!" Malcom yelled from across the dock. "We're heading out for the festivities at the San Remedios Church. Want to tag along?"

"I'll be along shortly," Jake said. "I need a shower and a shave first."

"Spiffing up for that young woman, right? Okay, we'll see you there," Malcom said.

It was almost two hours later when Jake approached the church. The crowd was huge and loud, and dozens of entrepreneurial vendors were plying their wares at their tables and carts serving all kinds of sliced fruits, fresh juices and charbroiled shish kabobs. Jake wore a pair of light grey tropical trousers, tan deck shoes, a buff-colored Manila-styled guayabera shirt, a Panama hat, dark Gucci sunglasses and his stainless steel Rolex Mariner chronometer on his left wrist. He looked like a prosperous landowner, or well-heeled tourist. He was handsome to boot, and he drew the attention of numerous women in the crowd.

Jake wove his way through the hundreds of people, making toward the entrance to the church. The crowd thickened as he closed with the concrete staircase, but he slowly ascended and entered into the interior of the church, removing his Panama hat and pushing his sunglasses atop his head. The ceremonies were over and the isles were filled with participants, including a dozen U.S. Marines in dress blues, one holding a staff with an American flag and the other holding a staff with the U.S. Marine Corps flag. Probably the honor guard, Jake thought.

Then he saw her. Facing in his direction but engrossed in conversation with a Marine officer whose back was turned to him, and several other well-dressed Saipanians. She wore a simply-cut white jacket, while silk blouse and a white skirt of the same material as the jacket. A bright red flower was tucked into her raven-black hair over her left ear. Her dark eyes were flashing and when she spoke, her lips moved expressively over beautiful white teeth. Jake was mesmerized.

Then, she saw him, and her eyes widened in surprise. At that very moment, Jake felt a hand on his shoulder and a voice from behind that said, "Sergeant Porter, I presume?" Jake turned and was flabbergasted to see Gunnery Sergeant Sweikert offering his hand. Sweikert was dressed in his Marine blues with all his medals. He had a serious look on his face.

"What the hell, gunny?' was the best Jake could do under the circumstances.

"I arrived on a military flight late last night," Gunny Sweikert said. "Stayed at the Hilton. I'm on the Corps' ceremonials list and I took advantage of the rechristening of the church to get a free ride here. I've brought bad news, I'm afraid. Let's step out front and find a spot to talk." He took Jake's arm and led him out the front of the church. Jake didn't even have a chance to look over his shoulder. If he had, he would have seen the gorgeous Chamorro woman tugging her mother's arm and speaking rapidly, looking and pointing in Jake's direction.

Outside on the lawn, Gunny Sweikert cut to the chase. "No easy way to say this, Jake, and I hate being the bearer of bad news, but here it is. Doctor Ambrose and Brenda Warren were murdered on board the *Sea Bones*."

It hit Jake deep in his gut. "What are you saying, Gunny? Murdered, why? When? Why hasn't Tag or Stacy called me?"

"It was Major Taggart who called me. The bodies were not discovered on *Sea Bones* until the week after you left with your boat for San Diego. No one could reach you while you were enroute across the Pacific. He asked me to bring the news to you if I could. He didn't want to do it by telephone. There are no answers at this time to your questions.

"The police don't have a clue. They didn't find the bodies until over a week after they were killed. The police are also trying to make a connection between the murders and two missing persons from Miami, one of them a private detective. Their car was found at a public boat ramp just down the river from the yacht club where the Doc had his boat. They had bought a rubber inflatable boat for reasons unknown and it's missing, too. Because of the proximity of the boat ramp to the yacht club, there's some speculation they may have purchased the inflatable to paddle up to the *Sea Bones*, and somehow are involved in the killings. But the investigation is just beginning."

Jake struggled to adjust his mind to the fact that Doctor Ambrose and Brenda were dead. Shot dead on the *Sea Bones*. He just couldn't believe it. And then it struck him that maybe his quest for the treasure had something to do with it, but he didn't see how. Yes, he'd used the Doc's Internet connection to do some research, but that was the only connection to the Doc. He had not even discussed his treasure quest with the Doc. Brenda, of course, was fully aware of what he was up to. Could she have talked to the wrong person?

"The police are looking for you, too, by the way," Sweikert continued. "Mainly because Ambrose was your employer and Brenda was your girlfriend, and the fact that you left town near the time of their deaths. Your encounter with the Haitians in the Bahamas has made the news, too. Seems a porno bimbo sold the story to a New York tabloid."

"Christ almighty, Gunny!" Jake said.

"And then there's this," Sweikert said, pulling a sealed envelope from inside his tunic and handing it to Jake. "Major Taggart swore me to secrecy and to deliver it to you with strict instruction to not disturb the seal. As you can see, the envelope is sealed as he gave it to me."

Jake took the envelope, folded it and placed it in a trouser pocket. His mind was numb, his emotions were shattered, and he could bear no more for the moment. "Thank you, gunny," he said. "I need some time to think this all through. My boat's at the Micro Beach Marina in Tanapag, about a 10 minute drive from here. If you can, I'd appreciate it if you could drop by before leaving Saipan. I may ask you to take a message to Tag and Stacy if that is possible."

"No problem, Sergeant," Sweikert said. "Sorry to have been the bearer of such bad news." He could see that Jake was stricken and at a loss for what to do next. He gave Jake a pat on the shoulder, then returned to the church.

Jake passed through the crowd in a daze. He walked back to the *Giggling Witch* oblivious to the happy, noisy throngs around him. He slid the companionway open, went down below and opened the salon skylight and a couple of ports to let in some fresh air, then sank onto the main salon settee to think. About an hour later, as distraught as ever, he sat up and went to the galley to retrieve a cold bottle of beer. He remembered the envelope and drew it from his trouser pocket, then sat down at the salon table and opened it. It read:

"Jake - Broke the code. Or maybe it was more Stacy's doing. She found Bustamente's family crest in a Spanish historical archive and that led to discovering that the cipher was his family's motto. Bustamente was tricky. The message was buried in the Latin text of his "confession," but the actual decrypted letters of the cipher were in the vernacular Spanish. Here's the message after translating it into English:

Concepcion of Manila lost. Cargo saved. Buried in cave.

Latitude 27º 15'N, Longitude 154W.

Congratulations! I know you must be thrilled. Your suspicions were right on. At least you now know for sure that the treasure was once on the island. Let's hope it's still there. Needless to say, mums the word as far as we are concerned.

"Call us if there is anything we can do to further the cause. Gunny Sweikert has volunteered to deliver this message to you. He has some other news that's not quite so happy and we extend our deepest sympathies. By the way, news of your Bahamian encounter with the Haitians is all over the local news. You got away just in time."

The letter was signed by both Tag and Stacy.

The worst of news and the best of news all on the same day! Jake's emotional system was shattered. And then there was the beautiful island girl at the church. Once again he had been thwarted in speaking with her. She had seen him in the church and knew that he had seen her. What must she think of his hasty exit without introducing himself? Frustrating was not the word for it. Jake went to the galley and popped another beer. He climbed the companionway stairs and sat on a cockpit cushion beneath the awning, gazing out on a sparkling sun-washed ocean, processing the day's events.

That was where he was sitting when he saw Gunny Sweikert and Sammy T from the *Titan III* coming down the dock. Sweikert had changed from his dress blues to khaki trousers, a colorful Hawaiian-style shirt and sandals. Sammy T was dressed in an orange Titan III tee-shirt, baggy shorts, flip-flops and the same Yankees ball cap, just like when he and Jake had first met at the marina in front of the Dai Ichi hotel; he was smiling broadly.

"Ahoy, Jake!" Sammy hailed. "Permission to come aboard?"

"Granted, Sammy," Jake said. "You, too, gunny. I'm still processing the news you brought."

"That's why we're here, Jake," Sammy T said. "We've come to invite you to our home for dinner tonight. Gunny Sweikert is a long time friend of our family. He knew our father in the Corps before he was killed. My family understands sadness and loss, Jake."

"Well, that's very kind of you, Sammy, but I..." Jake said before being interrupted by Gunny Sweikert.

"Besides, a young lady who wants to make your acquaintance will be there," Sweikert said with a thin smile.

"Yeah, Jake! You've been making eyes at my sister," Sammy T said, laughing.

"Your sister?" Jake said, thoroughly confused.

"That's right. Elena, my younger sister. She's a school teacher here. She saw you when she was in the memorial park putting some flowers on our grandfather's grave," Sammy T said.

"Your grandfather's grave?" Jake said, puzzled.

"The deLeon family is a family of warriors, Jake," Sweikert said. "Three generations of fighters. You'll be in good company. Elena's mother, Delilah, told me about Elena's encounter with you in the memorial park. She has made me promise to bring you to their home so she can meet you."

"Christ almighty! Gunny. Tell me you didn't say anything to them about Iraq or the Haitians," Jake said.

"Now how could I spare a family of warriors such tales of bravery and derring-do, Jake?" Sweikert laughed. "Not to worry. Like I said, you'll be in good company."

"Come on, Jake," Sammy T said. "We're not taking 'no' for an answer. You can mope around tomorrow if you want, but tonight we're *dancing*! Besides, Elena and my Mom will kill me if I show up without you."

They drove down the Beach Road toward Marpi Point in a well-kept Range Rover, Sammy T doing the driving, Jake sitting in the back. Sweikert, in the front passenger seat, kept his eyes on the road ahead and had little to say.

"After the next turn, Jake, my family's property begins on the right. We raise prime beef cattle, one of less than a half dozen Saipanian families that do. And we have a Chinese family on the property across the road that grows a large truck garden of fresh vegetables that we sell in Garapan's market. We're pretty much self-sufficient. My grandfather bought the ranch when he was a young man. When he went off to college and law school in Manila, the family kept everything together," Sammy T said with obvious pride.

The Range Rover slowed as they passed a pasture with twenty or thirty head of well-fed steers. They continued past a painted sign that said 'Marpi Point' and finally turned into a well-traveled dirt road heading toward the ocean. The road was lined with tall, swaying palm trees, their tops laden with thick clusters of dark brown coconuts. The fields left and right were tamed and manicured; bright vermillion trees were everywhere. As they neared the family compound, more than a dozen

319

cars were parked in among the foliage, and Jake could hear music in the distance.

"Here we are, Jake!" Sammy T said. They had parked some fifty feet away from a prosperous low-slung native home built of wood with a shiny aluminum roof. It was obvious they were expected. A group of over twenty Saipanians, plump women with wide smiles and small, dark brown men holding bottles of the local beer stood in the yard. A dozen or more children were scampering about and squealing, slowing only briefly to survey the new arrivals. From the doorway came the woman that Jake had seen with Elena in the church, and right behind her, Elena herself.

Jake sucked in his breath when he saw her. She was that perfect mixture of Chinese-Polynesian blood that produced women of extraordinary beauty with creamy skin color and full lips, ample breasts, tiny waists and the curvaceous shape that lured men to their marital doom.

Elena's mother gave Jake a tremendous family-style hug. "I am Delilah, Sammy's mother." She took his hand, then stepped back and smiling, said, "Welcome to our home, Jake. George Sweikert has told us all about you." Turning to Elena, she said, "This is my daughter, Elena, Jake." She took Elena's hand and tugged her gently forward. Elena was looking into Jake's eyes so intensely that he felt naked before them. Elena offered her free hand to Jake and said softly, "I saw you in the park."

"Yes, that was me," Jake said. Elena's hand was smooth, warm and firm. "I was playing with the children of friends of mine."

Elena's mother laughed. "Elena thought you were married and the children were yours."

"No, I am not married," Jake said. He smiled lamely, unable to break eye contact with Elena.

"You came to Saipan on your sailboat," Elena said, struggling to make conversation with this very handsome young man who had made her knees quiver in the park. The children with Jake had confused her, but there was no mistaking the feeling she had gotten when she first laid eyes on Jake. It was the sign her mother had said she would feel when she met the man of her life. And now, Elena made no effort to remove her hand from Jake's grip.

Earlier in the day at the church, when Sweikert returned from having taken Jake outside to tell him of the murder of Dr. Ambrose and Brenda, Sweikert had learned from Elena's mother of the memorial park encounter between Jake and Elena. He took the occasion to relate Jake's battlefield exploits in Iraq, and his slaughter of the Haitian pirates in the Bahamas, describing Jake as a 'warrior's warrior'. The mother and daughter had exchanged knowing glances, but said nothing.

"Yes. I arrived a couple of weeks ago," Jake said. "I met your brother, Sammy, in front of the Dai Ichi where he keeps the *Titan III*. He didn't say anything about a sister."

On that note, Elena's mother began waving to all of the guests to come and meet Jake. Sammy T brought Jake a cold beer, grinning at Jake's obvious discomfiture in the presence of his beautiful sister. "You look hungry, Jake. Elena! What are you doing just sitting there? Why don't you fix Jake a plate?" he said.

"Don't you move, Elena," said her mother. "I will fix plates for you and Jake. You just get to know each other." She waggled a finger at her son, Sammy, and told him to go find his wife and see that she and his children were fed.

The party lasted until almost midnight. Jake and Elena had sat together mostly undisturbed except for an occasional interruption by the children. They exchanged inconsequential small talk, each listening closely to the other, consumed by the closeness they were sharing. Elena explained that she had gone to the University of Manila to get her education to become a school teacher and was so happy to return to the quiet beauty of her island. Jake told her about joining the Marine Corps at the age of 17, then was extended because of the Gulf War in Iraq, and only recently finished his studies for a Bachelor's degree in Business by going to night classes while he drove a wealthy doctor's yacht. Elena asked, "How old are you, Jake?" immediately lowering her eyes in embarrassment at having asked such a personal question.

Jake smiled. "Thirty-one," he said.

"I'm twenty-three," Elena said quickly to counter any offense she may have incurred with her question. She paused then said, "Almost an old maid in my society."

Jake laughed. "There's time enough yet, Elena. And you are a most beautiful young woman." Then on a reckless impulse, he said "If your mother was not watching us so closely, I would sneak a kiss." He was amazed that he had said such a thing.

Elena beamed, gave a quick glance at her mother to see if she was watching, she was not, and before Jake knew it, he had received a soft kiss on his cheek. Then, with a mischievous smile, Elena said, "In my society, we're now almost engaged."

"My God! Things move fast here," Jake said. He laughed again, and said, "I think I'd better read up on the local traditions before I get into something I can't handle."

The music from the boom box was increasing in volume and some of the women began to dance the beautifully erotic dance similar to that of Tahiti and the Society Islands. Elena was pulled into the group and she began to rock her hips and rotate her shoulders and breasts in unison with the music. She never took her eyes off of Jake, and as she pumped her pelvis and shook her breasts, Jake had the distinct feeling that all the moves were for his benefit.

Gunny Sweikert and Sammy came over to sit down beside Jake and watch the dancing. Each was nursing a beer, as was Jake. "We gotta be cutting out, Jake," Sweikert said. "I leave on a MATS flight tomorrow coming in from Japan, that takes me to Hawaii for a short layover, then on to Dover Air Force Base. Long haul. Sammy is driving me to the Hyatt, then he's spending the night on *Titan III*. We thought we'd have breakfast, then do a short visit with you on your boat, then off to the airport."

The music had ended and Jake said, "Let me say goodnight to Elena and her mother.

"You're leaving?" Elena asked. She was perspiring from the frantic dancing, and radiant.

"Yes," Jake said. "Sammy is dropping me off at my boat. Maybe we can get together sometime this week and go for a sail on the *Giggling Witch*."

Elena's eyes brightened in excitement. "How about tomorrow?" she asked.

"Tomorrow is fine," Jake said. He wished it was already tomorrow. "Bring a bathing suit. We can anchor at Managaha Island and go for a swim and lunch."

"That will be very nice," Elena said as her mother walked up to say goodnight.

"What will be very nice?" Elena's mother asked.

"Jake invited me to go for a sail on his boat," Elena said, knowing what was coming.

"Oh, wonderful! I haven't been on a sailboat for years, except your brother's trimaran," Delilah said. "I'm quite a fisherman, Jake. I will catch a nice mahi mahi and cook it for our lunch."

"Okay, Jake. Let's hit the highway," Sammy T said. He gave his mother a

323

kiss on the cheek and Gunny Sweikert did the same. Elena tugged Jake's arm gently, and on tip toes, gave him a kiss on the cheek. Jake looked to her mother to see if he had violated any island protocol in accepting the kiss. The smile on Delilah's face assured him that all was well. She accepted his kiss as well.

Back on the *Giggling Witch*, Jake opened hatches and ports to air out the boat, then stretched out on the main salon settee. What a day! The death of two friends and the day-long encounter with Elena and her family. When sleep overtook him, his mind was still trying to process it all.

Jake woke to a tapping on his hull. "Captain Porter, Captain Porter, are you awake?" It was Tess. Jake stepped up the companionway. "You're invited to breakfast," she said. "And here's your first cup of coffee," she said, handing him a ceramic pot. "Mom's doing blueberry pancakes. They're the best ever!"

"Thanks, Tess. Just what I needed." Jake took the pot, poured coffee into a mug and returned the pot to Tess. "Let me comb my hair and I'll be right over."

"Hey!" Malcom yelled from the cockpit of his boat. "We saw you briefly at the church yesterday, but then you disappeared. We pigged-out on all the native snacks, and waddled back here late yesterday afternoon, but you had already taken off somewhere."

When he stepped into the cockpit of their boat, Jake told them all that had happened the day before with the exception of the news of the deaths of Doctor Ambrose and Brenda. No sense in spreading that gloom about. He mentioned that he was sailing the *Giggling Witch* over to Managaha Island for an afternoon of sailing and lunch and that he and Lizzie, Liam and Tess were invited to go along. Tess and Liam immediately squealed in delight and dashed down below to get their goggles and swim fins.

"They don't take much encouragement, do they?" Lizzie said, smiling.

"We accept the invitation. It will be good to get away from the dock and let someone else do the sailing."

"Honestly, I've been itching to sail with that Chinese rig, Jake," Malcom said.

"I'll show you the ropes," Jake said. "You won't believe how simple it is, really."

They finished their breakfast and were still sitting in the cockpit, when a little after ten o'clock in the morning Jake spied Elena, her mother, and two girls of about ten years of age coming down the dock. Elena was as breath-taking as ever. She wore a light pale yellow cotton shift tied at the waist, thin leather sandals and a broad-brimmed straw hat, and white plastic-framed sunglasses. She had a small woven-grass beach bag looped to one wrist.

Jake stepped onto the dock, gave a light kiss to everyone, starting with Delilah, then the girls, then Elena. God! How wonderfully she smelled and felt. Then Lizzie and Malcom came across the dock followed by Liam and Tess. Malcom and Lizzie had been on the island long enough to know that they were in the presence of Saipan royalty. Tess and Liam gave formal handshakes to Delilah and Elena, then struck up a relationship with the two girls of their age. Malcom and Lizzie were both blown away by the beauty of Elena, and kind of awed that Jake had connected so innocently with Elena's family.

They boarded the *Giggling Witch*, filling the cockpit. Malcom and Liam went forward and aft to cast off the dock lines. Jake powered gently aft, and they cleared the dock with ease. Once they passed the buoys and were outside the harbor reef, Malcom, under Jake's tutelage, raised the fully-battened Chinese lug rig's mainsail. Jake shut down the engine and the *Giggling Witch* heeled slightly to the morning breeze. No sooner than they were underway, a small proa of about seventeen feet in length zipped across their wake and Jake saw that it was Sammy T and his son. They hailed the boat, waved and yelled that they would meet them at Managaha Island.

It was a magical day. The *Giggling Witch* circled the small island several times to give Malcom, Liam, Elena, her mother, and anyone else so inclined, an opportunity to steer the boat and handle the sails. Everyone walked the decks from stem to stern and climbed out on the bowsprit to watch the *Giggling Witch's* curling bow wave. When they found a likely cove on the lee side of the island, Liam and Jake lowered the anchor after Malcom had doused the sails, then Jake and the kids put up the full deck awning to make a comfortable shade. Sammy T and his son, Eduardo, had beached their proa and swum out to the *Giggling Witch*. Sammy told Jake that Gunny Sweikert's military flight was delayed until tomorrow. He planned to come down to the marina later that evening.

Elena's mother had indeed caught a nice-sized mahi mahi while they were circling the island and it was now being prepped for the grill. Jake was surprised when Elena came from below in her bikini, wiggled a finger at him, then dove overboard and began swimming to the beach. He did not need any further encouragement. He dove in and came up behind her as she stepped out of the water and began to push her brother's proa off the beach into the water. "Let's go sailing Saipan style!" she said. Laughing, she jumped into the proa and Jake piled in right behind her. She pulled the sail sheet taunt, and off they went. Elena steered the boat around the end of the island and as soon as they could not be seen by anyone aboard the *Giggling Witch*, she leaned forward and gave Jake a hard kiss on the mouth. Jake took her hand, pulled her toward him and reciprocated. She was near naked in her bikini and overwhelmingly soft and beautiful. It was all Jake could do to not grab her in lust and have his way with her.

At that moment, Elena spun the proa around on the opposite tack, gave Jake a small push, and he toppled over the side into the ocean. She tacked the proa again and luffed up alongside him, laughing. "Come on! We've got to get back in view of my mother."

Jake flipped a leg over the proa's side and pulled himself aboard. Elena steered the boat expertly and in a moment, they were racing around the point and in full view of the *Giggling Witch*. Elena handed the tiller to Jake, then stretched out on her stomach atop a beach towel in the bottom of the proa, and Jake had a view that he would never forget as long as he lived. He also noticed a curious tattoo on the bottom of Elena'a foot.

When he came alongside the *Giggling Witch*, Elena dove over the side calling to Liam and Tess to jump in and climb aboard the proa with Jake. And so it went. Swimming, sailing, eating, laughing and finally some dancing. The two girls that had come with Elena and her mother were two of Elena's school students, and when Elena put on a tape of traditional dance music, the girls began to dance on the *Giggling Witch's* foredeck, and soon had Tess and her mother, Lizzie, joining in. The men and Liam clapped hands to the drumbeat, and when Delilah climbed out of the cockpit and began to dance, too, they whooped and hollered.

As twilight approached, Jake steered the *Giggling Witch* through Saipan's harbor entrance, then made a smooth turn toward Tanapag and the Micro Beach Marina. No one noticed the ugly, rusting Japanese long-liner that had entered the harbor earlier and was anchored off the commercial dock. Nor did they see the two heavily tattooed Japanese, the captain and his first mate, eyeing them through binoculars. One of them, the captain, lingered his gaze on the beautiful native girl in the white bikini, her arm resting on the shoulder of the round-eye steering the sailboat.

PIRATE'S ROUNDTABLE:

LAUNCH THE INTERCEPTION

Date: February 27, 2001

Lat. 46° 95' N, Long 7° 44' E .

Berne, Switzerland

(One)

As per protocol, the teleconference opened from the Switzerland terminal.

"Gentlemen, our quarry has arrived in Saipan, Marianas. We had an employee of our correspondent bank in Saipan take a stroll down to check the local marinas to see where Porter's boat, the *Giggling Witch*, is berthed. We have confirmation that she is at the government marina in Tanapag, and it appears Porter has arrived alone. We must now discuss our next move. Any comments?"

Monaco began: "He's a ballsy son-of-a-bitch, that Porter. Sailing across the Pacific by himself. Now the question is, does he have logistical support in Saipan? And where will he go after Saipan? It's a damn good thing that we can follow his boat's every move with the transponder. We've got to watch this guy very closely, and be ready to jump on the treasure when he reaches it. For all we know, his group has a boat and crew standing by to load the treasure once he makes its exact location."

"Who's going to close in on him?" Singapore asked. "What are our resources in that area? I'm too damn far away to get any of my equipment to sea on such a short notice. And as I recall, the last time we had an inventory check none of us had vessels anywhere near the Marianas."

Berne spoke up. "Your assessment of the current positions of our vessels is correct. Given that, I took the initiative to take a look at some of our contract people. You remember the Japanese long-liner that we contracted with to help with the salvage of that China Sea wreck several years ago? Well, I sent the owner a coded message via single-sideband and asked his location and availability. He's working out of the Kurile Islands north of the Sea of Japan at the moment, hauling something that he didn't specify. He'll be finished within ten days, he says, and he's available for charter. I didn't give him any additional information, but I sent a small retainer for his trouble and asked him to stand by."

"Kurile Islands?" Monaco said. "What a frigging end-of-the-world place to be in! Cold as a bitch this time of the year, too. Remote is not the word for it. Nothing but volcanoes and seals. That's where the Japanese hid their fleet for the attack on Pearl Harbor, you know? But the good news is that it's not much more than fifteen hundred nautical miles from Saipan. Those old long-liners can make twelve to fifteen knots if you push 'em, and they carry enough bunker to cross the Pacific twice without refueling. Back when they were fishing them, they could stay at sea for nine months or more at a time. They have huge cargo capacity, too. No trouble hauling that galleon's treasure. They can just turn off the refrigeration and use all the fish stalls."

"Of course we need to put one of our own aboard any vessel

participating in recovering the treasure to protect our interests," said Berne. "This Japanese long-liner is adequate for hauling the treasure, but we must be able to control all aspects of the operation once the recovery is underway. A second support vessel is needed to provide security personnel and any unexpected logistical support that may arise, and it must be faster than the long-liner. I'm thinking we should alert Johann, the Dutchman, and see if we can position his converted coastal patrol boat. That thing can make over thirty knots as I recall, and her hull is armored. She's too small to haul much cargo, but if the Japanese captain decides to get creative and make off with the treasure, Dutch's boat can easily overtake her. Any ideas along those lines?

"The Jap's crew can do the heavy lifting with loading the treasure. He'll probably have at least a half-dozen crew, and they will probably be armed," Monaco observed. "If Dutch takes the job, he should bring along at least ten well-armed crew to take care of any difficulties."

"Agreed," Berne said. "If there are no objections, I will arrange for the Japanese long-liner to proceed to Saipan, and keep Porter's boat under surveillance. No overt moves. Just keep an eye on the coming and goings of Porter, particularly if he begins to poke around in any specific area of the Marianas. However, I suspect his stop is only for re-provisioning. The Spanish treasure galleons tended to avoid the Marianas after losing two or three there. Too many reefs. They usually skirted north of the Marianas chain and continued to gain northing to intercept the trades, but Porter may have some information we don't. While the long-liner is making her way to Saipan, I'll contact Dutch and see what he's up to these days and if he's game to join our hunt."

"A good plan, I believe," said Singapore. "Actually, I might be available to join the long-liner to keep an eye on the Jap captain. As I recall, he was a Yakuza at one time, a Japanese Mafia hood tattooed from his ankles to his Adam's apple. Those characters are notorious for being devious and violent."

"Good," said Berne. "Having you aboard would make me feel better.

Okay, then. I'll dial all of you up when there's fresh news.

The teleconference monitor went blank.

(Two)

Shikotan Island, Kuril Island Group

43º 48' N Lat., 146º 45' E Long.

The *Taka Maru #17* tugged at her anchor chain under the press of an exceedingly cold forty-mile-an-hour wind, the bow of the 110 long-foot steel vessel rising and falling through an arc of 20 feet with the harbor's wind-driven white caps slapping loudly against her hull. A fierce storm front coming off the Siberian steppes was driving ambient temperatures to well below freezing, sleet was expected soon, and the night was still young.

The long-liner's anchorage off the east side of Shikotan Island was only moderately protected. On a clear night, the lights of Hokkaido, Japan's northern-most island, were visible to the naked eye; but not on this wintry evening. The thirty thousand Russian inhabitants of the eighteen islands making up the Kuril Island Group, including the 1,500 inhabitants of Shikotan Island, were huddled in their primitive homes, only 40 percent of them having indoor plumbing, enduring yet another night of miserable weather and crushing poverty.

The *Taka Maru #17* was a relic of the days when international fishing laws controlling fishing operations on the oceans of the world were non-existent, or shamefully inadequate, to protect species that were being decimated by over-fishing. When rigged for fishing giant migratory tuna, the *Taka Maru #17* could set up to 2,000 hooks, and keep a crew of twenty busy for daily 12-hour shifts hauling in the catch. Purpose-built, the *Taka Maru #17* was exceedingly ugly to all but the Japanese crewing on them. No effort by the Japanese naval architects who designed her gave any consideration to making her beautiful. Her lines were plain, and her superstructure mostly square. One hundred ten feet in length, drawing 22 feet below the waterline, with a hold capacity of nearly 500 metric tons of frozen fish, the *Taka Maru #17's* one-thousand-horsepower LH26G Hanshin Aineki diesel could drive her at a maximum speed of 20 knots, consuming only 2.0 Kiloliters per day. Her diesel bunkers of over 3,000 gallons permitted her to cruise and work at sea for almost a year without returning to port.

But the *Taka Maru #17* no longer chased fish. Her new cargo was contraband, usually Japanese consumer electronics smuggled into the contested waters of what the Japanese government called the Northern Territories, and the Russians claimed as their own by virtue of Stalin's Decree of Presidium of the Supreme Soviet in 1946. In fact, Japan and the Soviet Union, now Russia, never signed a peace treaty ending their World War II conflict.

The *Taka Maru #17* operated in the political vacuum that followed. Russia's president, Boris Yeltsin, attempted to liberate the Kuriles from Moscow politics and declare them a "free economic zone." He failed to persuade the Russian Duma to authorize it, but it became a *defacto* situation anyway that gave unfettered license to the likes of the *Taka Maru #17*. A brutal economic battlefield of thieves, smugglers and greedy Russian military was created that bred a savage breed of murderous pirates like Yoto Nakura, the Captain of the *Taka Maru #17,* and his Yakuza crew.

(Three)

Yoto Nakura was silent as Coronel Dimitri Markov drove the 4-door Russian UAZ Hunter from Shikotan's airstrip to the island's only commercial pier. In the back seat, three young Philippine women whispered quietly to each other, swaying from side to side as the nimble all-terrain vehicle negotiated the pot-holed roadway. The women had been provided with fur-lined jackets as they stepped off the plane, and given a warm chocolate drink laced with a mild opiate to calm any apprehensions they may have over their new environment. Through the rearview mirror, Coronel Markov was eyeing the women enviously between glances at the roadway's hazards.

"You will have them soon enough, Coronel, " Yoto Nakura said. "But tonight, they entertain my crew. In the morning, when we clear the harbor, they will be brought to the pier and taken to my club. Give them one day of rest and to settle into their quarters, then you and your men may take your pleasure. I will arrange with my club's manager for you to be first in line, and he will see that your bill is favorably adjusted."

"You are too kind, Captain," said Markov, reaching into an inner pocket of his military tunic. "And here are the residency permits for your new hostesses, as promised. They will not be troubled during their stay here in Shikotan."

Yoto Nakura took the permits, and seeing that they were almost to the pierhead, called his First Mate on his hand-held VHF. Matsu answered immediately from the bridge of the *Taka Maru #17*. Nakura ordered that the ship's dinghy meet them at the pier. In short order, the 25-foot Zodiac sportboat and its forty-horsepower Yamaha outboard were alongside the pier. Yoto Nakura and his First Mate settled the women into the dinghy and spun off into the dark, punching through the choppy harbor waters.

The women were shivering from the cold and wet ride when the dinghy rode up the *Taka Maru #17's* stern ramp. Nakura helped them out of the dinghy and instructed them to hold each other's hand while he led them down a companionway into the ship's interior. They went down a short companionway and Nakura opened a door, turning to direct the women inside a warm, ceramic-tiled bath area. Men's voices and splashing water could be heard from an adjoining compartment. Nakura opened a closet and brought out three white cotton robes and towels, handing them to the women. They understood immediately and began to undress. Nakura turned his back to them and went into the bath area where three of his off-duty crew were soaking in the hot bath. "Hai!" they said in unison, greeting their captain. Each crew member, like their captain, was heavily tattooed in the Yakuza fashion, with full-bodied murals depicting fiery dragons, violent seascapes and abstract designs encircling gang insignia. Shoulders, necks, chests and arms, backs and buttocks, armpit to ankle, the whole of it looking like a full suit of long underwear.

Acknowledging their greeting with only a nod of his head, Yoto Nakura went to the ceramic pot atop a kerosene-fired warmer and filled three small cups with warm sake. He took them to the women, who were no longer shivering, but understandably needing some fortification. They took the cups to their lips, smiling and giggling at each other. Yoto Nakura, satisfied, led them into the bath area. His crew whistled and laughed as the three curvaceous, bronze-skinned women shyly shed their robes and stepped into the bath.

Captain Yoto Nakura met his First Mate in the companionway outside the bath. The two of them went directly to the bridge where Nakura opened a large chart drawer and withdrew a British navigational chart depicting the western Pacific Ocean. He spread the chart across a table behind the steering station, placed his finger on the Kurile Islands, then slowly traced a path eastward stopping when his finger reached Saipan, Marianas. Matsu nodded in understanding, but said nothing.

"The round-eyes we worked for in the South China Sea recovering that cargo of Chinese porcelain have made contact. They require our services once more. They are once again seeking treasure, and again wish to intervene in the recovery operations of others," Nakura said. "I have taken their money and agreed. But this time will be different. We will not kill for them. We will not haul the treasure for them. We will not cover up the killings for them," Yoto Nakura said. "No, this time we will kill them all and keep the treasure for ourselves—all of it."

The viciousness in Nakura's voice chilled Matsu. But he knew the source of Nakura's bitterness. He had been aboard the *Taka Maru #17* when the crew had descended upon the Dutch recovery team working the South China Sea wreck site, machine-gunned to death all of them and sank their vessel. The bodies had been gathered and placed in one of the deep freezer compartments and covered with frozen tuna. Weeks later, after the Chinese porcelain had been recovered and stored aboard, the stiff frozen bodies were placed in a weighted fishing net and dumped overboard, sinking in several thousand feet of water. The porcelain was off-loaded and transported to a warehouse in Jakarta for auction. Yoto Nakura learned later that the precious cargo had sold for more than $20 million U.S. dollars. Nakura was paid only $350,000 for his participation. It infuriated him, but there was nothing he could do about it.

"Matsu, we make for Hokkaido on the tide," Yoto Nakura said. "Call the club and have the women picked up at first light. I will meet with my *oyabun* in Hokkaido for his blessing. We need ten solid yakuza to join our crew, and I will ask for his help in selecting them. We must assemble weapons. AK-47s for everyone, and they must be delivered offshore after we have cleared port inspections. I will take care of that. Food, fuel and water, that's your department. Then, we make for Saipan to get what is ours. Understood?" Matsu nodded vigorously and uttered a loyal "Hai!"

Seven days later, a fully-provisioned *Taka Maru #17* with Captain Yoto Nakura on the bridge and a well-armed crew totaling fifteen Yakuza aboard, motored at near maximum speed out of the Sea of Japan and set course for Saipan, Marianas.

LOVE'S LABOR LOST

March 19, 2001
Lat. 15º, 15′ North, Long. 145º, 45 East
Saipan, Northern Marianas

(One)

Barely one hour after the *Giggling Witch* had returned to the Micro Beach Marina from the day's sailing around Managaha Island, Gunny Sweikert came strolling down the dock in his green Marine fatigues and combat boots. He announced that his delayed MATS flight would depart Saipan in the morning, so this was a farewell visit. Jake fetched him a cold beer and introduced him to Malcolm and Lizzie and their children. Elena sat as close to Jake as decorum permitted, Sammy T's wife, Rosalita, and two sons had joined them earlier, and Delilah went to Jake's galley to fry some bananas and plantains for snacks. Finally, the party broke up and only Jake and Gunny Sweikert were left in the *Giggling Witch's* cockpit. Elena had left a kiss on Jake's cheek and whispered that she would see him tomorrow after her school's classes ended.

"Looks to me like Elena has taken a liking to you," Sweikert said. "As you know, I knew her father in Vietnam, and since he's not here to speak for her interests, may I ask just exactly what are you intentions toward this young lady?"

"I wish I knew, Gunny," Jake said. "I'm not sure I'm in the driver's seat actually. She wasn't part of my plan when I came to Saipan."

"I don't mean to pry, Sergeant, but just exactly what was your plan?" Sweikert asked. "Back when you were shooting up that old car at the county firing range in Gainesville, I asked Major Taggart what you were up to and he said he was sworn to secrecy. I told him I thought you'd make an excellent officer candidate for the Corps. He agreed, but said he thought you had a full plate and wouldn't consider reentering the Corps, even as an officer. Then, I get a phone call from him and he asks if I can take a message to you. The message is that two of your friends have been murdered. He also asks me to deliver a sealed envelope to you, and asks me on my honor to not open it. When I ask him where you are, he tells me, Saipan—the other side of the friggin' world! Now, I think you'll agree, I have good cause to ask what is this 'plan' of yours that involves people getting murdered, and your courting the innocent daughter of a Marine acquaintance of mine."

"It's a long story, Gunny, and I'm not sure I know all of it," Jake said. "I don't know why Doctor Ambrose and Brenda were killed. Ever since you brought that message, I have been scouring my brain to figure out any connection I may have had that would bring about such a disaster."

"Then, there's that incident in the Bahamas in which you are in the company of the same doctor and young woman, along with some other folks, and you kill four Haitian thugs. Right after that is when you take off on your boat. To tell you the truth, Sergeant, it leaves me with a bad taste in my mouth," Sweikert said.

"Yes, I can see that it would, gunny," Jake said, "but I have to be careful about what I say about my reasons for coming to Saipan. I don't want to be the cause of any more deaths. Here is what I can say: I'm following up on a find I made. I needed to conduct some research to determine its authenticity. That's why I asked you for the name of a Marine Corps intelligence officer. I was looking for someone who knew something about secret codes and how to break them. I used Doctor Ambrose's Internet connection on his boat to do some of the research. Brenda accompanied me when I went to visit Tag....uh, Major Taggart, in Gainesville. Brenda was fully aware of what I was looking into, doctor Ambrose was not. Unfortunately, Brenda was unable to keep her mouth shut, and when I found out she had breached our sworn agreement with Bahamian authorities, I trashed our relationship. Who she's told and what she's told, I am not sure. But it could be related to the murders. I just don't know."

"The New York tabloids and the local newspapers were filled with the Bahamas story," Sweikert said. "Lots of speculation about why you left town and where you were headed. You say you made a 'find.' Any amplification on that?"

"Here's where it gets sticky, gunny," Jake said. "Major Taggart and Stacy know where I am headed. That message you brought to me was them telling me they had broken the code. In a sense, my life is in their hands. If they are indiscreet and the wrong people find out where I am headed, my life is forfeit for sure."

Gunny Sweikert was dumbfounded. Were it not for the very real deaths of two people and the involvement of a Marine officer for whom he had the greatest respect, he would have discounted Jake Porter's story as pure fantasy. "So, Saipan is not your final stop then?" he asked cautiously.

"No, it isn't. I stopped here to take on water and food, and wait for a seasonal change in the weather. I need favorable winds to get where I'm going. Meeting Elena was totally unexpected. I can tell you truthfully, it wouldn't take much for me to abandon my plan and chase her instead," Jake said, smiling ruefully.

"Son of a bitch, Sergeant! Secret codes, multiple murders, the slaughter of four Haitians, and cross-Pacific sailing in search of a 'find'. You are a real piece of work, that's for sure," Sweikert said. "Now back to our first topic of conversation, what are your plans for Elena?"

"You tell me, Gunny," Jake said. "Like I said, she has hit me like a brick over the head. I've never met anyone even remotely like her. She's not only beautiful, she's smart as hell. How she got to be twenty-three years old and not be married with children I'll never know."

"There's a lot more to that young lady than you know, Sergeant," said Sweikert. "Her family carries a lot of responsibility on Saipan. Her older brother, Sammy, runs his charter business and does quite well. He's a smart business guy. I wouldn't be surprised if he ends up running for governor some day, and with his grandfather's name behind him, he'd probably win, too.

"Your situation with Elena will probably be resolved soon. Not to worry. She's leaving Saipan in a few weeks at the end of the school year. Delilah told me at the party the other night that Elena has won an all-expense paid scholarship for a Master's degree at the University of Auckland in New Zealand. I guess Elena didn't tell you that, did she?"

"No, she didn't, Gunny," Jake said. "We haven't had much opportunity to talk privately. There's always someone from the family, or several of her school students, around us. I appreciate you telling me. It takes some of the heat off."

"Okay, that about covers it then. I've got an early flight tomorrow."

"Before you go, Gunny, I have a question. You don't have to answer it, of course, but I'd appreciate your input," Jake said.

"Go ahead, Sergeant. I don't think you could have any greater surprises for me," Sweikert said.

"How do you feel about the Japanese, Gunny?"

Now what the hell? Gunny Sweikert thought. "Japs? Don't particularly care for them. Marines have good cause to despise them. They beheaded many of us during the war when we were helpless prisoners of war. Starved and tortured us. Then there's the senseless slaughter of thousands of civilians at Nanking, and the forcing of thousands of innocent women to become prostitutes for their troops. They called them 'comfort women.' 'Greater East Asia Co-Prosperity Sphere,' my ass! Fanatical racist bastards with no moral conscience. Loyal to their emperor, a murderous fraud who called himself a god. General McArthur should have hung the son-of-bitch for the war criminal he was. The atomic bomb didn't teach them a thing. They are as devious as ever, just more clever in their dealings these days. In general, that's how I feel. That what you wanted to hear?"

"No love lost then, right?" Jake smiled. "How about taking something from the Japs that might involve breaking a few laws in the process? No killing or anything like that. Just grabbing something that the Japs don't even know they have, something that they didn't earn and have no right to keep? Located in a place they stole in violation of a legitimate treaty."

"What the hell you talking about, Sergeant?" Sweikert asked.

"My 'find', gunny. The reason I sailed across the Pacific. Let me show you something," Jake said, rising to go down below and fetch the cargo manifest for the Manila galleon, *Nuestra Senora de la Concepcion.*

(Two)

As promised, Elena came down the Micro Beach Marina dock the following day. It was early afternoon and she was accompanied by three of her school's students. They were laughing and obviously enjoying a private joke, for when they came up to the *Giggling Witch*, they went silent as Elena hailed the boat.

Jake came topside with a broad smile across his face. The sight of Elena was uplifting, and for a moment he set aside the knowledge that she would soon be leaving Saipan. "Welcome aboard," he said. Elena, vibrant as ever, kicked off her sandals and stepped over the lifelines onto the deck and took Jake's hand. She leaned into him and kissed him on the mouth. Then, she turned to look at her students, then back to him. The students acknowledged the prearranged message, crossing the dock to strike up a conversation with Liam and Tess, who had been doing their correspondence school homework in the shade beneath the awning over the cockpit of their boat.

Elena gave Jake another kiss, then led him down the companionway steps to the *Giggling Witch's* salon. Jake followed as a sheep to slaughter. At the bottom of the stairs, Elena turned and threw her arms around Jake's neck. On tiptoes, she pulled herself tightly to his chest and kissed him again, longer and even more firmly. Overwhelmed, Jake let his arms drop to her tiny waist and pulled her fullness to him, feeling a swelling in his loins.

The two Yakuza from the *Taka Maru #17* stepped off the Beach Road and onto the Micro Beach Marina's dock. They wore what looked like black pajamas. They had locally-purchased straw hats on their bald heads and pink flip-flops on their feet. Their blue tattoos showed only on the tops of their feet and lower necks. They were moving slowly down the dock toward the *Giggling Witch* when the young Chamorro clerk from the marina office stepped out of her office and called to them. They turned reluctantly, the Chamorro clerk explaining the dock was for the owners of boats and their guests. One of the Yakuza spoke in Japanese, the Chamorro clerk replying that she didn't speak Japanese. She gestured indicating that the Yakuza must return to the Beach Road. The Yakuza spoke rapidly to each other in Japanese. They were under instructions to be invisible and cause no confrontations. They bowed politely, smiling to the Chamorro clerk, then left the dock.

Jake was breathless and his heart was pounding. He could see that Elena was also aroused. They both eased their grips on one another, and laughed together. "I'm not sure how much of this I can take," Jake said.

Elena looked at him curiously, not sure she understood.

"I mean, the stopping is killing me," Jake explained.

Elena laughed. "I have my reputation, you know. Besides the girls will be back in just a few minutes. I told them to come back in no more than twenty minutes."

"Why twenty minutes?" Jake asked, stroking Elena's arms and pulling her to him for a kiss on the forehead.

"I think twenty minutes in your hands is the maximum resistance I have before I take my clothes off and pull you into bed," Elena said.

Jake smiled and kissed her full on the lips. "Twenty minutes might be stretching it a bit. I'm good for about ten."

Elena laughed, kissed him hard on the mouth, then grabbed his hand and pulled him up the companionway to the cockpit. The girls were just crossing back over the dock with Liam and Tess in tow.

"Mom and Dad say come over for some lemonade. They said you both probably needed cooling off," little Tess said.

Jake and Elena laughed and crossed over the dock. Malcom and Lizzie gave them close scrutiny and correctly guessed that the temperature below decks on the *Giggling Witch* had indeed been elevated. Malcom announced that he and his family would be leaving Saipan within the week, continuing their voyage toward the Philippines.

Elena said there would have to be a going-away party, and she would take charge of arranging it. Then, she announced that she had to get her students to their homes and get back home herself. Laughing, she said her mother was watching her more closely than ever since Jake had showed up on Saipan. She gave Jake a kiss on the lips and said her goodbyes to everyone. Jake watched her swaying hips with longing as she strode down the dock.

"We have really enjoyed your company these past few weeks, Jake, and especially meeting Elena and her family. Our only regret is that we will miss the wedding."

"Wedding?" Jake asked with raised eyebrows.

"Elena has you hook, line and sinker, sailor boy," Lizzie said with a laugh.

"You never had a chance, Jake," Malcom said, joining with his wife. "That girl is something special, and I get the feeling she would sail with you anywhere you're heading. By the way, you've never said exactly where it is that you're headed after Saipan."

"I learned last night that Elena has won a scholarship in New Zealand to study for her Master's degree. Any sailing together we might do is going to have to be worked around that. So, I guess New Zealand might be a destination after Saipan, but who knows?" Jake was fast becoming artful in dodging questions about his plans.

(Three)

The next three weeks were the happiest in Jake's life. During the week, Elena came to the marina every day after school. Always with a couple of students, of course, but always managing to get them alone for precious minutes of breathless groping and passionate kissing. The last couple of times, she had let him push her blouse up and fondle her breasts. It nearly drove Jake crazy, hearing her moan then having to stop when the kids returned and jumped on the deck above.

Sometimes Sammy T came down to the dock with his wife, Rosita, and children. Elena almost always came with them, sitting skin-to-skin with Jake in the *Giggling Witch's* cockpit. They talked of life on Saipan, their family, and what the future might hold. It was Sammy T that sprung the question everyone had wanted to ask but didn't. "How did you happen to sail to Saipan, Jake? Do you have your next port in mind?"

Elena, Sammy T, and Rosita, looked closely at Jake to hear his reply.

Jake knew he must answer carefully. A great deal was at stake; he did not want to put his relationship with Elena at risk. At the same time, he didn't know how to mention his true mission: a quest for Spanish treasure buried on a Jap island . So, he danced around the question with a mixture of truth and deception. He regretted deeply that he couldn't be forthright.

"There's no easy answer to your first question, Sammy, and I don't know the answer to the second one," Jake began. "I became the owner of the *Giggling Witch* almost by accident. Fate, I guess you could say. I've been restless ever since I got out of the Marine Corps. I wanted to finish my college studies, and I did that. In the meanwhile, again with fateful intervention, I became the captain of a surgeon's fancy motor yacht. Life was good; lots of parties, trips to the Florida Keys and across the Gulf Stream to the Bahamas. Not much in the way of money, but there was nothing not to like. I got comfortable, but the itch to travel was always there.

"Finally, events unfolded that rocked my boat, so to speak. Gunny Sweikert told you about the doctor being murdered, along with a young woman I knew. Before he was killed, the doctor told me that because of the violence aboard his boat in the Bahamas, he was going to sell her. That would end my employment as Captain. I was feeling a need to move on anyway. I had spent time in Okinawa while I was in the Corps, and liked the island life. So, I took off heading west across the Pacific ocean, and here I am."

"The winds blew you to me," Elena said.

(Four)

Jake had paid no attention to the Jap long-liner anchored in Garapan. He did not even notice the Yakuza who loitered across the Beach Road from the entrance to the Micro Beach Marina. There was no reason to pay them any attention; they had cleverly covered up their tattoos, wearing long sleeved shirts and trousers. They dressed as tourists, with Nikons hanging around their necks, seeking to be as inconspicuous as possible. Jake was too preoccupied with Elena to notice much of anything else. He didn't even notice the *Taka Maru #17*'s Zodiac dinghy when it passed the marina dock at least once every day where the *Giggling Witch* was tied up, then spun away toward Managaha Island. Not until he began to move the *Giggling Witch* did he finally realize he was being watched.

344

It began with an innocent sail to the far side of Saipan's eastern shore. An overnight picnic of sorts with Elena's family. They were anchored in Magicienne Bay, the largest bay on the eastern side of Saipan Island. Sammy T had brought along some SCUBA gear from the *Titan III*; Sammy and Jake had gone spear fishing and returned not only with a large grouper, but a sack full of lobsters. Jake had just surfaced at the bow of his dinghy, and happened to look seaward. He spied a large inflatable dinghy ghosting around the bay's southern headland. Two persons aboard sitting low; then they moved behind the headland. After climbing aboard the *Giggling Witch*, Jake grabbed his binoculars for a closer look. The Zodiac was again poking its nose around the headland; one of the people was holding binoculars looking in the direction of the *Giggling Witch*. Suddenly, they came about and went behind the headland again. They had seen Jake watching them with binoculars and sped away.

A few days later with Elena's school closed for a long 4-day weekend in celebration of a Saipan government holiday, Jake decided to take a look at some of the islands just north of Saipan. The one that intrigued him the most was called Anatahan. Located eighty miles north of Saipan, it was six miles long and two miles wide, had an active volcano and was unpopulated. He had no trouble convincing Sammy T to accompany him and bring along some diving gear. Elena and her sister-in-law, Rosita, joined them. Elena's mother was detailed to stay at home and watch their children.

Arriving at Anatahan Island in the early evening after a full day of sailing, Jake anchored the *Giggling Witch* in twenty feet of water and payed out two hundred feet of chain rode. They went ashore the next morning and while stomping around the lava fields, they came to a rise that offered a fantastic view of the Philippine Sea side of the island. But on the horizon, Jake spied the ugly profile of the *Taka Maru #17*, and saw a familiar Zodiac inflatable sport boat exit the stern and head toward the island. Jake didn't have his binoculars with him, but he and Sammy T agreed that the long-liner was none other than the one that had been anchored at Garapan for the past few weeks.

When they returned to the *Giggling Witch,* Jake placed his binoculars in the cockpit. He asked Elena to scan the horizon from time to time and look for the inflatable sport boat. Then he and Sammy donned diving gear and went over the side to look for dinner. When they returned with a nice grouper and a couple of red snappers, Elena said she had not seen anything. They marinated and grilled the fish, married them with heaping servings of seasoned rice, and ate their dinner.

The inflatable sport boat never showed up. Instead, Jake was scanning Anatahan's shoreline with his binoculars at twilight and saw two dark shapes moving along the lava shelf opposite their anchorage. The fading evening sunlight reflected off their binoculars. The *Giggling Witch* was definitely under surveillance. Jake decided to try something. Once it was completely dark, he retrieved the *Giggling Witch's* anchor and motored slowly out of the cove with the navigation lights doused. He steered north for several miles before raising sails to take advantage of the northeast trade breeze, then steered for Sarigan, the next island up the Marianas chain.

They arrived at dawn, dropping anchor in thirty feet of water opposite the grey volcanic island. Only a small patch of green vegetation was visible on the north end of the island, the rest covered in grainy ash. Again, Jake and Sammy T took the dinghy ashore, but this time they skirted the island to land on the opposite side, then slogged through the ash to a height of maybe 300 feet.

There she was, the long-liner standing offshore maybe a mile away. If they had been looking from the *Giggling Witch's* deck at sea level, she would not have been visible. The Japs had followed them during the night! Jake and Sammy T conferred on what this meant: the long-liner was using satellite imagery, no doubt about it. The question was, how and why? They returned to their dinghy and sped for the *Giggling Witch.* They retrieved the anchor once again, and headed south, back toward Saipan. They looked over the stern all day for sight of the long-liner, but the horizon remained empty.

After returning to the dock at the Micro Beach Marina, Jake, Sammy T, Elena and Rosita waited for the long-liner to return to its anchorage in Garapan. They had no way of knowing it, but the *Taka Maru #17* had purposely stayed below the horizon to avoid detection. Instead, it had continued on to by-pass Saipan, and anchor at Tinian, three miles south and west of Saipan. Sammy T said he would contact some friends in the Saipan government and inquire about the Jap long-liner to see if he could figure out what they were up to. He said he would also ask some of the government's telecommunications technicians about satellite tracking. Elena was visibly upset over the development. The idea of Japanese following Jake was disturbing. She gave Jake an especially long kiss as she was leaving to go home.

In the late afternoon of the following day, Sammy T came down the Micro Beach Marina dock to give Jake a report on his findings. A cousin of his in the customs office pulled the paperwork and said the long-liner was home-ported in the Kurile Islands, a remote area contested by Japan and Russia. It was a haven for smugglers among other things. The customs officer who had boarded the long-liner when it first arrived said the crew were Yakuza, as evidenced by their heavy body tattoos. He said they were a rough-looking bunch, and the boat didn't look like it was doing any fishing either. The long-liner's captain said he was ferrying the boat to be sold by a ship's broker. He said they were in Saipan to await the arrival of a part for their engine before continuing.

Jake knew who Yakuza were and summed it up: "A Jap boat crewed by criminals, from a port known for smuggling, and capable of setting to sea to track the *Giggling Witch*, but claiming to need a vital engine part. What a crock of bullshit!"

"Yeah, real smelly, Jake," Sammy T said. "What's their game, do you think? What's their interest in you and the *Giggling Witch*? Using a vessel of more than one hundred feet in length with a crew of fifteen seems like overkill if you and the *Witch* are the only targets."

Jake couldn't say it out loud, but he knew in his gut that it had something to do with the treasure on Marcus Island. Somewhere along the way, he had made a mistake. Somehow he had alerted unknown persons of his quest. As thoughts churned in his mind, the only bright side that came to him was this: if they were *following* him, it meant they didn't know where the treasure was. They were depending on him to lead them to it. He smiled and thought: *And damned if I'm going to do that!*

It was the first round of a cat-and-mouse game. Jake moved the *Giggling Witch* frequently over the next two weeks, and made repeated forays to Anatahan Island to give the impression that he was exploring that area for the treasure. In case he was being watched through binoculars, he made a big show of strapping on SCUBA gear and making multiple dives around the island. The long-liner always followed. Never close enough to be seen, but there just the same, as evidenced by the ghostly presence of the big Zodiac. He needed no further evidence to know he was being tracked.

However, the seasonal change in the weather was upon him. He needed to depart soon for Marcus Island, but the ramifications of an unknown party capable of tracking him by satellite no matter where he went was more than unsettling. It was disastrous! No way could he head for Marcus Island and the treasure with them tracking the *Giggling Witch* every mile of the way. Sammy T said his friends in the government's telecommunications department told him it was unlikely that satellite photo-imagery was being used because it was so expensive. Probably data tracking from a transponder, they said.

Jake and Sammy T searched every square inch of the *Giggling Witch* looking for any kind of device that fit the description of a transponder. It had to be located externally in order to be solar-powered. They looked everywhere, from the tip of the bowsprit to the aft stern light housings. Jake used his bosun's chair and 4-part tackle to hoist himself up the mast. He unscrewed the masthead light and looked inside. He felt around the top of the masthead, but the thin profile of the transponder epoxied there gave no hint of its existence. Since the upper block of the bosun's chair's tackle prevented Jake from being able to rise high enough to look down on the masthead, he missed the transponder's presence. Besides, he could not think of any time the masthead had been exposed to tampering, and forgot about the mast being lowered for the transport across country to San Diego.

It left Jake in a real quandary. If the *Giggling Witch* was somehow compromised, how in hell was he going to proceed to Marcus Island? He had to find another boat. How was he going to do that on tiny Saipan, in the middle of the Pacific Ocean?

(Five)

The deLeon family was throwing a birthday party for Elena's mother, Delilah. Elena came by the Micro Beach Marina in the family's Range Rover to pick up Jake. She was as beautiful as ever, and excited to have Jake with her for the evening. They kissed passionately, Jake nudging her breasts with the back of his hand and feeling her nipples harden. She ran her tongue round his ear, nibbled on it and kissed him again and again. It was all she could do to grab the Rover's steering wheel and get them started down the road.

Jake stroked her leg and inner thigh until she grabbed his wrist and said he must stop or they would crash. He behaved himself for the rest of the drive, but made her stop when they turned into the family farm's road so he could kiss her one more time. They were interrupted by the honking of a horn from a car behind them. It was Sammy T, his wife, Rosita, and kids. Jake turned to look at them and saw that they were laughing; Sammy T pumping his arm outside his car's window. Elena cut a seductive look at Jake and laughed, too.

The tables were piled with food and fruit. A suckling pig was roasting in a pit out back of the house. Over thirty members of the deLeon family and their friends, men, women and children, danced to the music of the boombox, and sang old songs in the Chamorro language. Delilah greeted Jake with a big hug and a kiss on both cheeks. He returned the kisses with a kiss to Delilah's forehead and a gracious thanks for being invited to the party. Elena never let go of his hand and tugged him through the crowd to introduce him to everyone. Of course, everyone had already heard the stories about the handsome Marine's combat feats in Iraq, and saving the lives of those aboard the doctor's yacht by killing the pirates. He was accorded the greatest respect.

Speaking in Chamorro, the women chided Elena, wanting to know why it was taking her so long to land this hunk of a man. Before she could answer, Delilah called for silence and said she had an important announcement. Some thought it would be an engagement announcement for Elena, but everyone was surprised when Delilah said Elena had won a scholarship for her Master's degree studies at the University of Auckland. All eyes went to Elena and Jake. Elena did not know that Gunny Sweikert had already told Jake about the scholarship. She was relieved to see that he was smiling and clapping his hands like everyone else. Jake bent down and gave Elena a chaste congratulatory kiss on the forehead. Everyone clapped their hands and sang their praises for Elena's scholarship.

The party lasted late and Jake discovered that a hammock had been prepared for him. He was expected to stay overnight. That settled, he drank his share of beer, then retired for the night. Elena came along side the hammock, lifted one of his hands to touch her breast, then gave him a juicy goodnight kiss. The following morning, he awoke to the roosters crowing and the rattling of cooking pots in the kitchen. Elena appeared, all smiles and looking delicious. She handed Jake a cup of hot coffee and kissed him on the mouth. Jake looked around nervously to see if her mother was watching. Elena giggled. "Relax. You have Mama's approval. She's already named our first two children."

"Dear God," Jake said.

"I'm just teasing, silly," Elena said.

Delilah called out from the kitchen announcing breakfast was ready. Jake climbed out of the hammock, rinsed his face and hands in a nearby basin, and pawed his hair. At the table, Delilah asked about the Jap long-liner. Sammy had told her a little the night before, but she wanted the whole story. When Jake had finished with the details of the long-liner's tracking activities and was on his second cup of coffee, Delilah said, "We can rid ourselves of the Yakuza with no problem. I will speak to some government people and we'll send them on their way."

"I appreciate that, Delilah, but I'm thinking it might be better if we let them be for the moment," Jake said. "If they're tracking me by satellite, they can do that over the horizon and there's nothing we can do about it. They can float out there, or follow me for months. I've got to figure out how to give them the slip."

"Why are they following you, Jake?' Delilah asked. "You say you know for sure that they are following you. What do you have that is of interest to them?"

It was time to come clean. So, Jake told Delilah and Elena what he was up to. All of it, with the exception of naming Marcus Island, or giving any geographical clue to where he was headed. He had to keep that an absolute secret. His life depended upon it. Anyone who knew where he was headed would be in extreme danger from anyone wanting to intercept his treasure quest.

Elena was amazed to learn that Jake had crossed the Pacific Ocean single-handedly in search of Spanish treasure. Learning that Gunny Sweikert had brought a message from Jake's friends in Florida confirming the treasure's location made it all so very real, and left her speechless. Delilah was astounded in her own way. Her precious daughter had fallen helplessly in love with this handsome adventurer; she didn't know whether to laugh or cry.

Jake could see that the news of his true purpose in coming to Saipan was having mixed reviews. But before he could continue, Sammy showed up in the Range Rover. He had come to pick up Jake to ferry him back to the Micro Beach Marina. Delilah rose to fetch him a cup of coffee. Speaking rapidly in the Chamorro language, she told him Jake's revelations about his treasure quest.

"Holy smokes, Jake!" Sammy said. "Spanish gold! That explains why the long-liner and the Yakuza crew are not overkill at all. They're intending to get that treasure before you do."

"That's a definite possibility, Sammy," Jake said. "What's driving me nuts is trying to figure out how they got on to me. How did they even find out I was looking for treasure? How did they find me here in Saipan? That long-liner and those Yakuza came here from Russia, for Pete's sake. What's that all about? There's a bigger picture here that I'm not getting, and it's freaking me out."

"We know they're following the *Giggling Witch* for sure," Sammy said. "Wherever you go with your boat, they're going to be right behind you. Fifteen Yakuza criminals, man."

I know, I know," Jake said." I've got to find a way to give them the slip."

A smile crossed Delilah's face. Elena and Sammy saw it and exchanged glances. "You said you were going to recover only a small portion of the treasure, Jake, just what your boat could carry, then come back later for the rest of it. How much do you need to recover on the first trip?" Delilah asked.

"If I choose well, a few Chinese porcelain vases, some gold bars, jewelry and loose gem stones," Jake said. "I got some help from an antiquities expert in Florida, to identify the pieces that will sell for the most at auction. She showed me a porcelain vase that was not even a foot-and-a-half high that sold for over two million dollars."

Delilah clapped her hands. She looked at Sammy and Elena and said, "*Makena*!"

"Ho boy! Ho boy!" Sammy said with a whoop.

Elena was shocked. "Mama! You can't be serious!" She grabbed Jake's arm and pulled him to her.

"Why not?" Delilah said, smiling and rising to her feet. "Our ancestors crossed all of the Pacific in them. Come on, Jake, let's take a look," and she grabbed Jake's other arm, pulling him along down a descending path toward the ocean. Elena and Sammy followed, Sammy laughing and Elena fuming, saying "I can't believe this. I can't believe this."

When they reached the water's edge, there, poised atop three large logs lying parallel to the water's edge, was a thirty-five foot long Polynesian proa. Delilah led Jake alongside and said, "Hop in Jake. Try her on for size."

Jake threw a leg over the side of the proa's hull. A small wooden seat was wedged in the rear of the hull. He sat down and stretched his legs out in front of him. The proa's interior was deep and looked to be about three-and-a-half feet wide. The hull was close to two inches thick. Not a toy.

"Our family sails *Makena* every year in the inter-island regatta to Guam and back. Three hundred miles one way, and we always win," Sammy said. "My father and two of my uncles carved her. No seams to leak. Solid wood from stem to stern. Unsinkable, too."

"Sammy! I can't believe you're going along with this," Elena said.

Ignoring her, Sammy said, "She'll do twenty knots easy, Jake, more if the wind is right. More than three times faster than the *Giggling Witch* when she's making top speed. 'Have you to the treasure and back before you know it. Elena won't even miss you," he grinned.

Delilah put a hand on Jake's shoulder. "Give it some thought, Jake," she said. "No need to decide right now, but this is an option. *Makena* is every bit as sea-worthy as your sailboat. There are a few tricks to handling her, but Sammy and Elena are both experienced proa sailors. They can show you the ropes. *Makena* is heavy when she's on land, but once in the water she's light as a feather to handle. Just think about it." She gave a wave to Sammy and indicated that they should leave Jake and Elena alone to contemplate this new development.

(Six)

It came down to just not having any other viable options. Hard as it was to accept, the *Giggling Witch* was out of the race. If Malcom and Lizzie had still been around, he might have worked out some way to charter their boat, but they were long gone on their way to the Philippines. To continue his quest, Jake needed another boat, a tried-and-true sea boat, and like Delilah said, the proa had a thousand-year-old history of open-ocean voyaging. Sammy came by the marina to talk about the implications. He pointed out that the season was perfect, with very low odds of storms. Good foul-weather gear would keep him dry. Not as comfortable as a warm bunk on the *Giggling Witch*, but endurable. The *Makena* was a voyaging proa, designed to carry cargo, food and passengers on long inter-island cruises. She could carry plenty of treasure.

In the end, they decided to go for a sail on *Makena*— just to see how it felt. Delilah, Sammy, Elena and Jake pushed together and *Makena* slid off the logs that were keeping her high and dry. Jake, Sammy and Elena climbed into the proa, raised the sail and off they went. It was a good day to practice; the wind was light at about ten-to- twelve knots, and there was a small chop of about two feet. Sammy took the helm and began to explain the proa's particulars. Elena sat at the forward end behind Jake, rubbing his back, anxious over where all this was leading. After a while, Sammy shifted his position around Jake, letting Jake slip into the aft seat and take the helm. *Makena* was surging forward at more than 15 knots; she had the weight and shape to make her way easily. At Sammy's instructions, Jake put Makena through her paces. *I can do this*, he thought. *Damned if I can't*.

For the remainder of the week, everyday after Elena got home from teaching, she and Jake took Makena out for a sail. They sailed her around Marpi Point and down to the marina at Garapan where Sammy's trimaran, the *Titan III* was berthed. They luffed-up behind the big green trimaran and hailed Sammy. When he came on deck, Jake pronounced himself ready. Sammy gave a yell, dove in and climbed aboard *Makena* for the sail home.

Dinner talk that evening was all about preparing *Makena* for the upcoming voyage. Delilah and Elena both insisted on preserving some fruits and vegetables in sealed crockery. Jake could bring along some canned and freeze-dried stuff if he wanted, but they insisted they put together a healthier and more tasty menu. Jake began to prepare his list of necessities for navigating and digging up treasure: sextant, sight reduction tables, chronometer, stopwatch and charts; Marine Corps entrenching tool, binoculars, flashlight, spotlight, knife, canteen, rope, cooking utensils, fire-making stuff and the Air Force surplus desalinator for converting salt water to fresh water. He would carry water in plastic jugs, three of them of the 5-gallon size, and also bring water coconuts. All that he had read of Marcus Island indicated little or no water. Apart from pirates, it was his biggest concern. Hopefully, the desalinator that Archie McGruder had given him would prove adequate. Better than nothing, he thought. The last item on Jake's list to stow aboard *Makena* was the Haskins rifle; he made no mention of it to avoid alarming Elena.

On the evening before Jake's intended departure for Marcus Island, Elena put two soft packages in the bow of *Makena*, two water coconuts and a flashlight. Just a couple of hours before dark, they walked down the path to the ocean. *Makena* floated to her mooring ball just a few feet off the beach. Without saying anything, Elena waded out to *Makena* and climbed aboard. Jake followed her, climbed in, cast off the mooring line, raised the sail and steered *Makena* in the direction Elena was pointing. It was the most beautiful of evenings to sail, the sun low in the sky, a warm breeze blowing, and *Makena* slipping effortless forward.

Elena moved back to sit in between Jake's legs, her head resting on his lower chest, her hands on the top of his legs. After a short while, she lifted her head and pulled Jake down for a deep kiss. Without a word, she took his free hand and pushed it down inside her blouse atop one of her breasts and held it there by his wrist.

Jake gently squeezed her breast, slid his hand under it to cup it and moved his fingers softly over her already hardened nipple. He leaned forward and Elena turned her face upward to receive his kiss. Jake could have pole vaulted with his erection. Elena laid her back against it, and he knew she could feel it throbbing to his heartbeat.

Finally, Elena indicated a shallow cove protected by two lava outcroppings. Jake steered *Makena* into the cove and up onto the sandy beach. Elena rose, turned to kiss him, then pushed away to gather the two bundles in the bow. Without a word, she stepped onto the beach and went to two storm-bent palm trees to string up the large family-style hammock. From the other bundle she pulled out a light cotton blanket. The sun had set and the gauzy twilight was fading fast. Jake stood transfixed at the beautiful woman preparing their bed.

When the hammock was set, Elena turned to Jake, slipped out of her blouse to expose two of the most perfect breasts Jake had ever seen. She smiled, then stepped gracefully out of her skirt and climbed totally naked into the hammock. Jake needed no further encouragement. He stripped naked and climbed into heaven, Elena sliding a leg over his hip, laying a clear path to her dark warm delta. She took his hardened manhood in her hand and guided him in. Only the sea birds heard her moan when Jake entered her. She gave a small yelp when he broke her virginal hymen, then pulled Jake's buttocks to drive him home, again, again and again.

Jake gasped with surprise, then succumbed to Elena's wild and rhythmic pumping of her hips, breathing heavily into his ear and moaning in a way that made Jake plunge into her all the more fiercely. They stayed at it until Elena loosed a fragile scream and Jake exploded into her. They remained wrapped around each other motionless, throbbing in all the right places, hearts beating as one, while the warm tropical breeze rocked the hammock back and forth.

They kept at it all night. Totally lost to their lovemaking, totally disconnected from anything else. In between bouts, they strolled into the surf to wash off the sweat and love juices. The water was warm and refreshing. They splashed and swam, groped each other to the point they needed a horizontal surface and returned to the hammock for more. Finally, in the early morning just before dawn, they collapsed in exhaustion and slept, curled together, legs and arms entwined. By the time they woke, made love again and sailed *Makena* back to the family's mooring ball, it was midmorning and the de Leon home was vacant except for the chickens pecking around the front yard. Delilah had left a note on the kitchen table saying she was going to the Chang's across the road for some fresh vegetables. The coffee was fresh and on the stove. Just warm it up.

Elena fried some eggs and warmed some leftover pork ribs. They were sitting at the kitchen table finishing their breakfast when Delilah returned with two large straw baskets loaded with vegetables and fruit. One look at her daughter, the glow on her face and the reddish patches here and there on her body, and she knew the whole story. Jake was slow in making eye contact, so she went over and gave him a kiss on each cheek. Then, she took her daughter in her arms, squeezed her tightly and told her she loved her. Tears rolled down Elena's face, but she smiled and knew everything was going to be okay. She went over to Jake, put an arm inside his arm and kissed him openly and passionately.

How in the world he was going to leave his boat, the *Giggling Witch,* behind, part from this incredibly passionate lover who owned his heart, then sail across the Pacific Ocean in a native proa to search for Spanish treasure, he had no idea.

TREASURE ISLAND

Date: May 29, 2001

Lat. 22.17 N, Long. 153.58 E

Western North Pacific Ocean

(One)

Five days now since pushing off from Saipan. Five nights, too. Long nights filled with floating visions of Elena, her incredible smile, her soft nakedness in the hammock pressing against him, her giggles and playfulness in the dark tropical night that he had wished would never end. *Makena* surging eastward with a bone in her teeth, tearing along at something around 15 knots, maybe more. Exhilarating, but tiring, too. Jake had accommodated himself as comfortably as possible in the narrow, plunging hull. *Makena* rose confidently with each towering wave, then skated breathlessly down its face, only to surge upward as the trade wind pressed downward into the trough, filling her triangular sail. She was in her element, and mastering it.

It required no great effort on Jake's part to keep the proa flying eastward, but the speed and the sound of the ocean rushing past the hull made sleep impossible. It had become his routine now to round-up

Makena three times over the course of every twenty-four hours, heaving-to and letting *Makena* bob gently in the great Pacific swell while he slid down deeper into the hull and grabbed two or three hours of sleep. Upon awakening, he would eat a piece of fruit and take shallow swallows of water, then grab the sail's mainsheet, haul it toward him and resume his eastward trek.

It was proving to be very difficult to take his noon latitude sight because of *Makena's* motion. Jake had to wait for the proa to crest a wave then pull the sun down in the sextant's mirror before *Makena's* downward plunge began. If he missed it, he had to be ready for the next rise moments later. He did not have a lot of confidence in his sights for the last two days, and it was making him anxious. His plan was to sail north and east until he reached Marcus Island's latitude of 22 degrees, 17 minutes North, then sail directly East, holding to that latitude until he spied the island. If he was too far north or south of that latitude, he would miss the island completely and it would be impossible to turn around against the trade wind and sail back to the island. One shot, all or nothing.

As the new day's sun turned the far eastern horizon a lighter grey, Jake squinted, blinked twice, then smiled. There to starboard, not even a mile away, a stable brown smudge low in the water. Marcus, by god! He grabbed his binoculars for a closer look. When *Makena* rose to the top of a swell, Jake could see the heavy surf pounding the island's western shoreline, and beyond it the scruffy, uneven surface of the island. The vegetation seemed to consist of small trees and thick underbrush. Even though it was low-lying, Jake could not see all the way across the island. Closer at hand, off *Makena's* port side, Jake could see white water and the breaking surf of the off-lying reef to the island's northwest.

He hauled *Makena's* rudder and spun off to the southeast, rounding the island's southwestern point and steering to close with the beach. Now less than a quarter mile off the point, he could hear the thunderous roar of the huge waves pounding the western reef. It quickly became obvious that rounding the southwestern point was not going to provide much shelter from the press of wind and sea. *Makena* charged across the southern side of the island, skating only a few hundred yards offshore, giving Jake a closer look.

The reef projected out several hundred yards from the southwestern point, then pinched-in toward the beach between the southwestern point of the island and the farther southeastern point. Almost exactly in the middle of the two points, Jake could see what appeared to be a concrete pier, or the remnants of one, jutting out into the surf. Just inland from the pier, across the narrow beach, were two man-made abutments about two hundred feet apart. No idea as to their purpose. Beyond them, Jake could make out the rooftops of two buildings; probably the former Coast Guard station, now long-since abandoned. The surf was smashing violently over and across the concrete pier; definitely not a safe landing place.

Jake pointed *Makena* away from the inhospitable shore and steered for the far southeastern point, giving it 500 yards of clearance, remembering from the chart that the reef extended quite some distance seaward off the point. Once he cleared the point and could see down the full length of the eastern side of the island, he again closed with the beach staying just outside the reef. The lee side of the island was much calmer, the sea moderately choppy with waves little more than one foot in height.

As *Makena* neared the northeastern point of the island, Jake searched for the only other break in the island's deadly reef necklace. This one, he knew, would be off the end of the Jap-built runway. Then he saw it. A very narrow break of untroubled water with a lighter blue bottom and he steered *Makena* sharply to port. *Makena* darted through the hole in the reef and Jake rounded her up inside the lagoon's flat water, dropping the sail and tossing the anchor overboard. *Makena* fell obediently into line behind the anchor rode, coming to rest about 100 feet off the beach.

Jake reveled in the quiet and motionless lagoon. He watched some dark-colored sea birds circle high over the island, and saw land crabs scurrying across the beach sand. Looking down into the crystal-clear water, he could see two or three different kinds of fish swimming in the shadow beneath the proa. Looked like there would be no problem with food.

The beach was no more than fifty feet broad from the water's edge, and the island rose up steeply to more than one hundred feet, covered with a thick green foliage called ginkokai, that reminded him of kudzu. Looking down the beach toward the southeastern point, the height of the island fell away and appeared to be no more than 10 or twenty feet above the water. To his right, toward the northeastern point, the island continued high for a few hundred yards, then sloped downward toward the surf.

He leaned forward in the proa and pulled back the weather tarp revealing the narrow bundle that contained his Haskins sniper rifle, unwrapped it, screwed the barrel into the receiver and worked the bolt action. He also grabbed the 7x50 binoculars and a hand-held compass. Standard fare for a former Marine Corps sniper.

Further forward, on the starboard side of the proa's hull, he pulled out a web belt with a Ka-Bar combat knife attached along with an ammo pouch containing 5 rounds for the Haskins, and a 1-quart canteen of water. Wearing only khaki swim shorts, an olive drab Marine Corps tee-shirt, a floppy campaign hat and Reefwalkers on his feet, Jake eased himself over the side of the proa into waist-deep water. He held the Haskins and the web belt over his head to keep them dry and walked slowly up onto the beach — a Marine amphibious assault of one.

He slipped a round into the Haskin's chamber, then slung it over his shoulder by its strap. He snapped the web belt into place so that the Ka-Bar, ammo pouch and canteen rode comfortably across his hips, then hung the binoculars around his neck and began to walk along the water's edge toward the northeastern point.

The island's high embankment began to slope downward gradually as he approached the point. He spied a large chunk of concrete and steel rebar hanging down from the height, swinging gently. Jake recognized it as a piece of the Jap runway. It looked like a storm surge had undercut the land beneath the corner of the runway and it had collapsed of its own weight. As he clambered upward and made his way around it and up onto the runway itself, he was met by the full force of the wind. Twenty five to thirty knots, he estimated.

Jake saw that the Jap runway was in poor condition; pot holes and long erosion fissures snaking across from the edges were everywhere. The compass bearing numerals painted at the end of the runway were crossed-out with faded yellow paint. The international signal for an inoperative runway. He walked briskly down the length of the runway marveling at the huge surf being driven against the island's reef. To his left, looking toward the center of the island, all he could see was waist-high scrub bushes and a few dozen scraggly trees, none more than fifty feet in height, pulsating with the wind.

As he neared the end of the runway, he spied several rows of rusted military trucks, hundreds of 55-gallon drums stacked on top of one another, and a couple of rows of large propane gas tanks, their previously white surfaces now faded with dark brown rust stains.

Leading off from the left side of the runway was a broken path through the scrub brush and a clump of trees the other side of which Jake could see metal rooftops. But rather than take that path, he continued to the end of the runway and stepped down a 20-foot embankment to the beach. He now stood on the southwestern point of the island, the wind more to his back and the surf not quite so high as he turned to walk down the beach.

In short order he came upon the two concrete abutments and the concrete pier. He saw that each of the abutments had a massive iron ring attached facing the sea, and Jake surmised that they probably were used to secure lines from vessels docking at the pier. The pier itself was a wreck, twisted and sagging, its square concrete footings askew with large ragged gaps exposing rusting rebar. The surf battered the pier with blow after relentless blow, an endless battle by a merciless foe, the contest never in doubt. The pier had been out of service for a long time, maybe twenty or thirty years, Jake guessed, and its condition informed him that the island had served no commercial or military interest for at least that period of time. The island was truly abandoned.

Jake resisted the urge to walk inland and check out the buildings that were now within easy view. Instead, he continued along the beach, making his way to the southwestern point, then turning left to look down Marcus' eastern side. In the near distance, he could see *Makena* dancing behind her anchor just a few feet off the beach. He looked at his watch; not quite twenty minutes since he had left the proa and stepped onto the beach. *A damn small piece of real estate*, he thought. How the Japs crammed almost 3,000 troops, tanks and artillery on it was a mystery.

Jake continued his circumnavigation of the island to rejoin *Makena*, then turned to retrace his steps back to the concrete pier. This had obviously been the island's 'front door.' He turned to his right to walk inland. Going slightly uphill along a coral sand path some 20 feet wide, in short order he came upon the two metal-roofed buildings he had spied earlier. They were in an advanced state of deterioration and far worst condition than the photos he had viewed via the Internet websites. They were aluminum-sided with an aluminum roof and had no windows or doors; totally stripped. Evidence of concrete platforms for power generators were alongside each building, but all electrical equipment, cabling, power distribution panels, internal wiring and electrical outlets had been removed. The rooms within were totally bare, the floors covered with an inch or two of sand. Everything open to the weather, the trade wind whistling through the vacant spaces.

Outside, Jake strolled down the long line of old, rusting propane tanks and the dozens of WWII military trucks. The trucks rested on collapsed rubber tires and their metal rims, and when Jake lifted the hoods of several of them, saw that they, too, had been gutted of engines, pumps, alternators and anything else of value. Around and behind the trucks were hundreds of rusting 55-gallon fuel drums, stacked on top of each other, or lying on their sides.Moving beyond the big junk pile and heading toward the center of the island in expectation of finding the 'lagoon' described in some of the research material he had read, Jake found only a broad depression of darkly colored sand surrounded by scraggly waist-high bushes. The discoloration suggested that there had been water captured there in the past, but it was bone-dry now. Jake immediately thought of his precious supply of water onboard *Makena*. That was the weak link in his expedition. His time on the island was limited by the amount of water to sustain life.

Jake now turned his attention to the elevated end of the island. Standing in the flat lagoon, he estimated that the island gained perhaps 100 or more feet in altitude in that direction. This was where he concluded the most likely location of the treasure was, and it was also the nearest to the northeastern break in the reef. In his mind, the galleon had passed through or over the reef at this point and come to rest on the beach. Moving the treasure from the galleon's holds onto the beach and then into a cave would have been challenging, but not impossible.

But where was the cave? The island's substructure was cement-hard lava, and digging through that would have been nearly impossible. Marines fighting in the islands of the Pacific during WWII had a tough time with their entrenching tools trying to carve out even a shallow depression for protection from enemy rifle fire and mortar barrages. The lava substructure lay barely one or two feet beneath the coral sand covering it. Deeper than that and you were trying to punch through something as hard as granite, or reinforced concrete.

(*Two*)

So, what had happened to the cave and its entrance? Jake mused. He stomped across the elevated ridge, shoving stiff bushes aside and kicking at the kudzu-like ginkokai beneath them. The ginkokai lapped over the top edges of the ridge and draped down the seaward slope like rotten shag carpet. The view was magnificent; he could see the entire island and an unbroken vista of dark blue ocean surrounding it. Thousands of Japanese had lived on this island for years during the world war, and before that there had been a few minor encampments by bird feather hunters and guano gatherers, but none had been aware of any cave.

Two thoughts came to mind: no one was looking for a treasure or a cave; they were all completely distracted by whatever endeavor had brought them to the island. The bombing by the Americans had most certainly kept the Japs occupied with survival rather than thoughts of treasure hunting. The second thought: the cave entrance no longer existed; the passage of almost 400 years allowed for any one of a number of natural events to close, or obscure, the cave's entrance. Maybe a volcanic eruption or shift in the island's substructure, or a fierce tropical storm and ocean surge that came ashore to redefine the island's perimeter. No way to know, really.

From atop the ridge, Jake could see that the drop to the beach was near vertical. After dropping to one knee and sighting along the top of the ridge, he saw an almost imperceptible downward slant to the northeast, and it gave him the feeling of a ship's deck sinking by the starboard bow. What if over time the island had shifted and the cave's entrance was now below water? Not good news. But if the dome of the cave was still above water, it could be entered from the top. How much of the treasure could be recovered in such a scenario was difficult to calculate.

Without any further engineering thought, Jake decided to dig a grid of exploratory trenches across the brow and backside of the knoll. He would be looking for a seam, or a fracture, or any deformation that would suggest the dome of a cave. If he got lucky and the top of the entrance was still above water, maybe he would strike it. But if the trenching produced nothing, he would score the surface of the cliff facing the ocean, working from the top down.

365

As the day's light faded, Jake waded out to *Makena*, pulled himself aboard and rustled through his stores to find his fishing gear, and cooking utensils. Sitting on *Makena's* outrigger, he tossed his lure toward the reef and in short order was rewarded with a bright red reef snapper of about three pounds. He quickly cleaned it on the beach, built a fire of driftwood and roasted the fish to perfection. He chopped the top off a water coconut he had brought from Saipan and washed his meal down. He tossed the fish carcass down the beach and the land crabs swarmed furiously over it. Then he waded back out to *Makena*, climbed aboard, slipped under the covers and was quickly asleep.

(Three)

The eastern sky had only begun to lighten when Jake slipped over the side with his Marine Corps entrenching tool in hand, a ball of string, and a floppy campaign hat. It was the beginning of what would become weeks of hard labor with seemingly little reward for the effort. He climbed to the top of the ridge, stretched out the string between prominent bushes, then struck the ground beneath it to lay out the beginning of a trench.

Cutting through the ginkokai was the tough part; it was a thick, stringy mass over the island's sandy cover. He slashed, cut and dug from earliest light to fading twilight each and every day for the next two weeks. He deepened each trench until he struck the island's black lava substructure. It was ugly, dirty work. The toughest part was controlling his consumption of water. He had set up McGruder's surplus Air Force desalinator atop the hood of one of the old military trucks, and it faithfully turned out about a gallon of drinkable water each day. But the production was not keeping up with the consumption, hard as Jake tried. The water coconuts he was saving for the voyage to Hawaii.

At the beginning of the third week of digging, Jake decided to start a new trench just over the brow of the ridge. He had avoided this area earlier because the ginkokai was so thick and it was difficult maintaining a firm footing so close to the edge of the ridge. He was two hours into brute hacking at the roots of the ginkokai, down on his knees and working from his hips when he swung the entrenching tool down and struck something unexpected, then heard the ominous and unmistakable click of an explosives detonator. It is a sound unlike any other, and Jake's anti-mine experience in the Iraqi desert connected instantly to his nervous system. Without conscious thought, he threw himself over the lip of the ridge intending to roll down the 100-foot high embankment to the beach, but the timer had been set in April 1945 for a delayed 2.5 seconds, and when the 500-pound bomb exploded, Jake was barely three feet down the slope. But it was three feet that saved his life.

He was thrown high into the air, tumbling head over heels, already unconscious from the concussion of the bomb's explosion, and felt nothing when he landed upside down on his right shoulder on the hard sand beach, breaking his collarbone.

Jake had no way of knowing that the glowing dawn being revealed by his fluttering eye lids was the second day since the explosion, not the first. He had lain sprawled on the beach, his lower torso submerged at high tide, for two and a half days, his brain so thoroughly concussed that he was spared the pain of the broken collarbone. He attempted to push himself up, but was rewarded with a pain so unexpected that he screamed out loud, and dropped back down to the beach.

Several hours passed before he tried again, this time shifting to his left side and achieving a sitting up position facing the ocean. He saw land crabs scurry away, startled by his movements. He saw bloody tears on his hands where they had begun to pick at his flesh, thinking him dead. His rattled thoughts gave no hint of where he was, who he was, or what had happened to him. He just stared blankly at the surf breaking over the reef.

Later that evening, long after the pitch black sky had filled with stars, Jake got up on his knees, then stood unsteadily, gazing at the stars. He saw *Makena* down the beach and recognized her for the first time.

Shortly afterwards, his former life began to tumble into place, and by dawn, he knew where he was. His shoulder ached terribly, but he had already learned how to hold his right arm so that it didn't pull on the broken collarbone. He waded out to *Makena*, but discovered he couldn't climb aboard. She rode too high in the water and was shifting so much that the motion prevented him from getting a good handhold. He went back to the beach exhausted from the effort, and sat for several hours.

Then, he saw the solution. He pulled himself to *Makena's* bow and disconnected the anchor line, then let the rising tide lift her up and carry her onto the beach. He could now step over the outrigger and into the hull. He rummaged through his stores and came up with some over-the-counter pain-killer pills and stuffed a half dozen into his mouth, chewing them dry. That made him think of the desalinator, and he realized how thirsty he was. He lifted one of his stored bottles of water to his mouth and almost emptied it. Coughing, he turned with the near-emptied bottle to go check on the desalinator.

The desalinator was filled to capacity. Jake carefully, but shakily, emptied the fresh water into the bottle, and filled the reservoir with sea water to continue the desalination process. He looked to the ridge across the island, but in the darkness could see nothing unusual. Feeling exhausted and still disoriented, he sat down alongside the old military truck to rest, deciding to wait for the light of dawn.

With the new dawn, Jake awoke with a great hunger deep in his gut. He had not eaten for more than three days, but he decided to check out the ridge before going down to *Makena* for food. He crossed the darkened-sand lagoon and pushed his way through the brush to the top of the knoll and immediately saw the devastation caused by the explosion. There was a huge bowl-shaped depression, slanting down toward the northeastern point. In the middle of the depression there was a gaping fissure some three feet wide and over ten feet long. Jake approached it carefully, not knowing how solid was the rim around the fissure. He dropped to his knees, then lay prone and inched his way to the lip of the fissure. There was a hollowness and he sensed it was large, but the sun was still low in the sky and the hollowness was pitch black.

Jake pushed back from the edge, gained his feet and headed for *Makena*. Hunger moved to the back of his brain as he searched for and recovered his spotlight. He took another swallow of water, then proceeded back to the fissure atop the ridge. This time, as he shone the powerful light into the darkness, he saw grey box-like shapes, and big rope-tied packages with rounded edges. His heart leaped in excitement. "I'll be damned! I'll be double-damned!" he exclaimed. He rolled over onto his back to face the sun and laughed and laughed. Arguably the happiest man on earth.

(Four)

By mid-day, Jake had eaten and returned to the blasted fissure to figure out the next step. From the lip of the fissure to the top of the nearest treasure bundle, it appeared to be about twenty feet. He was very much aware of the disaster that awaited him if he should fall or descend into the fissure and have no secure way to get back to the surface. His busted collarbone was a major hindrance to his lifting or pulling strength.

After much thought, he decided to make a rope ladder with *Makena's* anchor line. Marines are taught all sorts of rope and mechanical leverage tricks for hauling or placing heavy field artillery pieces, or dislodging equipment from unimaginably difficult places. He had a rope ladder finished in little more than three hours, and anchored it by tying it to a truck wheel rim that he had rolled into one of the trenches he had dug. He slung his spotlight around his neck and lowered the ladder into the blackness of the fissure, then painfully began his descent using his legs and one good arm.

The sun was just past its zenith and the light passing through the ten-foot long fissure gave fairly good light. Jake stood on top of a high stack of soft, tightly-wrapped bundles. Probably silk skeins or tapestries, he thought, remembering Stacy's recounting from the cargo manifest. Not as exciting as gold bars and sparkling jewels. He shone his spotlight downward and could see it being reflected off water. The cave was flooded toward its seaward end. Jake made his way slowly and carefully down the stacks of soft bundles until he was just above the water. He spied a column of sea chests and pulled one off the top. The chest's curved top came loose from the rotten leather hinges attaching it to the trunk, and the top shelf spilled its contents.

Jake grabbed to catch the shelf and was rewarded with a black lacquered box that tumbled toward him. He lifted the box's lid and found a soft draw-string bag. He pulled it open and his hand was instantly filled with twenty or more sparkling diamonds, a half-dozen un-mounted rubies of various shapes, and three spun-gold broaches with a Christian cross atop their centers. Jake laughed heartily and pocketed the jewels, feeling every bit the victorious pirate.

For the next several hours, Jake moved cautiously in and around the anonymous treasure shapes, poking here and there with his Ka-Bar knife trying to get a feel for how the cave had been packed and in what order or type of cargo. In the darker, lower end of the cave he spied a wooden crate stuffed with what had once probably been hay and noticed stacks of shiny white porcelain. He used his K-Bar to pry loose one of the ends, and gently pulled a brightly painted vase from its four hundred year old resting place. Jake recognized a green-and-yellow stylized phoenix rising against a distant blue mountaintop. It was gorgeous, even to the unpracticed eye of a Marine sniper.

It was difficult to leave the treasure cave, but the light was fading fast. And Jake wanted to save the batteries in his spotlight. He carefully wrapped the porcelain vase in a piece of fabric torn from one of the soft bundles, tied it to the end of the rope ladder and began his ascent to the surface. It was not as easy as descending. He used mostly his legs for hauling his weight up, and used his good arm to pull himself close to the ladder to minimize the swaying. It was when he reached the rim that things became really difficult because of his broken collarbone.

By the time he was completely out of the cave and stretched out alongside the fissure, he was sweating profusely and his collarbone was broadcasting racking waves of intense pain across his back. He pulled the rope ladder to the surface, freed the Chinese porcelain vase, tucked it under his arm, and made his way back to *Makena*. He climbed into *Makena's* hull, washed down another mouthful of pain-killers and collapsed beneath covers too exhausted to eat, but deliriously happy. Oh! to have Elena at his side this night!

At first light, Jake hauled in his fishing line and harvested three medium-sized reef fish. He stepped out of *Makena's* hull, built a fire and voraciously consumed all three in minutes. He sipped a small amount of water and immediately thought of the emergency distiller. He set off with an empty container to tap the collected water. His shoulder ached deeply, and he was stiff all over from his exertions the day before climbing the rope ladder, but he was a happy man despite the difficulties.

He had found the treasure and that was all that mattered! When he reached the desalinator, he filled his empty container, poured in fresh seawater and closed the top. He walked up the hill to the treasure cave's opening and sat down on the edge of one of his trenches to ponder his situation.

His water was running low, and already he was not sure if the amount on hand would carry him to Hawaii. And there remained so much to do. It was a multi-level logistics problem. He would need to shift his belongings out of *Makena* to make room for treasure. Then rearrange his food, water, charts and navigation tools for easy access while at sea. The treasure itself loomed as the real challenge. From his first exploratory plunge into the cave, he had learned that the bulk of the treasure, the silk goods and porcelain, were the last to have been stored, and their considerable weight and bulk sat on top of everything else.

Apart from the size of the bundles, there was the problem of where to shift them out of the way after they had been inspected. The space within the cave was tight, and the effort needed to move them was going to be very difficult with his broken collarbone. He momentarily cursed his injury, but quickly realized that his injury could have been much worse; and after all, had there not been the help from the bomb, he would never have penetrated the cave's dome.

On his second visit to the treasure cave, Jake went straight to the bottom of the cave and the tall column of wooden chests. He began to pull them down one at a time. He used his Ka-Bar knife and entrenching tool to pry open or smash the trunks, and was quickly rewarded for his efforts. The favorite hideaway places of Manila's Spaniards seemed to be false bottoms, and hollow chest tops. The wood was in an advanced state of deterioration and offered little resistance to Jake's blows.

When a secret compartment collapsed, the loot tumbled out. Small gold bars of about 4 inches in length, 2 inches in width, and maybe one-half-inch thick became common. Each bar of gold was struck with some kind of symbol or number to identify its owner. In the same compartments, a wide variety of other treasure items revealed themselves, everything from jade-handled letter openers, carved apple-white jade statuettes of dragons clutching scantily-clad women, all sorts of be-jeweled brooches mounted with diamonds and precious stones, gold bracelets with precious and semi-precious stones, to a black lacquered box filled with perfectly shaped white pearls and shiny black pearls, all strung to perfection. Trying to get the debris out of the way to make more room for opening new trunks was a real problem.

Jake took a woman's silk blouse from one of the trunks and dumped the loose stones, jade carvings, jewelry and other treasure into it. He put the growing collection of gold bars into another blouse. The first blouse held probably 45-50 pounds of precious stones and jewelry, the second maybe 40 to 50 pounds of small gold bars. A nice haul, but modest compared to what he intended to extricate from the cave. Almost as an afterthought, he grabbed some of the hand-written letters and a Catholic missal from several of the chests and stuffed them in one of the blouses to serve as provenance.

Although he was just beginning to penetrate the treasure, he was aware that the more valuable portion as described by Stacy when she had read from the cargo manifest, was not yet discovered. He put the two treasure-laden blouses aside, and climbed cautiously across the top of the bundles toward what had been the entrance of the cave. The roof of the cave was sharply down-turning toward the ocean side. He slid down to water level and stepped into the cool salt water up to his knees, the water level obviously rising and falling with the tide from the look of the stains. He slid his bare feet carefully across the corrugated bottom and came to a series of porcelain-bearing crates that had partially collapsed of their own weight.

Bare-handedly, he pulled one of the crate's sideboards loose, and grabbed a piece of porcelain. It was a soup or gravy tureen with an elegantly shaped handle evolving into a plunging dolphin, the top rim having a shiny, metallic gleam to it. In the poor light at the bottom of the cave Jake couldn't tell if it was gold or silver. He set it aside and pulled himself along a narrow corridor between stacks of cargo and came to another stack of porcelain-bearing crates. These crates seemed more heavily constructed, and there was a purple ribbon wrapped cross the top of them.

With difficulty, Jake pried the top two planks loose from one side and reached through rotten hay to grab what turned out to be a rather large dinner plate. It was incredibly thin and light, and shone with a ghostly pale blue in the light of the spotlight. The rim had a broad silvery or gold band, and in the center, a multi-colored crest of some sort. The Pope's tableware! Jake was sure of it. He reached deeper toward the center of the crate, one level down and extracted ever so carefully what appeared to be a large serving platter with identical metallic trimming on the rim and a hand-painted crest. He wrapped each piece in some clothing from one of the chests he had pilfered earlier, and carried them carefully back to the top of the treasure bundles directly below the open fissure. In the sunlight from above, he examined the two pieces of porcelain and recognized the family crest of Pope Innocent XII that Stacy had shown him back in Florida.

Jake was overwhelmed by his find, and decided to call it a day; his shoulder was aching like hell anyway. He gathered the two blouses with their treasure, and wrapped the two pieces of the Pope's dinnerware in several layers of old clothes. All of it he tied together, then made his way painfully across the top of the soft bundles and attached them to the bottom of the rope ladder.

After regaining the top of the fissure, he gathered his treasure and made his way to *Makena*. There was still enough light in the day to begin the task of emptying the proa in preparation for receiving what Jake hoped would be a prodigious haul of incalculable value. He had not as yet found any of the cargo chests with the large inventory of gold chains, jewelry and other handcrafted items detailed in the cargo manifest. But he reasoned that tomorrow was another day, and starting fresh in the morning, he would finally penetrate the heart of the treasure hoard.

Unpacking *Makena* and stacking water bottles, water coconuts, sextant, stopwatch, charts, binoculars and all the rest of his gear, he came upon Tag's 35-millimeter camera. He had completely forgotten about it. In his somewhat rattled state of mind, he altered the coming day's plan to include a photo session of those items he would be unable to bring with him to Hawaii. Then, sheer exhaustion overtook him. He swallowed another mouthful of painkillers, spread a blanket over the bare hull bottom of the proa, climbed in and collapsed into restless abandon.

The wind was up when he awoke the next morning. The surf was booming against the reef, and although the water was calm between him and the reef, the ocean thundered menacingly, reminding him that he still had a long and dangerous voyage ahead of him. Once again, he gathered his entrenching tool, strapped on his canteen and Ka-Bar knife, and this time grabbed the 35-mm camera. His shoulder ached deeply despite his having strapped his right arm tightly to his body. He was also seriously concerned about his ability to get *Makena* off the beach, raise the sail and steer her twenty-four hours a day for thousands of miles of open ocean. Dwelling on it was not going to help matters, he knew, but the realities of the challenge loomed large in his mind.

Back at the fissure's lip, Jake slithered once again over the cave's rim and descended the rope ladder into the treasure cave. This time, he went directly to the lowest depth at the most seaward end of the cave where he had retrieved the Pope's porcelain pieces. When he stepped onto the "floor" of the cave, up to his knees in salt water, his feet again encountered the corrugated unevenness, but this time he stooped down to touch what was beneath his feet. He ran his fingers along strange creases and pulled up. To his amazement, he dislodged and brought up a gold bar. He had been walking on gold! He guessed the bar to weigh about ten pounds. He shined the weakening light of the spotlight on it and saw the impression of the Spanish royal crown.

Beneath his feet was the gold of Manila's royal treasury! According to the cargo manifest of *Nuestra Senora de la Concepcion*, there were twenty-five chests filled with it! Jake let out a whoop of joy! He began to lift bar after bar of the golden hoard, stacking them atop one of the porcelain crates. He loved to hear the metallic clinking sound as the bars struck one another.

By mid-afternoon, Jake had ferried over one hundred of the Spanish treasury's gold bars to the top of the bundles just beneath the cave's fissure. The pain from his shoulder was growing with each trip from the bottom of the cave. Ten gold bars amounted to a hundred pounds, and the strain on his shoulder from all that hauling was telling. He gathered the bars into clothing from the personal chests of Manila's Spaniards, knotted the cloth, then carried each improvised sack individually up the face of the treasure's crates and bundles to position them for lifting out of the cave. He took his first picture with the camera, focusing on the impressive stack of gold bars.

Returning to the bottom again, he pushed a little further between two columns of porcelain and stopped at a stack of 3 squat wooden crates and pried open the top of the uppermost crate. The crate held 4 large, brightly-painted porcelain vases with stylized handles on either side. Most interesting to Jake's first look was that the vases looked like vases-within-vases. There was a lattice-like outer shell over a second inner shell. Jake had never seen anything like them in all the museum pictures that Rebecca had shown him. He decided he would keep two of them to take to Makena, but would ferry all four to the top of the treasure closest to the cave's opening and take pictures of them.

Back to the bottom of the cave, Jake was again lifting chests when his spotlight began to flicker. Not much juice left in the batteries. He pried open the top of a chest in the dark, then gave a quick look with the fading spotlight. It was a cargo chest! The first thing he saw was rope-like chains of finely-crafted gold, looped back and forth in multiple layers. He grabbed a handful and began to pull in the dark while climbing back up the face of the treasure stacks. At the top, with natural light, he continued to pull the chains up and saw what he had: incredibly delicate gold chains, each individual chain of a different style. Jake laughed and laughed as he stuffed some of the chains into two of the recently recovered jugs. What a haul! He exulted in boundless joy.

Exhausted and in pain, but fired up by the new treasure discoveries, Jake made one last plunge to the bottom of the cave, gathering an assortment of new porcelain pieces, gold chains, and jewelry. He included several more pieces of the Pope's dinnerware, and a half dozen of the exotic Chinese vases and jugs. He spaced them out in a display, draping gold chains over the lot, with stacks of jewelry, crucifixes and silver candelabras and took multiple photos with the camera, close-ups of individual pieces and group shots. It was a shame that he couldn't bring it all with him, but *Makena's* hull would never hold it all, and besides, the proa needed to be relatively light to sail properly.

Once he had lifted the gold bars and the most recently recovered treasure from the cave, Jake began to make multiple trips down to the beach and *Makena*. He wobbled and stumbled, and nearly went head-over-heels as he came down the embankment at the end of the Jap runway. He was tired, thirsty, and in pain. His recovery from the concussion was still incomplete, and his thinking was not clear. After wrapping the porcelain pieces and stowing everything in its place aboard the proa, he intended to drag some of the ginkokai over the fissure and the trenches he had dug in an effort to reduce the visibility of his recovery efforts. It would quickly reset itself and grow; not that there was much chance of anyone visiting the island or stumbling over the cave's entrance. But whether he had the energy to do it was questionable.

Makena was completely empty and all of Jake's gear laid out on the beach. During the more than 3 weeks Jake had been on the island, *Makena* had shifted back and forth with the tide and had worked herself deep into the beach. The hull had to be freed before he could begin to load the treasure. But Jake couldn't budge the heavy wooden hull and its outrigger. He took his entrenching tool and began to dig out the hull around all sides hoping that on an incoming tide she would float. The digging of the heavy wet sand took its toll and finally he collapsed against the hull, laughing deliriously at his ridiculous predicament — the treasure ready to be loaded, and he a prisoner of the island!

Later that night, long after sunset, the rising tide washed up between his legs and woke him. He felt *Makena* move ever so slightly and pulled himself upright alongside the hull. The incoming tide had filled in the trench he had dug on either side, but it was loose watery sand. He went to the bow to shove. His shoulder screamed in pain at the effort. For a moment Jake thought he was going to faint. He moved along the hull to the outrigger, turned outboard and lifted the outrigger, using the leverage to rock *Makena*. Up and down, up and down, he pumped the outrigger. His shoulder howled in protest.

Just when he thought it was no use, a small wave on the incoming tide lifted *Makena's* heavy stern. Jake leaped to the bow and shoved with everything he had. *Makena's* stern lifted to the next wave and then slid into lagoon, now fully afloat. Jake grabbed the outrigger to hold her parallel to the beach, then tied the anchor line to the bow and staggered ashore. He collapsed in a heap, and had it not been for the aggressive land crabs, he would have slept where he had fallen. He used the outrigger to climb into *Makena's* hull after he had chewed some more of the painkillers, then covered himself with a piece of silk tapestry he had scavenged from the cave. He plunged into fitful sleep to the throbbing cadence of pain from his shoulder.

When he awoke, Jake pulled himself upright in the hull. He moaned at the pain in his shoulder and back. He felt weak and exhausted despite the night's sleep. He looked toward the beach and saw the jumble of treasure and his personal effects piled helter-skelter against the sandy cliff of the island. With great difficulty, he eased himself over the side of *Makena's* hull into the lagoon and waded ashore. He was hungry and thirsty, but he had forgotten to bait his hooks the day before.

His thinking continued to be scattered, and he was having difficulty in projecting future tasks. He dug through the pile, found a small jar of pickled pears that Elena had packed for him, then he stumbled off to the desalinator with an empty canteen. Half-way there, he suddenly stopped and realized that he would never be able to get the water out of the coconuts he had brought from Saipan. It was a two-handed affair with the machete to lop-off the top of a coconut, and with his injured collarbone he was down to one hand.

By the time he returned to *Makena* and the treasure, he had decided to open the coconuts on the beach where he could lodge them against the cliff and hack them open with the machete, then pour the precious liquid into the Chinese jugs. As an afterthought, he decided to fill the jugs part way with the loose stones and jewelry to control the sloshing of the water inside. But first, propelled by the deep grumbling in his stomach, he baited his hooks in hopes for fresh food before dark.

Jake eased the anchor line to allow *Makena* to float just a few feet off the surf's edge. One at a time, he placed the gold bars from Manila's royal treasury in the bottom of the hull, spreading their weight along the entire length. After three rows side by side, he began to string-out the gold chains in long rows alongside and atop the gold bars, then wedged-in the short gold bars he had found in the personal chests of *Concepcion's* passengers. Atop these he laid a layer of silk tapestry for padding, then placed the selected pieces of Chinese porcelain including the two pieces of the Pope's tableware, each wrapped securely in strips of silk tapestry. Inside of each porcelain vase he poured loose diamonds, rubies, pearls and smaller pieces of jewelry mostly broaches, rings, gold buttons and bracelets. In and around all of this Jake placed his sparse supply of food from Saipan, his sextant, binoculars, chronometer, reduction tables and charts. Standing on the beach, Jake observed *Makena* carefully. She seemed to be no lower in the water than when he had departed Saipan, and the load was balanced.

Pleased with himself, Jake turned to the last item on the beach: his Haskins sniper rifle. Bulky and twenty-three pounds in weight, he was going to have to leave it behind. He needed to find a secure place to hide it. He looked at his watch and considered his progress. Water was the main concern. He needed one more day of production from the desalinator. He needed to spread the ginkokai over his diggings and the cave's entrance. His concussed mind struggled to figure it out.

He picked up the Haskins, slung it over his good shoulder, and buckled on his canteen and Ka-Bar knife. Slowly and painfully, he made his way down the beach and around the southeastern point to the desalinator. He emptied the day's production, filling the canteen, and poured in what would be the last seawater he would purify. Then he went to the last truck in the front row, crawled under the engine compartment and laid the bundled Haskins inside the transmission tunnel. Close to total collapse, Jake chose to remain under the truck until after the mid-day heat.

It was his grumbling stomach that stirred him to activity. He returned to *Makena* and checked his fishing lines. Success! Two reef snappers. He built a fire and roasted them, then consumed them both in a matter of minutes. The closing chapter of his time on Marcus Island was slowly coming together in his mind. He would spend the remainder of the day dragging the ginkokai over the cave and surrounding trenches. He would replenish the desalinator and collect the last of the freshwater the next day, then launch *Makena* through the reef at dusk, wind and weather permitting, of course.

The wind moderated to something less than 15 knots, and the surf was parting gently at the entrance to the reef. Jake, exhausted from deploying the ginkokai and the walk to the desalinator, threw a leg onto the proa's outrigger and worked his way to *Makena's* hull. She seemed to dance with the excitement of returning to her element, but Jake was pressed hard to haul her bow around, raise the sail and steer for the center of the break in the reef. It was a relief to clear the narrow passage, shift the sail and bear away to the southeast. He watched numbly as the dark shadow of Marcus Island disappeared over the horizon.

His shoulder pained him beyond description, but with great effort he was able to position his compass in front of him and steer a course with his left arm, while pushing against the hull with his legs. How long he could bear the pain and summon the energy to steer, he did not know. But thinking of Elena and looking at the bundled treasure, he knew it was success or death. Nothing in between.

THE RETURN

Date: June 30, 2001

Lat. 21º .9' N, Long. 160º 149' W

Niihau Island, Hawaiian Island Group

(One)

Makena sped gracefully before the gentle ten-mile-per-hour wind, riding the small surf toward tiny Niihau Island's sparse and arid seventy acres, her captain only partially conscious from time to time. Jake had not eaten nor taken in water for seven days. It took an extreme effort to just lift his head, check that his treasure was undisturbed and that the sail was set properly. He had cinched the mainsail sheet to the rear outrigger many days earlier when he no longer had the strength or could bear the pain of hauling it. It was the crudest form of self-steering, but fortunately *Makena* was well-balanced and the sail properly trimmed for a downwind reach.

Makena was making perhaps 15 knots when, at full tilt, she drove up onto the white sand beach of Nonopapa Bay. She skidded to a stop abreast a line of swaying coconut palms some twenty feet beyond the surf's edge. Her captain registered only the slightest acknowledgement of their arrival; little more than a lifting of his chin from his chest and a draping of his left arm over the side of the proa's hull. No telling how long he might have remained there if left undisturbed; so little of life's spark left.

"Don't move, mister!" the Marine sentry commanded. He had spied the proa bearing down on the beach, radioed his sergeant, then raced at full gallop to intercept the interloper. He stood with his M-16 nestled into his shoulder, sighting down the barrel and pointing it at the slumped body lying in what looked like a Polynesian outrigger loaded with ominous-looking bundles that could easily be explosives. "This is a U.S. Government facility, mister, and you are in a whole lot of shit!" he said. The body made no move, its face obscured by a wrapping of cloth around and over the head.

The duty sergeant arrived on the run, his 9mm Beretta pistol drawn. "What 'cha got here, Walker? A lost tourist from Kauai, or what?" the sergeant said.

"Don't know, Sarge, but he's got a load of something in that boat," Private Walker said. "And he hasn't moved or said anything either."

"Keep a bead on him while I take a closer look," the sergeant ordered. "Hey, you! Look at me! What's your business here?" The sergeant squatted down to try to look at Jake's face.

Jake heard the voices, but had no idea what they were about. He shifted slowly and painfully, raising his left hand to pull off the Chinese cloth covering his head and face. The sun was blinding, and the heat on his sunburned face made him wince in discomfort. Then he heard a woman's voice.

"What's going on, Sergeant Lewis? Who's that in the proa?" The voice was that of an attractive 50s-something woman wearing a brightly colored Hawaiian Mumu. "He looks injured. Where did he come from?" she asked as she joined the two Marines. "Call my husband on your phone and tell him what you've found." As she said that, she took a few tentative steps toward the slumped figure in the proa and kneeled down to come eye-level with Jake's sun-ravaged face. "He's burned to a crisp!" she said. "Hand me your canteen, sergeant," she ordered.

The Marine sergeant obeyed the wife of his General, quickly passing his canteen to her outstretched hand. Simultaneously, he called the General's quarters asking the houseboy to make the connection. "General's already left for his conference, Sarge," the houseboy said.

"The General's already on his way to the conference, mam," the Sergeant relayed to the General's wife, but she was already holding up the interloper's head and helping him swallow water from the canteen. He gulped it down like he'd never tasted water before, and coughed several times. His eyes fluttered opened, and he smiled through cracked lips.

Thank you mam," Jake said. Then recognizing the two Marines in uniform, he added, "Sergeant Jake Porter, Second of the Fifth," and gave a weak salute with his left hand.

The sergeant cautiously lifted a corner of the tarp covering Jake's treasure and raised an eyebrow. "Chinese Jars, mam. That's what he's hauling," said the sergeant. "We should take a closer look at this stuff," he added, pulling back the tarp a little further revealing several more Chinese vases.

"Is Tony Perelli on duty, sergeant? Tell him to bring an IV and some sedatives, and salve for sunburn. Belay that search for now, Sergeant Lewis, until we see more of what this is all about," the General's wife ordered. "He's a Marine, you heard him say. One of ours."

"Yes, mam," the sergeant said, then radioed for Lance Corporal Perelli, the guard unit's corpsman, to come on the double.

By the time corpsman Perelli arrived with a green canvas bag containing the items the General's wife had ordered, Jake was sitting up straight in the proa and in weak, almost inaudible whispers had explained that he had a broken collarbone. Perelli installed the IV, gave Jake some triple-strength ibuprophen, then applied a cooling salve to his face, neck and arms. He then examined Jake's shoulder and confirmed his diagnosis. "A clean break from what I can tell," he said. "Must hurt like hell though. How long's it been broken, sir?"

"Couple of weeks," Jake said, wincing under Perelli probing.

"Let's get him to the house," the General's wife said. "Perelli, you get some bandaging so we can stabilize the shoulder." Many years before marrying a young Marine lieutenant who forty years later would become Commandant of the U.S. Marine Corps, Mary Winton had been a Navy nurse. She knew her stuff.

Realizing that they were going to separate him from the proa and the treasure, Jake croaked a desperate plea. "Mam, I am most grateful, but I can't leave my boat. I've got some valuable stuff in it."

"Sergeant Lewis, place a sentry on this boat. Make that two sentries. No one's to touch it. Understand? Not to peek inside, examine it, or move it in any way. Rotate the sentries every two hours and have the sergeant of the guard give me an update on any changes, understood? And keep trying to reach the General."

"Yes, mam," Sergeant Lewis said.

"You two men," the General's wife addressed the young Marine guards, "Help our guest to his feet, and give Corporal Perelli a hand with the IV." She led them up the beach and into a large lanai. She spoke to a steward in green Marine fatigues waiting at the top of the stairs. "Willie, call the kitchen. Have them fix a large bowl of chicken soup and bring it to me immediately." As Jake was hauled to the porch, the General's wife picked up a pitcher of iced lemonade, poured a glass and held it to Jake's parched lips. Jake could have cried for joy.

As they settled him onto a plump bed, Jake pulled his wallet from a hip pocket, extracted a slip of paper and handed it to the General's wife. "I have been out of touch with my friends for many weeks and I know they are worried. Would you please call these numbers and let them know I have returned?"

"Yes, of course," she said. "But you must lie still. I have some soup on the way." The list began with a Marine Corps major, a professor at the University of Florida, then a Marine Corps Gunnery Sergeant in Fort Lauderdale, Florida, whose name sounded familiar, then a Saipan telephone exchange for a school teacher, then an antiquities expert at a Palm Beach gallery. An intriguing list for sure, but she called each one in turn.

(Two)

Stacy answered the telephone and stood in shock as the female voice introduced herself as a Marine general's wife and announced that Jake had arrived in Hawaii on a native proa stuffed with Chinese vases. "Tag! Tag!" she called out to her husband. "Come quickly! Jake is in Hawaii, and he's okay, but has a broken collarbone!"

Bryce Taggart ran to the phone to listen in with Stacy. Stacy explained that her husband had just come to the phone and would she mind repeating the good news? Could they speak with Jake? The general's wife said that Jake was in an extreme state of exhaustion and suffering not only a broken collarbone, but was severely dehydrated. She suggested that he be given a few hours to rest and recover, then he could call them on her personal cell phone. She left the number with them. After the conversation was over, Stacy and Tag hugged each other and danced a little jig in the living room. Jake had done it! The world would stand still for them until they next heard Jake's voice. But no sooner had Tag mixed a couple of celebratory drinks for the two of them than the phone rang again. It was Gunnery Sergeant Sweikert calling from Fort Lauderdale, to tell them of his receiving a call from the wife of the Commandant of the Marine Corps.

Sweikert was laughing and cussing at the same time. "Of all the damn places in the whole wide world that son-of-a-bitch could wash onto a beach, he lands in the front yard of the Commandant of the Marine Corps. Can you believe that? And the Commandant's wife says his proa is loaded with Chinese vases. They've even got a Marine squad guarding it to keep it safe for him!" He laughed again, and Stacy and Tag Bryce laughed with him, but they were puzzled that Jake had arrived in a native proa rather than his steel sailboat. What was that all about? they asked Sweikert. "No idea," he said. "He was on his boat when I last saw him in Saipan. By the way, I'm acquainted with the Commandant. We served together," Sweikert said. "I'm thinking about putting in a call to him. Jake's on Niihau Island and may need someone to vouch for him. The Corps' top brass is pretty serious about any uninvited visitors to their Hawaii hideaway."

The General's wife, Mary Winton, skipped over Elena's name because, given the time zone of the Marianas, she considered it unconscionable to call a school teacher at three o'clock in the morning. Seven o'clock would be plenty early she decided, and instead called the Palm Beach, Florida, number for Rebecca Fontaine. Rebecca answered her cell phone and gasped at the news General Winton's wife relayed. After hearing that Jake was not in the best of shape, but was receiving medical care and resting, she asked Mary Winton to repeat the part about Jake arriving in a native proa filled with Chinese porcelain vases.

"Did you actually see the vases, Ms. Winton?" Rebecca asked.

"Oh, yes," Mary Winton said. "They are quite beautiful. Very colorful. And strange, too. Around the upper half of two of them, they had a lace-like layer over an inner vase. I've traveled with my husband to the Far East many times, but I've never seen anything like them."

Rebecca's hand holding the phone trembled, and she switched the phone to the other ear. "Ms. Winton, your description fits a style called 'reticulated', and it's very, very rare. In Jake's behalf, I ask that you do all that you can to keep those vases safe. They are valuable beyond imagining."

"Don't you worry, Rebecca," Mary Winton said. "Jake is being cared for and the vases as well. We have a Marine guard watching over the proa and its contents. Once Jake has recovered somewhat, I'm sure he will want to unload his proa, and we will all have a chance to see the vases. Believe me, I am as excited as you are. Do you have any idea where he obtained them?"

Rebecca said, "No. Jake was following some research being done by an academic team of treasure salvers. It is my understanding that he was involved in the treasure's recovery. May I come to see Jake?" Rebecca asked.

"That may be difficult, Rebecca," Mary Winton said. "Jake has landed on Niihau Island. It is a small, privately-owned island just across the Kaulakahi Channel from the island of Kauai. The Department of the Navy, specifically the United States Marine Corps, has a long-term lease on a few acres around Nonopapa Bay. It is designated as an R&R destination for very senior Marine Corps officers. They meet here not only to rest and recuperate from the stress of their responsibilities, they also use it to discuss very secret planning. I have a call in to my husband who is the Commandant of the Marine Corps. It is going to be up to him to decide how all this plays out. Jake has landed on sacred land, so to speak. I believe everything will work out okay, but as I say, my husband will handle it. Why don't you call Jake tomorrow and speak with him? Here is my cell phone number that he will be using."

"The first person Rebecca called after receiving the news of Jake's return was Hattie Heinz on Palm Beach. "Hattie, this is Rebecca at the Left Bank gallery. Grab a chair, honey. I've got some news that will definitely make you weak in the knees."

(Three)

General Lester A. Winton, Commandant of the United States Marine Corps, listened to his wife's description of the native proa that had landed on the beach at his compound at Nonopapa Bay. Her description of its sole occupant, a Marine Corps sergeant by the name of Jake Porter and the Chinese vases left him puzzled in the extreme. He told her his conference was completed, and he was on his way home. He instructed her to place a guard at Sergeant Porter's bedroom door, allow no one to interview him other than herself, and wait for his return. He grabbed his leather briefcase, his cover, and was on the way out the door when his clerk announced that he had a call from a Gunnery Sergeant by the name of George Washington Sweikert. A Marine Corp general meets a lot of people on his way up the career ladder, but few like Gunnery Sergeant Sweikert. Why do I have this feeling that Gunny Sweikert is involved in this proa business? he asked himself, taking the call in the ready room.

When the Commandant's khaki-painted Lincoln Continental pulled into the driveway, General Winton's wife, Mary, was waiting patiently at the foot of the stairs, barefoot and dressed in her favorite Mumu, a smile on her face and a flower in her hair. Willie, their steward, waited at the top of the stairs holding a serving tray with his General's favorite drink in the center, an ice-cold Tom Collins .

General Winton took his bride in his arms, gave her a firm kiss, and motioned Willie to bring the Tom Collins. "I want to see the proa first, Mary," he said, and steered her around toward the back of the lanai and to the beach. "How's the sergeant?"

"He's sleeping, Win," Mary said. "Corporal Perelli said he was not far from dying when he first examined him. Another day or two without water and he would have gone into systemic shock. We hydrated him, spread some salve on his sunburn and fed him a bowl of chicken soup. Corporal Perelli has put a plaster over his collarbone and wrapped it in a field dressing. So he's stabilized."

"Where the hell did he come from?" General Winton asked. "Does he have a passport?"

"Win, I could see the sergeant was in critical shape. I called Corporal Perelli to administer to his immediate health needs. I ordered a guard to be posted to protect the proa and its contents until you were apprised of the situation and came to take control," Mary Winton said.

General Winton smiled. "By the book, eh, sweetheart? You've done well. Now let's see what we have here." They had arrived at the proa, and the two sentries braced to attention. "Stand easy, men. Step off a few paces and give us some room to look things over," he said, and walked around *Makena* several times paying particular attention to her sailing rig. "Well built," he pronounced. "This is the real thing, Mary. What the Pacific islanders have used for a thousand years." He lifted the corner of one of the tarps covering the cargo. "Looks like Chinese vases," he said. "Wonder where he got them." He lifted one of the smaller vases and was surprised at its weight.

General Winton reached into the vase to see what was making it so heavy, and when he retrieved his hand, it was filled with loose diamonds, rubies and sapphires. "Holy Mother Mary," he said, holding them for Mary to see.

"Oh, my! Oh, my!" was all she could say at the moment. Then, as her husband dipped back into the vase and pulled out a fresh handful of the jewels sparkling brilliantly in the late Hawaiian afternoon sunlight, she said, "How beautiful! How beautiful! Win."

General Winton turned to the guards who were standing twenty feet away, watching but not watching. "Call the Duty Sergeant, and have him report here immediately."

"Aye, aye, sir," they responded in unison. One of them raised his VHF radio to his mouth and called for the Duty Sergeant. In less than 3 minutes, the sergeant arrived on the run and saluted his General.

"Sergeant, I want the guard doubled," General Winton barked. "Bring up some kerosene lamps and keep this site and that proa well-lit tonight. Anyone who touches the proa or its contents will be court-martialed and spend the next ten years in Fort Leavenworth. I suggest a ten-foot perimeter, two entries facing outward, and two inward. Anyone attempting to approach the proa, you are to arrest them and call me immediately. Understood?"

"Aye, aye, sir. Right away, sir," the Duty Sergeant said, giving a brisk salute before spinning on his heels to mount the guard.

General Winton turned to his wife and said, "Mary, let's go see your sergeant." He took her hand and they headed for the lanai. Enroute, the General chuckled and in a low whisper said, "I got a call from Master Gunnery Sergeant George Sweikert just before I left the office. Remember him from Iraq? Want to guess what the call was about?" Before Mary Winton could tell her husband that Gunny Sweikert was on the list of friends given her by Sergeant Porter to call, her husband answered his own question. "He was calling to present your sergeant's bonafides. Wanted me to know that your Sergeant Porter is the Marine sniper who knocked off Saddam Hussein's cousin, the Deputy Defense Minister during the first Iraq war. Porter was decorated by both the Saudi and Kuwaiti governments. We hung a few medals on him, too. Now he's in our backyard with a zillion bucks in jewels and Chinese vases.

"Gunny Sweikert also said that Sergeant Porter's fiancée is the closest thing to royalty on the island of Saipan, Her grandfather was the fellow who showed our Marines where the Japs were hiding during our invasion. He saved the lives of many Marines, and we decorated him for it. The father of Porter's fiancée was a Marine platoon sergeant who was killed in Vietnam while trying to drag two wounded Marines to cover. He was awarded the Silver Star posthumously. Her older brother served in the Corps and is back living with his family in Saipan. As if that were not enough, her younger brother is serving in the Corps now. A Marine Corps family across three generations, Mary, and a distinguished one at that. I have a feeling this is going to get real interesting."

The two of them, General Winton and his wife, stood in the doorway to observe Sergeant Jake Porter lying in bed asleep. "Damn! He's burned to a crisp," the General said in a lowered voice.

"That's what I said when I first saw him," Mary said. "But he's looking better already." She picked up a chart that Lance Corporal Perelli had left on a bedside table. "His temperature is only slightly elevated, his pulse a little high, too, but not so bad considering what he's been through," Mary said. "Corporal Perelli is monitoring the IV and administering some low-level painkillers to help with the broken collarbone. He's refreshing the sunburn ointment every four hours."

"When can I talk to him?" General Winton asked.

"Well, we need to feed him some more soup in a couple of hours. Why don't we have dinner, and then Perelli can wake him for the feeding?"

General Winton grunted in agreement, gave his wife a peck on the cheek and headed for the shower.

Four)

"How you feeling, sergeant?" General Winton asked as Lance Corporal Perelli wiped soup from Jake's chin, then retreated from the room with the soup dish and tray. His wife stood beside him and smiled in a motherly way.

"Stiff and sore, sir," Jake said, visibly uncomfortable that he couldn't stand in the presence of the Marine Corps' highest-ranked officer. General Winton was a legend in his own right, and the last time Jake saw an official Corps photograph of him, he had more ribbons on his tunic than Jake had ever seen.

"How long were you in that proa?" General Winton asked.

Jake squirmed a little at the question. He knew he was on thin ice. Perelli had told him he was on a privately-owned Hawaiian Island named Niihau, and had landed on property leased to the Marine Corps for its most senior officers. "I'm not sure, sir. At least two or three weeks, I think. I wasn't thinking too clearly the last part of the trip after I ran out of water. I didn't mean to land on this island, sir. My collarbone being broken, I didn't have the strength to steer. *Makena* was kinda on autopilot and I was passing out a lot."

"*Makena*? That the name of the proa? General Winton asked.

"Yes sir," Jake said. "She belongs to my fiancée's family. They loaned her to me. I departed from Saipan, sir."

General Winton thought about that for a moment. Almost three thousand miles of singled-handed ocean sailing in an open boat. Impressive.

"You understand we had to take a close look at your proa. All those bundles, you could have been hauling explosives, or some kind of contraband," the general said.

"Yes, sir, I understand, sir" Jake said, knowing what was coming next. They've seen the treasure, or at least part of it, and will want to know where it came from. But he was surprised at the general's next comment.

"I got a telephone call earlier from a Marine Corps gunnery sergeant that I spent some time with in Iraq. He cautioned me, respectfully of course, that I was not to call you 'Snapper.' General Winton smiled. "So, just to keep clear, I know all about you, Sergeant Jake Porter. After Gunny Sweikert's call, I had your complete service jacket forwarded to me by facsimile from Washington," General Winton said. "The only part that is missing is how you came to be sailing across the Pacific Ocean in a native proa filled with what I would guess to be several million dollars in treasure." It was an invitation for Jake to tell his story.

"Yes, sir," Jake said. "It's a long story, sir."

"My wife has already notified your friends of your safe return from wherever you've been," General Winton said. "At the moment, U.S.

taxpayers are footing the bill for the Marine Corps to guard your proa. That's an issue I've got to address, but it is not an insurmountable one, mainly a bit of creative paperwork. You are on a sensitive military installation, sergeant, and there are some ground rules. However, the Department of the Navy allows us, on a very limited basis, to invite and entertain civilians and dignitaries of various sorts. I am thinking that Mary and I may have an impromptu dinner party this weekend and invite your friends to attend a presentation of your ocean voyaging and treasuring hunting endeavors. Sort of a show-and-tell. What do you think of that arrangement. Sergeant Porter?"

Jake was flabbergasted. "It would be an honor, sir, mam," was all he could say.

"We will leave you to continue your recuperation, Jake," Mary Winton said. " Because of the time difference I have not called Elena, your fiancée. I thought you would like to do that yourself," she said handing Jake her cell phone.

"Thank you for everything, mam" Jake said.

"Get some rest, sergeant," General Winton said as he led his wife out of the room.

Jake immediately dialed Elena's telephone number in Saipan.

(Five)

The way it worked out, after everyone had had an opportunity to speak with Jake by phone and express their astonishment at his cross-Pacific feat, arrangements were made to fly everyone into Kauai by commercial air. Rebecca Fontaine, beside herself at the prospect of managing such a haul of treasure and beyond excited to see it for herself, made the airline and lodging arrangements for everyone. She put the tab on The Left Bank's credit card: first class airline seats and penthouse suites at Kauai's most luxurious beachside hotel, where they would await the arrival of Lena and her mother from Saipan. Rebecca also engaged the services of a local inter-island helicopter service to fly them all to Niihau Island the next day. The company's new Italian-built Augusta A109 had 8 seats, and would make short work of the 17-mile trip across Kaulakahi Channel to Nonopapa Bay.

While all of this was going on, Jake was slowly regaining his strength. He was being fed well, and Lance Corporal Perelli was checking his collarbone daily, monitoring his food and water intake, and continuing to apply ointments to Jake's sunburned face, neck and arms. Jake could see *Makena* and her Marine guard detail from his window, but he was disinclined to disturb the arrangement put in place by General Winton. Another day or two, Jake felt, and he would be his old self again.

The greater truth however, was that his mind was consumed with two pressing thoughts: he was now most likely a millionaire, but he was unsure how to think about that; secondly, he knew he had to go back to Marcus Island, and the logistics of returning to Marcus Island to recover the bulk of the treasure weighed heavily. He and *Makena* had made off with not even one percent of it. The remainder was totally unprotected and exposed to discovery by others. He thought of the stacks of gold bars, gold chains, jewelry and Chinese porcelain that he had piled atop the bundles of silk just before he left. He must act fast.

The main issue for a recovery of the remaining treasure was money. Jake had no idea as to the value of the Chinese porcelain and jewels he had loaded into *Makena*. It had been a haphazard selection on Marcus Island, but he knew it was worth a lot of money. He just didn't know how much, or how long it would take to convert it to cash, or whether it would cover the mounting of a large recovery operation. From his experience in the treasure cave, the bulk of the treasure was immense. It would take a half-dozen men several days to lift it to the surface and transfer it to an offshore vessel. That vessel would have to be a fairly large one, a commercial ocean-going freighter of some sort. How to locate such a vessel and the crew to operate it was beyond his competence. Finding a crew that could be trusted in the presence of hundreds of millions of treasure was a major problem, too, but a possible solution to that issue was already forming in his mind.

(Five)

Major Bryce Taggart (USMC, Ret.) and his fiancée, Dr. Stacy Burns, University of Florida professor of European History, Gunnery Sergeant George Sweikert, USMC Reserves, and Rebecca Fontaine, holding two bouquets of flowers, stood in a line alongside a white stretch-limousine watching the inter-island turbo-prop De Havilland, with Elena and her mother aboard, taxi to the terminal. Elena and her mother had flown from Saipan on a Pan American flight to Honolulu, then transferred to the turbo-De Havilland for the final leg to Kauai. Only Gunny Sweikert had previously met the two women, but as the passengers deplaned there was no mistaking them. Elena's mother came down the steps first, beaming in excitement upon seeing Gunny Sweikert, throwing open her arms in welcome. Elena descended behind her mother with the grace of a princess. Her posture was regal and she wore a perfectly-tailored, crème-colored two-piece suite with a colorful silk scarf around her neck, and her bare legs ended perfectly in polished red high heels. She was show-stopper beautiful. Her eyes were wide in anticipation, and she was smiling enthusiastically even though she knew she would not be reunited with Jake until tomorrow.

Gunny Sweikert made the introductions, and after a round of hugs, they boarded the limo and Rebecca broke out the champagne. At the hotel, they were treated like royalty and led to their rooms to freshen up. A short while later, they gathered in the hotel lobby and took their places at an elegant table on an outside patio overlooking the gleaming Pacific Ocean to begin a feast that they would remember to the day they died.

Bryce Taggart tapped on his water glass to gain the attention of everyone. "I thought it would be advisable to mention a couple of things before we begin to discuss Jake and his adventure in this rather public place. Stacy and I were sworn to secrecy by Jake and asked to not reveal anything about his quest for treasure. We have honored our promise to him. Jake made the point that there are people who would do anything to disrupt his efforts, and perhaps even kill him if he stood in the way of their seizing the treasure for themselves. I feel we should all recognize that Jake continues to be in great danger.

"His recovery of this small piece of the treasure exposes him—and his friends—to even greater risk if he is identified with this recent success. The death of two of Jake's dearest friends, along with recent activities in Saipan, have led Jake to believe that he is being watched very closely by an unknown group. The appearance of this small portion of the treasure on the open market at international auctions will create great curiosity. Many people will recognize that what is being sold is representative of only a tiny portion of the galleon's cargo. They will wonder where the rest of it is, and who is recovering it."

Rebecca Fontaine raised her hand and said, "Forgive me for interrupting, Tag. You are quite right about the need for secrecy. I thought all of you would like to hear this good news." Rebecca reached into her purse and brought out a facsimile transmission. "Jake and I met with a very, very wealthy collector of Chinese porcelain before he sailed to Saipan. She is a long-time customer of my family's business, and her private collection of Chinese artifacts rivals that of most museums. She has provided me with the authority," Rebecca said, waving the facsimile copy, "to spend up to 100 million U.S. dollars to purchase items that Jake has recovered. This arrangement will provide Jake with instant funds, and the sale can be kept totally private until Jake feels any danger is past."

Everyone at the table was floored by the size of the sale. Stacy spoke first. "Rebecca, that is astounding news. I can safely guess that Jake will be speechless when he hears it."

"And if I know Jake, as soon as he's able he will go after the remainder of the galleon's cargo," Tag said. "This is far from over."

"I am so happy that Jake has so many friends on his side," Elena said. Her voice was soft and melodious in the way of Pacific islanders.

Since her arrival at Kauai with her mother, Elena had probed everyone for any information about Jake. Tag, Stacy, Gunny Sweikert and Rebecca had each shared their personal stories of how they first met Jake. Rebecca had diplomatically left out the part where she and Jake had slept in the same bed at Hattie Heinz's mansion on Palm Beach. There had been no sex, so she didn't feel she was being less than honest by not relating the tale.

"Jake decided to use my family's proa because there was a Japanese fishing boat, what they call a 'long-liner', that showed up and anchored at Saipan. We discovered that every time we moved Jake's sailboat, the *Giggling Witch*, a crew boat from the long-liner, or the long-liner itself, followed us. And members of the crew strolled out to the marina in Tanapag, trying to look like they were just tourists on a holiday. But their tattoos marked them as Yakuza, a criminal group from Japan. Jake was sure they had somehow found a way to track the *Giggling Witch*. He searched everywhere to see if they had secreted a GPS transponder of some kind on his boat, but those things are so small he couldn't find one.

By taking the proa, Jake was able to shake off his pursuers. While he made his way to the treasure, my brother and I moved the *Giggling Witch* around some of the islands north of Saipan, pretending to conduct diving operations as though we were searching for a sunken galleon. My brother and several of his friends are sailing the *Giggling Witch* around the island right now to continue the deception, and it looks like we have them fooled. They are very clumsy in their surveillance, and we have many of our friends and family on the island watching them day and night."

"I don't think it's wise for you to return to Saipan any time soon, Elena," Gunny Sweikert said. "If those Japs really are involved in shadowing Jake and looking to grab the treasure, they are a real danger to you, too. Especially if they think you know anything important."

Elena smiled. "I am booked on a Pan Am flight back to my home the day after tomorrow." She emphasized the word 'home'. "I am a school teacher, and my students need me. The time is long gone when anyone on Saipan runs from Japanese. I want to see Jake and comfort him. There's been a hole in my life ever since he sailed away on *Makena*. When that is done, I must go. Jake will come to me in Saipan when this treasure business is behind us."

"I'll drink to that!" Rebecca said.

"Well said," Stacy said. She raised her glass and made a toast. "Here's to Jake and Elena." Everyone raised their glasses and levity was restored to their banquet.

(Six)

Jake watched the preparations for General and Mary Winton's impromptu lawn party with quiet amusement and considerable humility. A small field tent had been erected adjacent to *Makena* to provide shade and protection from the blustery Hawaiian sea breeze. On the opposite side of the proa, a light fly tent had been set up with metal folding lawn chairs. A large rubberized ground cloth had been spread alongside the proa to serve as a floor for treasure as it was removed from the proa.

Mary Winton had discussed how she thought the event should progress and asked for Jake's input. Jake thought the general's wife had planned it well. The guests would arrive by helicopter, landing just a few hundred feet from where the proa was situated. Jake would be there to greet them, along with her and the General. Then they would proceed to the chairs beneath the fly tent, iced tea and sandwiches would be served, and then Jake would begin to unload the proa of its precious cargo. Once the show-and-tell, as the General referred to it, was over, all of them would go to the Winton's lanai for a luau-style dinner. Before dark, the treasure would be loaded onto the helicopter and all the guests, including Jake would depart the island. It would be left to Jake to make whatever arrangements were necessary to move *Makena* to another place.

During his brief stay, Jake, General Winton and his wife Mary had reached an easy accommodation. With considerable effort General Winton had made no further inquiries into Jake's treasure quest, or where he had found the treasure. He was convinced beyond any doubt that Jake had not arrived at Nonopapa Bay on purpose. His physical condition of extreme dehydration, hunger and a broken collarbone coupled with weeks of single-handed steering of the proa made that highly unlikely. No, Jake was not an intruder. To that must be added the fact that he was a former Marine Corps sniper, and a highly decorated one at that.

Then, there was the fact that his fiancée was also a member of the Marine Corps family. Her grandfather won fame during the Marine Corp's invasion of Saipan in World War II, her father was in the Corps and lost his life in Vietnam. Her older brother had served in the Corps during the first Gulf War in Iraq, and she had a younger brother currently serving in the Corps. Impeccable credentials without question. To all of that, fate had delivered them to his front door. He did not intend to miss this remarkable opportunity to demonstrate Marine Corps hospitality and gratitude for their service to their country.

(Seven)

The Augusta A109 made two circumnavigations of Niihau island, giving the excited passengers a bird's-eye view of the tiny island. The helicopter pad was easily identified, and the beautifully landscaped grounds surrounding the General's lanai were just a few hundred feet away. Of greatest interest was the native proa next to the beach and the two tent-like structures next to it. As the helicopter swooped down in a gentle, curving descent and landed on the concrete helipad, its passengers could see the welcoming committee: a squad of armed Marines were clustered together in preparation for surrounding the helicopter, and three people in tropical attire braced against the wash of the helicopters' rotors. One of them had his right arm in a sling. He looked terribly thin, but he was smiling broadly.

The pilot braked the rotors and popped open the passenger door, followed by a hydraulically extending staircase. Master Gunnery Sergeant Sweikert was the first down the stairs, followed in turn by a matronly woman in colorful native dress, then Rebecca, then Elena, then Tag and Stacy. When Elena stepped onto the staircase, she locked onto the eyes of the young man with the sling, gave a squeal of pure joy, kicked off her shoes and ran barefooted to him. Careful of his arm, she grabbed Jake's face and pulled his lips to hers. Jake steadied the two of them with his good left arm and pulled Elena tightly against his chest.

"Now that's what I call a hero's welcome," General Winton laughed. His wife, Mary, turned to the other arriving guests, introduced herself and made them all welcome. She saw that everyone was having a hard time not looking at the proa, so she led them across the lawn for a closer look. Jake and Elena, hugging and holding hands, followed.

Makena sat just as she had when she skidded off the ocean onto Niihau Island's beach a week earlier. The sail swung easily to the wind, and the treasure was still beneath the tarps just as Jake had secured it for the trip from Marcus Island. The corner of the tarp that had been lifted by the Marine sentry for inspection had been tucked back inside the hull.

Elena's mother, Delilah, went to *Makena's* bow and bent to kiss it, giving it a brief blessing in her native Chamorro language. As she straightened, Gunny Sweikert took her hand and gave it a squeeze. "A job well done, *Makena*," he said.

Rebecca was so anxious to see what was below the tarps, she turned to Jake and said, Okay, sailor, let's see what you've got."

Jake and Elena approached the proa together, each with an arm around the other's waist. Jake turned to General Winton and Mary Winton. This was not exactly the way they had planned it, but Mary Winton smiled and nodded her head.

"Take a look for yourself, Rebecca," Jake said, smiling. "Just lift the front corner of the tarp and drag it aft." He really didn't want to let go of Elena anyway. They kissed again, bringing smiles to everyone's face.

Like a kid beneath the Christmas tree opening presents, Rebecca slowly tugged the tarp. As the tarp came off, the first thing Rebecca saw was two large Chinese porcelain vases, each lightly wrapped in old Chinese silk cloth. As she uncovered them, she swooned. "Oh, my God, oh my God!" She gently lifted the larger of the two and was immediately surprised at the weight. Puzzled, she reached into the vase and came out with a handful of precious stones, just as General Winton had done days earlier. Dumfounded, she didn't know what to say or do.

Jake stepped forward and picked up the script that Mary Winton and he had planned. He gently took the vase from Rebecca's hands and upended it. The jewels inside spilled onto the ground cloth that had been laid alongside the proa. He then handed the vase back to Rebecca. While she stood in awe of the pile of jewels at her feet, Jake grabbed a second vase upending it as well in a rainbow of sparkling brilliance. General Winton and his wife laughed and clapped their hands in appreciation of Jake's showmanship. Tag, Stacy, Elena's mother and Gunny Sweikert gasped in amazement. They, too, joined in the clapping of their hands.

Jake drew the tarp back even further, exposing anonymous lumps that turned out to be more vases. With Elena's help, he unwrapped each one, handing them to Rebecca, who by this time was speechless. The last vase Jake had handed her was reticulated and undeniably Shunzhi, priceless beyond calculation. She estimated that there were probably a half-dozen wealthy Chinese collectors who would gladly pay more than $50 million for just that one porcelain vase because of its rarity. Jake then reached down alongside the bottom of *Makena's* hull and grabbed a handful of gold chains and a bar of gold. These he handed to a dumbfounded Tag and Stacey. Before they could say a word, he reached back inside the hull and pulled out two more gold bars with the Spanish treasury's royal stamp and handed them to Gunny Sweikert. Finally, he extracted a twenty-foot long gold chain of exquisitely intricate design and draped it around Lena's mother's neck. She beamed and grabbed Jake's chin, pulling it toward her to give him a kiss.

Jake then selected a medium-sized bundle, transferred it to the ground alongside Makena and opened it. Out tumbled dozens and dozens of pieces of hand-crafted jewelry, rings, broaches, pendants, and bracelets, some in gold and some in silver. Most of the pieces were mounted with jade, or precious stones. In the pile was a small polished teak chest inlaid with mother-of-pearl. Jake opened the chest and pulled out letters and a Spanish family's Catholic missal. He handed the papers to a dazed Rebecca, saying "provenance." Then before she could respond, he grabbed a handful of the jewelry, each beautiful in its own right, and spread them out on the ground cloth. Everyone reached down to pick up a piece and examine it.

While they were occupied, Jake reached into *Makena's* hull and extracted two well-wrapped objects. He turned to Stacy and said, "The Pope's dinnerware."

Stacy was already in a state of speechless awe. Tag remembered Stacy's research that mentioned the Jesuits' gift to His Holiness the Pope. This was her research come to life, a magical moment for any academician. He watched his fiancée ever so carefully remove the wrapping to reveal the shimmering gold-trimmed porcelain dinner plate bearing Pope Innocent's family crest; fired in the Chinese Khan's private kilns almost 400 years ago. The other piece she had handed to Tag, and when he removed the wrapping, he held an equally beautiful serving platter, also bearing the Pope's crest. They held the two pieces in front of them for all to see. Mary Winton stepped forward to touch the plate that Stacy held. Stacy carefully passed it to her and she in turn handed it to General Winton.

For a finale to his "show-and-tell," Jake grabbed over two hundred feet of gold chains that he had strung out along the bottom of the proa and dragged them to the center of the tarp. For effect, he draped them across the Chinese vases. Then he and Elena, after another hasty kiss, tossed gold bar after gold bar, over twenty of them, onto the tarp.

Holding tightly to Elena, Jake addressed the gathering: "As you all know, my original plan was to bring back the treasure in my sailboat, the *Giggling Witch*. The presence of what I believe are Jap pirates forced me to switch to *Makena*. The *Witch* could have carried four or fives times the amount you see here. I'm afraid this is all I was able to stuff into *Makena*." Then, looking down at Elena, he added with a smile, "Anyway, I was in a hurry to get back to my real treasure." Elena pulled his face down to hers and gave him an extended kiss, Jake again holding her tightly against his chest. Everyone applauded again.

The only things left in the proa were Jake's sextant, charts, chronometer, binoculars and his camera. He picked up the camera and handed it to Rebecca. "Photos from the cave, and a hint of what's left. Hattie will probably flip when she sees what's left to buy. It's going to be one hell of a flea market," he said. But Rebecca continued to be speechless. Never, ever in her life had she been in the presence of such a fortune. To see it come tumbling out of a native proa on a tiny Hawaiian island, and realizing that she was commissioned to selling it, was just mind-numbing. It would bring the highest single-client commission in the history of her family's business. She couldn't wait to tell her father of her coup. And she was already relishing the phone call she would make to Hattie Heinz in Palm Beach, to tell her what was available for her to purchase.

The additions to Hattie's Chinese collection would make headlines throughout the world of art. Museum directors from Hong Kong to New York would be plying her for invitations to visit her and see the new additions to her private collection. It was the kind of attention that Hattie Heinz lived for.

General Winton's wife, Mary, addressed her guests, "I don't know about the rest of you, but I need to sit down for a spell and have a glass of iced tea." General Winton seconded the suggestion, and everyone except

Rebecca took seats under the fly tent. Rebecca was clearly undone. She held the reticulated Shunzhi vase in here arms like it was a newborn baby. It was simply the most wonderful thing. She brought it with her to sit beneath the fly tent with the others. She turned to General Winton and said softly, "This is more rare than anything in the world of antiquities with the possible exception of King Tut's death mask." General Winton nodded in astonishment.

After they had sat for awhile and had sandwiches and iced tea while gazing at the piles of treasure spread before them, Rebecca remembered that she had not yet told Jake of Hattie's authorization to spend 100 million dollars. She drew the facsimile from her purse and handed it to Jake. Elena kissed him on the ear while he read it.

Rebecca was on a roll. She pulled her cell phone from her purse. "I'm calling an insurance carrier in New York that I've done business with before. I'm buying a policy to cover what's out there on the lawn. I'm taking photos of your haul with my cell phone and forwarding them to the insurance people. I can only estimate the value at this point, but I'm going to ask coverage for $250 million. The two reticulated vases in my estimation are easily worth $100 million. I will arrange for a valuation by one or more international authorities and obtain written and certified assessments. I will arrange for our helicopter to be met tonight on Kauai by a bonded international courier firm.

"I will also have a private security firm provide security around the helicopter while we make the transfer of the treasure to the courier people. The courier firm's insurance will be on top of our own coverage. They will take possession of the treasure and convey it by private jet to my family's business in Palm Beach. We have a very secure vault, and I will have the external security tripled. Hattie is going to want to see what she has bought, and we can do that at The Left Bank, or we can take several pieces to her home for her inspection. There will be no public viewing, or any news release of a sale until you give us the word that all dangers of intervention are behind us."

Jake was a bit dazzled by how fast things were progressing. "So, I have access to $100 million? I mean, I can start spending it?" he asked.

"Tomorrow morning, as soon as the banks open on Kauai, I will exercise the power-of-attorney Hattie has given me and I will order the transfer of funds to any bank account of your choosing," Rebecca said. "You can then spend away."

Everyone under the tent heard the exchange between Jake and Rebecca. They were all in amazement at the amount of money being discussed. Each was wondering what Jake would do next. They weren't left wondering for long.

"Tag, Gunny, I need a freighter. Probably something around 100 to 200 feet. It has to be in service, complete with current documentation and flag of convenience, and ready to go. No time for repairs. A real bonus would be if it had an engineer aboard who knows the boat's electrical, mechanical and propulsion systems. We don't need a captain. I'll be doing the driving."

General Winton was observing Jake closely. Five days ago, Jake was at death's door. His shoulder was today still in a plaster, and his arm was in a sling. But here he was, directing operations and spelling out the drill to a Marine Corps major and a salty old Corps gunnery sergeant; the two of them listening intently to Jake and, from the looks of it, prepared to follow whatever orders he issued.

"The *Sea Bones* was registered with Lloyd's Register," Jake continued. "I saw her paper work, and as her captain I had to keep the registration up to date. It had a big impact on the annual insurance premium. Lloyd's is an international registry of all commercial vessels around the world. The directory provides all the details and specifications of each vessel, powerplant, tonnage, country of registry, builder and owner. It's a clearinghouse so to speak, and it carries announcements of vessels for sale and their present location. That's a good place to start looking for our boat. Focus on boats the nearest to Saipan. Time is of the essence."

"Forgive me for interrupting, Jake, but I might be of some assistance in that area," General Winton said. "The Marine Corps contracts with dozens of shipping firms all over the world to have our equipment hauled around and prepositioned as necessary to the political situation. We do a thorough background check of the vessels and their owners to make sure we know who we are doing business with. If you think it would be helpful, I could contact our logistics people in Washington and see if they have a line on any available tonnage."

"I'd be most grateful, General," Jake said. "It looks like I have enough money on hand to buy one, but maybe we could charter one like the Corps does."

"I'll look into it in the morning," General Winton said, "and I'll call you on your cell phone as soon as I hear something."

"Elena doesn't return to Saipan until the day after tomorrow, sir" Jake said. "So I have some catching up to do in that department, and it sounds like Rebecca is going to be pretty busy, too. I have a couple of other logistics projects that Tag and Gunny can take care of if they're willing."

"I have taken an extended vacation from the university," Tag said. "I didn't have any classes this semester anyway. Stacy has taken an emergency leave of absence, but she's covered. She has two excellent graduate interns to manage her classes. So we're at your disposal, Jake."

Jake laughed. "And you don't want to forget that you're both millionaires now. Neither of you have to work another day of your lives at anything you don't want to do.

"Well now, Jake, I don't think...," Tag began.

"Tag, I would never had been able to pull this off without Stacy's and your help. I said in the beginning that if I had an opportunity to make us all rich, I would," Jake said. "Well, our boat has come in, as they say."

"Besides, your help brought Jake to me in Saipan. That's worth more than a million dollars to me," Elena said hugging Jake tightly around his waist.

"Jake, I really don't know what to say," Tag said.

"Nor I, Jake," Stacy said, coming over to give Jake a kiss on the cheek. "Except thank you so very much. Tag and I haven't been the same since you and Brenda came to the university for that first visit. I don't think we've stopped thinking about the *Concepcion* and her treasure since that afternoon. For a college professor, it has been quite a ride."

"Why don't we go up to the main house and freshen up?" Mary Winton said. "Our household staff has been preparing a real feast for this very special occasion." Mary Winton and Jake exchanged furtive winks, and General Winton was unable to avoid giving Elena a quick glance.

After everyone had gone to a bathroom, then freshened themselves with the warm cotton towels handed them by the General's household staff, they entered the dining room. Warmly lit by lanterns and candles, the twenty-foot long table was topped by a honey-and-ginger glazed porker on a silver platter with a huge mango in its mouth and surrounded by tropical fruit. Platters of steaming rice, beans and potatoes, and all sorts of other dishes lined the middle of the table.

Everyone took their chairs, General Winton sitting at the head and his wife, Mary, to his right. The servants moved down behind the guests, pouring wine into sparkling crystal goblets. Jake and Elena sat next to each other, of course, and opposite them sat Delilah and Gunny Sweikert, and Major Bryce Taggart and Stacy facing each other across the table. Rebecca sat at the end of the table, still in a daze over the day's events, wondering if the treasure on the lawn was really safe.

General Winton rose, tapped on his wine glass and cleared his throat. "I have attended many a celebration and more dinners than you can count in the course of my forty-year-plus career in the Marine Corps. I can truthfully say that none has been more exciting than this one, or attended by more delightful and honored guests. The Marine Corps is proud to recognize the service of those around this table, especially the deLeon family of Saipan. I also have the honor tonight to invite one of our guests to make a special presentation. Sergeant Jake Porter, you have the floor." The General raised his glass to Jake and took his seat. Mary Winton and Delilah deLeon exchanged glances and smiles across the table. They knew what was coming.

Jake rose and raised his glass in toast. "General, I am most grateful for the hospitality which you and Mary have extended to me since my uninvited intrusion. In addition, to saving my life, you have made your home welcome to my friends. I will be forever grateful and in your debt. I would like to make this occasion even more special by sharing this moment with you." Jake turned to Elena, and eased his chair out from behind him. Elena looked up at him curiously, wondering what this was all about. Jake reached into his pocket and lowered himself to one knee. "Elena, you are my life. Back on Saipan, before I shoved off with *Makena*, I asked your mother if she would allow me to propose marriage to you and she said yes. My fortunes have improved considerably since then, and I was wondering if you would have me for a husband?"

Elena took Jake's face in her hands, a tear rolling down from the corners of both of her eyes, and said, "Yes, my love. Yes!"

Jake opened his hand, unfolded a dark velvet cloth and lifted a ring he had selected from the *Concepcion's* treasure, a flashing yellow diamond mounted atop a gold ring surrounded by tiny faceted rubies. He took her hand and slid the ring on to her finger, a perfect fit. Elena stood and

lifted him from his bended knee, throwing her arms around his neck and kissing him with unabashed passion.

General Winton stood, followed by everyone else, and said, "A toast to love and long life for Jake and Elena."

"Hear! Hear!" everyone said in unison. Then they all made their way to Elena and Jake to anoint them with congratulatory hugs and kisses.

The dinner was anti-climatic after that, though it was delicious beyond description. They finally made their way back down to the pile of treasure alongside *Makena*, and under Rebecca's strict directions, the porcelain vases, the Pope's tableware, the jewelry, the gold bars and everything else were placed into padded shipping covers that Rebecca had had the foresight to bring onboard the helicopter. When everything was secured, they gave General and Mary Winton hugs and handshakes, then boarded the helicopter for the return flight across Kaulakahi Channel to Kauai.

Following a protracted radio conversation between the pilot of the Augusta A109 helicopter and Kauai's airport control tower, they hovered to a soft landing at the far end of a taxi strip next to a darkened hangar. A dozen automobiles and vans with flashing red lights, surrounded by a small army of airport and private security people were there to meet them. Even before the rotors stopped, the helicopter was surrounded by some seriously armed people with Israeli machine pistols and semi-automatic 12-gage Remington shotguns.

Rebecca stood at the top of the helicopter's staircase and spoke with the head of the security detail and the courier people. Identifications were swapped and contracts were signed and counter-signed. The treasure was off-loaded piece-by-piece and escorted across the tarmac to the nearby hangar. On signal, the hangar door lifted revealing a gleaming Gulfstream IV, with the pilot, co-pilot and security personnel standing by its stairs. Each piece of the packaged treasure was inspected again and checked off the lists of the security people and the courier personnel. When everyone was satisfied, Rebecca came over to Jake and Elena to give them each a kiss.

"I have confirmation on the insurance. The courier's insurance policy kicked in when we each signed the contract. I'm going with the treasure to Palm Beach to see it safely into The Left Bank's vault. I would love to spend more time with you here in Hawaii, but business takes precedence. Jake, you can call or visit your bank in the morning. The money will be there. Call me if there are any questions, okay? I'm so excited, I think I may pee in my pants."

"Have a nice flight, Rebecca," Elena said. "We'll miss you, but I'm sure we'll be together again soon. You must visit us in Saipan. We are expecting you." Elena gave Rebecca a parting kiss on the cheek. "And tell Hattie Heinz that we would love to have her for a guest as well."

Everyone but Rebecca boarded a black limousine for the short ride to their hotel. Jake confessed that he was wiped out and was looking forward to a good night's sleep. Elena squeezed his knee, nuzzled his neck, and said, "We'll see about that."

PIRATE'S PROGRESS REPORT

Date: April 27, 2001

Lat. 14º 58' N, Long. 145º 37'E

Tinian Island, Northern Marianas

(One)

Yoto Nakura sat at the bridge of the *Taka Maru #17* fingering the microphone transmit button of the ship's single-sideband radio. He had been composing his message all morning, refining it to make sure it conveyed the right mix of his optimism toward discovering the location of the treasure, but also his increasing frustration over the time being spent tracking the round eye's sailboat, the *Giggling Witch*. He and his Yakuza crew had staked out the Tanapag marina where the *Giggling Witch* was berthed when she was in port. They watched the comings and goings of everyone visiting the yacht, especially the beautiful Chamorro woman who seemed to have joined the crew.

Every time the yacht left the marina, they followed. Since they were tracking the yacht by satellite, there was no need to follow too closely. The yacht could make a top speed of no more than 10 knots; the *Taka Maru 17#* could make 20. No contest if it came to a chase. When the yacht slowed or anchored, Yoto Nakura ordered the ship's Zodiac into the water to follow them and see what they were up to. The Zodiac had been seen by the yacht's crew, but Yoto Nakura, felt they were not particularly affected by the brief encounters. What had become interesting over the past few weeks was the continual return to Anatahan Island north of Saipan. Each return visit was longer in duration and members of the yacht's crew were seen donning SCUBA gear.

The latest development, the yacht had been joined by the big 70-foot trimaran, the *Titan III* from the Garapan marina. It appeared that the trimaran was being used as a diving platform. The owner chartered the boat for local diving expeditions, and had many air tanks on deck and a diesel-powered air compressor for filling the tanks. From all appearances, they were definitely onto something. The last time, there were about a half-dozen people putting on diving gear. Things seemed to be speeding up. Yoto Nakura decided he was prepared to radio Berne, Switzerland, for an update. He was also going to demand an additional payment toward his expenses.

(Two)

Lat. 46° 95' N, Long. 7° 44' E

Berne, Switzerland

Per protocol, the teleconference originated at 1200 hours Zulu, with Berne launching the meeting.

Berne: "Gentlemen, we seem to be back on course with the Florida-based treasure quest. I have just spoken to Captain Yoto Nakura by single-sideband radio. As you know, Jake Porter and his sailboat, the *Giggling Witch*, made it to Saipan. We launched a long-liner captained by Yoto Nakura, a former associate of ours at the South China Seas wreck of several years ago. Nakura's vessel is currently anchored at

Tinian Island, about three miles south and west of Saipan Island. Clearing the port every time Nakura needed to follow one of Porter's moves proved to be a real paperwork hassle with the port authorities, and also kept Nakura's long-liner in easy view of Porter. So, Nakura moved his long-liner from Saipan, to Tinian. This has not affected our monitoring of Porter's activities. Nakura's Zodiac tender speeds over to Saipan every day to check Porter's marina and look for any changes. We monitor Porter's boat's movements by satellite twenty-four hours a day, of course.

"Captain Nakura informs us that Porter has begun probing around the northern Marianas, particularly Anatahan Island. Anatahan is about eighty miles north of Saipan, an easy one-day sail for Porter. It's a damn small island, about six miles long and two miles wide, low-lying; exactly the kind of place that a Manila galleon might stumble over in the night, or during a storm. A recent development: After multiple solo vessel trips to Anatahan Island, Porter has recently been accompanied by a large trimaran with a lot of diving gear. A number of divers have been seen in dinghies and diving in the area.

"Captain Nakura is urging us to action. I have congratulated him on his patience, and informed him that we have a support vessel on its way. Johann, the Dutchman, and his armored patrol boat are enroute to Saipan as we speak. I also told Nakura that one of our consortium's partners would be joining him within the week and would remain aboard the long-liner throughout the term of recovery operations as specified in our contract. Nakura has demanded an additional deposit to cover operational expenses, and in light of these positive developments, I have forwarded the funds to him. I anticipate that once Dutch arrives with reinforcements, we can move in on the dive site at Anatahan Island and remove Porter from the picture. That eighty miles of ocean between Anatahan and Saipan is perfect for giving us the time and space to grab what's ours. I'll let you know when Johann arrives on the scene. That's it for now."

Transmission ended. Screens go blank.

(Three)

Lat. 14º 58' N, Long. 145º 37'E

Tinian Island, Northern Marianas

Captain Yoto Nakura called the crew of the *Taka Maru #17* to assemble topside on the after deck. They were a menacing-looking assembly; shaved heads and dark blue full-body tattoos gleaming in the sunlight, wearing only a cotton thong between their legs, .

"Our waiting time is coming to an end," Nakura began. He stood naked to the waist; his pants rolled up to his knees, his own tattoos pulsating with his muscular movements. "I have just received news that a support vessel will soon arrive. I know this vessel and her captain from a previous treasure recovery in the South China Sea. The vessel is a very fast, armored patrol boat that used to be in the Canadian Navy. The captain is a treacherous Dutchman whose word is worth nothing. He will bring a crew of armed murders with him. He is not our friend, or partner. He guards our recovery operations to protect his bosses' investment. At the proper time, we will kill this Dutchman and all of his soldiers. Their possessions and their share of this operation will be distributed among my Yakuza brothers.

"Also, one of the principal partners of this treasury recovery will be arriving to stay on our *Taka Maru #17* and watch the operations. Until I signal otherwise, this partner will be treated with respect. He will not be given any cause to doubt our dedication to his enterprise. But at the right moment, I will personally kill this partner who would deal with us as if we were fools. I will throw his body into the sea, and we will take the entire treasure for ourselves. No one comes out of this venture alive except you, my Yakuza brothers, and me.

"I am sending our Zodiac across the way to Saipan to pick up some Saipanian comfort women. We will drink warm Saki, relax in our hot baths, and fuck these women until our guest arrives. The women will be

414

paid handsomely and you will bring no harm to them. Just fuck them so that they remember when they last had Yakuza between their legs."

FORMING UP THE FLEET

Date: July 10, 2001

Lat. 09º 00' N, /Long. 80º 00'W

Panama Canal, Republic of Panama

(One)

After Elena and her mother, Delilah, had boarded the Pan American Flight from Honolulu, to Tokyo, then on to Saipan, Jake had called a meeting of Gunny Sweikert, Bryce Taggart and Stacy Burns. They met in Jake's suite at the Royal Hilton, and it would be fair to say that they were a happy group. Jake confirmed that his bank account's balance reflected the $100 million that Rebecca assured him would be there when he checked. He had immediately hired a private courier firm to deliver two cashier's checks, each for a million dollars, to Tag and Stacy's room in the hotel. They had called him on the hotel's phone system, telling him that they had no words to express the gratitude they were feeling.

Jake offered to discuss a fee with Gunny Sweikert in reward for his making the effort to come to Saipan, bringing both good and bad news. Sweikert demurred, saying Jake could make a donation to the Marine Corps Christmas Children's Fund if he liked. Jake agreed and saw that the transfer was made. A short while later, he handed Sweikert a bank transfer note confirming it. Sweikert whistled when he saw the amount: "Quarter of a million dollars. A lot of happy yuletide faces in that, Snapper," he said, deliberately using the nickname that Jake despised.

"I'm going after the rest of the *Concepcion's* treasure," Jake announced without fanfare. Of course, everyone already knew that. They sat on the edges of their chairs to see what role Jake had in mind for them. "There are some logistics that need to be taken care of. Time is of the essence, as they say. It's strictly volunteer. If we pull it off, the checks you just got will pale in comparison to the next payoff," Jake said. He reached across the table and picked up a nine-by-ten manila envelope, sliding out color photos. "These are the pictures I took in the cave. Rebecca had the film developed. I received these this morning by special courier. Rebecca enclosed a note that I will share with you in a moment because it bears directly on what we're discussing here today."

You could have heard a pin drop. The photos were passed around and Stacy was the first to speak. "I can't believe what I'm seeing, Jake," she said breathlessly. "Just look at them! All those porcelain vases. Every one of them almost four hundred years old, each worth tens of millions of dollars. Those squares stacked behind them. Gold bars? Unbelievable, Jake, unbelievable!"

"That stack is worth millions, Stacy. There are probably more than fifty more stacks just like it," Jake said, smiling. "Remember, I had a broken collarbone. That really slowed me down. But there was only so much that I could take in *Makena* anyway. I had to leave this behind. I had no choice. But now, I intend to go back and grab it. It's lying totally unprotected."

"Jake, I'm sold," Tag said. "This is so mind boggling. I can hardly believe

I'm a part of it. The amount of history in that cave could keep a professor writing for the next twenty years on. I will go to my grave remembering all of us sitting alongside *Makena* in General Winton's front yard on Niihau Island. You and Rebecca pulling those vases out and dumping those jewels on the ground; then the gold bars and the gold chains. Simply unbelievable, like Stacy says."

Cutting to the chase, Jake said, "In a nutshell, we need a big cargo boat, and we need some people to cover our backs. I've been thinking about it, but right now, I'd like to get some feedback from you on whether I'm thinking right. I figure it will take at least five guys to unload that cave and get the treasure transferred to a boat. No problem there; plenty of strong backs available, but these people must also be able to fight. They must be absolutely trustworthy." Jake paused for effect.

"Tag, Gunny, I want to know what you think about hiring some young Marines for the job. I'm thinking about the jarheads in your Marine Corps Reserves unit in Gainesville, Tag. If you have any likely candidates in your reserve unit in Fort Lauderdale, Gunny, pitch the deal to them. Strictly volunteer, as I said." Jake was interrupted by the hotel phone ringing.

"Colonel Parker, Mr. Porter," a deep voice said, "Calling from the Pentagon, sir. The Commandant asked me to check our list of chartered cargo vessels for any that are available. The general said you needed a dry bulk cargo carrier of about 100-feet in length, with an Engineer. I believe we're lucky, sir. There's a Finnish transport of that size currently hung up in the Panama Canal. Some sort of paperwork snafu. They're in ballast, anchored on Lake Gatun, and available for a charter as soon as they get a check to pay for their 'Canal transit. Here's the contact number for their agent in London. Will there be anything else, sir?"

"No, Colonel. That covers it. Please convey my appreciation to General Winton," Jake said, then hung up.

"Our boat," Jake said to Gunny, Tag and Stacy. "Waiting for us at the

Panama Canal," he smiled. "How's this sounding to you so far?"

"We going to war, Jake?" Gunny Sweikert asked. "Attack some Pacific island defended by Jap Yakuza fanatics? Maybe not fighting for their emperor, but something just as dangerous: money."

"If everything goes my way, Gunny, not a shot will be fired and no one hurt. I went to that island all by myself, grabbed some treasure, didn't see a soul coming or going," Jake said. "I'd like to repeat that. But the size of what we're going after is so large it can't be done by one person."

"What will we tell our Marines?" Bryce Taggart asked. "What is the mission? What is the payoff?"

Jake thought for a moment, then said, "No mention of treasure. They will find out about that soon enough when we pull up to Marcus Island. An ocean cruise, all expenses paid. If no one bothers us, we are simply going to go inside a cave, remove boxes and bundles, and load them onto our ship, then sail away."

"How long will all this take?" Stacy asked. "Most of the Marines in Tag's reserves detachment have jobs, or are attending college classes. I think they are definitely going to want to know how long they will be gone and what's in it for them."

"Good question, Stacy" Jake said. "An educated guess, I think from beginning to end it will take no longer than two months, hopefully half of that. Weather and a lot of other factors are involved. As to what's in it for them, let's keep it in their realm of thinking. In addition to all expenses paid, how about a 4-year college degree paid for, complete with books, tuition and living expenses, and a nice bonus check to boot when they graduate?"

"What if our little venture is interrupted by some bad boys wanting to take the treasure for themselves?" Gunny Sweikert asked.

"We deal with them the way good people always deal with thieves and crooks," Jake said. "They interfere at their own risk. If the intruders are legitimate Japanese government troops, that's a different story. They have the authority to stop, and even detain us. But from my visit to Marcus, it doesn't look like the Japanese government has any interest in Marcus Island, and I don't intend to give them any reason otherwise."

"So our Marines will be armed?" Sweikert asked.

"Absolutely," Jake said. "The stakes at risk are large, and the kind of people who would interfere are vicious take-no-prisoners people. We must be able to defend ourselves. Armed pirates are deadly, but our Marines are better trained. This is not a Sunday picnic. Ships transiting the Panama Canal have chandlery agents ashore who procure food, fuel, charts, medical supplies and anything else the vessel's captain requires. We will outfit our Marines with brand new weapons and plenty of ammunition. As a former Marine armourer, I believe I have a handle on that. Also, I left my fifty-caliber Haskins sniper rifle on Marcus, and I intend to retrieve it."

"It does sound like you're going to war, Jake," Stacy said. "I'm not sure I like the idea of Tag fighting Yakuza pirates on some Japanese island."

"I understand, Stacy," Jake said. "Like I said, this is strictly volunteer. For me, I can't stand the idea of leaving all that treasure for some bumbling idiot to stumble over. A lot of good can be done with that treasure. I'm a millionaire many times over right now. I can just go back to Saipan, marry Elena, pump out babies and live happily forever. But this is not about going after the money just for the sake of the money.

From the moment I discovered the English Lieutenant's sailing log, I have felt compelled in a fateful way. I have no idea how this will all play out. If you had told me I would abandon my beautiful steel sailboat and cross the Pacific in a wooden native proa loaded with Spanish treasure, I would have told you that you are crazy. The last night Elena and I were in bed together at the Hilton on Kauai, she asked me what I was going to

420

do with the money. I answered her truthfully, I really don't know. We agreed it was something we were going to have to give a lot of thought to."

"So, we recruit some young jarheads, where do we rendezvous and when," Gunny Sweikert asked. It was the first indication that he might be onboard with the venture.

"I'm going to call the London agent of our ship and make arrangements to take care of their financial problems, order the boat fueled and prepared for a two month cruise to a destination yet to be announced. Estimated passengers: eight. That's you, Tag, if you're in, you Gunny, me and five of our Marines. The Marines provide security and order aboard just like they do on a U.S. Navy vessel. When we make Marcus, they will put their backs into transferring the treasure to our ship while keeping an eye out for intruders. With luck, we're on Marcus for no more than five days, then back to Panama. We transfer the treasure in sealed boxes to the Zona LIbre in Panama, and Rebecca conducts an international on-line auction. The purchasers send their agents to pick up what they've bought, and Rebecca deposits the money into an offshore banking account. Then we all go our separate ways."

"Very neat, Jake, and very well thought out," Stacy said. "But if you and Tag think I am going to sit out this adventure in Gainesville waiting and wondering where you are and what's going on, you have gravely miscalculated. I'm going, too. And I'm not taking no for an answer. I'm a skilled photographer and research writer. All of this is ultimately going to be on television, and I want to document, write and produce the program."

The three men saw the serious frown across Stacy's face, looked at each other, then began laughing. Tag got up and went to his fiancée, giving her a kiss square on her lips.

"I was wondering when you were going to volunteer for something, Stacy," Jake said. "They have some terrific photographic equipment shops in Panama City. We'll have the ship's chandlery buy whatever you feel you need. Now let me call that agent in London and sew this thing up. Then, I want to tell you about Rebecca's note. It's important."

(Two)

They had the Hilton's Room Service bring up lunch. While they munched on delicate sandwiches and sliced fruit, Jake produced Rebecca's note and began. "Secrecy has always been our strongest suit. The only people who know the treasure is buried on Marcus Island, what the Japs call *Minami Torishima*, are in this room; four of us. Not even Elena, her mother, Delilah, or her brother Sammy T, or Rebecca have any idea. They are very curious, but they understand why I have not told them.

"We know there are some people who are aware that we have been looking for Spanish treasure. They are spending a lot of money following us. I am concerned about what will happen when portions of the treasure begin to appear on the market. Treasure hunters all over the planet will tune their antennas to pick up the slightest clues as to where the treasure has come from. The provenance I recovered will quickly reveal that it was aboard a Spanish galleon in the seventeenth century. Researchers will begin to comb archives everywhere to identify the vessel, and thus learn what the total cargo was. They will see that only a small portion is represented in what is being sold. They will wonder where is the rest of it.

"When Rebecca located a very wealthy buyer who could buy almost all of what I brought back the first time, I was hopeful that we would be able to go after the remainder before any great interest was stirred up. Rebecca's note has kind of dashed that possibility. It looks like the cat is out of the bag. Basically, what's she's telling me is that her buyer has already made calls to her fellow antiquities collectors to tell of her new acquisitions. She has invited the curator of New York's largest museum to visit her in Palm Beach to see her new Shunzhi porcelain vases. In a way, you can't blame her; she's spent over 100 million dollars. Fortunately, she has no idea the treasure was transported on a proa

422

that made landfall on a Hawaiian island. Rebecca is the cut-out on that piece of information.

"I have spoken at length with Rebecca, impressing upon her how important it is to never mention that the treasure arrived by proa, or that it passed through Niihau Island. I have stressed the need for absolute secrecy, and that lives are on the line, not to mention the considerable commission Rebecca would lose if pirates intercept us. Rebecca is going to maintain the professional silence of her role in the antiquities market. She will not reveal the identities of either buyer or seller of the treasure already in hand. She will raise no suspicions because that is a traditional practice. She is going to put the jewelry and some of the precious stones on display at The Left Bank in Palm Beach and go through the motions. She will entertain offers, provide provenance, host international jewelry assessor and all the other things that normally occur when a treasure find is brought to market.

"Only one piece of the Chinese porcelain will be put on display, and it will be marked 'Sold.' No doubt articles will appear in the newspapers and the professional collectors journals, and there will be all sorts of excitement and curiosity, but no hint will be given of where the treasure was discovered, or that any part of it remains in the original location. Speculation about the remainder of the cargo will be just that: speculation. It is the best that can be done under the circumstances. Rebecca understands that she and her family's business will lose millions of dollars in fees if there is any leak."

"We have to move fast, Jake," Stacy said.

"Amen to that. Your return plane tickets have already been purchased by Rebecca," Jake said. "I'm headed for Panama to prepare our boat. I leave it in your and Tag's hands to recruit our young Marines. Call Rebecca with their names, and she will have airline tickets issued for them. They can pick them up at airport when they show up for the flight. We rendezvous in Panama, hopefully within the next three to four days. The sooner the better. Call me if you hit any snags, okay?"

(Three)

Jake took an Air Panama flight from Honolulu, and arrived in Panama City, Panama, late that evening. He hired a taxi to take him to the Gatun Yacht Club, about halfway across the isthmus. He had learned from talking with the Finnish ship's agent that the vessel he was chartering was anchored on Lake Gatun, less than a quarter of a mile from the yacht club. The agent had radioed the vessel and arranged for Jake to be picked up. The ship's tender and a young crewman were waiting at the club's dock when Jake arrived. He tossed a single sport bag into the boat and they went directly to the ship. Although it was dark, the lighting around the club was enough for Jake to see that the ship was well-cared for; her sharply-pointed bow and well-designed bridge structure spoke well for the designer and builder.

The vessel was one hundred-seven feet in length, fifty-one feet in beam, drew twenty feet when on her lines, and powered by two huge MANN diesels. Designed by a German naval architecture firm, and built in a Dutch yard in Rotterdam. Jake climbed the boarding ladder and was met on the main deck by her captain, a forty-something bear of a man from Poland. He pulled a big briar pipe from his mouth, gave Jake a firm handshake and introduced himself as Captain Robert Krawczyk, native of Krakow. They went immediately to Captain Krawczyk's quarters. The captain picked up a telex sheet and handed it to Jake. It was confirmation from the vessel's owners of the transfer of funds from Jake's bank in payment of the deposit for the charter. The charter agreement lay on the captain's desk and Jake read it carefully before signing.

The captain had received notice from his office that the bunkering bill and transit fees in payment to the Panama Canal Commission were paid, and that the captain was to receive instructions from their charterer as to what direction they were headed, then apply to the Panama Canal Commission for a zarpe, then exit the Canal and anchor in the Bay of Panama's open roadstead. Once underway, he was to radio the home office and notify them of their destination and the cargo to be carried. The telex stressed that the charter was an open charter, and the client was at liberty to determine the destination and length of time involved. The captain, in turn, was empowered to refuse the client's orders if he felt the destination posed risks outside of normal operations. The ferrying of drugs, weapons or other types of dangerous cargo was strictly prohibited, and the captain was authorized to terminate the charter should any of those situations arise.

The terms were reasonable, but Jake could see that they might cause difficulties, particularly if armed pirates showed up at Marcus Island while they were recovering the treasure. The operative word was 'if.' If they could make their way to Marcus, and complete the recovery within the next 30 days, Jake was confident no pirate operation could respond in so short a time, particularly if they had yet to discover the treasure's location.

Jake assured Captain Krawczyk that the charter did not involve hauling dangerous cargo. He explained that he and his partners were simply transporting some antique decorative vases and textile goods that had a very high market value. After picking them up, they would return to Panama for transshipping to purchasers through the Zona Libre. He said that the other passengers for the voyage were college professors and a team of civilians with military backgrounds hired to protect the cargo in the event of piracy.

Captain Krawczyk sucked on his briar pipe, then nodded in agreement. He led Jake down a narrow passageway to Jake's cabin, and said there was no steward on board, so the passengers were going to have to fend for themselves during the voyage. This was a working cargo vessel, not a cruise liner. Jake said that would not present a problem. The passengers were a resourceful lot in his opinion, he assured the captain. Captain Krawczyk asked Jake how soon he felt he would be ready for sea. Jake said he expected the passengers to all be onboard within the next three to five days, and that some shopping had to be done in Panama City for some comfort items and photographic gear. He would attend to that himself. Again, Captain Krawczyk nodded in agreement. He left Jake to prepare his bunk, and said breakfast was possible if Jake could make his way to the bridge by seven AM.

(Four)

The next two days were hectic for Jake. He went ashore to the Gatun Yacht Club, explained to the secretary that he had a shopping list to fill, and asked for a taxi driver who could stick with him for the entire day. No problem there. A young Panamanian with a big 4-door Chevrolet Caprice arrived when called, and he and Jake headed for Panama City. Jake purchased dozens of categories of "comfort items," from a pair of twenty-gallon insulated water coolers and hammocks, to grapnels and rope-and-block tackle. He stopped at the ships chandlery to go over their lists of stores on hand and ordered food for everyone on board including Captain Krawczky, the ship's engineer and two deck hands. Frozen steaks, pork tenderloins, chicken, and the full range of fresh vegetables. A few cases of wine and beer were included, but no whisky. He also ordered a professionally assembled medical kit complete with morphine surrettes.

He then went to one of Panama City's largest water sports stores and bought four 10-foot Zodiac RIB inflatables at $3,500 each, and matching twenty-horsepower Mercury outboards along with auxiliary fuel containers. He purchased pistol flare guns and a selection of red, green and white flares. He next visited a sporting goods store and purchased seven Armalite M16AR automatic assault rifles in .223 caliber with full automatic function and complete with 30-round magazines and Nikon 12x telescopic sights, plus 300 boxes of ammunition, each box containing 100 rounds. He also bought eight Glock 37's chambered for the .45 GAP round with 230 grain soft-nosed bullets. The magazines held 15 rounds; a real handful of stopping power.

To round out the firepower, he selected a Baby Glock for Stacy, figuring she would feel left out otherwise. He then selected U.S. Marine Corps K-Bar knives, military-grade wristwatches with luminous compasses, and Mag-Lite aluminum flashlights for each of his Marines. He purchased everything in bond, what the Panamanian government called 'sin impuesto', no tax, and it was all to be delivered to the Zona Libre to be brought aboard when his ship cleared Panama.

As he was leaving the sporting goods store, his cell phone rang. It was Tag announcing that he had filled the quota for Marines. Laughing, he said every one of them had been at the firing range in Gainesville when Jake had blown up the old Buick with a single shot from his Haskins. Tag said his phone was still ringing from other young Marines in his unit asking to be put on stand-by in event of any cancellations. All of the selected Marines had completed bootcamp at Parris Island, and three of them had also completed summer training sessions in small unit combat tactics. All of them had qualified 'Expert' in marksmanship with the M-16. They were young, sharp and anxious to get into some action.

"Good job, Tag. I just hope everything goes this well. Give me their names and I'll have plane tickets prepared and sent to you for distribution," Jake said. "Our transport is top-drawer, by the way. One hundred-seven footer, German designed and Dutch built. When you and the guys arrive, and I guess that includes Stacy, just take a taxi from the airport to the Gatun Yacht Club. Call me on my cell and I'll come with the ship's tender to pick you up.

"I did some big-time shopping today. Got our 'tools of the trade' so-to-speak, some fast inflatables, and plenty of food. We'll eat well, but we'll probably have to do our own cooking. The captain has made it clear he's running a cargo vessel, not a 'Love Boat.' Crusty old Polish bastard, but he'll do. If he gives us any trouble, I'll just buy the goddam boat and fire his ass."

"Gunny wasn't happy that I filled our quota all by myself, but he's onboard with the project," Tag chuckled. "Said he was packing his bag as we spoke and would be ready to leave 'Lauderdale tomorrow and probably be in Panama by late afternoon."

"Good," Jake said. "I'll include his ticket along with yours, Stacy and our guys. They are all E-tickets; just present your driver's license at the ticket counter and pick them up at the airport. Just call Gunny and let him know that. Call me if there are any problems, okay? Tell Stacy she can hit the photography stores with a blank check as soon as she gets here. Have her shopping list prepared. We want to be underway as quickly as possible."

"Got it, Jake," Tag said. "See you in Panama."

SNAPPER TAKES A POKE

Date: December 1990

Lat. 28° 26'N, Long. 48° 30'W

Vicinity of Khafji, Saudi Arabia

(One)

The briefing with the battalion's intelligence officer (S-2) was thorough, but served only to heighten Jake's apprehension. The ops plan called for each of the three sniper teams to ride to their insertion points in separate Blackhawk helicopters. The Blackhawks would depart the division's headquarters area thirty miles south of the Kuwaiti border just after nightfall, fly fifty miles west before turning sharply north to cross over the border's minefields and Iraqi armor deployments. They would then descend to barely twenty feet above the desert floor and wheel to the right along an east-west line of insertion less than two miles south of the airport and Kuwait City.

The choppers would hover, not land, at the points of insertion, and after the 2-man sniper teams had exited at their respective drops, they would then scurry obliquely out of the area at low altitude. As a diversion, ten miles from where the snipers had exited, they would rise sharply to a height of 300 feet deploying flares and exercising their guns on nothing in particular to attract radar signatures while U.S. Air Force fighter-bombers simultaneously unloaded high-explosives north and east of

429

Kuwait City and Kuwait International Airport. The idea was to draw attention and hopefully mask the insertion of the sniper teams. An AWACS airborne battlefield command center would be cruising the vicinity at 40,000 feet to monitor the action and coordinate assets as the situation required.

The sniper teams were ordered to target aircraft and armored vehicles of all types including personnel carriers. They were shown infrared aerial photos of the dispositions of their targets and provided with GPS satellite coordinates. The battalion's G-2 laid it out for them. "We want havoc, men. We want explosions and personnel chaos. The Iraqis will have no battlefield info to indicate a major enemy presence. They will come out of their revetments to find and suppress the source of their pain. That movement will be observed by the AWAC, and Marine aviation will destroy it. This is a 'shoot and scoot' operation, Marines. Time between insertion and extraction is 2 hours. Read your 'prick' codes and make sure you have the Chemlite patterns down pat for signaling your extraction chopper."

Jake learned that he and his spotter were the team assigned to stir up the Kuwait airport. The roster showed he had been paired with Lance Corporal Jimmy Tremain, a short and lean 19-year old Southerner from Waycross, Georgia, with about two years in the Corps, who probably weighed less than 140 pounds. But Jake knew Tremain to be a no-nonsense Marine with an uncanny ability to provide accurate "dope" for a shoot in record time. Rather than binoculars, Tremain used a 20x-power Bauch & Lomb scope that he had "liberated" from the rifle range at Quantico. He had purchased a used 1950s-era German Leica 35-millimeter camera from a hockshop in Virginia Beach, and fashioned an attachment for marrying it to the spotter scope. He told his sniper buddies he wanted some combat photos to show his young wife back in Georgia.

Following the intelligence briefing, the newly-invested Sergeant Porter and his spotter, Lance Corporal Tremain, met at the battalion armory to draw their gear. Jake would carry his Haskins SOPMOD .50-caliber rifle, and Tremain an M-16. Both would also strap on shoulder holsters with 15-round M9 (9mm) Beretta semi-automatic pistols. Jake would bring

100 assorted rounds of ammo for the Haskins including depleted uranium, armor-piercing incendiary rounds and boat-tail ball rounds (highly accurate match-grade ammo) for enemy personnel, plus 30 rounds of 9mm ammo for his Beretta. Jimmy Tremain draped two bandoliers over his wiry shoulders for a total of 500 rounds (7.62 mm) for his M-16, plus 30 rounds for his pistol.

Each Marine attached four M67 fragmentation grenades to their fighting harnesses, along with two "willie peter" (white phosphorous) grenades, two smoke grenades and 3 green star clusters. They also had red and green Chemlite sticks for signaling their extraction helicopters. Jake would carry the team's patrol-order book and map inside a map case along with a compass and a GPS receiver. Lance Corporal Tremain would carry the "prick," the PRC-77 radio and codes. To top-off this back-breaking load, they each added four quarts of water in two canteens and two MREs even though extraction by the Blackhawks was supposed to happen within two hours of their insertion.

The Blackhawks swooped in from the west just after dark and settled in a blast of whirling sand. Sergeant Jake Porter and Lance Corporal Jimmy Tremain climbed aboard and grabbed hand-holds as the chopper lifted off immediately, turning back to the west. As the Blackhawk sped into the dark, hostile maw of the desert night, Jake became aware of his rising heartbeat and knew that he was already running on a high dose of adrenalin. When he turned to look at his spotter, he saw Tremain's jaw working and his adams-apple bobbing up and down. *Both of us scared shitless. All the fucking Navy ships, airplanes, thousands of Army troops and tanks, and they send in six jarheads with rifles to slug it out with Saddam because they don't want to tear-up some goddamn Kuwaiti buildings. Fucking Marine Corps!*

(Two)

It was a short ride. When the Blackhawk dipped to hover at the insertion point, Jake stepped onto the skid then dropped the couple of feet to land on crusty sand. Tremain piled out behind him, landing with a grunt. And then the chopper was gone, leaving them in black silence. Both snipers went prone, and Jake checked the GPS. Comparing the coordinates with his map, he saw that they were some 200 yards south of a 150-foot high sand berm that ran east and west not quite a mile south of the Kuwait International Airport. *Right up the Iraqis' fucking asshole, plum smack in the middle of the enemy's backyard, and me with a fucking single-shot rifle!*

Jake hand-signaled Tremain to begin a low-crouch scurry toward the berm, its crest faintly outlined by the distant lights of the Kuwait City airport on the other side. The desert night was cold, but the sand still retained some heat from the day's sun.

When they crested the berm, the lights of the airport shone brightly before them, and the eastern horizon glowed a soft yellow in the direction of Kuwait City. "Holy shit, Jake. Will you look at that?" Tremain said as he took in the huge expanse of the airport. Several large passenger aircraft were visible on the tarmac, their tails facing the snipers, but given the distance they seemed like toys to the naked eye.

"Yeah," Jake said. "Let's get that scope out and survey the pickings. We got less than 20 minutes to kickoff." Jake realized he was making a real effort to sound calm and collected for the younger Marine. He had already shifted the Haskins from his back, slipped the thin plastic dust cover off of it, removed the weather caps from both ends of the telescopic sight, and slipped an armor-piercing incendiary round into the chamber.

"Man, oh man!" Tremain whispered excitedly. He had buried the tripod of the Bauch & Lomb scope into the soft sand atop the berm and was moving it slowly left to right. "Let's use the control tower right center of the perimeter lights for reference, okay?" he said as he began to identify targets and estimate ranges. "Nine o'clock we got two four-engine aircraft at the near edge, range 1,400 yards. At nine o'clock beyond those aircraft, three Hind-34 choppers, range 1,600 yards. At 10 o'clock, on the near edge, one smaller twin-engine passenger jet. Then we got another passenger jet facing to our left, with a boarding ramp in place and ground support attached." Tremain called out each of the targets in a slow sing-song chant with only a hint of tension. "At 11 o'clock, we got the rear of a hangar, contents not observable. And...whoa! two—no, make it three

432

T-72 battle tanks against the side of the hangar and a whole slew of BTR-60s (Russian-built wheeled armored personnel carriers). Looks like...hmm, five of 'em, range 1,600 yards."

As Tremain continued with his targeting, Jake followed his sweep through the Haskin's telescopic sight. His rifle's sight picture was narrower than Tremain's spotter scope, but more powerful. He was able to also see a small number of personnel moving about the airport. He paused to look at the smaller passenger jet with the attached boarding ramp. It looked like it was being readied for flight. The two larger 4-engine aircraft looked like Lockheed 1011s, and were parked with their wheels chocked. The Russian-made Hind-34 helicopter gunships were buttoned-down for the night, their rotor blades secured with tie-downs. But if their crews were nearby, it wouldn't take much time for them to get airborne. They would bear watching.

By the time his spotter had scanned and reported their entire kill-zone, Jake knew there were more targets than he'd ever have time to hit, and if the concentration of armor that Tremain had scoped was duplicated in any other areas of the airport which were outside their kill-zone, then they were truly "poking" a beehive as Captain Murray had said.

It was also very clear to Jake that when the "bees" hauled out of their nest, they would come with a vengeance—and in force. He and his spotter were on foot in a barren, featureless desert with only darkness for cover. Thermal gunsights on the Iraqis' armor would have no trouble finding them. "Shoot and scoot," they called it. But "scoot" to where? Jake was thinking. Everything depended on the Warthogs and Apache gunships to knock out the big armor, and give cover to the Blackhawks coming to take them home.

In that moment it came to Jake as clear as a bell: his life rested on events totally out of his personal control. With that sobering thought in mind, he rolled onto his stomach, lifted the Haskin's butt to his shoulder, and became what the Marine Corps had trained him to be—a cold-blooded killer.

(Three)

As if from a great distance, he heard his spotter activate the "prick," then key three short and two long clicks to signal the airborne AWAC command center that their team had received the 'Go' command. Through the Haskin's telescopic sight Jake saw movement on the ramp leading up to the cabin door of the small twin-engine passenger jet. At the top of the ramp stood a crew member, the pilot maybe, who was talking to a group of four uniformed Iraqis standing at the base of the ramp.

Someone in Arab dress crossed the tarmac toward the plane and the four saluted him as he stepped onto the ramp to board the aircraft. That was enough for Jake. He worked the bolt action to eject the armor piercing round he had inserted earlier and replaced it with a boat-tail round. By the time Jake had the aircraft back in his cross-hairs, the Arab now stood at the top of the ramp and turned as Jake lowered the Haskin's cross-hairs to rest on the Arab's upper chest. The Haskins jumped as the .50-caliber projectile left the muzzle. Immediately, Jake chambered an armor-piercing incendiary round and swung the cross-hairs to the plane's tail section centering on the port engine nacelle, sending off the second round before the group of four at the base of the ramp could respond to the violent and unexplainable disappearance of the Arab at the top of the ramp. To them, he had seemed to have leaped backwards through the plane's cabin door.

But when the engine nacelle exploded, the four Iraqis jumped away from the plane in confusion. They had heard no gunfire, saw only the aircraft's engine suddenly disintegrate in a white flash of piercing metallic scream. Just then, a figure in a white shirt with striped shoulder epaulets appeared in the plane's cabin doorway followed by another crewmember. They looked aft at the flame-engulfed engine on the tail. Meanwhile Jake had already loaded another boat tail round and was centering crosshairs on the upper torso of the pilot who was now coming down the ramp in a panic taking three steps at a time. The Haskins recoiled once, then twice as Jake brought down both crew. He saw their upper torsos explode and slam violently against the ramp stairs.

The tail section of the jet was now a growing mass of flames, attracting a dozen or more uniformed troops who were running from the nearby hangar to the burning plane. One was carrying a portable fire extinguisher. They were making wild gestures and clearly did not understand why the plane was on fire. And the sight of the bloody mess of the crew on the ramp did not help matters. It was all too confusing. There had been no sound of gunfire, no speeding vehicles or combatants running about. Then, as they stood gaping at the unexplainable horror in front of them, the port under-wing engine of the big Lockheed passenger jet behind them suddenly exploded in flames. No sooner had they spun around and jumped back in fright at this new development, one of the engines on the second jet parked next to it also exploded. Flames and smoke began to envelop both planes. That was all the Iraqi troops needed to convince themselves to run for cover.

Jake chambered another armor-piercing incendiary round and sent it on its way to the smaller passenger jet at the far left edge of the tarmac. It hit the starboard wing's fuel cell and erupted in a massive orange fireball. Barely a minute had elapsed since Jake's first shot. Four aircraft were aflame, at least three Iraqis were dead and the airport was waking up. In the clear desert night, Jake could hear a faint wailing sound of sirens. No time to waste.

Lance Corporal Jimmy Tremain, his eye glued to his scope, was marveling at the smooth, rapid way in which Jake was chambering rounds and finding his targets. The carnage he was witnessing was like nothing the young Southerner had ever seen. He reached for his Leica and snapped it onto the scope just as a large spotlight atop the airport's control tower came on and began to light up the corner of the airport tarmac where the planes were burning.

"Might want to mess up that control tower, Jake," he said just as Jake put an incendiary round through one of the tower's large slanted glass panes. A bright orange flash came from the interior of the control tower, and a second round from the Haskins was followed by a great spray of glass, then a swirling cloud of smoke pouring from the tower's interior. The spotlight remained on, but its movement had stopped.

"Nine o'clock!" Tremain yelled. "Vehicles heading for the choppers."

Jake swung the Haskins back to his left and picked up the vehicles in the scope. They were piled with aircrew. Pilots and mechanics leaped from their vehicles and ran to the three Hind-34 gunships and began to rapidly clear the rotor blade tie-downs and remove the covers over the pitot tubes. Jake chambered one of the uranium-depleted armor-piercing incendiary rounds and took sight on the lower rear of one of the ramp vehicles just about where the fuel tank would be and fired. The truck's fuel tank erupted in a fiery blast, lifting the half-ton vehicle in the air and flipping it forward to collide with one of the Hind-34 choppers, setting it on fire and carrying a number of Iraqis to a flaming death.

Even before the vehicle had bounced off the Russian chopper, Jake loosed another round, this time into the starboard engine nacelle of the nearest Hind-34, setting it afire. At this point there was no doubt in the Iraqis' minds that they were under hostile fire. But awareness of the threat was of no comfort. They were terrified and confused because there were no sounds of gunfire, engines, rotors or anything of their combat experience to explain the source of the devastating gunfire. Marine sniper Jake Porter and his noise-suppressed Haskins rifle were almost a mile away and totally silent at that distance.

Some of the aircrew jumped into the two other gunships and Jake saw the rotorblades of the most distant Hind gunship begin to turn. Jake laid the Haskins' telescopic sight's crosshairs on its cockpit and sent an armor-piercing round into it. Through the Haskin's scope a muted flash, almost like a spark, could be seen for an instant then wisps of smoke began to rise from the interior. *Scratch one, maybe two pilots.* By this time, in little more than 30 or 40 seconds from the time he had hit the first Hind gunship, Jake brought the Haskins to bear on the third Hind, centering again on one of the engine nacelles. In quick succession, he placed additional armor-piercing incendiary rounds into the tail-rotor systems of each gunship. None of the deadly choppers would be doing any flying any time soon.

"Armor on the move! Eleven o'clock, 1,600 yards. Three BTRs and a T-72 coming through the fence," Tremain sang out excitedly.

Jake felt his heart skip a beat. The element of surprise was waning fast. And he was under no illusions. The targets thus far had been large and mostly static. More importantly, they hadn't been looking for him or shooting back. He knew with a certainty that that comfortable scenario would soon be coming to an end.

And he also knew that the only Iraqi armored units with the newer Russian-built T-72s were Republican Guards, Saddam's best. All the other units had Vietnam-era T-55s. The only target on a T-72 that was vulnerable to a .50-caliber round from Jake's Haskins rifle was the tank's thermal sight system, and that was what Jake took out on the T-72 as it passed through the airport's perimeter fence.

The tank, suddenly blind in the desert darkness, skewed to the left and the tank commander's head popped out of the top of the turret to see what had happened to the sighting system. The message he took below to the crew was the top two-thirds of his headless torso spewing arterial blood everywhere. That was all that remained after taking a .50-caliber round from Jake's Haskins in his upper chest at shoulder-level. There are no words to describe the psychological shock of being in the tight confines of a tank and having one of your closest buddies drop into your midst minus his head, jerking like a chicken with a wrung neck and spraying everyone and everything with volumes of pulsating arterial blood.

Two of the BTRs in front of the T-72 turned left after passing through the airport's perimeter fence and headed away from the two Marine Corps snipers, unaware that the T-72 had taken fire. The third one turned right to parallel the fence, a gunner topside manning the twin 20-mm machine guns also unaware the T-72 behind him had stalled. From almost a mile away, Jake tracked the moving target with the Haskins rifle, leading the gunner's body to compensate for the vehicle's speed. It was a classic right-to-left broadside shot. The Haskins' recoil punched into Jake's shoulder and the .50-caliber boat-tail round entered the gunner's left shoulder less than one and a half seconds later, virtually cutting him in half. As his shattered remains sunk behind his guns, Jake chambered the Haskin's armor-piercing incendiary round that was designed especially for taking out lightly armored vehicles like the BTR-

60. In quick succession he put five evenly-spaced rounds into the personnel compartment. The projectiles were designed to shatter into dozens of pieces of ricocheting, personnel-maiming steel once penetrating the vehicle's armor, and the incendiary charge to ignite fuel or ammo.

The BTR came to a halt and the rear door swung open. Half a dozen Iraqi soldiers piled out, some of them limping, two crawling on hands and knees and one dragging a comrade. They dove for cover on the opposite side of their disabled vehicle. For the Iraqis, there was no question the enemy fire was coming from the south in the direction of the berm, but where exactly and how many of the enemy might be deployed there was not knowable. They could not see the distant berm in the darkness, and they could not hear the report of gunfire.

"Armor on the move!," Jake's spotter yelled again. "T-72s coming through the fence and turning north to the disabled BTR. Range 1,600 yards," Jimmy Tremain said, barely containing the adrenalin-induced squeak in his voice. "Got three more BTRs right behind them," he added.

The tactical situation was collapsing fast. The element of surprise was over. The enemy was now responding with a fury. All they were missing was a precise location of their enemy's position, and they were spreading out abreast of one another scanning the dark desert right up to the berm looking for thermal signatures. But they were also stupid. Two of the tank commanders stood upright in their turrets, and Jake ended both of their lives. Because of the third tank's wild maneuvering, it took Jake two shots to disable its thermal sighting system.

"Holy shit, Jake! Nine o'clock, 1,600 yards, "Tremain yelled. "Three more T-72s coming from the north outside the perimeter." A pause, then, "Fire engines at the aircraft, Jake. Nine o'clock, 1,400 yards."

"Give the AWACS command center a call," Jake said evenly. "See if they got the armor movement on their scopes, and advise our situation is deteriorating fast. Get an update on our extraction."

No sooner had Jake spoken than he heard the unmistakable chatter of helicopter rotor blades. *Marine Corps to the rescue!* But he spoke too soon. The sound belonged to two Hind-34 gunships that had taken off from some other part of the airport. They were a little less than a mile away, flying low and abreast of one another behind the exiting BTRs, but still north of the berm where Jake and Tremain were hunkered down. It would not take them long to scour the narrow one-mile swath between the berm and the airport's perimeter with their thermal sights.

Certain death for the two Marine snipers was only minutes away when Jake turned the Haskins rifle on the port engine of the nearest Hind-34. It was a tough shot to make. The Hind was a fast-moving target, tracking right to left, rising and falling in an evasive maneuver and the target area was a minuscule three-foot wide opening in the engine nacelle behind which spun the engine's turbine blades. It took three shots.

"He's flaming, Jake," Tremain yelled. "Get the other son of a bitch before he turns on us!" Tremain was pulling his M-16 off his back, giving little thought to the fact that the M-16's 7.62 mm round was impotent against the Hind's armored fuselage.

Jake saw the first Hind gunship falter, then set down roughly on the desert floor with fire and smoke pouring from the engine and rotor system. Before he could target the second airborne Hind, the gunship's waist gunner began to hose down the top of the berm some 300 yards east of them. They were firing wildly, but it was heart-numbing to hear the deep thunder of the machine guns and the sand being blasted away. Jake chambered another armor-piercing round and aimed for the pilot-side of the cockpit. The Haskins rifle bucked and the chopper suddenly reared upward and backward, recovered level flight for a moment, then dropped out of control to strike the desert floor and explode.

But Jake and his spotter had no time to enjoy the pyrotechnics. A violent blast only a few dozen feet from them blew them down from their perch on the top backside of the berm. Both snipers lost their sense of hearing and suffered disorientation from the concussion of what had been a round fired from the lead T-72 tank that Tremain had spotted coming down the outside of the airport perimeter.

It was a blessing in disguise. Immediately following the blast, the berm was raked by heavy machine-gun fire, cutting through the berm ten feet below the crest where Jake and Jimmy Tremain had been only moments before. The machine-gun rounds drove clear through the berm and had the two Marines not been sent tumbling down the backside of the berm, they would have been reduced to little more than shredded flesh.

Unable to hear and his head pounding from the concussion, Jake scrambled in the dark to find his Haskins rifle. It helped that the long, fluted barrel was more than a little warm from the firing it had been doing. Jake pulled the Haskins to him, and squatting, he tapped the barrel to clear any sand that may have entered it, worked the bolt action to extract the spent shell casing and slipped another round into the chamber. Iraqi machine-gun and cannon fire from the T-72s were blasting up and down the berm. It was clear that the Iraqis did not know exactly where their enemy was, but fire-and-maneuver tactics would soon flush them.

Because he could no longer hear, Jake was unaware of the arrival of the Marine Corps Apache gunships until he saw a huge orange and white fireball lighting up the sky from the other side of the berm; the first of the Iraqi T-72s succumbing to an Apache's Stinger anti-tank missile. Still not sure of what he was experiencing, Jake looked at his spotter and saw Tremain was grinning, pointing south behind them. Jake rolled over on his back and saw a near-solid stream of red tracer rounds spewing from a low-flying A-10 Warthog, followed by multiple fireballs on the other side of the berm.

Jake gave the hand signal to Tremain to haul-ass away from the berm. The two snipers flipped out Chemlite sticks as they ran to make sure the aviation boys didn't mistake them for fleeing Iraqis. Five hundred yards south of the berm, they laid out the prescribed Chemlite pattern for their extraction. A Blackhawk appeared out of the dark, swooped to a near-hover and the two Marines flung themselves aboard.

(Four)

It took the better part of two days for Sergeant Jake Porter to regain his hearing. During his recovery, he and Lance Corporal Tremain occupied side-by-side hospital beds in the battalion's field hospital, receiving intravenous fluids, hot meals and far more attention from the medical staff than their medical condition deserved. Everyone wanted to see the two Marine snipers who had killed Saddam Hussein's first cousin, the Iraqi deputy defense minister.

The AWACS command center aircraft orbiting over the Kuwaiti Airport had picked up the frantic wailing of Iraqis identifying the Arab that Jake had nailed at the top of the boarding ramp. The battlefield intelligence team had also noted the impressive destruction wreaked by the two-man Marine sniper team: 2 Lockheed L-1011 passenger jets, 1 each DeHaviland DH-125 twin-engine executive jet, 1 each twin-engine Sabreliner executive jet, 5 Russian-built Hind-34 helicopter gunships, 1 each Russian-built BTR-60 armored personnel carrier, the disabling of two Russian-built T-72 battle tanks, and the destruction of a half-ton vehicle. In addition, an estimated 20 or more Iraqis had perished from direct fire of Jake's Haskins rifle.

Jimmy Tremain had regained his hearing before Jake, and was entertaining the medical staff and ward visitors with lurid descriptions of deadly Sergeant Jake Porter in action. "Snap! Snap! Snap! One round after another. Every time Jake snapped back the bolt of that Haskins rifle, somebody died," he said. "We didn't know that Arab getting on the plane was Saddam's cousin, of course, but he was dead the minute 'ole Snapper laid them cross-hairs on him."

And the name stuck. From that time on, anyone who wanted to know which of the ward's patients was the sniper that got Saddam's cousin, the reply was, "Snapper's in Ward A, Bed 12."

The battalion's Command Sergeant Major came down from headquarters to pick them up at the hospital and drive them back to their company's bivouac. He greeted them with a proud smile and a crushing handshake. "Well done, Marines. You're both up for Purple Hearts, and maybe a Bronze Star, too," he announced. "No guarantees, of course. But damn, Porter, you two sure as hell tore up some expensive property in a mighty short time. And the Marine aviation that came in to clean up what you left for them had a field day. Knocking off Saddam's cousin was just cream on the pudding."

Marine Corps sniper Jake Porter was so grateful to just be alive that he paid little attention to the Command Sergeant Major's praise. *I'll gladly trade the medals for a ticket out of this fucking place!* But the U.S. Marine Corps has a time-honored ritual for recognizing the battlefield exploits of its own, and neither Sergeant Porter or his spotter, Lance Corporal Tremain would escape it.

After a week of light duty, during which time the battle photos taken by Tremain through his spotter's scope were developed and the prints distributed all the way to General Swartzkopf at CENTCOM headquarters, Jake and his spotter received word that Division had approved both a Bronze Star for valor and a Purple Heart for each of them. There was also some scuttlebutt that Jake would be put up for the Marine Corps' Medal for Gallantry as well. Wearing impeccably starched utilities and soft covers on their heads, the two snipers were brought before the Division commander.

With the camcorders of the Stars & Stripes Magazine rolling and their cameras flashing, the two Marines received their awards for combat valor that was still being reported around the world. The news item was fueled by a rumor that Saddam Hussein had snarled malevolently when informed of the loss of his cousin to the infidel Marines. He promised they would pay for the spilling of a martyr's blood. In response, Saudi Arabia's King Faisal announced that his country was awarding the two Marine Corps snipers with the Golden Eagle Award, Saudi Arabia's highest medal for battlefield bravery given to non-Arabs. Shortly thereafter, the emir of Kuwait announced that General Norman Swartzkopf and the two Marine heroes would be the first to receive his country's new Kuwaiti Liberation Medal. Rumor had it that it had four ounces of pure gold in it.

THE BATTLE FOR MARCUS ISLAND

Date: July 15, 2001
Lat. 15º, 15' N, Long. 145º, 45 E
Tinian Island, Northern Marianas

(One)

Yoto Nakura answered the single-sideband radio per the prearranged scheduled. It was Berne, Switzerland, calling, and the tone of voice was not pleasant.

"Captain Nakura, I have some disturbing news. Treasure from the Manila galleon, *Nuestra Senora de la Concepcion,* is on the market. As you know, that was the object of Porter and his boat the *Giggling Witch*. We are completely baffled by this development because we were under the impression that you had Porter under close surveillance. When was the last time you saw Porter in Saipan?"

"I receive the same satellite tracking information that you do," Nakura responded irritably. "Porter's boat, the *Giggling Witch* is berthed at the Tanapag marina. The last time the boat moved was five days ago. It went to Anatahan Island and was there for three days. There was more diving activity. As you know, I have urged action for many weeks now. I believe they continue to go to Anatahan Island because that is where their information has told them to search. Any treasure that is for sale did not get there by the *Giggling Witch*."

"No, but they may have recovered a few pieces, then shipped them to Palm Beach by air from Saipan. Did you see Porter himself at Anatahan Island ?"

"No, but that doesn't mean he's not there. We have to maintain a distance from them to avoid being detected." Nakura did not mention that the clumsiness of his men and his own surveillance methods in general had probably already alerted Porter to the fact he was being watched. "My understanding was that Porter's boat was the object of our surveillance. I also reported to you that he had recruited a large seventy-foot trimaran with a lot of diving gear to support his search."

"Well, the son-of-a-bitch has given us the slip, or he has assets that we don't know about. Treasure from the *Concepcion* is being sold as we speak. It is being sold from a small boutique in Palm Beach, Florida; not an international auction firm. This suggests that only a portion of the treasure has been recovered, although we have no way of knowing the extent of the recovery. But something is up. There are rumors that an antiquities curator from the Metropolitan Museum of Arts in New York has been seen in Palm Beach.

"Only one piece of Chinese porcelain is on display, everything else is jewelry, jade carvings and so on. The provenance that is being displayed to authenticate the treasure consists of various letters written by passengers. The letters indicate that the passengers were aboard a Manila galleon bound for Acapulco in 1698. We are checking the passenger lists of the galleon to see if there is a match of the names."

"So, what are my instructions?" Nakura asked. The bitterness and frustration were evident in his tone of voice.

"I understand you are still anchored at Tinian. Send some of your people to Saipan. See if you can locate Porter. Get close to the *Giggling Witch*. See if you can learn anything. Has John, our partner, arrived yet?"

"Yes, he arrived yesterday and is aboard now. He came all the way from Singapore, and is resting. Shall I call him?"

"No need at the moment. Let him rest. We are going to do some investigating on our end to try to find out more about the treasure that was recovered. That is all for now."

(Two)

Elena and her mother, Delilah, finished preparing food to take to the *Giggling Witch*. It had been almost a week since Elena and her brother, Sammy T, had taken Jake's boat to Anatahan Island. The Japanese long-liner had followed, as evidenced by the presence of her Zodiac sport boat. Elena and her family felt that they were protecting Jake by diverting the Jap's attention away from Jake's progress toward Marcus Island. Elena missed Jake terribly. Since giving him a farewell kiss at the Honolulu airport, she was experiencing a vacuum in her life like nothing she had ever known.

When she and her mother returned to Saipan, she had gone to the Micro Beach Marina and slept aboard the *Giggling Witch* in Jake's bunk. It made her feel closer to him, but also reminded her that he was a great distance from her. Now, she and Sammy were going to sail up to Anatahan Island again for two or three days of diversionary tactics, waiting to hear from Jake that he had recovered the remainder of the Spanish treasure from some place that she and her brother had no knowledge of.

Elena's mother drove her to the Micro Beach marina and accompanied her down the dock to the *Giggling Witch*. Sammy was already there. He had removed the awning and sail covers, and was ready to shove off. Sammy kissed his mom, Elena kissed her as well then climbed aboard, and they motored away from the dock. Delilah stood on the end of the dock until she saw the sails go up and the *Giggling Witch* lean into the wind, bearing north toward Anatahan Island.

(Three)

Captain Yoto Nakura called Matsu to the bridge. Matsu stood stiffly, bowing his head respectfully and said, "Hai"

"Matsu, we have been deceived somehow. The treasure we have been following is appearing on the market in the United States. You and I know it was not recovered by Porter here in Saipan. I want you to go to the marina in Tanapag and find Porter. I want to verify that he is here. I know his boat is here, but I want to know if Porter himself is here. If he is gone, then we are wasting our time in Saipan. Take the Zodiac, land at Garapan. Walk to the Micro Beach marina in Tanapag. Find Porter, if he is to found."

"Hai!" Matsu bowed and left quickly.

Nakura watched the Zodiac speed away to transit the three miles to Saipan. The single-sideband radio chirruped. It was Berne, Switzerland, again.

"Forget looking for Porter, Captain Nakura. This Porter is one clever bastard. From the beginning, we followed his Internet inquiries when he was contacting the *Archivo General de las Indias* in Seville, Spain. He began by saying he was looking for information about a vessel named the *San Pedro*. Shortly after that, he switched to looking at Spanish galleons lost in the late 17th century. Finally, he narrowed his inquiries to the Manila galleon, *Concepcion*. We followed those efforts of his because we have a resource working for us at the *Archivo* in Seville.

"We missed completely the possibility that Porter might have made earlier research inquiries at different institutions. We now know that he actually began his research looking for the ship's log of an English man-o-war called *HMS Cygnet*, but for some reason didn't pursue it. We have a part-time associate in the British War Museum, and he, belatedly, tells us of Porter's inquiries about the British warship.

"We have only recently learned of this. We had our resource in the British War Museum locate the ship's log for the *HMS Cygnet* and scour it for the years that Porter's Manila galleons went missing. Lo and behold, the British warship rescued a Spanish castaway on an uncharted north Pacific island on May 24th, 1699. The *Concepcion* had departed Manila eight months earlier, and probably ran aground on the island. The Spanish castaway's name was Don Emilio Bustamente de la Vega, and he was a passenger aboard the *Concepcion* when she was lost. The treasure is almost certainly buried on that island.

"The Japanese name for the island is Minami Torishima, formerly Marcus Island. The precise location is Lat. 22º 17' N, Long. 153º 58' E. You are to proceed immediately to that location, and if Porter is there attempting to recover the treasure, you know what to do. Dutch, the captain of your support vessel, is underway at this very moment. It's a long haul, but he'll proceed at best speed. He will rendezvous there to give you any support you may need. Understood?"

Captain Yoto Nakura absorbed all that had been said, and realized that he had been duped by not only Porter, but whoever was operating the *Giggling Witch* as a diversion. It had all been a ruse to distract him while Porter made off with the treasure. How Porter got from Saipan to the treasure without the *Giggling Witch*, he had no idea. Then he thought of the New Zealand sailboat that had shared the dock with the *Giggling Witch* for many weeks. Could the tricky round-eye have borrowed or chartered that boat to go to the treasure while his friends deceived him into believing there was treasure at Anatahan Island? Yoto Nakura fumed, and the more he thought of how cleverly he had been tricked, the more incensed he became. He grabbed the VHF radio's microphone and hailed Matsu, who had just made it to Saipan in the Zodiac.

When Matsu answered, Nakura gave him orders to return immediately to the Taka Maru#17. Matsu responded by saying that the *Giggling Witch* was pulling away from the dock and heading north, apparently to

Anatahan Island. "Forget the sailboat," Nakura said. Then a thin smile spread across his face.

(Four)

They anchored the *Giggling Witch* in the same bay at Anatahan Island as before. Sammy lowered and secured the sails, set the anchor, then shut down the engine. Elena was putting their dinner on plates and preparing to take them to the cockpit, when she heard the roar of the Zodiac's outboard. The big sportboat came along side in a swoosh, five near-naked Yakuza aboard, their head-to-toe tattoos giving them the appearance of scaly reptiles. Three of the Yakuza grabbed the *Giggling Witch's* lifelines and climbed aboard. When Sammy turned to protest, he was punched in the throat and went to his knees struggling to breathe. Elena came up the companionway and screamed when she saw the Yakuza strike her brother. Two Yakuza grabbed her arms and yanked her into the cockpit, then threw her into the arms of a Yakuza standing in the Zodiac.

Once Elena was in the Zodiac, the Yakuzas on board the *Giggling Witch* grabbed a piece of line and tied the semi-conscious Sammy T to the base of the main mast. They raised the anchor and using the Zodiac like a tugboat, pushed the *Giggling Witch* away from the island into deeper water. A quarter mile off Anatahan Island, the ocean bottom was over one thousand feet deep.

One of the Yakuza went down below, removed the hoses from the seacocks and opened the valves. Water began to rush inside the *Giggling Witch's* hull. The Yakuzas jumped from the deck into the Zodiac. The last sight Elena had of her brother was him tied to the mast of the sinking boat. She screamed, "Sammy! Sammy!" One of the Yakuza reached across and gave her a hard, open-handed slap across her face. She was unconscious when the Yakuza stuck his hand down

inside her blouse and squeezed her breast. Mercifully, she did not see the *Giggling Witch* sink beneath the ocean's surface, her brother struggling helplessly against his bonds.

Yoto Nakura watched with satisfaction when the Zodiac returned with the Chamorro woman, lying limp in the bottom of the sportboat. The pirate consortium's partner, who had introduced himself only as 'John' when he first came aboard the *Taka Maru #17* at Tinian Island, stood beside him at the rail. When he asked Nakura what this was all about and who was the woman, Nakura turned to him and said, "This is done at my orders. I am the captain of this vessel. But if you must know, this woman was a spy who caused us a lot of delay. She is connected to the leader of the group attempting to recover treasure at Minami Torishima. She may have value if we need to barter. Do you question my orders?" Nakura asked with a hard tone in his voice.

"No, of course not, Captain," John replied. "What must be done, must be done."

One of the Yakuza who had been in the Zodiac reported to Matsu, assuring him that the sailboat was now on the ocean's bottom. Matsu went directly to the bridge of the *Taka Maru #17* passing the information to Yoto Nakura. "Well done, Matsu. Now we steer for what is ours. Set the course for Minami Torishima, maximum cruise speed," Nakura ordered. He then went down to the aft deck where the Zodiac had been recovered. He ordered the Chamorro woman manacled, hands and feet, and secured to a bunk. A watch was to be set to keep an eye on her. She was not to be touched. Anyone who disobeyed that order would be food for the fish.

(Five)

Date: July 19, 2000

Lat. 09º 00' N, /Long. 80º 00'W

Panama Canal, Republic of Panama

Jake smiled when he rode his ship's tender to the Gatun Yacht Club dock and saw his crew assembled, all smiles and filled with excitement, their duffle bags at their feet. Stacy was grinning from ear to ear, clearly on the adventure of her lifetime. Tag and Gunny Sweikert stood beside her looking steady and ready. The five young Marines knew Jake immediately from the demonstration of his Haskins sniper rifle at the Gainesville firing range. They shouted loud hoots in recognition. Looking at them, Jake remembered when he was seventeen years old and a Marine recruit, filled with piss and vinegar. Japanese pirates were no match for these young men, he knew. Guadalcanal, Tarawa, Saipan, Iwo Jima, and Okinawa were ample testimony to that. He just hoped fate would favor their endeavor and see them all home safe and sound.

Jake stepped up onto the yacht club dock and gave everyone a handshake. Then they piled their gear into the tender and motored out to the ship that would ferry them to the treasure on the far side of the Pacific Ocean. Captain Krawczyk had already obtained their *zarpe* and permission to complete their transit of the Panama Canal. He called the chandlery to order the delivery of all stores held in bond.

ake in the meanwhile took everyone on a tour of the ship, showing them where they would bunk and the location of the nearest head for showering and relieving themselves. He explained that they were aboard a cargo vessel not a cruise ship, and that they would have to share in the cooking and general housekeeping chores. The ship's crew was reduced to the Captain, the engineer, and two deckhands. So, there might be occasions when they would be called upon to do bosun deck work, too.

One of the young Marines, a hulk of a guy at two hundred fifty pounds that everyone called 'Tank', announced that he had been a short order cook at a Waffle House Restaurant and would have no problem cranking out the meals. Stacy said she had a few culinary talents of her own and wouldn't mind helping out in the galley. Jake said that he would serve as armorer, and announced his purchase of the new Armalite M-16s and the Glock pistols. The Marines, including Gunny Sweikert and Major Taggart, nodded their heads in appreciation of the selections in weaponry. Stacy's face clouded over a bit at the mention of the weapons, so Jake took the occasion to announce for the first time to the young Marines that the mission was to recover and protect a cargo of very valuable art objects. He explained that because of the enormous value of the cargo, there were some unfriendly people who might try to intervene. If they were lucky, not a shot would be fired, but they must be prepared for any eventuality.

One of the Marines, a stocky fellow with a closely-cropped Marine-style haircut that everyone called 'Buzz', asked, "May I ask where are we headed, sir? Where the cargo is located?"

"Buzz, the location has been kept secret for obvious reasons. But I can tell you that the cargo was deposited on a small volcanic island in the north Pacific almost 400 years ago. I was on this island just a few weeks ago, located the cargo, and brought a small portion of it back aboard my sailboat. I left ninety-nine point-nine percent of it behind because my boat was so small. I have assembled this expedition to recover what I couldn't carry the first time around."

"So, this is like treasure, sir?" another of the Marines asked.

"Yes," Jake said. "The island is incredibly remote. It has been abandoned for a long time. It is uninhabited and has no fresh water, only some brackish rainwater on occasion. Our plan is to pull up alongside the island, launch boats to go ashore and transfer the cargo, treasure If you will, to our ship and leave. Our ship will not even anchor; just stand offshore during the transfer. I estimate it will take a maximum of five days to make the transfer. We will then return to Panama, where our antiquities expert will conduct an international auction."

Jake heard the big MANN diesels start up, and the rumbling of anchor chain in the hawse as the anchor was being raised. He excused himself and went topside to see what was going on. Captain Krawczyk announced that the Panama Canal pilot had come aboard and they were being directed to the locks for lowering to the Miraflores locks and onto the Pacific Ocean. He also handed Jake a copy of the delivery slip from the chandlery, indicating that everything had been accounted for and was now in the forward hold. "There are some interesting items in your cargo that I think we should talk about when we have an opportunity. Specifically, the weaponry and ammunition," he said, lighting his black briar pipe."

"No problem, Captain," Jake answered. "I also have a telex from your company that I would like to share with you. I believe in keeping all cards on the table. Why don't we have a skull session when we reach the roadstead in Panama Bay?

Captain Krawczyk nodded his head in agreement. "I must join the Canal pilot on the bridge as we finish our transit. We should be in the roadstead in about four hours."

Tank and Stacy prepared a meal that was fit for a visiting head of state; everything from steak, veggies and a cold salad, to chilled Portuguese table wine. Captain Krawczyk complimented Jake on his shopping, and expressed his thanks to the two chefs. Then he gave a nod to Jake and the two of them left the table and went topside to the bridge. The ship rode gently at her anchorage in the open roadstead. Krawczyk opened the conversation asking about the military-style equipment and the weapons that Jake had brought aboard, reminding Jake of his company's strict rules against ferrying weapons, explosives, or dangerous cargo.

"Captain, I have spoken frankly to you and I have signed your company's charter agreement. I told you that we were going to be carrying very valuable cargo, and that there are some dangerous people who would like to take it from us. I explained that the passengers you were taking on board were academic types and some civilians with military backgrounds. All of that is true. The weapons and ammunition we have brought on board do not constitute cargo. They are the personal effects of the young security guards you met at dinner, and are considered the tools of their trade. We must protect the cargo and ourselves, and that includes you and your ship. Pirates make no distinction among the people aboard a vessel they capture; they kill them all if they wish."

"Exactly where are we headed, Mr. Porter?" Captain Krawczyk asked.

"I am prepared to give you that information, Captain, once I am assured that you consent to participate in our voyage," Jake said. "The first thing I want you to know is that our destination is remote and uninhabited. There is no port to clear into. There will be no processing of arrival or departure documentation. Secondly, to keep everything as legal as possible with regard to you and your ship, you will not anchor. Technically and officially, you will neither arrive or depart. Your vessel will remain offshore. You personally and your Engineer and deckhands, will not leave your ship and go ashore anywhere." Jake reached into his shirt pocket and brought out a thin telex message.

"We may conduct this voyage in strict accordance with your company's charter contract, but with some flexibility. I cannot compromise my responsibility to protect our cargo, or our personal safety. I am prepared to offer you a handsome performance bonus for your cooperation. If what I have outlined to you is unacceptable, I understand. You have only to say no, and pack your bags. Jake handed the telex message to Captain Krawczyk.

Krawczyk pulled his briar pipe from his shirt pocket and filled the bowl with a dark Turkish blend. He put his reading glasses on, turned the telex to the light and read the message. Basically, the message said that the company had been offered a most attractive price to buy his ship outright, and the company had agreed to sell. All that was needed was the signing of a sales agreement and a transfer of funds. Captain Krawczyk was free to work out a contract with the new owner, or return to Finland at the company's expense for further instructions.

"What is the amount of the performance bonus, Mr. Porter," Captain Krawczyk asked.

"Two hundred fifty thousand U.S dollars paid immediately to any bank of your choosing. Fifty thousand to your Engineer, and twenty-five thousand to each of your deck crew."

Captain Krawczyk studied the telex once more, then said "The Bank of West Hampton, Essex, England. I will check with the Engineer and my crew for theirs."

Do you have a small scale chart of the Pacific Ocean, Captain?" Jake asked.

"I do," Krawczyk said, pulling a chart from a drawer.

"Marcus Island, Captain," Jake said, laying his finger on the chart beneath the tiny island. "Latitude 22º 17' N, Longitude 153º 58' E. for an immediate departure and at your best speed. We have not a minute to spare. I will call my bank while we are still within cell phone range of Panama City. I would appreciate an estimated time of arrival at your earliest convenience, Captain." Jake stood and offered his hand. "No radio communications of any kind, Captain. Our position and destination are to be known only to us."

Captain Krawczyk smiled and sucked deeply on his pipe, giving Jake a firm handshake in return. He seemed pleased with his new employment arrangement. He called down to the engine room and advised the Engineer that they were weighing anchor. He called the deckhands over the ship's intercom and ordered the weighing of the anchor immediately. Once the anchor was up, Captain Krawczyk set the course and telegraphed to the engine room for full speed. The lights of Panama City soon disappeared as they plunged into the early evening darkness heading west by northwest, aiming for a minuscule half-acre of coral atoll.

(Six)

Date: July 24 , 2001

Lat. 22º 17' N, Long. 153º 58' E.

Marcus Island/Minami Torishima

454

Yoto Nakura was more than pleased. They had sighted Minami Torishima's low profile just before dusk on the third day full day of sailing out of Saipan. He had breathed a sigh of relief when he saw that the ocean surrounding the tiny island was free of any other ship. His only concern now was whether or not Porter had preceded him and made off with the remainder of the treasure. He would know the answer to that soon enough.

The next step was to send his Yakuza ashore and search the island for any sign of digging. The timing was unfortunate only in the sense that the Taka Maru#17 must be held offshore until dawn, a twelve-hour delay. There were strong currents in and around the island, and the island was surrounded by coral reef. If the Taka Maru#17 was accidently set onto the reef, it would be a disaster, and most probably the end of their lives. He called Matsu to the bridge, gave him his instructions, then went below to check on the Chamorro woman.

Elena heard the click of the stateroom door handle. She tensed in fear every time the door opened. So far, the sound of the door handle only announced the arrival of a food tray. But the trays were carried by grossly tattooed Japanese Yakuza, naked except for a white thong between their legs. Their black eyes danced in excitement as they scanned her body, and it was no secret what the Yakuza were thinking. But this time, it was Nakura, the captain. He frightened her most of all because she knew he held her life in his hands. He had ordered the murder of her brother, Sammy. Helpless though she was, Elena knew she would not hesitate to kill this bastard from hell if ever given the chance.

"We have arrived," Nakura announced, smiling down at the beautiful Chamorro woman, her hands and feet manacled to the metal bunk. "Your Porter is nowhere to be seen. I will know in the morning whether he has come and gone. For you, it makes no difference. You will join your brother soon. But before you leave us, I will fuck you. I will fuck you many times, all the way to Shikotan, then hand you over to my Yakuza. They have not had a woman for more than a week, and I know

455

they hunger for you. You are all they talk about. Shall we see what they will receive?" Nakura grabbed Elena's blouse with both hands and yanked it off violently, leaving her naked above the waist. "Very nice, my pretty Chamarro whore," Nakura said in Japanese, taking one of Elena's breast in his hand.

Elena screamed and struggled against the metal chains binding her arms and legs, but it was of no use. No one on the Taka Maru#17 would come to her aid. This tattooed monster could do anything he wanted with her.

Yoto Nakura felt his groin grow tense and struggle against the thong between his legs. Smiling, he freed it, allowing it to grow even bigger. He saw the fright in the Chamorro woman's eyes, and grinned. He grabbed Elena's skirt and ripped it off, then her panties, leaving him an unobstructed view of the dark delta between her legs. "Perhaps we could have a sample right now? I am free for the evening," Nakura laughed. He was reaching to massage one of Elena's breasts when there was a rapid knocking at the stateroom door. Nakura straightened his thong to cover his erection and went to the door. "What is it that you interrupt me?" he asked in a menacing tone of voice. From the other side of the door, a crewman answered timidly. "Matsu sent me, sir. There is a radar contact."

From the Taka Maru#17's bridge, Captain Yoto Nakura studied the radar image. It indicated a vessel steaming east at about twelve knots. If she kept to her present course, she would pass Minami Torishima to the north by ten or twelve miles. "Coffee, Matsu," he ordered. "I will stay until first light. Get your rest. We have a big day tomorrow." And it will end with a sound fucking of the Chamorro whore before sunset, he thought with pleasure.

At dawn, Captain Nakura ordered the Zodiac sportboat and a search crew of six Yakuza to head for the landing alongside Minami Torishima's wrecked pier. Their orders were to fan out over the island and search every square foot for any disturbance that suggested digging. Nakura sat at the bridge along with 'John', the pirate consortium partner. He watched his Yakuza swarm up and down the beach. It didn't take long.

The depression created by the five hundred pound bomb was easily spotted despite Jake's attempt to conceal it with ginkokai. The two Yakuza who spied it first excitedly pulled the ginkokai aside and looked down through the fissure. They saw the pile of Chinese porcelain and gold bars that Jake had stacked on top of the big bundles of silk tapestries. One of the Yakuza radioed the Taka Maru#17 with his VHF hand-held radio and announced excitedly, "We have it!"

"Let's go take a look, John, what do you say?" Nakura said. He ordered the Zodiac to return to the ship. When it arrived at the Taka Maru#17's stern ramp, Nakura and the pirate consortium's representative, 'John,' jumped in. Once on the beach, Nakura led the way to the treasure pit. All of the Yakuza that had come ashore on the island for the search were now standing in a circle around the big fissure, and very excited.

Nakura leaned over the edge of the fissure and smiled with deep satisfaction. He had beaten Porter to the treasure! The treasure was his! He ordered two Yakuza to return to the Taka Maru#17 and bring a steel ladder, rope and spotlights. The remaining Yakuza stood respectfully around the fissure waiting for any orders from their captain. Speaking in Japanese, Nakura said, "You have done well and your reward is at hand. At Tinian, I told you that the treasure is ours alone. I told you that this piece of lying shit," he indicated 'John' standing alongside him oblivious to what was being said in Japanese, "I would kill myself, and that the only survivors would be you, my Yakuza brothers, and me."

Nakura lifted an automatic pistol from his pants pocket, pressed it against the back of John's head and pulled the trigger. A burst of blood and brain exited the front of his face carrying his eyes and nose with it. John collapsed, dead before he hit the ground. "Throw him over the bank to the beach. The tide will carry him away," Nakura ordered.

When the Zodiac returned, three Yakuza hauled a ladder, two coils of rope, and a spotlight to the cave. The ladder was lowered to set atop the soft bundles, and Nakura went down first. His heart was pounding as he lifted one of the Chinese porcelain vases, then some of the gold chains and bars of gold. He shined the flashlight down into the depths of the cave and saw for the first time the bulk of the treasure. Hundred of millions of Yen! Enough to live as a king for the rest of his life. He radioed his bosun aboard the Taka Maru#17, saying he needed material for building an 'A' frame to position over the fissure, plus an eight-part block-and-tackle to lift the treasure to the surface. This was going to be a laborious and time-consuming job. He had no idea where Porter was, or even if he was coming at all, but he wanted the treasure safely aboard his ship and to be well away from the island as soon as possible. As an afterthought, he ordered a small gas-powered generator and lights be brought to the cave; they would work round the clock, day and night.

(Seven)

Jake, Major Taggart and Gunny Sweikert stood out on the starboard wing of the bridge taking in the progress of their ship toward Marcus Island. By Captain Krawczyk's estimate, with favorable wind and current, they would arrive at the tiny atoll within nine days of their departure from Panama. They were making a steady thirty knots, and he had given the Engineer permission to push for extra engine RPMs and speed if possible.

Earlier, Jake had asked that the two senior Marines, Taggart and Sweikert, take over the training and battle preparations for Marcus. Between the two of them, he argued, they had far more combat and small unit tactical experience than he did as a Marine Staff Sergeant and sniper. He felt more comfortable taking his tactical orders from them, and since they had a common goal, it would be good to present a unified front to the young Marines. Surprised at this voluntary suspending of his authority, the two senior Marines admired Jake's wisdom and agreed with his decision.

Taggart, Sweikert and Jake had already spent some time studying the satellite photos of Marcus Island. Jake, of course, had walked all over the island just a few weeks earlier. He had a fresh, ground-level perspective of what the island terrain offered in the way of cover. He took satellite photo printouts and with red and black colored pens marked-in the features he felt were most important. He indicated the old military truck at the end of the first line of trucks as the one where he had hidden his Haskins sniper rifle. He made the point that he thought recovering the Haskins was a priority because of the destructive firepower it could be bring to bear on enemy forces. He described the old Coast Guard building as nothing more than light aluminum framework offering no cover from concentrated rifle fire. A round fired from one of the Armalite M-16s would go clear through them.

The island cupped in the middle, and the high ground was on the surrounding ridgeline. The old military trucks offered good cover to whoever got control of them first. As far as landing the Zodiacs, they would be restricted to the two breaks in the reef.

Major Bryce Taggart and Gunny Sweikert took it all in, studied the photos, and developed several scenarios, depending on whether the island had remained uninhabited since Jake's visit, or if there was an occupying force defending it. They also took into account the logistics of transferring the treasure from the island to their ship. Over the next several days, as their ship plowed ahead at maximum speed across the Pacific toward Marcus Island, the two officers held planning sessions with the five young Marines to drive home the basics and explain what they were up against.

With the permission of Taggart and Sweikert, Jake issued the new Armalite rifles and Glock pistols to his Marines. Stacy was tickled to receive the Baby Glock that Jake had purchased for her. He conducted familiarization sessions on both weapons, demonstrating field stripping and cleaning. He announced that Major Taggart would be directing target practice, and that Gunny Sweikert would be conducting PT and hand-to-hand combat sessions to keep everyone loosened up. He inflated one of the Zodiac sport boats to familiarize them with the process. The Zodiacs were RIB types with hard, fiberglass bottoms for landing on coral or rough beaches. He broke one of the Mercury outboards out of its packaging and ran the Marines through the operating instructions in the Owner's Manual.

They placed mattresses on the afterdeck to soften their hand-to-hand sessions with Gunny Sweikert. He covered all of the basic moves to disarm and disable including the strategic application of the K-Bar knife into the vitals of an enemy. Major Taggart set up targets on a wooden pedestal he had rigged up, and everyone zeroed in their firearms including Stacy. Stacy proved to be a good shot, and the Marines applauded her performance with such exuberance that she blushed deeply.

When Captain Krawczyk finally called Major Taggart to the bridge to announce that Marcus Island would be visible on radar that evening about eight o'clock, Taggart passed the word to Gunny Sweikert, then he informed Jake and the Marines. Taggart called for a tactical session following dinner. Captain Krawczyk asked if he could sit in, and his request was approved. It proved to be a wise decision because Krawczyk pointed out that his radar transmissions would alert any vessel anchored at Marcus. If he came within line-of-sight of Marcus, his own ship's image would reveal their presence on the other vessel's radar screen. If they intended to make a totally secret trip to the island in the dark, then his vessel should stay below the horizon. The Marines could approach the island in their Zodiacs undetected, he suggested, particularly if the island was between them and an anchored vessel. The sea state at the moment was almost flat calm, winds under eight miles per hour; a good night for skulking around on the water.

Jake still hoped that Marcus was uninhabited, and that they would find a deserted island just as he had left it. But a lot could have happened in the weeks since he left Marcus in the proa. His last phone call from Panama to Elena, it was her mother, Delilah, who had answered. She said that Elena and Sammy had sailed the *Giggling Witch* earlier that day to Anatahan Island to continue to decoy the Jap long-liner. It was

460

not what Jake wanted to hear. He had asked Elena to stay close to home until he returned. But Elena was head strong, and she wanted to help protect Jake. It was no use arguing with her; she was going to do whatever she decided.

Taggart and Gunny Sweikert decided to take Captain Krawczyk's information into their calculations. They had no reason to believe that there was a vessel anchored at Marcus with radar, but why take the chance and lose the element of surprise? They decided to launch the Zodiacs and travel the last 15 miles to Marcus under cover of darkness. If the island was clear, they would radio Captain Krawczyk to close with the island and stand off until dawn. The Marines in the Zodiacs would follow Jake ashore to secure the treasure site.

It was decided that Major Taggart would remain on their ship, much to Stacy's relief. His role was to monitor the approach to Marcus, and be ready to order an evacuation, or direct their ship to Marcus as a back-up to the landing force. He was Mission Control, so to speak, and would keep Captain Krawczyk in the loop as necessary.

The Mercury outboards were secured to the Zodiacs, a five-gallon container with extra fuel was included. Three of the four Zodiacs, carrying the five young Marines, Gunny Sweikert and Jake, plus their rifles, pistols, ammo and VHF hand-held radios aboard were lowered over the side with the ship's cargo crane. The fourth Zodiac was rigged with motor and fuel, but held in reserve for Taggart. Sweikert led the way; he and his Marine powered off followed closely by the other Zodiacs. The Zodiacs could plane at 10 knot, so Marcus's dark profile came into view rather quickly.

As they closed with the island, a bright light was seen shining from the island, and Jake's heart sank when he saw the shadowy outline of a ship's upper structure on the far side of the island. He double-clicked his VHF hand-held radio, the signal to stop and regroup. All of the Zodiacs circled together and held onto each other's lines.

461

Jake and Sweikert had Nikon 7x50 binoculars, and each was scanning the island, focusing especially on the bright light at the northern end. They could see figures moving around, but couldn't see what they were up to. They could also see a huge pile of boxes and bundles piled up to one side of the light being back-lighted by the bright light. It was an unhappy scenario. Jake leaned over to Sweikert, saying "Gunny, we don't know who these people are. We can't just go ashore and kill them. Hell, they may be employees of the Japanese government. I need a closer look at that vessel anchored on the other side. What do you think?" Jake asked, acceding to Gunny Sweikert's leadership.

"Agreed, Jake," Sweikert said. "Go check it out. They can't see us this far offshore, so we'll just hang out here."

Jake broke loose from the ring of Zodiacs and sped away toward Marcus, but keeping well offshore and noting his reciprocal bearing for returning to the floating island of Marines. Thankfully, it was a dark night. When he rounded the southeastern point, he had a full unobstructed view of the ship and recognized its profile immediately. The Jap long-liner from Saipan! No doubt about it. It was too damn ugly to be anything other. The bastards digging up the treasure were Yakuza!

Jake powered-down the Zodiac and skirted the Jap long-liner, making his way around the southeastern point until he was abreast of the bright light onshore. He scanned the activity ashore with his binoculars and saw that they were lifting treasure with an A-frame and tackle. The boxes were being dragged away from the fissure and stacked. From the size of the stack, they had been at it for at least several days. Jake immediately wondered how much of it, if any, had already been transferred to the long-liner. He angled away from the island and headed back for Gunny Sweikert and the other Marines.

"Yakuza!" Jake said when he rejoined Sweikert. "No doubt about it, Gunny. There are at least ten or fifteen of them on the island. The vessel on the other side of the island is the Jap long-liner from Saipan. I'd recognize that ugly piece of crap anywhere. It looks like they have been recovering treasure for several days. They're lifting it out with block-and-tackle. A slow process. No way to tell how far along they are, or how much treasure has already been transferred to their ship. As I see it, Gunny, we've got two targets, the treasure site and the long-liner."

"Got it, Jake. Let's put our heads together and think this one through. Biggest mistake Custer made at the Little Big Horn was dividing his forces before the battle, and underestimating the number of the enemy he was going to fight. Let's bring the Major in on this one." Sweikert called Major Taggart and laid out the situation for him. Taggart asked for a couple of minutes to review the satellite photos of the island. Then he came back on the phone.

"If we own their boat, they aren't going anywhere. We've got them and the treasure. But it wouldn't hurt to put some flanking pressure on them on the island. We don't know how many Yakuza are on the boat, or how many are on the island. And then there's the long-liner's captain. Is he on the island, or on the boat? We take him, the rest of the Yakuza will fold. Let's get Jake on the island to recover his Haskins. That multiplies our firepower. Have him find a place where he can bring the Haskins to bear on the treasure pit as well as the Jap boat. Gunny, you and the rest of our Marines take the Jap boat. Do it as quickly and as quietly as you can. If the Yakuza on the island hear gunfire coming from their boat, be prepared to repel boarders. Jake will provide covering fire with his Haskins."

"Got it, sir," Sweikert said. "We're rolling. I'll keep you up to speed. Out."

"Okay, Jake," Sweikert said. You're cleared to go get your Haskins. Set up to cover the treasure pit and the Jap long-liner. Keep Buzz with you to cover your back. Don't start any wars until we've got the long-liner secured, okay? Keep your VHF on so we can coordinate. Use your ear piece."

"One last thought, Gunny, but it's an important one," Jake said. "We should make every effort to avoid shooting into the stacks of cargo. A single bullet could shatter a Chinese vase worth millions of dollars. If the Yakuza take shelter behind the stacks of cargo, we've got to draw them out. Not try to shoot through the treasure. okay?"

Sweikert turned to the Marines and said, "Got that, men? No firing into the treasure. Flush 'em then shoot them." Sweikert reached across from his Zodiac to shake Jake's and Buzz's hands. Jake turned away, throttled-up the outboard and headed for Marcus, figuring to land just inside the southwestern tip at the end of the old Jap runway. The night was pitch black, and the Yakuza were standing in bright light with their backs to the ocean, their attention focused on raising the treasure. Surprise should be complete.

Sweikert set the assault plan for the taking of the Jap long-liner, made sure his Marines understood, then they motored off abreast of one another. Enroute, Sweikert studied the Taka Maru#17 through his binoculars, looking for lights or movement above decks. The ship was dark except for a small light in the bridge area. He saw no one moving about topside. The ship was anchored, bow facing the island's beach. Anyone standing watch would probably be looking toward the brightly-lit treasure pit and all the activity there. Sweikert scanned the bridge and forward area closely, but saw no movement. He led the other Zodiacs with their Marines around the stern of the ship, signaling for the outboard motors to be shut off and switching to oars.

They rowed slowly to a spot below the transom, threw padded grapnels to snag the deck rail and quickly climbed hand-over-hand to the deck. Within three minutes, all four Marines and Sweikert were on the *Taka Maru#17's* deck. Crouching, moving quickly but silently along the port side of the ship, they worked their way in the darkness toward the bridge and bow.

(Eight)

Yoto Nakura was a happy man. His fortune and future were secure. He had spent the day alongside the treasure pit directing his men in their labors to raise the treasure from the depths of the pit to the surface. Each time a load was brought to the surface, he directed it to be swung aside and dragged alongside the other boxes, chests and bundles of silk tapestries. He opened the personal chests of the Concepcion's passengers, plowing through the various drawers and compartments searching for jewelry and precious stones. He passed out these small pieces of the treasure to his crew, much to their delight. He was like a kid beneath the Christmas tree.

The most valuable items were the Chinese porcelain vases, he knew. Unfortunately, the wooden crates holding them were rotten, and could not be trusted to stay together for the hauling to the surface. At the same time, it was too time-consuming to bring up each vase one at a time. So a lot of time was spent in building a platform to stack them on, or bundling them in scraps of silk.

After a day in the sun, Yoto Nakura decided to return to the Taka Maru#17, take a shower and go play with the Chamorro woman. The excitement of the treasure had diverted his attention these past several days, and he was yet to have his pleasure with her. She would fight him, he knew, but that only excited him the more. Tonight he would spread her legs and have her in whatever way he wished.

"Matsu, take over. I'm going to the boat for a shower," Nakura ordered. "Keep an eye out to seaward. That bastard Dutch and his crew may come over the horizon at any time. Remember our plan. We get them on the island, show them the treasure, and while they are looking, we kill them all. Understand?"

"Hai!" Matsu said obediently. He directed one of the Yakuza to take Nakura to the Taka Maru#17 and return with the Zodiac. He was leaving only one Yakuza on the vessel, keeping all the rest on the island to recover the treasure. They were moving tons of stuff, and needed every strong back at their disposal. The crewman on the boat was there solely for anchor watch to make sure the Taka Mru#17's anchor was not

465

dragging.

Nakura had just finished his shower and was standing naked outside the doorway to the compartment where he held the Chamorro woman when he heard the rifle shot from topside.

(Nine)

Jake and Buzz shut down the outboard motor and rowed the last hundred yards to the beach. They dragged the Zodiac up onto the beach, and pulled it on top of a bed of dark kelp. The kelp broke up the Zodiac's profile and provided a bit of camouflage. It would be hard to see in the dark from the island's interior. They climbed the twenty-foot high coral sand embankment, Jake leading the way, and pushed through knee-high brush toward the line of rusting military trucks. Jake dropped down and rolled beneath the truck on the nearest end and fished inside the transmission tunnel, pulling out his Haskins sniper rifle.

"All right!" Buzz whispered, a smile stretching across his face. He remembered well the final shot Jake had taken with the Haskins during his demonstration at the county firing range in Gainesville, Florida. He had destroyed an old shot-up Buick with an armor-piercing incendiary round, leaving nothing but a flaming hulk bearing no resemblance to an automobile.

Jake removed the covering from his rifle, satisfied that the oiling-down and the thick wrapping had kept moisture at bay. He snapped the barrel into the receiver, inserted the bolt and a loaded 5-round magazine. Five more magazines, oiled and individually wrapped lay alongside the Utel telescope. Jake slid the scope into the grooves on top of the receiver. Locked and loaded, as they say. He handed his Armalite M-16 rifle to Buzz, who checked its magazine, ratcheted the action to insert a round into the chamber, then flipped it into safety mode, ready to go. His own Armalite was already set to fire if the safety was taken off.

In a muffled voice, Jake oriented Buzz to their location, explaining he was going to set up in the bed of the truck, the Haskin's bi-pod resting on top of the truck's cab while he, Jake, would stand in the bed of the truck. The truck was high enough to see the long-liner anchored just off the beach. Swinging the barrel to his left, he could see the treasure pit, the stack of treasure alongside, and the Yakuza standing around in the light from the generator. No one was looking his way. The Yakuza had no idea what was about to happen to them. That was when he heard the rifle shot coming from the long-liner.

The Yakuza gathered around the treasure pit heard it, too. They stopped what they were doing and turned to look in the direction of their long-liner. They couldn't see the Marines' Zodiacs tied to the stern of the Taka Maru#17. It was too dark to make out what might be happening, but the sound of the gunshot was enough to galvanize them. A half-dozen of the Yakuza grabbed up their AK-47's and ran to the beach to jump into their Zodiac. They fired up the big Yamaha outboard and roared off to the long-liner to see what was happening.

Jake spoke calmly to Buzz, "The Yakuza at the pit will be heading our way once I open up with the Haskins. They all have AK-47s, so it's going to get real hot. Start taking 'em out as soon as you have a shot. Remember, these are Jap criminals and they intend to kill us. They won't be taking any prisoners. Got that?"

"Got it, Sarge," Buzz said. "I'm on full auto, and I got plenty of ammo."

Jake watched the Yakuza's Zodiac heading for the long-liner. They outnumbered the Marines on the Jap boat by two to one at least. Jake swung the Haskin seaward, put his eye to the scope, centered the crosshairs of the scope on the big Yamaha outboard, purposely aiming a bit high to make sure he got a hit somewhere along the length of the Zodiac, and fired his first shot. The sound of the Haskins roared across the island and the Yakuza at the treasure pit all hit the deck, trying to figure out what was going on. Several fired probing rounds in Jake's general direction, but none of the rounds even hit the truck.

Jake missed the Yamaha, but the round punched a hole through the

467

Zodiac's fiberglass hull, and seawater immediately began to rush into the inflatable. For his second shot, Jake aimed at the three men sitting on the starboard inflation tube and fired. The Haskins roared again and Jake saw that all three of the Yakuza were gone. He had apparently also punctured the inflation chamber they were sitting on. Driven by the Yamaha, making almost ten knots, the Zodiac skewed to the right when the starboard inflation chamber deflated. The Zodiac almost flipped over, but the Yakuza driving it chopped the power.

The remaining three Yakuza were looking toward the island holding their AK-47s and trying to figure out the situation, confused as to who might be shooting at them. They had had the island to themselves for days. It was located in the middle of nowhere. Where did these people come from? Who were they? How did they get here? Where was their boat?

The only answer they received to their questions was another round from the Haskins. This one struck the Yamaha outboard igniting the motor's gasoline tank, exploding it into flaming shrapnel that blew the remaining Yakuzas into the water. The Zodiac went adrift, and with the next shot shattering its remaining inflation chamber, began to sink. Jake thought he saw one Yakuza swimming toward the shore holding his AK-47 out of the water, but that was a minor concern because the Yakuzas at the treasure pit had begun spreading out and were frantically hosing down the darkness with their AK-47s in the direction of the sound of the Haskins.

Buzz caught two Yakuzas between him and the light at the treasure pit. He squeezed off two short three-round bursts from his Armalite assault rifle and watched them spin and drop. Jake spun the Haskins to point toward the treasure pit and shot through the A-frame, reducing it to splinters. One of the Yakuzas was smart enough to shut off the generator and douse the light. Jake heard some soft shuffling along the line of trucks, and drew his Glock 45GAP pistol. He tapped Buzz on the shoulder to warn him, holding a finger to his mouth for silence. The Yakuza walked past the end of the truck bed looking for his enemy. Jake leveled the Glock to the center of his back, one foot beneath his head and squeezed off a round that drove the Yakuza to the ground with an exit hole in his chest that you could fit a basketball into.

Fire and maneuver, fire and maneuver. That was the small unit tactic beat into the brain of every Marine, so Jake and Buzz abandoned their hide in the old truck. They slipped to the ground and crawled away toward the beach and the end of the old Jap runway. Familiar territory for Jake. He led Buzz down alongside the runway, his Haskins slung over his shoulder, but also carrying his Armalite, and the Glock stuck in pants behind his belt. They came to the end of the runway, crossed over it, now crawling, they closed on the treasure pit. The question was how many Yakuza were left and where in the dark of Marcus Island were they?

(Ten)

Gunny Sweikert couldn't believe their luck. The Yakuza he had surprised at the bow and shot dead as he turned with his AK-47 leveled, was the only Yakuza on the boat. At least that was what a quick search revealed. Plenty of hiding spaces left because it was a big boat, but from the looks of it, the dead Yakuza was the anchor watch. So that meant the captain was probably ashore at the treasure pit taking care of business. Then he had seen the big Zodiac heading his way with at least a half-dozen Yakuza. But before he could even become concerned with the threat, he watched the Zodiac explode. By the time Jake and his Haskins were finished, all Sweikert could see was a sole Yakuza holding his AK-47 over his head, side-stroking for the beach. Sweikert pinpointed the target and two of his Marines laced the water around the Yakuza with automatic fire from their new Armalites. Scanning the ocean with his binoculars, Sweikert was sure the Yakuza didn't make it to the beach.

Sweikert ordered his Marines to their Zodiacs for a beach assault to support Jake and Buzz. He saw them over the side, then radioed Jake to let him know friendly Marines would be moving about and be careful to not shoot them. Jake acknowledged with two clicks of his microphone.

Apparently he was closing with the enemy and unable to speak aloud. Gunny Sweikert then radioed Major Taggart. "We're in possession of the Jap long-liner, sir" he said when Taggart answered. "Jake took out a load of Yakuzas in their Zodiac. That Haskins is a piece of work. He and Buzz have been tearing up the island. There's maybe another eight to ten Yakuza on the island. I've sent my Marines to the beach to give Jake a hand. We should be closing everything down soon. Dawn is coming in a couple of hours. I think you could ask Captain Krawczyk to close with the island now. We want to get the treasure on board ASAP. The Yakuzas have done a lot of our work for us. There's a really big pile already on the surface. Over."

"Good job, Gunny," Taggart said. "The Captain is right here on the bridge, and he's firing up the revolutions. We should be there in less than twenty minutes. Keep your eyes open, Gunny. It's not over 'til it's over, you know. Out"

(Eleven)

When Yoto Nakura heard the single rifle shot topside, he knew it came from the bow section in front of the bridge. Probably his Yakuza anchor watch taking a hit. Definitely not his AK-47 firing. So that means there's an enemy on board, an armed enemy. Where did they come from? They must have arrived in a small boat. Where is their mother ship? Who *are* these people? As he struggled to calculate the situation, Nakura heard the unmistakable report of a large caliber rifle in the distance, probably fifty caliber. Four or five shots. Who was shooting and what were the targets? He went to the crew quarters where he had the Chamorro woman manacled. She sat up abruptly, eyes wide in fear. He gave her a hard slap across the face, then gagged her.

Elena had heard the first rifle shot, too, then the sounds of more gunfire. What was happening? Were the Yakuza killing someone? Then, when the Yakuza captain burst through the door holding a pistol, her first thought was that he had just killed someone and was now coming to kill her. But instead, he struck her hard across the face, stunning her.

When she regained clarity, her mouth was stuffed with a rag that was held in place with another rag tied around and behind her head. She was helpless and feared she would soon die at the hands of this tattooed animal.

Yoto Nakura did not dare climb to the bridge or deck level since he had no way of knowing how many of the enemy were aboard his long-liner. He felt sure his Yakuza brothers on the island would come to his rescue, but the large caliber rifle fire had him worried. A waiting game was best, he decided. He moved quietly down the companionway and slipped in behind a stairwell where he squatted invisibly in the dark. Anyone descending the stairs would have their backs to him. He would have the advantage of surprise.

(Twelve)

Captain Krawczyk brought his freighter into the lee of Marcus Island, slowing, then stopping to ride just behind the Jap long-liner. He could see the Gunny Sergeant waving from the bridge, signaling an all clear. Taggart spoke to Sweikert by VHF, then Taggart announced that he was going to board the Jap long-liner. Stacy Burns said she was going with him. Taggart said no, not until the island was secured and all Yakuza were accounted for. But Stacy was willful and insisted. She reached into her pants pocket and produced her Baby Glock. "I'm covering your back, Tag," she smiled. "I've got too much invested in you, sweetheart. The ship has been secured. Gunny Sweikert is aboard. Surely I will be safe in the company of two senior combat-tested Marines," she said.

Taggart was not in a mood to argue. He wanted to get onboard the long-liner as soon as possible. "All right Stacy, dammit. Just keep close to me and try not to shoot me in the back with that pistol, okay?"

The two of them descended the boarding ladder and jumped into the spare Zodiac. They motored over to the Jap long-liner, and Sweikert lowered the long-liner's boarding ladder. He didn't know how to operate the boat's hydraulic stern ramp. They met at the top of the ladder.

"Glad to see you're still in one piece, Gunny," Taggart said, extending a hand. "Stacy insisted in coming over so she can cover our backs."

"We can always use an extra Marine, sir," Sweikert said with a wink in Stacy's direction. "But the island is not cleared yet, sir. There's been gunfire. I think Jake and our Marines are finishing up. We should know soon." Just as he said that, a burst of AK-47 fire erupted on the island, followed by M-16 rifle fire from more than one rifle. "Let's get inside the bridge, sir. No sense in getting hit by stray fire." The three of them moved inside the bridge and closed the door.

"Jake knows the island well enough to figure out all the hidey holes the Yakuza might use," Taggart said. "He and our Marines will do a thorough search and a body count to make sure we have them all. No prisoners to worry about. The Yakuza aren't surrendering. As soon as Jake gives us the all clear, we'll start moving the treasure to our freighter. Captain Krawczyk is already rigging the crane and cargo nets."

While they were talking, Stacy inched over to look at the Yakuza body on the foredeck. A thick pool of blood had spread out beneath his body. He was very, very dead. His AK-47 was still lying alongside his body. She turned to the doorway leading off the bridge, opened it and peered down the companionway. Not a soul stirred.

It was like a ghost ship. Stacy had never been aboard a large vessel like this one, and the fact that it was Japanese made it even more intriguing. Her husband and Gunny Sweikert were occupied with communicating with Jake on the island and paying her no attention. Sweikert was suggesting that he leave Taggart and Stacy to themselves so that he could join in the mopping up operations on the island. Apparently they agreed, because she saw Sweikert go over the side to the Zodiac. So, she thought, that must mean the long-liner was secured. Just her and her husband in charge.

Stacy closed the door behind her and descended the companionway steps to the next deck level. She had no warning of Yoto Nakura springing from behind the steps. Nakura gave her a hard blow across the back of her head with his pistol. Stacy collapsed to the deck unconscious.

"A woman!" Nakura said to himself. "What is happening? Who are these people that bring a woman onto his ship?" He reached down and grabbed Stacy by the collar of her shirt and dragged her down the companionway to the room where he held the Chamorro woman. *Two women to bargain with, if necessary,* he thought. But where were his Yakuza brothers? There were fifteen of them. What were they doing?

The gunfire he had heard was a mix of calibers, the AK-47s having a distinct sound. He was not hearing any firing now. He dragged Stacy into the room with the Chamorro woman, grabbed a piece of line and tied her hands and feet. He left her next to the bunk to which Stacy was manacled. He made a fierce snarl at Stacy, grabbed his crotch, and drew his finger across his throat. The message was clear: one sound and he would slit her throat. Stacy's, too, no doubt. He left and closed the door.

Jake and Buzz hooked up with the Marines that had come ashore from the long-liner. They were now flushing the Yakuza with concentrated automatic rifle fire, driving them toward the old Coast Guard buildings. By Jake's count, there were less than four or five of them left. Buzz let off a burst of fire from his M-16, and Jake thought, make that three or four. Buzz was one hell of a shot, and a cool cucumber to boot.

Elena couldn't believe her eyes! Stacy! What was she doing here? Where was her husband, Tag? How could she be on this Japanese ship with her in the middle of the ocean? It made no sense whatsoever! The last time Elena had seen Stacy was on Kauai, in Hawaii. Elena had waved good-bye to Stacy, Tag and Jake as she and her mother boarded a flight to return to Saipan. This was all so unbelievable! The gag on her mouth prevented her from speaking to Stacy, or rousing her to consciousness. What had that Yakuza animal done to her? There was blood oozing from Stacy's scalp. running down over her ear. How long would it be before she regained consciousness? *Jake, Jake, my love. Where are you? Come to me, I need you.*

Gunny Sweikert eased his Zodiac up onto Marcus's beach next to the old concrete pier. He heard two or more AK-47s firing, and a lot of return fire from the M-16s, but he had no idea where everybody was. The far eastern horizon was beginning to lighten, and that was good news. Just as he stepped from the Zodiac, he heard the sound of running feet and back-stepped into the ocean, slipping behind one of the pier's twisted columns. Three Yakuza, naked except for thongs and their blue tattoos, came down the path from the old Coast Guard buildings, AK-47s in their hands. They saw Sweikert's Zodiac, but too late. Sweikert stepped from behind the pier and mowed them down with full automatic fire from his M-16. The Yakuza tumbled to the beach, twitching only briefly in their final death spasms.

Buzz came down the path in a low crouch, spied Sweikert and grinned. He then saw the Yakuzas bleeding out on the beach and said, "Hey, Gunny, you took away all my fun!" Jake came up behind him and gave Sweikert a wave. "I believe that's all of them, Gunny," Jake said. "We'll give it another look, but we spread across the island and flushed them all in this direction. They just ran out of island." The happy rendezvous ended when they heard distant gunfire. Rapid multiple shots. One after the other without pause. Eight or nine shots. The Marines all looked at one another. The shots had come from the Jap long-liner, no doubt.

"Damn!" Sweikert yelled. "The Major and Stacy!"

They piled into Sweikert's Zodiac, Jake and Sweikert and Buzz, Jake operating the Mercury outboard. As they sped away from the beach, two Marines stepped onto the beach behind them wondering what the hell was going on. Sweikert radioed Taggart on his VHF, "Major Taggart! Major Taggart! Are you there sir? Over." Silence. "What's going on, sir? Are you in trouble? We're coming alongside now, sir."

Jake, Sweikert and Buzz scrambled out of the Zodiac and up the Jap long-liner's boarding ladder. Major Taggart had not shown himself all the while they were approaching the boat. A bad sign. Where the hell was Taggart and where the hell was Stacy, and who was doing all the shooting? They entered the bridge area, weapons at the ready. They moved down the companionway stairs leading off the bridge and worked their way slowly down the hallway. They could see an open doorway and heard conversation.

"Major! That you in there?" Sweikert yelled.

"Yes, in here, Gunny!" Taggart answered.

When Jake and Sweikert entered, Buzz remaining outside to cover their backs, the sight before them was beyond comprehension. Taggart was cutting Stacy's bonds, and Elena was still manacled to the bunk, naked, holding Stacy's Baby Glock in her hand. On the floor was a Yakuza, tattooed from head to toe, missing the front right side of his head, a huge blob of grey brain matter dribbling onto his shoulder. His torso was riddled with bullet holes, each seeping copious amounts of dark blood.

Jake and Elena saw each other at the same time. Jake leaped across the space separating them, embracing her and kissing her all over her face, saying, "Baby, baby, Jesus Christ almighty! What are you doing here?"

She smiled a weary smile and said, "What took you so long, my love?" Then she said, ever so calmly, "Please free me so I can give you a proper hug."

Jake found the keys to the manacles and freed Elena, taking her into his arms immediately, rocking back and forth, stroking her arms and back and legs. "Dear God, I love you, Elena."

Bryce Taggart scooped Stacy up into his arms and carried her down the hallway and up the companionway stair to the bridge, then out into the morning sunlight. Sweikert had grabbed the First Aid kit mounted on the bridge's bulkhead, broken out some alcohol, gauze swabs and a bottle of iodine. He was still cleaning Stacy's head wound when Jake joined them carrying Elena in his arms wrapped in a sheet. Elena had her arms around Jake's neck and her head rested on his shoulder.

Once everyone was stabilized, Sweikert called across to Captain Krawczyk to give him a situation report and to prepare to take on cargo. He used the VHF to call his Marines on the island to order them to gather the Yakuza bodies and their weapons for transport to the Taka Maru#17. Following that, they were to go to the treasure pit and begin moving the treasure to the beach. He cautioned that a guard must be posted just in case.

By noon, treasure was being stacked on the beach and two Zodiacs plus Krawczyk 's tender, a twenty-foot long aluminum boat with a small internal diesel engine, were hauling the treasure to their ship. Taggart said he wanted to move Stacy off the long-liner. He announced that he was taking a Zodiac. Jake said he and Elena would come as well, but after they had crossed over and Tag and Stacy had climbed onto their ship's boarding ladder, Elena took Jake's hand in hers and said, "Please. May we go to your treasure island? I have something important to tell you." Jake agreed without hesitation, kissing her softly on her forehead.

Jake looked into Elena's eyes with great concern. There was a light, an electricity of some kind, that was missing. She had yet to speak of what happened on the long-liner. He knew from his combat experience that it was best to let it all come out on its own. Some of the dark stuff would never get out. It wasn't something you could rush. He would give Elena the rest of his life for her to come to grips with what happened on that Jap long-liner.

Jake nosed the Zodiac onto Marcus Island, shut down the outboard motor, stood and lifted Elena to her feet by her elbow. She stepped gingerly onto the beach, slipping on her sandals, then raised Jake's hand to her lips and kissed it. Jake bent down and kissed her full on the lips, holding her close.

"Show me where you landed when you first got here after leaving Saipan, she asked.

Jake put his arm around her shoulders and said, "This way. There are only two breaks in the reef. I passed through the one on the other side. It's a short walk, and it's a beautiful day." Jake led her around the southeastern point of Marcus Island and up to the break in the reef where he first anchored *Makena*. He described for her how lonely he had felt at that moment, all alone on the island, but also how excited he was to reach the place he had been reading about in the young English lieutenant's log book, and the note from Bryce Taggart that Gunny Sweikert had brought to him on Saipan confirming that the Spaniard castaway, Bustamente, had buried the *Concepcion's* cargo in a cave on this island.

"Did you think of me at all?" Elena asked, looking up at him.

"Elena, you have no idea how close I came to abandoning the whole thing because of you. Leaving you behind when I sailed away on *Makena* was the hardest thing I have ever done. It was the prospect of returning to you that kept me together."

Elena squeezed his hand. "You say the nicest things, my love." She paused, looking out on the breaking reef. It was such a beautiful day. "Now, I must tell you something that is very unhappy. Forgive me for ruining this moment of triumph for you, but until now I have not had an opportunity to share this with anyone else. I will have to tell my mother soon, and it will break her heart, I know."

Jake found his own heart was constricting as he waited. He could sense profound pain in her voice, but could not imagine its source.

Elena said it quickly and plainly: "My brother, Sammy, is dead. He was murdered by the Yakuza at Anatahan Island. They tied Sammy to the mast of the *Giggling Witch* and sank her."

Jake was struck dumb. He didn't know what to say. The vision of Elena's brother tied to his boat's mast and the boat sunk was too horrific to imagine. Elena slipped from his arms in a faint, but Jake caught her, holding her as tightly as he could, allowing her to sink to her knees. He sat down beside her, kissing her hands, taking her by her shoulders and squeezing her to him. He rubbed her back, kissed the back of her neck. Tears welled in his eyes when he thought of smiling, happy-go-lucky Sammy, his beautiful wife and two young sons.

"Elena, Elena, I am so sorry to hear this. I cannot imagine it. It is too, too terrible! What an evil thing the Yakuza have done. And you have had to keep this to yourself, all the while a captive of the evil bastard who ordered it. I don't know how you have borne it and kept your sanity."

"The Yakuza on the long-liner where you found me and Stacy. That was the Yakuza captain. I shot him with Stacy's pistol until there were no more bullets in it."

"Dear God, dear God!" Jake said. This soft, loving, precious young woman, so innocent when he first met her. Now she must live forever the dark memory of her brother's murder, and her own killing of a monster. They sat together for a long while, then Jake rose and helped Elena to her feet. He draped his arm about her shoulders, and they continued their circuit of Marcus Island's beach.

As they came full circle, activity at the concrete pier was something to behold. Marines were carrying boxes and bundles down to the beach like busy ants at a summer picnic. The Zodiacs and the ship's tender were going back and forth like water beetles. Captain Krawczyk had come ashore, rolled up his trousers and was standing in the surf directing his two deckhands in the loading of the tender.

Late that afternoon, Jake and Elena walked up to the treasure pit. A new A-frame had been built and the last of the treasure was being brought to the surface. Elena wanted to go down inside it to see what Jake had experienced. They went down in a sling and stood aside while treasure was being lifted to the surface. Jake separated himself from Elena and went down to the lowest part of the cave, the part nearest to the ocean. The cave seemed much larger now that most of the treasure had been removed. Only a few boxes were left, and he noticed something shining. He waded across to it and was surprised to discover that it was a heavy battle sword in a sheath, lying atop a lacquered box with a handwritten letter. It was too dark to read the letter. It was probably in Spanish anyway, so he tucked it into his shirt pocket, then hefted the sword and climbed back to Elena.

"You found a sword?" Elena observed.

"Yeah. Might make a good souvenir to hang over my mantle in Saipan."

Elena smiled. "You are thinking of having a mantle in Saipan?"

"Oh, yes, my island princess," Jake said, "and a whole lot more." He bent to give her a full kiss on the mouth.

They returned to the beach hand-in-hand, caught a ride on one of the Zodiacs to Captain Krawczyk' freighter, then went looking for Stacy and Tag to see how they were doing. They met Tag coming across the deck. He had a concerned look on his face. "Stacy's in our stateroom taking a nap. I've tried to talk to her about what happened on the Jap long-liner, but she doesn't remember much. No recollection at all of being hit on the head. She has only a vague memory of the gunfire. She knows it was not her that shot the Yakuza captain, but she doesn't remember how Elena got her pistol. It was pretty traumatic for sure. Elena, how are you doing? It is wonderful to see you again even under these terrible circumstances. Is this a good time for me to ask how in the world you came to be on the long-liner?"

Jake answered for her. "Even more bad news, Tag. That Jap bastard killed her brother, Sammy. Tied him to the mast of my boat and sank the boat. Kidnapped Elena."

"Dear God!" Tag said, reaching across to touch Elena's shoulder. "How terrible, how terrible!"

Elena said, "The hardest part is yet to come. I must tell my mother."

"Let's get you to a bunk for a little rest. I'll have Captain Krawczyk set up a satellite phone connect to Saipan," Jake said.

"If it's all right, I'd like to go see Stacy for just a few minutes," Elena said. "We haven't spoken since we were captives of the Yakuza captain."

"Absolutely, Elena," Tag said. He turned to lead them to their stateroom.

Jake left Elena in the company of Tag and went aft to join the Marines. The five of them were standing in a group enthusiastically recounting their individual experiences on Marcus Island. For each of them it was the closest thing to real combat they had ever encountered. The enemy had been real, and there was no doubt that the Yakuza were bent on killing anyone interfering with their venture.

"A job well done, men," Jake said in greeting. "Thank God nobody got hit despite all that AK-47 fire. Believe me, this was not at all what I had planned. As you know, my fiancée was a prisoner of the Yakuza captain. I owe you my thanks for the magnificent way you fought these Jap bastards and assisted in saving Elena's life."

"Sarge, that Haskins is just too much!" Buzz said. "I was just telling the guys how you took out that Zodiac filled with those tattooed bastards."

"In case anyone is interested." Jake said, "right after dinner tonight I am going to auction-off the Haskins. One of you will be the lucky winner."

"Oh, man! Let it be me!" Tank said, clapping his hands.

At that moment, Gunny Sweikert exited from the bridge. "Listen up, men. Clean-up time. Then, we're on our way to Panama and paycheck time. Let's do one more sweep of the island for any weapons or bodies. Then, we'll form up on the beach and go out to the long-liner. The long-liner is going to be scuttled along with the Yakuza bodies. 'Best we can, let's leave no trace of what happened here, okay? Okay, move it!" The

480

young Marines piled into a Zodiac and headed for the beach. Each had his Armalite M-16 slung over a shoulder.

"Jake," Sweikert said, "How about you and me go over to the Jap long-liner, do a quick reconnaissance, look for any treasure that may have made its way to the boat, then drag the Yakuza down a hatch and prepare to scuttle the damn thing. Captain Krawczyk is going to send his two bosun mates over to open some seacocks. They know where they are located and how to do it. It's almost three thousand feet to the bottom here. Krawczyk will tow the long-liner out a few hundred yards to let her sink."

"Let's do it," Jake said. "Give me a minute to let Elena know what's up, okay?" Jake found Elena sitting with Stacy, holding her hand, the two of them talking quietly. "I'm going over to the long-liner with Gunny Sweikert. We're cleaning house, and going to sink her. You might want to watch that from here. Closing a ugly chapter in your life. Also, Captain Krawczyk is ready to make a satellite hook-up so you can talk with your Mom in Saipan. I'll be back in an hour or two, okay? Stacy, you hanging in there? Sorry I haven't spoken with you since we got you and Elena off the Jap's boat. We're really humping it to clear out of here. Tag will not leave the boat again. Our Marines are sanitizing the island. We'll have all of this behind us shortly, then we can relax and repair our fences."

"Elena rose and beckoned Jake to come to her. She put her arms around his neck and kissed him. "I will be all right, my love," she said. "I love you. Be careful."

Jake and Sweikert crossed over to the Jap long-liner, boarded her, went to the after deck and dragged the Yakuza bodies to an open deck hatch, dropped them through it and secured the hatch to keep the bodies from floating out. Then they went forward and down to the refrigerated hold to search for any treasure that might have been brought aboard. The refrigeration was off and the area smelled of rotten fish and ammonia. But, no treasure. It looked like the Yakuza were going to sort through the treasure before transferring it to their boat.

The two bosun mates arrived and after a quick conference with Gunny Sweikert, went to the forward and aft bilge areas and the engine room to open seacocks. Seawater began to rush in by the thousands of gallons per minute. The long-liner would go under in a very short while.

Satisfied with their work, they reported to Sweikert, then returned to their ship. They were still stacking and securing treasure below decks for the return trip to Panama. Sweikert and Jake returned to Captain Krawczyk 's freighter just as the Marines were coming back from Marcus. They had found only one AK-47, and no more bodies. They were a really excited bunch of guys.

Once all was secured, Captain Krawczyk ordered his two bosun's mates to go to the Jap long-liner a final time to raise its anchor; that done, they brought a line over and Krawczyk backed-down his freighter to tow the Taka Maru#17 clear of Marcus Island. The Jap long-liner was already sitting low in the water, and it looked like she would go down by the bow. Everyone came to the rail to watch the sinking. Major Bryce Taggart, his fiancée, Stacy, Jake and Elena, Gunny Sweikert, and the five young Marines lined the rail to cheer their victory.

Captain Krawczyk reversed his freighter and pulled slowly away, then ordered the casting off of the towline, spun the helm and began to depart Marcus Island. The last sight they had as they went over the horizon was the stern of Taka Maru#17 lifting almost vertical as she plunged to the bottom of the sea.

(Thirteen)

Krawczyk's freighter had not been below the horizon more than two hours, making 27 knots toward Panama, when a low, sleek vessel approached Marcus Island from the southwest. Dutch and his former patrol vessel had been delayed by engine trouble caused by contaminated fuel, but now as they came upon the low-lying island just before dusk, they were disappointed to see no other ship; not the Taka

Maru#17, or any other vessel that might be pursuing treasure. Dutch had been in contact with Berne, Switzerland, and knew that they had not had any contact with Yoto Nakura for over forty-eight hours. The unspoken fear was that Nakura had recovered the treasure and was now headed at breakneck speed back to his base in the Kurile Islands.

Dutch put a launch over the side and sent a half-dozen of his men to the island to look for any clues. The crew chief radioed back saying, "Dutch, this place looks like Iwo Jima, after the battle. There's blood on the beach and in a dozen other places all over the island, but not a body anywhere. The island is covered with spent shells from AK-47s, M-16s and 9-mm pistols. There was a hell of a firefight here. We found a big hole, sort of a cave, with some bundles of old silk piled around it and down inside it. Rotten shit. Worthless. No sign of any treasure. Looks like somebody else got here before us."

"That fucking Jap Yakuza!" Dutch cursed. "Bring the boat. I want to take a look for myself," Dutch ordered. Berne, Switzerland was not going to like hearing this news.

ZONA LIBRE - THE AUCTION

Date: August 9, 2001

Lat. 09º 00' N, /Long. 80º 00'W

Panama Canal, Republic of Panama

(One)

When Jake and Tag came onto the bridge, Captain Krawczyk was puffing away on his big briar pipe chatting with Gunny Sweikert. "How're the women doing, Mr. Porter?" he asked with genuine concern. Earlier, once they had cleared Marcus Island and were well on their way, Jake had told Captain Krawczyk how he and Major Taggart had found their women. He described the unbelievable scene, Stacy barely conscious and bleeding from the head, Elena naked and shackled to a bunk holding the Glock automatic pistol, and the bullet-riddled body of the Japanese Yakuza captain on the floor.

"They're a bit out of it, Captain," Jake said. "But I believe they'll pull out of it okay."

Jake and Tag had concluded that Stacy and Elena were both

experiencing symptoms of post-traumatic syndrome. The mental trauma that had been inflicted upon them by Yoto Nakura on board the Taka Maru#17 was definitely affecting their mood and attention span. They seemed oblivious to the ship and its surroundings and the other people on the ship. Jake did not think it was a good time for Elena to call her mother in Saipan to tell her of Sammy's death. It should be done soon, of course, because Delilah was almost certainly frantic over the disappearance of her two children for almost two weeks. But it was just more trauma for Elena to handle. Jake felt the phone call could be put on hold.

Jake decided to make a call over the ship's satellite radio to Rebecca in Palm Beach, to give her a heads up and make arrangements for the rendezvous in Panama. When Rebecca answered the phone, it was with an obvious burst of relief.

"How are you, Jake? We've all been holding our breath waiting for word from you. Where are you?"

"On our way to Panama with the goodies, Rebecca," Jake said. "Enough Chinese vases and artifacts to keep you busy for quite a while, I imagine. I'm calling to give you our ETA, and see what we might do enroute to help you set up in the Zona Libre in Panama."

"Oh, Jake!" Rebecca squealed. "This is the most exciting day of my life to date! Just so you will know, everything you brought back the first time around is sold or consigned. I've got antiquities dealers from Hong Kong to Amsterdam calling me wanting a piece of the action, and asking where is the rest of the treasure? Hattie Heinz, by the way, is doing back-flips! And here is the real news. She anted up an additional twenty million to cover her purchases from your first load. I've already deposited that in your Panama bank account, by the way. Hattie bought every one of the porcelain vases, and quite a few of the jade items, and a few pieces of the jewelry, too. Now, she has deposited another one hundred million dollars in an escrow account at the The Left Bank as a deposit against the next load you bring in. I tell you, Jake, she is aiming to have the greatest Chinese porcelain collection in the world. And she doesn't give a damn what it will cost!

"Also, she had the curator of the New York Metropolitan Museum of Art down for a visit to her Palm Beach mansion to take a look at the vases you brought back on your first load. I was invited along for the tour. The curator gave me his card and indicated that the museum was interested in purchasing as well. Those four reticulated Shunzhi pieces are so rare that they almost gave him a heart attack. Hattie's negotiating with the museum to put together a year-long exhibit of her collection. Right now, she's the darling of the art world, and loving every minute of it. She'll be written-up in every art world magazine around the globe. A couple of Texas billionaires have offered to marry her, if you can believe that!"

"Well, when she sees the stuff in this next load, you may have to get a wheelchair for her. There's tons of it, Rebecca, and don't forget the Pope's dinnerware setting. We've got it onboard, too. So, what's the plan now for Panama?

"I will be in Panama, when you arrive, I will have suites set up for all of you at the Hilton International, Jake. How long before you arrive?"

"The Captain estimates seven to eight more days. It's a long haul. Over eight thousand miles," Jake said.

"I need to get the marketing ball rolling, Jake. Get the publicity out there and fire-up the buyers. Can you take some pictures of individual vases and artifacts with your cell phone and send them to me? And pictures of the Pope's dinnerware, too?

"I think we can do better than that," Jake said. "We have an accomplished photographer and multi-lingual PhD. on board with a brand new Nikon digital SLR."

"Jake, you are beyond amazing! You are referring to Stacy, I imagine. Transmit those photos and descriptions to me and I'll get the ball rolling!"

"Rebecca, I'd like to refresh on some of the ground rules. I expect you to follow them to the letter, okay? As before, you must not under any circumstances mention my name in connection with the treasure. That goes for Tag, Stacy and Elena, too. Also, I have never told you where the treasure was located. That must also remain a total secret. Here is what you can say: the treasure is from a Manila galleon named Nuestra Senora de la Concepcion. She sailed from Manila, Philippines, in August 1698, with over seven hundred people aboard and was never heard from again. That's it. We have plenty of provenance to establish the identity of the find. You place all of us in mortal danger if you reveal our association with the treasure.

"Do you understand that, Rebecca? The governments of China, Spain and God only knows who else are going to be real pissed that they didn't get a piece of this action. You can be sure the IRS is going to be taking a close look at The Left Bank's bank deposits and money transfers in the coming months."

"Absolutely! I understand completely!" Rebecca said. "What you have just told me is more than enough for the press and general public to know. Besides, once the academics and news hounds get that little piece of information, they will scour the libraries and historical repositories of the world to fill in the story anyway. Your secret is safe with me. And not to worry about the IRS. The money transfers have been going through our numbered account in Switzerland, into your numbered offshore account in Panama. We've been trading internationally for many years, and we know the ropes.

By the way, Papa wants to meet you. He is beyond excited about this treasure recovery. It is the dream of every antiquities dealer in the world. The Left Bank will soon have a world-wide reputation. Once Papa learned that you have found the love of your life in Elena and are not a threat to running off with me, he wants to make your acquaintance. How is Elena anyway?"

"She's with me, Rebecca," Jake said. "Long story to that. I'll fill you in when we meet in Panama. I'll get the photos off to you no later than tomorrow. Captain Krawczyk will give you the satellite phone connect so you can call if you need to between now and our arrival. Bye for now." Jake passed the phone to Captain Krawczyk.

Jake filled in Tag on Rebecca's news, then said that he thought Stacy and Elena should be given some task, some kind of activity to occupy their minds. Tag agreed. Jake suggested that Stacy and Elena be put to work organizing and photographing the treasure. Stacy could use her new camera and Elena could prepare a brief written description to accompany each photograph.

When they proposed the idea to the two women, and took them down into the hold to look at the treasure, Jake and Tag were surprised at how enthusiastically they took to the project. He breathed a sigh of relief when he took Elena in his arms. "We'll call your Mama a little later today. I'll sit in with you if you want me to, okay?" Elena took his face in her hands and kissed him deeply.

Tag detailed two of the young Marines to help Stacy and Elena set up the pieces of treasure for photographing. Tank prepared lemonade and sandwiches and brought it down to them. The Marines detailed to work with the two beautiful women went to work with gusto. Stacey told them what to look for, cautioned them to be very, very careful in handling anything. It was all four hundred years old, and very fragile, and worth millions, she told them. They were to focus on the Chinese porcelain first. The smaller artifacts would come later. Elena helped her set up a platform and drape a piece of Chinese tapestry as a backdrop.

Elena examined each piece as it was placed on the platform for a photograph, numbering it and writing a brief description of the piece, examining the bottom for inscriptions, and measuring its dimensions with a ruler. She was building a detailed catalog.

Sometimes Elena would pause, turning a particularly spectacular piece in her hands, remarking on it to Stacy. They would pass the porcelain piece back and forth, noting its finer points. Stacy, calling upon her cross-cultural education, would explain some of the history behind the artistic imagery. It was a healing therapy, and every now and then the two women would look up from their work, and realize they were in the cargo hold of an ocean-going freighter in the presence of an unprecedented collection of ancient beauty making its way across the Pacific Ocean. In words unspoken, the artistic endeavors of countless Chinese artisans centuries earlier were modulating the darkness Stacy and Elena had experienced at the hands of the Yakuza.

When Elena lifted a porcelain piece that appeared to have functioned as a chamber pot, she saw the intricately drawn picture of a Chinese courtesan grasping the enormous erection of a Samurai while he reached inside her kimono to massage her breast, Elena burst into laughter and showed it to Stacy. Both women were laughing when Jake and Tag came down the ladder to the cargo hold. Hearing their women laugh so heartily was a more than welcome sound. It lifted their hearts and gave them hope for a full recovery.

When Elena showed the pornographic chamberpot to Jake, his eyebrows arched and he smiled broadly. "I'm thinking it might be time for a nap."

"Yes, this art conservatory work is very wearying, and also kind of dirty," Elena said, picking up on Jake's suggestion. "I could use a hot shower."

"I could scrub your back," Jake said.

"Oh, that would be very nice," Elena said. "Besides, we need to get ready for our celebratory dinner tonight. Tank says it's Porterhouse steaks to order and baked potatoes."

(Two)

The dinner was sumptuous to say the least. Tank had prepared a feast that featured the promised porterhouse steaks and baked potatoes, but also included fresh-baked bread and a huge salad. They all sat at the main galley table, Gunny Sweikert, Tag, Stacy, Jake, Elena and the five Marines. Captain Krawczyk made a brief appearance, but had to return to the bridge. His freighter was plowing ahead at breakneck speed toward the Panama Canal. He had left his two bosuns on the bridge to watch for other shops for safety's sake. After he left, Jake rose to announce the drawing of the raffle for his Haskins sniper rifle. Each of the five Marines had put their names on a slip of paper and put it in a bowl. Stacy did the honors in drawing.

"And the winner is…." she announced, drawing out the moment as much as she could, "Buzz!"

Jake picked up the twenty-three pound rifle, complete with flash and sound suppressor, and the Utel scope, and handed it to Buzz, who was all smiles. His fellow Marines booed in jest, then slapped him on the back to congratulate him on his good fortune.

Gunny Sweikert stood up and called the meeting to order. "Gentlemen, we have one more order of business before we call it a day. Take your seats please. Major Taggart, the floor is yours."

Major Bryce Taggart stood at the head of the table, lifted a wine glass in toast. "To these two beautiful women in our company, and to the futures of each of you. A job well done, Marines!"

Everyone stood, Stacy and Elena both blushing a little, and took a sip of their wine.

"Men," Taggart began, "I don't have to tell you how unusual this mission was. As Jake has said, we had no intention to hurt anyone and every hope of avoiding any confrontation. If we had arrived at the treasure site before the Yakuza, we could have scooped up the treasure and been gone without a shot being fired. But that was not meant to be. It was Jake who originally discovered the treasure site. The treasure legitimately belonged to him, if anyone. Jake discovered he was being followed by the Jap boat you saw. He first saw it in Saipan. We have since learned that the Yakuza captain of that boat murdered Elena's brother. As you all know, Elena was kidnapped at Saipan, and held captive by that Yakuza captain. The Yakuza also struck my fiancée, Stacy, knocking her unconscious, and tied her up. You must have no doubt in your minds that the killing we did on that island was justified in every sense of the word. We rid the world of some truly vicious, evil people."

The meeting erupted in cheers, the young Marines all stood up and a toast was proposed to Stacy and Elena for their bravery, and to the memory of Elena's brother.

"Now, to our final order of business," Major Taggart said. "We will now take a solemn oath of brotherhood. Each of us holds in his hands the life of the others gathered here. Let us swear that we will never reveal our participation in this venture. We will keep it hidden in our breasts and take it to our graves. Never will we mention our actions to anyone who is not present at this table tonight. It is our secret and our secret alone. No mother, no girlfriend, no buddy of ours will ever hear of this from our lips. By so swearing, we protect each other lives and secure our future. Do you all so swear?"

In unison, all said "We so swear!"

(Three)

Elena, with great dread, made her call to Saipan to speak with her mother and to tell her that her oldest child, Sammy, was dead. She and Jake had gone to the freighter's bridge to speak by satellite phone. Much to her surprise, a male answered the phone. "Who is this?" she asked.

"Elena? Is that you? This is Tony. Where in hell are you? Mama is near an emotional collapse. You've been gone for almost two weeks! Where's Sammy? His wife is going nuts."

"Tony?" Elena said. Tony was her youngest brother, still in the Marine Corps and serving in Iraq. "What are you doing home, Tony? I thought you were in Iraq."

"I'm on a thirty-day separation leave. I report back to Pendleton for four months of duty and separation. The war is over for me, thank God. Iraq is a pit, believe me. But you haven't answered my question. Where are you and why haven't you called Mama?"

"Tony, I thank God you are there with Mama. I have some terrible news. Our brother, Sammy, is dead. He was murdered by Japanese Yakuza at Anatahan Island. The Yakuza kidnapped me."

"What? What are you saying, Elena? Jap Yakuza? Sammy dead? You're not making any sense. Mama has gone to her sister's house for the day. She won't be back until this evening. Now give this all to me again, I can't believe what you're telling me! Sammy dead? Son of a bitch!"

It took a while, but with Elena crying, and relaying all that had happened since she and Sammy sailed away to Anatahan Island, it was reliving it all over again. Finally, the call was over. It was agreed that Tony would break the news to their mother. For that, Elena was grateful. She would call her mother tomorrow to speak with her personally. She turned to Jake, placing her head on his chest, sobbing quietly.

Jake placed his mouth close to her ear and spoke softly. "Your brother, Anthony, is home? That's good news, sweetheart. It will be much better for him to tell your mother about Sammy than for you to tell her over the phone. Actually, I have an idea. Why don't we fly your Mom and Tony to Panama? It will be good for you to spend some time with her. Tony said he was on separation leave. He could get a compassionate leave because of his brother's death. Why don't I have Gunny Sweikert call his buddies in the Pentagon and get that rolling? And look, why don't we have Sammy's widow, Rosalita, and their children come along with them. They all need a break from this sadness. You and I can entertain them, and help deal with this stuff."

"I love you, Jake" Elena said. "You are a wonderful man. I am so proud of you. Yes, ask Gunny for his help."

(Four)

Jake handed the letter from the treasure cave to Stacy. Fluent in Spanish, she would be able to read it. He explained how he had found it in the treasure cave on Marcus Island, and that it was accompanied by a heavy Chinese battle sword. He showed her the sword.

Stacy took the letter, studied it at length then announced that it was written by none other than Don Emilio Bustamente de la Vega. Yes, the very same castaway that had been saved by the English warship in 1699! She read the letter aloud, haltingly as she struggled with the four hundred year old vernacular. She and Jake were in astonishment. The excitement in Stacy's voice grew as she plowed through the letter to its end. She looked up from the letter, and she and Jake shared a moment of incredulity.

Jake then pointed to the drawing in the lower left corner of the letter. The letter had explained that this symbol was tattooed to the instep of Bustamente's children so they could be identified if ever they were separated from their parents. He explained that his wife was Chinese, and had been supplied to him by a Chinese trader, a junk captain named Ling Po, in reward for saving his life. He suspected that the Chinese trader was the father of his wife. Bustamente wrote that his wife had insisted that his three daughters receive the tattoo just as their mother had in China.

Jake asked Stacy, "Have you ever seen this tattoo?"

"No," Stacy said. "Should I have?" She was puzzled by Jake's question.

"Come with me," Jake said. He led Stacy to his stateroom where Elena was resting after the trauma of speaking with her brother. He opened the door quietly so as not to disturb her. Elena was asleep, covered with a sheet. Jake slowly lifted one corner of the sheet to expose Elena's left foot. Stacy gasped. The tattoo was the same as in Bustamente's letter! Jake lowered the sheet and the two of them left the stateroom without disturbing Elena.

"What does this men, Jake?" Stacy asked with an almost uncontainable excitement.

"It means, Stacy," Jake said with a broad grin across his face, "that Elena is a direct descendant of Don Bustamente. Bustamente was entrusted with the safe-keeping of the treasure aboard the Nuestra Senora de la Concepcion. And, actually, he owned a small portion of the treasure for himself and this Chinese trader, Ling Po. It means the disposition of the treasure of the Concepcion belongs to Elena."

"Dear lord!" Stacy exclaimed. "This is beyond imagining! It is simply too, too fantastic! Let's go tell Tag!"

Major Bryce Taggart was equally stunned by the news. "Damnedest thing I've ever heard! That poor girl! Responsible for those millions. I wonder what she will say when she finds out. When do you intend to tell her, Jake?"

"Well, the secret is almost 400 years old. I think it'll keep until we get to Panama," Jake said. "You know, Elena's Mom probably has the tattoo, too. A family tradition across four centuries! I've suggested to Elena that she invite her Mom, her brother, Tony, Sammy's widow, Rosalita, and their children to fly to Panama, and join in our celebration. Maybe knowing about the treasure and her heritage will soften the loss of Sammy. What do you think?"

"A good idea, Jake," Stacy said, and Tag agreed. It was going to be hard to keep such a secret, but they would be in Panama in just a few days. "You think we should bring Gunny Sweikert in on this?"

"Absolutely," Jake said. "Gunny knew Elena's father when he was in Vietnam. He's very protective of Elena. Ran me through the wringer in Saipan when he saw Elena was taking a liking to me. This little piece of news will blow his socks off."

(Five)

Jake transmitted to Rebecca the digital photos that Stacy had taken of the treasure. Chinese porcelain of every description, the entire collection of Pope Innocent's tableware, and dozens of different kinds of antiquities, from jade and ivory carvings, to incredibly beautiful jewelry had been photographed, measured and described by Stacy and Elena.

When Rebecca looked at the digital photo files for the first time and saw the breath of the treasure, and the fact that almost all of it was from the Shunzhu and Qing eras, she was once again speechless. "Jake, my heart is beating like a teenage lover! You have no idea, no idea the impact this find is going to have on the world antiquities market! I will release these photos immediately to the major dealers and auction houses around the world. I'll set up shop in the Zona Libre. I'll invite some of the Chinese porcelain and antiquities experts from Sotheby's and Christie's to help me show it. It's going to be the biggest party you've ever imagined! I can't wait to hear what the Vatican will say!"

(Six)

Captain Krawczyk brought his ship to anchor in the open roadstead of the Bay of Panama, opposite the entrance to the Panama Canal. He had radioed ahead to his ship's chandlery agent to notify them that his entire cargo was to be declared in bond and arrangements made for its transfer to the Zona Libre. Customs agents and Immigration officials came out in launches to clear the boat. Once all the paperwork was done, Captain Krawczyk received permission to come alongside the dock so the transfer of the cargo could begin. The customs dock was a restricted area, so Rebecca had to wait for Jake to come get her. She had called him by her cell phone, and her excitement was palatable.

"Jake! Jake! Over here!" she yelled from a limousine parked up against the gate. She was elegantly dressed for the warm tropical climate of Panama. She threw her arms around Jake's neck and gave him a big kiss on the mouth.

"I hope Elena wasn't able to see that," she said with a laugh.

"Let me get you a dock pass and you can bring the limo down to our freighter," Jake said. "We can all pile in and head for the hotel. It'll be nice to have roomy quarters for a change."

Rebecca giggled like a school girl. "You and Elena have the penthouse suite at two thousand dollars a day. I think you'll find your new quarters adequate. Tag and Stacy have the same size suite, but it's one floor down, and Gunny's suite is right next to theirs. Your Marines each have a double with a wet bar. The hotel has a five-star restaurant and the chef awaits your orders."

"You're the best, Rebecca," Jake said. "The treasure is being off-loaded as we speak. It will be accompanied by armed Adjuana all the way, right into the Zona Libre. Have you made arrangements for a shop in the Zone to handle the sales show?"

"You betcha," Rebecca said. "The TV broadcast equipment is being set up right now. All of the production staff are here and on the job. We'll need half a day to organize and set things up. Julie Franz from Christie's is already here. She's staying at the Hilton International, too. I think Dottie Simms from Sotheby's lands at the airport tonight. She's flying in from London. So, it's all coming together."

"Okay," Jake said, "here's the dock pass. One final thing before we go pick-up everybody and settle in. Elena and Stacy are very fragile at the moment, Rebecca. Elena was kidnapped by Jap Yakuza in Saipan. She was chained to a bunk and stripped naked. Her brother was murdered by the Yakuza. Stacy was slugged from behind by a Yakuza. A nasty blow that left her unconscious. Elena got hold of a pistol and shot the Yakuza dead. Blew off his face and riddled his body with bullets until the bullets were all gone. They've been through hell, Rebecca. Let's don't mention this, but I wanted you to know in case Stacy and Elena seem a bit out of it, okay?"

Rebecca said nothing for a moment, so stunned by what Jake had told her. It was like something out of crime novel, or movie. "Jake, I don't know what to say!"

"Let's don't say anything at the moment, Rebecca. There'll come a time when we can share all of it together and you'll be able to talk with them about it. But right now, let's focus on the upside of things."

"Yes, yes, of course." Rebecca said. "Thank you for telling me, Jake. How awful for you and Tag, too. We'll just have to work together and make sure it all turns out okay, right?"

"Right," Jake said. "Now, let's go get everybody and hit that hotel for hot showers and some fine dining."

(Seven)

The international auction was in full swing for a fourth day when Jake and Elena went to Panama's Tocumen International airport to meet the flight that was bringing Elena's mother, Delilah, her younger brother, Tony, her sister-in-law, Rosalita, and her two children from Saipan.

Gunny Sweikert, Tag and Stacy decided to wait at the Hilton International and greet the new arrivals there. Everyone was sensitive to the issue of Sammy's death and its impact on the deLeon family.

For the past four days, everyone had gathered in a special suite where they could watch the on-line auction as it was unfolding. Gunny Sweikert said it felt like a presidential staff sitting in a hotel room with the candidate watching the votes being counted. Rebecca Fontaine hosted the auction and got lots of coverage for The Left bank, but the item-by-item selling was handled by the two experts from Sotheby's and Christie's auction houses. The treasure was sold by blind bidding. All of the bids were received by international telephone, but none of the bidders were identified for the audience. Hundreds of individually wealthy collectors, museums and auction houses around the world were bidding.

Hattie Heinz matched the highest price bid on any of the pieces that she wanted for her collection in Palm Beach. She spent almost three hundred thousand dollars in the first two days of the auction. Her purchases were instantly insured, securely packaged against damage, then escorted out of the Zona Libre by the Panamanian Adjuana to a waiting aircraft to be flown non-stop to Fort Lauderdale, then transported by armored truck to her mansion on Palm Beach.

The security force at her home was doubled during the transfer. Headlines of the Palm Beaches' local newspaper raved over her new acquisitions from the sunken Manila galleon, *Nuestra Senora de la Concepcion*, and speculated over the identity of the mysterious recovery team. No one had any idea where the treasure had been found. It made for exciting reading. A photograph of a smiling Hattie Heinz holding one of the priceless reticulated Shunzhu vases accompanied the article. The story was picked up by dozens of other news agencies and broadcast around the world. Hattie Heinz was a household name in the art world, and she was loving every minute of it.

Jake was already learning the advantages of being wealthy. He arranged for a local customs agency to have Delilah and her family's luggage removed from the plane's general cargo immediately upon arrival, taken through customs and delivered to their limousine. Delilah, Tony, Rosalita and her children were met at the gate by friendly and solicitous airline representatives, who escorted them to a VIP room where waited a tearful Elena and a solemn Jake. It took a while for the first wave of emotions to subside. An attendant brought fresh chilled orange juice and coffee on a rolling cart, and warm cotton towelettes.

Delilah hugged Jake, and thanked him for taking care of Elena. She introduced her youngest son, Tony, and Jake took the hard hand of Elena's remaining brother. Although Tony was not in uniform, Jake recognized the ramrod straight posture and haircut of an active duty Marine. Delilah had already told Tony all about the former Marine who had sailed single-handedly across the Pacific Ocean to Saipan in search of lost Spanish treasure—and swept Elena off her feet. She told him how Jake as a Marine Corps sniper had killed Hussein's cousin, the deputy defense minister of Iraq, and how he killed four Haitian pirates to protect the passengers on a wealthy doctor's yacht in the Bahamas.

She told him about *Makena*, too, and her meeting the Commandant of the Marine Corps on Niihau Island in Hawaii, and the pile of treasure that Jake had recovered. Just turning twenty-one years old, it was a lot for a young man to digest, but Tony took an instant liking to the former Marine who was now engaged to his sister, Elena. He was looking forward to spending time with him.

The ride to the International Hilton from Panama's airport was a short one, and they were met by Gunny Sweikert, Tag and Stacy standing in front of the hotel's entrance. After greetings were exchanged, they repaired to Elena and Jake's suite where a light seafood luncheon of Alaskan king crab legs, local spiny lobster tails and freshly-caught shrimp had been prepared by the hotel's kitchen. Hotel staff seated everyone, poured wine, or their choice of drinks, then left graciously.

Gunny Sweikert offered a toast to Delilah and her family, including the memory of Sammy. A knock came at the door, and it was a smiling Rebecca. She went immediately to Delilah, whom she had not seen since they were guests of General and Mary Winton on Niihau Island. It was a tearful meeting when Rebecca was told about Sammy's death. Although Jake had already told her, Rebecca shed genuine tears of sympathy and hugged Delilah closely. She then turned to Elena and Stacy for a hug. Elena introduced her sister-in-law, Rosalita, Sammy's two sons, and finally, her brother Tony.

Rebecca joined in with a glass of wine, and bought everyone up to date on the auction. That evening a special feature sponsored by the National Geographic Society would be broadcast in which three of the personal chests of the Concepcion's passengers would be opened live on camera. Audiences around the world would watch as the chests were opened for the first time in almost four centuries and their contents displayed. The three major TV networks plus cable networks had anted-up big time bucks to broadcast the once-in-a-lifetime event.

Word of the fabulous treasure that had recently been recovered was headline news around the world. Moving on with her report, Rebecca announced that revenue from the auction had reached almost half a billion dollars earlier that day. Jake was a fabulously wealthy man, she said!

Hearing Rebecca say that, Jake looked at Tag and Stacy. They both met his glance and nodded their heads, grinning together. Jake went to the bedroom, took Bustamente's sword from a closet, and grabbed Bustamente's letter. When he returned, all eyes were on the heavy battle sword he held in his hand, wondering what he intended. Jake walked across the room and pulled Elena to her feet. He kissed her on her forehead and put his arm around her shoulders. "Delilah, your daughter, Elena, my island princess, has a very distinctive tattoo on the bottom of her left foot. Would it be too indelicate of me to ask you the significance of that tattoo and how it happens to be on her foot?

Delilah smiled broadly. "All of the deLeon children have the tattoo, Jake. Even Tony. Show him, Tony."

Tony deLeon, a bit self-consciously, slipped off his dress shoe and sock, lifted his foot and showed the tattoo.

"It is a tradition of my family," Delilah said. "I have one on my foot, and my mother and grandmother had one on theirs. Why do you ask, Jake?"

Jake turned to Stacy. "Stacy, would you please translate this letter for everyone?"

Stacy's audience was both puzzled and transfixed. She began by announcing that the author of the letter she was about to read was none other than Don Emilio Bustamente de la Vega, a member of a prominent Spanish Andalusian family and former Capitan of the Militia of Manila, Philippines, who had been rescued by an English warship after the *Concepcion* was lost. Don Bustamente, she explained, left the geographical location of this immense treasure embedded in a coded message in a young English lieutenant's sailing log that Jake had found almost four centuries later.

When Stacy reached the end of the letter in which Bustamente was explaining that the drawing at the bottom of the letter was the image that his Chinese wife had tattooed on the bottom of their children's feet, she turned the letter so everyone could see Bustamente's drawing of the tattoo. There was a collective gasp.

Jake took the moment to speak. He leaned down and kissed Elena lightly on her lips. "Elena and the deLeon family are descendants of Spanish nobility and the Bustamente blood line. As you heard in the letter, Bustamente was sent against his will to sail on the *Concepcion* with responsibility for representing the investments of Manila citizenry and, indirectly, the Spanish crown. By all rights, the deLeon family are the rightful heirs to the treasure and solely responsible for its disposition."

"Dear Lord! Is it true?" Delilah exclaimed, her eyes wide in amazement.

Elena looked up into Jake's face smiling, and pulled him down for a deep kiss. "Don't worry, my love, I will take care of you." Then she giggled, and was joined in laughter by everyone else in the room.

Rebecca was again speechless. Never in her life had she played a role in something of this magnitude. It was a real life fairy tale. It was the adventure of her life!

They spent the rest of the afternoon talking about the revelations of Bustamente's letter, having Stacy re-read parts of it. Rebecca called everyone to attention when the time came for the National Geographic broadcast to begin. The host announced the program and explained that the owners of these chests had gone to sea on the ill-fated Spanish galleon in 1698, bound for Acapulco, and were dead now for almost four centuries. With great fanfare, audiences around the world watched the dramatic opening of the chests, the experts' carefully examining and holding up the contents for all to see: clothes, hairbrushes, the handfuls of jewels, jade and pearls tumbling out of secret compartments, then reading the touching personal letters to family and friends that were never sent or received.

The show was a dramatic success, and the number of participants in the on-going auction grew in proportion. By prearrangement, the Sotheby's auctioneer announced that the thousands of pieces of Chinese-crafted jewelry and precious stones aboard the *Concepcion* were going to be divided into several hundred packages and distributed to fine jewelry stores and antiquities dealers around the world for local auctions and sales so that everyone would have an opportunity to own a piece of the *Concepcion's* treasure. It was a marketing coup to end all coups! Rebecca was beside herself with the success of it all.

After five days of sumptuous luxury at the Hilton International, the five young Marines packed their bags and headed for home in Florida. The day before they left, Jake and Gunny Sweikert accompanied them to Jake's Panamanian bank where they learned that a trust fund in the amount of one million dollars had been set up for each of them. The promised scholarship fund was already in place.

Jake reminded them of their sworn oath, and said the trust funds would disappear if it was discovered that they had not remained faithful to their oath. All of the Marines nodded solemnly at the warning, but assured Jake and Sweikert that their lips were sealed. They were blown away by Jake's generosity. Jake invited them to come visit him and Elena in Saipan. He said there were some unbelievably beautiful young women in Saipan, and the surfing there was great, too. Broad grins

crossed the young Marines' faces; each promised to take Jake and Elena up on the offer.

On the first of September, Gunny Sweikert, Tag and Stacy also said their goodbyes. Sweikert had to get back to his duties at the Marine Corps Reserve Center in Fort Lauderdale. Tag and Stacy had talked late into the night several times and Tag was leaning toward terminating his employment at the University of Florida, to free up some time for writing. Stacy had been approached by Elena's mother, Delilah, to participate in the organizing and administration of a number of foundations. Delilah wanted to fund some academic scholarships in memory of Sammy, and also establish some children's organizations in the Third World. Stacy saw it as a wonderful opportunity to travel, communicate and make a contribution. Delilah insisted that the position have a very lucrative salary and expense account.

Jake and Elena went with them to the airport. Stacy and Elena separated themselves from the others for a short while, holding hands, putting their foreheads together, and hugging one another. Finally they all boarded the flight to Miami, waving and smiling. Jake and Elena stayed in the terminal to watch the plane take-off. It was the closing of a major chapter in their lives. Elena had her arm around Jake's waist, and he draped an arm over her shoulders.

When the plane disappeared in the bright, cloudless blue of a sunny Panamanian sky, Elena wiped a tear from the corner of an eye. She stood on tip-toes to give Jake a kiss, wrapped her arms around his waist and pulled herself tightly against him. They walked hand-in-hand through the busy international terminal and returned to Rebecca's limo for the ride back to the hotel.

Jake's cell phone rang while they were in the limo. It was Rebecca announcing breathessly that she had received a call from a Monsignor Peroni at the Vatican in Rome. Peroni said he was calling to arrange for Pope Innocent's dinnerware to be picked up. No mention of buying it; just assuming it was a mere formality to claim what was rightfully theirs. Rebecca laughed. "I told him that I believed it was already consigned to a Chinese investment firm in Taiwan, but the deal was not yet concluded, or shipped. You should have heard him squeal and bluster! Said I would be hearing from the Vatican's lawyers. I reminded him of our many years in the antiquities trade and assured him the Vatican's claim would fall on deaf ears. I told him once the Pope's dinnerware passed into the possession of the Chinese investment firm, there would be little that the Catholic Church could do but offer to buy it, and I suspected the price would be considerably higher than if bought directly from the treasure consortium. I urged him to forego the legal path and make a direct offer for outright purchase as quickly as he could. He hung up on me!"

"I can tell you're loving it, Rebecca," Jake said. "Elena and I are in the limo on the way to the hotel. We just saw Gunny, Tag and Stacy off. We're going to hook up with Elena's family, have a nice dinner and maybe go to a club for some dancing. Probably in the next day or so, we're all going to fly back to Saipan. I arranged with a shipping company to pick-up *Makena* in Hawaii and transport her back to Saipan. I'd like to be there when she arrives; kinda coming full circle, if you know what I mean."

"Yes, I can imagine, Jake. What a ride you've had these past few months!" Rebecca said. "It has been beyond fantastic for me. I am forever in your debt. By the way, Papa has offered to hook-up you and the deLeon family with some really great financial advisors and legal people. He was a banker himself in Lebanon before the civil war there. He knows some very powerful financial management and investment people all over the world. Do you think you could take a quick side trip to Palm Beach to meet him? And I know Hattie would love to see you again, too, and to meet Elena."

"Thank you for the offer. It sounds like a good idea. I'll run it past Elena and Delilah. Rosalita's children want to go to DisneyWorld while they're so close, so maybe it'll happen. We have to go through Miami International anyway. I'll call you and let you know. We're pulling into the hotel right now. Join us for dinner if you can spare the time away from the auction."

(Eight)

The way it worked out, Rebecca turned over the day-to-day running of

504

the auction, packed her bags and joined Jake and Elena for a flight to Miami, then on to West Palm Beach International. The rest of the deLeon family changed planes at Miami for Orlando, Florida, and a visit to DisneyWorld. Rosalita was frequenty in tears as she watched her two fatherless children chatter excitedly about the upcoming adventure. Delilah consoled her as best she could. Tony promised his two nephews that he would ride every ride in the park with them.

Rebecca's father met them at the West Palm Beach airport in a stretch limo complete with a bottle of France's best champagne. A cultured gentleman of Europe's business world, he was a most gracious host. They drove immediately to Palm Beach and The Breakers restaurant for a mid-afternoon lunch. It was a memorable feast. The Fontaine family was treated like the royalty. Elena's beauty caught the eye of everyone in the restaurant.

No one would have guessed from her modest demeanor that she was well on her way to becoming a billionaire. Rebecca's father announced that Rebecca's penthouse condo was appropriated for Elena and Jake. Rebecca would be staying in her parent's condo. When Elena protested at displacing Rebecca, 'Papa' Fontaine clucked his tongue in dismissal. "Rebecca will sleep in the bedroom she grew up in." It was no inconvenience at all, he insisted. It was for only one night anyway since he understood that Jake and Elena were returning to Saipan.

After lunch, they drove to Hattie Heinz's stately mansion. She greeted them with open arms. "Jake! You handsome thing you! Give me a hug. And this must be Elena. My God, how beautiful you are! What adventures you have had! Rebecca has told me practically nothing. Come, let's go into my Florida Room. I have presents for both of you."

When they were seated, Hattie handed a small box to Elena, and a rather heavy one to Jake. "There's really nothing I can say to you, Jake, that would be sufficient to express my gratitude for your assistance in growing my Chinese porcelain collection. I want you to know that you and Elena are welcome in my home any time. Elena, I know I don't have to tell you that you are a most fortunate woman to have the love of this amazing young man."

Elena smiled shyly and said, "Thank you. I first saw Jake in the American Memorial Park on Saipan, and I knew immediately that he was very special. May I open my present?"

"Of course! Do it now. I see that Jake has given you a very impressive engagement ring. But a woman never has enough jewelry," Hattie said with a chuckle.

"Yes, this ring is from the treasure galleon. Jake selected it when he proposed to me in Hawaii," Elena said. She leaned over and gave Jake a kiss on the cheek. When she opened the box Hattie had given her, she gasped at the beauty of the golden ring inside.

"I have it on good authority," Hattie said, "provenance and all of that, that your new ring was once owned by none other than Cleopatra, the last pharaoh of Egypt.. It's estimated to be over 2,000 years old. The image inscribed on the top is RA, the Egyptian god of Life."

"Oh, it is so beautiful," Elena exclaimed, sliding the ring onto a finger on her right hand.

"Now yours, Jake," Hattie said.

Jake open his box and removed a highly polished mahogany box, opened the top and found a gleaming gold-plated U.S. Army Colt .45 caliber automatic pistol. Engraved on the slide was a dedication from the President of the Philippines to General Douglas McArthur commemorating his return to the Philippines during World War II.

"It's a limited edition, Jake, only one hundred made for distribution among the heavy hitters of the U.S. Military and political leaders of World War II," Hattie said. "Something for the guy who has everything," she chuckled.

"Thank you, Hattie," Jake said, leaning over to give Hattie a peck on the cheek.

"Jake can keep it alongside the Chinese battle sword that he recovered," Elena said.

"Chinese battle sword?" Hattie said.

Rebecca jumped into the conversation and told the story of Don Emilio Bustamente de la Vega, his letter, and the tattoo that identified Elena as a descendant, and her family's ownership of the treasure.

"Mercy! What an incredible story! " Hattie exclaimed. "So you are a billionaire, Elena, and Jake, you are a kept man!" Hattie laughed.

"Well," Elena said with a soft smile, "He owns my heart, so that makes him a billionaire, too, don't you think?"

"Absolutely!" Hattie said, reaching across to squeeze her hand.

After a tour of Hattie's latest Chinese porcelain acquisitions, including the four reticulated ones enjoying special prominence in her bedroom and parlor on the second floor, they parted and Rebecca, her father, Jake and Elena went to Rebecca's penthouse condominium. The following morning, after a flawless breakfast of Jamaican Blue Mountain coffee, rum-laced banana waffles and Canadian bacon prepared by Rebecca's father, Rebecca ushered Jake and Elena to her Bentley for the drive to Orlando. She had insisted on driving them there because she also wanted to see Delilah one more time. The Bentley was a dream ride, and with the top down beneath a cloudless sky, it ended too soon for everyone.

The deLeon family was staying at one of the 5-bedroom condos located on the DisneyWorld property. No automobile was needed. Shuttle buses made regular rounds to take guests to all park locations for entertainment and dining. Daily maid service kept the condo spotless, and the kitchen was kept well-stocked with all the necessities. Since arriving, it had been one continuous safari to all the major attractions.

Delilah, Tony, Rosalita and her two sons, hit every attraction offered. When they received the telephone call from Elena that she, Jake and Rebecca were on their way in Rebecca's Bentley, Delilah made it a point to be at the condo when they arrived.

"Welcome! Welcome, everyone!" Delilah greeted them at the door, immediately kissing her daughter and squeezing her with both arms. She gave Jake a kiss on both cheeks and hugged Rebecca. "Rosalita and the boys and Tony are making one more round of the rides today. They should be back in an hour or so."

Elena asked, "How are the boys, and Rosalita, Mama?"

"Rosalita is coming to terms with the loss of Sammy, but it will take a while, years I think. The boys have been told their daddy has gone to heaven, but I don't think they will realize the finality of that until we return to Saipan and they see that he is truly gone. The trip to Panama, this visit to the United States, and this stay at DisneyWorld have been good therapy for the boys. Truthfully, it has been good for me, too," Delilah said.

"It will all work out, Mama," Elena said. "Jake and I will be able to help, and Tony will be home from the Marine Corps in less than four months. The boys will be surrounded by love."

"Jake, you are going to live with us in Saipan?" Delilah asked.

"I can't think of a better place, Delilah, Jake said. "I've had no home other than the Corps and the *Giggling Witch*. Elena says that even though I am just a poor vagabond sailor, she'll take care of me."

Everyone laughed at that.

"We are very proud to have you for a member of our family, Jake. Make no mistake about that. I must tell you that I am intimidated by the responsibility of administering the funds generated from the sale of the *Concepcion's* treasure. It will take some careful thinking and planning.

508

Your help along those lines will be greatly appreciated. I believe there are also some excellent business opportunities to be had in Saipan. You can put that business administration degree to work, and I'm confident you will not lack for financial support when you launch the business. But what I really want is more grandchildren," Delilah said.

"We'll do our best," Elena said, pulling Jake to her and kissing him on the mouth. "We have to get married first, mama, and you're in charge of that. Rosalita can help, too."

At that moment the phone rang. It was Bryce Taggart calling from Gainesville, Florida.

"Hello, Jake. Hope I've caught you at a convenient time?" he said.

"A good a time as any, Tag. The deLeon women are sitting here planning my wedding!" Jake said.

"Well, Stacy and I plan to attend that event for sure!" Taggart said. He gave a hearty laugh. "But on a less happy note, I wanted to call you because I heard from Gunny Sweikert in Fort Lauderdale. The local newspaper is reporting what looks like a breakthrough in the murder of Doctor Ambrose and Brenda Warren. Seems the missing detective's secretary has told the police all about why her boss went to Fort Lauderdale. He was working on a contract from a European firm in Switzerland, I believe. The police, with some help from INTERPOL, have traced payments to the detective's firm in Miami. A transfer of funds from the Banco Santander in Spain, and another funds transfer from a numbered account in Lichtenstein.

"Her boss, a guy named Benito Garcia, was tight-lipped about the investigation he was hired for, but the secretary remembers that Garcia was going to check on some university people in Gainesville, and a doctor on a yacht in Fort Lauderdale. He took a video camera and his computer with him. Also, he was accompanied by the secretary's nephew, who has a sleazy background and was involved in a bash-up at a local Latino club and bar. Needless to say, Stacy and I are wondering if we are the 'university people' he was checking out. Our only connection to Ambrose and Brenda are through you and research on the *Concepcion*. Any ideas on that?"

"You're blowing me away, Tag," Jake said. "I've had this feeling all along that there were some people, unknown to me, who were following our research. When I discovered that the *Giggling Witch* was compromised, I racked my brain trying to figure out how anyone could know I was looking for treasure. I am convinced they put a transponder on my boat so they could follow me. Then, when the Jap long-liner began following me, I knew for a fact that I was being tracked. Sammy did some legwork in Saipan, and we discovered that the long-liner was home-based in the Kurile Islands north of Japan. I've asked myself a thousand times, why is a Jap long-liner from Russia, traveling to Saipan, specifically to watch me? Who's giving them their orders? And who's paying for it? They had fifteen people on that long-liner, for Christ's sake! Somebody was spending a lot of bucks."

"Well, maybe we'll soon know," Tag said. "The investigation is heating up in Florida, and they've got INTERPOL involved. Change of subject. What are your plans these days?"

"Everything's in a flux, Tag. Rebecca is here at DisneyWorld with us; she's turned the daily auction duties over to colleagues. We visited Hattie Heinz, the wealthy lady from Palm Beach, who was buying everything in sight from the *Concepcion* haul. Elena's mom, her sister-in-law, Rosalita and her two sons, and her younger brother, Tony have been taking in the DisneyWorld entertainment, but I think we'll all head for Saipan in the next day or so."

"Well, I'm glad to see things are returning to some sort of normal. Stacy is coming along fine, and I think the encounter with the Yakuza pirate will fade in time. She's in contact with Delilah, and I wouldn't be surprised if she shows up in Saipan, to plot and plan some ways to spend all that money. I'll probably tag along, too. So you may see me sooner than you think. How's Elena doing?"

"Pretty good, I think," Jake said. The loss of her brother, Sammy, and the Yakuza stuff have taken their toll. Time heals all wounds, they say, and I am hopeful that will be the case here. I think getting back to Saipan, will be good for everyone."

"Okay, Jake," Tag said. "Stay in touch and give everyone in the deLeon family our love, okay?"

"Will do, Tag. Don't spend all your money in one place!" Jake hung up the phone and realized that everyone had been following his conversation with Tag.

Elena asked, "Stacy is doing okay?"

"Yes. Tag sends his love to all of you," Jake said.

Delilah said, "We heard your talk about the investigation. That's good news. To find out who is behind all of this. While you were talking, Jake, we have decided we are ready to leave. Rebecca has volunteered to handle our travel arrangements."

"Great!" Jake said. "I'm ready for some island time with my Chamorro lover." He pulled Elena to him and was rewarded with a long kiss.

(Nine)

On September 3rd, the deLeon family, with Jake Porter in tow, departed Miami International for a non-stop trans-Pacific flight to Tokyo, then a flight change for a non-stop to Saipan. Despite the jet-lag, everyone was delighted to see so many deLeon family and island friends meeting them at the airport. The news about Sammy's death at Anatahan Island and Elena's kidnapping by Japanese Yakuza had spread quickly among Saipan's Chamorro community. But the question for them was why? Why did the Yakuza do such a thing? Delilah had not told anyone about Jake's quest for Spanish treasure. Nor had she told them of the fabulous wealth now possessed by the deLeon family. All that would come later. For now, tears must be reserved for Sammy, Rosalita and Sammy's two sons.

They went to the deLeon home on the north end of the island in a long parade of vehicles, the newly arrived and their luggage dispersed among the many vehicles. The mood was a mixed one of joy and sadness. The women immediately took over Delilah's kitchen and began to prepare food. They had bought fresh fruit and fish from the morning market in Tanapag; the fruit was quickly sliced and the fish put in ceramic pans for marinating. Fresh pots of iced tea and hot coffee were brought to the table. Several portable iceboxes with cold beer were brought into the shade under the front porch roof. The chatter from the women was voluminous, but only once did anyone mention *Makena*, the missing deLeon family proa. Delilah quickly dismissed the topic and launched another line of conversation.

On September 7th, *Makena* arrived as deck cargo on an inter-island freighter from Guam. One of Sammy's cousins who worked in the customs office cleared the paperwork. He could not help but notice that *Makena* was being shipped from Hawaii. Now, how in the world did *Makena* get from Saipan to Hawaii, he mused. None of the deLeon family had been gone from the island for any length of time, certainly not Delilah, or Sammy, or Elena. Who could have sailed the proa across the Pacific to Hawaii? Process of elimination left only one suspect: Jake Porter. Everyone knew Porter and Elena deLeon had paired up. Their love affair had been the talk of the island for quite a while.

After checking with another cousin, this one working in the Immigrations department, he discovered that Porter had cleared Saipan immigrations on May 23rd, and indicated that he was leaving by boat. He had arrived by boat, and apparently Immigrations assumed he was leaving by the same boat. But the boat that Porter had arrived on was named the *Giggling Witch*. Interesting. Now, where exactly was the *Giggling Witch* if Porter had departed on *Makena*? This would bear some looking into. It got even more interesting when his cousin in Immigrations called to say that Delilah, Rosalita, her two sons, and Tony deLeon had all flown out of Saipan bound for of all places, the Republic of Panama. When they had returned to Saipan, all of their passports reflected immigration stamps from Miami, Florida. On further examination, after reviewing photocopies of their passports, Delilah and Elena had flown to Hawaii several weeks earlier than their trip to Panama, then returned to Saipan. Very interesting, thought both cousins. *Makena* was being shipped to Saipan, from Hawaii, and Delilah and Elena had been in Hawaii. Did Porter sail *Makena* from Saipan, to Hawaii? If he did, why would he do that when he had his own boat, the *Giggling Witch*?

When the phone call from the Customs Office came announcing the arrival of *Makena*, Jake and Elena held a hasty conference with Delilah, and it was decided that Tony would drive Jake and Elena to take delivery of the proa. Jake and Elena would then sail *Makena* to the deLeon ranch at Marpi Point. It was the first time Tony had been alone with Jake and his sister since returning to Saipan. He had a lot of questions about the whole Japanese Yakuza thing, the recovery of the treasure at Marcus Island, and especially Elena's encounter with the Japanese Yakuza captain.

Elena described the Yakuza assault on her and Sammy at Anatahan Island. Tears streamed down her faced as she relived the lost of her brother. Jake intervened and suggested they talk about it later, but Elena said it was best to tell it all. Then she told what even Jake had not heard—her shooting of the Yakuza captain with Stacy's Baby Glock pistol. Stacy was barely conscious when the Yakuza captain drug her into the compartment where he had Elena shackled. When he left, Elena tried to talk to Stacy, but Stacy was in shock. "She kept saying 'Glock in pocket, Glock in pocket!' I had no idea what she meant. It sounded like 'glockenpoket'; it made no sense to me. I had never heard of a Glock pistol. I thought she was just delirious. Then she said, 'Glock pistol. Shoot Jap bastard!' Now, *that* I understood. But it was very difficult to get to Stacy's pocket. Stacy was tied hand and foot, but she was able to get up on her elbows and knees alongside the bunk and that raised her pocket to a level I could reach. Stacy said there was a bullet in the chamber and that the safety catch was in the trigger. All I had to do was pull the trigger, she said. I raised the pistol and held it concealed in my hair next to where I was shackled. When the Yakuza captain returned, he leaned over me, grinning, and shoved his hand between my legs. I just brought the pistol from behind my hair and shot him in the face. He slumped to the floor, and I rolled onto my left hip and shot him again and again until the bullets ran out."

When they arrived at the Customs House, they signed the paperwork and walked down to the dock where *Makena* was tied up. It took only a few minutes to set up the mast and sail. Elena gave Tony a kiss on the cheek and said they would talk more soon. She and Jake climbed into *Makena's* hull, and sailed away.

Two days later on September 7th, Delilah, Rosalita, her two sons, Tony, Jake and Elena boarded Sammy's trimaran, the Titan III, for a sail to Anatahan Island. Elena had suggested they visit the place where Sammy was murdered and place a wreath on the water. Delilah immediately approved the idea, and Rosalita thought it would be good for the boys, too. Elena wanted her own closure as well. The Titan III was roomy, with plenty of bunks for everyone, and she was stocked with food and water. Delilah assured them she would catch a nice mahi mahi for their first night's dinner.

They anchored in the same place where the *Giggling Witch* had anchored before the arrival of the Yakuza. It was a beautiful tropical night, a new moon shining overhead, and a soft breeze blowing across the deck. They ate Delilah's promised mahi mahi, and the adults shared a couple of bottles of wine. They would lay the wreath over Sammy's watery grave in the morning.

They ended up spending two days and nights at Anatahan Island, relishing in the quiet and the closeness to Sammy. Everyone but Delilah dove into the ocean for a swim, and later Jake, Tony and Rosalita's two boys swam over to the island's shoreline. Elena took the opportunity of their absence to tell Delilah of her killing of the Yakuza captain, and her mother cried along with her. Their lives would never be the same, they knew, but they also acknowledged how much they had to live for.

"Mama, Jake has not said anything to me about what happened on the treasure island. I think he is almost ashamed of the killing he has done in his lifetime even though every time it was thrust upon him. He killed even more men, the Yakuzas, on the treasure island. Stacy told me what her fiancée, Tag, said about the fight on the island. Jake killed another half-dozen men. Tag and Gunny Sweikert say Jake is an awesome fighter, a natural warrior, but I think Jake does not like that role. More than anything, I long for peace and quiet for Jake and me. I would like to build a house on our family property near the ocean cliff, and make babies with Jake."

"I know just the spot," Delilah said, smiling. "When we return to our island, let's go take a look. We can have your Uncle Tooney survey it and lay out a house plan. Okay?"

They laid Sammy's wreath of beautiful island flowers in the Titan III's wake as they sailed away to the south for Saipan. Everyone on board was relaxed, and they took turns singing old island songs. Elena stayed snuggled up next to Jake and saw that he never lacked for food or drink or a passionate kiss. Rosalita's boys had taken a liking to Jake, and at one point during the homeward sail the youngest even climbed into his lap and went to sleep.

When they made up the Titan III's lines to the dock in Garapan, a half-dozen Deleon family members came down the dock all excited and animated. Had they heard the news? Terrorists had blown-up the Twin Towers in New York! The President had declared war! He said the terrorists would be pursued no matter where they were. Iraq was going to feel the wrath of the U.S. military might! And Tony, there's a telegram from the Marine Corps waiting for you. You must hurry home to read it.

515

After the quiet and tranquility of Anatahan Island, it was almost too much to bear. They all piled into the Range Rover and headed for home. There were more deLeon family members awaiting their arrival, and Delilah's kitchen table was already covered with food. A suckling pig was roasting on the pit out back, and the men were frequenting the ice chests for a cold one. Tony retrieved his letter, and as expected, it announced the termination of his leave with orders to report to the Pendleton Marine Barracks in California, by the earliest and fastest mode of transportation. There was a telephone number he was to call immediately to confirm receipt of his orders.

Jake got Tony's attention and led him away from the crowd of well-wishing relatives. "Life's a bitch, Tony," Jake said. "I've been down this road myself, and you can bet that the Marine Corps will use this opportunity to extend your enlistment. So, don't be surprised when it happens, okay? They tacked a year onto my enlistment when Saddam invaded Kuwait. Blowing up the Twin Towers on U.S. soil is going to draw a far stronger response than the invasion of Kuwait, believe me. Just keep your head down, Tony, and go with the flow. The Iraqis can't hold a candle to our firepower; they'll fight in the beginning, but when things heat up, they'll fold up their tents and raise their hands in surrender. It won't last long, you can bet on that."

"Thanks for the pep talk, Jake," Tony said. "Just knowing you're here to take care of my sister and my family makes it a lot easier to go."

A day later, they saw Tony off at the Saipan International Airport, the women crying as expected and the men giving Tony pats on the back, wishing him good luck. After the plane had disappeared into the Eastern sky, they all returned to Delilah's and drank and sang into the early morning hours.

(Ten)

The next two weeks were some of the happiest for Jake. He and Elena made love morning, noon and night. She squealed in ecstasy when she

516

reached orgasm, wrapping her beautiful legs around his waist and riding his erection until Jake could delay his ejaculation no longer. They giggled and laughed at their sexual antics, took a shower and usually went at it again until exhausted.

Delilah interrupted one of their love-making sessions on the Titan III, where they had spent the night to get away from the constant crowd at the deLeon home. She called on Jake's cell phone to announce that a team of financial advisers was arriving the next day to begin developing investment strategies for the hundreds of millions of dollars that Jake had transferred from his Panama bank account into Delilah's account. Would it be possible for Jake and Elena to attend? she asked. The meeting would be held in a conference room at the Hilton Hotel.

Slightly breathless, and still firmly in the saddle with Elena, who was giggling at Jake's effort to calm his voice, he agreed to attend. "I'll be there, Delilah, and Elena is nodding her head to say she will be there, too," Jake said.

"Good. Just so you will know, Jake, I sent ten million dollars back to your account in Panama, so you can keep my daughter in the manner to which she is accustomed. I don't believe she will be returning to teaching any time soon. By the way, Stacy is coming for a visit next week to help me with setting up an educational foundation honoring Sammy's memory. Unfortunately, Tag won't be coming along with her. His Marine Corps Reserve unit has been activated, and he's headed to Arizona for desert combat training."

"Delilah, he's a millionaire for Pete's sake! Why doesn't he resign his commission and become a full-time writer like he's always wanted. He's done his bit for his country, and took Iraqi shrapnel in the ass for the effort. I can't believe Stacy is letting him do that!"

"Well, it must be contagious, because I got a call from Gunny Seikert, too, and he told me pretty much the same thing. George is in his fifties, you know. But his unit has been mobilized. They completed their desert training last year and will be deploying for Iraq within the next few weeks. They're waiting for weapons upgrading and scheduling for the inoculations they all have to take. I hope they don't have the same reaction to the shots that Tony did. He got really sick, and spent a week in bed recovering."

"Yeah, they hit you for everything from the Nile virus, to cholera and smallpox all at once," Jake said.

"Give my daughter a kiss for me, and get back to whatever it was that had you so breathless," Delilah laughed and hung up the phone.

The investment and financial advisors from New York, two men and a woman, stretched their time on Saipan as much as they could; so taken by the beauty of the island. Delilah had them to her home for some authentic Chamarro cooking, and Jake and Elena took them sailing around the island on the Titan III. They were delighted when Stacy arrived just before they were to leave and Delilah asked them to stay for a couple of extra days to bring Stacy up to speed on technical aspects of gratuity trusts and international money transfer regulations.

Jake and Elena picked up Stacy at Saipan's international airport. The two women raced into each other's arms and Jake could see that a special bond had been forged between them as a result of their encounter with the Yakuza at Marcus Island. Stacy gave Jake kisses on both cheeks and thanked him for the additional five million dollars he had deposited in her and Tag's bank accounts.

Jake just smiled and said, "Well, like I said in Hawaii, if we pulled off the recovery of the remainder of the *Concepcion's* treasure, your next paycheck would make the first pale in comparison. I am very sorry that it came with such a high price, Stacy. But now you will have an opportunity to spread all those millions around and do some good with it. I believe Delilah already has a dozen different charities and children's' homes lined up to receive donations."

"Tag asked me to convey his gratitude, too," Stacy said. "But you know,

Jake, he is a Marine through and through, and I don't believe the money will change a single thing about him. His Marine Corps reserve unit is in Arizona as we speak. He's not allowed to use his cell phone or make private communications while they are in the desert, but I expect to hear from him next week. I fear he will soon be sent to Iraq. The Twin Towers destruction at the hands of terrorists has changed the world forever, I'm afraid. There will be no end to religious fanaticism and racial hatred. It is a world war without end or borders. So sad, so sad."

"My brother, Tony, was recalled from his separation leave and we have learned that the Marine Corps has extended his enlistment. They will probably be sending him back to Iraq," Elena said.

"Let's hit the road, you two," Jake said. "Delilah is waiting to see you, and I believe Rosalita and her boys will be there, too. We'll have something to talk about other than doom and destruction. And Elena can show you the homesite she and her mom have picked for our new home. Incredible view of the ocean from a thousand-foot cliff. Delilah is campaigning for a bunch of grandkids, and she wants them all right next door. It's going to be a chore meeting her expectations."

"I am going to help, my love," Elena said softly, pulling his head down for a kiss.

CALL TO DUTY

Date: December 24, 2001

Lat. 15º, 15' North, Long. 145º, 45 East
Saipan, Northern Marianas

(One)

News of the death of a loved one is never easy to bear, Jake thought. But surely, the cruelest time of all is Christmas. Tony deLeon died in a midnight mortar attack on the small provincial compound he and his squad were guarding at a nameless highway intersection in southern Iraq. The news was brought to the deLeon home by the Governor of the island, and two Marine Corps reservists in full dress blues. Jake cursed the fact that he and Elena were not there at the time, but were sailing *Makena* with Rosalita's two boys, trying to fill in for their deceased father, Sammy.

When they arrived at Delilah's home, the yard and road were packed with vehicles and a crowd of dozens and dozens of islanders. Elena immediately sensed something was wrong. The crowd parted, allowing Elena to move quickly to the house where she found her mother sobbing softly and dabbing at her eyes with a handkerchief. The dreaded telegraph lay on the table. Elena went to her knees in front of her mom, and all Delilah could say was 'Tony.' Elena picked up the telegram, read it, then joined in the crying with her mother.

Jake came into the room already knowing what awaited him. One of the deLeon family had whispered the terrible news to him as he approached the house. A burning anger welled up in his chest as he came to sit by Elena and her mother, Delilah. He fumed in silent frustration over the senselessness of it all; the feeling of helplessness in responding to such a tragedy. These soft island people giving up their precious children to maniacal jihadists on the other side of the world. He thought, too, of the almost three thousand people murdered in the destruction of the Twin Towers in New York. Fathers, mothers, sons and daughters who had done nothing other than gone to work to earn a living on that fateful day.

Rosalita came into the room crying, wailing really, and Jake took the opportunity to step outside to grab a breath of fresh air and clear his thinking. He reached into his pocket and pulled out his cell phone. He dialed Gunny Sweikert in Fort Lauderdale, hoping his unit had not yet deployed to Iraq.

"What's up, Snapper?" Sweikert answered abruptly, reading Jake's name on his cell phone's screen.

For once, Jake was not put off by being called 'Snapper.' "What's the status on that Officer Candidate School deal for former Marine enlisted people?"

"The Corps is always looking for a few good men, Snapper," Sweikert laughed. "You figuring to even things up with the Twin Towers jihadists?"

"Tony deLeon is coming home in a casket from Iraq, Gunny. Delilah got the telegram earlier today."

"Damn! I'm sorry to hear that, Jake. Truly, I am," Sweikert said. "I'll give her a day, then call her and Elena."

"I'm sure they will appreciate that," Jake said.

"So, you want me to put you in for OCS?" Sweikert asked. "Assuming you can pass a physical, I'm sure your combat record and a couple of recommendations from me and Major Taggart will get you in the door. We could call in the heavy artillery and let General Winton, the Commandant, know what's going on, too."

"No politics, Gunny," Jake said firmly. "If they won't take me as I am, then fuck 'em."

"Right. Right," Sweikert said. "Frankly, you don't even need my and Taggart's recommendations. You can stand on your record. Our recommendations will probably do little more than speed up your selection. I'll notify our Selection Board and put in your request. I'm putting the forms and paperwork in an envelope right now and you should have it in four to five days. To save time, facsimile the completed forms back to me and I'll get the ball rolling. Welcome aboard, sir. Semper Fi!"

"Thanks, Gunny," Jake answered and hung up the phone. Now, all he had to do was break the news to Elena.

The emotional turmoil of Tony's death, and the expectation of the arrival of his casket prevented Jake from talking with Elena about his re-entering the Marine Corps. She and Rosalita attended to their mother daily, cooking her meals, making beds, and greeting the endless stream of extended family and islanders stopping by to express their condolences. Jake gathered up Rosalita's two sons and entertained them with sailing, building a kite, fishing and playing with a Frisbee in the American Memorial Park. The boys were having a hard time dealing with the loss of their favorite uncle so soon after the loss of their father. It was upsetting for them to see their mother crying so much. They stayed very close to Jake, and took his hand wherever they went.

With the arrival of Tony's casket, the Marine Corps funeral ceremonies that followed, and burial on the deLeon ranch, a week passed before an opportunity presented itself to talk with Elena about his decision to re-enter the Marine Corps. The Officer Candidate School application forms that Gunny Sweikert had sent arrived on the same day as Tony's casket. The irony was not lost on Jake.

Now, a week after Tony's burial, Jake and Elena were standing among the surveying stakes that had been laid out for their new home. Elena's Uncle Toomey had just left after showing them a rough sketch of the house he was going to build, and they had walked hand-in-hand to the cliff's edge to look out on the beautiful blue of the Pacific Ocean.

"I don't think I have ever been in a more beautiful place," Jake said, his arm around Elena's shoulders. "And I know I have never been happier in my life since meeting you."

"And that's why you are signing up with the Marine Corps again," Elena said with a smile.

"How the hell?..." Jake said in exasperation.

"I saw the papers that Gunny Sweikert sent to you. You left them on the Titan's galley table. And Stacy called to tell me that Tag had called her from Arizona. He said that Gunny Sweikert had called him to say you were asking about the officer candidate school."

"Looks like the cat's out of the bag," Jake said. "But the papers aren't signed, Elena, and I had no intention of making that move without discussing it first with you. Sometimes I feel like I've brought nothing but trouble to you and the deLeon family ever since I arrived on Saipan. Sammy died because of my pursuit of the treasure, and I damn near got you and Stacy killed, too. I've certainly brought a lot of sadness to your Mom and Rosalita. I never intended any of it, of course, but nevertheless, I am at the center of it all."

"So you thought you'd balance things out by going back into the Marine Corps?"

"I don't know if 'balancing it out' is the right expression, Elena. It just seems like the right thing to do. I sure as hell don't want to endure the Iraqi desert again, and I don't like the idea of people trying to kill me either. I didn't go looking for trouble with the Yakuza, but they messed with me, and they paid the price. The Iraqis have messed with me by coming to my country and killing my countrymen, and killing your brother, Tony. I'm just not inclined to let them get away scot free with that."

"My grandfather risked his life and the happiness of his family when he went to the beaches of Saipan during the American invasion in World War Two," Elena said. "He showed the Marines where the Japs were hiding. They say his selfless service saved hundreds of lives. My father volunteered for Vietnam. The Viet Cong shot him in the back while he was dragging two wounded Marines to cover. The Yakuza killed my brother, kidnapped me and almost killed Stacy. Now, the Iraqis have killed my last brother, Tony. I, too, have an accounting sheet that needs balancing, Jake."

"So, what do you think I should do, Elena?" Jake asked turning to look deeply into her eyes.

"I think we should go talk to Mama," Elena said with a smile. "Mothers know best, and my mama is the best."

They found Delilah at her kitchen table with stacks of legal documents surrounding her. She looked up when Jake and Elena came in. She seemed tired around the eyes, but nevertheless gave a broad smile. "I've begun spending that treasure money, Jake. Those investment people have given me the ground rules, and Stacy is helping, too. We've started with funding some orphanages around the world. I thought focusing on children in the beginning would be a good place to start. Here's a list of the first fifty orphanages and the organizations that will administer the funding to make sure it's spent correctly." She handed the list to Elena.

Elena gave the list a quick look, then handed it to Jake. She pointed to five of the orphanages on the list, and Jake saw that they were all located in Iraq. They were followed by orphanages in Iran, Afghanistan and several of the old Soviet republics with large Muslim populations. Delilah had her own way of dealing with Muslim fundamentalism.

"Rosalita and I have decided it's time to tattoo the boys," Delilah announced. "We were wondering if you and Jake would like to attend. It stings a bit, and I was thinking, Jake, that you and Elena might have a calming effect on the boys."

"Of course, Delilah," Jake said immediately. Elena took Jake's arm in hers and tiptoed to give him a kiss. "You're such a sweetie, my love."

The following day, Rosalita brought her two sons to the deLeon home at Marpi Point. Delilah had already prepared the ink and needles. The youngest son volunteered to go first if he could sit in Jake's lap while it happened. With just a little bit of whimpering and considerable squirming, the job was soon finished. He was rewarded with a frozen homemade mango juice popsicle. His mother, Rosalita, held an ice cube to the new tattoo.

Then, Eduardo stepped forward bravely and announced that he wanted Elena to hold one of his hands, and Jake the other. When Delilah finished and rewarded him with a popsicle, she turned to Jake and said, "You're next, Jake. No popsicle. Elena will take care of your reward later," she chuckled.

Jake was taken aback. He didn't know if she was serious, or just joking.

Elena leaned over his shoulder with a mischievous smile. "We invite you to join the deLeons' warrior society, my love. It's centuries old, and you'll be in good company. It's also better than dog tags in a combat zone." She giggled and kissed him on the ear.

Well, why not? Jake kicked off his sandals and lifted his left foot for Delilah.

(Two)

A week later, Major Bryce Taggart, recently returned from the Arizona desert with his Gainesville Marine Corps reserve unit, called to say congratulations to Jake for his acceptance to the Corps' Officer Candidate School. Jake was surprised because he had not yet heard anything from the application he had forwarded to Gunny Sweikert. "Gunny called me a few minutes ago to tell me of your selection. He said the Corps waived your interview with the Selection Officer and the essay requirement, probably because of your combat record. All you have to do is pass the physical when you arrive at Quantico. Sweikert's got more connections at Marine Corps headquarters than the President of the United States, I think. Anyway, you'll receive official notice within the next day by telegram. Your report date is two weeks from today, so pack your bags, amigo."

"Thanks for the heads up, Major," Jake said. "How's Stacy doing? Delilah raves about the assistance she has been providing with the investment research. Between them, I believe they are spending some big time money, and it looks like the world is going to be a better place for it."

"Stacy is doing well," Taggart replied. "The flight out to Saipan and the couple of weeks with Delilah, Elena and Rosalita has occupied her completely. She's on the telephone every day talking with private foundations and help organizations, and loving every minute of it."

"Great," Jake said. "Maybe we will be able to get together as soon as I finish the OCS program."

"You won't have any trouble with the OCS program, Jake. But it's ten weeks of hell and harassment at the hands of some demented senior Marine Corps sergeants and mean-assed officers. After graduation, you will be sent to what's called The Basic School (TBS), where you will be taught leadership Marine Corps-style. It's a bitch, too, but you're a Second Lieutenant at that point, and I know you have all the qualities the Corps expects in a Marine officer. After that, it's probably Iraq."

"Sounds like a well-planned future, Major," Jake said. He chuckled under his breath. "I'm already doing some PT and distance running around the island. I'm not a 17-year old anymore, you know. Humping a fully-loaded rucksack for twenty miles is going to be a challenge."

"Tell me about it, mate. I just got back from the Arizona desert and we had PT at four o-clock in the morning before the sun heated up the desert, then all day skirmishing with mock enemy troops under the heat of the sun. I lost fifteen pounds that I didn't know I had to lose," Taggart laughed.

"Thanks again for the heads-up, sir. Talk with you soon."

(Three)

The ten-week OCS training at Brown Field at Marine Corps Base Quantico was everything Taggart had described, and more. The instructors, enlisted and officer-alike, were a sadistic bunch in Jake's opinion, and clearly enjoyed inflicting physical and psychological pain on the young officer candidates. Of the 127 who entered the program, only 79 were left at graduation. Jake earned the admiration of instructors and fellow officer candidates with his near-perfect scores on the firing range. He was a killer shot. He was outstanding on the self-defense course, too. Jake had picked up on some karate moves while stationed on Okinawa, birthplace of karate.

On one of the hand-to-hand sessions involving the use of knives, hard rubber ones but still painful if they made it to their intended target, Jake was paired with a huge ex-NFL tackle who was a former graduate of a naval ROTC program at an Ivy league university. Out-weighing Jake easily by seventy pounds and looming over him with huge shoulders and arms, the money was not on Jake. But when the guy rushed Jake, screaming fiercely as they had been taught, everyone had to blink twice when they saw Jake drop effortlessly to the ground, sweep the guy's feet from under him, then bound up alongside him leveraging the arm with the knife from the elbow, twisting it then bringing the arm down on a knee, taking the knife like candy from a baby. The instructor was suitably impressed to the extent that he ordered Jake to repeat the move in slow motion for the edification of the rest of the class.

It was no surprise that when it came time for the officer candidates to elect their Brigade Commander, Jake was selected. It was a signal honor, and recognition of not only his professional performance during the OCS program, but the easy manner in which he won their respect and friendship. Jake had helped many of the candidates over some tough bumps in the program. They called him 'The Old Man' because at almost thirty-two years of age, Jake was the oldest officer candidate in the class. At formation, he would now stand in front and apart from the rest of the brigade. Orders of the day also called for all former Marine enlisted personnel to wear any medals they had been awarded while serving in the Marine Corps. Jaws dropped when Jake appeared with his Bronze Star, the Marine Corps Medal for Gallantry, the gaudy gold Kuwaiti Liberation Medal and the 4-inch diameter gold disk and colored sash that had been presented to him by the Saudi government. Jake felt like he resembled a Middle Eastern potentate, but orders were orders.

Jake mentioned none of this to Elena, who had traveled to Quantico with him and waited patiently for each of the three brief weekend leaves he was granted during OCS. She had rented a spacious and beautifully decorated hotel suite nearby. She also leased a bright red Maserati convertible from a local dealership, and when she picked him up at the Quantico gate, Jake's fellow officer candidates were blown away by the incredibly beautiful Polynesian woman at the wheel. She even got a higher eyeball rating than the Maserati, and everyone wanted to know more about her. The only ground that Jake would give was a promise that she would be at the graduation dance and available to dance.

Elena drove him immediately and at a high rate of speed to their hotel where she pulled him into their room and jumped onto the king-size bed, flipping up her skirt to show that she wore no panties. She squealed in mock fright when Jake dropped his trousers exposing a rapidly growing erection while she frantically unbuttoned her blouse to reveal two flawless breasts. "We have two hours before Room Service brings us our lunch," she gasped breathlessly taking his erection in her hand and throwing a leg over his hip.

In the Marine Corps, unsubstantiated rumors are called 'scuttlebutt', and during the final week of OCS the scuttlebutt was that the Commandant of the Marine Corps would be attending their class' graduation parade. It was unprecedented; surely the Marine Corps' highest-ranking officer had more pressing issues than to attend the graduation of a bunch of new lieutenants. Scuttlebutt also said Quantico's Commanding Officer, and several special guests would be on the reviewing stand as well. Speculation ran high as to who those guests might be.

As it developed, the entire population of trainees at Quantico turned out for the Pass in Review, led by the new graduates of the Officer Candidate School. The Commandant of the Marine Corps was indeed on the Reviewing Stand, and that was why every training unit, all 650 Marines in full dress blues, was participating. Jake led his class onto the parade grounds, following the Marine Corps band, making one pass before the Reviewing Stand and saluting the colors, before positioning his fellow candidates in front of the Reviewing Stand as he had been instructed. He was stunned to see Delilah and Elena on the Reviewing Stand. *What the hell?*

Once all the units had passed in review and taken their assigned places, they were called to 'Parade Rest', and Quantico's Commanding Officer stepped to the microphone. "We are assembled here today to congratulate the graduating class of the Officer Candidate School, and say 'Well Done!' We are honored to have the Commandant of the United States Marine Corps as a special guest, and also two very beautiful young women with a very personal connection to the United States Marine Corps. I give over the podium to the Commandant of the United States Marine Corps, General Walter A. Winton. Atten-hut!" The assembled Marines snapped to attention in perfect symmetry.

"At ease, Marines," General Winton ordered, and the assembled Marines stood at an easy parade rest. "It is my honor today to not only recognize your achievements, but to introduce to you two people who are the very epitome of what the Corps is all about: dedication and fidelity in the face of all obstacles. The two women you see on this stage are Marine Corps family through and through. Delilah deLeon's grandfather gave great service to the Marine Corps during our invasion of Saipan during World War Two. Unarmed, he led our Marines to where the Japanese Imperial Army's troops were hiding, saving hundreds of lives. Delilah's husband served in Vietnam, and was machine-gunned in the back by North Vietnamese while he was dragging two fellow Marines to safety. Delilah's oldest son, a former Marine, was murdered by Japanese Yakuza criminals with no moral character or value for human life. Delilah's youngest son, a Lance Corporal in the Corps and deployed to Iraq, gave his life barely two months ago in the service of his country, the casualty of an insurgent mortar attack.

"But Delilah has not been defeated by these indescribable losses. She and her family have created a number of trusts and foundations designed to make this world a better place, especially for the children around the world. Delilah, the stage is yours."

Delilah, dressed in a colorful tropical dress and large woven straw hat, a soft yellow flower over her left ear, stepped to the microphone. "Hello, fellow Marines! Yes, that's right. Fellow Marines. As General Winton mentioned, my husband and my two sons were both United States Marines. My message to you today on this graduation day is short and simple: Love your country. Do your duty. Remain true to the values that make the United States the most envied country on this planet. We have a long history of generosity and assisting the less fortunate around the world.

Today I want to announce the formation of The deLeon Foundation in the memory of my grandfather, my husband and my two sons with a gift of five million dollars to the United States Marine Corps Children's Christmas Fund. Now, I would like to introduce you to my daughter, Elena, who has lost her father and two brothers, all former Marines. Elena has been a school teacher on our home island of Saipan. She has accepted the proposal of marriage from a United States Marine, and I could not be happier. She will present him with his officer's saber."

Elena stood gracefully and crossed the stage. Dressed in a white two-piece suit, her raven black hair parting to hang over one shoulder, a bright red flower over her left ear, she was breathtakingly beautiful. "The sword that I am presenting to the new Marine Corps officer whom you have selected to be your brigade commander has a long and storied history. It once belonged to an ancestor of mine, Don Emilio Bustamente de la Vega, a member of the Spanish aristocracy, and Capitan of the Military Garrison of Manila, Philippines. It is a sword honorably bloodied, and was presented to Don Bustamente in gratitude for saving the life of its owner over four hundred years ago. I present it now to your brigade commander so that it may continue its illustrious and honorable career."

General Winton rose, took the sword and its gleaming sheath from his aide-de-camp and offered his arm to Elena. They strode from the Reviewing Stand and came to stand in front of soon-to-be Second Lieutenant Jake Porter. Jake snapped to attention. General Winton handed the sword to Elena, and she in turn handed it to Jake. Jake took the sword and fastened the sheath to his belt, then withdrew the sword and saluted by bringing it to his chin. He then placed it against his right shoulder.

Elena stepped up to him and placed a kiss on his cheek. She whispered softly, but loudly enough for General Winton to hear. "We will have a son in September."

"Well done, Lieutenant. Well done indeed." General Winton said, a broad smile crossing his face.

AFTERWORD

Date: March 1, 2002

Lat. 38º 52' North, Long. 77º 29' West
Marine Barracks, Quantico, Virginia

Nothing travels faster in the Marine Corps than scuttlebutt, especially when the topic is about the Corps' Commandant. Some of the recent scuttlebutt was almost beyond belief; word had it that the Commandant had attended a graduation party celebrating the commissioning of 79 new Second Lieutenants at Quantico, that he had removed his tunic with all his medals and four stars signaling that he was to be considered just one of the boys, then was seen participating in a wildly exotic native dance with a stunningly beautiful South Pacific islander.

And there was more: the Commandant's wife was escorted to the dance floor by the newly-graduated lieutenant who had been selected by his fellow officer candidates to be their brigade commander, and the four of them had danced to an ancient tribal beat calling for outrageously-suggestive hip thrusting and butt-waving.

Also, true to his promise, Jake permitted his fellow Marine officers to dance with his voluptuous fiancée. It was reported to have been a party to end all parties.

After the Commandant and his wife had left the festivities late that evening, the officers were called to order and the Commandant's aide passed out the duty orders for the new lieutenants. Each young Second Lieutenant, some accompanied by their wives or girl friends, opened the envelopes containing the deployments that would launch their careers as Marine Corps officers.

Second Lieutenant Jake Porter received his envelope and handed it to Elena, giving her a kiss. Elena opened the envelope and read Jake's orders. She smiled, her eyes dancing in delight. No Afghanistan for Jake; at least not for now. He was being assigned to fill a Major's billet, to direct the daily operations of the Marine Corps' marksmanship and sniper school at Quantico. Jake kissed Elena, pulled her close to him, knowing how thrilled she was to know that he would be in her bed every night for at least the next couple of years, and that he would be with her when their son was born.

Date: April 11, 2002

Lat. 46° 95' N, Long 7° 44' E .

Berne, Switzerland

The hour was late when the office buzzer sounded. The duty officer in the lobby said that there were three police officers wanting to see him. He said they had warrants; warrants to search and a warrant for his arrest. One of them showed identification from INTERPOL, the other two flashed their gold Swiss Securité badges.

He was not in the least surprised. For several weeks now, ever since he had received the single-sideband radiotelephone message from Dutch at Marcus Island, telling him the treasure cave was gutted, he suspected it was the beginning of the end. Dutch had found the body of their pirating partner, John, dead from a large caliber bullet hole in the back of his head, beach crabs feasting on his body at the base of the cliff beneath the treasure cave's entrance.

At first, he was sure the Yakuza had ripped him off, but then Dutch and his crew had found thousands of spent AK-47, AR-15, and 9mm automatic pistol shells scattered all across tiny Marcos Island. It was clear that a furious battle had been fought between the Yakuza and some unknown force. The Yakuza's long liner and crew never returned to the Kurile Islands, nor were they ever seen anywhere else. Scuttled off Marcus Island, and sent to the bottom of the Pacific Ocean, he was convinced. The treasure hauled off by the unknowns.

"Send them up," he told the building security officer, then went to the office door and unlocked it.

The warrant for his arrest specified his communications with a private detective agency in Miami, Florida, USA, and bank transfers in payment for breaking and entering into a motor yacht named the *Sea Bones*. Then, the two murders aboard the yacht at the hands of the hired private investigators. Additional digital data and satellite telecommunication records had been recovered relating to efforts to intercept a salvage operation. Japanese naval personnel had recently visited an island in the north Pacific, and discovered evidence of a gunfight there. Sonar surveillance in the surrounding ocean depths indicated a steel vessel of some 200 feet in length was lying on the bottom just offshore of the tiny island, some 2,300 feet down. A mini-sub was being loaned by the U.S. Navy to check it out.

The handcuffs clicked shut around his wrists, and he was led from the building to a waiting police van with barred windows.

Date: August 22, 2002

Lat. 16° 58' S, Long 179° 18' E .

Vanua Levu, Republic of Fiji Islands, Pacific Ocean

Archie McGruder's *Waltz'n* rode easily to her anchor in Fawn Harbor, the salty old French sailboat's wooden deck staying cool beneath the white cotton awning that stretched from the mainmast to the mizzen mast. Vanua Levu was the second largest of the 322 islands in the Fiji group, and Fawn Harbor offered calm, weather-protected anchoring for cruising sailboats. The native market for fresh vegetables, fruit and catch-of-the-day from local fishermen was only a five-minute walk from the sandy beach.

Archie was stretched out in a multi-colored hammock that swung gently beneath the awning's shade. He watched the approaching native rowboat, a curvaceous and smiling Fijian woman softly stroking an oar with a skill learned from when she was just beginning to walk. Archie raised an arm in greeting, and stepped out of the hammock to take the boat's painter and tie it to a deck cleat. He took several small net bags filled with fruit and vegetables that she handed up to him, then grabbed the tail of a gutted yellow fin tuna minus its head, and swung it aboard.

"How is your mother, love?" Archie asked. Tatia's mother was getting on in years and complaining of a backache.

"She is better," Tatia answered, climbing through the lifelines to *Waltz'n deck*. She bestowed a light kiss to Archie's cheek, gathered up her purchases and went below to the galley. Archie followed behind her,

admiring the soft rhythms of her trim body and sweet perfume, counting himself exceedingly fortunate to have won her affections.

"I met the American couple from the catamaran at the market. They gave me a couple of women's fashion magazines and an old issue of the

Wall Street Journal for you. I invited them over for dinner and drinks tonight. Is that okay with you?" Tatia asked.

"Of course," Archie MsGruder said, rolling up the tattered issue of the Wall Street Journal and heading back to his hammock. He heard a bottle cap pop, turned and saw that Tatia had a cold beer for him.

"You are a keeper, love. Now, I'm going to catch up on the news," he said, taking the beer and kissing her hand.

In the hammock, Archie opened the well-read copy of the Journal, and turned a few pages. When he reached a feature article describing the incredible recovery of a Manila galleon's treasure lost in the late Seventeenth Century, his jaw dropped. A picture of a smiling Jake Porter with a voluptuous native island woman standing next to him, a flower in her hair over an ear, and the two of them holding a large Chinese vase. According to the article, an American named Jake Porter was credited with the discovery of the treasure, valued in the hundreds of millions of dollars, but a family from the island of Saipan was dispensing the wealth through charities around the world. Porter was now a United States Marine Corps officer, married to a young woman from Saipan, and they were expecting a baby in the next few weeks.

"Good on you, Jake," Archie said, taking a deep swallow of his beer. "Good on you."

FINIS

ABOUT THE AUTHOR

Author Robbie Johnson is an ocean-going sailor, aircraft and helicopter pilot, SCUBA diver and sport parachutist. He gained his FAA Private Pilot's license at the age of 16, and his Commercial Pilot's license at the age of eighteen. He is licensed to fly both fixed-wing aircraft and helicopters and worked as a crop-dusting pilot. He is a sport parachutist and was a member of the first Parachute Club of America's chapter in Florida.

He has lived aboard ocean-going sailboats for the past thirty-five years, twenty of those years outside the United States, and presently makes his year 'round home aboard one of the most famous sailboats ever designed, a steel gaff-rigged Tahiti Ketch.

Robbie earned his Bachelor's degree from Mercer University, Atlanta/Macon, GA, and his Master's degree from California State University, Dominguez Hills ((Los Angeles) graduating with highest academic distinction (Summa cum laude), and was elected to Phi Kappa Phi, our nation's oldest and most prestigious academic honor society.

Robbie has lived an adventurous life that includes being one of two principal divers who recovered four priceless bronze cannons from a depth of 120 feet off Terceira Island, Azores, for the Portuguese government. He was also a principal diver in an Oxford University-sponsored expedition to find the lead coffin of Sir Frances Drake, off Portobelo, Republic of Panama. Queen Elizabeth's husband, Prince Philip, wished the expedition luck, but said he preferred to "let sleeping dogs lie."